ADVISORY BOARD

THE WESLEYAN EDITION OF THE
WORKS OF HENRY FIELDING

———

JOSEPH ANDREWS

Oxford University Press, Ely House, London W.1

GLASGOW NEW YORK TORONTO MELBOURNE WELLINGTON
CAPE TOWN SALISBURY IBADAN NAIROBI LUSAKA ADDIS ABABA
BOMBAY CALCUTTA MADRAS KARACHI LAHORE DACCA
KUALA LUMPUR HONG KONG TOKYO

HENRY FIELDING

Joseph Andrews

EDITED BY

MARTIN C. BATTESTIN

OXFORD
AT THE CLARENDON PRESS
1967

© *Martin C. Battestin 1967*

PRINTED IN GREAT BRITAIN

TO LOUIS LANDA

Yet *some* there were, among the *sounder Few*
Of those who *less presum'd,* and *better knew,*
Who durst assert the *juster Ancient Cause,*
And here *restor'd* Wit's *Fundamental Laws.*

PREFACE

THE Wesleyan edition[1] of *Joseph Andrews* is primarily a textual edition. It is designed to furnish scholars and other interested readers both with a reliable text and with all other materials relevant to the history and essential meaning of the text. The principles and procedures followed in preparing the text and the textual apparatus are described at length by Professor Bowers immediately following the General Introduction. Included as a special feature of the appendixes is a discussion of the priority and authority of the 'Murphy editions', which have served as the basis for many modern reprints of the novel.

The Introduction itself is historical rather than critical: emphasis is on the making of the novel—the circumstances of its genesis and composition, and the facts of its printing and publication—rather than on its larger meanings.[2] *Joseph Andrews* is a rich and various work whose significance and abundant life are inexhaustible; certainly, if it were not presumptuous, it would be impossible here to attempt a critical 'explication' of the novel that would be definitive. The aim of the Introduction and the explanatory annotations is, therefore, to provide the reader with the basic information necessary for him to form his own conclusions about Fielding's intentions in *Joseph Andrews*. Whereas the Introduction sketches the general background, discussing Fielding's activities during the period immediately preceding the publication of the novel and identifying the originals of certain characters, the annotations identify and explain the numerous historical references and literary allusions that occur in the text itself. Though I have, of course, tried to avoid irrelevancies, the notes in some instances are quite full: *Joseph Andrews* is a highly topical book, often alluding to matters of contemporary history once familiar but now virtually forgotten; a certain amplitude is required in

[1] Although the present edition of Fielding is being published jointly by the Wesleyan University Press and the Clarendon Press, the designation 'Wesleyan edition' will be used both for the purpose of convenient reference and to acknowledge the fact that the project was initially encouraged and supported by Wesleyan.

[2] My own interpretation of the meaning and structure of *Joseph Andrews* is set forth in *The Moral Basis of Fielding's Art: A Study of 'Joseph Andrews'* (Wesleyan University Press: Middletown, Conn., 1959).

order to refresh the reader's memory and to establish obscure frames of reference without which Fielding's meaning in a given passage can be grasped only imperfectly, if at all.

Those who aided me in the preparation of this volume, which required more years to complete than I care to remember, are too many to have justice done them in this brief notice. I began to study Fielding, and in particular *Joseph Andrews*, intensively in 1956, as Peter H. B. Frelinghuysen Fellow at Princeton. My research for this edition, however, did not begin in earnest until 1960, with my appointment as a Fellow of the American Council of Learned Societies and a sabbatical leave from my teaching duties at Wesleyan University. Subsequent grants, both from the University of Virginia and from the American Philosophical Society (in the summer of 1962), enabled me to continue my research and to complete the preparation of the manuscript. I am grateful to all these institutions, without whose generous support the present work would still be in process.

My labours were eased considerably by the always courteous co-operation of librarians on both sides of the Atlantic. I wish to thank the staffs of the British Museum, the Bodleian Library, the Victoria and Albert Museum, and the New York Public Library; of Princeton, Columbia, Wesleyan, and Yale Universities; and of the University of Virginia. I am particularly grateful to Mr. Herman W. Liebert of Yale and to Mr. William H. Runge of Virginia.

It is, of course, impossible fully to acknowledge my obligations to those scholars, living and dead, who have contributed so much to our knowledge of Fielding and his writings: it will be evident, I trust, that in preparing the Introduction and annotations I had occasion to draw upon the works of Cross, Blanchard, McKillop, Woods, Miller, and many others; and, despite its imperfections, J. Paul de Castro's edition of *Joseph Andrews* (Scholartis Press, 1929), the only previous attempt to annotate the novel at length, helped to simplify my own task.

Among others who assisted me in various capacities, I am especially indebted to Miss Clodagh Harvey, who helped with the collation of the texts; to Professor William McCulloh, who is responsible for whatever accuracy there may be in my translations of Greek and Latin; and to Professor William B. Todd, Mr. E. G. W. Bill, and Mr. W. S. Hiscock, who contributed to the

solving of specific problems of interpretation. At the eleventh hour
I was able to check the annotations dealing with legal matters
against the commentary of Hugh Amory, who allowed me to
consult relevant portions of his doctoral dissertation, 'Law and
the Structure of Fielding's Novels' (Columbia University, 1964).
Dean Irby B. Cauthen, Jr., my colleague and fellow admirer of
Fielding, kindly made the resources of his own library available
to me; and on more than one occasion another colleague, Professor Lester A. Beaurline, helped me to penetrate the mysteries
of bibliography. To my associates, the editors and advisers of the
Wesleyan edition, I am indebted for many helpful suggestions:
thanks are due to John Butt, James L. Clifford, W. B. Coley, Arthur
Friedman, Richard L. Greene, Allen T. Hazen, Alan D. McKillop,
Henry K. Miller, and Charles B. Woods—all of whom read the
manuscript at various stages. That such a distinguished company
of scholars should have been willing to contribute their time and
advice to the improvement of this volume is a privilege which I
am pleased to acknowledge. It is a special pleasure, however, to
declare my profound obligations—and my sincere gratitude—to
Louis Landa, who first encouraged my interest in Fielding
and who, whenever I have sought his aid or counsel, has given
generously of his time, knowledge, and wisdom.

In particular, I wish to acknowledge the invaluable assistance
of Fredson Bowers. In his several publications Professor Bowers
established the textual and bibliographical principles which I
followed in preparing this edition; what is more, his personal
advice and careful criticism of the manuscript are largely responsible for whatever virtues the present text may possess. The
faults, I need hardly add, are entirely my own.

To my wife Ruthe—who accompanied me through the
drudgery of collation and the reading of proof, whose good
taste prevented more than one catastrophe of style, and whose
wit and affection have sustained me—I owe my gratitude, and
much more.

LIST OF CONTENTS

GENERAL INTRODUCTION

IT is a commonplace among historians of the novel that Fielding began *Joseph Andrews* in amused exasperation at the astonishing vogue of Richardson's *Pamela: or, Virtue Rewarded.* If not the 'lewd and ungenerous engraftment' that Fielding's disgruntled rival would have it,[1] *Joseph Andrews* was certainly prompted by the fact and fame of Richardson's book. Published on 6 November 1740, *Pamela* almost overnight became a sensation: it ran through six editions in little more than a year, achieving a popularity so vast and vociferous that Fielding's Parson Oliver described the commotion as an 'epidemical Phrenzy'.[2] By January 1741 *The Gentleman's Magazine* could observe that it was already *'in Town as great a Sign of Want of Curiosity not to have read* Pamela, *as not to have seen the* French *and* Italian *Dancers'.*[3] The simple, as well as the sophisticated, took Richardson's servant girl to heart, trembling over her trials as she withstood the assaults and clumsy intrigues of her ardent master, and exulting in her triumph as she brought him at last to his knees in capitulation and marriage. In the country, so tradition has it, the villagers of Slough gathered at the smithy to hear her story read aloud, and they communally celebrated her wedding by ringing the church bells. 'Like the snow, that lay last week, upon the earth and all her products,' wrote Aaron Hill to Richardson barely two months after the novel had appeared, '[Pamela] covers every other image with her own unbounded whiteness.'[4] A host of opportunists rushed to take advantage of the book's popularity: Pamela was portrayed on fans and in waxworks, and there were attempts, mostly abortive, at dramatic and operatic versions of her story. As early as May 1741 a certain John Kelly had written *Pamela's Conduct in High Life,* the first of the spurious continuations that angered Richardson and set him reluctantly to work on his own

---

[1] *The Correspondence of Samuel Richardson,* ed. Anna Laetitia Barbauld (1804), iv. 286.

[2] See Oliver's first letter in *Shamela* (1741).

[3] *The Gentleman's Magazine,* xi (January 1741), 56.

[4] Letter of 29 December 1740 (*The Works of the Late Aaron Hill, Esq.,* 2nd ed. [1754], ii. 130).

General Introduction

authentic sequel, published in December. Indeed, in a letter at the close of the year, Solomon Lowe called upon his friend Richardson (rather superfluously) to 'witness the Labours of the Press in Piracies, in Criticisms, in Cavils, in Panegyrics, in Supplements, in Imitations, in Transformations, in Translations, &c, beyond anything I know of'.[1]

It was, however, the claim represented in Aaron Hill's letter —the 'whiteness', the moral purity, of Richardson's heroine, whose chastity proves so profitable to her—that especially irked Fielding. Even the clergy, the custodians of the public morality, were broadcasting their approval: Dr. Benjamin Slocock, for example, had sounded Pamela's praises from the pulpit of St. Saviour's, Southwark, as if, it may have seemed to Fielding, Richardson had written not a mere romance after all, but another book of Scripture. Even Alexander Pope had been impressed by Pamela's 'virtue': the novel, he was reported about town as saying, would do more good than many volumes of sermons. In the midst of this uproar Fielding found it impossible to hold his peace. A book in his opinion technically inept and morally mercenary had taken the public fancy as few books had ever done, and, in the interests of good taste and good sense, it needed to be shown for what he believed it was: an absurd and pretentious performance, the most notable example in fiction of what Fielding was to call 'the true Ridiculous'. In his brilliant parody, *Shamela* (April 1741), he set about the destructive task of exposing, hilariously, the more vulnerable sides of Richardson's work. In *Joseph Andrews* (February 1742) he offered his own alternative conception of the art and purpose of the novel.

Although Fielding, in writing first *Shamela* and then *Joseph Andrews*, was thus eager to introduce a measure of sanity into the hysteria over *Pamela*, to laugh the public into good sense and to furnish a new, and a better, 'species of writing', there were other more practical motives for his novel. A review of Fielding's circumstances and the variety of his activities during this period will clarify these reasons and help to define the climate, at once brisk and sombre, in which he wrote. In the case of a book as topical

---

[1] Quoted in Alan Dugald McKillop, *Samuel Richardson, Printer and Novelist* (University of North Carolina Press: Chapel Hill, 1936), p. 67. For full accounts of the reception of *Pamela* and of the abundant literature the book occasioned, see McKillop and Bernard Kreissman, *Pamela-Shamela: A Study of the criticisms, burlesques, parodies, and adaptations of Richardson's 'Pamela'* (University of Nebraska Press: n.p., 1960).

and allusive as *Joseph Andrews* this background is especially relevant; as Fielding himself advised his readers, 'every thing is copied from the Book of Nature, and scarce a Character or Action produced which I have not taken from my own Observations and Experience'.

The history of *Joseph Andrews* properly begins with the passage of the theatrical Licensing Act of 1737, for which Fielding's scathing satires of the Walpole administration were largely responsible. 'Like another *Erostratus*', sneered Colley Cibber with metaphors typically mixed, Fielding 'set Fire to his Stage, by writing up to an Act of Parliament to demolish it'.[1] When the doors of the Little Theatre in the Haymarket closed on 24 June, Fielding was forced to abandon the lucrative business of writing for the stage and to look elsewhere—principally to the profession of the law—for the means to support his wife and family. Financially, these were difficult, perhaps even desperate, days for him. In November 1739, in order to supplement his income, Fielding spared time enough from his law studies to commence hackney author in earnest and to resume his labours—now as Hercules Vinegar, editor of *The Champion*—on behalf of the Opposition. In June of the following year he was called to the bar at the Middle Temple, but despite his attendance at Westminster Hall in term time and his diligence on the Western Circuit, he had few briefs and those not very profitable. Perhaps, as with his own Mr. Wilson, his clients feared he would turn their deeds into plays. That his need was urgent is evident from a flurry of fugitive writing, much of it political in nature. In October appeared *The Military History of Charles XII*, which Fielding, at least in part, translated from the French.[2] In January 1741 he published two poems: *Of True Greatness*, an epistle addressed rather obsequiously to the 'Boy Patriot', George Bubb Dodington; and *The Vernoniad*, a mock-epic praising Admiral Vernon, hero of the Opposition, and criticizing Walpole's languid pursuit of the war with Spain. In April *Shamela* appeared, as Fielding uproariously began the fun at Richardson's expense. Also published in April was *The Crisis: A Sermon*, an electioneering tract which most scholars attribute to Fielding. This writing was done concurrently with

---

[1] *An Apology for the Life of Mr. Colley Cibber, Comedian*, 2nd ed. (1740), p. 231.
[2] See John E. Wells, 'Henry Fielding and the History of Charles XII', *JEGP*, xi (1912), 603–13.

his occasional contributions to *The Champion*, an association that he irregularly maintained until June, and with his composition of at least some of the pieces included in the *Miscellanies* (1743). In December he produced still another political piece, *The Opposition: A Vision*, this time in satiric reproof of his old party.

It seems clear that none of these ephemeral productions did more than interrupt the steady decline of his fortunes. In the invaluable Preface to the *Miscellanies* is a pathetic apology for *The Wedding Day* (1743) that doubtless has a wider application to much of Fielding's hackney writing in 1741: he had suffered this imperfect piece to be produced not from the hope of augmenting his reputation, but from 'a much more solid, and in my unhappy Situation, a much more urgent Motive'. The records of the Court of Common Pleas further testify that on 27 March 1741, at the height of his fugitive writing, Fielding's poverty had driven him to borrow £197, payable on demand, from one Joseph King, who subsequently sued to recover the debt during Trinity Term of the following year.[1] In June 1741, moreover, the death of Fielding's father, whose early promise of a £200 allowance was never fulfilled,[2] only added to his misfortunes without increasing his income. In general, Fielding's implicit description of himself in *The Opposition* as a shabby and impecunious Patriot drudge was not much exaggerated.

In the winter Fielding's financial difficulties were rendered more acute by the sickness that ravaged his family and eventually, in March 1742, took the life of his favourite daughter, Charlotte.[3] The delay in the publication of the *Miscellanies*, he announced in *The Daily Post* of 5 June 1742, was owing to 'the Author's Indisposition last Winter, and a Train of melancholy Accidents scarce to be parallell'd'. In the Preface to these volumes may be found a more eloquent and explicit account of the situation:

Indeed when I look a Year or two backwards, and survey the Accidents which have befallen me, and the Distresses I have waded through whilst I have been engaged in these Works, I could almost challenge some Philosophy to myself, for having been able to finish them as I have. . . .

. . . I was last Winter [i.e. 1741–2] laid up in the Gout, with a favourite Child dying on one Bed, and my Wife in a Condition very little better on

---

[1] See Wilbur L. Cross, *The History of Henry Fielding* (Yale University Press: New Haven, 1918), i. 376.

[2] Cross, i. 57–58.   [3] Cross, i. 351.

another, attended with Circumstances which served as very proper Decorations to such a Scene. . . .

It is likely that the darkness of those grim months was brightened a little by assistance from the outside. In *Joseph Andrews* (III. i), for instance, the praise of the nameless peer (probably Chesterfield) may have been Fielding's grateful acknowledgement of favours received. Furthermore, one current story had it that Ralph Allen, pleased with something Fielding had written, began their friendship by making him a present of £200.[1] To judge from the warm compliments twice paid to Allen's charity and hospitality in *Joseph Andrews* (III. i, vi), and from other evidence, it does indeed appear that some time after 27 October 1741 Fielding, in the company of Pope, had been 'courteously entertained' in Allen's newly built Palladian mansion at Prior Park, near Bath.[2] The visit marks the beginning both of Fielding's personal relations with the poet and, more important, of his lasting friendship with his most generous patron, the man who was to serve as a model for Squire Allworthy of *Tom Jones*. But the extent of Allen's benefactions, if any, can only be surmised, and alone they were unable to offset the 'Train of melancholy Accidents' of which Fielding complained.

There is considerable circumstantial evidence to suggest that he was driven to seek further assistance from a source far less likely than Ralph Allen—namely, Sir Robert Walpole. In June Fielding had made a puzzling decision when he severed his long-standing connexion with *The Champion*, and also, it seems, with the Opposition, whose cause that journal was supporting.[3] This was a crucial election year in England, and the Patriots were marshalling all their forces in an effort—successful, as it proved in February of 1742—to depose the Minister. In February 1741, at a strategic moment before the spring elections, Carteret and Samuel Sandys rose in Parliament to move Walpole's impeachment; in May the Opposition protested at the Army's interference in the Westminster elections; and in the summer, after news of the military débâcle at Carthagena had been published, the cry

[1] See Samuel Derrick's letter from Bath, 10 May 1763. (*Letters* [Dublin, 1767], ii. 57–58.)

[2] For a full discussion of the evidence, see Battestin, 'Lord Hervey's Role in *Joseph Andrews*', *PQ*, xlii (1963), 235–9.

[3] See the Preface to the *Miscellanies* and G. M. Godden, *Henry Fielding: A Memoir* (1910), pp. 115–16.

against ministerial malfeasance and mismanagement resounded throughout the town. The reasons for Fielding's break with his former party at a time when he urgently needed money and when his services would have been most useful to them are difficult to determine, but one inference seems inevitable. As the signs of their eventual victory became clear, the Patriots were fast forgetting their grand professions and entering instead upon a furious race for power and place in government; what is more, they were not adequately rewarding him for his labours on their behalf. They had proved themselves hypocrites and ingrates, and Fielding could no longer afford to sacrifice the interests of himself and his family in a bad cause. If we read carefully, his disaffection with the Opposition is implicit in an obscure, but interesting, episode in *Joseph Andrews* (II. vii–ix), a kind of political parable in which Parson Adams encounters a blustering fellow who speaks out vehemently against the Standing Army and against the ineffectual pursuit of the war with Spain; the gentleman's loud protestations of valour and self-sacrifice for one's country soon prove empty, however, as he flees in fear of his life at the first hint of real danger. Fielding's readers would have been sure to penetrate the thin veil of this allegory and to associate this man of false courage with those Patriots (with a capital *P*) whose principles he shares and whose perfidious conduct he emulates. Appropriately delivered to this same gentleman, Adams's 'notable Dissertation' on his political adventures reveals that the parson, as well as his author, has previously experienced the hypocrisy and thanklessness of those members of the Country Party whom he helped to elect.

The situation is even clearer in the curious sixpenny pamphlet, *The Opposition: A Vision*, which Fielding, interrupting work on *Joseph Andrews*, published in December, just as the new Parliament was meeting to decide Walpole's fate: in this satire Fielding acidly rebuked his former allies for double-dealing and ingratitude, and, stranger still, he complimented his old enemy, the Prime Minister, for his generosity and good intentions. Had Fielding, then, changed his politics altogether and accepted Walpole's patronage in an effort to provide for his family? There is evidence to suggest that he had.[1] Walpole and his party do not,

---

[1] See Battestin, 'Fielding's Changing Politics and *Joseph Andrews*', PQ, xxxix (1960), 39–55. In reference to his quitting *The Champion* Fielding's enemies could thus accuse him

of course, escape criticism in *Joseph Andrews*: consider the wry allusion to the 'Trade' of prime-ministering (II. i), or the ale-house-keeper's impassioned outburst against *The Daily Gazetteer* (II. xvii), or the contemptuous caricature of Beau Didapper (i.e. John, Lord Hervey), who abjectly serves his Great Man 'at the Expence of his Conscience, his Honour, and of his Country' (IV. ix).¹ It is thus clear that Fielding's disenchantment with the Opposition did not entail his approval of the questionable political ethics of the administration. As he himself implied in the revised opening to Book II, Chapter x, both parties were, after all, 'riflers' of their country. Without doubt, in *Jonathan Wild* (IV. iii) the address of the 'very grave Man' to the debtors of Newgate mirrors Fielding's true political convictions: 'it is better to shake the Plunder off than to exchange the Plunderer.' The behaviour of the Opposition after the spring elections had proved to him that corruption and hypocrisy were not confined to one party. When the Patriots, whose cause he had worked to promote, proved ungrateful, he turned elsewhere to meet very pressing financial exigencies.

Politics and patrons, even *Pamela* for that matter, by no means exhaust the contemporary issues, people, events which affected Fielding's life and thought during this period, and which find their place in *Joseph Andrews*. Indeed, one sign of Fielding's power as a novelist is his ability to shape the private and the local into a larger design of universal relevance; to transform, as it were, the idiosyncratic into the symbolic. The creation of Parson Adams is a case in point. Within the context of the Christian and comic traditions that Fielding draws upon, Adams owes most to his namesake, the patriarch Abraham, and to Cervantes's errant knight, Don Quixote; for many of his most memorable characteristics, however, the good parson is indebted to an original in real life—namely, Fielding's friend, the very learned and forgetful Dorsetshire curate, William Young.² Similarly, the journey

---

of having taken 'a small pecuniary Gratuity to betray his Paymasters and the Paper, out of which he had for sometime extracted a precarious Subsistence . . .' (*Old England*, 5 August 1749).

¹ See below, p. xxiii, n. 2.

² William Young (1702 ?–57) was originally from Hannington, Wilts. On 15 July 1727, in his twenty-fifth year, he matriculated at St. John's College, Oxford. From 1731 to 1740 he served as curate of East Stour (a chapelry of Gillingham), the village in Dorset where Fielding grew up. An accomplished classicist, he edited Ainsworth's *Dictionary of the*

Adams takes with Joseph carries them away from London toward Dorsetshire[1] along a real English highway at a particular moment of English history, the autumn of 1741, though it is at the same time a symbolic and ageless progress from the City of this World, the very type and habitation of vanity, toward a better country.

Fielding's personal interests and the particular shape and pressure of his circumstances are, indeed, everywhere apparent in *Joseph Andrews*: at times they enter the novel casually, in the merely private or topical allusion; but often, as we have seen, they are made to serve quite functional purposes, affecting the choice of character, action, setting. Parson Adams, for instance, discloses that he was originally lured towards the Great City by an

Latin Tongue and Hederich's *Greek Lexicon*, and collaborated with Fielding in a translation of Aristophanes' *Plutus*, published in May 1742; in 1752 the two friends projected, but never finished, a translation of Lucian. Young died on 30 August 1757.

It was common knowledge about town that Young was the original of Parson Adams (though, according to one story, he threatened to knock a man down who mentioned it to him). One contemporary account, written 18 December 1742, is especially valuable as background to Fielding's characterization of Adams: 'Parson Young was a Dorsetshire parson of great parts and learning, an absent man and of no great knowledge of the world. Fielding has drawn his character in "The Adventures of Joseph Andrews" under the feigned name of Abraham Adams. He had a wife, six children, and a curacy of about 30*l.* a year. The following story shows him honest, simple, and without guile. Jointly with Fielding he translated Aristophanes' "Plutus" or God of Riches. Lord Talbot, to whom it is dedicated, sent Young five guineas, as a gratuity, but he for a long time refused it, because it did not belong to him, he having no hand in the dedication. At last he took it, but not for himself, but Fielding, who writ the dedication. He saw him daily for five days, but still forgot the five guineas. At last, upon a dispute, he pulled out the money to lay a wager; being questioned about it, he said 'twas Χρυσος Αριστοφανικος [*sic*] and belonged to Fielding: and so told the manner of his coming by it. 'Twas with great difficulty he could be persuaded to take any part of it, but at last, they, upon the judgment of the company, divided it; but he still insisted upon paying Fielding's reckoning out of his share. He is now [18 December 1742] tutor to a young Gentleman at 70*l.* a year. Before he entered on this service, he endeavoured by a feigned letter to himself to get leave of his patron to spend a fortnight in the country; but this letter, containing the pretended invitation, he put into his patron's hand sealed and unopened, which piece of absence discovered the scheme, so little was he able to act this little piece of disingenuity. Mr. Young was curate of Gillingham, and formerly Schoolmaster at Romsey, where he was so careless a man as to run into every tradesman's debt, and had went to gaol if Sir J. St. B.—, Mr. Thomas, and others had not raised money to redeem him. All he knew of the matter was, he wanted the goods and had 'em.' (From the original manuscript as recorded in the *Salisbury and Wiltshire Herald*, 25 February 1837; quoted in J. Paul de Castro, 'Fielding's "Parson Adams"', *N & Q*, 12th ser., i [18 March 1916], 224–5 and, somewhat altered and abridged, in de Castro's edition of *Joseph Andrews* [1929], pp. 383–4.)

[1] Although Fielding, perhaps to conceal the identities of his characters, places Sir Thomas Booby's country seat, and hence Adams's parish, in Somerset, the location described in the novel is probably East Stour, Dorset, where Fielding lived as a young man and where William Young had his cure. (See *Joseph Andrews*, ed. de Castro, pp. 403–4.)

actual advertisement of the Society of Booksellers for Promoting Learning; and he has read with care and approbation Bishop Hoadly's controversial work on the eucharist. Joseph meets an innkeeper, 'plain Tim', whom Fielding knew; and at Lady Booby's table he has overheard Pope's compliments to Ralph Allen and the Man of Ross. There is further talk of the recent military fiasco at Carthagena, of *The Daily Gazetteer* and of Pope's *Homer*, of Hogarth, of 'Mother' Haywood's brothel, of John Wesley and George Whitefield. Indeed, in *Joseph Andrews* Fielding or his characters refer to a host of actual people of every description—highwaymen and freethinkers, actors and actresses, preachers and playwrights, toymakers and auctioneers, philanthropists and peers. Most prominent of these is Colley Cibber, whose recent autobiography, *An Apology for the Life of Mr. Colley Cibber, Comedian* (1740), had not only offended Fielding's taste by the violence it committed upon the English language, but had also revived their old quarrel by calling him names. What is still more to the point, besides William Young at least two and possibly three others of Fielding's contemporaries served as models for principal characters in the novel: namely, Peter Walter, the miser and money-lender of Stalbridge Park, who sat for the portrait of the predatory Peter Pounce;[1] John, Lord Hervey, the effeminate courtier who provided some salient features in the characterization of Beau Didapper;[2] and John, Duke of

[1] Peter Walter (1664 ?–1746) of Stalbridge Park, Dorset, some four miles from Fielding's residence in East Stour, was a money scrivener infamous for his unscrupulous and usurious practices. A 'dextrous attorney' and Land Steward to the Duke of Newcastle, among others, he acquired much property in the country, including Fielding's own estate, and cut down the timber for profit. From 1715 to 1727 he was Member of Parliament for Bridport. According to *The Gentleman's Magazine*, at the time of his death on 19 January 1746 he was worth some £300,000.

For Pope and Swift, as well as for Fielding, Walter was the very type of grasping avarice. For other references to Walter in Fielding's works see *The Champion* (31 May 1740) and the following from the *Miscellanies* of 1743: 'An Essay on Conversation', 'Epigram on One Who Invited Many Gentlemen to a Small Dinner', 'Some Papers Proper to be Read before the Royal Society', and *Jonathan Wild* (II. vii).

[2] John, Lord Hervey, Baron Ickworth (1696–1743)—the little, foppish, philandering courtier who was Queen Caroline's favourite and Sir Robert Walpole's chief instrument in the House of Lords. Hervey's sinecures at court included his appointments as Vice-Chamberlain (1730) and as Lord Privy Seal (1740). His health always delicate, Hervey painted his face with cosmetics to disguise his ghastly pallor, and he observed a strict regimen, drinking no wine or strong liquor. He was a thorough francophile, who loved French clothes and French songs, as well as the Italian opera; his professed ignorance of Latin, on the other hand, made him a public jest, especially after he had attempted a clumsy epitaph for the

Montagu, the notorious practical joker who may have been the inspiration for the 'roasting' squire.[1] Clearly, this is a work of art firmly rooted in the soil of contemporary life.

2. DATE OF COMPOSITION

Of the numerous topical references in *Joseph Andrews* only a few offer assistance in fixing a date of composition. Considering the pace of Fielding's life during 1741, it is unlikely that he could have begun the novel much before the late summer or early autumn: work on *The Champion*, together with considerable miscellaneous writing, engaged his attention until June, after which he would have resumed his travels on the Western Circuit. Internal evidence tends to confirm this supposition.

queen. A wit and a skilful mimic, by indulging his talent for ridicule at Pope's expense, he became the target of some of the poet's most vicious, and brilliant, satiric verses, especially the portrait of Sporus (Hervey also had a reputation for homosexuality) in the *Epistle to Dr. Arbuthnot*. In 1741 Hervey was again the talk of the town when Conyers Middleton made him the subject of a fulsome dedication in *The Life of Cicero*; Fielding, both amused and annoyed, parodied this performance in *Shamela* and resumed the attack in *Joseph Andrews*. (See 'Lord Hervey's Role in *Joseph Andrews*', PQ xlii [1963], 226–41.)

[1] John, Second Duke of Montagu (1688 ?–1749), a courtier who enjoyed various sinecures and distinctions, was a member of the Cabinet Council under Walpole. Aurélien Digeon was the first to propose that Montagu was the original of the 'roasting' squire, and his view has been generally accepted. (See *Les Romans de Fielding* [Paris, 1923], p. 88 n.— Digeon confuses Montagu and Charles Lennox, Duke of Richmond; *Joseph Andrews*, ed. de Castro, pp. 392–3, and F. Homes Dudden, *Henry Fielding: His Life, Works, and Times* [Oxford, 1952], i. 372.) The evidence, however, is either contradictory or inconclusive. Unlike the squire, who is a bachelor about forty years of age, Montagu was married (to the youngest daughter of the Duke of Marlborough, Lady Mary Churchill) and in 1741 would have been in his early fifties. On the other hand, Montagu, who was notorious for his pranks, was a likely model for Fielding's practical joker. In 1740 his mother-in-law, the Duchess-Dowager of Marlborough, wrote of him: 'All his talents lie in things only natural in boys of fifteen years old, and he is about two and fifty; to get people into his garden and wet them with squirts, and to invite people to his country houses, and put things into their beds to make them itch, and twenty such pretty fancies like these.' (*Opinions* [1788], p. 58.) The case for Montagu as the original of the 'roasting' squire is finally based upon the following experience of Montesquieu, identical with the climactic joke upon Adams: Montagu, writes Montesquieu, 'was one of the most extraordinary characters I ever met with; endowed with the most excellent sense, his singularity knew no bounds. Only think! at my first acquaintance with him, having invited me to his country seat, before I had leisure to get into any sort of intimacy, he practised on me that whimsical trick which undoubtedly you have either experienced, or heard of; under the idea of playing the play of an introduction of ambassadors, he soused me over head and ears into a tub of cold water.' (Quoted in Francis Hardy, *Memoirs of the Political and Private Life of James Caulfield, Earl of Charlemont*, 2nd ed. [1812], i. 65.) As Montesquieu himself indicates, however, this prank was a familiar one; there is no clear evidence that it was Montagu, and not some other 'roaster', whom Fielding meant to satirize.

From several allusions in *Joseph Andrews* March of 1741 seems the earliest *possible* time that Fielding could have begun writing. At the very start of the novel (i. i) he wryly alludes to Richardson's vanity in publishing those 'excellent Essays or Letters prefixed to the second and subsequent Editions' of *Pamela*. Clearly, as he began to write, Fielding was aware of at least the third edition of Richardson's novel (published in March), and, more probably, the fourth (May) or even the fifth (October). 'Subsequent' instead of 'third', let us say, implies at least two editions after the second. The beginning of March is also the earliest possible date for Parson Adams's statement that his journey toward London to sell his sermons was prompted 'by an Advertisement lately set forth by a Society of Booksellers, who proposed to purchase any Copies offered to them at a Price to be settled by two Persons' (i. xv). Adams here refers to announcements by the Society of Booksellers for Promoting Learning which began appearing in the newspapers on 4 March and were carried continuously until well into August.[1] Another allusion, to the public enthusiasm over the fiery evangelist, George Whitefield (i. xvii), may further corroborate a terminus in March: although Whitefield had earlier secured a large following, he had for some months been in America, out of the public eye; he returned to London from South Carolina on 15 March, at which time he began to preach and proselytize in earnest.[2] Taken together, these bits of evidence suggest that Fielding could not have written the early chapters of his novel before March; they in no way preclude a later date.

Other references to events that can be dated with some confidence indicate that by mid-June—and probably somewhat later —Fielding was at least half-way into Book II. There, in the episode satirizing the Patriots, the man of courage angrily denounces the cowardly conduct of the Army at Carthagena (ii. vii). News of the British defeat at Carthagena did not reach London until 19 June,[3] public discussion of the fiasco becoming most vehement during July and August. The strong anti-Patriot bias of these chapters (ii. vii–ix) suggests, furthermore, that Fielding

[1] See *The Daily Post* of 4 March and *The Craftsman* of 8 August; during this period the advertisement was carried in various newspapers, including Fielding's *Champion*.

[2] See *The Gentleman's Magazine*, xi (March 1741), 162.

[3] See *The London Gazette*, 16–20 June 1741.

wrote them some time after his defection from the Opposition, a break that can conveniently be placed in late June, when he finally abandoned *The Champion*.

But, as we have seen, Fielding could have had little leisure to work on the novel before autumn. The narrative itself is set in the first weeks of that season, when the night air was chill enough for greatcoats (I. xii) and when sudden showers of rain surprised travellers on the road (II. xii). More specifically, from the date of that ludicrous deposition of Lawyer Scout and Thomas Trotter (IV. v), we may infer that the day after the company returned to Lady Booby's country seat was a Sunday in October, some twelve days after Joseph had set out on his journey from London. Although Fielding could not actually have been as far into his novel as this, so early in the autumn, it may well be that he was here adjusting the chronology of the narrative to conform to a time in September or October when he was beginning the account of Joseph's adventures on the road. Unfortunately, however, the time-scheme of *Joseph Andrews* is not nearly so carefully plotted and consistent as that of *Tom Jones*. Characters in the novel twice contradict the necessary facts of the book's chronology,[1] and Fielding himself errs when he declares that the Tuesday in October on which the banns of marriage for Joseph and Fanny were published a second time (IV. iv) was a 'Holiday': in that month, in 1741, St. Luke's Day fell on a Sunday (the 18th) and St. Simon and St. Jude's Day on a Wednesday (the 28th).

What is perhaps our most helpful evidence indicates that Fielding, even in late autumn, was no more than half-way through the novel. We recall that at some time during the period from 27 October to the beginning of January—most probably in November—Fielding, together with Pope, had been 'courteously entertained' at Ralph Allen's 'stately House' at Prior Park. Complimentary allusions both to Pope (III. ii, vi) and to Allen's generosity and hospitality were in all likelihood inspired by this visit. It would seem, then, that Fielding did not begin work on the opening chapters of Book III until November at the earliest. Since his manuscript was in the hands of the printer early in January,[2] it follows that he required not more than two months to finish the second half of the novel. Assuming a similar rate of composition for Books I and II, we may conjecture that *Joseph*

[1] See p. 31, n. 1, p. 297, n. 1.   [2] See below, p. xxix.

Andrews was written in about four months, or during the period from September through December 1741.

In debt and neglected by his former friends among the Patriots, his wife ill and his daughter dying, Fielding laboured late in 1741, with incredible detachment, to write the first masterful comic novel in English. Constrained by these distressing circumstances, he doubtless wrote steadily, though not without interruption, to finish the book; the minor inconsistencies of detail in his narrative attest its hasty composition.[1] Other commitments prevented him from giving his attention exclusively to the novel: some time had to be spared for a cursory revision of *Shamela* for the second edition in November; and during December he paused to write *The Opposition* and, perhaps, to draft at least part of *A Journey from This World to the Next*. Near the turn of the new year, however, he had finished his manuscript and completed arrangements for its publication.

3. HISTORY OF PUBLICATION

The publication of *Joseph Andrews* by Andrew Millar marks the beginning (so far as is known with certainty)[2] of Fielding's friendly association with one of the most prominent and generous members of the London Trade.[3] Exactly when and how the two

---

[1] Fielding corrected some of these slips in revision (see pp. 50. 10, 75. 25, 101. 21, 235. 23, 269. 15); others that he overlooked have been pointed out in the notes (see p. 31, n. 1, p. 48, n. 1, p. 49, n. 1, p. 49, n. 3, p. 67, n. 1, p. 112, n. 1, p. 161, n. 1, p. 297, n. 1, p. 309, n. 2).

[2] Fielding took at least some part in the translation of Gustaf Adlerfeld's *Military History of Charles XII*, which was published jointly by members of the Trade, including Millar, in 1740. (See J. E. Wells, 'Henry Fielding and the History of Charles XII', *JEGP*, xi [1912], 603–13; and Cross, i. 284–7.) But, as the receipt for an advance payment indicates, Fielding was then working for John Nourse. There is little foundation for Cross's surmise that Fielding supervised the translation of the Abbé Banier's *Mythology and Fables of the Ancients, Explain'd from History*, brought out by Millar in instalments, 1739–41. (See Cross, ii. 106, n., and iii. 336.)

[3] From 1728 to 1768 Andrew Millar (1706–68) enjoyed a prosperous career as a London bookseller and publisher. He had a reputation for dealing honestly and generously with his authors: as Dr. Johnson remarked, Millar 'raised the price of literature'. After his arrival from Edinburgh one of his earliest ventures was the purchase of Thomson's tragedy, *Sophonisba*, and his poem, *Spring*; he continued to publish for Thomson such works as *Liberty* and *The Seasons*. He was one of the chief sponsors of Johnson's *Dictionary* and brought out the histories of Robertson and Hume. Beginning with *Joseph Andrews*, Millar published all of Fielding's novels and much of his other work. His relations with the novelist were more than merely professional. (See Austin Dobson, 'Fielding and Andrew Millar', *The Library*, 3rd ser., vii [1916], 177–90.)

men met and struck the bargain that was to launch Fielding on his career as a novelist remains obscure; according to a pleasant tradition, however, it was the poet, James Thomson, who brought them together.[1] As the story goes, Fielding, anxious as usual to discharge a debt, was prepared to give his manuscript into the hands of one reluctant bookseller for only £25. Meeting Thomson in the meanwhile, who had read the manuscript and recognized its merit, Fielding upon his advice rescued the novel from the bookseller and submitted it instead to Thomson's publisher, Millar. Some days later (dutifully heeding the recommendation of his wife) Millar agreed to purchase it. With Thomson assisting, negotiations were opened at a coffee-house in the Strand, after a good dinner and two bottles of port:

'I am a man,' said Millar, 'of few words, and fond of coming to the point; but really, after giving every consideration I am able to your novel, I do not think I can afford to give you more than 200*l*. for it.' 'What!' exclaimed Fielding, 'two hundred pounds!' 'Indeed, Mr. Fielding,' returned Millar, 'indeed I am sensible of your talents; but my mind is made up.' 'Two hundred pounds!' continued Fielding in a tone of perfect astonishment; '*two hundred pounds* did you say?' 'Upon my word, Sir, I mean no disparagement to the writer or his great merit; but my mind is made up, and I cannot give one farthing more.' 'Allow me to ask you,' continued Fielding with undiminished surprise, 'allow me, Mr. Millar, to ask you, whether you are *serious*?' 'Never more so,' replied Millar, 'in all my life; and I hope you will candidly acquit me of every intention to injure your feelings, or depreciate your abilities, when I repeat that I positively cannot afford you more than two hundred pounds for your novel.' 'Then, my good Sir,' said Fielding, recovering himself from this unexpected stroke of fortune, 'give me your hand; the book is yours.'[2]

The details of the anecdote are suspiciously elaborate, but the story itself may well be faithful, essentially, to the facts. Although no evidence that Fielding knew Thomson personally has survived, their acquaintance is not unlikely: for one thing, both writers had been active in the literary opposition to Walpole; for another, Fielding's unusually ardent praise of Thomson's poetry, though it occurs some years later in *The Jacobite's Journal* (4 June

---

[1] The story, mistakenly told of *Tom Jones*, may be found in Charles F. Partington, *The British Cyclopædia of Biography* (London, 1837), i. 706. As Frederick Lawrence long ago pointed out, the circumstances, if true at all, could relate only to the sale of *Joseph Andrews*. (*The Life of Henry Fielding* [London, 1855], p. 164 n.)

[2] Partington, i. 706.

1748), suggests the puffing of a friend more than the cool judgement of a critic. The amount of the bargain, as we shall see, is close to the actual figure. Even the statement that, in accepting the book, Millar acted upon the advice of his wife squares with what seems to have been his usual practice.[1]

However doubtful this story may be, it is certain that arrangements for publishing *Joseph Andrews* had been completed by early January 1742, for, according to an announcement in *The Champion*, the novel was 'In the Press' on the 12th of that month.[2] An item in the ledger of Henry Woodfall the elder, to whom Millar assigned the printing of the first two editions, reveals that 1,500 sets of the novel, perhaps briefly delayed owing to 'alterations' that Fielding appears to have made in press, had been run off by mid-February:

> Feb. 15, 1741/2. History of the Adventures of Joseph Andrews, &c., 12mo., in 2 vols., No. 1500, with alterations.[3]

Heralded by advertisements in the newspapers, the first edition '(*In two neat Pocket Volumes, Price bound 6s.*)' reached the bookstalls a week later, on Monday, 22 February.[4] Fielding's name did not appear on the title-page until the third edition, but his authorship, as well as the nature of his subject, was an open secret even before the novel had been officially issued. As far away as Bath, Dr. George Cheyne had heard the news and wrote to Richardson requesting that a copy of the book be sent to him: 'I beg as soon as you get Fieldings Joseph Andrews, I fear in Ridicule of your Pamela and of Virtue in the Notion of Don Quixotes Manner, you would send it me by the very first Coach

---

[1] Professor McKillop has called my attention to the entry for 13 June 1773 in *James Beattie's London Diary 1773*, ed. Ralph S. Walker (Aberdeen, 1946), where Mrs. Millar, after Thomson's death, is said to have made her husband exclude from a new edition of *The Seasons* several corrections and revisions which the poet himself had made in collaboration with Lyttelton. Mrs. Millar declared 'that she preferred the old expressions to the new ones. The old were accordingly retained, and the corrections unhappily lost; for Miller durst not contradict his wife in any thing' (p. 53).

[2] *The Champion*, 12 January 1741/2. Similar advertisements appeared in *The Daily Post* for 23, 25, 26 January and in *The London Evening-Post* for 23–26 January.

[3] P. T. P., 'Woodfall's Ledger, 1734–1747', *N & Q*, 1st ser., xi (2 June 1855), 419.

[4] Advertisements promising the publication of the first edition on Monday, 22 February 1742, were carried in *The Champion* (11, 13, 16, 18, 20 February) and in *The Daily Post* (11, 12, 13, 15, 16, 17 February). The novel was duly announced in *The Daily Post* for 22 February as published that day; *The Champion*, which was not issued on Mondays, carried the notice on Tuesday the 23rd.

it is to be publish't the 22ᵈ and perhaps if your People be artful they may procure it of the Trade on Saturday and send it by the Monday's Coach for Bath.'[1] Dr. Cheyne's eagerness to have this best of all the anti-*Pamela*'s must have piqued his friend; it suggests, and subsequent events prove, that a considerable audience was waiting to share the laugh on Richardson and to judge for themselves the merits of Fielding's 'new species of writing'.

The arrangements with Millar were doubtless roughly defined before *Joseph Andrews* went to press, but for some reason the formal assignment of the copyright was postponed until 13 April. On that date, in a document written throughout in his own hand, Fielding signed over to Millar all rights and titles to three very different works: namely, *A Full Vindication of the Dutchess Dowager of Marlborough*, *Miss Lucy in Town*, and *Joseph Andrews*. In return he received £199. 6s., which, as Millar's note on the back of the assignment indicates, was the sum of these individual payments: £5. 5s. for the pamphlet, £10. 10s. for the farce, and £183. 11s. for the novel. Once Fielding's reputation as a novelist had been established, Millar was to pay much more for *Tom Jones* (£600) and *Amelia* (£800–1,000); furthermore, there is no reason to believe that he later added a supplementary payment, as he appears to have done in the case of *Tom Jones* when the book proved popular. The amount paid for *Joseph Andrews* was nevertheless quite liberal for a first novel—indeed, about three times what Goldsmith probably received for *The Vicar of Wakefield* some twenty years later. Of the two witnesses to the sale, one, appropriately, was the Reverend Mr. William Young, the original of Parson Adams. Couched in the tautological legal jargon that Fielding loved to ridicule, the full text of the agreement is as follows:

Know all Men by these Presents that I Henry Fielding of the Middle Temple Esqʳ for and in Consideration of the Sum of one hundred ninety nine Pounds six Shillings of lawful Money of Great Britain to me in Hand paid by Andrew Millar of Sᵗ Clementˢ Danes in the Strand Bookseller, the Receipt whereof is hereby acknowledged, and of which I do acquit the said Andrew Millar his Execrs and Assigns have bargained sold delivered assigned and set over, and by these Pres[ents] do bargain sell deliver assign and set over all that my Title Right and Property in and to a certain Book

[1] In Alan D. McKillop, 'The Personal Relations between Fielding and Richardson', *MP*, xxviii (1931), 424–5.

printed in two Volumes known and called by the Name and Title of the History of the Adventures of Joseph Andrews and of his Friend Mr Abraham Adams written in Imitation of the Manner of Cervantes Author of Don Quixotte, and also in and to a certain Farce called by the Name of Miss Lucy in Town a Sequel to the Virgin unmasqued, and also in and to a certain Pamphlet called a full Vindication of the Dutchess Dowager of Marlborough [&c] with all Improvements, Additions or Alterations whatsoever which now are or hereafter shall at any time be made by me or any one else by my Authority to the said Book Farce or Pamphlet, to have and to hold the said bargained Premises unto the said Andrew Millar his Exrs Admrs or Assigns to the only proper Use and Behoof of the said Andrew Millar his Exrs Admrs or Assigns for ever, and I do hereby covenant and with the said Andrew Millar his Exrs Admrs and Assigns that I the said Henry Fielding the Author of the said bargained Premises have not at any time heretofore done committed or suffered any Act or thing whatsoever by means whereof the said bargained Premises or any Part thereof is or shall be impeached or incumbered in any wise and I the said Henry Fielding for myself my Exrs Admrs and Assigns shall warrant and defend the s^d bargained Premises f[or] ever against all Persons whatsoever claiming under me my Exrs Admrs or Assigns. In witness whereof I have hereunto set my Hand and Seal this 13 of April 1742.

Signed sealed and delivered by the
within named Hcn: Fielding the
Day and year within mentioned
in the Presence of   Wm Young   Hen. Fielding
                     Wm Hawkes   [Seal][1]

Although *Joseph Andrews* did not match the astonishing vogue of *Pamela*, it was none the less an immediate success. By May a second edition was called for, and Fielding, with the craftsman's wish to polish and perfect his work, began to revise the novel —correcting several inconsistencies in detail, smoothing syntax, filling out scenes and characters, sharpening his satire. Even though (if the terms of the agreement with Millar were strictly observed) he was not paid for his trouble, his revisions are nevertheless remarkably thorough, always shrewd. Missing from the novel as it first appeared were a number of its most humorous and skilful passages. Many features of the memorable figure of Parson Adams and of Mrs. Tow-wouse, as well as lively strokes in the depiction of almost every other major character, were lacking;

---

[1] Transcribed from the manuscript in the Forster Collection, the Victoria and Albert Museum, South Kensington.

long dramatic passages at the beginning and end of the central
narrative were as yet unwritten, leaving the opportunity of those
crucial structural positions unrealized; and ridicule of the clergy,
lawyers, and politicians was under-developed.[1] Fielding's first
readers found a book in many ways less finished, less effective,
than the one shortly to be published. The second edition of *Joseph
Andrews*—thus 'Revised and Corrected with *Alterations* and *Additions* by the AUTHOR'—was through the press by 31 May;
encouraged by the initial reception of the novel, Millar had increased by 500 the number of sets ordered. The entry in Woodfall's ledger reads:

> May 31, 1742. The 2nd edit. of Joseph Andrews, 12mo., No. 2000,
> 27 shts.[2]

According to *The Daily Post*, the second edition was published
on Thursday, 10 June,[3] the same day on which Millar entered
the work in the Stationers' Register.

Early in the following year Millar projected a third edition,
completely reset in smaller type and 'illustrated with CUTS' (that
is, twelve rather undistinguished copper plates) by James Hulett.
The title-page of this edition, the first to declare Fielding's authorship, is silent about any further revisions; but of the 186 new
substantive readings that occur, many are striking enough to
indicate that Fielding again retouched his work before allowing
it to go to press—this time, however, with nothing like the
thoroughness of his labours for the second edition. To illustrate
the nature of these changes, the following examples may serve,
each implying a knowledge of such matters as characterization
and narrative context that it is unreasonable to attribute to a
compositor, or even to some hypothetical printing-house editor:
thus, among other slight alterations of a passage in III. xii, Fielding underscores the hypocrisy of Peter Pounce by observing that
Parson Adams was respectful, not of the miser's 'Goodness', of

---

[1] For a full analysis of Fielding's changes in the second and subsequent editions, see
Battestin, 'Fielding's Revisions of *Joseph Andrews*', *Studies in Bibliography*, xvi (1963),
81–117.

[2] *N & Q*, 1st ser., xi (1855), 419.

[3] See also *The Daily Post* for 11, 12, 15 June; *The London Evening-Post* for 12–15 June;
and *The Universal Spectator, and Weekly Journal* for 17 July. The second edition was not
listed in *The Gentleman's Magazine* and *The London Magazine* until August; but, since
the edition was through Woodfall's press by 31 May, a date of publication in June is quite
likely.

which he has none at all, but rather of his 'seeming Goodness' (p. 270, l. 10); the incompetent and capricious Justice Trolick of editions 1–2 is now more appropriately named 'Frolick' (p. 285, l. 29); Pamela's vanity is further exposed when she is made to refer to herself as the 'Lady', rather than merely the 'Wife', of Squire Booby (p. 302, l. 35); and the substitution of the word 'Error' for the phrase 'mutual Deceit' eliminates a false impression that the confusion in the amorous combat between Mrs. Slipslop and Beau Didapper was somehow deliberate (p. 331, l. 12). It would, of course, be too much to say that Fielding was behind all the substantive changes that occur; a number suggest the compositorial variation normally to be expected in a reprint. That Fielding was responsible for somewhat more than half of the verbal changes is, however, equally clear. And this conclusion, based on the examination of the text itself, is further supported by the evidence of a unique series of advertisements carried more than two years later in Fielding's own *True Patriot*: notices in that journal describe the third edition as 'Revised and Corrected with Alterations and Additions by the Author'.[1]

Millar assigned the printing of the edition, as well as of the fourth and fifth, to William Strahan. Strahan's records reveal that the third edition, amounting to 3,000 sets, was through the press by 20 February 1743, at a cost to Millar of £45:

> February 20, 1743 For printing the Adventures of Joseph Andrews
> 20 Sheets Small Pica 12ᵐᵒ. Nº. 3000 @ £2: 5 p Sheet
>
> £   s   d
> 45/ /   [2]

The date of publication for this edition must remain approximate: although it is tempting to follow *The Daily Post*, which began advertising publication on Thursday, 24 March, conflicting notices in other newspapers place the time as early as Monday, 21 March, or as late as Monday, 28 March.[3]

---

[1] *The True Patriot*, 26 November and 3, 10, 24 December 1745.

[2] British Museum Add. MS. 48800. Millar paid the charges on 11 May 1744. For a discussion of Strahan's accounts as they relate to Fielding's works, see J. Paul de Castro, 'The Printing of Fielding's Works', *The Library*, 4th ser., i (1921), 257–70. De Castro, however, is sometimes inaccurate in citing Strahan's entries.

[3] During the week of Tuesday, 15 March, to Saturday, 19 March 1743, advertisements in *The General Evening Post* promised that the edition would be published 'On Monday next' (i.e. on 21 March); publication was accordingly announced in both *The General Evening*

The fact that three editions of *Joseph Andrews*, together amounting to 6,500 sets, were published in a little more than a year helps to measure the success of Fielding's first venture as a novelist. This supply was sufficient to meet the demands of the public for five years before a fourth edition of 2,000 copies, and later a fifth, again of 2,000 copies, were required. In June 1748 Strahan charged Millar £36 for 'Joseph Andrews, 20 Sheets Nº. 2000 @ £1 : 16 : p Sheet'. The nature of several of the substantive variants reveals that this edition, the fourth, was cursorily revised by Fielding, perhaps by means of a list of about twenty readings sent to the publisher for incorporation. This, indeed, is the last edition of *Joseph Andrews* that can be considered at all authoritative. Of the 120 new substantive readings, the great majority may be attributed to the compositor; a few, however, are clearly authorial. In the first of these, for instance, the addition of a word ('privately') prevents Adams from publicly decrying the ignorance of Sir Thomas Booby and others of the gentry (p. 23, l. 31); this slight change thus serves to distinguish the parson from such officious clergymen as Richardson's Arthur Williams, whose inability to keep the secrets of his superiors Fielding had ridiculed in *Shamela*. Although the same inconsistency was overlooked elsewhere in the novel (i. xv), another revision corrects from three to nine the number of those volumes of sermons which Adams intended to publish in London (p. 75, l. 25); a third prevents the usually good-natured Mr. Wilson from expressing too callously his relief at the death of a jealous mistress (p. 211, l. 30); a fourth more appropriately reveals the Christian emphasis of Adams's theoretical stoicism (p. 265, l. 16); a fifth, by the inclusion of one of Fielding's favourite descriptive words ('violent') and by the deletion of a superfluous article of clothing (since Adams has on 'neither Breeches nor Stockings' the earlier statement that he also lacked garters may have seemed redundant), serves to improve the vividness and economy of an amusing passage (p. 270, ll. 18–19). In comparison with his revision of the second, and even of the third,

---

Post and *The St. James Evening Post* (not published on Mondays) for Tuesday, 22 March–Thursday, 24 March. But the same pattern of advertisements was followed in *The London Daily Post, and General Advertiser* exactly one week later: the numbers for Friday and Saturday, 25 and 26 March, declare that the edition would be published 'On Monday next' (i.e. on 28 March), on which date publication is duly noticed.

edition, Fielding's changes here are, as one would suppose, not extensive; they amount to no more than one-sixth of the total number of new substantive readings. But in such passages as those considered above there are clear signs of an author's care. Corroborative evidence to this effect is found in the advertisements for the edition. Announcing publication on Saturday, 29 October 1748 (the title-page reads 1749), notices in *The General Advertiser* include this helpful statement, prominently displayed: '*The Fourth Edition. Revis'd and Corrected by the Author.*'[1]

Early in the following year, *Tom Jones* appeared. The enthusiastic reception of Fielding's masterpiece may well have stimulated renewed interest in his first novel, for a fifth edition of *Joseph Andrews*, the last to be published by Millar in Fielding's lifetime, was through the press in April 1751.[2] The entry in Strahan's ledgers is identical with that for the fourth edition: 'Joseph Andrews, 20 Sheets N°. 2000 @ £1: 16: p Sheet.' Millar withheld publication for some months, finally releasing the book simultaneously with *Amelia* on Thursday, 19 December.[3] Although, as the title-page states, this edition was also 'Revised and Corrected', the substantive changes here are far less frequent and striking and are almost certainly the work of the compositor. There is little reason to believe that Fielding authorized the few new readings that occur.[4]

Since it has already been told at length in Frederick T. Blanchard's exhaustive study,[5] there is no need to rehearse the story of the reception of *Joseph Andrews*. In view of the novel's history

[1] *The General Advertiser* carried notices of the edition both before and after, as well as on, the date of publication, 29 October 1748: see the numbers for 22, 24–29, 31 October, 1–5 November. Advertisements in *The London Evening-Post*, Tuesday–Saturday, 18–22 October, promised publication the following week and also stated that the work was '*Revis'd and Corrected by the* AUTHOR'. Fielding's paper, *The Jacobite's Journal*, did not advertise the edition until Saturday 5 November.

[2] De Castro misread the date in Strahan's ledger as April 1750. (See *The Library*, 4th ser., i [1921], 266, and the 'Bibliographical Note' to his edition of *Joseph Andrews* [1929].) Before his death Millar issued three other editions: the sixth in 1762, the year of Arthur Murphy's edition of Fielding's *Works*; the seventh in 1764; and the eighth in 1768.

[3] See *The General Advertiser*, 19 December 1751. Notice began in *The London Daily Advertiser* a day later.

[4] Only three of these readings seem to be improvements, and these could well be the result of a compositor's lucky misreading of the text (see Historical Collation, 61. 35, 180. 38, 247. 39).

[5] See *Fielding the Novelist: A Study in Historical Criticism* (Yale University Press: New Haven, 1927), pp. 1–25 and *passim*.

of publication, however, it would appear that Professor Blanchard, in evaluating his evidence, made rather too much of the indifference or hostility of Fielding's first readers. Besides the five authorized editions of *Joseph Andrews*, other editions appearing during Fielding's lifetime further suggest that, both in Great Britain and on the Continent, demand for the novel was keen. In October 1742 Sir Dudley Ryder had to be engaged (presumably by Millar) 'to rescue Jos. Andrews and Parson Adams out of the hands of pirates'.[1] But in Dublin, beyond the reach of the Copyright Law, unauthorized editions were printed in 1742 and 1747 for George Ewing, William Smith, and George Faulkner. Within a decade of its first appearance, moreover, *Joseph Andrews* had been rendered into French, German, Danish, and Italian.

The earliest of these foreign versions, based upon the third edition and published in 1743, includes an explanatory epistle by the translator, the Abbé des Fontaines.[2] This remarkable essay, too long neglected, stands as the first of many critical discussions of *Joseph Andrews*. Posing as an English lady writing to recommend the novel to a friend in France, the abbé compares Fielding's achievement to that of Cervantes and to the paintings of the Dutch school; he praises *l'honnêteté* of Fielding's images and style, his skill at dramatic dialogue, and his ability to create and to sustain memorable characters, Parson Adams in particular. Against those too fastidious readers who might be disposed to criticize the novel as 'low' and immoral, the abbé defends the didactic value of Fielding's situation by reference to the biblical account of Joseph and Potiphar's wife and its representation in Christian art. *Joseph Andrews*, he asserts, is 'un Livre le plus

---

[1] Quoted in Cross, i. 355. In the following year A. Merryman, printer of *All-Alive and Merry; or, The London Daily Post*, made a casual, and slovenly, attempt to reprint at least a portion of the novel: *All-Alive and Merry* for 20 April 1743 carries some 350 words relating to 'The History of Betty the Chambermaid' (*Joseph Andrews*, I. xvii–xviii). Since no excerpt from *Joseph Andrews* appears in Merryman's journal for 7 April (the only other extant number for 1743), it is clear that no attempt was made to serialize the entire novel. (See R. M. Wiles, *Serial Publication in England before 1750* [Cambridge University Press, 1957], pp. 49–50.)

[2] The title-page of this translation reads: *Les Avantures de Joseph Andrews, et du ministre Abraham Adams, publiées en Anglois, en 1742, par M. Feilding* [sic]*; et traduites en françois, à Londres, par une dame angloise, sur la troisiéme édition* (Londres, 1743). The epistle, entitled 'Lettre d'une dame angloise à Madame *** Maitresse des Comptes de Montpellier', was also included in later editions appearing in 1744 and 1750.

ingénieux & le plus agréable que notre Angleterre ait produit.
. . . Ce n'est point un Livre de simple amusement pour les gens
du monde: c'est un Livre de science & de morale familière, à la
portée de tout le monde, & de plus un Livre, où l'on puise la
connoissance de la manière dont on vit en Angleterre.'

What prevents us from accepting the abbé's remarks as typical
of contemporary reaction to *Joseph Andrews* is not so much his
delight in Fielding's performance as the subtlety and astuteness
of his critical judgements. Although Fielding in moments of
depression could complain that his works were ill received and
affect to despise the insubstantial favours of the Muse,[1] it seems
clear that his first published novel found a numerous and, for the
most part, an appreciative audience.

MARTIN C. BATTESTIN

[1] See Fielding's Preface to Sarah Fielding's *Adventures of David Simple*, 2nd ed. (1744).

TEXTUAL INTRODUCTION

THIS edition offers a critical unmodernized text of *Joseph Andrews*. The text is critical in that it has been established by the application of analytical criticism to the evidence of the various early documentary forms in which the novel appeared. It is unmodernized in that every effort has been made to present the text in as close a form to Fielding's own inscription and successive revisions as the surviving documents permit, subject to normal editorial regulation.

I. THE COPY-TEXT AND ITS TREATMENT

Since the formal assignment of copyright from Fielding to his publisher Millar is extant, no doubt can exist as to the authoritative nature of the manuscript of *Joseph Andrews* that was sent to the press. The first edition, therefore, was printed almost certainly from holograph and in that respect remains the only text with an overall authority. But as Dr. Battestin has shown, Fielding made a very thorough revision of this text in preparation for the second edition, which was set from a copy of the first edition that Fielding had annotated with the additions and alterations that he wished to appear. This second edition represents the only real reworking that Fielding gave to his novel. For the third edition he corrected or polished various readings by marking a copy of the revised second edition. Later he cursorily read over the third printing and made a very few minor alterations to send to the press as copy for the fourth edition. With this version of his text he apparently remained content; the variant readings that occur in the fifth edition, the last to appear in his lifetime, appear to have no authority.

In a situation of this sort textual critics recognize a double authority.[1] For an unmodernized edition the most authentic form of what are known as the 'accidentals' of a text—that is, the

---

[1] Sir Walter Greg, 'The Rationale of Copy-Text', *Studies in Bibliography*, iii (1950), 19–36, is the main authority. See also F. Bowers, 'Current Theories of Copy-Text, with an Illustration from Dryden', *Modern Philology*, xlviii (1950), 12–20; 'Established Texts and Definitive Editions', *Philological Quarterly*, xli (1962), 1–17; 'Textual Criticism', in *The Aims and Methods of Scholarship in Modern Languages and Literatures* (Modern Language Association of America, 1963), pp. 23–42.

spelling, punctuation, capitalization, word-division, and such typographical matters as the use of italicized words—can be transmitted only in the document that lies nearest to the lost holograph, that is, in the first edition, the one printing that was set direct from manuscript. An editor will understand that the first edition by no means represents a diplomatic reprint of the manuscript and that in many respects the accidentals are a mixture of the author's and the compositors'. But whatever the relative impurity, the first edition stands nearest to the author's own characteristics and represents the only authority in these matters that has been preserved for the texture in which his words were originally clothed. It may be remarked that Fielding was accustomed, as authors still are, to the styling of his work for the press; but since we must presume that he read proof for the first edition, he had the opportunity, if he chose, to alter any compositorial intervention that did not suit his convictions.

On the other hand, when he sent the marked-up pages of the first edition to the press as copy for the second printing, there is no evidence that in any major respect he altered the accidentals that had passed his scrutiny in the original proof sheets. The odds do not favour an author of the time tinkering extensively with the accidentals of printed copy so long as his meaning had not been altered as a result of house-styling, and all seemed reasonably in order. Thus despite the numerous authoritative changes that Fielding made in the words, or 'substantives', for the second edition, the few corrections or alterations in the styling that evidence suggests actually took place do not alter the fact that the vast majority of the changes in the accidentals represent merely the normal compositorial differences characteristic of reprints of the time.

In this respect, in the second edition the authority of the substantives and of the accidentals splits. Given the thoroughgoing nature of the literary revision, almost all of the changes in the words must be accepted as authorial, whereas almost all of the changes in the texture of the accidentals must be labelled as compositorial and hence unauthoritative. If this be so for the second edition, which Fielding looked over with particular care, the differentiation between the two authorities necessarily increases in the third edition, in which Fielding's alterations were markedly less extensive, and in the fourth edition wherein the authorial verbal changes were casual indeed. Under these circumstances Sir Walter Greg's classic theory of copy-text must hold. That is, a critical editor chooses as his copy-text—the basic authority for his old-spelling edition—that document which can be isolated as the supreme authority for the accidentals. In this respect, then, he comes as close as documentary evidence permits to the desirable reproduction of authorial characteristics in spelling, pointing, and the like. In this authoritative texture of the first edition, then, he inserts those verbal changes in later editions that in his estimate represent authorial correction or revision, and not compositorial variation and corruption. By this procedure an editor of *Joseph Andrews* substantially reproduces the marked copy that was given to the press for the second edition, which was in the main followed by the printer in respect to the wording but was casually varied in the accidentals. Successively thereafter he attempts to recover the markings in the second edition that served as printer's copy for the third, and then the markings in the third that served the printer for the fourth edition. This is a critical process almost exclusively in which the editor shoulders his proper responsibility to separate the author's intended alterations from the increasing verbal corruption that inevitably accompanies the transmission of a text through a series of reprints. Unfortunately, there is no short cut. The fourth edition, although it represents Fielding's final revision, cannot be the supreme authority for the substantives that the first edition represents for the accidentals. As the appendix Historical Collation demonstrates, Fielding's correction and casual revision of the third and fourth editions (probably without proof-reading) failed to remove a number of printer's errors that had entered the mainstream of his text—corruptions that, in the fourth edition at least, far outnumbered the authoritative changes that he made. Verbally, therefore, the fourth is the most untrustworthy of all the revised editions.

When the textual situation as in *Joseph Andrews* dictates this critical treatment of the copy-text, the main editorial problem centres on the identification of authorial revision. Here certain logical rules of textual criticism are of some assistance. That is, the part is always surveyed in relation to the whole so that the circumstances surrounding the production of any given edition can be used as evidence, or at least as suggesting a 'climate of opinion', when an individual reading is under scrutiny. For example, the careful and extensive revision of the second edition, as an entity, shifts the weight of critical opinion in favour of the altered readings. Since so many are manifestly authorial, the 'indifferent' variant is more likely to be the author's, too, than a compositorial corruption. This would be especially true if Fielding had read proof on the sheets of the second edition, although we have no evidence to support even speculation in this matter.

Dr. Battestin, therefore, has very properly admitted all substantive variants in the second edition as authorial save only recognizable printer's errors and such semi-orthographic variants as the change of 'farther' to 'further', or of 'thrashed' to 'threshed', which appear to be compositorial since they either contradict Fielding's known habits of diction or of style, or else fail to improve the sense. Since the critical editor acts as a judge in this editorial winnowing of evidence, it is proper to say that in *Joseph Andrews* all substantive variants in the second edition have been presumed to be innocent unless the editor to his satisfaction could prove them guilty as printer's corruption.

On the other hand, when in the third, and even more in the fourth, edition Fielding is concerned with relatively minor matters of style or of correction, and even these chiefly in isolated cases, the editorial climate of opinion necessarily shifts with the evidence. The verbal variants grow increasingly 'indifferent' and more and more suspicious, on the whole, and the clear evidence for authorial intervention that had characterized the majority of the second-edition changes is increasingly wanting. Under these conditions, which more and more parallel the nature of the variants in the demonstrably unauthoritative posthumous Murphy edition, the editorial judgement alters in its point of view. A variant in the third and, especially, in the fourth edition must show cause why it should be accepted, and therefore must pass a more stringent test of authority than is necessary or advisable in the largely revised second edition. Dr. Battestin, as a consequence, has rejected the majority of the indifferent variant readings in the third and fourth editions and has concentrated on those few that offer positive evidence that they are authorial. To be accepted, a variant must successfully pass certain tests of probability. Is the change consistent with Fielding's usual practice? Without suggesting the sophistication of printing-house editor or compositor, does it improve the syntax, style, or sense? Does it in any way enhance the narrative or the description? These critical tests may perhaps have excluded a handful of Fielding's changes for which adequate reasons were hard to find, but they have successfully barred from the present attempt at an established text what is surely the vast majority of printing-house errors, whether of inadvertence or of sophistication, that demonstrably plague the later transmission in print of any text, and which in *Joseph Andrews* cannot be imputed to Fielding's authority. The Wesleyan edition, therefore, offers an eclectic text that in its representation of the author's final intentions for his novel is as pure as the logic of textual criticism and the intimate acquaintance of its editor with the substance and expression of Fielding's thought can produce.

As the final operation in the recovery of this Fielding text and its presentation in critical form, Dr. Battestin has altered the accidentals of the first edition, on the authority of the second, third, or fourth, in any case in which it seemed likely that Fielding had made the change, or in which—although the agent could scarcely be determined—the change seemed desirable as restoring Fielding's general stylistic habits. These changes have been made cautiously and in some small part with the convenience of the reader in view when marked anomalies might have distracted the attention. Correspondingly, on his own authority the editor has made a few alterations to remove patent error or striking inconsistency which had been allowed to stand in these editions, so long as the changes conformed to Fielding's usual characteristics or to the standards of the copy-text itself. In this process Dr. Battestin has not tried to achieve an unnatural consistency in spelling, capitalization, or punctuation: wanting the manuscript, no editor could determine whether the compositor(s) or Fielding himself was responsible for the casual variation that is normal in the period. However, with four exceptions (p. 61, l. 35, p. 131, l. 2, p. 174, l. 7, p. 180, l. 38) the editor did not find it necessary to emend any substantive reading in the copy-text except by the progressively rigorous choice of authority from among the variants of the three succeeding revised editions.

With few exceptions, all accidental as well as all substantive alterations have been recorded in the textual apparatus so that a critic may reconstruct the copy-text in detail as well as the substantive variation from it in the second, third, fourth, and fifth editions. However, in a few purely formal matters the following editorial changes have been made silently. (1) Typographical errors such as turned letters or wrong fount are not recorded, and (2) the small capitals that in the original begin each paragraph have been ignored. (3) The running quotation marks in the left margin have been omitted and quotations have been indicated according to the modern custom. Throughout, necessary opening or closing quotation marks in dialogue have been supplied silently. (4) The placement of punctuation in relation to quotation marks, chiefly in dialogue, has been normalized according to the common practice of the copy-text. (5) Simple arabic numbers have been spelled out and such abbreviations as 'Chap.' for 'Chapter' and the conventional ampersand have been expanded. (6) When the apostrophe and roman 's' follows an italicized name, the roman is retained only when it indicates the contraction for 'is' but is normalized to italic when the possessive case is required. (7) The fount of punctuation is normalized without regard for the variable practice of the original. Pointing within an italic passage is italicized; but pointing following an italicized word that is succeeded by roman text is silently placed in roman. (8) In this novel Fielding sometimes identifies his speakers within round brackets in the midst of quoted speech, as ' "To your Invention rather, (said the Doctor) your Memory will be . . .".' Although his usual practice is represented in this example, he occasionally adds quotation marks, as in ' "To your Invention rather," (said the Doctor) "your Memory will be . . .".' Such intrusive quotation marks, by the standards of this text, have been silently removed. (9) Fielding frequently treated indirect quotations as if they were direct, and introduced such passages sometimes with a capital but more frequently with a lower-case letter. In this edition all such quotations are silently normalized to lower case, as in 'and told the Coachman, "he was certain there was a *dead* Man . . .".'

2. THE APPARATUS

All the textual apparatus is placed in appendixes where it may be consulted at leisure by those who wish to analyse the total evidence on which the present text has been established. In the first appears the List of Substantive Emendations. All verbal variation has been recorded here, but to the substantives have been added some examples of variant readings in the accidentals when these have influenced meaning in a semi-substantive manner. Since the purpose of this list is to present at a view the major editorial departures from the copy-text first edition, only the earliest source of the approved variant is recorded together with the history of the copy-text reading up to its accepted emendation in the earliest source. The subsequent history of the variant will be found in the Historical Collation. As early sources of emendation, only the authoritative second, third, and fourth editions are listed (except for two necessary corrections drawn from the unauthoritative fifth edition). Two other emendations are assigned to W, representing the present edition, whether or not they actually originated here or with some preceding editor. By their nature they cannot be authoritative, even though they have proved to be necessary, and hence a more precise record would serve little purpose, especially since little independent emendation has proved necessary in the substantives themselves. The basic note provides, first, the page—line reference and the precise form of the emended reading in the present text. Following the square bracket appears the identification of the earliest source of the emendation in the editions collated. A semicolon succeeds this notation, and following this appears the rejected copy-text reading with the sigla of the editions that provide its history up to the point of emendation. In these notations certain arbitrary symbols appear. When the variant to be noted is one of punctuation, a wavy dash ~ takes the place of the repeated word associated with the pointing. An inferior caret ₐ calls attention to the absence of punctuation either in the copy-text or in the early edition from which the alteration was drawn. Three dots indicate one or more omitted words in a series.

The List of Accidentals Emendations follows on the record of substantive and semi-substantive emendation, and conforms to the same rules. The list includes all changes made in the copy-text except for those described as silently normalized. A list of word-divisions holds information about hyphenated compounds that will lead to an accurate reconstruction of the copy-text from the modern print. The reader may take it that any word hyphenated at the end of a line in the present text has been broken by the modern printer and that the hyphenation was not present in the copy-text unless it is separately listed and confirmed here.

Correspondingly, when a word is hyphenated at the end of the line in the copy-text, the editor has been charged with ascertaining whether it is a true hyphenated compound or else an unhyphenated word that has been broken; if the former, an entry will be found in this list noting the fact that a hyphenated word within the line of the present edition was broken and hyphenated at the line-ending in the copy-text. Although certain of the editorial decisions in the matter of these compounds approach the level of emendation, no record has been made of their treatment in editions other than the copy-text.

In all entries in the accidentals list, the forms of the accidentals to the right as well as to the left of the bracket accord with the system of silent normalization adopted for the edited text. Moreover, no record is made of variation in the accidentals that is not the matter being recorded. That is, if a punctuation variant alone is in question, the lemma of the word to which the pointing refers will take the form of the accidentals of the copy-text regardless of the spelling or capitalization of the word in the edition from which the punctuation variant was drawn. In this respect, then, the wavy dash to the right of the bracket signifies only the substantive and not its accidentals form in any edition other than the copy-text.

The Historical Collation of readings is keyed to the present edited text, not to the precise readings of the first-edition copy-text, and is confined to the variants in the five editions published during Fielding's lifetime. This collation contains (1) all rejected first-edition substantive and semi-substantive readings listed in the first or substantive appendix, with the record of variation carried through the fifth edition and, if necessary, to the present text. (2) All rejected substantive variants in the second, third, fourth, and fifth editions. (3) All rejected semi-substantive variants in the second, third, fourth, and fifth editions that have an important effect on the meaning comparable to that of a verbal change. In this Historical Collation the reading of an edition is to be taken as agreeing with that of the present text, to the left of the bracket, unless a variant is specifically recorded for it following the bracket. The accidentals of the word to the left of the bracket are those of the edition from which it was drawn. To the right of the bracket the accidentals will be those of the earliest edition noted; variation in the accidentals of later editions from this are not recorded.

3. COLLATION

In his preparation of the present text Dr. Battestin collated the following copies of the first edition: British Museum (C. 95. a. 6), Bodleian Library (Don. f. 191), Princeton University Library, and the University of Virginia Library. In the last, gathering D of the first volume is from the second edition. For the second edition, British Museum (635. c. 9) provided the basic text, but its variants from the copy-text that have been recorded were checked against the Princeton University Library copy and Dr. Battestin's own. The third-edition copy used for collation was British Museum (12612. ccc. 1) checked against the copies in the libraries of Princeton and of Yale Universities. The fourth edition was British Museum (12612. cc. 14) checked against the Yale copy. The unauthoritative fifth edition was collated in British Museum (12614. b. 24) checked against the Yale copy. The Murphy edition had its octavo in the Fielding Collection of Yale University collated against the copy of the quarto in the University of Virginia Library. No press-variants were discovered in the four collated copies of the first edition.

FREDSON BOWERS

THE
HISTORY
OF THE
ADVENTURES
OF
JOSEPH ANDREWS,
And of his FRIEND
Mr. *ABRAHAM ADAMS.*

Written in Imitation of
The *Manner* of CERVANTES,
Author of *Don Quixote.*

IN TWO VOLUMES.

VOL. I.

LONDON:
Printed for A. MILLAR, over-againſt
St. Clement's Church, in the *Strand.*
M.DCC.XLII.

PREFACE

As it is possible the mere *English* Reader may have a different Idea of Romance with the Author of these little Volumes;[1] and may consequently expect a kind of Entertainment, not to be found, nor which was even intended, in the following Pages; it may not be improper to premise a few Words concerning this kind of Writing, which I do not remember to have seen hitherto attempted in our Language.

The EPIC as well as the DRAMA is divided into Tragedy and Comedy. *Homer*, who was the Father of this Species of Poetry, gave us a Pattern of both these,[2] tho' that of the latter kind is entirely lost; which *Aristotle* tells us,[3] bore the same relation to Comedy which his *Iliad* bears to Tragedy. And perhaps, that we have no more Instances of it among the Writers of Antiquity, is owing to the Loss of this great Pattern, which, had it survived, would have found its Imitators equally with the other Poems of this great Original.

And farther, as this Poetry may be Tragic or Comic, I will not scruple to say it may be likewise either in Verse or Prose: for tho' it wants one particular, which the Critic enumerates in the constituent Parts of an Epic Poem, namely Metre; yet, when any kind of Writing contains all its other Parts, such as Fable, Action, Characters, Sentiments, and Diction, and is deficient in Metre only; it seems, I think, reasonable to refer it to the Epic; at least, as no Critic hath thought proper to range it under any other Head, nor to assign it a particular Name to itself.

Thus the *Telemachus*[4] of the Arch-Bishop of *Cambray* appears to me of the Epic Kind, as well as the *Odyssey* of *Homer*; indeed, it is much fairer and more reasonable to give it a Name common with that Species from which it differs only in a single Instance, than to confound it with those which it resembles in no other.

[1] *Joseph Andrews* was originally published in two volumes.

[2] The *Margites*, a satirical epic having a fool (*margos*) as hero, was attributed to Homer by both Aristotle and Zeno.

[3] *Poetics*, iv. 12. (References to the *Poetics* are to the Loeb Classical Library translation [London, 1927].)

[4] *Les Avantures de Télémaque fils d'Ulysse* (1699), a popular prose epic having as its theme the education of a prince, was written by the French theologian, François de Salignac de la Mothe-Fénelon (1651–1715). Fénelon was named Archbishop of Cambrai in 1695.

Such are those voluminous Works commonly called *Romances*, namely, *Clelia*, *Cleopatra*, *Astræa*, *Cassandra*, the *Grand Cyrus*,[1] and innumerable others which contain, as I apprehend, very little Instruction or Entertainment.

Now a comic Romance is a comic Epic-Poem in Prose; differing from Comedy, as the serious Epic from Tragedy: its Action being more extended and comprehensive; containing a much larger Circle of Incidents, and introducing a greater Variety of Characters. It differs from the serious Romance in its Fable and Action, in this; that as in the one these are grave and solemn, so in the other they are light and ridiculous: it differs in its Characters, by introducing Persons of inferiour Rank, and consequently of inferiour Manners, whereas the grave Romance, sets the highest before us; lastly in its Sentiments and Diction, by preserving the Ludicrous instead of the Sublime. In the Diction I think, Burlesque itself may be sometimes admitted; of which many Instances will occur in this Work, as in the Descriptions of the Battles, and some other Places, not necessary to be pointed out to the Classical Reader; for whose Entertainment those Parodies or Burlesque Imitations are chiefly calculated.

But tho' we have sometimes admitted this in our Diction, we have carefully excluded it from our Sentiments and Characters: for there it is never properly introduced, unless in Writings of the Burlesque kind, which this is not intended to be. Indeed, no two Species of Writing can differ more widely than the Comic and the Burlesque: for as the latter is ever the Exhibition of what is monstrous and unnatural, and where our Delight, if we examine it, arises from the surprizing Absurdity, as in appropriating the Manners of the highest to the lowest, or *è converso*; so in the former, we should ever confine ourselves strictly to Nature from the just Imitation of which, will flow all the Pleasure we can this way convey to a sensible Reader. And perhaps, there is one Reason, why a Comic Writer should of all others be the least excused for deviating from Nature, since it may not be always so easy

---

1 These voluminous French romances were translated into English during the seventeenth century by John Davies, Sir Charles Cotterel, and others, and were very much in vogue; Mr. Spectator discovered them in the library of the fashionable Leonora (*Spectator*, no. 37 [12 April 1711]). *Astrée*, the several parts of which were issued 1607–28, is by Honoré d'Urfé (1567–1625); *Cassandre* (1644–50) in 10 vols. and *Cléopâtre* (1647–56) in 12 vols. are by Gauthier de Costes de la Calprenède (1614–63); *Clélie* (1654–60) and *Artamène, ou le Grand Cyrus* (1649–53), both in 10 vols., are by Mlle Madeleine de Scudéry (1607–1701).

for a serious Poet to meet with the Great and the Admirable; but Life every where furnishes an accurate Observer with the Ridiculous.

I have hinted this little, concerning Burlesque; because, I have often heard that Name given to Performances, which have been truly of the Comic kind, from the Author's having sometimes admitted it in his Diction only; which as it is the Dress of Poetry, doth like the Dress of Men establish Characters, (the one of the whole Poem, and the other of the whole Man,) in vulgar Opinion, beyond any of their greater Excellencies: But surely, a certain Drollery in Style, where the Characters and Sentiments are perfectly natural, no more constitutes the Burlesque, than an empty Pomp and Dignity of Words, where every thing else is mean and low, can entitle any Performance to the Appellation of the true Sublime.

And I apprehend, my Lord *Shaftesbury's* Opinion of mere Burlesque[1] agrees with mine, when he asserts, 'There is no such Thing to be found in the Writings of the Antients.' But perhaps, I have less Abhorrence than he professes for it: and that not because I have had some little Success on the Stage this way;[2] but rather, as it contributes more to exquisite Mirth and Laughter than any other; and these are probably more wholesome Physic for the Mind, and conduce better to purge away Spleen, Melancholy and ill Affections, than is generally imagined. Nay, I will appeal to common Observation, whether the same Companies are not found more full of Good-Humour and Benevolence, after they have been sweeten'd for two or three Hours with Entertainments of this kind, than when soured by a Tragedy or a grave Lecture.

[1] Anthony Ashley Cooper, third Earl of Shaftesbury (1671–1713). In Part I, Section 4, of *Sensus Communis: An Essay on the Freedom of Wit and Humour* (first published in 1709 and later included in the *Characteristics* [1711]), Shaftesbury remarks that buffoonery and burlesque flourish best in those countries where tyranny prohibits the free expression of serious thought; thus the Italians surpass the English in ridicule and raillery. In Section 5 he continues: ' 'Tis for this reason, I verily believe, that the Antients discover so little of this Spirit, and that there is hardly such a thing found as mere *Burlesque* in any Authors of the politer Ages' (5th ed. [1732], i. 73).

[2] Fielding's burlesque dramas include *Tom Thumb* (1730), *The Covent-Garden Tragedy* (1732), and *Tumble-Down Dick; or, Phaeton in the Suds* (1736). The first of these, a brilliant travesty of heroic tragedy, had an initial run of 'upwards of Forty Nights, to the politest Audiences'. (Preface to *The Tragedy of Tragedies; or, The Life and Death of Tom Thumb the Great* [1731].)

But to illustrate all this by another Science, in which, perhaps, we shall see the Distinction more clearly and plainly: Let us examine the Works of a Comic History-Painter, with those Performances which the *Italians* call *Caricatura*; where we shall find the true Excellence of the former, to consist in the exactest copying of Nature; insomuch, that a judicious Eye instantly rejects any thing *outré*; any Liberty which the Painter hath taken with the Features of that *Alma Mater*.—Whereas in the *Caricatura* we allow all Licence. Its Aim is to exhibit Monsters, not Men; and all Distortions and Exaggerations whatever are within its proper Province.

Now what *Caricatura* is in Painting, Burlesque is in Writing; and in the same manner the Comic Writer and Painter correlate to each other. And here I shall observe, that as in the former, the Painter seems to have the Advantage; so it is in the latter infinitely on the side of the Writer: for the *Monstrous* is much easier to paint than describe, and the *Ridiculous* to describe than paint.

And tho' perhaps this latter Species doth not in either Science so strongly affect and agitate the Muscles as the other; yet it will be owned, I believe, that a more rational and useful Pleasure arises to us from it. He who should call the Ingenious *Hogarth*[1] a Burlesque Painter, would, in my Opinion, do him very little Honour: for sure it is much easier, much less the Subject of Admiration, to paint a Man with a Nose, or any other Feature of a preposterous

---

[1] Fielding's good friend, William Hogarth (1697–1764), is the 'History-Painter' to whose work Fielding refers in distinguishing between comic art and caricature. Hogarth himself illustrated the difference in *Characters and Caricaturas* (1743), and returned Fielding's compliment with this advice to the curious: '*For a farther explanation of the difference betwixt* "Character *and* Caricatura, *see* y^e *Preface to* Jo^h *Andrews.*" ' (John Ireland, *A Supplement to Hogarth Illustrated* [1798], p. 342.) Fielding's great admiration for Hogarth's work may be seen in this passage from *The Champion*, 10 June 1740: 'I esteem the ingenious Mr. *Hogarth* as one of the most useful Satyrists any Age hath produced. In his excellent Works you see the delusive Scene exposed with all the Force of Humour, and, on casting your Eyes on another Picture, you behold the dreadful and fatal Consequence. I almost dare affirm that those two Works of his, which he calls the *Rake's* and the *Harlot's Progress*, are calculated more to serve the Cause of Virtue, and for the Preservation of Mankind, than all the *Folio's* of Morality which have been ever written; and a sober Family should no more be without them, than without the *Whole Duty of Man* in their House.' In *Tom Jones* Fielding directs his readers to specific paintings by Hogarth to clarify the description of Bridget Allworthy (I. xi), Mrs. Partridge (II. iii), and Thwackum (III. vi). Other complimentary references to Hogarth or his works occur in *The Vernoniad*, *An Essay on Conversation*, *Amelia*, *The Covent-Garden Journal*, and *The Journal of a Voyage to Lisbon*. Appropriately, it is to Hogarth that we owe the only known portrait of Fielding, drawn as the frontispiece to Arthur Murphy's edition of the *Works* (1762).

Size, or to expose him in some absurd or monstrous Attitude, than to express the Affections of Men on Canvas. It hath been thought a vast Commendation of a Painter, to say his Figures *seem to breathe*; but surely, it is a much greater and nobler Applause, *that they appear to think*.

But to return—The Ridiculous only, as I have before said, falls within my Province in the present Work.—Nor will some Explanation of this Word be thought impertinent by the Reader, if he considers how wonderfully it hath been mistaken, even by Writers who have profess'd it: for to what but such a Mistake, can we attribute the many Attempts to ridicule the blackest Villanies; and what is yet worse, the most dreadful Calamities? What could exceed the Absurdity of an Author, who should write *the Comedy of* Nero, *with the merry Incident of ripping up his Mother's Belly*;[1] or what would give a greater Shock to Humanity, than an Attempt to expose the Miseries of Poverty and Distress to Ridicule? And yet, the Reader will not want much Learning to suggest such Instances to himself.

Besides, it may seem remarkable, that *Aristotle*, who is so fond and free of Definitions, hath not thought proper to define the Ridiculous. Indeed, where he tells us it is proper to Comedy, he hath remarked that Villany is not its Object:[2] but he hath not, as I remember, positively asserted what is. Nor doth the *Abbé Bellegarde*, who hath writ a Treatise on this Subject,[3] tho' he shews us many Species of it, once trace it to its Fountain.

The only Source of the true Ridiculous (as it appears to me) is Affectation.[4] But tho' it arises from one Spring only, when we

---

[1] In A.D. 59 Nero (A.D. 37–68) ordered the assassination of his mother Agrippina, who, in a gesture of repudiation of her son, preferred her womb to the sword and was stabbed to death. (See Tacitus, *Annals*, XIII. 8.) In *The Jacobite's Journal* (26 March 1748) Fielding used the same illustration in declaring his intention to abandon ridicule as a weapon against the Jacobites who were trying to overthrow the government: 'To consider such Attempts as these in a ludicrous Light, would be as absurd as the Conceit of a Fellow in *Bartholomew-Fair*, who exhibited the comical Humours of *Nero* ripping up his Mother's Belly. . . .'

[2] *Poetics*, v. 1–2.

[3] *Reflexions sur le ridicule, et sur les moyens de l'éviter* (1696) by Jean Baptiste Morvan de Bellegarde (1648–1734). Affectation, vanity, and imposture are among the varieties of ridiculous behaviour which the Abbé Bellegarde warns his readers to avoid. When Fielding resumed discussion of this subject in *The Covent-Garden Journal* (18 and 25 July 1752), he praised 'the judicious Abbé Bellegarde' and earnestly recommended his 'excellent Lessons on the Ridiculous'.

[4] Though he seems to imply as much, Fielding is by no means the first, even among his more immediate contemporaries, to analyse the Ridiculous. To mention only two of many

consider the infinite Streams into which this one branches, we shall presently cease to admire at the copious Field it affords to an Observer. Now Affectation proceeds from one of these two Causes, Vanity, or Hypocrisy: for as Vanity puts us on affecting false Characters, in order to purchase Applause; so Hypocrisy sets us on an Endeavour to avoid Censure by concealing our Vices under an Appearance of their opposite Virtues. And tho' these two Causes are often confounded, (for there is some Difficulty in distinguishing them) yet, as they proceed from very different Motives, so they are as clearly distinct in their Operations: for indeed, the Affectation which arises from Vanity is nearer to Truth than the other; as it hath not that violent Repugnancy of Nature to struggle with, which that of the Hypocrite hath. It may be likewise noted, that Affectation doth not imply an absolute Negation of those Qualities which are affected: and therefore, tho', when it proceeds from Hypocrisy, it be nearly allied to Deceit; yet when it comes from Vanity only, it partakes of the Nature of Ostentation: for instance, the Affectation of Liberality in a vain Man, differs visibly from the same Affectation in the Avaricious; for tho' the vain Man is not what he would appear, or hath not the Virtue he affects, to the degree he would be thought to have it; yet it sits less aukwardly on him than on the avaricious Man, who *is* the very Reverse of what he would *seem* to be.

From the Discovery of this Affectation arises the Ridiculous— which always strikes the Reader with Surprize and Pleasure; and that in a higher and stronger Degree when the Affectation arises

precursors: 'A Dissertation upon Laughter' had appeared anonymously in *The Publick Register: or, The Weekly Magazine, etc.* during January 1741, in which we are said to laugh because of the incongruity between our expectations of how a person will behave and his actual behaviour; earlier, in two essays in *Common Sense* (3 and 10 September 1737), the writer—whom at least one scholar wished to identify with Fielding because of the similarity of their views (see Cross, i. 334)—follows La Rochefoucauld in tracing the Ridiculous to its causes in affectation and vanity (but not in hypocrisy, which is said to provoke indignation rather than amusement).

Fielding himself had attempted to locate the sources of the Ridiculous before he wrote the Preface, and he returned to the subject more than once. In *The Champion* (15 April 1740) he stated that 'Vanity is the true Source of Ridicule,' and in the leader for 20 November 1739 he had found much ridiculous behaviour to arise from a common vice, hypocrisy. Toward the end of his career he devoted space in *The Covent-Garden Journal* to a fresh consideration of the subject: at this time he attributed the Ridiculous to the triumph of 'Humour' over good-breeding, which is in turn simply the observance of 'the most golden of all Rules' (18 July 1752); and, he continued, one of the chief reasons for such behaviour is the lack of proper methods of education (25 July 1752).

from Hypocrisy, than when from Vanity: for to discover any one to be the exact Reverse of what he affects, is more surprizing, and consequently more ridiculous, than to find him a little deficient in the Quality he desires the Reputation of. I might observe that our *Ben Johnson*,[1] who of all Men understood the *Ridiculous* the best, hath chiefly used the hypocritical Affectation.

Now from Affectation only, the Misfortunes and Calamities of Life, or the Imperfections of Nature, may become the Objects of Ridicule. Surely he hath a very ill-framed Mind, who can look on Ugliness, Infirmity, or Poverty, as ridiculous in themselves: nor do I believe any Man living who meets a dirty Fellow riding through the Streets in a Cart, is struck with an Idea of the Ridiculous from it; but if he should see the same Figure descend from his Coach and Six, or bolt from his Chair with his Hat under his Arm, he would then begin to laugh, and with justice. In the same manner, were we to enter a poor House, and behold a wretched Family shivering with Cold and languishing with Hunger, it would not incline us to Laughter, (at least we must have very diabolical Natures, if it would:) but should we discover there a Grate, instead of Coals, adorned with Flowers, empty Plate or China Dishes on the Side-board, or any other Affectation of Riches and Finery either on their Persons or in their Furniture; we might then indeed be excused, for ridiculing so fantastical an Appearance. Much less are natural Imperfections the Objects of Derision: but when Ugliness aims at the Applause of Beauty, or Lameness endeavours to display Agility; it is then that these unfortunate Circumstances, which at first moved our Compassion, tend only to raise our Mirth.[2]

The Poet[3] carries this very far;

> *None are for being what they are in Fault,*
> *But for not being what they would be thought.*

---

[1] Fielding greatly admired Ben Jonson (1572–1637). In stating his later view that humours are the source of the Ridiculous, Fielding quotes at length from a relevant passage in *Every Man Out of His Humour* (*Covent-Garden Journal*, 18 July 1752).

[2] Cf. the first of William Wycherly's 'Maxims and Moral Reflections' in *Posthumous Works* (1728), p. 9: 'OUR Natural Imperfections are never more our Shame, than when by Art we endeavour to hide them, or improve them into Perfections: For we are pitied, while we go lame because we can't help it; but laugh'd at for pretending to dance, when we are oblig'd to hobble.'

[3] William Congreve (1670–1729). The verses are from his poem, 'Of Pleasing; An Epistle to Sir Richard Temple', ll. 63–64.

Where if the Metre would suffer the Word *Ridiculous* to close the first Line, the Thought would be rather more proper. Great Vices are the proper Objects of our Detestation, smaller Faults of our Pity: but Affectation appears to me the only true Source of the Ridiculous.

But perhaps it may be objected to me, that I have against my own Rules introduced Vices, and of a very black Kind into this Work. To which I shall answer: First, that it is very difficult to pursue a Series of human Actions and keep clear from them. Secondly, That the Vices to be found here, are rather the accidental Consequences of some human Frailty, or Foible, than Causes habitually existing in the Mind. Thirdly, That they are never set forth as the Objects of Ridicule but Detestation. Fourthly, That they are never the principal Figure at that Time on the Scene; and lastly, they never produce the intended Evil.

Having thus distinguished *Joseph Andrews* from the Productions of Romance Writers on the one hand, and Burlesque Writers on the other, and given some few very short Hints (for I intended no more) of this Species of writing, which I have affirmed to be hitherto unattempted in our Language; I shall leave to my good-natur'd Reader to apply my Piece to my Observations, and will detain him no longer than with a Word concerning the Characters in this Work.

And here I solemnly protest, I have no Intention to vilify or asperse any one: for tho' every thing is copied from the Book of Nature, and scarce a Character or Action produced which I have not taken from my own Observations and Experience, yet I have used the utmost Care to obscure the Persons by such different Circumstances, Degrees, and Colours, that it will be impossible to guess at them with any degree of Certainty; and if it ever happens otherwise, it is only where the Failure characterized is so minute, that it is a Foible only which the Party himself may laugh at as well as any other.

As to the Character of *Adams*, as it is the most glaring in the whole, so I conceive it is not to be found in any Book now extant. It is designed a Character of perfect Simplicity; and as the Goodness of his Heart will recommend him to the Good-natur'd; so I hope it will excuse me to the Gentlemen of his Cloth; for whom, while they are worthy of their sacred Order, no Man can possibly have a greater Respect. They will therefore excuse me, notwith-standing the low Adventures in which he is engaged, that I have made him a Clergyman; since no other Office could have given him so many Opportunities of displaying his worthy Inclinations.

CONTENTS

BOOK I

BOOK II

BOOK III

BOOK IV

The History of the Adventures of
JOSEPH ANDREWS,
and of his Friend Mr. *Abraham Adams*

BOOK I

CHAPTER I

Of writing Lives in general, and particularly of Pamela; *with a Word by the bye of* Colley Cibber *and others.*

IT is a trite but true Observation, that Examples work more forcibly on the Mind than Precepts: And if this be just in what is odious and blameable, it is more strongly so in what is amiable and praise-worthy. Here Emulation most effectually operates upon us, and inspires our Imitation in an irresistible manner. A good Man therefore is a standing Lesson to all his Acquaintance, and of far greater use in that narrow Circle than a good Book.

But as it often happens that the best Men are but little known, and consequently cannot extend the Usefulness of their Examples a great way; the Writer may be called in aid to spread their History farther, and to present the amiable Pictures to those who have not the Happiness of knowing the Originals; and so, by communicating such valuable Patterns to the World, he may perhaps do a more extensive Service to Mankind than the Person whose Life originally afforded the Pattern.

In this Light I have always regarded those Biographers who have recorded the Actions of great and worthy Persons of both Sexes. Not to mention those antient Writers which of late days are little read, being written in obsolete, and, as they are generally thought, unintelligible Languages; such as *Plutarch, Nepos,*[1] and

[1] Fielding more than once praised Plutarch (*c.* A.D. 46–after 120), whom he called in *Tom Jones* (XVII. ii) 'one of the best of our Brother Historians', and he regretted that his writings were neglected in favour of modern wits and scribblers. In *The Covent-Garden Journal* (4 February 1752) he declared: 'I have not read even Lucian himself with more Delight than I have Plutarch.' The principal work of the Roman historian and biographer, Cornelius Nepos (*c.* 99–*c.* 24 B.C.), was *De Viris Illustribus.*

C

others which I heard of in my Youth; our own Language affords many of excellent Use and Instruction, finely calculated to sow the Seeds of Virtue in Youth, and very easy to be comprehended by Persons of moderate Capacity. Such are the History of *John* the Great, who, by his brave and heroic Actions against Men of large and athletic Bodies, obtained the glorious Appellation of the Giant-killer; that of an Earl of *Warwick*, whose Christian Name was *Guy*; the Lives of *Argalus* and *Parthenia*, and above all, the History of those seven worthy Personages, the Champions of Christendom.[1] In all these, Delight is mixed with Instruction, and the Reader is almost as much improved as entertained.

But I pass by these and many others, to mention two Books lately published, which represent an admirable Pattern of the Amiable in either Sex. The former of these which deals in Male-Virtue, was written by the great Person himself, who lived the Life he hath recorded, and is by many thought to have lived such a Life only in order to write it. The other is communicated to us by an Historian who borrows his Lights, as the common Method is, from authentic Papers and Records.[2] The Reader, I believe, already conjectures, I mean, the Lives of Mr. *Colley Cibber*,[3] and

[1] Fielding facetiously refers to some popular penny romances that were hawked about by chapmen: *The History of Jack and the Giants, The History of Guy, Earl of Warwick, The Unfortunate Lovers: The History of Argalus and Parthenia,* and *The Most Famous History of the Seven Champions of Christendom: Saint George of England, Saint Denis of France, Saint James of Spain, Saint Anthony of Italy, Saint Andrew of Scotland, Saint Patrick of Ireland, and Saint David of Wales,* the first written version of which was done in 1596 by Richard Johnson. Later, in ridiculing Thomas Carte's *General History of England* for its Jacobitical bias, Fielding used these same romances in contrast to true history and biography (see *The Jacobite's Journal,* 27 February 1748).

[2] Richardson posed as the editor, not the author, of Pamela's private correspondence.

[3] *An Apology for the Life of Mr. Colley Cibber, Comedian, and Late Patentee of the Theatre-Royal. With an Historical View of the Stage during his Own Time. Written by Himself* was first published in April 1740. Colley Cibber (1671–1757), actor, playwright, and poet laureate, had once been on friendly terms with Fielding. He accepted Fielding's first play, *Love in Several Masques* (1728), for the Drury Lane Theatre and acted the role of Rattle, for which Fielding praised him in the Preface to the published version. But Cibber rejected Fielding's next piece and was thereupon satirized as Marplay in *The Author's Farce* (1730). The success of such plays as *Tom Thumb* (1730) may have helped to heal this breach, for Fielding was soon at Drury Lane, where, during the first six months of 1732, Cibber and his son Theophilus produced five of his comedies. In the following year, however, the rift became irreparable, Fielding perhaps sharing a widespread sentiment that the Cibbers had dealt unfairly with John Highmore, patentee of Drury Lane. From this time on Cibber was a standing target for Fielding's ridicule—in the revised version of *The Author's Farce* (1734), for instance, and as Ground-Ivy in *The Historical Register for 1736*. Although incidental hits at Cibber's incompetence as a stylist and a playwright, and at

of Mrs. *Pamela Andrews*. How artfully doth the former, by in-
sinuating that he *escaped* being promoted to the highest Stations
in Church and State, teach us a Contempt of worldly Grandeur!
how strongly doth he inculcate an absolute Submission to our
Superiors! Lastly, how completely doth he arm us against so
uneasy, so wretched a Passion as the Fear of Shame; how clearly
doth he expose the Emptiness and Vanity of that Fantom, Reputation![1]

What the Female Readers are taught by the Memoirs of
Mrs. *Andrews*, is so well set forth in the excellent Essays or
Letters prefixed to the second and subsequent Editions[2] of that
Work, that it would be here a needless Repetition. The authentic

his jealous discouragement of promising young actors, occur early in *The Champion* (see
the numbers for 17, 20 November and 25 December 1739), it was the publication of the
Apology that prompted Fielding to renew his attacks in earnest. For one thing, Cibber, by
defending the theatrical Licensing Act and dismissing the Opposition wits as disappointed
placemen, had clearly associated himself with Walpole—a fact noticed by the author of *The
Laureat: or, The Right Side of Colley Cibber, Esq.* (1740) and reiterated in such Patriot
journals as *Common Sense* (see the numbers for 13 December 1740 and 17 January 1741).
More specifically, however, Cibber had contemptuously alluded to Fielding as 'a broken
Wit', representing him as a mercenary scribbler whose scurrilous satires against 'Religion,
Laws, Government, Priests, Judges, and Ministers' caused a justly incensed legislature to
censor the stage. (*Apology*, 2nd ed. [1740], pp. 231–3.) In *The Champion* Fielding retaliated
with a vengeance, ridiculing Cibber's poems, plays, and politics, scoffing at his vanity, and
hauling him before the bench of the Court of Censorial Inquiry on the charge of murdering
the English language. (See especially the numbers for 22, 29 April, 3, 6, 17 May 1740.)
In the following year he continued the attack in *The Vernoniad* (January), *Shamela* (April),
and *The Opposition* (December); indeed, Fielding was still jibing at Cibber at the very end
of his career, in *The Journal of a Voyage to Lisbon*.

1 In general Fielding ridicules Cibber's vanity and the fulsome tone of his addresses to
his superiors; but he was especially amused by a passage from Chapter iii of the *Apology*:
'I AM now come to that Crisis of my Life, when Fortune seem'd to be at a Loss what she
should do with me. Had she favour'd my Father's first Designation of me, he might then,
perhaps, have had as sanguine Hopes of my being a Bishop, as I afterwards conceived of my
being a General, when I first took Arms, at the Revolution. Nay, after that, I had a third
Chance too, equally as good, of becoming an Under-propper of the State' (2nd ed., p. 47).
Cibber thus gratefully attributed his successful career in the theatre to a benevolent Providence, which rescued him from these other employments to which he was less well suited.
In *The Champion* (6 May 1740) Fielding had similarly referred to this passage, in which the
comedian implies 'That he narrowly escaped being a General or a Bishop'. Later, in *The
Covent-Garden Journal* (28 April 1752) he again ironically applauded 'our worthy
Laureat', who 'in the excellent Apology for his Life, gave Thanks to Providence that he did
not in his Youth betake himself either to the Gown or the Sword'. See also *A Journey from
This World to the Next*, I. vi.

2 In the first edition of *Pamela* Richardson had allowed two commendatory letters to be
prefixed to his work; in the second edition he inserted twenty-four additional pages of these
'puffs', including a poem. Fielding had previously parodied this practice in *Shamela*.

History with which I now present the public, is an Instance of the great Good that Book is likely to do, and of the Prevalence of Example which I have just observed: since it will appear that it was by keeping the excellent Pattern of his Sister's Virtues before his Eyes, that Mr. *Joseph Andrews* was chiefly enabled to preserve his Purity in the midst of such great Temptations; I shall only add, that this Character of Male-Chastity, tho' doubtless as desirable and becoming in one Part of the human Species, as in the other, is almost the only Virtue which the great Apologist hath not given himself for the sake of giving the Example to his Readers.

CHAPTER II

Of Mr. Joseph Andrews *his Birth, Parentage, Education, and great Endowments, with a Word or two concerning Ancestors.*

Mr. *Joseph Andrews*, the Hero of our ensuing History, was esteemed to be the only Son of Gaffar and Gammer *Andrews*, and Brother to the illustrious *Pamela*, whose Virtue is at present so famous. As to his Ancestors, we have searched with great Diligence, but little Success: being unable to trace them farther than his Great Grandfather, who, as an elderly Person in the Parish remembers to have heard his Father say, was an excellent Cudgel-player. Whether he had any Ancestors before this, we must leave to the Opinion of our curious Reader, finding nothing of sufficient Certainty to relie on. However, we cannot omit inserting an Epitaph which an ingenious Friend of ours hath communicated.

> *Stay Traveller, for underneath this Pew*
> *Lies fast asleep that merry Man* Andrew;
> *When the last Day's great Sun shall gild the Skies,*
> *Then he shall from his Tomb get up and rise.*
> *Be merry while thou can'st: for surely thou*
> *Shall shortly be as sad as he is now.*

The Words are almost out of the Stone with Antiquity. But it is needless to observe, that *Andrew* here is writ without an *s*, and is

besides a Christian Name. My Friend moreover conjectures this
to have been the Founder of that Sect of laughing Philosophers,
since called *Merry Andrews*.

To wave therefore a Circumstance, which, tho' mentioned
in conformity to the exact Rules of Biography, is not greatly
material; I proceed to things of more consequence. Indeed it is
sufficiently certain, that he had as many Ancestors, as the best
Man living; and perhaps, if we look five or six hundred Years
backwards, might be related to some Persons of very great
Figure at present, whose Ancestors within half the last Century
are buried in as great Obscurity. But suppose for Argument's
sake we should admit that he had no Ancestors at all, but had
sprung up, according to the modern Phrase, out of a Dunghill,
as the *Athenians* pretended they themselves did from the Earth,[1]
would not this *Autokopros have been justly entitled to all the
Praise arising from his own Virtues? Would it not be hard, that
a Man who hath no Ancestors should therefore be render'd incapable of acquiring Honour, when we see so many who have
no Virtues, enjoying the Honour of their Forefathers? At ten
Years old (by which Time his Education was advanced to Writing
and Reading) he was bound an Apprentice, according to the
Statute,[2] to Sir *Thomas Booby*, an Uncle of Mr. *Booby's* by the
Father's side. Sir *Thomas* having then an Estate in his own hands,
the young *Andrews* was at first employed in what in the Country
they call *keeping Birds*. His Office was to perform the Part the
Antients assigned to the God *Priapus*,[3] which Deity the Moderns
call by the Name of *Jack-o'-Lent*:[4] but his Voice being so extremely musical, that it rather allured the Birds than terrified
them, he was soon transplanted from the Fields into the Dog-
kennel, where he was placed under the Huntsman, and made
what Sportsmen term a *Whipper-in*.[5] For this Place likewise the

* In *English*, sprung from a Dunghil.

---

[1] Claiming descent from Cecrops and Ericthonius, the Athenians called themselves
autochthones (sprung from the earth).

[2] 5 Elizabeth, cap. 4, known as 'the Statute of Apprentices'. According to Section VII of
this statute, however, one could not be bound as an apprentice before the age of twelve.

[3] The Greek god of fertility and the guardian deity of gardens. His statue, a grotesque
little figure with an enormous phallus, was placed in gardens as a kind of scarecrow. (See
Jonathan Wild, I. iii.)

[4] Usually a human effigy to be thrown at, a butt; but here apparently a scarecrow.

[5] A huntsman's assistant who keeps the hounds from straying from the main pack.

Sweetness of his Voice disqualified him: the Dogs preferring the Melody of his chiding to all the alluring Notes of the Huntsman, who soon became so incensed at it, that he desired Sir *Thomas* to provide otherwise for him; and constantly laid every Fault the Dogs were at, to the Account of the poor Boy, who was now transplanted to the Stable. Here he soon gave Proofs of Strength and Agility, beyond his Years, and constantly rode the most spirited and vicious Horses to water with an Intrepidity which surprized every one. While he was in this Station, he rode several Races for Sir *Thomas,* and this with such Expertness and Success, that the neighbouring Gentlemen frequently solicited the Knight, to permit little *Joey* (for so he was called) to ride their Matches. The best Gamesters, before they laid their Money, always enquired which Horse little *Joey* was to ride, and the Betts were rather proportioned by the Rider than by the Horse himself; especially after he had scornfully refused a considerable Bribe to play booty[1] on such an Occasion. This extremely raised his Character, and so pleased the Lady *Booby,* that she desired to have him (being now seventeen Years of Age) for her own Foot-boy.

Joey was now preferred from the Stable to attend on his Lady; to go on her Errands, stand behind her Chair, wait at her Tea-table, and carry her Prayer-Book to Church; at which Place, his Voice gave him an Opportunity of distinguishing himself by singing Psalms: he behaved likewise in every other respect so well at divine Service, that it recommended him to the Notice of Mr. *Abraham Adams* the Curate; who took an Opportunity one Day, as he was drinking a Cup of Ale in Sir *Thomas's* Kitchin, to ask the young Man several Questions concerning Religion; with his Answers to which he was wonderfully pleased.

CHAPTER III

Of Mr. Abraham Adams *the Curate,* Mrs. Slipslop *the Chambermaid, and others.*

M R. *Abraham Adams* was an excellent Scholar. He was a perfect Master of the *Greek* and *Latin* Languages; to which he added a

[1] To lose the race deliberately for profit.

great Share of Knowledge in the Oriental Tongues, and could read and translate *French*, *Italian* and *Spanish*. He had applied many Years to the most severe Study, and had treasured up a Fund of Learning rarely to be met with in a University. He was besides a Man of good Sense, good Parts, and good Nature; but was at the same time as entirely ignorant of the Ways of this World, as an Infant just entered into it could possibly be. As he had never any Intention to deceive, so he never suspected such a Design in others. He was generous, friendly and brave to an Excess; but Simplicity was his Characteristic: he did, no more than Mr. *Colley Cibber*, apprehend any such Passions as Malice and Envy to exist in Mankind,[1] which was indeed less remarkable in a Country Parson than in a Gentleman who hath past his Life behind the Scenes, a Place which hath been seldom thought the School of Innocence; and where a very little Observation would have convinced the great Apologist, that those Passions have a real Existence in the human Mind.

His Virtue and his other Qualifications, as they rendered him equal to his Office, so they made him an agreeable and valuable Companion, and had so much endeared and well recommended him to a Bishop, that at the Age of Fifty, he was provided with a handsome Income of twenty-three Pounds a Year; which however, he could not make any great Figure with: because he lived in a dear Country,[2] and was a little incumbered with a Wife and six Children.

It was this Gentleman, who, having, as I have said, observed the singular Devotion of young *Andrews*, had found means to question him, concerning several Particulars; as how many Books there were in the New Testament? which were they? how many Chapters they contained? and such like; to all which Mr. *Adams* privately said, he answer'd much better than Sir *Thomas*, or two other neighbouring Justices of the Peace could probably have done.

Mr. *Adams* was wonderfully sollicitous to know at what Time, and by what Opportunity the Youth became acquainted with

[1] In the *Apology*, Chapter I, Cibber writes: 'My Ignorance, and want of Jealousy of Mankind has been so strong, that it is with Reluctance I even yet believe any Person, I am acquainted with, can be capable of Envy, Malice, or Ingratitude . . .' (2nd ed., p. 7).

[2] A recurring topic in the Opposition newspapers during 1741 was the suffering of the poor in the provinces owing to the rising cost of living; the price of provisions in some areas had more than doubled. (See *Common Sense*, 21 February and 28 March 1741.)

these Matters: *Joey* told him, that he had very early learnt to read
and write by the Goodness of his Father, who, though he had
not Interest enough to get him into a Charity School,[1] because a
Cousin of his Father's Landlord did not vote on the right side
for a Church-warden in a Borough Town, yet had been himself
at the Expence of Sixpence a Week for his Learning. He told
him likewise, that ever since he was in Sir *Thomas's* Family, he
had employed all his Hours of Leisure in reading good Books;
that he had read the Bible, the *Whole Duty of Man*,[2] and *Thomas
à Kempis*;[3] and that as often as he could, without being perceived,
he had studied a great good Book which lay open in the Hall
Window, where he had read, *as how the Devil carried away half
a Church in Sermon-time, without hurting one of the Congregation*;
and *as how a Field of Corn ran away down a Hill with all the
Trees upon it, and covered another Man's Meadow*. This sufficiently
assured Mr. *Adams*, that the good Book meant could be no other
than *Baker's* Chronicle.[4]

The Curate, surprized to find such Instances of Industry and
Application in a young Man, who had never met with the least
Encouragement, asked him, if he did not extremely regret the
want of a liberal Education, and the not having been born of
Parents, who might have indulged his Talents and Desire of
Knowledge? To which he answered, 'he hoped he had profited
somewhat better from the Books he had read, than to lament his
Condition in this World. That for his part, he was perfectly con-
tent with the State to which he was called, that he should en-

---

[1] Established by the Society for the Promotion of Christian Knowledge at their first
meeting (8 March 1699), charity schools offered vocational training and moral instruction
for the children of the poor.

[2] *The Whole Duty of Man* (1658), probably written by Richard Allestree (1619–81),
chaplain to the King and provost of Eton, was a favourite devotional work analysing the
individual's duty to God and his neighbour. As a boy at Eton, Fielding heard passages from
the book read aloud every Sunday afternoon (Cross, i. 48).

[3] Thomas à Kempis—Thomas Haemmerlein or Hemercker of Kempen (1380–1471)—
was an Augustinian monk and the supposed author of the *Imitation of Christ* (1441).

[4] *A Chronicle of the Kings of England, From the time of the Romans Government Unto
the Death of King James* (1643), by Sir Richard Baker (1568–1645). In *The Covent-Garden
Journal* (11 February 1752) Fielding again cited the first of the passages in italics and
called Baker's work 'the great Favourite of my Youth'; it was a favourite, too, of Sir
Roger de Coverley, who, like Sir Thomas Booby, kept it in his hall window (*Spectator*, nos.
269 and 329 [8 January and 18 March 1712]). The passages to which Joseph Andrews
alludes may be found in the *Chronicle* under the headings, 'Casualties happening in [the]
time' of Henry IV and Queen Elizabeth.

deavour to improve his Talent,[1] which was all required of him, but not repine at his own Lot, nor envy those of his Betters.' 'Well said, my Lad,' reply'd the Curate, 'and I wish some who have read many more good Books, nay and some who have written good Books themselves, had profited so much by them.'

Adams had no nearer Access to Sir *Thomas*, or my Lady, than through the Waiting-Gentlewoman: For Sir *Thomas* was too apt to estimate Men merely by their Dress, or Fortune; and my Lady was a Woman of Gaiety, who had been bless'd with a Town-Education, and never spoke of any of her Country Neighbours, by any other Appellation than that of *The Brutes*. They both regarded the Curate as a kind of Domestic only, belonging to the Parson of the Parish, who was at this time at variance with the Knight; for the Parson had for many Years lived in a constant State of Civil War, or, which is perhaps as bad, of Civil Law, with Sir *Thomas* himself and the Tenants of his Manor. The Foundation of this Quarrel was a Modus,[2] by setting which aside, an Advantage of several Shillings *per Annum* would have accrued to the Rector: but he had not yet been able to accomplish his Purpose; and had reaped hitherto nothing better from the Suits than the Pleasure (which he used indeed frequently to say was no small one) of reflecting that he had utterly undone many of the poor Tenants, tho' he had at the same time greatly impoverish'd himself.

Mrs. *Slipslop* the Waiting-Gentlewoman, being herself the Daughter of a Curate, preserved some Respect for *Adams*; she professed great Regard for his Learning, and would frequently dispute with him on Points of Theology; but always insisted on a Deference to be paid to her Understanding, as she had been frequently at *London*, and knew more of the World than a Country Parson could pretend to.

---

[1] Cf. Matthew xxv. 14–30. The parable of the talents was frequently used by divines to inculcate the lesson that one must submit to the divine will, accepting without envy one's station in society and labouring to act well in it. (See Isaac Barrow, 'Of Industry in Our General Calling as Christians', *Theological Works*, ed. Alexander Napier [Cambridge, 1859], iii. 411–17; and Samuel Clarke, 'Of Resignation to the Divine Will in Affliction', *Sermons*, ed. John Clarke, 2nd ed. [1730], vi. 254–5, 263–6.)

[2] A modus substituted a fixed money payment for the tithe of the produce (and other titheable objects) that parishioners were expected to pay the Church. Over the years the value of the produce tended to increase, but the amount of the modus remained as originally fixed, thus, in effect, gradually diminishing the real income of the clergyman.

She had in these Disputes a particular Advantage over *Adams*: for she was a mighty Affecter of hard Words, which she used in such a manner, that the Parson, who durst not offend her, by calling her Words in question, was frequently at some loss to guess her meaning, and would have been much less puzzled by an *Arabian* Manuscript.

Adams therefore took an Opportunity one day, after a pretty long Discourse with her on the *Essence*, (or, as she pleased to term it, the *Incense*) of Matter, to mention the Case of young *Andrews*; desiring her to recommend him to her Lady as a Youth very susceptible of Learning, and one, whose Instruction in *Latin* he would himself undertake; by which means he might be qualified for a higher Station than that of a Footman: and added, she knew it was in his Master's power easily to provide for him in a better manner. He therefore desired, that the Boy might be left behind under his Care.

'La Mr. *Adams*,' said Mrs. *Slipslop*, 'do you think my Lady will suffer any *Preambles* about any such Matter? She is going to *London* very *concisely*, and I am *confidous* would not leave *Joey* behind her on any account; for he is one of the genteelest young Fellows you may see in a Summer's Day, and I am *confidous* she would as soon think of parting with a Pair of her Grey-Mares: for she values herself as much on one as the other.' *Adams* would have interrupted, but she proceeded: 'And why is *Latin* more *necessitous* for a Footman than a Gentleman? It is very proper that you Clargymen must learn it, because you can't preach without it: but I have heard Gentlemen say in *London*, that it is fit for no body else. I am *confidous* my Lady would be angry with me for mentioning it, and I shall draw myself into no such *Delemy*.' At which words her Lady's Bell rung, and Mr. *Adams* was forced to retire; nor could he gain a second Opportunity with her before their *London* Journey, which happened a few Days afterwards. However, *Andrews* behaved very thankfully and gratefully to him for his intended Kindness, which he told him he never would forget, and at the same time received from the good Man many Admonitions concerning the Regulation of his future Conduct, and his Perseverance in Innocence and Industry.

CHAPTER IV

What happened after their Journey to London.

No sooner was young *Andrews* arrived at *London*, than he began to scrape an Acquaintance with his party-colour'd Brethren, who endeavour'd to make him despise his former Course of Life. His Hair was cut after the newest Fashion, and became his chief Care. He went abroad with it all the Morning in Papers, and drest it out in the Afternoon; they could not however teach him to game, swear, drink, nor any other genteel Vice the Town abounded with. He applied most of his leisure Hours to Music, in which he greatly improved himself, and became so perfect a Connoisseur in that Art, that he led the Opinion of all the other Footmen at an Opera, and they never condemned or applauded a single Song contrary to his Approbation or Dislike. He was a little too forward in Riots at the Play-Houses and Assemblies; and when he attended his Lady at Church (which was but seldom) he behaved with less seeming Devotion than formerly: however, if he was outwardly a pretty Fellow, his Morals remained entirely uncorrupted, tho' he was at the same time smarter and genteeler, than any of the Beaus in Town, either in or out of Livery.

His Lady, who had often said of him that *Joey* was the handsomest and genteelest Footman in the Kingdom, but that it was pity he wanted Spirit, began now to find that Fault no longer; on the contrary, she was frequently heard to cry out, *Aye, there is some Life in this Fellow.* She plainly saw the Effects which Town-Air hath on the soberest Constitutions. She would now walk out with him into *Hyde-Park* in a Morning, and when tired, which happened almost every Minute, would lean on his Arm, and converse with him in great Familiarity. Whenever she stept out of her Coach she would take him by the Hand, and sometimes, for fear of stumbling, press it very hard; she admitted him to deliver Messages at her Bed-side in a Morning, leered at him at Table, and indulged him in all those innocent Freedoms which Women of Figure may permit without the least sully of their Virtue.

But tho' their Virtue remains unsullied, yet now and then some small Arrows will glance on the Shadow of it, their Reputation;

and so it fell out to Lady *Booby*, who happened to be walking Arm in Arm with *Joey* one Morning in *Hyde-Park*, when Lady *Tittle* and Lady *Tattle* came accidentally by in their Coach. *Bless me*, says Lady *Tittle, can I believe my Eyes? Is that Lady* Booby? *Surely*, says *Tattle. But what makes you surprized? Why is not that her Footman?* reply'd *Tittle*. At which *Tattle* laughed and cryed, *An old Business, I assure you, is it possible you should not have heard it? The whole Town hath known it this half Year.* The Consequence of this Interview was a Whisper through a hundred Visits, which were separately performed by the two Ladies* the same Afternoon, and might have had a mischievous Effect, had it not been stopt by two fresh Reputations which were published the Day afterwards, and engrossed the whole Talk of the Town.

But whatever Opinion or Suspicion the scandalous Inclination of Defamers might entertain of Lady *Booby's* innocent Freedoms, it is certain they made no Impression on young *Andrews*, who never offered to encroach beyond the Liberties which his Lady allowed him. A Behaviour which she imputed to the violent Respect he preserved for her, and which served only to heighten a something she began to conceive, and which the next Chapter will open a little farther.

CHAPTER V

The Death of Sir Thomas Booby, *with the affectionate and mournful Behaviour of his Widow, and the great Purity of* Joseph Andrews.

A T this Time, an Accident happened which put a stop to these agreeable Walks, which probably would have soon puffed up the Cheeks of Fame,[1] and caused her to blow her brazen Trumpet through the Town, and this was no other than the Death of Sir *Thomas Booby*, who departing this Life, left his disconsolate Lady

---

* It may seem an Absurdity that *Tattle* should visit, as she actually did, to spread a known Scandal: but the Reader may reconcile this, by supposing with me, that, notwithstanding what she says, this was her first Acquaintance with it.

---

[1] After Dido indulged her passion for Aeneas, the goddess Fame published the scandal throughout Libya (*Aeneid*, iv. 173 ff.).

confined to her House as closely as if she herself had been attacked by some violent Disease. During the first six Days the poor Lady admitted none but Mrs. *Slipslop* and three Female Friends who made a Party at Cards: but on the seventh she ordered *Joey*, whom for a good Reason we shall hereafter call JOSEPH,[1] to bring up her Tea-kettle. The Lady being in Bed, called *Joseph* to her, bad him sit down, and having accidentally laid her hand on his, she asked him, *if he had never been in Love? Joseph* answered, with some Confusion, 'it was time enough for one so young as himself to think on such things.' 'As young as you are,' reply'd the Lady, 'I am convinced you are no Stranger to that Passion; Come *Joey*,' says she, 'tell me truly, who is the happy Girl whose Eyes have made a Conquest of you?' *Joseph* returned, 'that all Women he had ever seen were equally indifferent to him.' 'O then,' said the Lady, 'you are a general Lover. Indeed you handsome Fellows, like handsome Women, are very long and difficult in fixing: but yet you shall never persuade me that your Heart is so insusceptible of Affection; I rather impute what you say to your Secrecy, a very commendable Quality, and what I am far from being angry with you for. Nothing can be more unworthy in a young Man than to betray any Intimacies with the Ladies.' *Ladies! Madam*, said *Joseph, I am sure I never had the Impudence to think of any that deserve that Name.* 'Don't pretend to too much Modesty,' said she, 'for that sometimes may be impertinent: but pray, answer me this Question, Suppose a Lady should happen to like you, suppose she should prefer you to all your Sex, and admit you to the same Familiarities as you might have hoped for, if you had been born her equal, are you certain that no Vanity could tempt you to discover her? Answer me honestly, *Joseph*, Have you so much more Sense and so much more Virtue than you handsome young Fellows generally have, who make no scruple of sacrificing our dear Reputation to your Pride, without considering the great Obligation we lay on you, by our Condescension and Confidence? Can you keep a Secret, my *Joey*?' 'Madam,' says he, 'I hope your Ladyship can't tax me with ever betraying the Secrets of the Family, and I hope, if you was to turn me away, I might have that Character of you.' 'I don't intend to turn you away, *Joey*,' said she, and sighed,

---

[1] An allusion to the chastity of the biblical Joseph, who resisted the solicitations of Potiphar's wife (Genesis xxxix. 7–20).

'I am afraid it is not in my power.' She then raised herself a little in her Bed, and discovered one of the whitest Necks that ever was seen; at which *Joseph* blushed. 'La!' says she, in an affected Surprize, 'what am I doing? I have trusted myself with a Man alone, naked in Bed; suppose you should have any wicked Intentions upon my Honour, how should I defend myself?' *Joseph* protested that he never had the least evil Design against her. 'No,' says she, 'perhaps you may not call your Designs wicked, and perhaps they are not so.'—He swore they were not. 'You misunderstand me,' says she, 'I mean if they were against my Honour, they may not be wicked, but the World calls them so. But then, say you, the World will never know any thing of the Matter, yet would not that be trusting to your Secrecy? Must not my Reputation be then in your power? Would you not then be my Master?' *Joseph* begged her Ladyship to be comforted, for that he would never imagine the least wicked thing against her, and that he had rather die a thousand Deaths than give her any reason to suspect him. 'Yes,' said she, 'I must have Reason to suspect you. Are you not a Man? and without Vanity I may pretend to some Charms. But perhaps you may fear I should prosecute you; indeed I hope you do, and yet Heaven knows I should never have the Confidence to appear before a Court of Justice, and you know, *Joey*, I am of a forgiving Temper. Tell me *Joey*, don't you think I should forgive you?' 'Indeed Madam,' says *Joseph*, 'I will never do any thing to disoblige your Ladyship.' 'How,' says she, 'do you think it would not disoblige me then? Do you think I would willingly suffer you?' 'I don't understand you, Madam,' says *Joseph*. 'Don't you?' said she, 'then you are either a Fool or pretend to be so, I find I was mistaken in you, so get you down Stairs, and never let me see your Face again: your pretended Innocence cannot impose on me.' 'Madam,' said *Joseph*, 'I would not have your Ladyship think any Evil of me. I have always endeavoured to be a dutiful Servant both to you and my Master.' 'O thou Villain,' answered my Lady, 'Why did'st thou mention the Name of that dear Man, unless to torment me, to bring his precious Memory to my Mind, (*and then she burst into a Fit of Tears.*) Get thee from my Sight, I shall never endure thee more.' At which Words she turned away from him, and *Joseph* retreated from the Room in a most disconsolate Condition, and writ that Letter which the Reader will find in the next Chapter.

CHAPTER VI

How Joseph Andrews *writ a Letter to his Sister* Pamela.

To Mrs. *Pamela Andrews*, living with Squire *Booby*.
'*Dear Sister*,

'Since I received your Letter of your good Lady's Death, we
have had a Misfortune of the same kind in our Family. My worthy
Master, Sir *Thomas*, died about four Days ago,[1] and what is
worse, my poor Lady is certainly gone distracted. None of the
Servants expected her to take it so to heart, because they quar-
relled almost every day of their Lives: but no more of that,
because you know, *Pamela*, I never loved to tell the Secrets of my
Master's Family;[2] but to be sure you must have known they
never loved one another, and I have heard her Ladyship wish his
Honour dead above a thousand times: but no body knows what
it is to lose a Friend till they have lost him.

'Don't tell any body what I write, because I should not care to
have Folks say I discover what passes in our Family: but if it
had not been so great a Lady, I should have thought she had
had a mind to me. Dear *Pamela*, don't tell any body: but she
ordered me to sit down by her Bed-side, when she was in naked
Bed; and she held my Hand, and talked exactly as a Lady does
to her Sweetheart in a Stage-Play, which I have seen in *Covent-
Garden*, while she wanted him to be no better than he should be.

'If Madam be mad, I shall not care for staying long in the
Family; so I heartily wish you could get me a Place either at the
Squire's, or some other neighbouring Gentleman's, unless it be
true that you are going to be married to Parson *Williams*, as
Folks talk, and then I should be very willing to be his Clerk: for
which you know I am qualified, being able to read, and to set a
Psalm.

'I fancy, I shall be discharged very soon; and the Moment
I am, unless I hear from you, I shall return to my old Master's

[1] According to the chronology of the preceding chapter, Joseph is writing this letter on
the seventh day after his master's death.
[2] Among Parson Oliver's concluding observations in *Shamela*, the third of the immoral
tendencies of Richardson's novel is that 'All Chambermaids . . . are countenanced in Impertinence to their Superiors, and in betraying the Secrets of Families.'

Country Seat, if it be only to see Parson *Adams,* who is the best
Man in the World. *London* is a bad Place, and there is so little
good Fellowship, that next-door Neighbours don't know one
another. Pray give my Service to all Friends that enquire for
me; so I rest

Your Loving Brother,
Joseph Andrews.'

As soon as *Joseph* had sealed and directed this Letter, he
walked down Stairs, where he met Mrs. *Slipslop,* with whom
we shall take this Opportunity to bring the Reader a little better
acquainted. She was a Maiden Gentlewoman of about Forty-
five Years of Age, who having made a small Slip in her Youth
had continued a good Maid ever since. She was not at this time
remarkably handsome; being very short, and rather too corpulent
in Body, and somewhat red, with the Addition of Pimples in the
Face. Her Nose was likewise rather too large, and her Eyes too
little; nor did she resemble a Cow so much in her Breath, as in
two brown Globes which she carried before her; one of her Legs
was also a little shorter than the other, which occasioned her to
limp as she walked. This fair Creature had long cast the Eyes of
Affection on *Joseph,* in which she had not met with quite so good
Success as she probably wished, tho' besides the Allurements of her
native Charms, she had given him Tea, Sweetmeats, Wine, and
many other Delicacies, of which by keeping the Keys, she had the
absolute Command. *Joseph* however, had not returned the least
Gratitude to all these Favours, not even so much as a Kiss; tho'
I would not insinuate she was so easily to be satisfied: for surely
then he would have been highly blameable. The truth is, she was
arrived at an Age when she thought she might indulge herself
in any Liberties with a Man, without the danger of bringing a
third Person into the World to betray them. She imagined, that
by so long a Self-denial, she had not only made amends for the
small Slip of her Youth above hinted at: but had likewise laid up
a Quantity of Merit to excuse any future Failings. In a word, she
resolved to give a loose to her amorous Inclinations, and pay off
the Debt of Pleasure which she found she owed herself, as fast as
possible.

With these Charms of Person, and in this Disposition of Mind,
she encountered poor *Joseph* at the Bottom of the Stairs, and asked
him if he would drink a Glass of something good this Morning.

Joseph, whose Spirits were not a little cast down, very readily and thankfully accepted the Offer; and together they went into a Closet, where having delivered him a full Glass of Ratifia, and desired him to sit down, Mrs. *Slipslop* thus began:

'Sure nothing can be a more simple *Contract* in a Woman, than to place her Affections on a Boy. If I had ever thought it would have been my Fate, I should have wished to die a thousand Deaths rather than live to see that Day. If we like a Man, the lightest Hint *sophisticates*. Whereas a Boy *proposes* upon us to break through all the *Regulations* of Modesty, before we can make any *Oppression* upon him.' *Joseph*, who did not understand a Word she said, answered, '*Yes Madam;*—' 'Yes Madam!' reply'd Mrs. *Slipslop* with some Warmth, 'Do you intend to *result* my Passion? Is it not enough, ungrateful as you are, to make no Return to all the Favours I have done you: but you must treat me with *Ironing?* Barbarous Monster! how have I deserved that my Passion should be *resulted* and treated with *Ironing?*' 'Madam,' answered *Joseph*, 'I don't understand your hard Words: but I am certain, you have no Occasion to call me ungrateful: for so far from intending you any Wrong, I have always loved you as well as if you had been my own Mother.' 'How, Sirrah!' says Mrs. *Slipslop* in a Rage: 'Your own Mother! Do you *assinuate* that I am old enough to be your Mother? I don't know what a Stripling may think: but I believe a Man would *refer* me to any Green-Sickness silly Girl *whatsomdever*: but I ought to despise you rather than be angry with you, for *referring* the Conversation of Girls to that of a Woman of Sense.' 'Madam,' says *Joseph*, 'I am sure I have always valued the Honour you did me by your Conversation; for I know you are a Woman of Learning.' 'Yes but, *Joseph*,' said she a little softened by the Compliment to her Learning, 'If you had a Value for me, you certainly would have found some Method of shewing it me; for I am *convicted* you must see the Value I have for you. Yes, *Joseph*, my Eyes whether I would or no, must have declared a Passion I cannot conquer.—Oh! *Joseph!*—'

As when a hungry Tygress, who long had traversed the Woods in fruitless search, sees within the Reach of her Claws a Lamb, she prepares to leap on her Prey; or as a voracious Pike, of immense Size, surveys through the liquid Element a Roach or Gudgeon which cannot escape her Jaws, opens them wide to swallow the little Fish: so did Mrs. *Slipslop* prepare to lay her

violent amorous Hands on the poor *Joseph*, when luckily her
Mistress's Bell rung, and delivered the intended Martyr from her
Clutches. She was obliged to leave him abruptly, and defer the
Execution of her Purpose to some other Time. We shall there-
fore return to the Lady *Booby*, and give our Reader some Account
of her Behaviour, after she was left by *Joseph* in a Temper of
Mind not greatly different from that of the inflamed *Slipslop*.

CHAPTER VII

Sayings of wise Men. A Dialogue between the Lady and her
Maid, and a Panegyric or rather Satire on the Passion
of Love, in the sublime Style.

IT is the Observation of some antient Sage, whose Name I have
forgot, that Passions operate differently on the human Mind, as
Diseases on the Body, in proportion to the Strength or Weakness,
Soundness or Rottenness of the one and the other.

We hope therefore, a judicious Reader will give himself some
Pains to observe, what we have so greatly laboured to describe,
the different Operations of this Passion of Love in the gentle and
cultivated Mind of the Lady *Booby*, from those which it effected
in the less polished and coarser Disposition of Mrs. *Slipslop*.

Another Philosopher, whose Name also at present escapes my
Memory, hath somewhere said, that Resolutions taken in the
Absence of the beloved Object are very apt to vanish in its
Presence; on both which wise Sayings the following Chapter
may serve as a Comment.

No sooner had *Joseph* left the Room in the Manner we have
before related, than the Lady, enraged at her Disappointment,
began to reflect with Severity on her Conduct. Her Love was
now changed to Disdain, which Pride assisted to torment her.
She despised herself for the Meanness of her Passion, and *Joseph*
for its ill Success. However, she had now got the better of it in
her own Opinion, and determined immediately to dismiss the
Object. After much tossing and turning in her Bed, and many
Soliloquies, which, if we had no better Matter for our Reader,
we would give him; she at last rung the Bell as above-mentioned,

and was presently attended by Mrs. *Slipslop*, who was not much better pleased with *Joseph*, than the Lady herself.

Slipslop, said Lady *Booby*, *when did you see* Joseph? The poor Woman was so surprized at the unexpected Sound of his Name, at so critical a time, that she had the greatest Difficulty to conceal the Confusion she was under from her Mistress, whom she answered nevertheless, with pretty good Confidence, though not entirely void of Fear of Suspicion, that she had not seen him that Morning. 'I am afraid,' said Lady *Booby*, 'he is a wild young Fellow.' 'That he is,' said *Slipslop*, 'and a wicked one too. To my knowledge he games, drinks, swears and fights eternally: besides he is horribly *indicted* to Wenching.' 'Ay!' said the Lady, 'I never heard that of him.' 'O Madam,' answered the other, 'he is so lewd a Rascal that if your Ladyship keeps him much longer, you will not have one Virgin in your House except myself. And yet I can't conceive what the Wenches see in him, to be so foolishly fond as they are; in my Eyes he is as ugly a Scarecrow as I ever *upheld*.' 'Nay,' said the Lady, 'the Boy is well enough.'— 'La Ma'am,' cries *Slipslop*, 'I think him the *ragmaticallest* Fellow in the Family.' 'Sure, *Slipslop*,' says she, 'you are mistaken: but which of the Women do you most suspect?' 'Madam,' says *Slipslop*, 'there is *Betty* the Chamber-Maid, I am almost *convicted*, is with Child by him.' 'Ay!' says the Lady, 'then pray pay her her Wages instantly. I will keep no such Sluts in my Family. And as for *Joseph*, you may discard him too.' 'Would your Ladyship have him paid off immediately?' cries *Slipslop*, 'for perhaps, when *Betty* is gone, he may mend; and really the Boy is a good Servant, and a strong healthy *luscious* Boy enough.' 'This Morning,' answered the Lady with some Vehemence. 'I wish Madam,' cries *Slipslop*, 'your Ladyship would be so good as to try him a little longer.' 'I will not have my Commands disputed,' said the Lady, 'sure you are not fond of him yourself.' 'I Madam?' cries *Slipslop*, reddening, if not blushing, 'I should be sorry to think your Ladyship had any reason to *respect* me of Fondness for a Fellow; and if it be your Pleasure, I shall fulfill it with as much *reluctance* as possible.' 'As little, I suppose you mean,' said the Lady; 'and so about it instantly.' Mrs. *Slipslop* went out, and the Lady had scarce taken two turns before she fell to knocking and ringing with great Violence. *Slipslop*, who did not travel post-haste, soon returned, and was countermanded as to *Joseph*, but ordered to send *Betty* about her Business without delay. She went out a second time with much greater alacrity than before; when the Lady began immediately to accuse herself of Want of Resolution, and to apprehend the Return of her Affection with its pernicious Consequences: she therefore applied herself again to the Bell, and resummoned Mrs. *Slipslop* into her Presence; who again returned, and was told by her Mistress, that she had consider'd better of the Matter, and was absolutely resolved to turn away *Joseph*; which she ordered her to do immediately. *Slipslop*, who knew the Violence of her Lady's Temper, and would not venture her Place for any *Adonis* or *Hercules* in the Universe, left her a third time; which she had no sooner done, than the little God *Cupid*, fearing he had not yet done the Lady's Business, took a fresh Arrow with the sharpest Point out of his Quiver, and shot it directly into her Heart: in other and plainer Language, the Lady's Passion got the better of her Reason. She called back *Slipslop* once more, and told her, she had resolved to see the Boy, and examine him herself; therefore bid her send him up. This wavering in her Mistress's Temper probably put something into the Waiting-Gentlewoman's Head, not necessary to mention to the sagacious Reader.

Lady *Booby* was going to call her back again, but could not prevail with herself. The next Consideration therefore was, how she should behave to *Joseph* when he came in. She resolved to preserve all the Dignity of the Woman of Fashion to her Servant, and to indulge herself in this last View of *Joseph* (for that she was most certainly resolved it should be) at his own Expence, by first insulting, and then discarding him.

O Love, what monstrous Tricks dost thou play with thy Votaries of both Sexes! How dost thou deceive them, and make them deceive themselves! Their Follies are thy Delight! Their Sighs make thee laugh, and their Pangs are thy Merriment!

Not the Great *Rich*, who turns Men into Monkeys, Wheel-barrows, and whatever else best humours his Fancy, hath so strangely metamorphosed the human Shape;[1] nor the Great

---

[1] John Rich (1682 ?–1761) was theatrical manager first at Lincoln's Inn Fields and later (after 1732) at the New Theatre in Covent Garden. Rich was largely responsible for the enormous contemporary vogue of pantomimes and 'entertainments', in which, under the name of 'Lun', he made famous the role of Harlequin, astonishing audiences with spectacular tricks and stage effects. He was satirized by Pope in *The Dunciad* (iii. 252–64) for vulgarizing and debasing the theatres.

Fielding ridiculed Rich in several plays and farces—most notably as Harlequin in

Cibber, who confounds all Number, Gender, and breaks through every Rule of Grammar at his Will, hath so distorted the *English* Language,[1] as thou dost metamorphose and distort the human Senses.

Thou puttest out our Eyes, stoppest up our Ears, and takest away the power of our Nostrils; so that we can neither see the largest Object, hear the loudest Noise, nor smell the most poignant Perfume. Again, when thou pleasest, thou can'st make a Mole-hill appear as a Mountain; a *Jew's*-Harp sound like a Trumpet; and a Dazy smell like a Violet. Thou can'st make Cowardice brave, Avarice generous, Pride humble, and Cruelty tender-hearted. In short, thou turnest the Heart of Man inside-out, as a Juggler doth a Petticoat, and bringest whatsoever pleaseth thee out from it. If there be any one who doubts all this, let him read the next Chapter.

CHAPTER VIII

In which, after some very fine Writing, the History goes on, and relates the Interview between the Lady and Joseph; *where the latter hath set an Example, which we despair of seeing followed by his Sex, in this vicious Age.*

Now the Rake *Hesperus* had called for his Breeches, and having well rubbed his drowsy Eyes, prepared to dress himself for all

Pasquin (1736), which Rich had earlier refused for Covent Garden, and as Harlequin and Mr. Machine in *Tumble-Down Dick* (1736), the published version of which Fielding ironically dedicated to 'Mr. John Lun'. Both Pope and Fielding particularly scored Rich's favourite practice of exhibiting monstrous transformations and other unnatural effects. In *Tumble-Down Dick* the Genius of Gin thus addresses Harlequin:

> Take, *Harlequin*, this Magick Wand,
> All things shall yield to thy Command:
> Whether you wou'd appear Incog,
> In Shape of Monkey, Cat, or Dog;
> Or else to shew your Wit, transform
> Your Mistress to a Butter-Churn;
> Or else, what no Magician can,
> Into a Wheel-barrow turn a Man. . . .

Rich is again ridiculed in *The Champion* (3 May 1740), where Fielding observes that in the theatre 'the dexterous Harlequin of sooty Countenance, long time prevails, turns all things topsy-turvy, subverts the Order of Nature, and makes the human Puppet Man dance Jiggs upon his Head . . . .' (See also the issues for 22 April and 24 May 1740, and *Tom Jones*, v. i.)   [1] See p. 18, n. 3.

Night; by whose Example his Brother Rakes on Earth likewise leave those Beds, in which they had slept away the Day. Now *Thetis* the good Housewife began to put on the Pot in order to regale the good Man *Phœbus*, after his daily Labours were over. In vulgar Language, it was in the Evening when *Joseph* attended his Lady's Orders.

But as it becomes us to preserve the Character of this Lady, who is the Heroine of our Tale; and as we have naturally a wonderful Tenderness for that beautiful Part of the human Species, called the Fair Sex; before we discover too much of her Frailty to our Reader, it will be proper to give him a lively Idea of that vast Temptation, which overcame all the Efforts of a modest and virtuous Mind; and then we humbly hope his Good-nature will rather pity than condemn the Imperfection of human Virtue.

Nay, the Ladies themselves will, we hope, be induced, by considering the uncommon Variety of Charms, which united in this young Man's Person, to bridle their rampant Passion for Chastity, and be at least, as mild as their violent Modesty and Virtue will permit them, in censuring the Conduct of a Woman, who, perhaps, was in her own Disposition as chaste as those pure and sanctified Virgins, who, after a Life innocently spent in the Gaieties of the Town, begin about Fifty to attend twice *per diem*, at the polite Churches and Chapels, to return Thanks for the Grace which preserved them formerly amongst Beaus from Temptations, perhaps less powerful than what now attacked the Lady *Booby*.

Mr. *Joseph Andrews* was now in the one and twentieth Year of his Age. He was of the highest Degree of middle Stature. His Limbs were put together with great Elegance and no less Strength. His Legs and Thighs were formed in the exactest Proportion. His Shoulders were broad and brawny, but yet his Arms hung so easily, that he had all the Symptoms of Strength without the least clumsiness. His Hair was of a nut-brown Colour, and was displayed in wanton Ringlets down his Back. His Forehead was high, his Eyes dark, and as full of Sweetness as of Fire. His Nose a little inclined to the Roman. His Teeth white and even. His Lips full, red, and soft. His Beard was only rough on his Chin and upper Lip; but his Cheeks, in which his Blood glowed, were overspread with a thick Down. His Countenance had a Tenderness joined with a Sensibility inexpressible. Add to this the most perfect Neatness in his Dress, and an Air, which to those who have not seen many Noblemen, would give an Idea of Nobility.

Such was the Person who now appeared before the Lady. She viewed him some time in Silence, and twice or thrice before she spake, changed her Mind as to the manner in which she should begin. At length, she said to him, '*Joseph*, I am sorry to hear such Complaints against you; I am told you behave so rudely to the Maids, that they cannot do their Business in quiet; I mean those who are not wicked enough to hearken to your Solicitations. As to others, they may not, perhaps, call you rude: for there are wicked Sluts who make one ashamed of one's own Sex; and are as ready to admit any nauseous Familiarity as Fellows to offer it; nay, there are such in my Family: but they shall not stay in it; that impudent Trollop, who is with Child by you, is discharged by this time.'

As a Person who is struck through the Heart with a Thunderbolt, looks extremely surprised, nay, and perhaps is so too.—Thus the poor *Joseph* received the false Accusation of his Mistress; he blushed and looked confounded, which she misinterpreted to be Symptoms of his Guilt, and thus went on.

'Come hither, *Joseph*: another Mistress might discard you for these Offences; But I have a Compassion for your Youth, and if I could be certain you would be no more guilty—Consider, Child, (*laying her Hand carelessly upon his*) you are a handsome young Fellow, and might do better; you might make your Fortune—.' 'Madam,' said *Joseph*, 'I do assure your Ladyship, I don't know whether any Maid in the House is Man or Woman —.' 'Oh fie! *Joseph*,' answer'd the Lady, 'don't commit another Crime in denying the Truth. I could pardon the first; but I hate a Lyar.' 'Madam,' cries *Joseph*, 'I hope your Ladyship will not be offended at my asserting my Innocence: for by all that is Sacred, I have never offered more than Kissing.' 'Kissing!' said the Lady, with great Discomposure of Countenance, and more Redness in her Cheeks, than Anger in her Eyes, 'do you call that no Crime? Kissing, *Joseph*, is as a Prologue to a Play.[1] Can I believe a young Fellow of your Age and Complexion will be

---

[1] Cf. *The Merry Wives of Windsor*, III. v. 75. Falstaff's overtures to Mistress Ford were interrupted: 'after we had embrac'd, kiss'd, protested, and, as it were, spoke the prologue of our comedy . . . .'

content with Kissing? No, *Joseph*, there is no Woman who grants
that but will grant more, and I am deceived greatly in you, if you
would not put her closely to it. What would you think, *Joseph*,
if I admitted you to kiss me?' *Joseph* reply'd, 'he would sooner
die than have any such Thought.' 'And yet, *Joseph*,' returned she,
'Ladies have admitted their Footmen to such Familiarities; and
Footmen, I confess to you, much less deserving them; Fellows
without half your Charms: for such might almost excuse the
Crime. Tell me, therefore, *Joseph*, if I should admit you to such
Freedom, what would you think of me?—tell me freely.' 'Madam,'
said *Joseph*, 'I should think your Ladyship condescended a great
deal below yourself.' 'Pugh!' said she, 'that I am to answer to
myself: but would not you insist on more? Would you be contented with a Kiss? Would not your Inclinations be all on fire
rather by such a Favour?' 'Madam,' said *Joseph*, 'if they were,
I hope I should be able to controll them, without suffering them
to get the better of my Virtue.'—You have heard, Reader, Poets
talk of the *Statue of Surprize*;[1] you have heard likewise, or else
you have heard very little, how Surprize made one of the Sons
of *Cræsus* speak tho' he was dumb.[2] You have seen the Faces, in
the Eighteen-penny Gallery, when through the Trap-Door, to
soft or no Musick, Mr. *Bridgewater*, Mr. *William Mills*,[3] or some
other of ghostly Appearance, hath ascended with a Face all pale
with Powder, and a Shirt all bloody with Ribbons; but from

[1] Cf. Ovid, *Metamorphoses*, iii. 418–19; or Shakespeare's *Richard III* (III. vii), which in
Cibber's version reads: 'each like statues fix'd, / Speechless and pale, star'd in his fellow's
face . . .'; or Lewis Theobald's *Persian Princess* (IV. ii): 'And turn me to a Statue with
Confusion'; or Edward Young's *Busiris* (IV): '—*Passion choaks / Their Words, and they're
the Statues of Despair.*' The last reference is quoted by Fielding in *The Tragedy of Tragedies*,
II. viii, note k, to illustrate one of the trite conventions of heroic tragedy.

[2] Crœsus, King of Lydia (*c.* 560–546 B.C.), had two sons: one was accidentally killed;
the other was mute. During the capture of Crœsus's citadel by the army of Cyrus, a Persian
soldier approached Crœsus to kill him. Seeing his intention, Crœsus's son was shocked by
fear into uttering his first words: 'Fellow, slay not Crœsus.' (*Herodotus*, i. 85.)

[3] Actors who performed in Fielding's plays. Bridgewater (d. 26 August 1754) often
played the ghost of Hamlet's father. Fielding was especially fond of 'Honest Billy Mills'
(d. 17 April 1750), who frequently acted the part of Banquo, and who appeared as the
ghost of Gaffer Thumb in the Drury Lane production of *The Tragedy of Tragedies* (May
1732). Mills was a good man, if no very good actor; when his fortunes declined, Fielding
devoted space in *The Jacobite's Journal* (23 April 1748) to urging attendance at his benefit
night. In tragedy, Fielding remarked, Mills 'is thought of all others to have made the best
Appearance through a Trap-Door: for which Reason those Characters which are in some
Part of the Play to enter upon the Stage Head-foremost, generally fell to his Lot.' Mills
is again complimented in *Tom Jones* (VII. i).

none of these, nor from *Phidias*, or *Praxiteles*, if they should return to Life—no, not from the inimitable Pencil of my Friend *Hogarth*,[1] could you receive such an Idea of Surprize, as would have entered in at your Eyes, had they beheld the Lady *Booby*, when those last Words issued out from the Lips of *Joseph*.— 'Your Virtue! (said the Lady recovering after a Silence of two Minutes) I shall never survive it. Your Virtue! Intolerable Confidence! Have you the Assurance to pretend, that when a Lady demeans herself to throw aside the Rules of Decency, in order to honour you with the highest Favour in her Power, your Virtue should resist her Inclination? That when she had conquer'd her own Virtue, she should find an Obstruction in yours?' 'Madam,' said *Joseph*, 'I can't see why her having no Virtue should be a Reason against my having any. Or why, because I am a Man, or because I am poor, my Virtue must be subservient to her Pleasures.' 'I am out of patience,' cries the Lady: 'Did ever Mortal hear of a Man's Virtue! Did ever the greatest, or the gravest Men pretend to any of this Kind! Will Magistrates who punish Lewdness, or Parsons, who preach against it, make any scruple of committing it? And can a Boy, a Stripling, have the Confidence to talk of his Virtue?' 'Madam,' says *Joseph*, 'that Boy is the Brother of *Pamela*, and would be ashamed, that the Chastity of his Family, which is preserved in her, should be stained in him. If there are such Men as your Ladyship mentions, I am sorry for it, and I wish they had an Opportunity of reading over those Letters, which my Father hath sent me of my Sister *Pamela's*, nor do I doubt but such an Example would amend them.' 'You impudent Villain,' cries the Lady in a Rage, 'Do you insult me with the Follies of my Relation, who hath exposed himself all over the Country upon your Sister's account? a little Vixen, whom I have always wondered my late Lady *John Booby* ever kept in her House. Sirrah! get out of my sight, and prepare to set out this Night, for I will order you your Wages immediately, and you shall be stripped and turned away.—' 'Madam,' says *Joseph*, 'I am sorry I have offended your Ladyship, I am sure I never intended it.' 'Yes, Sirrah,' cries she, 'you have had the Vanity to misconstrue the little innocent Freedom I took in order to try, whether what I had heard was true. O' my Conscience, you have had the Assurance to imagine, I was fond of you myself.' *Joseph*

[1] See p. 6, n. 1.

answered, he had only spoke out of Tenderness for his Virtue; at which Words she flew into a violent Passion, and refusing to hear more, ordered him instantly to leave the Room.

He was no sooner gone, than she burst forth into the following Exclamation: 'Whither doth this violent Passion hurry us? What Meannesses do we submit to from its Impulse? Wisely we resist its first and least Approaches; for it is then only we can assure ourselves the Victory. No Woman could ever safely say, *so far only will I go.* Have I not exposed myself to the Refusal of my Footman? I cannot bear the Reflection.' Upon which she applied herself to the Bell, and rung it with infinite more Violence than was necessary; the faithful *Slipslop* attending near at hand: To say the truth, she had conceived a Suspicion at her last Interview with her Mistress; and had waited ever since in the Antichamber, having carefully applied her Ears to the Key-Hole during the whole time, that the preceeding Conversation passed between *Joseph* and the Lady.

CHAPTER IX

What passed between the Lady and Mrs. Slipslop, *in which we prophesy there are some Strokes which every one will not truly comprehend at the first Reading.*

'SLIPSLOP,' said the Lady, 'I find too much Reason to believe all thou hast told me of this wicked *Joseph*; I have determined to part with him instantly; so go you to the Steward, and bid him pay him his Wages.' *Slipslop*, who had preserved hitherto a Distance to her Lady, rather out of Necessity than Inclination, and who thought the Knowledge of this Secret had thrown down all Distinction between them, answered her Mistress very pertly, 'she wished she knew her own Mind; and that she was certain she would call her back again, before she was got half way down stairs.' The Lady replied, 'she had taken a Resolution, and was resolved to keep it.' 'I am sorry for it,' cries *Slipslop*; 'and if I had known you would have punished the poor Lad so severely, you should never have heard a *Particle* of the Matter. Here's a Fuss indeed, about nothing.' 'Nothing!' returned my Lady; 'Do you think I will countenance Lewdness in my House?' 'If you will turn away every Footman,' said *Slipslop*, 'that is a lover of the Sport, you must soon open the Coach-Door yourself, or get a Sett of *Mophrodites* to wait upon you; and I am sure I hated the Sight of them even singing in an Opera.' 'Do as I bid you,' says my Lady, 'and don't shock my Ears with your beastly Language.' 'Marry-come-up,' cries *Slipslop*, 'People's Ears are sometimes the nicest Part about them.'

The Lady, who began to admire the new Style in which her Waiting-Gentlewoman delivered herself, and by the Conclusion of her Speech, suspected somewhat of the Truth, called her back, and desired to know what she meant by that extraordinary degree of Freedom in which she thought proper to indulge her Tongue. 'Freedom!' says *Slipslop*, 'I don't know what you call Freedom, Madam; Servants have Tongues as well as their Mistresses.' 'Yes, and saucy ones too,' answered the Lady: 'but I assure you I shall bear no such Impertinence.' 'Impertinence! I don't know that I am impertinent,' says *Slipslop*. 'Yes indeed you are,' cries my Lady; 'and unless you mend your Manners, this House is no Place for you.' 'Manners!' cries *Slipslop*, 'I never was thought to want Manners *nor Modesty neither*; and for Places, there are more Places than one; and I know what I know.' 'What do you know, Mistress?' answered the Lady. 'I am not obliged to tell that to every body,' says *Slipslop*, 'any more than I am obliged to keep it a Secret.' 'I desire you would provide yourself,' answered the Lady. 'With all my heart,' replied the Waiting-Gentlewoman; and so departed in a Passion, and slapped the Door after her.

The Lady too plainly perceived that her Waiting-Gentlewoman knew more than she would willingly have had her acquainted with; and this she imputed to *Joseph's* having discovered to her what past at the first Interview. This therefore blew up her Rage against him, and confirmed her in a Resolution of parting with him.

But the dismissing Mrs. *Slipslop* was a Point not so easily to be resolved upon: she had the utmost Tenderness for her Reputation, as she knew on that depended many of the most valuable Blessings of Life; particularly Cards, making Court'sies in public Places, and above all, the Pleasure of demolishing the Reputations of others, in which innocent Amusement she had an extraordinary Delight. She therefore determined to submit to any Insult from a Servant, rather than run a Risque of losing the Title to so many great Privileges.

She therefore sent for her Steward, Mr. *Peter Pounce*; and ordered him to pay *Joseph* his Wages, to strip off his Livery and turn him out of the House that Evening.

She then called *Slipslop* up, and after refreshing her Spirits with a small Cordial which she kept in her Closet, she began in the following manner:

'*Slipslop*, why will you, who know my passionate Temper, attempt to provoke me by your Answers? I am convinced you are an honest Servant, and should be very unwilling to part with you. I believe likewise, you have found me an indulgent Mistress on many Occasions, and have as little Reason on your side to desire a change. I can't help being surprized therefore, that you will take the surest Method to offend me. I mean repeating my Words, which you know I have always detested.'

The prudent Waiting-Gentlewoman, had duly weighed the whole Matter, and found on mature Deliberation, that a good Place in Possession was better than one in Expectation; as she found her Mistress therefore inclined to relent, she thought proper also to put on some small Condescension; which was as readily accepted: and so the Affair was reconciled, all Offences forgiven, and a Present of a Gown and Petticoat made her as an Instance of her Lady's future Favour.

She offered once or twice to speak in favour of *Joseph*: but found her Lady's Heart so obdurate, that she prudently dropt all such Efforts. She considered there were more Footmen in the House, and some as stout Fellows, tho' not quite so handsome as *Joseph*: besides, the Reader hath already seen her tender Advances had not met with the Encouragement she might have reasonably expected. She thought she had thrown away a great deal of Sack and Sweet-meats on an ungrateful Rascal; and being a little inclined to the Opinion of that female Sect, who hold one lusty young Fellow to be near as good as another lusty young Fellow, she at last gave up *Joseph* and his Cause, and with a Triumph over her Passion highly commendable, walked off with her Present, and with great Tranquility paid a visit to a Stone-Bottle, which is of sovereign Use to a Philosophical Temper.

She left not her Mistress so easy. The poor Lady could not reflect, without Agony, that her dear Reputation was in the power of her Servants. All her Comfort, as to *Joseph* was, that she hoped he did not understand her Meaning; at least, she could say for herself, she had not plainly express'd any thing to him; and as to Mrs. *Slipslop*, she imagined she could bribe her to Secrecy.

But what hurt her most was, that in reality she had not so entirely conquered her Passion; the little God lay lurking in her Heart, tho' Anger and Disdain so hoodwinked her, that she could not see him. She was a thousand times on the very Brink of revoking the Sentence she had passed against the poor Youth. Love became his Advocate, and whispered many things in his favour. Honour likewise endeavoured to vindicate his Crime, and Pity to mitigate his Punishment; on the other side, Pride and Revenge spoke as loudly against him: and thus the poor Lady was tortured with Perplexity; opposite Passions distracting and tearing her Mind different ways.

So have I seen, in the Hall of *Westminster*; where Serjeant *Bramble* hath been retained on the right Side, and Serjeant *Puzzle* on the left; the Balance of Opinion (so equal were their Fees) alternately incline to either Scale. Now *Bramble* throws in an Argument, and *Puzzle's* Scale strikes the Beam; again, *Bramble* shares the like Fate, overpowered by the Weight of *Puzzle*. Here *Bramble* hits, there *Puzzle* strikes; here one has you, there t'other has you; 'till at last all becomes one Scene of Confusion in the tortured Minds of the Hearers; equal Wagers are laid on the Success, and neither Judge nor Jury can possibly make any thing of the Matter; all Things are so enveloped by the careful Serjeants in Doubt and Obscurity.

Or as it happens in the Conscience, where Honour and Honesty pull one way, and a Bribe and Necessity another.—If it was only our present Business to make Similies, we could produce many more to this Purpose: but a Similie (as well as a Word) to the Wise. We shall therefore see a little after our Hero, for whom the Reader is doubtless in some pain.

CHAPTER X

Joseph *writes another Letter: His Transactions with* Mr. Peter Pounce, *&c. with his Departure from* Lady Booby.

THE disconsolate *Joseph*, would not have had an Understanding sufficient for the principal Subject of such a Book as this, if he had any longer misunderstood the Drift of his Mistress; and indeed that he did not discern it sooner, the Reader will be pleased to apply to an Unwillingness in him to discover what he must condemn in her as a Fault. Having therefore quitted her Presence, he retired into his own Garret, and entered himself into an Ejaculation on the numberless Calamities which attended Beauty, and the Misfortune it was to be handsomer than one's Neighbours.

He then sat down and addressed himself to his Sister *Pamela*, in the following Words:

'*Dear Sister* Pamela,

'Hoping you are well, what News have I to tell you! O *Pamela*, my Mistress is fallen in love with me—That is, what great Folks call falling in love, she has a mind to ruin me; but I hope, I shall have more Resolution and more Grace[1] than to part with my Virtue to any Lady upon Earth.

'Mr. *Adams* hath often told me, that Chastity is as great a Virtue in a Man as in a Woman. He says he never knew any more than his Wife, and I shall endeavour to follow his Example. Indeed, it is owing entirely to his excellent Sermons and Advice, together with your Letters, that I have been able to resist a Temptation, which he says no Man complies with, but he repents in this World, or is damned for it in the next; and why should I trust to Repentance on my Death-bed, since I may die in my sleep? What fine things are good Advice and good Examples! But I am glad she turned me out of the Chamber as she did: for

[1] As is evident in *Shamela*, where the absurd Parson Tickletext is made to praise *Pamela* for inculcating 'the useful and truly religious Doctrine of *Grace*', Fielding associated the religion of Richardson's heroine with the Methodism of George Whitefield, whose Antinomian stress upon the efficacy of faith and grace rather than good works Fielding deplored. (See p. 79, n. 1; p. 82, n. 2.)

I had once almost forgotten every word Parson *Adams* had ever said to me.

'I don't doubt, dear Sister, but you will have Grace to preserve your Virtue against all Trials; and I beg you earnestly to pray, I may be enabled to preserve mine: for truly, it is very severely attacked by more than one: but, I hope I shall copy your Example, and that of *Joseph*, my Name's-sake;[1] and maintain my Virtue against all Temptations.'

Joseph had not finished his Letter, when he was summoned down stairs by Mr. *Peter Pounce*, to receive his Wages: for, besides that out of eight Pounds a Year, he allowed his Father and Mother four, he had been obliged, in order to furnish himself with musical Instruments, to apply to the Generosity of the aforesaid *Peter*, who, on urgent Occasions, used to advance the Servants their Wages: not before they were due, but before they were payable; that is, perhaps, half a Year after they were due, and this at the moderate *Premiums* of fifty *per Cent.*[2] or a little more; by which charitable Methods, together with lending Money to other People, and even to his own Master and Mistress, the honest Man had, from nothing, in a few Years amassed a small Sum of twenty thousand Pounds or thereabouts.

Joseph having received his little Remainder of Wages, and having stript off his Livery, was forced to borrow a Frock and Breeches of one of the Servants: (for he was so beloved in the Family, that they would all have lent him any thing) and being told by *Peter*, that he must not stay a Moment longer in the House, than was necessary to pack up his Linnen, which he easily did in a very narrow Compass; he took a melancholy Leave of his Fellow-Servants, and set out at seven in the Evening.

He had proceeded the length of two or three Streets, before he absolutely determined with himself, whether he should leave the Town that Night, or procuring a Lodging, wait 'till the Morning. At last, the Moon, shining very bright, helped him to come to a Resolution of beginning his Journey immediately, to which likewise he had some other Inducements which the Reader, without being a Conjurer, cannot possibly guess; 'till we have given him those hints, which it may be now proper to open.

[1] See p. 29, n. 1.
[2] By an act of 1713 (12 Anne, cap. 16) the allowable rate of usury had been reduced to 5 per cent.

CHAPTER XI

Of several new Matters not expected.

IT is an Observation sometimes made, that to indicate our Idea of a simple Fellow, we say, *He is easily to be seen through*: Nor do I believe it a more improper Denotation of a simple Book. Instead of applying this to any particular Performance, we chuse rather to remark the contrary in this History, where the Scene opens itself by small degrees, and he is a sagacious Reader who can see two Chapters before him.

For this reason, we have not hitherto hinted a Matter which now seems necessary to be explained; since it may be wondered at, first, that *Joseph* made such extraordinary haste out of Town, which hath been already shewn; and secondly, which will be now shewn, that instead of proceeding to the Habitation of his Father and Mother, or to his beloved Sister *Pamela*, he chose rather to set out full speed to the Lady *Booby's* Country Seat, which he had left on his Journey to *London*.

Be it known then, that in the same Parish where this Seat stood, there lived a young Girl whom *Joseph* (tho' the best of Sons and Brothers) longed more impatiently to see than his Parents or his Sister. She was a poor Girl, who had been formerly bred up in Sir *John's*[1] Family; whence a little before the Journey to *London*, she had been discarded by Mrs. *Slipslop* on account of her extraordinary Beauty: for I never could find any other reason.

This young Creature (who now lived with a Farmer in the Parish) had been always beloved by *Joseph*, and returned his Affection. She was two Years only younger than our Hero. They had been acquainted from their Infancy, and had conceived a very early liking for each other, which had grown to such a degree of Affection, that Mr. *Adams* had with much ado prevented them from marrying; and persuaded them to wait, 'till a few Years Service and Thrift had a little improved their Experience, and enabled them to live comfortably together.

They followed this good Man's Advice; as indeed his Word was little less than a Law in his Parish: for as he had shewn his Parishioners by a uniform Behaviour of thirty-five Years dura-

---

[1] Fielding's error for 'Sir Thomas's'.

tion,[1] that he had their Good entirely at heart; so they consulted him on every Occasion, and very seldom acted contrary to his Opinion.

Nothing can be imagined more tender than was the parting between these two Lovers. A thousand Sighs heaved the Bosom of *Joseph*; a thousand Tears distilled from the lovely Eyes of *Fanny*, (for that was her Name.) Tho' her Modesty would only suffer her to admit his eager Kisses, her violent Love made her more than passive in his Embraces; and she often pulled him to her Breast with a soft Pressure, which, tho' perhaps it would not have squeezed an Insect to death, caused more Emotion in the Heart of *Joseph*, than the closest *Cornish* Hug[2] could have done.

The Reader may perhaps wonder, that so fond a Pair should during a Twelve-month's Absence[3] never converse with one another; indeed there was but one Reason which did, or could have prevented them; and this was, that poor *Fanny* could neither write nor read, nor could she be prevailed upon to transmit the Delicacies of her tender and chaste Passion, by the Hands of an Amanuensis.

They contented themselves therefore with frequent Enquiries after each other's Health, with a mutual Confidence in each other's Fidelity, and the Prospect of their future Happiness.

Having explained these Matters to our Reader, and, as far as possible, satisfied all his Doubts, we return to honest *Joseph*, whom we left just set out on his Travels by the Light of the Moon.

Those who have read any Romance or Poetry antient or modern, must have been informed, that Love hath Wings; by which they are not to understand, as some young Ladies by mistake have done, that a Lover can fly: the Writers, by this ingenious Allegory, intending to insinuate no more, than that Lovers do not march like Horse-Guards; in short, that they put the best Leg foremost, which our lusty Youth, who could walk with any Man, did so heartily on this Occasion, that within four Hours, he reached a famous House of Hospitality well known to the Western Traveller. It presents you a Lion on the Sign-Post: and the Master, who was christened *Timotheus*, is commonly

[1] Fielding apparently forgets that in I. iii, Adams is said to be just fifty years old.
[2] The wrestlers of Cornwall were famous.
[3] Earlier in this chapter we were told that Fanny had been discarded by Slipslop 'a little before the Journey to *London*'.

called plain *Tim*.[1] Some have conceived that he hath particularly chosen the Lion for his Sign, as he doth in Countenance greatly resemble that magnanimous Beast, tho' his Disposition savours more of the Sweetness of the Lamb. He is a Person well received among all sorts of Men, being qualified to render himself agreeable to any; as he is well versed in History and Politicks, hath a smattering in Law and Divinity, cracks a good Jest, and plays wonderfully well on the *French* Horn.

A violent Storm of Hail forced *Joseph* to take Shelter in this Inn, where he remembered Sir *Thomas* had dined in his way to Town. *Joseph* had no sooner seated himself by the Kitchin-Fire, than *Timotheus*, observing his Livery, began to condole the loss of his late Master; who was, he said, his very particular and intimate Acquaintance, with whom he had cracked many a merry Bottle, aye many a dozen in his Time. He then remarked that all those Things were over now, all past, and just as if they had never been; and concluded with an excellent Observation on the Certainty of Death, which his Wife said was indeed very true. A Fellow now arrived at the same Inn with two Horses, one of which he was leading farther down into the Country to meet his Master; these he put into the Stable, and came and took his Place by *Joseph's* Side, who immediately knew him to be the Servant of a neighbouring Gentleman, who used to visit at their House.

This Fellow was likewise forced in by the Storm; for he had Orders to go twenty Miles farther that Evening, and luckily on the same Road which *Joseph* himself intended to take. He therefore embraced this Opportunity of complimenting his Friend with his Master's Horses, (notwithstanding he had received express commands to the contrary) which was readily accepted: and so after they had drank a loving Pot, and the Storm was over, they set out together.

[1] Doubtless Timothy Harris, the 'publican of good taste' whom Fielding compliments in *Tom Jones* (VIII. viii). Harris, who died in 1748, was the prosperous keeper of 'The Red Lion' inn at Egham, Surrey. His wife's name was Elizabeth. (See his will, probated Prerogative Court of Canterbury, on file at Somerset House, London: Strahan. Folio 329. 1748.)

CHAPTER XII

Containing many surprizing Adventures, which Joseph
Andrews *met with on the Road, scarce credible to those
who have never travelled in a Stage-Coach.*

NOTHING remarkable happened on the Road, 'till their arrival
at the Inn, to which the Horses were ordered; whither they came
about two in the Morning. The Moon then shone very bright,
and *Joseph* making his Friend a present of a Pint of Wine, and
thanking him for the favour of his Horse, notwithstanding all
Entreaties to the contrary, proceeded on his Journey on foot.

He had not gone above two Miles, charmed with the hopes of
shortly seeing his beloved *Fanny*, when he was met by two Fellows
in a narrow Lane, and ordered to stand and deliver. He readily
gave them all the Money he had, which was somewhat less than
two Pounds; and told them he hoped they would be so generous
as to return him a few Shillings, to defray his Charges on his way
home.

One of the Ruffians answered with an Oath, *Yes, we'll give
you something presently: but first strip and be d—n'd to you.—Strip,*
cry'd the other, *or I'll blow your Brains to the Devil. Joseph,* remembring that he had borrowed his Coat and Breeches of a
Friend; and that he should be ashamed of making any Excuse
for not returning them, reply'd, he hoped they would not insist
on his Clothes, which were not worth much; but consider the
Coldness of the Night. *You are cold, are you, you Rascal!* says one
of the Robbers, *I'll warm you with a Vengeance*; and damning his
Eyes, snapt a Pistol at his Head: which he had no sooner done,
than the other levelled a Blow at him with his Stick, which
Joseph, who was expert at Cudgel-playing, caught with his, and
returned the Favour so successfully on his Adversary, that he laid
him sprawling at his Feet, and at the same Instant received a Blow
from behind, with the Butt-end of a Pistol from the other Villain,
which felled him to the Ground, and totally deprived him of his
Senses.

The Thief, who had been knocked down, had now recovered
himself; and both together fell to be-labouring poor *Joseph* with

their Sticks, till they were convinced they had put an end to his miserable Being: They then stript him entirely naked, threw him into a Ditch, and departed with their Booty.

The poor Wretch, who lay motionless a long time, just began to recover his Senses as a Stage-Coach came by. The Postillion hearing a Man's Groans, stopt his Horses, and told the Coachman, 'he was certain there was a *dead* Man lying in the Ditch, for he heard him groan.' 'Go on, Sirrah,' says the Coachman, 'we are confounded late, and have no time to look after dead Men.' A Lady, who heard what the Postillion said, and likewise heard the Groan, called eagerly to the Coachman, 'to stop and see what was the matter.' Upon which he bid the Postillion 'alight, and look into the Ditch.' He did so, and returned, 'that there was a Man sitting upright as naked as ever he was born.'—'O *J-sus*,' cry'd the Lady, 'A naked Man! Dear Coachman, drive on and leave him.' Upon this the Gentlemen got out of the Coach; and *Joseph* begged them, 'to have Mercy upon him: For that he had been robbed, and almost beaten to death.' 'Robbed,' cries an old Gentleman; 'Let us make all the haste imaginable, or we shall be robbed too.' A young Man, who belonged to the Law answered, 'he wished they had past by without taking any Notice: But that now they might be proved to have been *last in his Company*; if he should die, they might be called to some account for his Murther. He therefore thought it adviseable to save the poor Creature's Life, for their own sakes, if possible; at least, if he died, to prevent the Jury's finding *that they fled for it*.[1] He was therefore *of Opinion*, to take the Man into the Coach, and carry him to the next Inn.' The Lady insisted, 'that he should not come into the Coach. That if they lifted him in, she would herself alight: for she had rather stay in that Place to all Eternity, than ride with a naked Man.' The Coachman objected, 'that he could not suffer him to be taken in, unless some body would pay a Shilling for his Carriage the four Miles.' Which the two Gentlemen refused to do; but the Lawyer, who was afraid of some Mischief happening to himself if the Wretch was left behind in that Condition, saying, 'no Man could be too cautious in these Matters, and that he remembered very extraordinary Cases in the

---

[1] Fleeing the scene of a capital crime was an offence for which the fugitive, even if subsequently acquitted of the crime itself, was liable to forfeit all his goods. (See Giles Jacob, *New Law-Dictionary*, 4th ed. [1739], s.v. *'fugam fecit'*.)

Books,' threatned the Coachman, and bid him deny taking him up at his Peril; 'for that if he died, he should be indicted for his Murther, and if he lived, and brought an Action against him, he would willingly take a Brief in it.' These Words had a sensible Effect on the Coachman, who was well acquainted with the Person who spoke them; and the old Gentleman abovementioned, thinking the naked Man would afford him frequent Opportunities of shewing his Wit to the Lady, offered to join with the Company in giving a Mug of Beer for his Fare; till partly alarmed by the Threats of the one, and partly by the Promises of the other, and being perhaps *a little* moved with Compassion at the poor Creature's Condition, who stood bleeding and shivering with the Cold, he at length agreed; and *Joseph* was now advancing to the Coach, where seeing the Lady, who held the Sticks of her Fan before her Eyes, he absolutely refused, miserable as he was, to enter, unless he was furnished with sufficient Covering, to prevent giving the least Offence to Decency. So perfectly modest was this young Man; such mighty Effects had the spotless Example of the amiable *Pamela*, and the excellent Sermons of Mr. *Adams* wrought upon him.

Though there were several great Coats about the Coach, it was not easy to get over this Difficulty which *Joseph* had started. The two Gentlemen complained they were cold, and could not spare a Rag; the Man of Wit saying, with a Laugh, *that Charity began at home*; and the Coachman, who had two great Coats spread under him, refused to lend either, lest they should be made bloody; the Lady's Footman desired to be excused for the same Reason, which the Lady herself, notwithstanding her Abhorence of a naked Man, approved: and it is more than probable, poor *Joseph*, who obstinately adhered to his modest Resolution, must have perished, unless the Postillion, (a Lad who hath been since transported for robbing a Hen-roost) had voluntarily stript off a great Coat, his only Garment, at the same time swearing a great Oath, (for which he was rebuked by the Passengers) 'that he would rather ride in his Shirt all his Life, than suffer a Fellow-Creature to lie in so miserable a Condition.'

Joseph, having put on the great Coat, was lifted into the Coach, which now proceeded on its Journey. He declared himself almost dead with the Cold, which gave the Man of Wit an occasion to ask the Lady, if she could not accommodate him with a Dram. She

answered with some Resentment, 'she wondered at his asking her
such a Question;' but assured him, 'she never tasted any such thing.'

The Lawyer was enquiring into the Circumstances of the
Robbery, when the Coach stopt, and one of the Ruffians, putting
a Pistol in, demanded their Money of the Passengers; who
readily gave it them; and the Lady, in her Fright, delivered up a
little silver Bottle, of about a half-pint Size, which, the Rogue
clapping it to his Mouth, and drinking her Health, declared held
some of the best *Nantes*[1] he had ever tasted: this the Lady afterwards assured the Company was the Mistake of her Maid, for
that she had ordered her to fill the Bottle with *Hungary* Water.[2]

As soon as the Fellows were departed, the Lawyer, who had,
it seems, a Case of Pistols in the Seat of the Coach, informed the
Company, that if it had been Day-light, and he could have come
at his Pistols, he would not have submitted to the Robbery; he
likewise set forth, that he had often met Highwaymen when he
travelled on horseback, but none ever durst attack him; concluding, that if he had not been more afraid for the Lady than for
himself, he should not have now parted with his Money so easily.

As Wit is generally observed to love to reside in empty
Pockets; so the Gentleman, whose Ingenuity we have above
remark'd, as soon as he had parted with his Money, began to
grow wonderfully facetious. He made frequent Allusions to
Adam and *Eve*, and said many excellent things on Figs and Fig-
Leaves; which perhaps gave more Offence to *Joseph* than to any
other in the Company.

The Lawyer likewise made several very pretty Jests, without
departing from his Profession. He said, 'if *Joseph* and the Lady
were alone, he would be the more capable of making a *Conveyance* to her, as his *Affairs* were not *fettered* with any *Incumbrance*;
he'd warrant, he soon suffered a *Recovery* by a Writ of *Entry*,
which was the proper way to create *Heirs in Tail*; that for his own
part, he would engage to make so *firm a Settlement* in a Coach,
that there should be no Danger of an *Ejectment*;'[3] with an Inun-
dation of the like Gibbrish, which he continued to vent till the
Coach arrived at an Inn, where one Servant-Maid only was up in

---

[1] Brandy.   [2] A distilled water made of rosemary flowers and spirit of wine.
[3] The bawdy *double ententes* in this passage depend upon the jargon of real property
law. The less obvious terms are as follows: a *conveyance* is the lawful transference of property from one person to another, usually by deed; an *incumbrance* is a burden on property,
such as a mortgage; an *heir in tail* is a person who succeeds to an estate by virtue of a deed

readiness to attend the Coachman, and furnish him with cold
Meat and a Dram. *Joseph* desired to alight, and that he might
have a Bed prepared for him, which the Maid readily promised to
perform; and being a good-natur'd Wench, and not so squeamish
as the Lady had been, she clapt a large Faggot on the Fire, and
furnishing *Joseph* with a great Coat belonging to one of the Host-
lers, desired him to sit down and warm himself, whilst she made
his Bed. The Coachman, in the mean time, took an Opportunity
to call up a Surgeon, who lived within a few Doors: after which,
he reminded his Passengers how late they were, and after they
had taken Leave of *Joseph*, hurried them off as fast as he could.

The Wench soon got *Joseph* to bed, and promised to use her
Interest to borrow him a Shirt; but imagined, as she afterwards
said, by his being so bloody, that he must be a dead Man: she
ran with all speed to hasten the Surgeon, who was more than half
drest, apprehending that the Coach had been overturned and
some Gentleman or Lady hurt. As soon as the Wench had informed him at his Window, that it was a poor foot Passenger who
had been stripped of all he had, and almost murdered; he chid her
for disturbing him so early, slipped off his Clothes again, and
very quietly returned to bed and to sleep.

Aurora now began to shew her blooming Cheeks over the
Hills, whilst ten Millions of feathered Songsters, in jocund
Chorus, repeated Odes a thousand times sweeter than those of our
Laureate, and sung both *the Day and the Song*;[1] when the Master

of entail, whereby the estate is settled on a number of specific persons in succession; an
ejectment is the process of expelling a person from his holding.

[1] Cibber succeeded Laurence Eusden as Poet Laureate in 1730; his odes, composed to be
sung annually on the occasions of the New Year and the King's birthday, were a standing
jest. Typically in these poems, Cibber would celebrate the day and the song, as in these
concluding lines from *An Ode for His Majesty's Birth-Day, October 30, 1731*:

> With Song, ye BRITONS, lead the Day!
> Sing! sing the Morn, that gave him Breath,
> Whose Virtues never shall decay,
> No, never, never taste of Death.

In *The Historical Register for the Year 1736* (I. i) Fielding parodied a Cibberian 'Ode to the
New Year', choosing as his refrain:

> Then sing the Day,
> And sing the Song;
> And thus be merry
> All Day long.

But the allusion in *Joseph Andrews* brings this general background into specific focus by

of the Inn, Mr. *Tow-wouse*, arose, and learning from his Maid an Account of the Robbery, and the Situation of his poor naked Guest, he shook his Head, and cried, *Good-lack-a-day!* and then ordered the Girl to carry him one of his own Shirts.

Mrs. *Tow-wouse* was just awake, and had stretched out her Arms in vain to fold her departed Husband, when the Maid entered the Room. 'Who's there? *Betty?*' 'Yes Madam.' 'Where's your Master?' 'He's without, Madam; he hath sent me for a Shirt to lend a poor naked Man, who hath been robbed and murdered.' 'Touch one, if you dare, you Slut,' said Mrs. *Tow-wouse*, 'your Master is a pretty sort of a Man to take in naked Vagabonds, and clothe them with his own Clothes. I shall have no such Doings.—If you offer to touch any thing, I will throw the Chamber-Pot at your Head. Go, send your Master to me.' 'Yes Madam,' answered *Betty*. As soon as he came in, she thus began: 'What the Devil do you mean by this, Mr. *Tow-wouse?* Am I to buy Shirts to lend to a sett of scabby Rascals?' 'My Dear,' said Mr. *Tow-wouse*, 'this is a poor Wretch.' 'Yes,' says she, 'I know it is a poor Wretch, but what the Devil have we to do with poor Wretches? The Law makes us provide for too many already.[1] We shall have thirty or forty poor Wretches in red Coats shortly.' 'My Dear,' cries *Tow-wouse*, 'this Man hath been robbed of all he hath.' 'Well then,' says she, 'where's his Money to pay his Reckoning? Why doth not such a Fellow go to an Ale-house? I shall send him packing as soon as I am up, I assure you.' 'My Dear,' said he, 'common Charity won't suffer you to do that.' 'Common Charity, a F—t!' says she, 'Common Charity teaches us to provide for ourselves, and our Families; and I and mine won't be ruined by your Charity, I assure you.' 'Well,' says he, 'my Dear, do as you will when you are up, you know I never contradict you.' 'No,' says she, 'if the Devil was to contradict me, I would make the House too hot to hold him.'

With such like Discourses they consumed near half an Hour,

evoking a passage in the *Apology* in which Cibber, commenting upon his first schoolboy effort as an occasional poet, compares it to Fielding's travesty: 'I cannot say it was much above the merry Style of *Sing! Sing the Day, and sing the Song*, in the Farce . . .' (2nd ed., p. 29). Fielding also rallies Cibber on his bad verse in *Pasquin* (II. i) and *The Vernoniad* (1741).

[1] Barracks were scarce in England. By law (I George, cap. 3) soldiers were billeted on the keepers of inns, livery stables, and alehouses, who were compelled to supply lodging, food, and small beer for four pence a day.

whilst *Betty* provided a Shirt from the Hostler, who was one of her Sweethearts, and put it on poor *Joseph*. The Surgeon had likewise at last visited him, had washed and drest his Wounds, and was now come to acquaint Mr. *Tow-wouse*, that his Guest was in such extreme danger of his Life, that he scarce saw any hopes of his Recovery.—'Here's a pretty Kettle of Fish,' cries Mrs. *Tow-wouse*, 'you have brought upon us! We are like to have a Funeral at our own expence.' *Tow-wouse*, (who notwithstanding his Charity, would have given his Vote as freely as he ever did at an Election, that any other House in the Kingdom, should have had quiet Possession of his Guest) answered, 'My Dear, I am not to blame: he was brought hither by the Stage-Coach; and *Betty* had put him to bed before I was stirring.' 'I'll *Betty* her,' says she—At which, with half her Garments on, the other half under her Arm, she sallied out in quest of the unfortunate *Betty*, whilst *Tow-wouse* and the Surgeon went to pay a Visit to poor *Joseph*, and enquire into the Circumstance of this melancholy Affair.

CHAPTER XIII

What happened to Joseph *during his Sickness at the Inn, with the curious Discourse between him and Mr.* Barnabas *the Parson of the Parish.*

As soon as *Joseph* had communicated a particular History of the Robbery, together with a short Account of himself, and his intended Journey, he asked the Surgeon 'if he apprehended him to be in any Danger:' To which the Surgeon very honestly answered, 'he feared he was; for that his Pulse was very exalted and feverish, and if his Fever should prove more than *Symptomatick*, it would be impossible to save him.' *Joseph*, fetching a deep Sigh, cried, '*Poor* Fanny, *I would I could have lived to see thee! but* G—'s *Will be done.*'

The Surgeon then advised him, 'if he had any worldly Affairs to settle, that he would do it as soon as possible; for though he hoped he might recover, yet he thought himself obliged to acquaint him he was in great danger, and if the malign Concoction of his Humours[1] should cause a suscitation of his Fever, he might soon grow delirious, and incapable to make his Will.' *Joseph* answered, 'that it was impossible for any Creature in the Universe to be in a poorer Condition than himself: for since the Robbery he had not one thing of any kind whatever, which he could call his own.' *I had*, said he, *a poor little Piece of Gold which they took away, that would have been a Comfort to me in all my Afflictions; but surely*, Fanny, *I want nothing to remind me of thee. I have thy dear Image in my Heart, and no Villain can ever tear it thence.*

Joseph desired Paper and Pens to write a Letter, but they were refused him; and he was advised to use all his Endeavours to compose himself. They then left him; and Mr. *Tow-wouse* sent to a Clergyman to come and administer his good Offices to the Soul of poor *Joseph*, since the Surgeon despaired of making any successful Applications to his Body.

Mr. *Barnabas* (for that was the Clergyman's Name) came as soon as sent for, and having first drank a Dish of Tea with the Landlady, and afterwards a Bowl of Punch with the Landlord, he walked up to the Room where *Joseph* lay: but, finding him asleep, returned to take the other Sneaker,[2] which when he had finished, he again crept softly up to the Chamber-Door, and, having opened it, heard the Sick Man talking to himself in the following manner:

'O most adorable *Pamela*! most virtuous Sister, whose Example could alone enable me to withstand all the Temptations of Riches and Beauty, and to preserve my Virtue pure and chaste, for the Arms of my dear *Fanny*, if it had pleased Heaven that I should ever have come unto them. What Riches, or Honours, or Pleasures can make us amends for the Loss of Innocence? Doth not that alone afford us more Consolation, than all worldly Acquisitions? What but Innocence and Virtue could give any Comfort to such a miserable Wretch as I am? Yet these can make me prefer this sick and painful Bed to all the Pleasures I should

[1] Medicine in the eighteenth century was still very much under the influence of the humoral pathology of Hippocrates (c. 460–355 B.C.)—'the divine Hippocrates', as Fielding's contemporary, Robert James, called him, 'to whom we are obliged for most Things in Medicine' (*A Medicinal Dictionary* [1743–5], I. xcvi). According to this doctrine, health depends upon the perfect mingling of the four basic humours: blood, phlegm, yellow bile, and black bile. When one of these elements predominates or is deficient, sickness results.
[2] A small bowl of punch.

have found in my Lady's. These can make me face Death without
Fear; and though I love my *Fanny* more than ever Man loved
a Woman; these can teach me to resign myself to the Divine
Will without repining. O thou delightful charming Creature,
if Heaven had indulged thee to my Arms, the poorest, humblest
State would have been a Paradise; I could have lived with thee in
the lowest Cottage, without envying the Palaces, the Dainties,
or the Riches of any Man breathing. But I must leave thee, leave
thee for ever, my dearest Angel, I must think of another World,
and I heartily pray thou may'st meet Comfort in this.'—*Barnabas*
thought he had heard enough; so down stairs he went, and told
Tow-wouse he could do his Guest no Service: for that he was very
light-headed, and had uttered nothing but a Rhapsody of Nonsense all the time he stayed in the Room.

The Surgeon returned in the Afternoon, and found his Patient
in a higher Fever, as he said, than when he left him, though not
delirious: for notwithstanding Mr. *Barnabas's* Opinion, he had
not been once out of his Senses since his arrival at the Inn.

Mr. *Barnabas* was again sent for, and with much difficulty
prevailed on to make another Visit. As soon as he entered the
Room, he told *Joseph*, 'he was come to pray by him, and to prepare him for another World: In the first place therefore, he hoped
he had repented of all his Sins?' *Joseph* answered, 'he hoped he
had: but there was one thing which he knew not whether he
should call a Sin; if it was, he feared he should die in the Commission of it, and that was the Regret of parting with a young
Woman, whom he loved as tenderly as he did his Heartstrings?'
Barnabas bad him be assured, 'that any Repining at the Divine
Will, was one of the greatest Sins he could commit; that he ought
to forget all carnal Affections, and think of better things.' *Joseph*
said, 'that neither in this World nor the next, he could forget his
Fanny, and that the Thought, however grievous, of parting from
her for ever, was not half so tormenting, as the Fear of what she
would suffer when she knew his Misfortune.' *Barnabas* said,
'that such Fears argued a Diffidence and Despondence very
criminal; that he must divest himself of all human Passion, and
fix his Heart above.' *Joseph* answered, 'that was what he desired
to do, and should be obliged to him, if he would enable him to
accomplish it.' *Barnabas* replied, 'That must be done by Grace.'
Joseph besought him to discover how he might attain it. *Barnabas*

answered, 'By Prayer and Faith.' He then questioned him concerning his Forgiveness of the Thieves. *Joseph* answered, 'he feared, that was more than he could do: for nothing would give him more Pleasure than to hear they were taken.' 'That,' cries *Barnabas*, 'is for the sake of Justice.' 'Yes,' said *Joseph*, 'but if I was to meet them again, I am afraid I should attack them, and kill them too, if I could.' 'Doubtless,' answered *Barnabas*, 'it is lawful to kill a Thief: but can you say, you forgive them as a Christian ought?' *Joseph* desired to know what that Forgiveness was. 'That is,' answered *Barnabas*, 'to forgive them as—as—it is to forgive them as—in short, it is to forgive them as a Christian.' *Joseph* reply'd, 'he forgave them as much as he could.' 'Well, well,' said *Barnabas*, 'that will do.' He then demanded of him, 'if he remembered any more Sins unrepented of; and if he did, he desired him to make haste and repent of them as fast as he could: that they might repeat over a few Prayers together.' *Joseph* answered, 'he could not recollect any great Crimes he had been guilty of, and that those he had committed, he was sincerely sorry for.' *Barnabas* said that was enough, and then proceeded to Prayer with all the expedition he was master of: Some Company then waiting for him below in the Parlour, where the Ingredients for Punch were all in Readiness; but no one would squeeze the Oranges till he came.

Joseph complained he was dry, and desired a little Tea; which *Barnabas* reported to Mrs. *Tow-wouse*, who answered, 'she had just done drinking it, and could not be slopping all day;' but ordered *Betty* to carry him up some Small Beer.

Betty obeyed her Mistress's Commands; but *Joseph*, as soon as he had tasted it, said, he feared it would encrease his Fever, and that he longed very much for Tea: To which the good-natured *Betty* answered, he should have Tea, if there was any in the Land; she accordingly went and bought him some herself, and attended him with it; where we will leave her and *Joseph* together for some time, to entertain the Reader with other Matters.

CHAPTER XIV

*Being very full of Adventures, which succeeded each
other at the Inn.*

IT was now the Dusk of the Evening, when a grave Person rode
into the Inn, and committing his Horse to the Hostler, went
directly into the Kitchin, and having called for a Pipe of Tobacco,
took his place by the Fire-side; where several other Persons were
likewise assembled.

The Discourse ran altogether on the Robbery which was committed the Night before, and on the poor Wretch, who lay above
in the dreadful Condition, in which we have already seen him.
Mrs. *Tow-wouse* said, 'she wondered what the devil *Tom Whipwell* meant by bringing such Guests to her House, when there
were so many Ale-houses on the Road proper for their Reception?
But she assured him, if he died, the Parish should be at the
Expence of the Funeral.' She added, 'nothing would serve the
Fellow's Turn but Tea, she would assure him.' *Betty*, who was
just returned from her charitable Office, answered, she believed
he was a Gentleman: for she never saw a finer Skin in her Life.
'Pox on his Skin,' replied Mrs. *Tow-wouse*, 'I suppose, that is all
we are like to have for the Reckoning. I desire no such Gentle-
men should ever call at the *Dragon*;' (which it seems was the
Sign of the Inn.)

The Gentleman lately arrived discovered a great deal of Emo-
tion at the Distress of this poor Creature, whom he observed not
to be fallen into the most compassionate Hands. And indeed, if
Mrs. *Tow-wouse* had given no Utterance to the Sweetness of her
Temper, Nature had taken such Pains in her Countenance, that
Hogarth himself never gave more Expression to a Picture.

Her Person was short, thin, and crooked. Her Forehead projected in the middle, and thence descended in a Declivity to the
Top of her Nose, which was sharp and red, and would have hung
over her Lips, had not Nature turned up the end of it. Her Lips
were two Bits of Skin, which, whenever she spoke, she drew
together in a Purse. Her Chin was peeked,[1] and at the upper end

[1] In this rare instance the unauthoritative fifth edition probably restores Fielding's
meaning. 'Peeked' (or 'peaked', as Murphy has it) is usual in such a context: consider, for

of that Skin, which composed her Cheeks, stood two Bones, that almost hid a Pair of small red Eyes. Add to this, a Voice most wonderfully adapted to the Sentiments it was to convey, being both loud and hoarse.

It is not easy to say, whether the Gentleman had conceived a greater Dislike for his Landlady, or Compassion for her unhappy Guest. He enquired very earnestly of the Surgeon, who was now come into the Kitchin, 'whether he had any hopes of his Recovery?' he begged him, to use all possible means towards it, telling him, 'it was the duty of Men of all Professions, to apply their Skill *gratis* for the Relief of the Poor and Necessitous.' The Surgeon answered, 'he should take proper care: but he defied all the Surgeons in *London* to do him any good.' 'Pray, Sir,' said the Gentleman, 'What are his Wounds?'—'Why, do you know any thing of Wounds?' says the Surgeon, (winking upon Mrs. *Towwouse*.) 'Sir, I have a small smattering in Surgery,' answered the Gentleman. 'A smattering,—ho, ho, ho!' said the Surgeon, 'I believe it is a smattering indeed.'

The Company were all attentive, expecting to hear the Doctor, who was what they call a dry Fellow, expose the Gentleman.

He began therefore with an Air of Triumph: 'I suppose, Sir, you have travelled.'[1] 'No really, Sir,' said the Gentleman. 'Ho! then you have practised in the Hospitals, perhaps.'—'No, Sir.' 'Hum! not that neither? Whence, Sir, then, if I may be so bold to enquire, have you got your Knowledge in Surgery?' 'Sir,' answered the Gentleman, 'I do not pretend to much; but, the little I know I have from Books.' 'Books!' cries the Doctor.— 'What, I suppose you have read *Galen* and *Hippocrates*!' 'No, Sir,' said the Gentleman. 'How! you understand Surgery,' answers the Doctor, 'and not read *Galen* and *Hippocrates*!' 'Sir,' cries the other, 'I believe there are many Surgeons who have never read these Authors.' 'I believe so too,' says the Doctor, 'more shame for them: but thanks to my Education: I have them by

example, the old usurer in Smollett's *Roderick Random*, Chapter XI, whose chin is 'peaked and prominent'. The original compositor may have misread the manuscript or have used type from a fouled case.

[1] Travel abroad as a means of improving one's knowledge of medicine was recommended by several eminent physicians of the period, among them Sir Hans Sloane, Dr. Richard Mead, and Dr. John Radcliffe. By the terms of his will (1714) Radcliffe left his Yorkshire estate to the Master and Fellows of University College, Oxford, for the foundation of two travelling medical fellowships.

heart, and very seldom go without them both in my Pocket.'
'They are pretty large Books,' said the Gentleman. 'Aye,' said
the Doctor, 'I believe I know how large they are better than you,'
(at which he fell a winking, and the whole Company burst into
a Laugh.)

The Doctor pursuing his Triumph, asked the Gentleman, 'if
he did not understand Physick as well as Surgery.' 'Rather
better,' answered the Gentleman. 'Aye, like enough,' cries the
Doctor, with a wink. 'Why, I know a little of Physick too.'
'I wish I knew half so much,' said *Tow-wouse*, 'I'd never wear
an Apron again.' 'Why, I believe, Landlord,' cries the Doctor,
'there are few Men, tho' I say it, within twelve Miles of the Place,
that handle a Fever better.—*Veniente occurrite Morbo*:[1] That is
my Method.—I suppose Brother, you understand *Latin*?' 'A
little,' says the Gentleman. 'Aye, and *Greek* now I'll warrant you:
Ton dapomibominos poluflosboio Thalasses.[2] But I have almost forgot these things, I could have repeated *Homer* by heart once.'—
'Efags! the Gentleman has caught a *Traytor*,'[3] says Mrs. *Tow-
wouse*; at which they all fell a laughing.

The Gentleman, who had not the least affection for joking,
very contentedly suffered the Doctor to enjoy his Victory; which
he did with no small Satisfaction: and having sufficiently sounded
his Depth, told him, 'he was thoroughly convinced of his great
Learning and Abilities; and that he would be obliged to him, if
he would let him know his opinion of his Patient's Case above
stairs.' 'Sir,' says the Doctor, 'his Case is that of a dead Man.—
The Contusion on his Head has *perforated* the *internal Membrane*
of the *Occiput*, and *divellicated* that *radical* small *minute* invisible
Nerve, which *coheres* to the *Pericranium*; and this was attended
with a Fever at first *symptomatick*, then *pneumatick*, and he is at
length *grown deliruus*, or delirious, as the Vulgar express it.'

He was proceeding in this learned manner, when a mighty

[1] Persius, *Satires*, iii. 64: 'Oppose the disease at its first approach.' Since the surgeon is
not remarkable for his knowledge of the classical languages, Fielding may have intended
the corruption introduced into the second edition.

[2] Two unrelated phrases from the *Iliad*: '*Ton dapomibominos*' ('answering him') and
'*poluflosboio Thalasses*' ('of the loud sounding sea').

[3] Considering the context and the reaction of the company, *traitor* makes little sense
and may be a printer's error for *Tartar*. The slang phrase, 'to catch a Tartar', was applied
to one who finds himself caught in a trap he has laid for another. It is curious, however,
that Fielding, in altering the phrase for the second edition, should have overlooked the
error; perhaps he meant Mrs. Tow-wouse to commit a rare malapropism.

Noise interrupted him. Some young Fellows in the Neighbourhood had taken one of the Thieves, and were bringing him into
the Inn. *Betty* ran up Stairs with this News to *Joseph*; who begged
they might search for a little piece of broken Gold, which had a
Ribband tied to it, and which he could swear to amongst all the
Hoards of the richest Men in the Universe.

Notwithstanding the Fellow's persisting in his Innocence, the
Mob were very busy in searching him, and presently, among
other things, pulled out the Piece of Gold just mentioned; which
Betty no sooner saw, than she laid violent hands on it, and conveyed it up to *Joseph*, who received it with raptures of Joy, and
hugging it in his Bosom declared, *he could now die contented*.

Within a few Minutes afterwards, came in some other Fellows,
with a Bundle which they had found in a Ditch; and which was
indeed the Clothes which had been stripped off from *Joseph*, and
the other things they had taken from him.

The Gentleman no sooner saw the Coat, than he declared he
knew the Livery; and if it had been taken from the poor Creature
above stairs, desired he might see him: for that he was very well
acquainted with the Family to whom that Livery belonged.

He was accordingly conducted up by *Betty*: but what, Reader,
was the surprize on both sides, when he saw *Joseph* was the Person
in Bed; and when *Joseph* discovered the Face of his good Friend
Mr. *Abraham Adams*.

It would be impertinent to insert a Discourse which chiefly
turned on the relation of Matters already well known to the
Reader: for as soon as the Curate had satisfied *Joseph* concerning
the perfect Health of his *Fanny*, he was on his side very inquisitive
into all the Particulars which had produced this unfortunate
Accident.

To return therefore to the Kitchin, where a great variety of
Company were now assembled from all the Rooms of the House,
as well as the Neighbourhood: so much delight do Men take
in contemplating the Countenance of a Thief:

Mr. *Tow-wouse* began to rub his Hands with pleasure, at seeing
so large an Assembly; who would, he hoped, shortly adjourn into
several Apartments, in order to discourse over the Robbery; and
drink a Health to all honest Men: but Mrs. *Tow-wouse*, whose
Misfortune it was commonly to see things a little perversly, began
to rail at those who brought the Fellow into her House; telling

her Husband, 'they were very likely to thrive, who kept a House of entertainment for Beggars and Thieves.'

The Mob had now finished their search; and could find nothing about the Captive likely to prove any Evidence: for as to the Clothes, tho' the Mob were very well satisfied with that Proof; yet, as the Surgeon observed, they could not convict him, because they were not found in his Custody; to which *Barnabas* agreed: and added, that these were *Bona Waviata*,[1] and belonged to the Lord of the Manor.

'How,' says the Surgeon, 'do you say these Goods belong to the Lord of the Manor?' 'I do,' cried *Barnabas*. 'Then I deny it,' says the Surgeon. 'What can the Lord of the Manor have to do in the Case? Will any one attempt to persuade me that what a Man finds is not his own?' 'I have heard, (says an old Fellow in the Corner) Justice *Wise-one* say, that if every Man had his right, whatever is found belongs to the King of *London*.'[2] 'That may be true,' says *Barnabas*, 'in some sense: for the Law makes a difference between things stolen, and things found: for a thing may be stolen that never is found; and a thing may be found that never was stolen. Now Goods that are both stolen and found are *Waviata*; and they belong to the Lord of the Manor.' 'So the Lord of the Manor is the Receiver of stolen Goods:' (says the Doctor) at which there was a universal Laugh, being first begun by himself.

While the Prisoner, by persisting in his Innocence, had almost (as there was no Evidence against him) brought over *Barnabas*, the Surgeon, *Tow-wouse*, and several others to his side; *Betty* informed them, that they had over-looked a little Piece of Gold, which she had carried up to the Man in bed; and which he offered to swear to amongst a Million, aye, amongst ten Thousand. This immediately turned the Scale against the Prisoner; and every one now concluded him guilty. It was resolved therefore,

[1] In disputes about the law, Barnabas 'trusted entirely to *Wood's Institutes*' (I. xv), which contains the following definition: '*Waifs (Bona Waviata)* are Goods which are stolen and waived upon Pursuit (for fear of being Apprehended) by the Thief in his Flight, and upon that Account forfeited to the Lord of the Manor. The Reason of this Forfeiture is as a Punishment of the Owner of the Goods, for not Pursuing and Bringing the Thief to be Attainted. If the Thief had not the Goods in Possession upon Pursuit, there is no Forfeiture; and then the Owner may seise them where He finds them, without any fresh Pursuit.' (Thomas Wood, *An Institute of the Laws of England*, 3rd ed. [1724], p. 213.)

[2] According to Jacob's *New Law-Dictionary*, the goods of felons and fugitives are forfeit to the king. (4th ed. [1739]; s.v. 'King's Prerogative'.)

to keep him secured that Night, and early in the Morning to carry him before a Justice.

CHAPTER XV

Shewing how Mrs. Tow-wouse *was a little mollified; and how officious Mr.* Barnabas *and the Surgeon were to prosecute the Thief: With a Dissertation accounting for their Zeal; and that of many other Persons not mentioned in this History.*

BETTY told her Mistress, she believed the Man in Bed was a greater Man than they took him for: for besides the extreme Whiteness of his Skin, and the Softness of his Hands; she observed a very great Familiarity between the Gentleman and him; and added, she was certain they were intimate Acquaintance, if not Relations.

This somewhat abated the severity of Mrs. *Tow-wouse's* Countenance. She said, 'God forbid she should not discharge the duty of a Christian, since the poor Gentleman was brought to her House. She had a natural antipathy to Vagabonds: but could pity the Misfortunes of a Christian as soon as another.' *Tow-wouse* said, 'If the Traveller be a Gentleman, tho' he hath no Money about him now, we shall most likely be paid hereafter; so you may begin to score whenever you will.' Mrs. *Tow-wouse* answered, 'Hold your simple Tongue, and don't instruct me in my Business. I am sure I am sorry for the Gentleman's Misfortune with all my heart, and I hope the Villain who hath used him so barbarously will be hanged. *Betty*, go, see what he wants. G— forbid he should want any thing in my House.'

Barnabas, and the Surgeon went up to *Joseph*, to satisfy themselves concerning the piece of Gold. *Joseph* was with difficulty prevailed upon to shew it them; but would by no Entreaties be brought to deliver it out of his own Possession. He, however, attested this to be the same which had been taken from him; and *Betty* was ready to swear to the finding it on the Thief.

The only Difficulty that remained, was how to produce this Gold before the Justice: for as to carrying *Joseph* himself, it seemed impossible; nor was there any greater likelihood of obtain-

ing it from him: for he had fastened it with a Ribband to his
Arm, and solemnly vowed, that nothing but irresistible Force
should ever separate them; in which Resolution, Mr. *Adams*,
clenching a Fist rather less than the Knuckle of an Ox, declared
he would support him.

A Dispute arose on this Occasion concerning Evidence, not
very necessary to be related here; after which the Surgeon dress'd
Mr. *Joseph's* Head; still persisting in the imminent Danger in
which his Patient lay: but concluding with a very important
Look, 'that he began to have some hopes; that he should send
him a *Sanative soporiferous* Draught, and would see him in the
Morning.' After which *Barnabas* and he departed, and left Mr.
Joseph and Mr. *Adams* together.

Adams informed *Joseph* of the occasion of this Journey which
he was making to *London*, namely to publish three[1] Volumes of
Sermons; being encouraged, he said, by an Advertisement lately
set forth by a Society of Booksellers, who proposed to purchase
any Copies offered to them at a Price to be settled by two Persons:[2] but tho' he imagined he should get a considerable Sum of
Money on this occasion, which his Family were in urgent need of;
he protested, 'he would not leave *Joseph* in his present Condition:'
finally, he told him, 'he had nine Shillings and three-pence-half-
penny in his Pocket, which he was welcome to use as he pleased.'

This Goodness of Parson *Adams* brought Tears into *Joseph's*
Eyes; he declared 'he had now a second Reason to desire life,
that he might shew his Gratitude to such a Friend.' *Adams* bad
him 'be chearful, for that he plainly saw the Surgeon, besides
his Ignorance, desired to make a Merit of curing him, tho' the
Wounds in his Head, he perceived, were by no means dangerous;
that he was convinced he had no Fever, and doubted not but he
would be able to travel in a day or two.'

---

[1] Fielding overlooked this slip in revision. In Chapter XVI and thereafter, they are nine
volumes.

[2] Thomas Osborne, a friend of Richardson's, was the founder of 'the Society of Booksellers for promoting of Learning, by purchasing of Manuscripts, Copies, &c. design'd for
the Press'. The advertisement that tempted Adams toward London appeared in the newspapers, including Fielding's *Champion*, from 4 March to 8 August 1741. Adams refers to
the Society's proposal: 'That they will give ready Money to any Author or Proprietor of
a Work, which shall be approv'd of by two Persons of Judgment, to be nominated one by
the Author, the other by the Society, who shall also fix the Price to be given, on the Author's
conveying to the said Society his Right and Interest in such Copy.' (From *The Champion*,
24 March 1740/1.) Or the author might choose instead to settle for half the profits.

These Words infused a Spirit into *Joseph*; he said, 'he found himself very sore from the Bruises, but had no reason to think any of his Bones injured, or that he had received any Harm in his Inside; unless that he felt something very odd in his Stomach: but he knew not whether that might not arise from not having eaten one Morsel for above twenty-four Hours.' Being then asked, if he had any Inclination to eat, he answered in the Affirmative; then Parson *Adams* desired him to name what he had the greatest fancy for; whether a poached Egg, or Chicken-broth: he answered, 'he could eat both very well; but that he seemed to have the greatest Appetite for a piece of boiled Beef and Cabbage.'

Adams was pleased with so perfect a Confirmation that he had not the least Fever: but advised him to a lighter Diet, for that Evening. He accordingly eat either a Rabbit or a Fowl, I never could with any tolerable Certainty discover which; after this he was by Mrs. *Tow-wouse's* order conveyed into a better Bed, and equipped with one of her Husband's Shirts.

In the Morning early, *Barnabas* and the Surgeon came to the Inn, in order to see the Thief conveyed before the Justice. They had consumed the whole Night in debating what Measures they should take to produce the Piece of Gold in Evidence against him: for they were both extremely zealous in the Business, tho' neither of them were in the least interested in the Prosecution; neither of them had ever received any private Injury from the Fellow, nor had either of them ever been suspected of loving the Publick well enough, to give them a Sermon or a Dose of Physick for nothing.

To help our Reader therefore as much as possible to account for this Zeal, we must inform him, that as this Parish was so unfortunate as to have no Lawyer in it; there had been a constant Contention between the two Doctors, spiritual and physical, concerning their Abilities in a Science, in which, as neither of them professed it, they had equal Pretensions to dispute each other's Opinions. These Disputes were carried on with great Contempt on both sides, and had almost divided the Parish; Mr. *Tow-wouse* and one half of the Neighbours inclining to the Surgeon, and Mrs. *Tow-wouse* with the other half to the Parson. The Surgeon drew his Knowledge from those inestimable Fountains, called the *Attorney's Pocket-Companion*, and Mr. *Jacob's Law-*

Tables; *Barnabas* trusted entirely to *Wood's Institutes*.[1] It happened on this Occasion, as was pretty frequently the Case, that these two learned Men differed about the sufficiency of Evidence: the Doctor being of opinion, that the Maid's Oath would convict the Prisoner without producing the Gold;[2] the Parson, *è contra, totis viribus*.[3] To display their Parts therefore before the Justice and the Parish was the sole Motive, which we can discover, to this Zeal, which both of them pretended to be for publick Justice.

O Vanity! How little is thy Force acknowledged, or thy Operations discerned? How wantonly dost thou deceive Mankind under different Disguises? Sometimes thou dost wear the Face of Pity, sometimes of Generosity: nay, thou hast the Assurance even to put on those glorious Ornaments which belong only to heroick Virtue. Thou odious, deformed Monster! whom Priests have railed at, Philosophers despised, and Poets ridiculed: Is there a Wretch so abandoned as to own thee for an Acquaintance in publick? yet, how few will refuse to enjoy thee in private? nay, thou art the Pursuit of most Men through their Lives. The greatest Villanies are daily practised to please thee: nor is the meanest Thief below, or the greatest Hero above thy notice. Thy Embraces are often the sole Aim and sole Reward of the private Robbery, and the plundered Province. It is, to pamper up thee, thou Harlot, that we attempt to withdraw from others what we do not want, or to with-hold from them what they do. All our Passions are thy Slaves. Avarice itself is often no more than thy Hand-maid, and even Lust thy Pimp. The Bully Fear like a Coward, flies before thee, and Joy and Grief hide their Heads in thy Presence.

---

[1] Three legal handbooks of the period—*The Attorney's Pocket Companion; or, A Guide to the Practisers of the Law*, by John Mallory of the Inner Temple; *The Statute-Law Common-plac'd: or, A General Table to the Statutes*, by Giles Jacob (1686–1744); and *An Institute of the Laws of England; or, The Laws of England in their Natural Order, according to Common Use*, by Thomas Wood (1661–1722). On Giles Jacob, see *The Champion*, 25 December 1739 and 12 February 1739/40; in the former number it is asserted, ironically, that 'a very competent Knowledge of the Law is to be met with in *Jacob's* Dictionary [i.e. the *New Law-Dictionary*], and the other *legal* Works of that learned Author'.

[2] The testimony of one witness was sufficient evidence, except in cases of treason, where two were required. For a conviction for felony, proof was required that the thief had taken the goods and at some time had them in his possession. (See Wood's *Institutes*, 3rd ed. [1724], pp. 643, 369–70.)

[3] 'Mightily of the opposite opinion.'

I know thou wilt think, that whilst I abuse thee, I court thee; and that thy Love hath inspired me to write this sarcastical Pane-gyrick on thee: but thou art deceived, I value thee not of a far-thing; nor will it give me any Pain, if thou should'st prevail on the Reader to censure this Digression as errant Nonsense: for know to thy Confusion, that I have introduced thee for no other Purpose than to lengthen out a short Chapter; and so I return to my History.

CHAPTER XVI

The Escape of the Thief. Mr. Adams's *Disappointment. The Arrival of two very extraordinary Personages, and the Introduction of Parson* Adams *to Parson* Barnabas.

BARNABAS and the Surgeon being returned, as we have said, to the Inn, in order to convey the Thief before the Justice, were greatly concerned to find a small Accident had happened which some-what disconcerted them; and this was no other than the Thief's Escape, who had modestly withdrawn himself by Night, declin-ing all Ostentation, and not chusing, in imitation of some great Men, to distinguish himself at the Expence of being pointed at.

When the Company had retired the Evening before, the Thief was detained in a Room where the Constable, and one of the young Fellows who took him, were planted as his Guard. About the second Watch, a general Complaint of Drowth was made both by the Prisoner and his Keepers. Among whom it was at last agreed, that the Constable should remain on Duty, and the young Fellow call up the Tapster; in which Disposition the latter appre-hended not the least Danger, as the Constable was well armed, and could besides easily summon him back to his Assistance, if the Prisoner made the least Attempt to gain his Liberty.

The young Fellow had not long left the Room, before it came into the Constable's Head, that the Prisoner might leap on him by surprize, and thereby, preventing him of the use of his Weapons, especially the long Staff in which he chiefly confided, might reduce the Success of a Struggle to an equal Chance. He wisely therefore, to prevent this Inconvenience, slipt out of the

Room himself and locked the Door, waiting without with his Staff in his Hand, ready lifted to fell the unhappy Prisoner, if by ill Fortune he should attempt to break out.

But human Life, as hath been discovered by some great Man or other, (for I would by no means be understood to affect the Honour of making any such Discovery) very much resembles a Game at *Chess*: for, as in the latter, while a Gamester is too attentive to secure himself very strongly on one side the Board, he is apt to leave an unguarded Opening on the other; so doth it often happen in Life; and so did it happen on this Occasion: for whilst the cautious Constable with such wonderful Sagacity had possessed himself of the Door, he most unhappily forgot the Window.

The Thief who played on the other side, no sooner perceived this Opening, than he began to move that way; and finding the Passage easy, he took with him the young Fellow's Hat; and without any Ceremony, stepped into the Street, and made the best of his Way.

The young Fellow returning with a double Mug of Strong Beer was a little surprized to find the Constable at the Door: but much more so, when, the Door being opened, he perceived the Prisoner had made his Escape, and which way: he threw down the Beer, and without uttering any thing to the Constable, except a hearty Curse or two, he nimbly leapt out at the Window, and went again in pursuit of his Prey: being very unwilling to lose the Reward[1] which he had assured himself of.

The Constable hath not been discharged of Suspicion on this account: It hath been said, that not being concerned in the taking the Thief, he could not have been entitled to any part of the Reward, if he had been convicted. That the Thief had several Guineas in his Pocket; that it was very unlikely he should have been guilty of such an Oversight. That his Pretence for leaving the Room was absurd: that it was his constant Maxim, that a wise Man never refused Money on any Conditions: That at every Election, he always had sold his Vote to both Parties, *&c.*

But notwithstanding these and many other such Allegations, I am sufficiently convinced of his Innocence; having been

[1] By law (4 & 5 William & Mary, cap. 8) the reward for capturing a highwayman and prosecuting him to conviction was £40, together with his horse, arms, money, and any other goods taken with him—provided, of course, that these last were not claimed by the thief's victims.

positively assured of it, by those who received their Informations
from his own Mouth; which, in the Opinion of some Moderns,
is the best and indeed only Evidence.

All the Family were now up, and with many others assembled
in the Kitchin, where Mr. *Tow-wouse* was in some Tribulation;
the Surgeon having declared, that by Law, he was liable to be
indicted for the Thief's Escape, as it was out of his House: He
was a little comforted however by Mr. *Barnabas's* Opinion, that
as the Escape was by Night, the Indictment would not lie.[1]

Mrs. *Tow-wouse* delivered herself in the following Words:
'Sure never was such a Fool as my Husband! would any other
Person living have left a Man in the Custody of such a drunken,
drowsy Blockhead as *Tom Suckbribe?*' (which was the Constable's
Name) 'and if he could be indicted without any harm to his Wife
and Children, I should be glad of it.' (Then the Bell rung in
Joseph's Room.) 'Why *Betty*, *John Chamberlain*, where the Devil
are you all? Have you no Ears, or no Conscience, not to tend the
Sick better?—See what the Gentleman wants; why don't you go
yourself, Mr. *Tow-wouse?* but any one may die for you; you have
no more feeling than a Deal-Board. If a Man lived a Fortnight
in your House without spending a Penny, you would never put
him in mind of it. See whether he drinks Tea or Coffee for Breakfast.' 'Yes, my Dear,' cry'd *Tow-wouse*. She then asked the Doctor
and Mr. *Barnabas* what Morning's Draught they chose, who
answered, they had a Pot of *Syder-and*,[2] at the Fire; which we will
leave them merry over, and return to *Joseph*.

He had rose pretty early this Morning: but tho' his Wounds
were far from threatning any danger, he was so sore with the
Bruises, that it was impossible for him to think of undertaking a
Journey yet; Mr. *Adams* therefore, whose Stock was visibly
decreased with the Expences of Supper and Breakfast, and which
could not survive that Day's Scoring, began to consider how it was
possible to recruit it. At last he cry'd, 'he had luckily hit on a sure

[1] Since the thief was lawfully held in his house, Mr. Tow-wouse could be legally considered as jailer and his house a prison. For allowing a prisoner to escape, the jailer could be
charged with a misdemeanour (if he was merely negligent) or with a felony (if he acted
voluntarily). The punishment for negligence was a fine; for voluntary complicity the jailer
was judged guilty of the crime for which the prisoner was being detained. Negligence could
not be charged, however, for failing to 'guard the country' or to pursue a criminal at night.
(Wood's *Institutes*, 7th ed. [1745], pp. 369–70, 392.)
[2] A hot drink made of brandy, cider, spices, and sugar.

Method, and though it would oblige him to return himself home together with *Joseph*, it mattered not much.' He then sent for *Tow-wouse*, and taking him into another Room, told him, 'he wanted to borrow three Guineas, for which he would put ample Security into his Hands.' *Tow-wouse* who expected a Watch, or Ring, or something of double the Value, answered, 'he believed he could furnish him.' Upon which *Adams* pointing to his Saddle-Bag told him with a Face and Voice full of Solemnity, 'that there were in that Bag no less than nine Volumes of Manuscript Sermons, as well worth a hundred Pound as a Shilling was worth twelve Pence, and that he would deposite one of the Volumes in his Hands by way of Pledge; not doubting but that he would have the Honesty to return it on his Repayment of the Money: for otherwise he must be a very great loser, seeing that every Volume would at least bring him ten Pounds, as he had been informed by a neighbouring Clergyman in the Country: for, (said he) as to my own part, having never yet dealt in Printing, I do not pretend to ascertain the exact Value of such things.'

Tow-wouse, who was a little surprized at the Pawn, said (and not without some Truth) 'that he was no Judge of the Price of such kind of Goods; and as for Money, he really was very short.' *Adams* answered, 'certainly he would not scruple to lend him three Guineas, on what was undoubtedly worth at least ten.' The Landlord replied, 'he did not believe he had so much Money in the House, and besides he was to make up a Sum.¹ He was very confident the Books were of much higher Value, and heartily sorry it did not suit him.' He then cry'd out, *Coming Sir!* though no body called, and ran down Stairs without any Fear of breaking his Neck.

Poor *Adams* was extremely dejected at this Disappointment, nor knew he what farther Stratagem to try. He immediately apply'd to his Pipe, his constant Friend and Comfort in his Afflictions; and leaning over the Rails, he devoted himself to Meditation, assisted by the inspiring Fumes of Tobacco.

He had on a Night-Cap drawn over his Wig, and a short great Coat, which half covered his Cassock; a Dress, which added to something comical enough in his Countenance, composed a Figure likely to attract the Eyes of those who were not over-given to Observation.

¹ He owed a sum of money due on a certain date.

Whilst he was smoaking his Pipe in this Posture, a Coach and Six, with a numerous Attendance, drove into the Inn. There alighted from the Coach a young Fellow, and a Brace of Pointers, after which another young Fellow leapt from the Box, and shook the former by the hand, and both together with the Dogs were instantly conducted by Mr. *Tow-wouse* into an Apartment; whither as they passed, they entertained themselves with the following short facetious Dialogue.

'You are a pretty Fellow for a Coachman, *Jack*!' says he from the Coach, 'you had almost overturned us just now.' 'Pox take you,' says the Coachman, 'if I had only broke your Neck, it would have been saving somebody else the trouble: but I should have been sorry for the Pointers.' 'Why, you Son of a B—,' answered the other, 'if no body could shoot better than you, the Pointers would be of no use.' 'D—n me,' says the Coachman, 'I will shoot with you, five Guineas a Shot.' 'You be hang'd,' says the other, 'for five Guineas you shall shoot at my A—.' 'Done,' says the Coachman, 'I'll pepper you better than ever you was peppered by *Jenny Bouncer*.' 'Pepper your Grand-mother,' says the other, 'here's *Tow-wouse* will let you shoot at him for a Shilling a time.' 'I know his Honour better,' cries *Tow-wouse*, 'I never saw a surer shot at a Partridge. Every Man misses now and then; but if I could shoot half as well as his Honour, I would desire no better Livelihood than I could get by my Gun.' 'Pox on you,' said the Coachman, 'you demolish more Game now than your Head's worth. There's a Bitch, *Tow-wouse*, by G— she never *blinked** a Bird in her Life.' 'I have a Puppy, not a Year old, shall hunt with her for a hundred,' cries the other Gentleman. 'Done,' says the Coachman, 'but you will be pox'd before you make the Bett. If you have a mind for a Bett,' cries the Coachman, 'I will match my spotted Dog with your white Bitch for a hundred, play or pay.' 'Done,' says the other, 'and I'll run *Baldface* against *Slouch* with you for another.' 'No,' cries he from the Box, 'but I'll venture *Miss Jenny* against *Baldface*, or *Hannibal* either.' 'Go to the Devil,' cries he from the Coach, 'I will make every Bett your own way, to be sure! I will match *Hannibal* with *Slouch* for a thousand, if you dare, and I say done first.'

They were now arrived, and the Reader will be very contented to leave them, and repair to the Kitchin, where *Barnabas*, the

* To *blink* is a Term used to signify the Dog's passing by a Bird without pointing at it.

Surgeon, and an Exciseman were smoaking their Pipes over some *Syder-and*, and where the Servants, who attended the two noble Gentlemen we have just seen alight, were now arrived.

'*Tom*,' cries one of the Footmen, 'there's Parson *Adams* smoaking his Pipe in the Gallery.' 'Yes,' says *Tom*, 'I pulled off my Hat to him, and the Parson spoke to me.'

'Is the Gentleman a Clergyman then?' says *Barnabas*, (for his Cassock had been tied up when first he arrived.) 'Yes, Sir,' answered the Footman, 'and one there be but few like.' 'Ay,' said *Barnabas*, 'if I had known it sooner, I should have desired his Company; I would always shew a proper Respect for the Cloth; but what say you, Doctor, shall we adjourn into a Room, and invite him to take part of a Bowl of Punch?'

This Proposal was immediately agreed to, and executed; and Parson *Adams* accepting the Invitation; much Civility passed between the two Clergymen, who both declared the great Honour they had for the Cloth. They had not been long together before they entered into a Discourse on small Tithes, which continued a full Hour, without the Doctor or the Exciseman's having one Opportunity to offer a Word.

It was then proposed to begin a general Conversation, and the Exciseman opened on foreign Affairs: but a Word unluckily dropping from one of them introduced a Dissertation on the Hardships suffered by the inferiour Clergy;[1] which, after a long Duration, concluded with bringing the nine Volumes of Sermons on the Carpet.

Barnabas greatly discouraged poor *Adams*; he said, 'The Age was so wicked, that no body read Sermons: Would you think it, Mr. *Adams*, (said he) I once intended to print a Volume of Sermons myself, and they had the Approbation of two or three Bishops: but what do you think a Bookseller offered me?' 'Twelve Guineas perhaps (cried *Adams*.)' 'Not Twelve Pence, I assure you,' answered *Barnabas*, 'nay the Dog refused me a Concordance in Exchange.—At last, I offered to give him the printing

[1] Perhaps a reference to Thomas Stackhouse's work, *The Miseries and Great Hardships of the Inferior Clergy; and a Modest Plea for their Rights and better Usage*, a subject in which Fielding was keenly interested (consider, for example, his series, 'An Apology for the Clergy', in *The Champion*, 29 March, 5, 12, 19 April 1740). Stackhouse's book was originally published in 1722, but advertisements in *The Craftsman* (10 October 1741) and in *Common Sense* (17 October 1741) indicate that it was reissued at about the time that *Joseph Andrews* was being written.

them, for the sake of dedicating them to that very Gentleman who just now drove his own Coach into the Inn, and I assure you, he had the Impudence to refuse my Offer: by which means I lost a good Living, that was afterwards given away in exchange for a Pointer, to one who—but I will not say any thing against the Cloth. So you may guess, Mr. *Adams*, what you are to expect; for if Sermons would have gone down, I believe—I will not be vain: but to be concise with you, three Bishops said, they were the best that ever were writ: but indeed there are a pretty moderate number printed already, and not all sold yet.'—'Pray, Sir,' said *Adams*, 'to what do you think the Numbers may amount?' 'Sir,' answered *Barnabas*, 'a Bookseller told me he believed five thousand Volumes at least.'[1] 'Five thousand!' quoth the Surgeon, 'what can they be writ upon? I remember, when I was a Boy, I used to read one *Tillotson's* Sermons;[2] and I am sure, if a Man practised half so much as is in one of those Sermons, he will go to Heaven.' 'Doctor,' cried *Barnabas*, 'you have a profane way of talking, for which I must reprove you. A Man can never have his Duty too frequently inculcated into him. And as for *Tillotson*, to be sure he was a good Writer, and said things very well: but Comparisons are odious, another Man may write as well as he—I believe there are some of my Sermons,'—and then he apply'd the Candle to his Pipe.—'And I believe there are some of my Discourses,' cries *Adams*, 'which the Bishops would not think totally unworthy of being printed; and I have been informed, I might procure a very large Sum (indeed an immense one) on

---

[1] According to *An Index to the Sermons, Published since the Restoration*, by S. Letsome, more than 8,300 sermons had been printed by the mid 1730's (Part I, 1734; Part II, 1738); and this catalogue, by the author's own admission, is incomplete. The 1751 edition of the *Index*, in the possession of the British Museum, lists close to a thousand additional items. Since a volume would generally contain several sermons, the bookseller's estimate seems liberal, but not by very much.

[2] John Tillotson (1630–94), Archbishop of Canterbury, was a leader of the latitudinarians, who stressed the importance of morality and good works, believing that the fundamental principle of the Reformation, the doctrine of justification by faith alone, had been carried too far. Because of his 'natural and easy' style Tillotson's sermons were universally admired and widely imitated. (See, for example, Henry Felton, *A Dissertation on Reading the Classics, and Forming a Just Style*, 5th ed. [1753], pp. 178–9.) Fielding had great respect for Tillotson, and for such other latitudinarian divines as Isaac Barrow, Samuel Clarke, and Benjamin Hoadly (see p. 82, nn. 1–2; p. 83, n. 1, p. 274, n. 1); references to his work occur in *The Champion* (22 January and 15 March 1739/40), *The Covent-Garden Journal* (14 January 1752), and *A Proposal for Making an Effectual Provision for the Poor* (1753).

them.' 'I doubt that;' answered *Barnabas*: 'however, if you desire to make some Money of them, perhaps you may sell them by advertising *the Manuscript Sermons of a Clergyman lately deceased, all warranted Originals, and never printed.*[1] And now I think of it, I should be obliged to you, if there be ever a Funeral one among them, to lend it me: for I am this very day to preach a Funeral Sermon, for which I have not penned a Line, though I am to have a double Price.' *Adams* answered, 'he had but one, which he feared would not serve his purpose, being sacred to the Memory of a Magistrate, who had exerted himself very singularly in the Preservation of the Morality of his Neighbours, insomuch, that he had neither Ale-house, nor lewd Woman in the Parish where he lived.'—'No,' replied *Barnabas*, 'that will not do quite so well; for the Deceased, upon whose Virtues I am to harangue, was a little too much addicted to Liquor, and publickly kept a Mistress.—I believe I must take a common Sermon, and trust to my Memory to introduce something handsome on him.'—'To your Invention rather, (said the Doctor) your Memory will be apter to put you out: for no Man living remembers any thing good of him.'

With such kind of spiritual Discourse, they emptied the Bowl of Punch, paid their Reckoning, and separated: *Adams* and the Doctor went up to *Joseph*; Parson *Barnabas* departed to celebrate the aforesaid Deceased, and the Exciseman descended into the Cellar to gage the Vessels.

Joseph was now ready to sit down to a Loin of Mutton, and waited for Mr. *Adams*, when he and the Doctor came in. The Doctor having felt his Pulse, and examined his Wounds, declared him much better, which he imputed to *that Sanative soporiferous Draught*, a Medicine, 'whose Virtues,' he said, 'were never to be sufficiently extolled:' And great indeed they must be, if *Joseph* was so much indebted to them as the Doctor imagined, since nothing more than those Effluvia, which escaped the Cork, could

[1] Fielding, of course, is mocking the general practice of 'puffing' sermons, but he may here have had in mind the phrasing of a specific advertisement which the bookseller Thomas Osborne ran in *Common Sense* (13 and 20 December 1740); '*To be Dispos'd of,* / A Choice Collection of MANUSCRIPT SERMONS of an eminent Divine lately deceas'd. In this Collection there is a Discourse suited for every Sunday in the Year, and an Account when and where preached, which will be warranted Originals.' An advertisement for the sermons of John Sharp, late Lord Archbishop of York, also illustrates the practice, reading: 'Never before printed, and now publish'd from his own Papers.' (*The Craftsman*, 16 March 1733/4.)

have contributed to his Recovery: for the Medicine had stood untouched in the Window ever since its arrival.

Joseph passed that day and the three following with his Friend *Adams*, in which nothing so remarkable happened as the swift Progress of his Recovery. As he had an excellent Habit of Body, his Wounds were now almost healed, and his Bruises gave him so little uneasiness, that he pressed Mr. *Adams* to let him depart, told him he should never be able to return sufficient Thanks for all his Favours; but begged that he might no longer delay his Journey to *London*.

Adams, notwithstanding the Ignorance, as he conceived it, of Mr. *Tow-wouse*, and the Envy (for such he thought it) of Mr. *Barnabas*, had great Expectations from his Sermons: seeing therefore *Joseph* in so good a way, he told him he would agree to his setting out the next Morning in the Stage-Coach, that he believed he should have sufficient after the Reckoning paid, to procure him one Day's Conveyance in it, and afterwards he would be able to get on, on foot, or might be favoured with a lift in some Neighbour's Waggon, especially as there was then to be a Fair in the Town whither the Coach would carry him, to which Numbers from his Parish resorted.—And as to himself, he agreed to proceed to the great City.

They were now walking in the Inn Yard, when a fat, fair, short Person rode in, and alighting from his Horse went directly up to *Barnabas*, who was smoking his Pipe on a Bench. The Parson and the Stranger shook one another very lovingly by the Hand, and went into a Room together.

The Evening now coming on, *Joseph* retired to his Chamber, whither the good *Adams* accompanied him; and took this Opportunity to expatiate on the great Mercies God had lately shewn him, of which he ought not only to have the deepest inward Sense; but likewise to express outward Thankfulness for them. They therefore fell both on their Knees, and spent a considerable time in Prayer and Thanksgiving.

They had just finished, when *Betty* came in and told Mr. *Adams*, Mr. *Barnabas* desired to speak to him on some Business of Consequence below Stairs. *Joseph* desired, if it was likely to detain him long, he would let him know it, that he might go to Bed, which *Adams* promised, and in that Case, they wished one another good Night.

CHAPTER XVII

*A pleasant Discourse between the two Parsons and the
Bookseller, which was broke off by an unlucky
Accident happening in the Inn, which produced a
Dialogue between Mrs.* Tow-wouse *and her Maid
of no gentle kind.*

As soon as *Adams* came into the Room, Mr. *Barnabas* introduced
him to the Stranger, who was, he told him, a Bookseller, and
would be as likely to deal with him for his Sermons as any Man
whatever. *Adams,* saluting the Stranger, answered *Barnabas,* that
he was very much obliged to him, that nothing could be more
convenient, for he had no other Business to the great City, and
was heartily desirous of returning with the young Man who was
just recovered of his Misfortune. He then snapt his Fingers (as
was usual with him) and took two or three turns about the Room
in an Extasy.—And to induce the Bookseller to be as expeditious
as possible, as likewise to offer him a better Price for his Com-
modity, he assured him, their meeting was extremely lucky to
himself: for that he had the most pressing Occasion for Money
at that time, his own being almost spent, and having a Friend
then in the same Inn who was just recovered from some Wounds
he had received from Robbers, and was in a most indigent
Condition. 'So that nothing,' says he, 'could be so opportune, for
the supplying both our Necessities, as my making an immediate
Bargain with you.'

As soon as he had seated himself, the Stranger began in these
Words, 'Sir, I do not care absolutely to deny engaging in what
my Friend Mr. *Barnabas* recommends: but Sermons are mere
Drugs. The Trade is so vastly stocked with them, that really
unless they come out with the Name of *Whitfield* or *Westley,*[1]
or some other such great Man, as a Bishop, or those sort of People,
I don't care to touch, unless now it was a Sermon preached on the

[1] George Whitefield (1714–70) and John Wesley (1703–91), the great evangelists who
about 1738, in an effort to reform the apathy and worldliness within the Church of England,
began the popular movement known as Methodism. Though the two had been associated
since their membership in the original 'Methodist Society' at Oxford, Whitefield's strongly
Calvinistic bias eventually caused him to break with Wesley.

30th of January,[1] or we could say in the Title Page, published at the *earnest Request* of the Congregation, or the Inhabitants:[2] but truly for a dry Piece of Sermons, I had rather be excused; especially as my Hands are so full at present. However, Sir, as Mr. *Barnabas* mentioned them to me, I will, if you please, take the Manuscript with me to Town, and send you my Opinion of it in a very short time.'

'O,' said *Adams*, 'if you desire it, I will read two or three Discourses as a Specimen.' This *Barnabas*, who loved Sermons no better than a Grocer doth Figs, immediately objected to, and advised *Adams* to let the Bookseller have his Sermons; telling him, if he gave him a Direction, he might be certain of a speedy Answer: Adding, he need not scruple trusting them in his Possession. 'No,' said the Bookseller, 'if it was a Play that had been acted twenty Nights together, I believe it would be safe.'

Adams did not at all relish the last Expression; he said, he was sorry to hear Sermons compared to Plays. 'Not by me, I assure you,' cry'd the Bookseller, 'though I don't know whether the licensing Act[3] may not shortly bring them to the same footing: but I have formerly known a hundred Guineas given for a Play ——.' 'More shame for those who gave it,' cry'd *Barnabas*. 'Why so?' said the Bookseller, 'for they got hundreds by it.' 'But is there no difference between conveying good or ill Instructions to Mankind?' said *Adams*; 'would not an honest Mind rather lose Money by the one, than gain it by the other?' 'If you can find any such, I will not be their Hinderance,' answered the Bookseller, 'but I think those Persons who get by preaching Sermons, are the properest to lose by printing them: for my part, the Copy

---

[1] The anniversary of the execution of Charles I in 1649; sermons preached on this date, a holy day, were therefore usually political. According to Letsome's *Index*, more than 230 of these had been printed since the Restoration.

[2] A typical device of the booksellers for promoting the sale of sermons. Consider, for example, the following lines from advertisements in *Common Sense* (e.g. 8 November 1740) and *The Universal Spectator* (27 December 1740 and 31 January 1741): 'Delivered in the Parish of St. Martin's, and publish'd at the unanimous Request of the Congregation'; 'publish'd at the Request of a Friend'; 'Publish'd by Command of his Grace the Lord Archbishop of Canterbury'; or 'Publish'd at the Desire of the Masters of the Bench of the Two Honourable Societies'.

[3] Designed by Walpole to curb the licentiousness of the stage and to silence, in particular, Fielding's popular dramatic satires against the government, the theatrical Licensing Act was passed on 21 June 1737. By the terms of the act, all unlicensed theatres, including Fielding's own Little Theatre in the Haymarket, were closed, and new plays had to be submitted to the Lord Chamberlain for censorship.

that sells best, will be always the best Copy in my Opinion; I am no Enemy to Sermons but because they don't sell: for I would as soon print one of *Whitfield's*, as any Farce whatever.'[1]

'Whoever prints such Heterodox Stuff, ought to be hanged,' says *Barnabas*. 'Sir,' said he, turning to *Adams*, 'this Fellow's Writings (I know not whether you have seen them) are levelled at the Clergy. He would reduce us to the Example of the Primitive Ages forsooth! and would insinuate to the People, that a Clergyman ought to be always preaching and praying. He pretends to understand the Scripture literally, and would make Mankind believe, that the Poverty and low Estate, which was recommended to the Church in its Infancy, and was only temporary Doctrine adapted to her under Persecution, was to be preserved in her flourishing and established State.[2] Sir, the Principles of *Toland*, *Woolston*, and all the Free-Thinkers,[3] are not calculated to do half the Mischief, as those professed by this Fellow and his Followers.'

[1] The demand for his sermons was so great that Whitefield believed his bookseller had already 'got some *hundreds* by me'. (Letter to Mr. J— H— [25 March 1741]; *The Works of the Reverend George Whitefield* [1771–2], i. 256.)

[2] In his sermons Whitefield zealously denounced 'the indolent, earthly-minded, pleasure-taking clergy of the church of *England*', and stressed the need to 'restore the church to its primitive dignity'. (*Works*, v. 155; vi. 96.) In 1739 he was reproved for such views by Joseph Trapp, who, taking his text from Ecclesiastes vii. 16, accused Whitefield of being 'righteous overmuch'. In his reply Whitefield represented such 'polite gentlemen' as Trapp (and Parson Barnabas) as indignantly asking, ' "Are we to be always upon our knees ? Would you have us be always at prayer, and reading or hearing the word of God ?" ' ('The Folly and Danger of being not righteous enough', *Works*, v. 130.) In another sermon he spoke directly against 'the supposition, now current among us [cf. Barnabas's views], that most of what is contained in the gospel of Jesus Christ, was designed only for our Lord's first and immediate followers, and consequently calculated but for one or two hundred years'. (*Works*, vi. 89.) In *The Champion* for 5 April 1740 Fielding, siding with Whitefield for once, alludes to this controversy in remarking that some clergymen (like Barnabas) do not receive Christ's injunction to poverty 'in a strict, literal, practical Sense: . . . without *being righteous over much*, we may, I think, conclude, that if the Clergy are not to abandon all they have to their Ministry, neither are they to get immense Estates by it; and I would recommend it to the Consideration of those who do, whether they do not make a Trade of Divinity ?'

[3] John Toland (1670–1722) and Thomas Woolston (1670–1733) were among the most notorious of the Freethinkers, a term virtually synonymous with Deists, who disputed the orthodox doctrine of the Church and the authenticity of a religion based on claims of a special revelation as distinct from the evidence of the natural creation and the dictates of reason. Toland's *Christianity Not Mysterious* (1696) inaugurated a heated dispute between orthodoxy and Deism that lasted a generation. As a result of his equally controversial *Discourses on the Miracles of our Saviour* (1727–9), Woolston was found guilty of blasphemy, fined, and imprisoned for a year.

'Sir,' answered *Adams*, 'if Mr. *Whitfield* had carried his Doctrine no farther than you mention, I should have remained, as I once was, his Well-Wisher. I am myself as great an Enemy to the Luxury and Splendour of the Clergy as he can be. I do not, more than he, by the flourishing Estate of the Church, understand the Palaces, Equipages, Dress, Furniture, rich Dainties, and vast Fortunes of her Ministers. Surely those things, which savour so strongly of this World, become not the Servants of one who professed his Kingdom was not of it:[1] but when he began to call Nonsense and Enthusiasm to his Aid, and to set up the detestable Doctrine of Faith against good Works, I was his Friend no longer; for surely, that Doctrine was coined in Hell, and one would think none but the Devil himself could have the Confidence to preach it. For can any thing be more derogatory to the Honour of God, than for Men to imagine that the All-wise Being will hereafter say to the Good and Virtuous, *Notwithstanding the Purity of thy Life, notwithstanding that constant Rule of Virtue and Goodness in which you walked upon Earth, still as thou did'st not believe every thing in the true Orthodox manner, thy want of Faith shall condemn thee?* Or on the other side, can any Doctrine have a more pernicious Influence on Society than a Persuasion, that it will be a good Plea for the Villain at the last day; *Lord, it is true I never obeyed one of thy Commandments, yet punish me not, for I believe them all?*' 'I suppose, Sir,' said the Bookseller, 'your Sermons are of a different Kind.' 'Ay, Sir,' said *Adams*, 'the contrary, I thank Heaven, is inculcated in almost every Page, or I should belye my own Opinion, which hath always been, that a virtuous and good *Turk*, or Heathen, are more acceptable in the sight of their Creator, than a vicious and wicked Christian, tho' his Faith was as perfectly Orthodox as St. *Paul's* himself.'[2]—

---

[1] Perhaps a reflection of Bishop Hoadly's famous sermon, 'The Nature of the Kingdom, or the Church, of Christ' (31 March 1717), which began the Bangorian controversy. In this discourse Hoadly, whose theology Fielding admired despite the prelate's being himself a rather worldly pluralist (see p. 83, n. 1), insisted that religion was a matter of sincerity, not of external forms of worship. The Church of Christ, whose kingdom was not of this world, was the whole community of Christians.

[2] In replying to Joseph Trapp, in 'The Folly and Danger of being not righteous enough', Whitefield defended himself from the accusation of 'enthusiasm and madness', insisting that in religion 'we must feel that Spirit upon our hearts'. (*Works*, v. 125.) Invoking St. Paul and Articles XI–XIII of the Church, he declared in countless sermons that justification was by faith only and that good works were insufficient to salvation. The latitudinarian divines (such as John Tillotson) he accused of being 'mere moralists' (*Works*, iv. 19); he was in turn charged with Antinomianism and his message popularly represented as: ' "So

'I wish you Success,' says the Bookseller, 'but must beg to be excused, as my Hands are so very full at present; and indeed I am afraid, you will find a Backwardness in the Trade, to engage in a Book which the Clergy would be certain to cry down.' 'God forbid,' says *Adams*, 'any Books should be propagated which the Clergy would cry down: but if you mean by the Clergy, some few designing factious Men, who have it at Heart to establish some favourite Schemes at the Price of the Liberty of Mankind, and the very Essence of Religion, it is not in the power of such Persons to decry any Book they please; witness that excellent Book called, *A Plain Account of the Nature and End of the Sacrament*; a Book written (if I may venture on the Expression) with the Pen of an Angel, and calculated to restore the true Use of Christianity, and of that Sacred Institution: for what could tend more to the noble Purposes of Religion, than frequent cheerful Meetings among the Members of a Society, in which they should in the Presence of one another, and in the Service of the supreme Being, make Promises of being good, friendly and benevolent to each other? Now this excellent Book was attacked by a Party, but unsuccessfully.'[1] At these Words *Barnabas* fell a ringing with

you say you believe in the Lord Jesus Christ, you may live the life of devils." ' (*Works*, v. 135.) Stressing the supreme importance of good works, Parson Adams echoes a passage from a sermon by Fielding's admired Bishop Hoadly: 'We may be . . . certain, That an honest *Heathen* is much more acceptable to [God], than a dishonest and deceitful *Christian*; and that a charitable and good-natured *Pagan* has a better Title to his Favour, than a cruel and barbarous *Christian*; let him be never so orthodox in his Faith.' ('The Good Samaritan', *Twenty Sermons* [1755], p. 332.) From *The Champion* (24 May 1740) and *Shamela* through *Tom Jones* (VIII. viii; XVIII, xiii) and *Amelia* (I. iv), Fielding continued to attack Whitefield's form of Methodism.

[1] *A Plain Account of the Nature and End of the Sacrament of the Lord's Supper* (1735) was a rational, mystery-dispelling analysis of the eucharist by Benjamin Hoadly (1676–1761), the latitudinarian Bishop of Winchester. To Hoadly, who claimed to be representing 'One of our Lord's *Institutions*, in its original *Simplicity*' (p. viii), uncorrupted by the private interpretations of later commentators, the sacrament was merely an outward memorial of Christ's sacrifice, an occasion for communicants to reaffirm their brotherhood in Christ and their moral obligations to one another: 'by our partaking of the *Lord's Supper*, according to the Nature and Design of it, We profess our selves *Christ's* Disciples; and acknowledge our obligation to live according to *his* Laws: that by this We are led to a serious Consideration of the Tenor and Design of his Holy Religion; and to the sincerest Thankfulness for all that He did and suffered for Us; as well as to the most proper Dispositions and Resolutions of behaving Ourselves as becomes Us, in our Relation to *Him* as our *Head*, and to our *Brethren* as *Fellow-Members* with Us of the same *Body*. This is therefore, an effectual Acknowledgment of our strict Obligation to all Instances of *Piety*, and *Virtue*' (p. 155).

The heretical import of this work caused it to be attacked by a host of clergymen,

all the Violence imaginable, upon which a Servant attending, he
bid him 'bring a Bill immediately: for that he was in Company,
for aught he knew, with the Devil himself; and he expected to
hear the Alcoran, the *Leviathan*, or *Woolston*[1] commended, if he
staid a few Minutes longer.' *Adams* desired, 'as he was so much
moved at his mentioning a Book, which he did without apprehending any possibility of Offence, that he would be so kind to
propose any Objections he had to it, which he would endeavour
to answer.' 'I propose Objections!' said *Barnabas*, 'I never read
a Syllable in any such wicked Book; I never saw it in my Life,
I assure you.'—*Adams* was going to answer, when a most hideous
Uproar began in the Inn. Mrs. *Tow-wouse*, Mr. *Tow-wouse*, and
Betty, all lifting up their Voices together: but Mrs. *Tow-wouse's*
Voice, like a Bass Viol in a Concert, was clearly and distinctly distin-
guished among the rest, and was heard to articulate the following
Sounds.—'O you damn'd Villain, is this the Return to all the Care
I have taken of your Family? This the Reward of my Virtue? Is
this the manner in which you behave to one who brought you a
Fortune, and preferred you to so many Matches, all your Betters?
To abuse my Bed, my own Bed, with my own Servant: but I'll
maul the Slut, I'll tear her nasty Eyes out; was ever such a pitiful
Dog, to take up with such a mean Trollop? If she had been a
Gentlewoman like my self, it had been some excuse, but a beg-
garly saucy dirty Servant-Maid. Get you out of my House, you
Whore.' To which, she added another Name, which we do not
care to stain our Paper with.—It was a monosyllable, beginning
with a B—, and indeed was the same, as if she had pronounced

including Brett, Warren, Stebbing, Wheatly, Ridley, Leslie, Skelton, Johnson, and William
Law. Fielding knew at least two of these attacks at first hand: Thomas Bowyer's *A True
Account of the Nature, end, and efficacy of the Sacrament of the Lords Supper; being a Full
answer to the Plain Account, Shewing the Agreement of these plain Notions with the Socinians,
and their disagreement with the Church of England* (1736) is included in Shamela's library;
in another favourite book of Shamela's, *A Short Account of God's Dealings with the Reverend
Mr. George Whitefield* (1740), Whitefield remarked upon 'the miserable Delusion of the
Author of . . . the plain Account of the Sacrament' and predicted that Hoadly would be
damned for his views (pp. 45–46).
 Fielding's high regard for Hoadly, both personally and as a theologian, is well attested:
in *Of True Greatness* (1741) he is represented as the exemplary divine, and in *Tom Jones*
(II. vii) his 'great Reputation' in divinity is noticed.
 [1] *The Leviathan: or the Matter, Form, and Power of a Commonwealth, Ecclesiastical and
Civil* (1651), by Thomas Hobbes (1588–1679), defined man as a rapacious creature motivated by self-interest and pride, and it subordinated Church to State; for these reasons the
book and its author were universally decried by the clergy. For Woolston, see p. 81, n. 3.

the Words, *She-Dog*. Which Term, we shall, to avoid Offence, use on this Occasion, tho' indeed both the Mistress and Maid uttered the above-mentioned B——, a Word extremely disgustful to Females of the lower sort. *Betty* had borne all hitherto with Patience, and had uttered only Lamentations: but the last Appellation stung her to the Quick, 'I am a Woman as well as yourself,' she roared out, 'and no She-Dog, and if I have been a little naughty, I am not the first; if I have been no better than I should be,' cries she sobbing, 'that's no Reason you should call me out of my Name; my Be——Betters are wo——worse than me.' 'Huzzy, huzzy,' says Mrs. *Tow-wouse*, 'have you the Impudence to answer me? Did I not catch you, you saucy——' and then again repeated the terrible word so odious to Female Ears. 'I can't bear that Name,' answered *Betty*, 'if I have been wicked, I am to answer for it myself in the other World, but I have done nothing that's unnatural, and I will go out of your House this Moment: for I will never be called *She-Dog*, by any Mistress in *England*.' Mrs. *Tow-wouse* then armed herself with the Spit: but was prevented from executing any dreadful Purpose by Mr. *Adams*, who confined her Arms with the Strength of a Wrist, which *Hercules* would not have been ashamed of. Mr. *Tow-wouse* being caught, as our Lawyers express it, with the Manner,[1] and having no Defence to make, very prudently withdrew himself, and *Betty* committed herself to the Protection of the Hostler, who, though she could not conceive him pleased with what had happened, was in her Opinion rather a gentler Beast than her Mistress.

Mrs. *Tow-wouse*, at the Intercession of Mr. *Adams*, and finding the Enemy vanished, began to compose herself, and at length recovered the usual Serenity of her Temper, in which we will leave her, to open to the Reader the Steps which led to a Catastrophe, common enough, and comical enough too, perhaps in modern History, yet often fatal to the Repose and Well-being of Families, and the Subject of many Tragedies, both in Life and on the Stage.

---

[1] 'To be *Taken with the Manner*, is where a Thief having stolen any Thing, is taken with the same about him, as it were in his *Hands*; which is called *Flagrante delicto*.' (Jacob, *New Law-Dictionary*, 4th ed. [1739]; s.v. 'Manner'.) In *The Covent-Garden Journal* (28 October 1752) Fielding defines this phrase and uses it in a similar context.

CHAPTER XVIII

The History of Betty *the Chambermaid, and an Account of what occasioned the violent Scene in the preceding Chapter.*

BETTY, who was the Occasion of all this Hurry, had some good Qualities. She had Good-nature, Generosity and Compassion, but unfortunately her Constitution was composed of those warm Ingredients, which, though the Purity of Courts or Nunneries might have happily controuled them, were by no means able to endure the ticklish Situation of a Chamber-maid at an Inn, who is daily liable to the Solicitations of Lovers of all Complexions, to the dangerous Addresses of fine Gentlemen of the Army, who sometimes are obliged to reside with them a whole Year together, and above all are exposed to the Caresses of Footmen, Stage-Coachmen, and Drawers; all of whom employ the whole Artillery of kissing, flattering, bribing, and every other Weapon which is to be found in the whole Armory of Love, against them.

Betty, who was but one and twenty, had now lived three Years in this dangerous Situation, during which she had escaped pretty well. An Ensign of Foot was the first Person who made any Impression on her Heart; he did indeed raise a Flame in her, which required the Care of a Surgeon to cool.

While she burnt for him, several others burnt for her. Officers of the Army, young Gentlemen travelling the Western Circuit,[1] inoffensive Squires, and some of graver Character were set afire by her Charms!

At length, having perfectly recovered the Effects of her first unhappy Passion, she seemed to have vowed a State of perpetual Chastity. She was long deaf to all the Sufferings of her Lovers, till one day at a neighbouring Fair, the Rhetorick of *John* the Hostler, with a new Straw Hat, and a Pint of Wine, made a second Conquest over her.

[1] One of the eight districts in England and Wales through which judges and barristers travelled twice a year (usually after Hilary and Trinity terms) to hold court. The itinerary for the Summer Assizes in 1741 (7 July–8 August) was as follows: Southampton (Hampshire), New Sarum (Wilts), Dorchester (Dorset), Exeter (Devon), Bodmin (Cornwall), Wells (Somerset), and Bristol.

She did not however feel any of those Flames on this Occasion, which had been the Consequence of her former Amour; nor indeed those other ill Effects, which prudent young Women very justly apprehend from too absolute an Indulgence to the pressing Endearments of their Lovers. This latter, perhaps, was a little owing to her not being entirely constant to *John*, with whom she permitted *Tom Whipwell* the Stage-Coachman, and now and then a handsome young Traveller, to share her Favours.

Mr. *Tow-wouse* had for some time cast the languishing Eyes of Affection on this young Maiden. He had laid hold on every Opportunity of saying tender things to her, squeezing her by the Hand, and sometimes of kissing her Lips: for as the Violence of his Passion had considerably abated to Mrs. *Tow-wouse*; so like Water, which is stopt from its usual Current in one Place, it naturally sought a vent in another. Mrs. *Tow-wouse* is thought to have perceived this Abatement, and probably it added very little to the natural Sweetness of her Temper: for tho' she was as true to her Husband, as the Dial to the Sun,[1] she was rather more desirous of being shone on, as being more capable of feeling his Warmth.

Ever since *Joseph's* arrival, *Betty* had conceived an extraordinary Liking to him, which discovered itself more and more, as he grew better and better; till that fatal Evening, when, as she was warming his Bed, her Passion grew to such a Height, and so perfectly mastered both her Modesty and her Reason, that after many fruitless Hints, and sly Insinuations, she at last threw down the Warming-Pan, and embracing him with great Eagerness, swore he was the handsomest Creature she had ever seen.

Joseph in great Confusion leapt from her, and told her, he was sorry to see a young Woman cast off all Regard to Modesty: but she had gone too far to recede, and grew so very indecent, that *Joseph* was obliged, contrary to his Inclination, to use some Violence to her, and taking her in his Arms, he shut her out of the Room, and locked the Door.

How ought Man to rejoice, that his Chastity is always in his own power, that if he hath sufficient Strength of Mind, he hath always a competent Strength of Body to defend himself: and cannot, like a poor weak Woman, be ravished against his Will.

[1] Cf. Butler's *Hudibras*, III. ii. 175–6: 'True as a Dial to the Sun, / Although it be not shin'd upon.'

Betty was in the most violent Agitation at this Disappointment. Rage and Lust pulled her Heart, as with two Strings, two different Ways; one Moment she thought of stabbing *Joseph*, the next, of taking him in her Arms, and devouring him with Kisses; but the latter Passion was far more prevalent. Then she thought of revenging his Refusal on herself: but whilst she was engaged in this Meditation, happily Death presented himself to her in so many Shapes of drowning, hanging, poisoning, &c. that her distracted Mind could resolve on none. In this Perturbation of Spirit, it accidentally occurred to her Memory, that her Master's Bed was not made, she therefore went directly to his Room; where he happened at that time to be engaged at his Bureau. As soon as she saw him, she attempted to retire: but he called her back, and taking her by the hand, squeezed her so tenderly, at the same time whispering so many soft things into her Ears, and, then pressed her so closely with his Kisses, that the vanquished Fair-One, whose Passions were already raised, and which were not so whimsically capricious that one Man only could lay them, though perhaps, she would have rather preferred that one: The vanquished Fair-One quietly submitted, I say, to her Master's Will, who had just attained the Accomplishment of his Bliss, when Mrs. *Tow-wouse* unexpectedly entered the Room, and caused all that Confusion which we have before seen, and which it is not necessary at present to take any farther Notice of: Since without the Assistance of a single Hint from us, every Reader of any Speculation, or Experience, though not married himself, may easily conjecture, that it concluded with the Discharge of *Betty*, the Submission of Mr. *Tow-wouse*, with some things to be performed on his side by way of Gratitude for his Wife's Goodness in being reconciled to him, with many hearty Promises never to offend any more in the like manner: and lastly, his quietly and contentedly bearing to be reminded of his Transgressions, as a kind of Penance, once or twice a Day, during the Residue of his Life.

The History of the Adventures of

JOSEPH ANDREWS,

and of his Friend Mr. *Abraham Adams*

BOOK II

CHAPTER I

Of Divisions in Authors.

THERE are certain Mysteries or Secrets in all Trades from the highest to the lowest, from that of *Prime Ministring* to this of *Authoring*, which are seldom discovered, unless to Members of the same Calling. Among those used by us Gentlemen of the latter Occupation, I take this of dividing our Works into Books and Chapters to be none of the least considerable. Now for want of being truly acquainted with this Secret, common Readers imagine, that by this Art of dividing, we mean only to swell our Works to a much larger Bulk than they would otherwise be extended to. These several Places therefore in our Paper, which are filled with our Books and Chapters, are understood as so much Buckram, Stays, and Stay-tape in a Taylor's Bill, serving only to make up the Sum Total, commonly found at the Bottom of our first Page, and of his last.

But in reality the Case is otherwise, and in this, as well as all other Instances, we consult the Advantage of our Reader, not our own; and indeed many notable Uses arise to him from this Method: for first, those little Spaces between our Chapters may be looked upon as an Inn or Resting-Place, where he may stop and take a Glass, or any other Refreshment, as it pleases him. Nay, our fine Readers will, perhaps, be scarce able to travel farther than through one of them in a Day. As to those vacant Pages which are placed between our Books, they are to be regarded as those Stages, where, in long Journeys, the Traveller stays some time to repose himself, and consider of what he hath seen in the Parts he hath already past through; a Consideration which I take the Liberty to recommend a little to the Reader: for however swift his Capacity may be, I would not advise him to travel through these Pages too fast: for if he doth, he may probably miss the seeing some curious Productions of Nature which will be observed by the slower and more accurate Reader. A Volume without any such Places of Rest resembles the Opening of Wilds or Seas, which tires the Eye and fatigues the Spirit when entered upon.

Secondly, What are the Contents prefixed to every Chapter, but so many Inscriptions over the Gates of Inns (to continue the same Metaphor,) informing the Reader what Entertainment he is to expect, which if he likes not, he may travel on to the next: for in Biography, as we are not tied down to an exact Concatenation equally with other Historians; so a Chapter or two (for Instance this I am now writing) may be often pass'd over without any Injury to the Whole. And in these Inscriptions I have been as faithful as possible, not imitating the celebrated *Montagne*, who promises you one thing and gives you another;[1] nor some Title-Page Authors, who promise a great deal, and produce nothing at all.

There are, besides these more obvious Benefits, several others which our Readers enjoy from this Art of dividing; tho' perhaps most of them too mysterious to be presently understood, by any who are not initiated into the Science of *Authoring*. To mention therefore but one which is most obvious, it prevents spoiling the Beauty of a Book by turning down its Leaves, a Method otherwise necessary to those Readers, who, (tho' they read with great Improvement and Advantage) are apt, when they return to their Study, after half an Hour's Absence, to forget where they left off.

These Divisions have the Sanction of great Antiquity. *Homer* not only divided his great Work into twenty-four Books, (in

---

[1] The *Essais* of Michel Eyquem de Montaigne (1533–92) were first published in 1580. Montaigne frequently digresses, in a kind of conversational manner, from the subject indicated in his titles (e.g. 'Of Coaches', 'Of the Resemblance of Children to Their Parents', or 'Of Lame People'). As we know from *The Champion* (31 May 1740), Fielding had read Charles Cotton's translation, where, in the introductory essay, 'A Vindication of Montaigne's Essays', this perplexing method of composition is discussed at length: 'several of his Discourses', writes the author, 'do contain quite different Things from what is promis'd in the Titles . . . .' (Cotton, trans. *Montaigne's Essays in Three Books*, 5th ed. [1738], i. 4.)

Compliment perhaps to the twenty-four Letters[1] to which he had
very particular Obligations) but, according to the Opinion of
some very sagacious Critics, hawked them all separately,[2] delivering only one Book at a Time, (probably by Subscription). He was
the first Inventor of the Art which hath so long lain dormant, of
publishing by Numbers, an Art now brought to such Perfection,
that even Dictionaries are divided and exhibited piece-meal to the
Public; nay, one Bookseller hath (*to encourage Learning and ease the
Public*) contrived to give them a Dictionary in this divided Manner
for only fifteen Shillings more than it would have cost entire.[3]

---

[1] Cf. Thomas Parnell's statement, in 'An Essay on the Life, Writings, and Learning of
Homer', that Pisistratus, when publishing Homer's epics, 'distinguish'd each . . . into
twenty four Books, to which were afterwards prefix'd the twenty four Letters'. (In Pope's
Iliad [1715], i. 38.)

[2] An allusion to a theory first found in Aelian and given currency by Rapin's *Observations on the Poems of Homer and Virgil* (trans. John Davies, 1672). Some critics, such as
Richard Bentley, asserted that Homer 'wrote a sequel of Songs and Rhapsodies, to be
sung by himself for small earnings and good cheer, at Festivals and other days of Merriment; the *Ilias* he made for the Men, and the *Odysseis* for the other Sex. These loose Songs
were not collected together in the form of an Epic Poem till *Pisistratus's* Time, above 500
years after.' (Bentley, 'Remarks upon a Late Discourse of Free-Thinking in a Letter to
F. H. D.D.' [1713], in *Enchiridion Theologicum* [Oxford, 1792], v. 94.) Others, such as Mme
Dacier and Henry Felton, maintained that Homer's epics were written 'all in one Piece,
and not at all divided into Books' until long after his death. (Mme Dacier, Preface, *The
Iliad of Homer, Translated from the Greek into Blank Verse, by Mr. Ozell, Mr. Broom, and
Mr. Oldisworth*, 3rd ed. [1734], p. xlvii.) In *A Journey from This World to the Next* (i. viii)
Fielding ridicules the view of Bentley and his school by having Homer, with Mme Dacier
sitting in his lap, himself point out the 'Connection' in his *Iliad*.

[3] For a full discussion of the practice of publishing by numbers, see R. M. Wiles, *Serial
Publication in England before 1750* (Cambridge University Press, 1957). In glossing this
passage, the Abbé des Fontaines implied that Fielding was referring to the translation of
Bayle's dictionary (i.e. *A General Dictionary, Historical and Critical: In which a New and
Accurate Translation of that of the Celebrated Mr. Bayle . . . is included* [1734–41]), which
began to be issued by numbers in 1733. This work does seem to have achieved some
notoriety: it was cited in *The Grub-Street Journal* (19 September 1734) as an example of
'that strange Madness of publishing Books by piece-meal' (reprinted in *The Gentleman's
Magazine*, iv [September 1734], 489–90); and in the revised version of *The Author's Farce*
(II. iv) Fielding himself satirically alluded to it. However, not one bookseller was responsible for this venture, but several, Andrew Millar among them; and the work had been
completed by January 1741 (see *The Daily Post*, 13 January 1740/1), thus making Fielding's
use of the conditional tense ('would have cost') inappropriate.

Several other dictionaries were published this way, but Fielding probably had in mind
the first publication of the Society of Booksellers for Promoting Learning (see p. 67,
n. 2), Robert James's *Medicinal Dictionary*, the proposals for which appeared in June
1741, though publication did not begin until the following January. Richardson's friend,
Thomas Osborne, was the bookseller in question, who, while claiming to be 'among the
Benefactors to the Public', apologized for releasing the work by numbers at the unusually
high price of a shilling for five sheets—'for the better Accommodation of the Purchasers'.

Virgil hath given us his Poem in twelve Books, an Argument of his Modesty; for by that doubtless he would insinuate that he pretends to no more than half the Merit of the *Greek*: for the same Reason, our *Milton* went originally no farther than ten;[1] 'till being puffed up by the Praise of his Friends, he put himself on the same footing with the *Roman* Poet.

I shall not however enter so deep into this Matter as some very learned Criticks have done; who have with infinite Labour and acute Discernment discovered what Books are proper for Embellishment, and what require Simplicity only, particularly with regard to Similies, which I think are now generally agreed to become any Book but the first.[2]

I will dismiss this Chapter with the following Observation: That it becomes an Author generally to divide a Book, as it doth a Butcher to joint his Meat, for such Assistance is of great Help to both the Reader and the Carver. And now having indulged myself a little, I will endeavour to indulge the Curiosity of my Reader, who is no doubt impatient to know what he will find in the subsequent Chapters of this Book.

CHAPTER II

A surprizing Instance of Mr. Adams's *short Memory, with the unfortunate Consequences which it brought on* Joseph.

M R. *Adams* and *Joseph* were now ready to depart different ways, when an Accident determined the former to return with his Friend, which *Tow-wouse*, *Barnabas*, and the Bookseller had not been able to do. This Accident was, that those Sermons, which the Parson was travelling to *London* to publish, were, O my good Reader, left behind; what he had mistaken for them in the Saddle-Bags being no other than three Shirts, a pair of Shoes, and some

[1] *Paradise Lost* (1667) originally contained ten books only; not until the second edition in 1674 did it appear in its final form of twelve books.

[2] According to a precept of Aristotle (*Poetics* xxiv. 23) the diction of an epic poem should be varied, admitting embellishment in descriptive passages where action lags, but maintaining simplicity at other times. According to another principle, this time found in Horace, the opening or exordium should be couched in modest, unadorned language.

other Necessaries, which Mrs. *Adams*, who thought her Husband
would want Shirts more than Sermons on his Journey, had carefully provided him.

This Discovery was now luckily owing to the Presence of
Joseph at the opening the Saddle-Bags; who having heard his
Friend say, he carried with him nine Volumes of Sermons, and
not being of that Sect of Philosophers, who can reduce all the
Matter of the World into a Nut-shell, seeing there was no room
for them in the Bags, where the Parson had said they were deposited, had the Curiosity to cry out, 'Bless me, Sir, where are
your Sermons?' The Parson answer'd, 'There, there, Child, there
they are, under my Shirts.' Now it happened that he had taken
forth his last Shirt, and the Vehicle remained visibly empty.
'Sure, Sir,' says *Joseph*, 'there is nothing in the Bags.' Upon
which *Adams* starting, and testifying some Surprize, cry'd, 'Hey!
fie, fie upon it; they are not here sure enough. Ay, they are certainly left behind.'

Joseph was greatly concerned at the Uneasiness which he
apprehended his Friend must feel from this Disappointment: he
begged him to pursue his Journey, and promised he would himself return with the Books to him, with the utmost Expedition.
'No, thank you, Child,' answered *Adams*, 'it shall not be so. What
would it avail me, to tarry in the Great City, unless I had my
Discourses with me, which are, *ut ita dicam*,[1] the sole Cause, the
Aitia monotate of my Peregrination. No, Child, as this Accident
hath happened, I am resolved to return back to my Cure, together
with you; which indeed my Inclination sufficiently leads me to.
This Disappointment may, perhaps, be intended for my Good.'
He concluded with a Verse out of *Theocritus*, which signifies no
more than, *that sometimes it rains and sometimes the Sun shines*.[2]

Joseph bowed with Obedience, and Thankfulness for the Inclination which the Parson express'd of returning with him; and
now the Bill was called for, which, on Examination, amounted
within a Shilling to the Sum Mr. *Adams* had in his Pocket. Perhaps the Reader may wonder how he was able to produce a
sufficient Sum for so many Days: that he may not be surprised,

[1] 'So to speak.'

[2] In Theocritus, *Idyll IV*, 41–43, Corydon consoles Battus for the loss of his love: 'Soft
you, good Battus; be comforted. Good luck comes with another morn; while there's life
there's hope; rain one day, shine the next.' (J. M. Edmonds, trans.; Loeb Classical Library
[New York, 1912].)

therefore, it cannot be unnecessary to acquaint him, that he had borrowed a Guinea of a Servant belonging to the Coach and Six, who had been formerly one of his Parishioners, and whose Master, the Owner of the Coach, then lived within three Miles of him: for so good was the Credit of Mr. *Adams*, that even Mr. *Peter* the Lady *Booby's* Steward, would have lent him a Guinea with very little Security.

Mr. *Adams* discharged the Bill, and they were both setting out, having agreed *to ride and tie*: a Method of Travelling much used by Persons who have but one Horse between them, and is thus performed. The two Travellers set out together, one on horseback, the other on foot: Now as it generally happens that he on horseback out-goes him on foot, the Custom is, that when he arrives at the Distance agreed on, he is to dismount, tie the Horse to some Gate, Tree, Post, or other thing, and then proceed on foot; when the other comes up to the Horse, he unties him, mounts and gallops on, 'till having passed by his Fellow-Traveller, he likewise arrives at the Place of tying. And this is that Method of Travelling so much in use among our prudent Ancestors, who knew that Horses had Mouths as well as Legs, and that they could not use the latter, without being at the Expence of suffering the Beasts themselves to use the former. This was the Method in use in those Days: when, instead of a Coach and Six, a Member of Parliament's Lady used to mount a Pillion behind her Husband; and a grave Serjeant at Law condescended to amble to *Westminster* on an easy Pad, with his Clerk kicking his Heels behind him.

Adams was now gone some Minutes, having insisted on *Joseph's* beginning the Journey on horseback, and *Joseph* had his Foot in the Stirrup, when the Hostler presented him a Bill for the Horse's Board during his Residence at the Inn. *Joseph* said Mr. *Adams* had paid all; but this Matter being referred to Mr. *Tow-wouse* was by him decided in favour of the Hostler, and indeed with Truth and Justice: for this was a fresh Instance of that shortness of Memory which did not arise from want of Parts, but that continual Hurry in which Parson *Adams* was always involved.

Joseph was now reduced to a Dilemma which extremely puzzled him. The Sum due for Horse-meat was twelve Shillings, (for *Adams* who had borrowed the Beast of his Clerk, had ordered

him to be fed as well as they could feed him) and the Cash in his
Pocket amounted to Sixpence, (for *Adams* had divided the last
Shilling with him). Now, tho' there have been some ingenious
Persons who have contrived to pay twelve Shillings with Six-
pence, *Joseph* was not one of them. He had never contracted a
Debt in his Life, and was consequently the less ready at an Expedient to extricate himself. *Tow-wouse* was willing to give him
Credit 'till next time, to which Mrs. *Tow-wouse* would probably
have consented (for such was *Joseph's* Beauty, that it had made
some Impression even on that Piece of Flint which that good
Woman wore in her Bosom by way of heart.) *Joseph* would have
found therefore, very likely, the Passage free, had he not, when
he honestly discovered the Nakedness of his Pockets, pulled out
that little Piece of Gold which we have mentioned before. This
caused Mrs. *Tow-wouse's* Eyes to water; she told *Joseph*, she did
not conceive a Man could want Money whilst he had Gold in his
Pocket. *Joseph* answered, he had such a Value for that little Piece
of Gold, that he would not part with it for a hundred times the
Riches which the greatest Esquire in the County was worth. 'A
pretty Way indeed,' said Mrs. *Tow-wouse*, 'to run in debt, and
then refuse to part with your Money, because you have a Value
for it. I never knew any Piece of Gold of more Value than as many
Shillings as it would change for.' 'Not to preserve my Life from
starving, nor to redeem it from a Robber, would I part with this
dear Piece,' answered *Joseph*. 'What (says Mrs. *Tow-wouse*) I
suppose, it was given you by some vile Trollop, some Miss or
other; if it had been the Present of a virtuous Woman, you would
not have had such a Value for it. My Husband is a Fool if he
parts with the Horse, without being paid for him.' 'No, no, I can't
part with the Horse indeed, till I have the Money,' cried *Tow-
wouse*. A Resolution highly commended by a Lawyer then in the
Yard, who declared Mr. *Tow-wouse* might justify the Detainer.

As we cannot therefore at present get Mr. *Joseph* out of the
Inn, we shall leave him in it, and carry our Reader on after Parson *Adams*, who, his Mind being perfectly at ease, fell into a Contemplation on a Passage in *Æschylus*, which entertained him for
three Miles together, without suffering him once to reflect on his
Fellow-Traveller.

At length having spun out this Thread, and being now at the
Summit of a Hill, he cast his Eyes backwards, and wondered that

he could not see any sign of *Joseph*. As he left him ready to mount the Horse, he could not apprehend any Mischief had happened, neither could he suspect that he had miss'd his Way, it being so broad and plain: the only Reason which presented itself to him, was that he had met with an Acquaintance who had prevailed with him to delay some time in Discourse.

He therefore resolved to proceed slowly forwards, not doubting but that he should be shortly overtaken, and soon came to a large Water, which filling the whole Road, he saw no Method of passing unless by wading through, which he accordingly did up to his Middle; but was no sooner got to the other Side, than he perceived, if he had looked over the Hedge, he would have found a Foot-Path capable of conducting him without wetting his Shoes.

His Surprize at *Joseph's* not coming up grew now very troublesome: he began to fear he knew not what, and as he determined, to move no farther; and, if he did not shortly overtake him, to return back; he wished to find a House of publick Entertainment where he might dry his Clothes and refresh himself with a Pint: but seeing no such (for no other Reason than because he did not cast his Eyes a hundred Yards forwards) he sat himself down on a Stile, and pulled out his *Æschylus*.

A Fellow passing presently by, *Adams* asked him, if he could direct him to an Alehouse. The Fellow who had just left it, and perceived the House and Sign to be within sight, thinking he had jeered him, and being of a morose Temper, bad him *follow his Nose and be d—n'd*. *Adams* told him he was a *saucy Jackanapes*; upon which the Fellow turned about angrily: but perceiving *Adams* clench his Fist he thought proper to go on without taking any farther notice.

A Horseman following immediately after, and being asked the same Question, answered, 'Friend, there is one within a Stone's-Throw; I believe you may see it before you.' *Adams* lifting up his Eyes, cry'd, 'I protest and so there is;' and thanking his Informer proceeded directly to it.

CHAPTER III

The Opinion of two Lawyers concerning the same
Gentleman, with Mr. Adams's Enquiry into the
Religion of his Host.

H E had just entered the House, had called for his Pint and seated
himself, when two Horsemen came to the Door, and fastening
their Horses to the Rails, alighted. They said there was a violent
Shower of Rain coming on, which they intended to weather there,
and went into a little Room by themselves, not perceiving Mr.
Adams.

One of these immediately asked the other, if he had seen a
more comical Adventure a great while? Upon which the other
said, 'he doubted whether by Law, the Landlord could justify
detaining the Horse for his Corn and Hay.' But the former
answered, 'Undoubtedly he can: it is an adjudged Case, and I
have known it tried.'[1]

Adams, who tho' he was, as the Reader may suspect, a little
inclined to Forgetfulness, never wanted more than a Hint to
remind him, over-hearing their Discourse, immediately suggested to himself that this was his own Horse, and that he had
forgot to pay for him, which upon enquiry, he was certified of
by the Gentlemen; who added, that the Horse was likely to have
more Rest than Food, unless he was paid for.

The poor Parson resolved to return presently to the Inn, tho'
he knew no more than *Joseph*, how to procure his Horse his
Liberty: he was however prevailed on to stay under Covert, 'till
the Shower which was now very violent, was over.

The three Travellers then sat down together over a Mug of

---

[1] Tow-wouse was legally within his rights in detaining Adams's horse. Giles Jacob puts
the case as follows: 'By the Custom of the Realm, if a Man lies in an *Inn* one Night, the
Inn-keeper may detain his Horses until he is paid for the Expences. . . . A Person brings his
Horse to an *Inn*, and leaves him in the Stable there; the *Inn-keeper* may keep him 'till the
Owner pay for the Keeping: And if he eat out as much as he is worth, the Master of the
Inn after a reasonable Appraisement, may sell the Horse and pay himself' (*New Law-
Dictionary*, 4th ed. [1739], s.v. 'Inns'). As Dr. Amory suggests ('Law and the Structure
of Fielding's Novels' [unpublished Ph.D. dissertation, Columbia University, 1964], p. 49,
n. 1), Fielding may have remembered the 'adjudged Case' of *Yorke* v. *Grenaugh* (L. Raym.,
866, 92 E.R. 79 [K.B., 1703]), in which his grandfather Gould was a member of the Court.

good Beer; when *Adams*, who had observed a Gentleman's House
as he passed along the Road, enquired to whom it belonged: one
of the Horsemen had no sooner mentioned the Owner's Name,
than the other began to revile him in the most opprobrious Terms.
The *English* Language scarce affords a single reproachful Word,
which he did not vent on this Occasion. He charged him likewise
with many particular Facts. He said,—'he no more regarded a
Field of Wheat when he was hunting, than he did the High-way;
that he had injured several poor Farmers by trampling their Corn
under his Horse's Heels; and if any of them begged him with the
utmost Submission to refrain, his Horse-whip was always ready
to do them justice.' He said, 'that he was the greatest Tyrant to
the Neighbours in every other Instance, and would not suffer a
Farmer to keep a Gun, tho' he might justify it by Law; and in his
own Family so cruel a Master, that he never kept a Servant a
Twelve-month. In his Capacity as a Justice,' continued he, 'he
behaves so partially, that he commits or acquits just as he is in
the humour, without any regard to Truth or Evidence: The
Devil may carry any one before him for me; I would rather be
tried before some Judges than be a Prosecutor before him: If
I had an Estate in the Neighbourhood, I would sell it for half the
Value, rather than live near him.' *Adams* shook his Head, and
said, 'he was sorry such Men were suffered to proceed with
Impunity, and that Riches could set any Man above Law.' The
Reviler a little after retiring into the Yard, the Gentleman, who
had first mentioned his Name to *Adams*, began to assure him,
'that his Companion was a prejudiced Person. It is true,' says he,
'perhaps, that he may have sometimes pursued his Game over a
Field of Corn, but he hath always made the Party ample Satisfaction; that so far from tyrannizing over his Neighbours, or
taking away their Guns, he himself knew several Farmers not
qualified, who not only kept Guns, but killed Game with them.
That he was the best of Masters to his Servants, and several of
them had grown old in his Service. That he was the best Justice
of Peace in the Kingdom, and to his certain knowledge had decided many difficult Points, which were referred to him, with the
greatest Equity, and the highest Wisdom. And he verily believed,
several Persons would give a Year's Purchase more for an Estate
near him, than under the Wings of any other great Man.' He
had just finished his Encomium, when his Companion returned

and acquainted him the Storm was over. Upon which, they presently mounted their Horses and departed.

Adams, who was in the utmost Anxiety at those different Characters of the same Person, asked his Host if he knew the Gentleman: for he began to imagine they had by mistake been speaking of two several Gentlemen. 'No, no, Master!' answered the Host, a shrewd cunning Fellow, 'I know the Gentleman very well of whom they have been speaking, as I do the Gentlemen who spoke of him. As for riding over other Men's Corn, to my knowledge he hath not been on horseback these two Years. I never heard he did any Injury of that kind; and as to making Reparation, he is not so free of his Money as that comes to neither. Nor did I ever hear of his taking away any Man's Gun; nay, I know several who have Guns in their Houses: but as for killing Game with them, no Man is stricter; and I believe he would ruin any who did. You heard one of the Gentlemen say, he was the worst Master in the World, and the other that he is the best: but as for my own part, I know all his Servants, and never heard from any of them that he was either one or the other.——' 'Aye, aye,' says *Adams*, 'and how doth he behave as a Justice, pray?' 'Faith, Friend,' answered the Host, 'I question whether he is in the Commission: the only Cause I have heard he hath decided a great while, was one between those very two Persons who just went out of this House; and I am sure he determined that justly, for I heard the whole matter.' 'Which did he decide it in favour of?' quoth *Adams*. 'I think I need not answer that Question,' cried the Host, 'after the different Characters you have heard of him. It is not my Business to contradict Gentlemen, while they are drinking in my House: but I knew neither of them spoke a Syllable of Truth.' 'God forbid! (said *Adams*,) that Men should arrive at such a Pitch of Wickedness, to be-lye the Character of their Neighbour from a little private Affection, or what is infinitely worse, a private Spite. I rather believe we have mistaken them, and they mean two other Persons: for there are many Houses on the Road.' 'Why prithee, Friend,' cries the Host, 'dost thou pretend never to have told a lye in thy Life?' 'Never a malicious one, I am certain,' answered *Adams*; 'nor with a Design to injure the Reputation of any Man living.' 'Pugh, malicious! no, no,' replied the Host; 'not malicious with a Design to hang a Man, or bring him into Trouble: but surely out of love to one's self,

one must speak better of a Friend than an Enemy.' 'Out of love
to your self, you should confine yourself to Truth,' says *Adams*,
'for by doing otherwise, you injure the noblest Part of yourself,
your immortal Soul. I can hardly believe any Man such an Idiot
to risque the Loss of that by any trifling Gain, and the greatest
Gain in this World is but Dirt in comparison of what shall be
revealed hereafter.' Upon which the Host taking up the Cup,
with a Smile drank a Health to Hereafter: adding, 'he was for
something present.' 'Why,' says *Adams* very gravely, 'Do not you
believe another World?' To which the Host answered, 'yes, he
was no Atheist.' 'And you believe you have an immortal Soul?'
cries *Adams*: He answered, 'God forbid he should not.' 'And
Heaven and Hell?' said the Parson. The Host then bid him 'not
to prophane: for those were Things not to be mentioned nor
thought of but in Church.' *Adams* asked him, 'why he went to
Church, if what he learned there had no Influence on his Conduct
in Life?' 'I go to Church,' answered the Host, 'to say my Prayers
and behave godly.' 'And dost not thou,' cry'd *Adams*, 'believe
what thou hearest at Church?' 'Most part of it, Master,' returned
the Host. 'And dost not thou then tremble,' cries *Adams*, 'at the
Thought of eternal Punishment?' 'As for that, Master,' said he,
'I never once thought about it: but what signifies talking about
matters so far off? the Mug is out, shall I draw another?'

Whilst he was gone for that purpose, a Stage-Coach drove up
to the Door. The Coachman coming into the House, was asked
by the Mistress, what Passengers he had in his Coach? 'A Parcel
of *Squinny-gut* B—s, (says he) I have a good mind to overturn
them; you won't prevail upon them to drink any thing I assure
you.' *Adams* asked him, if he had not seen a young Man on
Horse-back on the Road, (describing *Joseph*). 'Aye,' said the
Coachman, 'a Gentlewoman in my Coach that is his Acquaintance
redeemed him and his Horse; he would have been here before
this time, had not the Storm driven him to shelter.' 'God bless
her,' said *Adams* in a Rapture; nor could he delay walking out to
satisfy himself who this charitable Woman was; but what was
his surprize, when he saw his old Acquaintance, Madam *Slipslop*?
Her's indeed was not so great, because she had been informed by
Joseph, that he was on the Road. Very civil were the Salutations
on both sides; and Mrs. *Slipslop* rebuked the Hostess for denying
the Gentleman to be there when she asked for him: but indeed

the poor Woman had not erred designedly: for Mrs. *Slipslop* asked for a Clergyman; and she had unhappily mistaken *Adams* for a Person travelling to a neighbouring Fair with the Thimble and Button,[1] or some other such Operation: for he marched in a swinging great, but short, white Coat with black Buttons, a short Wig, and a Hat, which so far from having a black Hatband, had nothing black about it.

Joseph was now come up, and Mrs. *Slipslop* would have had him quit his Horse to the Parson, and come himself into the Coach: but he absolutely refused, saying he thanked Heaven he was well enough recovered to be very able to ride, and added, he hoped he knew his Duty better than to ride in a Coach while Mr. *Adams* was on horseback.

Mrs. *Slipslop* would have persisted longer, had not a Lady in the Coach put a short End to the Dispute, by refusing to suffer a Fellow in a Livery to ride in the same Coach with herself: so it was at length agreed that *Adams* should fill the vacant Place in the Coach, and *Joseph* should proceed on horseback.

They had not proceeded far before Mrs. *Slipslop*, addressing herself to the Parson, spoke thus: 'There hath been a strange Alteration in our Family, Mr. *Adams*, since Sir *Thomas's* Death.' 'A strange Alteration indeed!' says *Adams*, 'as I gather from some Hints which have dropped from *Joseph*.' 'Aye,' says she, 'I could never have believed it, but the longer one lives in the World, the more one sees. So *Joseph* hath given you Hints.'—'But of what Nature, will always remain a perfect Secret with me,' cries the Parson; 'he forced me to promise before he would communicate any thing. I am indeed concerned to find her Ladyship behave in so unbecoming a manner. I always thought her in the main, a good Lady, and should never have suspected her of Thoughts so unworthy a Christian, and with a young Lad her own Servant.' 'These things are no Secrets to me, I assure you,' cries *Slipslop*; 'and I believe, they will be none any where shortly: for ever since the Boy's Departure she hath behaved more like a mad Woman than any thing else.' 'Truly, I am heartily concerned,' says *Adams*, 'for she was a good sort of a Lady; indeed I have often wished she had attended a little more constantly at the Service, but she hath done a great deal of Good in the Parish.' 'O Mr. *Adams*!'

[1] The ancestor of the shell game, practised by a professional sharper called a 'thimble-rigger'.

says *Slipslop*, 'People that don't see all, often know nothing. Many Things have been given away in our Family, I do assure you, without her knowledge. I have heard you say in the Pulpit, we ought not to brag: but indeed I can't avoid saying, if she had kept the Keys herself, the Poor would have wanted many a Cordial which I have let them have. As for my late Master, he was as worthy a Man as ever lived, and would have done infinite Good if he had not been controlled: but he loved a quiet Life, Heavens rest his Soul! I am confident he is there, and enjoys a quiet Life, which some Folks would not allow him here.' *Adams* answered, 'he had never heard this before, and was mistaken, if she herself,' (for he remembered she used to commend her Mistress and blame her Master,) 'had not formerly been of another Opinion.' 'I don't know, (replied she,) what I might once think: but now I am *confidous* Matters are as I tell you: The World will shortly see who hath been deceived; for my part I say nothing, but that it is *wondersome* how some People can carry all things with a grave Face.'

Thus Mr. *Adams* and she discoursed: 'till they came opposite to a great House which stood at some distance from the Road; a Lady in the Coach spying it, cry'd, 'Yonder lives the unfortunate *Leonora*, if one can justly call a Woman unfortunate, whom we must own at the same time guilty, and the Author of her own Calamity.' This was abundantly sufficient to awaken the Curiosity of Mr. *Adams*, as indeed it did that of the whole Company, who jointly solicited the Lady to acquaint them with *Leonora's* History, since it seemed, by what she had said, to contain something remarkable.

The Lady, who was perfectly well bred, did not require many Entreaties, and having only wished their Entertainment might make amends for the Company's Attention, she began in the following manner.

CHAPTER IV

The History of Leonora, *or the Unfortunate Jilt*.

LEONORA was the Daughter of a Gentleman of Fortune; she was tall and well-shaped, with a Sprightliness in her Countenance, which often attracts beyond more regular Features joined with an insipid Air; nor is this kind of Beauty less apt to deceive than allure; the Good-Humour which it indicates, being often mistaken for Good-Nature, and the Vivacity for true Understanding.

Leonora, who was now at the Age of Eighteen, lived with an Aunt of her's in a Town in the North of *England*. She was an extreme Lover of Gaiety, and very rarely missed a Ball or any other publick Assembly; where she had frequent Opportunities of satisfying a greedy Appetite of Vanity with the Preference which was given her by the Men to almost every other Woman present.

Among many young Fellows who were particular in their Gallantries towards her, *Horatio* soon distinguished himself in her Eyes beyond all his Competitors; she danced with more than ordinary Gaiety when he happened to be her Partner; neither the Fairness of the Evening nor the Musick of the Nightingale, could lengthen her Walk like his Company. She affected no longer to understand the Civilities of others: whilst she inclined so attentive an Ear to every Compliment of *Horatio*, that she often smiled even when it was too delicate for her Comprehension.

'Pray, Madam,' says *Adams*, 'who was this Squire *Horatio*?'

Horatio, says the Lady, was a young Gentleman of a good Family, bred to the Law, and had been some few Years called to the Degree of a Barrister. His Face and Person were such as the Generality allowed handsome: but he had a Dignity in his Air very rarely to be seen. His Temper was of the saturnine Complexion, but without the least Taint of Moroseness. He had Wit and Humour with an Inclination to Satire, which he indulged rather too much.

This Gentleman, who had contracted the most violent Passion for *Leonora*, was the last Person who perceived the Probability of its Success. The whole Town had made the Match for him, before he himself had drawn a Confidence from her Actions sufficient to mention his Passion to her; for it was his Opinion, (and perhaps he was there in the right) that it is highly impolitick to talk seriously of Love to a Woman before you have made such a Progress in her Affections, that she herself expects and desires to hear it.

But whatever Diffidence the Fears of a Lover may create, which are apt to magnify every Favour conferred on a Rival, and to see the little Advances towards themselves through the other End of the Perspective; it was impossible that *Horatio's* Passion should so blind his Discernment, as to prevent his conceiving Hopes from the Behaviour of *Leonora*; whose Fondness for him was now as visible to an indifferent Person in their Company, as his for her.

'I never knew any of these forward Sluts come to good, (says the Lady, who refused *Joseph's* Entrance into the Coach,) nor shall I wonder at any thing she doth in the Sequel.'

The Lady proceeded in her Story thus: It was in the Midst of a gay Conversation in the Walks one Evening, when *Horatio* whispered *Leonora*, 'that he was desirous to take a Turn or two with her in private; for that he had something to communicate to her of great Consequence.' 'Are you sure it is of Consequence?' said she, smiling.—'I hope,' answered he, 'you will think so too, since the whole future Happiness of my Life must depend on the Event.'

Leonora, who very much suspected what was coming, would have deferred it 'till another Time: but *Horatio*, who had more than half conquered the Difficulty of speaking by the first Motion, was so very importunate, that she at last yielded, and leaving the rest of the Company, they turned aside into an unfrequented Walk.

They had retired far out of the sight of the Company, both maintaining a strict Silence. At last *Horatio* made a full Stop, and taking *Leonora*, who stood pale and trembling, gently by the Hand, he fetched a deep Sigh, and then looking on her Eyes with all the Tenderness imaginable, he cried out in a faltering Accent; 'O *Leonora*! is it necessary for me to declare to you on what the future Happiness of my Life must be founded! Must I say, there is something belonging to you which is a Bar to my Happiness, and which unless you will part with, I must be miserable?' 'What can that be?' replied *Leonora*.—'No wonder,' said he, 'you are surprized, that I should make an Objection to any thing which is yours, yet sure you may guess, since it is the only one which the Riches of the World, if they were mine, should purchase of me.— O it is that which you must part with, to bestow all the rest! Can *Leonora*, or rather will she doubt longer?—Let me then whisper it in her Ears,—It is your Name, Madam. It is by parting with that, by your Condescension to be for ever mine, which must at once prevent me from being the most miserable, and will render me the happiest of Mankind.' *Leonora*, covered with Blushes, and with as angry a Look as she could possibly put on, told him, 'that had she suspected what his Declaration would have been, he should not have decoyed her from her Company; that he had so surprized and frighted her, that she begged him to convey her back as quick as possible;' which he, trembling very near as much as herself, did.

'More Fool he,' cried *Slipslop*, 'it is a sign he knew very little of our *Sect.*' 'Truly, Madam,' said *Adams*, 'I think you are in the right, I should have insisted to know a piece of her Mind, when I had carried matters so far.' But Mrs. *Grave-airs* desired the Lady to omit all such fulsome Stuff in her Story: for that it made her sick.

Well then, Madam, to be as concise as possible, said the Lady, many Weeks had not past after this Interview, before *Horatio* and *Leonora* were what they call on a good footing together. All Ceremonies except the last were now over; the Writings were now drawn, and every thing was in the utmost forwardness preparative to the putting *Horatio* in possession of all his Wishes. I will if you please repeat you a Letter from each of them which I have got by heart, and which will give you no small Idea of their Passion on both sides.

Mrs. *Grave-airs* objected to hearing these Letters: but being put to the Vote, it was carried against her by all the rest in the Coach; Parson *Adams* contending for it with the utmost Vehemence.

HORATIO *to* LEONORA

How vain, most adorable Creature, is the Pursuit of Pleasure in the absence of an Object to which the Mind is entirely devoted, unless it have some Relation to that Object! I was last Night condemned to the Society of Men of Wit and Learning, which, however agreeable it might have formerly been to me, now only gave me a Suspicion that they imputed my Absence in Conversation to the true Cause. For which Reason, when your Engagements forbid me the extatic Happiness of seeing you, I am always desirous to be alone; since my Sentiments for *Leonora* are so delicate, that I cannot bear the Apprehension of another's prying into those delightful Endearments with which the warm Imagination of a Lover will sometimes indulge him, and which

I suspect my Eyes then betray. To fear this Discovery of our Thoughts, may perhaps appear too ridiculous a Nicety to Minds, not susceptible of all the Tendernesses of this delicate Passion. And surely we shall suspect there are few such, when we consider that it requires every human Virtue to exert itself in its full Extent. Since the Beloved whose Happiness it ultimately respects, may give us charming Opportunities of being brave in her Defence, generous to her Wants, compassionate to her Afflictions, grateful to her Kindness, and, in the same manner, of exercising every other Virtue, which he who would not do to any Degree, and that with the utmost Rapture, can never deserve the Name of a Lover: It is therefore with a View to the delicate Modesty of your Mind that I cultivate it so purely in my own, and it is that which will sufficiently suggest to you the Uneasiness I bear from those Liberties which Men to whom the World allow Politeness will sometimes give themselves on these Occasions.

Can I tell you with what Eagerness I expect the Arrival of that blest Day, when I shall experience the Falshood of a common Assertion that the greatest human Happiness consists in Hope? A Doctrine which no Person had ever stronger Reason to believe than myself at present, since none ever tasted such Bliss as fires my Bosom with the Thoughts of spending my future Days with such a Companion, and that every Action of my Life will have the glorious Satisfaction of conducing to your Happiness.

Leonora to Horatio

The Refinement of your Mind has been so evidently proved, by every Word and Action ever since I had first the Pleasure of knowing you, that I thought it impossible my good Opinion of *Horatio* could have been heightened by any additional Proof of Merit. This very Thought was my Amusement when I received your last Letter, which, when I opened, I confess I was surprized to find the delicate Sentiments expressed there, so far exceeded what I thought could come even from you, (altho' I know all the generous Principles human Nature is capable of, are centered in your Breast) that Words cannot paint what I feel on the Reflec-

---

* This Letter was written by a young Lady on reading the former.[1]

[1] Probably by Fielding's sister Sarah (1710–68), who turned novelist herself in 1744 with *The Adventures of David Simple*, to which her brother contributed a Preface.

tion, that my Happiness shall be the ultimate End of all your Actions.

Oh *Horatio*! what a Life must that be, where the meanest domestick Cares are sweetened by the pleasing Consideration that the Man on Earth who best deserves, and to whom you are most inclined to give your Affections, is to reap either Profit or Pleasure from all you do! In such a Case, Toils must be turned into Diversions, and nothing but the unavoidable Inconveniences of Life can make us remember that we are mortal.

If the solitary Turn of your Thoughts, and the Desire of keeping them undiscovered, makes even the Conversation of Men of Wit and Learning tedious to you, what anxious Hours must I spend who am condemn'd by Custom to the Conversation of Women, whose natural Curiosity leads them to pry into all my Thoughts, and whose Envy can never suffer *Horatio's* Heart to be possessed by any one without forcing them into malicious Designs, against the Person who is so happy as to possess it: but indeed, if ever Envy can possibly have any Excuse, or even Alleviation, it is in this Case, where the Good is so great, that it must be equally natural to all to wish it for themselves, nor am I ashamed to own it: and to your Merit, *Horatio*, I am obliged, that prevents my being in that most uneasy of all the Situations I can figure in my Imagination, of being led by Inclination to love the Person whom my own Judgment forces me to condemn.

Matters were in so great forwardness between this fond Couple, that the Day was fixed for their Marriage, and was now within a Fortnight, when the Sessions chanced to be held for that County in a Town about twenty Miles distance from that which is the Scene of our Story. It seems, it is usual for the young Gentlemen of the Bar to repair to these Sessions, not so much for the sake of Profit, as to shew their Parts and learn the Law of the Justices of Peace: for which purpose one of the wisest and gravest of all the Justices is appointed Speaker or Chairman, as they modestly call it, and he reads them a Lecture, and instructs them in the true Knowledge of the Law.

'You are here guilty of a little Mistake,' says *Adams*, 'which if you please I will correct; I have attended at one of these Quarter Sessions, where I observed the Counsel taught the Justices, instead of learning any thing of them.'

It is not very material, said the Lady: hither repaired *Horatio*, who as he hoped by his Profession to advance his Fortune, which was not at present very large, for the sake of his dear *Leonora*, he resolved to spare no Pains, nor lose any Opportunity of improving or advancing himself in it.

The same Afternoon in which he left the Town, as *Leonora* stood at her Window, a Coach and Six passed by: which she declared to be the completest, genteelest, prettiest Equipage she ever saw; adding these remarkable Words, *O I am in love with that Equipage!* which, tho' her Friend *Florella* at that time did not greatly regard, she hath since remembered.

In the Evening an Assembly was held, which *Leonora* honoured with her Company: but intended to pay her dear *Horatio* the Compliment of refusing to dance in his Absence.

O Why have not Women as good Resolution to maintain their Vows, as they have often good Inclinations in making them!

The Gentleman who owned the Coach and Six, came to the Assembly. His Clothes were as remarkably fine as his Equipage could be. He soon attracted the Eyes of the Company; all the Smarts, all the Silk Waistcoats with Silver and Gold Edgings, were eclipsed in an instant.

'Madam,' said *Adams*, 'if it be not impertinent, I should be glad to know how this Gentleman was drest.'

Sir, answered the Lady, I have been told, he had on a Cut-Velvet Coat of a Cinnamon Colour, lined with a Pink Satten, embroidered all over with Gold; his Waistcoat, which was Cloth of Silver, was embroidered with Gold likewise. I cannot be particular as to the rest of his Dress: but it was all in the *French* Fashion, for *Bellarmine*, (that was his Name) was just arrived from *Paris*.

This fine Figure did not more entirely engage the Eyes of every Lady in the Assembly, than *Leonora* did his. He had scarce beheld her, but he stood motionless and fixed as a Statue, or at least would have done so, if Good-Breeding had permitted him. However, he carried it so far before he had power to correct himself, that every Person in the Room easily discovered where his Admiration was settled. The other Ladies began to single out their former Partners, all perceiving who would be *Bellarmine's* Choice; which they however endeavoured, by all possible means, to prevent: Many of them saying to *Leonora*, 'O Madam, I suppose we shan't have the pleasure of seeing you dance To-Night;' and then crying out in *Bellarmine's* hearing, 'O *Leonora* will not dance, I assure you; her Partner is not here.' One maliciously attempted to prevent her, by sending a disagreeable Fellow to ask her, that so she might be obliged either to dance with him, or sit down: but this Scheme proved abortive.

Leonora saw herself admired by the fine Stranger, and envied by every Woman present. Her little Heart began to flutter within her, and her Head was agitated with a convulsive Motion; she seemed as if she would speak to several of her Acquaintance, but had nothing to say: for as she would not mention her present Triumph, so she could not disengage her Thoughts one moment from the Contemplation of it: She had never tasted any thing like this Happiness. She had before known what it was to torment a single Woman; but to be hated and secretly cursed by a whole Assembly, was a Joy reserved for this blessed Moment. As this vast Profusion of Ecstasy had confounded her Understanding, so there was nothing so foolish as her Behaviour; she played a thousand childish Tricks, distorted her Person into several Shapes, and her Face into several Laughs, without any Reason. In a word, her Carriage was as absurd as her Desires, which were to affect an Insensibility of the Stranger's Admiration, and at the same time a Triumph from that Admiration over every Woman in the Room.

In this Temper of Mind, *Bellarmine*, having enquired who she was, advanced to her, and with a low Bow, begged the Honour of dancing with her, which she with as low a Curt'sy immediately granted. She danced with him all Night, and enjoyed perhaps the highest Pleasure, which she was capable of feeling.

At these Words, *Adams* fetched a deep Groan, which frighted the Ladies, who told him, 'they hoped he was not ill.' He answered, 'he groaned only for the Folly of *Leonora*.'

Leonora retired, (continued the Lady) about Six in the Morning, but not to Rest. She tumbled and tossed in her Bed, with very short Intervals of Sleep, and those entirely filled with Dreams of the Equipage and fine Clothes she had seen, and the Balls, Operas and Ridotto's, which had been the Subject of their Conversation.

In the Afternoon *Bellarmine*, in the dear Coach and Six, came to wait on her. He was indeed charmed with her Person, and was, on Enquiry, so well pleased with the Circumstances of her Father, (for he himself, notwithstanding all his Finery, was not quite so rich as a *Crœsus* or an *Attālus*.)[1] '*Attălus*,' says Mr. *Adams*, 'but pray how came you acquainted with these Names?' The Lady smiled at the Question, and proceeded—He was so pleased, I say, that he resolved to make his Addresses to her directly. He did so accordingly, and that with so much warmth and briskness, that he quickly baffled her weak Repulses, and obliged the Lady to refer him to her Father, who, she knew, would quickly declare in favour of a Coach and Six.

Thus, what *Horatio* had by Sighs and Tears, Love and Tenderness, been so long obtaining, the *French-English Bellarmine* with Gaiety and Gallantry possessed himself of in an instant. In other words, what Modesty had employed a full Year in raising, Impudence demolished in twenty-four Hours.

Here *Adams* groaned a second time, but the Ladies, who began to smoke him, took no Notice.

From the Opening of the Assembly 'till the End of *Bellarmine's* Visit, *Leonora* had scarce once thought of *Horatio*: but he now began, tho' an unwelcome Guest, to enter into her Mind. She wished she had seen the charming *Bellarmine* and his charming Equipage before Matters had gone so far. 'Yet, why (says she) should I wish to have seen him before, or what signifies it that I have seen him now? Is not *Horatio* my Lover? almost my Husband? Is he not as handsome, nay handsomer than *Bellarmine*? Aye, but *Bellarmine* is the genteeler and the finer Man; yes, that he must be allowed. Yes, yes, he is that certainly. But did not I no longer ago than yesterday love *Horatio* more than all the World? aye, but yesterday I had not seen *Bellarmine*. But doth not *Horatio* doat on me, and may he not in despair break his Heart if I abandon him? Well, and hath not *Bellarmine* a Heart to break too? Yes, but I promised *Horatio* first; but that was poor *Bellarmine's* Misfortune, if I had seen him first, I should certainly have preferred him. Did not the dear Creature prefer me to every Woman in the Assembly, when every She was laying out for him? When was it in *Horatio's* power to give me such an Instance of

[1] The wealth of the Attalids, kings of Pergamon (269–133 B.C.), was proverbial. In particular, the 'Testament of Attalus [III]' (*c.* 170–133 B.C.), bequeathing his kingdom to Rome, was celebrated by the poets as the type of lucrative good fortune (e.g. Horace, *Odes*, II. xviii. 5–6).

Affection? Can he give me an Equipage or any of those Things which *Bellarmine* will make me Mistress of? How vast is the Difference between being the Wife of a poor Counsellor, and the Wife of one of *Bellarmine's* Fortune! If I marry *Horatio*, I shall triumph over no more than one Rival: but by marrying *Bellarmine*, I shall be the Envy of all my Acquaintance. What Happiness!—But can I suffer *Horatio* to die? for he hath sworn he cannot survive my Loss: but perhaps he may not die; if he should, can I prevent it? Must I sacrifice my self to him? besides, *Bellarmine* may be as miserable for me too.' She was thus arguing with herself, when some young Ladies called her to the Walks, and a little relieved her Anxiety for the present.

The next Morning *Bellarmine* breakfasted with her in presence of her Aunt, whom he sufficiently informed of his Passion for *Leonora*; he was no sooner withdrawn, than the old Lady began to advise her Niece on this Occasion.—'You see, Child, (says she) what Fortune hath thrown in your way, and I hope you will not withstand your own Preferments.' *Leonora* sighing, 'begged her not to mention any such thing, when she knew her Engagements to *Horatio*.' 'Engagements to a Fig,' cry'd the Aunt, 'you should thank Heaven on your Knees that you have it yet in your power to break them. Will any Woman hesitate a Moment, whether she shall ride in a Coach or walk on Foot all the Days of her Life?—But *Bellarmine* drives six, and *Horatio* not even a Pair.' 'Yes, but, Madam, what will the World say?' answered *Leonora*; 'will not they condemn me?' 'The World is always on the side of Prudence,' cries the Aunt, 'and would surely condemn you if you sacrificed your Interest to any Motive whatever. O, I know the World very well, and you shew your own Ignorance, my Dear, by your Objection. O' my Conscience the World is wiser. I have lived longer in it than you, and I assure you there is not any thing worth our Regard besides Money: nor did I ever know one Person who married from other Considerations, who did not afterwards heartily repent it. Besides, if we examine the two Men, can you prefer a sneaking Fellow, who hath been bred at a University, to a fine Gentleman just come from his Travels?—All the World must allow *Bellarmine* to be a fine Gentleman, positively a fine Gentleman, and a handsome Man.—' 'Perhaps, Madam, I should not doubt, if I knew how to be handsomely off with the other.' 'O leave that to me,' says the Aunt. 'You know your

Father hath not been acquainted with the Affair.[1] Indeed, for my part, I thought it might do well enough, not dreaming of such an Offer: but I'll disengage you, leave me to give the Fellow an Answer. I warrant you shall have no farther Trouble.'

Leonora was at length satisfied with her Aunt's Reasoning; and *Bellarmine* supping with her that Evening, it was agreed he should the next Morning go to her Father and propose the Match, which she consented should be consummated at his Return.

The Aunt retired soon after Supper, and the Lovers being left together, *Bellarmine* began in the following manner: 'Yes, Madam, this Coat I assure you was made at *Paris*, and I defy the best *English* Taylor even to imitate it. There is not one of them can cut, Madam, they can't cut. If you observe how this Skirt is turned, and this Sleeve, a clumsy *English* Rascal can do nothing like it.—Pray how do you like my Liveries?' *Leonora* answered, 'she thought them very pretty.' 'All *French*,' says he, 'I assure you, except the Great Coats; I never trust any thing more than a Great Coat to an *Englishman*; you know one must encourage our own People what one can, especially as, before I had a Place, I was in the Country Interest,[2] he, he, he! but for myself, I would see the dirty Island at the bottom of the Sea, rather than wear a single Rag of *English* Work about me, and I am sure after you have made one Tour to *Paris*, you will be of the same Opinion with regard to your own Clothes. You can't conceive what an Addition a *French* Dress would be to your Beauty; I positively assure you, at the first Opera I saw since I came over, I mistook the *English* Ladies for Chambermaids, he he, he!'[3]

---

[1] Fielding forgets that earlier in the chapter we were told that 'the Writings' between Leonora and Horatio had been formally drawn.

[2] The Country Interest was another name for the Country Party or the Patriots, who opposed Walpole's administration. By inserting this brief passage into the second edition (June 1742), after the Patriots had unseated Walpole, Fielding was satirizing his old party, and especially Pulteney and Carteret, for precisely the same hypocritical self-indulgence at the expense of their country that they had decried in Walpole's courtiers (see p. 140, n. 1).

[3] Fielding's satire against Bellarmine is here more pointed than might at first appear. The decline of the English woollen industry was at this time a *cause célèbre* in the Opposition journals. In *The Champion* for 14 and 28 February 1739/40 Fielding himself had expressed his concern. On 28 March 1741 *Common Sense* congratulated those of the nobility who, 'sensible at last of the Injury done their Country by the Mode introduced of late Years of cloathing themselves in the Manufactures of France, have resolv'd to lay aside all their Cloaths made in that Country; and, for the future, not only to appear no more in such Manufactures themselves, but to discourage and discountenance, as much as lyes in

With such sort of polite Discourse did the gay *Bellarmine* entertain his beloved *Leonora*, when the Door opened on a sudden, and *Horatio* entered the Room. Here 'tis impossible to express the Surprize of *Leonora*.

'Poor Woman,' says Mrs. *Slipslop*, 'what a terrible *Quandary* she must be in!' 'Not at all,' says Miss *Grave-airs*, 'such Sluts can never be confounded.' 'She must have then more than *Corinthian* Assurance,' said *Adams*; 'ay, more than *Lais* herself.'[1]

A long Silence, continued the Lady, prevailed in the whole Company: If the familiar Entrance of *Horatio* struck the greatest Astonishment into *Bellarmine*, the unexpected Presence of *Bellarmine* no less surprized *Horatio*. At length *Leonora* collecting all the Spirits she was Mistress of, addressed herself to the latter, and pretended to wonder at the Reason of so late a Visit. 'I should, indeed,' answered he, 'have made some Apology for disturbing you at this Hour, had not my finding you in Company assured me I do not break in on your Repose.' *Bellarmine* rose from his Chair, traversed the Room in a Minuet Step, and humm'd an Opera Tune, while *Horatio* advancing to *Leonora* ask'd her in a Whisper, if that Gentleman was not a Relation of her's; to which she answered with a Smile, or rather Sneer, 'No, he is no Relation of mine yet;' adding, 'she could not guess the Meaning of his

their Power, the wearing of them in others'. Walpole, of course, was the villain who, by maintaining a large Standing Army and by fitting out expensive squadrons of ships, had forced taxes up, and with them the cost of English woollens. (See *Common Sense*, 27 June 1741). The issue was brought to climax in November, when it was discovered that more than 130 suits of French clothes had been imported surreptitiously to grace Walpole's courtiers at the King's birthday ball. In *The Champion* for 1 December an irate clothier railed at 'our *Frenchify'd* Monsters' for 'employing *French* Weavers, Spinners, Carders, Combers, Sheermen, Millers, Dyers, Carriers, Embroiderers, Lace-makers, Taylors, Button-makers, and a long *Et cetera*. All whose Gains by cloathing our abandoned Countrymen, is a downright Robbery of our own Poor, and, by these Means, starving Manufacturers . . . .' A foil to Walpole, the hero of the Opposition was the Prince of Wales, who forbade his servants to wear anything but English clothes and set the example himself. (See also *The Champion* for 31 October, and 7, 17, 26 November 1741.)

[1] Fielding may be allowed his own gloss on Parson Adams's allusion, which was inserted in the second edition at what must have been nearly the same time that Fielding and William Young were finishing their translation of Aristophanes' *Plutus* (published 31 May 1742). A note to Act I, scene ii of the play reads as follows: 'There was, according to *Strabo*, at *Corinth* a Temple dedicated to *Venus*, in which were contained more than a thousand Women, who were prostituted to all Persons who would come up to their Prices, which at last grew so exorbitant, that it became proverbial. *Every Man is not capable of going to* Corinth. There are many Names of the more Famous remembred; but none equal to *Lais*, whose Story is well known.'

Question.' *Horatio* told her softly, 'it did not arise from Jealousy.' 'Jealousy!' cries she, 'I assure you;—it would be very strange in a common Acquaintance to give himself any of those Airs.' These Words a little surprized *Horatio*, but before he had time to answer, *Bellarmine* danced up to the Lady, and told her, 'he feared he interrupted some Business between her and the Gentleman.' 'I can have no Business,' said she, 'with the Gentleman, nor any other, which need be any Secret to you.'

'You'll pardon me,' said *Horatio*, 'if I desire to know who this Gentleman is, who is to be intrusted with all our Secrets.' 'You'll know soon enough,' cries *Leonora*, 'but I can't guess what Secrets can ever pass between us of such mighty Consequence.' 'No Madam!' cries *Horatio*, 'I'm sure you would not have me understand you in earnest.' ''Tis indifferent to me,' says she, 'how you understand me; but I think so unseasonable a Visit is difficult to be understood at all, at least when People find one engaged, though one's Servants do not deny one, one may expect a well-bred Person should soon take the Hint.' 'Madam,' said *Horatio*, 'I did not imagine any Engagement with a Stranger, as it seems this Gentleman is, would have made my Visit impertinent, or that any such Ceremonies were to be preserved between Persons in our Situation.' 'Sure you are in a Dream,' says she, 'or would persuade me that I am in one. I know no pretensions a common Acquaintance can have to lay aside the Ceremonies of Good-Breeding.' 'Sure,' said he, 'I am in a Dream; for it is impossible I should be really esteemed a common Acquaintance by *Leonora*, after what has passed between us!' 'Passed between us! Do you intend to affront me before this Gentleman?' 'D—n me, affront the Lady,' says *Bellarmine*, cocking his Hat and strutting up to *Horatio*, 'does any Man dare affront this Lady before me, d—n me?' 'Harkee, Sir,' says *Horatio*, 'I would advise you to lay aside that fierce Air; for I am mightily deceived, if this Lady has not a violent Desire to get your Worship a good drubbing.' 'Sir,' said *Bellarmine*, 'I have the Honour to be her Protector, and d—n me, if I understand your Meaning.' 'Sir,' answered *Horatio*, 'she is rather your Protectress: but give yourself no more Airs, for you see I am prepared for you,' (shaking his Whip at him.) 'Oh! *Serviteur tres humble*,' says *Bellarmine*, '*Je Vous entend parfaitement bien*.' At which time the Aunt, who had heard of *Horatio's* Visit, entered the Room and soon satisfied all his

Doubts. She convinced him that he was never more awake in his
Life, and that nothing more extraordinary had happened in his
three days Absence, than a small Alteration in the Affections of
Leonora: who now burst into Tears, and wondered what Reason
she had given him to use her in so barbarous a Manner. *Horatio*
desired *Bellarmine* to withdraw with him: but the Ladies prevented it by laying violent Hands on the latter; upon which,
the former took his Leave without any great Ceremony, and
departed, leaving the Lady with his Rival to consult for his
Safety, which *Leonora* feared her Indiscretion might have en-
dangered: but the Aunt comforted her with Assurances, that
Horatio would not venture his Person against so accomplished a
Cavalier as *Bellarmine*, and that being a Lawyer, he would seek
Revenge in his own way, and the most they had to apprehend
from him was an Action.

They at length therefore agreed to permit *Bellarmine* to retire
to his Lodgings, having first settled all Matters relating to the
Journey which he was to undertake in the Morning, and their
Preparations for the Nuptials at his return.

But alas! as wise Men have observed, the Seat of Valour is not
the Countenance, and many a grave and plain Man, will, on a
just Provocation, betake himself to that mischievous Metal, cold
Iron; while Men of a fiercer Brow, and sometimes with that
Emblem of Courage, a Cockade, will more prudently decline it.

Leonora was waked in the Morning, from a Visionary Coach
and Six, with the dismal Account, that *Bellarmine* was run through
the Body by *Horatio*, that he lay languishing at an Inn, and the
Surgeons had declared the Wound mortal. She immediately
leap'd out of the Bed, danced about the Room in a frantic manner,
tore her Hair and beat her Breast in all the Agonies of Despair;
in which sad Condition her Aunt, who likewise arose at the News,
found her. The good old Lady applied her utmost Art to comfort
her Niece. She told her, 'while there was Life, there was Hope:
but that if he should die, her Affliction would be of no service to
Bellarmine, and would only expose herself, which might probably
keep her some time without any future Offer; that as Matters
had happened, her wisest way would be to think no more of
Bellarmine, but to endeavour to regain the Affections of *Horatio*.'
'Speak not to me,' cry'd the disconsolate *Leonora*, 'is it not owing
to me, that poor *Bellarmine* has lost his Life? have not these

cursed Charms' (at which Words she looked stedfastly in the Glass,) 'been the Ruin of the most charming Man of this Age? Can I ever bear to contemplate my own Face again?' (with her Eyes still fixed on the Glass.) 'Am I not the Murderess of the finest Gentleman? No other Woman in the Town could have made any Impression on him.' 'Never think of Things passed,' cries the Aunt, 'think of regaining the Affections of *Horatio*.' 'What Reason,' said the Niece, 'have I to hope he would forgive me? no, I have lost him as well as the other, and it was your wicked Advice which was the Occasion of all; you seduced me, contrary to my Inclinations, to abandon poor *Horatio*,' at which Words she burst into Tears; 'you prevailed upon me, whether I would or no, to give up my Affections for him; had it not been for you, *Bellarmine* never would have entered into my Thoughts; had not his Addresses been backed by your Persuasions, they never would have made any Impression on me; I should have defied all the Fortune and Equipage in the World: but it was you, it was you, who got the better of my Youth and Simplicity, and forced me to lose my dear *Horatio* for ever.'

The Aunt was almost borne down with this Torrent of Words, she however rallied all the Strength she could, and drawing her Mouth up in a Purse, began: 'I am not surprized, Niece, at this Ingratitude. Those who advise young Women for their Interest, must always expect such a Return: I am convinced my Brother will thank me for breaking off your Match with *Horatio* at any rate.' 'That may not be in your power yet,' answered *Leonora*; 'tho' it is very ungrateful in you to desire or attempt it, after the Presents you have received from him.' (For indeed true it is, that many Presents, and some pretty valuable ones, had passed from *Horatio* to the old Lady: but as true it is, that *Bellarmine* when he breakfasted with her and her Niece, had complimented her with a Brilliant from his Finger, of much greater Value than all she had touched of the other.)

The Aunt's Gall was on float to reply, when a Servant brought a Letter into the Room; which *Leonora* hearing it came from *Bellarmine*, with great Eagerness opened, and read as follows:

'*Most Divine Creature,*

The Wound which I fear you have heard I received from my Rival, is not like to be so fatal as those shot into my Heart, which have been fired from your Eyes, *tout-brilliant*. Those are the only Cannons by which I am to fall: for my Surgeon gives me Hopes of being soon able to attend your *Ruelle*; 'till when, unless you would do me an Honour which I have scarce the *Hardiesse* to think of, your Absence will be the greatest Anguish which can be felt by,

Madam,

Avec tout le respecte *in the World*,

Your most Obedient, most Absolute

Devoté,

Bellarmine'

As soon as *Leonora* perceived such Hopes of *Bellarmine's* Recovery, and that the Gossip Fame had, according to Custom, so enlarged his Danger, she presently abandoned all farther Thoughts of *Horatio*, and was soon reconciled to her Aunt, who received her again into Favour, with a more Christian Forgiveness than we generally meet with. Indeed it is possible she might be a little alarmed at the Hints which her Niece had given her concerning the Presents. She might apprehend such Rumours, should they get abroad, might injure a Reputation, which by frequenting Church twice a day, and preserving the utmost Rigour and Strictness in her Countenance and Behaviour for many Years, she had established.

Leonora's Passion returned now for *Bellarmine* with greater Force after its small Relaxation than ever. She proposed to her Aunt to make him a Visit in his Confinement, which the old Lady, with great and commendable Prudence advised her to decline: 'For,' says she, 'should any Accident intervene to prevent your intended Match, too forward a Behaviour with this Lover may injure you in the Eyes of others. Every Woman 'till she is married ought to consider of and provide against the Possibility of the Affair's breaking off.' *Leonora* said, 'she should be indifferent to whatever might happen in such a Case: for she had now so absolutely placed her Affections on this dear Man (so she called him) that, if it was her misfortune to lose him, she should for ever abandon all Thoughts of Mankind.' She therefore resolved to visit him, notwithstanding all the prudent Advice of her Aunt to the contrary, and that very Afternoon executed her Resolution.

The Lady was proceeding in her Story, when the Coach drove into the Inn where the Company were to dine, sorely to the dissatisfaction of Mr. *Adams*, whose Ears were the most hungry Part about him; he being, as the Reader may perhaps guess, of an insatiable Curiosity, and heartily desirous of hearing the End of this Amour, tho' he professed he could scarce wish Success to a Lady of so inconstant a Disposition.

CHAPTER V

A dreadful Quarrel which happened at the Inn where the Company dined, with its bloody Consequences to Mr. Adams.

As soon as the Passengers had alighted from the Coach, Mr. *Adams*, as was his Custom, made directly to the Kitchin, where he found *Joseph* sitting by the Fire and the Hostess anointing his Leg: for the Horse which Mr. *Adams* had borrowed of his Clerk, had so violent a Propensity to kneeling, that one would have thought it had been his Trade as well as his Master's: nor would he always give any notice of such his Intention; he was often found on his Knees, when the Rider least expected it. This Foible however was of no great Inconvenience to the Parson, who was accustomed to it, and as his Legs almost touched the Ground when he bestrode the Beast, had but a little way to fall, and threw himself forward on such Occasions with so much dexterity, that he never received any Mischief; the Horse and he frequently rolling many Paces distance, and afterwards both getting up and meeting as good Friends as ever.

Poor *Joseph*, who had not been used to such kind of Cattle, tho' an excellent Horseman, did not so happily disengage himself: but falling with his Leg under the Beast, received a violent Contusion, to which the good Woman was, as we have said, applying a warm Hand with some camphirated Spirits just at the time when the Parson entered the Kitchin.

He had scarce express'd his Concern for *Joseph's* Misfortune, before the Host likewise entered. He was by no means of Mr.

Tow-wouse's gentle Disposition, and was indeed perfect Master of his House and every thing in it but his Guests.

This surly Fellow, who always proportioned his Respect to the Appearance of a Traveller, from *God bless your Honour*, down to plain *Coming presently*, observing his Wife on her Knees to a Footman, cried out, without considering his Circumstances, 'What a Pox is the Woman about? why don't you mind the Company in the Coach? Go and ask them what they will have for Dinner?' 'My Dear,' says she, 'you know they can have nothing but what is at the Fire, which will be ready presently; and really the poor young Man's Leg is very much bruised.' At which Words, she fell to chafing more violently than before: the Bell then happening to ring, he damn'd his Wife, and bid her go in to the Company, and not stand rubbing there all day: for he did not believe the young Fellow's Leg was so bad as he pretended; and if it was, within twenty Miles he would find a Surgeon to cut it off. Upon these Words, *Adams* fetched two Strides across the Room; and snapping his Fingers over his Head muttered aloud, 'he would excommunicate such a Wretch for a Farthing: for he believed the Devil had more Humanity.' These Words occasioned a Dialogue between *Adams* and the Host, in which there were two or three sharp Replies, 'till *Joseph* bad the latter know how to behave himself to his Betters. At which the Host, (having first strictly surveyed *Adams*) scornfully repeating the Word *Betters*, flew into a Rage, and telling *Joseph* he was as able to walk out of his House as he had been to walk into it, offered to lay violent Hands on him; which perceiving, *Adams* dealt him so sound a Compliment over his Face with his Fist, that the Blood immediately gushed out of his Nose in a Stream. The Host being unwilling to be outdone in Courtesy, especially by a Person of *Adams's* Figure, returned the Favour with so much Gratitude, that the Parson's Nostrils likewise began to look a little redder than usual. Upon which he again assailed his Antagonist, and with another stroke laid him sprawling on the Floor.

The Hostess, who was a better Wife than so surly a Husband deserved, seeing her Husband all bloody and stretched along, hastened presently to his assistance, or rather to revenge the Blow which to all appearance was the last he would ever receive; when, lo! a Pan full of Hog's-Blood, which unluckily stood on the Dresser, presented itself first to her Hands. She seized it in her

Fury, and without any Reflection discharged it into the Parson's Face, and with so good an Aim, that much the greater part first saluted his Countenance, and trickled thence in so large a current down his Beard, and over his Garments, that a more horrible Spectacle was hardly to be seen or even imagined. All which was perceived by Mrs. *Slipslop*, who entered the Kitchin at that Instant. This good Gentlewoman, not being of a Temper so extremely cool and patient as perhaps was required to ask many Questions on this Occasion; flew with great Impetuosity at the Hostess's Cap, which, together with some of her Hair, she plucked from her Head in a moment, giving her at the same time several hearty Cuffs in the Face, which by frequent Practice on the inferiour Servants, she had learned an excellent Knack of delivering with a good Grace. Poor *Joseph* could hardly rise from his Chair; the Parson was employed in wiping the Blood from his Eyes, which had intirely blinded him, and the Landlord was but just beginning to stir, whilst Mrs. *Slipslop* holding down the Landlady's Face with her Left Hand, made so dextrous a use of her Right, that the poor Woman began to roar in a Key, which alarmed all the Company in the Inn.

There happened to be in the Inn at this time, besides the Ladies who arrived in the Stage-Coach, the two Gentlemen who were present at Mr. *Tow-wouse's* when *Joseph* was detained for his Horse's-Meat, and whom we have before mentioned to have stopt at the Alehouse with *Adams*. There was likewise a Gentleman just returned from his Travels to *Italy*; all whom the horrid Outcry of Murther, presently brought into the Kitchin, where the several Combatants were found in the Postures already described.

It was now no difficulty to put an end to the Fray, the Conquerors being satisfied with the Vengeance they had taken, and the Conquered having no Appetite to renew the Fight. The principal Figure, and which engaged the Eyes of all was *Adams*, who was all over covered with Blood, which the whole Company concluded to be his own; and consequently imagined him no longer for this World. But the Host, who had now recovered from his Blow, and was risen from the Ground, soon delivered them from this Apprehension, by damning his Wife, for wasting the Hog's Puddings, and telling her all would have been very well if she had not intermeddled like a B— as she was; adding, he was very glad the Gentlewoman had paid her, tho' not half what she deserved.

The poor Woman had indeed fared much the worst, having, besides the unmerciful Cuffs received, lost a Quantity of Hair which Mrs. *Slipslop* in Triumph held in her left Hand.

The Traveller, addressing himself to Miss *Grave-airs*, desired her not to be frightened: for here had been only a little Boxing, which he said to their *Disgracia* the *English* were *accustomata* to; adding, it must be however a Sight somewhat strange to him, who was just come from *Italy*, the *Italians* not being addicted to the *Cuffardo*, but *Bastonza*, says he. He then went up to *Adams*, and telling him he looked liked the Ghost of *Othello*, bid him *not shake his gory Locks at him, for he could not say he did it*.[1] *Adams* very innocently answered, *Sir, I am far from accusing you*. He then returned to the Lady, and cried, 'I find the bloody Gentleman is *uno insipido del nullo senso. Damnata di me*, if I have seen such a *spectaculo* in my way from *Viterbo*.'

One of the Gentlemen having learnt from the Host the Occasion of this Bustle, and being assured by him that *Adams* had struck the first Blow, whispered in his Ear: 'he'd warrant he would *recover*.' 'Recover! Master,' said the Host, smiling: 'Yes, yes, I am not afraid of dying with a Blow or two neither; I am not such a Chicken as that.' 'Pugh!' said the Gentleman, 'I mean you will recover Damages, in that Action which undoubtedly you intend to bring, as soon as a Writ can be returned from *London*; for you look like a Man of too much Spirit and Courage to suffer any one to beat you without bringing your Action against him: He must be a scandalous Fellow indeed, who would put up a Drubbing whilst the Law is open to revenge it; besides, he hath drawn Blood from you and spoiled your Coat, and the Jury will give Damages for that too. An excellent new Coat upon my Word, and now not worth a Shilling!

'I don't care,' continued he, 'to intermeddle in these Cases: but you have a Right to my Evidence; and if I am sworn, I must speak the Truth. I saw you sprawling on the Floor, and the Blood gushing from your Nostrils. You may take your own Opinion; but was I in your Circumstances, every Drop of my Blood should convey an Ounce of Gold into my Pocket: remember I don't advise you to go to Law, but if your Jury were Christians, they must give swinging Damages, that's all.' 'Master,' cry'd the

[1] Macbeth to the ghost of Banquo: 'Thou canst not say I did it. Never shake / Thy gory locks at me' (III. iv. 50–51).

Host, scratching his Head, 'I have no stomach to Law, I thank you. I have seen enough of that in the Parish, where two of my Neighbours have been at Law about a House, 'till they have both lawed themselves into a Goal.' At which Words he turned about, and began to enquire again after his Hog's Puddings, nor would it probably have been a sufficient Excuse for his Wife that she spilt them in his Defence, had not some Awe of the Company, especially of the *Italian* Traveller, who was a Person of great Dignity, with-held his Rage. Whilst one of the above-mentioned Gentlemen was employed, as we have seen him, on the behalf of the Landlord, the other was no less hearty on the side of Mr. *Adams*, whom he advised to bring his Action immediately. He said the Assault of the Wife was in Law the Assault of the Husband; for they were but one Person; and he was liable to pay Damages, which he said must be considerable, where so bloody a Disposition appeared. *Adams* answered, if it was true that they were but one Person he had assaulted the Wife; for he was sorry to own he had struck the Husband the first Blow. 'I am sorry you own it too,' cries the Gentleman; 'for it could not possibly appear to the Court: for here was no Evidence present but the lame Man in the Chair, whom I suppose to be your Friend, and would consequently say nothing but what made for you.' 'How, Sir,' says *Adams*, 'do you take me for a Villain, who would prosecute Revenge in cold Blood, and use unjustifiable Means to obtain it? If you knew me and my Order, I should think you affronted both.' At the word Order, the Gentleman stared, (for he was too bloody to be of any modern Order of Knights,) and turning hastily about, said, every Man knew his own Business.

Matters being now composed, the Company retired to their several Apartments, the two Gentlemen congratulating each other on the Success of their good Offices, in procuring a perfect Reconciliation between the contending Parties; and the Traveller went to his Repast, crying, as the *Italian* Poet says,

> '*Je voi* very well, *que tutta e pace*,
> So send up Dinner, good *Boniface*.'[1]

The Coachman began now to grow importunate with his Passengers, whose Entrance into the Coach was retarded by Miss

---

[1] After the character in Farquhar's *Beaux' Stratagem* (1707), the name given to an innkeeper.

Grave-airs insisting, against the Remonstrances of all the rest, that she would not admit a Footman into the Coach: for poor *Joseph* was too lame to mount a Horse. A young Lady, who was, as it seems, an Earl's Grand Daughter, begged it with almost Tears in her Eyes; Mr. *Adams* prayed, and Mrs. *Slipslop* scolded, but all to no purpose. She said, 'she would not demean herself to ride with a Footman: that there were Waggons on the Road: that if the Master of the Coach desired it, she would pay for two Places: but would suffer no such Fellow to come in.' 'Madam,' says *Slipslop*, 'I am sure no one can refuse another coming into a Stage-Coach.' 'I don't know, Madam,' says the Lady, 'I am not much used to Stage-Coaches, I seldom travel in them.' 'That may be, Madam,' replied *Slipslop*, 'very good People do, and some People's Betters, for aught I know.' Miss *Grave-airs* said, 'some Folks, might sometimes give their Tongues a liberty, to some People that were their Betters, which did not become them: for her part, she was not used to converse with Servants.' *Slipslop* returned, 'some People kept no Servants to converse with: for her part, she thanked Heaven, she lived in a Family where there were a great many; and had more under her own Command, than any paultry little Gentlewoman in the Kingdom.' Miss *Grave-airs* cry'd, 'she believed, her Mistress would not encourage such Sauciness to her Betters.' 'My Betters,' says *Slipslop*, 'who is my Betters, pray?' 'I am your Betters,' answered Miss *Grave-airs*, 'and I'll acquaint your Mistress.'—At which Mrs. *Slipslop* laughed aloud, and told her, 'her Lady was one of the great Gentry, and such little paultry Gentlewomen, as some Folks who travelled in Stage-Coaches, would not easily come at her.'

This smart Dialogue between some People, and some Folks, was going on at the Coach-Door, when a solemn Person riding into the Inn, and seeing Miss *Grave-airs*, immediately accosted her with, 'Dear Child, how do you?' She presently answered, 'O! Papa, I am glad you have overtaken me.' 'So am I,' answered he: 'for one of our Coaches is just at hand; and there being room for you in it, you shall go no farther in the Stage, unless you desire it.' 'How can you imagine I should desire it?' says she; so bidding *Slipslop*, 'ride with her Fellow, if she pleased;' she took her Father by the Hand, who was just alighted, and walked with him into a Room.

Adams instantly asked the Coachman in a Whisper, if he knew who the Gentleman was? The Coachman answered, he was now a Gentleman, and kept his Horse and Man: 'but Times are altered, Master,' said he, 'I remember, when he was no better born than myself.' 'Aye, aye,' says *Adams*. 'My Father drove the Squire's Coach,' answered he, 'when that very Man rode Postilion; but he is now his Steward, and a great Gentleman.' *Adams* then snapped his Fingers, and cry'd, he thought *she was some such Trollop.*

Adams made haste to acquaint Mrs. *Slipslop* with this good News, as he imagined it; but it found a Reception different from what he expected. That prudent Gentlewoman, who despised the Anger of Miss *Grave-airs*, whilst she conceived her the Daughter of a Gentleman of small Fortune, now she heard her Alliance with the upper Servants of a great Family in her Neighbourhood, began to fear her Interest with the Mistress. She wished she had not carried the Dispute so far, and began to think of endeavouring to reconcile herself to the young Lady before she left the Inn; when luckily, the Scene at *London*, which the Reader can scarce have forgotten, presented itself to her Mind, and comforted her with such Assurance, that she no longer apprehended any Enemy with her Mistress.

Every thing being now adjusted, the Company entered the Coach, which was just on its Departure, when one Lady recollected she had left her Fan, a second her Gloves, a third a Snuff-Box, and a fourth a Smelling-Bottle behind her; to find all which, occasioned some Delay, and much swearing of the Coachman.

As soon as the Coach had left the Inn, the Women all together fell to the Character of Miss *Grave-airs*, whom one of them declared she had suspected to be some low Creature from the beginning of their Journey; and another affirmed had not even the Looks of a Gentlewoman; a third warranted she was no better than she should be, and turning to the Lady who had related the Story in the Coach, said, 'Did you ever hear, Madam, any thing so prudish as her Remarks? Well, deliver me from the Censoriousness of such a Prude.' The fourth added, 'O Madam! all these Creatures are censorious: but for my part, I wonder where the Wretch was bred; indeed I must own I have seldom conversed with these mean kind of People, so that it may appear stranger to me; but to refuse the general Desire of a whole Company, hath something in it so astonishing, that, for my part, I own I should hardly believe it, if my own Ears had not been Witnesses to it.' 'Yes, and so handsome a young Fellow,' cries *Slipslop*, 'the Woman must have no Compassion[1] in her, I believe she is more of a *Turk* than a Christian; I am certain if she had any Christian Woman's Blood in her Veins, the Sight of such a young Fellow must have warm'd it. Indeed there are some wretched, miserable old Objects that turn one's Stomach, I should not wonder if she had refused such a one; I am as nice as herself, and should have cared no more than herself for the Company of *stinking* old Fellows: but hold up thy Head, *Joseph*, thou art none of those, and she who hath no *Compulsion* for thee is a *Myhummetman*, and I will maintain it.' This Conversation made *Joseph* uneasy, as well as the Ladies; who perceiving the Spirits which Mrs. *Slipslop* was in, (for indeed she was not a Cup too low) began to fear the Consequence; one of them therefore desired the Lady to conclude the Story—'Ay Madam,' said *Slipslop*, 'I beg your Ladyship to give us that Story you *commencated* in the Morning,' which Request that well-bred Woman immediately complied with.

CHAPTER VI

Conclusion of the Unfortunate Jilt.

LEONORA having once broke through the Bounds which Custom and Modesty impose on her Sex, soon gave an unbridled Indulgence to her Passion. Her Visits to *Bellarmine* were more constant, as well as longer, than his Surgeon's; in a word, she became absolutely his Nurse, made his Water-gruel, administred him his Medicines, and, notwithstanding the prudent Advice of her Aunt to the contrary, almost intirely resided in her wounded Lover's Apartment.

The Ladies of the Town began to take her Conduct under consideration; it was the chief Topick of Discourse at their Tea-Tables, and was very severely censured by the most part; especially by *Lindamira*, a Lady whose discreet and starch Carriage, together with a constant Attendance at Church three times a day,

---

[1] Fielding, or his printer, is responsible for this inconsistency (which Murphy corrected in 1762): later in this same passage Mrs. Slipslop, in a characteristic malapropism, confuses *compassion* and *compulsion*.

had utterly defeated many malicious Attacks on her own Reputation: for such was the Envy that *Lindamira's* Virtue had attracted, that notwithstanding her own strict Behaviour and strict Enquiry into the Lives of others, she had not been able to escape being the Mark of some Arrows herself, which however did her no Injury; a Blessing perhaps owed by her to the Clergy, who were her chief male Companions, and with two or three of whom she had been barbarously and unjustly calumniated.

'Not so unjustly neither perhaps,' says *Slipslop*, 'for the Clergy are Men as well as other Folks.'

The extreme Delicacy of *Lindamira's* Virtue was cruelly hurt by these Freedoms which *Leonora* allowed herself; she said, 'it was an Affront to her Sex, that she did not imagine it consistent with any Woman's Honour to speak to the Creature, or to be seen in her Company; and that, for her part, she should always refuse to dance at an Assembly with her, for fear of Contamination, by taking her by the Hand.'

But to return to my Story: As soon as *Bellarmine* was recovered, which was somewhat within a Month from his receiving the Wound, he set out, according to Agreement, for *Leonora's* Father's, in order to propose the Match and settle all Matters with him touching Settlements, and the like.

A little before his Arrival, the old Gentleman had received an Intimation of the Affair by the following Letter; which I can repeat *verbatim*, and which they say was written neither by *Leonora* nor her Aunt, tho' it was in a Woman's Hand. The Letter was in these Words:

'*Sir*,

I am sorry to acquaint you that your Daughter *Leonora* hath acted one of the basest, as well as most simple Parts with a young Gentleman to whom she had engaged herself, and whom she hath (pardon the Word) jilted for another of inferiour Fortune, notwithstanding his superiour Figure. You may take what Measures you please on this Occasion; I have performed what I thought my Duty, as I have, tho' unknown to you, a very great Respect for your Family.'

The old Gentleman did not give himself the trouble to answer this kind Epistle, nor did he take any notice of it after he had read it, 'till he saw *Bellarmine*. He was, to say the truth, one of those Fathers who look on Children as an unhappy Consequence of their youthful Pleasures; which as he would have been delighted not to have had attended them, so was he no less pleased with any opportunity to rid himself of the Incumbrance. He pass'd in the World's Language as an exceeding good Father, being not only so rapacious as to rob and plunder all Mankind to the utmost of his power, but even to deny himself the Conveniencies and almost Necessaries of Life; which his Neighbours attributed to a desire of raising immense Fortunes for his Children: but in fact it was not so, he heaped up Money for its own sake only, and looked on his Children as his Rivals, who were to enjoy his beloved Mistress, when he was incapable of possessing her, and which he would have been much more charmed with the Power of carrying along with him: nor had his Children any other Security of being his Heirs, than that the Law would constitute them such without a Will, and that he had not Affection enough for any one living to take the trouble of writing one.

To this Gentleman came *Bellarmine* on the Errand I have mentioned. His Person, his Equipage, his Family and his Estate seemed to the Father to make him an advantageous Match for his Daughter; he therefore very readily accepted his Proposals: but when *Bellarmine* imagined the principal Affair concluded, and began to open the incidental Matters of Fortune; the old Gentleman presently changed his Countenance, saying, 'he resolved never to marry his Daughter on a *Smithfield* Match;[1] that whoever had Love for her to take her, would, when he died, find her Share of his Fortune in his Coffers: but he had seen such Examples of Undutifulness happen from the too early Generosity of Parents, that he had made a Vow never to part with a Shilling whilst he lived.' He commended the Saying of *Solomon*,[2] *he that spareth the Rod, spoileth the Child*: but added, 'he might have likewise asserted, that *he that spareth the Purse, saveth the Child.*' He then ran into a Discourse on the Extravagance of the Youth of the Age; whence he launched into a Dissertation on Horses, and came at length to commend those *Bellarmine* drove. That fine Gentleman, who at another Season would have been well enough pleased to dwell a little on that Subject, was now very eager to resume the Circumstance of Fortune. He said, 'he had a very high value for the young Lady, and would receive

[1] A marriage for money.   [2] Cf. Proverbs xiii. 24.

her with less than he would any other whatever; but that even his Love to her made some Regard to worldly Matters necessary; for it would be a most distracting Sight for him to see her, when he had the Honour to be her Husband, in less than a Coach and Six.' The old Gentleman answer'd, 'Four will do, Four will do;' and then took a turn from Horses to Extravagance, and from Extravagance to Horses, till he came round to the Equipage again, whither he was no sooner arrived, than *Bellarmine* brought him back to the Point; but all to no purpose, he made his Escape from that Subject in a Minute, till at last the Lover declared, 'that in the present Situation of his Affairs it was impossible for him, though he loved *Leonora* more than *tout le monde*, to marry her without any Fortune.' To which the Father answered, 'he was sorry then his Daughter must lose so valuable a Match; that if he had an Inclination at present, it was not in his power to advance a Shilling: that he had had great Losses and been at great Expences on Projects, which, though he had great Expectation from them, had yet produced him nothing: that he did not know what might happen hereafter, as on the Birth of a Son, or such Accident, but he would make no promise, or enter into any Article: for he would not break his Vow for all the Daughters in the World.'

In short, Ladies, to keep you no longer in suspense, *Bellarmine* having tried every Argument and Persuasion which he could invent, and finding them all ineffectual, at length took his leave, but not in order to return to *Leonora*; he proceeded directly to his own Seat, whence after a few Days stay, he returned to *Paris*, to the great delight of the *French*, and the honour of the *English* Nation.

But as soon as he arrived at his home, he presently dispatched a Messenger, with the following Epistle to *Leonora*.

'*Adorable* and *Charmante*,

I am sorry to have the Honour to tell you I am not the *heureux* Person destined for your divine Arms. Your Papa hath told me so with a *Politesse* not often seen on this side *Paris*. You may perhaps guess his manner of refusing me—*Ah mon Dieu!* You will certainly believe me, Madam, incapable of my self delivering this *triste* Message: Which I intend to try the *French* Air to cure the Consequences of—*Ah jamais! Cœur! Ange!*—*Ah Diable!*—If your Papa obliges you to a Marriage, I hope we shall see you at *Paris*, till when the Wind that flows from thence will be the warmest *dans le Monde*: for it will consist almost entirely of my Sighs. *Adieu, ma Princesse! Ah L'Amour!*

Bellarmine'

I shall not attempt Ladies, to describe *Leonora's* Condition when she received this Letter. It is a Picture of Horrour, which I should have as little pleasure in drawing as you in beholding. She immediately left the Place, where she was the Subject of Conversation and Ridicule, and retired to that House I shewed you when I began the Story, where she hath ever since led a disconsolate Life, and deserves perhaps Pity for her Misfortunes more than our Censure, for a Behaviour to which the Artifices of her Aunt very probably contributed, and to which very young Women are often rendered too liable, by that blameable Levity in the Education of our Sex.

'If I was inclined to pity her,' said a young Lady in the Coach, 'it would be for the Loss of *Horatio*; for I cannot discern any Misfortune in her missing such a Husband as *Bellarmine*.'

'Why I must own,' says *Slipslop*, 'the Gentleman was a little false-hearted: but *howsumever* it was hard to have two Lovers, and get never a Husband at all—But pray, Madam, what became of *Ourasho*?'

He remains, said the Lady, still unmarried, and hath applied himself so strictly to his Business, that he hath raised I hear a very considerable Fortune. And what is remarkable, they say, he never hears the name of *Leonora* without a Sigh, nor hath ever uttered one Syllable to charge her with her ill Conduct towards him.

CHAPTER VII

A very short Chapter, in which Parson Adams *went a great Way.*

THE Lady having finished her Story received the Thanks of the Company, and now *Joseph* putting his Head out of the Coach, cried out, 'Never believe me, if yonder be not our Parson *Adams* walking along without his Horse.' 'On my Word, and so he is,' says *Slipslop*; 'and as sure as Two-pence, he hath left him behind at the Inn.' Indeed, true it is, the Parson had exhibited a fresh Instance of his Absence of Mind: for he was so pleased with having got *Joseph* into the Coach, that he never once thought of the Beast in the Stable; and finding his Legs as nimble as he desired, he sallied out brandishing a Crabstick, and had kept on before the Coach, mending and slackening his Pace occasionally, so that he had never been much more or less than a Quarter of a Mile distant from it.

Mrs. *Slipslop* desired the Coachman to overtake him, which he attempted, but in vain: for the faster he drove, the faster ran the Parson, often crying out, *Aye, aye, catch me if you can*: 'till at length the Coachman swore he would as soon attempt to drive after a Greyhound; and giving the Parson two or three hearty Curses, he cry'd, 'Softly, softly Boys,' to his Horses, which the civil Beasts immediately obeyed.

But we will be more courteous to our Reader than he was to Mrs. *Slipslop*, and leaving the Coach and its Company to pursue their Journey, we will carry our Reader on after Parson *Adams*, who stretched forwards without once looking behind him, 'till having left the Coach full three Miles in his Rear, he came to a Place, where by keeping the extremest Track to the Right, it was just barely possible for a human Creature to miss his Way. This Track however did he keep, as indeed he had a wonderful Capacity at these kinds of bare Possibilities; and travelling in it about three Miles over the Plain, he arrived at the Summit of a Hill, whence looking a great way backwards, and perceiving no Coach in sight, he sat himself down on the Turf, and pulling out his *Æschylus* determined to wait here for its Arrival.

He had not sat long here, before a Gun going off very near, a little startled him; he looked up, and saw a Gentleman within a hundred Paces taking up a Partridge, which he had just shot.

Adams stood up, and presented a Figure to the Gentleman which would have moved Laughter in many: for his Cassock had just again fallen down below his great Coat, that is to say, it reached his Knees; whereas, the Skirts of his great Coat descended no lower than half way down his Thighs: but the Gentleman's Mirth gave way to his Surprize, at beholding such a Personage in such a Place.

Adams advancing to the Gentleman told him he hoped he had good Sport; to which the other answered, 'Very little.'[1] 'I see, Sir,' says *Adams*, 'you have *smote* one Partridge:' to which the Sportsman made no Reply, but proceeded to charge his Piece.

Whilst the Gun was charging, *Adams* remained in Silence, which he at last broke, by observing that it was a delightful Evening. The Gentleman, who had at first sight conceived a very distasteful Opinion of the Parson, began, on perceiving a Book in his Hand, and smoking likewise the Information of the Cassock, to change his Thoughts, and made a small Advance to Conversation on his side, by saying, *Sir, I suppose you are not one of these Parts?*

Adams immediately told him, No; that he was a Traveller, and invited by the Beauty of the Evening and the Place to repose a little, and amuse himself with reading. 'I may as well repose myself too,' said the Sportsman; 'for I have been out this whole Afternoon, and the Devil a Bird have I seen 'till I came hither.'

'Perhaps then the Game is not very plenty hereabouts,' cries *Adams*. 'No, Sir,' said the Gentleman, 'the Soldiers, who are quartered in the Neighbourhood, have killed it all.'[2] 'It is very probable,' cries *Adams*, 'for Shooting is their Profession.' 'Ay, shooting the Game,' answered the other, 'but I don't see they are so forward to shoot our Enemies. I don't like that Affair of *Carthagena*;[3] if I had been there, I believe I should have done otherguess things, d—n me; what's a Man's Life when his Country demands it; a Man who won't sacrifice his Life for his Country

---

[1] The form of the text here has been emended in accord with Fielding's usual treatment of direct quotations. From the context it seems clear that these words are the gentleman's spoken reply to Adams and are not adverbial modifiers of 'answered'.

[2] It was unlawful for soldiers to kill game without permission; those who did were liable to a fine of £5 for each partridge killed (7 George II, cap. 2).

[3] In the spring of 1741 the British attacked the Spanish stronghold of Carthagena in the West Indies, but the assault was entrusted to raw, undisciplined troops, and it was badly mismanaged by General Wentworth. What at first seemed certain victory for the English was turned into a disaster, news of which reached London on 19 June (*The London Gazette*, 16–20 June 1741). The Opposition made the defeat into a political issue, blaming Walpole for maintaining a large Standing Army at public expense to intimidate the electorate at home (in May the army had interfered in the election of the court candidate for Westminster), while he entrusted the war against Spain to '*raw, new-raised Corps*, who had not Time to be taught Half their Business. . .' (*The Craftsman*, 1 August 1741). From June through December, when the new Parliament sat, Patriot journalists kept the subject ringing in the public ear. (See *The Craftsman*, 27 June, 11, 18 July, 1, 8, 22 August; *Common Sense*, 27 June, 19 December; *The Champion*, 21, 28 November.)

deserves to be hanged, d——n me.' Which Words he spoke with so violent a Gesture, so loud a Voice, so strong an Accent, and so fierce a Countenance, that he might have frightned a Captain of Trained-Bands at the Head of his Company; but Mr. *Adams* was not greatly subject to Fear, he told him intrepidly that he very much approved his Virtue, but disliked his Swearing, and begged him not to addict himself to so bad a Custom, without which he said he might fight as bravely as *Achilles* did. Indeed he was charm'd with this Discourse, he told the Gentleman he would willingly have gone many Miles to have met a Man of his generous Way of thinking; that if he pleased to sit down, he should be greatly delighted to commune with him: for tho' he was a Clergy-man, he would himself be ready, if thereto called, to lay down his Life for his Country.

The Gentleman sat down and *Adams* by him, and then the latter began, as in the following Chapter, a Discourse which we have placed by itself, as it is not only the most curious in this, but perhaps in any other Book.

CHAPTER VIII

A notable Dissertation, by Mr. Abraham Adams;
wherein that Gentleman appears in a political Light.

'I do assure you, Sir,' says he, taking the Gentleman by the Hand, 'I am heartily glad to meet with a Man of your Kidney: for tho' I am a poor Parson, I will be bold to say, I am an honest Man, and would not do an ill Thing to be made a Bishop: Nay, tho' it hath not fallen in my way to offer so noble a Sacrifice, I have not been without Opportunities of suffering for the sake of my Conscience, I thank Heaven for them: for I have had Relations, tho' I say it, who made some Figure in the World; particularly a Nephew, who was a Shopkeeper, and an Alderman of a Cor-poration. He was a good Lad, and was under my Care when a Boy, and I believe would do what I bad him to his dying Day. Indeed, it looks like extreme Vanity in me, to affect being a Man of such Consequence, as to have so great an Interest in an Alder-man; but others have thought so too, as manifestly appeared by the Rector, whose Curate I formerly was, sending for me on the

Approach of an Election, and telling me if I expected to continue
in his Cure, that I must bring my Nephew to vote for one Colonel
Courtly, a Gentleman whom I had never heard Tidings of 'till
that Instant. I told the Rector, I had no power over my Nephew's
Vote, (God forgive me for such Prevarication!) That I supposed
he would give it according to his Conscience, that I would by
no means endeavour to influence him to give it otherwise. He
told me it was in vain to equivocate: that he knew I had already
spoke to him in favour of Esquire *Fickle* my Neighbour, and
indeed it was true I had: for it was at a Season when the *Church
was in Danger*,[1] and when all good Men expected they knew not
what would happen to us all. I then answered boldly, If he
thought I had given my Promise, he affronted me, in proposing
any Breach of it. Not to be too prolix: I persevered, and so did
my Nephew, in the Esquire's Interest, who was chose chiefly
through his Means, and so I lost my Curacy. Well, Sir, but do
you think the Esquire ever mentioned a Word of the Church?
Ne verbum quidem, ut ita dicam;[2] within two Years he got a Place,
and hath ever since lived in *London*; where I have been informed,
(but G— forbid I should believe that) that he never so much as
goeth to Church. I remained, Sir, a considerable Time without
any Cure, and lived a full Month on one Funeral Sermon, which
I preached on the Indisposition of a Clergyman: but this by
the Bye. At last, when Mr. *Fickle* got his Place, Colonel *Courtly*
stood again; and who should make Interest for him, but Mr.
Fickle himself: that very identical Mr. *Fickle*, who had formerly
told me, the Colonel was an Enemy to both the Church and State,
had the Confidence to sollicite my Nephew for him, and the
Colonel himself offered me to make me Chaplain to his Regiment,

---

1 'The Church in Danger' was a cry raised repeatedly by the clergy during the early
years of the eighteenth century. For the most part it was directed by High Churchmen,
such as Sacheverell and Atterbury, against the principles of latitudinarianism and the
incursions of nonconformists and dissenters. Though the cry continued to be heard from
time to time, the last occasion on which it was invoked with any force was during the
elections of 1722, when the High Churchmen attacked the Court Party for its Whiggism
and willingness to compromise with dissenters. But the lack of specific references in the
passage suggests that Fielding merely intends to recall the general political antagonism
between these two factions. Adams's inconsistency is amusing: he embraces, intellectually,
the extreme latitudinarianism of Bishop Hoadly (I. xvii), yet is here seen to act politically
upon principles most frequently associated with those strong churchmen who opposed
toleration (see, too, his later impatient reference to Presbyterianism [III. v]).

2 'Not so much as a word, so to speak.'

which I refused in favour of Sir *Oliver Hearty*, who told us, he would sacrifice every thing to his Country; and I believe he would, except his Hunting, which he stuck so close to, that in five Years together, he went but twice up to Parliament; and one of those Times, I have been told, never was within sight of the House. However, he was a worthy Man, and the best Friend I ever had: for by his Interest with a Bishop, he got me replaced into my Curacy, and gave me eight Pounds out of his own Pocket to buy me a Gown and Cassock, and furnish my House. He had our Interest while he lived, which was not many Years. On his Death, I had fresh Applications made to me; for all the World knew the Interest I had in my good Nephew, who now was a leading Man in the Corporation; and Sir *Thomas Booby*, buying the Estate which had been Sir *Oliver's*, proposed himself a Candidate. He was then a young Gentleman just come from his Travels; and it did me good to hear him discourse on Affairs, which for my part I knew nothing of. If I had been Master of a thousand Votes, he should have had them all. I engaged my Nephew in his Interest, and he was elected, and a very fine Parliament-Man he was. They tell me he made Speeches of an Hour long; and I have been told very fine ones: but he could never persuade the Parliament to be of his Opinion.—*Non omnia possumus omnes.*[1] He promised me a Living, poor Man; and I believe I should have had it, but an Accident happened; which was, that my Lady had promised it before unknown to him. This indeed I never heard 'till afterwards: for my Nephew, who died about a Month before the Incumbent, always told me I might be assured of it. Since that Time, Sir *Thomas*, poor Man, had always so much Business, that he never could find Leisure to see me. I believe it was partly my Lady's fault too: who did not think my Dress good enough for the Gentry at her Table. However, I must do him the Justice to say, he never was ungrateful; and I have always found his Kitchin, and his Cellar too, open to me; many a time after Service on a *Sunday*, for I preach at four Churches, have I recruited my Spirits with a Glass of his Ale. Since my Nephew's Death, the Corporation is in other hands; and I am not a Man of that Consequence I was formerly. I have now no longer any Talents to lay out[2] in the Service of my Country; and to whom

---

[1] 'All things are not in the power of all' (Virgil, *Eclogues*, viii. 63).
[2] Cf. Matthew xxv. 14–30.

nothing is given, of him can nothing be required.[1] However, on all proper Seasons, such as the Approach of an Election, I throw a suitable Dash or two into my Sermons; which I have the pleasure to hear is not disagreeable to Sir *Thomas*, and the other honest Gentlemen my Neighbours, who have all promised me these five Years, to procure an Ordination for a Son of mine, who is now near Thirty, hath an infinite Stock of Learning, and is, I thank Heaven, of an unexceptionable Life; tho', as he was never at an University, the Bishop refuses to ordain him. Too much Care cannot indeed be taken in admitting any to the sacred Office; tho' I hope he will never act so as to be a Disgrace to any Order: but will serve his God and his Country to the utmost of his power, as I have endeavoured to do before him; nay, and will lay down his Life whenever called to that purpose. I am sure I have educated him in those Principles; so that I have acquitted my Duty, and shall have nothing to answer for on that account: but I do not distrust him; for he is a good Boy; and if Providence should throw it in his way, to be of as much consequence in a public Light, as his Father once was, I can answer for him, he will use his Talents as honestly as I have done.'

CHAPTER IX

In which the Gentleman descants on Bravery and heroic Virtue, 'till an unlucky Accident puts an end to the Discourse.

THE Gentleman highly commended Mr. *Adams* for his good Resolutions, and told him, 'he hoped his Son would tread in his Steps;' adding, 'that if he would not die for his Country, he would not be worthy to live in it; I'd make no more of shooting a Man that would not die for his Country, than ——

'Sir,' said he, 'I have disinherited a Nephew who is in the Army, because he would not exchange his Commission, and go to the *West-Indies*. I believe the Rascal is a Coward, tho' he pretends to be in love forsooth. I would have all such Fellows hanged, Sir, I would have them hanged.' *Adams* answered, 'that would be

[1] Cf. Luke xii. 48.

too severe: That Men did not make themselves; and if Fear had too much Ascendance in the Mind, the Man was rather to be pitied than abhorred: That Reason and Time might teach him to subdue it.' He said, 'a Man might be a Coward at one time, and brave at another. *Homer*,' says he, 'who so well understood and copied Nature, hath taught us this Lesson: for *Paris* fights, and *Hector* runs away:[1] nay, we have a mighty Instance of this in the History of later Ages, no longer ago, than the 705th Year of *Rome*, when the Great *Pompey*, who had won so many Battles, and been honoured with so many Triumphs, and of whose Valour, several Authors, especially *Cicero* and *Paterculus*, have formed such Elogiums;[2] this very *Pompey* left the Battle of *Pharsalia* before he had lost it, and retreated to his Tent, where he sat like the most pusillanimous Rascal in a Fit of Despair, and yielded a Victory, which was to determine the Empire of the World, to *Cæsar*.[3] I am not much travelled in the History of modern Times, that is to say, these last thousand Years: but those who are, can, I make no question, furnish you with parallel Instances.' He concluded therefore, that had he taken any such hasty Resolutions against his Nephew, he hoped he would consider better and retract them. The Gentleman answered with great Warmth, and talked much of Courage and his Country, 'till perceiving it grew late, he asked *Adams*, 'what Place he intended for that Night?' He told him, 'he waited there for the Stage-Coach.' 'The Stage-Coach! Sir,' said the Gentleman, 'they are all past by long ago. You may see the last yourself, almost three Miles before us.' 'I protest and so they are,' cries *Adams*, 'then I must make haste and follow them.' The Gentleman told him, 'he would hardly be able to overtake them; and that if he did not know his Way, he would be in danger of losing himself on the Downs; for it would be presently dark; and he might ramble about all Night, and perhaps, find himself farther from his Journey's End in the Morning than he was now. He advised him therefore to accompany him to his House, which was very little out of his way,' assuring him, 'that he would find some Country-Fellow in his

---

[1] In the *Iliad*, xi, Paris wounds Diomedes and others of the Greeks; in xxii Hector turns and flees as Achilles approaches the gates of Troy.

[2] See Cicero, 'On the Manilian Law', and Paterculus, *Roman History*, II. xxix.

[3] When Pompey's cavalry broke before Caesar's charge at the Battle of Pharsalia (48 B.C.) he retired to his tent in a fit of grief and shame. (See Plutarch's 'Life of Pompey'.)

Parish, who would conduct him for Sixpence to the City, where
he was going.' *Adams* accepted this Proposal, and on they
travelled, the Gentleman renewing his Discourse on Courage, and
the Infamy of not being ready at all times to sacrifice our Lives
to our Country. Night overtook them much about the same time
as they arrived near some Bushes: whence, on a sudden, they
heard the most violent Shrieks imaginable in a female Voice.
Adams offered to snatch the Gun out of his Companion's Hand.
'What are you doing?' said he. 'Doing!' says *Adams*, 'I am hasten-
ing to the Assistance of the poor Creature whom some Villains
are murdering.' 'You are not mad enough, I hope,' says the
Gentleman, trembling: 'Do you consider this Gun is only charged
with Shot, and that the Robbers are most probably furnished
with Pistols loaded with Bullets? This is no Business of ours; let
us make as much haste as possible out of the way, or we may fall
into their hands ourselves.' The Shrieks now encreasing, *Adams*
made no Answer, but snapt his Fingers, and brandishing his
Crabstick, made directly to the Place whence the Voice issued;
and the Man of Courage made as much Expedition towards his
own Home, whither he escaped in a very short time without once
looking behind him: where we will leave him, to contemplate
his own Bravery, and to censure the want of it in others; and
return to the good *Adams*, who, on coming up to the Place whence
the Noise proceeded, found a Woman struggling with a Man,
who had thrown her on the Ground, and had almost overpowered
her. The great Abilities of Mr. *Adams* were not necessary to
have formed a right Judgment of this Affair, on the first sight.
He did not therefore want the Entreaties of the poor Wretch to
assist her, but lifting up his Crabstick, he immediately levelled
a Blow at that Part of the Ravisher's Head, where, according to
the Opinion of the Ancients, the Brains of some Persons are
deposited, and which he had undoubtedly let forth, had not
Nature, (who, as wise Men have observed, equips all Creatures
with what is most expedient for them;) taken a provident Care,
(as she always doth with those she intends for Encounters) to
make this part of the Head three times as thick as those of ordinary Men, who are designed to exercise Talents which are vulgarly called rational, and for whom, as Brains are necessary, she
is obliged to leave some room for them in the Cavity of the Skull:
whereas, those Ingredients being entirely useless to Persons of

the heroic Calling, she hath an Opportunity of thickening the Bone, so as to make it less subject to any Impression or liable to be cracked or broken; and indeed, in some who are predestined to the Command of Armies and Empires, she is supposed sometimes to make that Part perfectly solid.

As a Game-Cock when engaged in amorous Toying with a Hen, if perchance he espies another Cock at hand, immediately quits his Female, and opposes himself to his Rival; so did the Ravisher, on the Information of the Crabstick, immediately leap from the Woman, and hasten to assail the Man. He had no Weapons but what Nature had furnished him with. However, he clenched his Fist, and presently darted it at that Part of *Adams's* Breast where the Heart is lodged. *Adams* staggered at the Violence of the Blow, when throwing away his Staff, he likewise clenched that Fist which we have before commemorated, and would have discharged it full in the Breast of his Antagonist, had he not dexterously caught it with his left Hand, at the same time darting his Head, (which some modern Heroes, of the lower Class, use like the Battering-Ram of the Ancients, for a Weapon of Offence; another Reason to admire the Cunningness of Nature, in composing it of those impenetrable Materials) dashing his Head, I say, into the Stomach of *Adams*, he tumbled him on his Back, and not having any regard to the Laws of Heroism, which would have restrained him from any farther Attack on his Enemy, 'till he was again on his Legs, he threw himself upon him, and laying hold on the Ground with his left Hand, he with his right belaboured the Body of *Adams* 'till he was weary, and indeed, 'till he concluded (to use the Language of fighting) *that he had done his Business*; or, in the Language of Poetry, *that he had sent him to the Shades below*; in plain *English, that he was dead.*

But *Adams*, who was no Chicken, and could bear a drubbing as well as any boxing Champion in the Universe, lay still only to watch his Opportunity; and now perceiving his Antagonist to pant with his Labours, he exerted his utmost Force at once, and with such Success, that he overturned him and became his Superiour; when fixing one of his Knees in his Breast, he cried out in an exulting Voice, *It is my turn now*: and after a few Minutes constant Application, he gave him so dextrous a Blow just under his Chin, that the Fellow no longer retained any Motion, and *Adams* began to fear he had struck him once too often; for he often asserted, 'he should be concerned to have the Blood of even the Wicked upon him.'

Adams got up, and called aloud to the young Woman,—'Be of good cheer, Damsel,' said he, 'you are no longer in danger of your Ravisher, who, I am terribly afraid, lies dead at my Feet; but G— forgive me what I have done in Defence of Innocence.' The poor Wretch, who had been some time in recovering Strength enough to rise, and had afterwards, during the Engagement, stood trembling, being disabled by Fear, even from running away, hearing her Champion was victorious, came up to him, but not without Apprehensions, even of her Deliverer; which, however, she was soon relieved from, by his courteous Behaviour and gentle Words. They were both standing by the Body, which lay motionless on the Ground, and which *Adams* wished to see stir much more than the Woman did, when he earnestly begged her to tell him 'by what Misfortune she came, at such a time of Night, into so lonely a Place?' She acquainted him, 'she was travelling towards *London*, and had accidentally met with the Person from whom he had delivered her, who told her he was likewise on his Journey to the same Place, and would keep her Company; an Offer which, suspecting no harm, she had accepted; that he told her, they were at a small distance from an Inn where she might take up her Lodging that Evening, and he would show her a nearer way to it than by following the Road. That if she had suspected him, (which she did not, he spoke so kindly to her,) being alone on these Downs in the dark, she had no human Means to avoid him; that therefore she put her whole Trust in Providence, and walk'd on, expecting every Moment to arrive at the Inn; when, on a sudden, being come to those Bushes, he desired her to stop, and after some rude Kisses, which she resisted, and some Entreaties, which she rejected, he laid violent hands on her, and was attempting to execute his wicked Will, when, she thanked G—, he timely came up and prevented him.' *Adams* encouraged her for saying, she had put her whole Trust in Providence, and told her 'he doubted not but Providence had sent him to her Deliverance, as a Reward for that Trust. He wished indeed he had not deprived the wicked Wretch of Life, but G—'s Will be done;' he said, 'he hoped the Goodness of his Intention would excuse him in the next World, and he trusted in her Evidence to acquit him in this.' He was then silent, and began to consider with himself, whether it would be properer to make his Escape, or to deliver himself into the hands of Justice; which Meditation ended, as the Reader will see in the next Chapter.

CHAPTER X

Giving an Account of the strange Catastrophe of the preceding Adventure, which drew poor Adams into fresh Calamities; and who the Woman was who owed the Preservation of her Chastity to his victorious Arm.

T H E Silence of *Adams*, added to the Darkness of the Night, and Loneliness of the Place, struck dreadful Apprehensions into the poor Woman's Mind: She began to fear as great an Enemy in her Deliverer, as he had delivered her from; and as she had not Light enough to discover the Age of *Adams*, and the Benevolence visible in his Countenance, she suspected he had used her as some very honest Men have used their Country; and had rescued her out of the hands of one Rifler, in order to rifle her himself.[1] Such were the Suspicions she drew from his Silence: but indeed they were ill-grounded. He stood over his vanquished Enemy, wisely weighing in his Mind the Objections which might be made to either of the two Methods of proceeding mentioned in the last Chapter, his Judgment sometimes inclining to the one and some-times to the other; for both seemed to him so equally adviseable, and so equally dangerous, that probably he would have ended his Days, at least two or three of them, on that very Spot, before he had taken any Resolution: At length he lifted up his Eyes, and spied a Light at a distance, to which he instantly addressed him-self with *Heus tu, Traveller, heus tu!*[2] He presently heard several

[1] This passage, added to the second edition, squints at the treachery of Fielding's former party, the so-called Patriots, who began scrambling for places in the government as soon as Walpole fell from power in February 1742; Pulteney, Carteret, and Sandys were among the most notorious of these. General allusions to this hypocritical behaviour are frequent in Fielding's writings of the period: see, for example, *The Opposition: A Vision, A Journey from This World to the Next* (I. vii), and *Jonathan Wild*. In a note to *Plutus* (II. v) Fielding remarks: 'TO MAKE USE OF POPULAR INTEREST, AND THE CHARACTER OF PATRIOTISM, IN ORDER TO BETRAY ONE'S COUNTRY, is perhaps the most flagitious of all Crimes.'
[2] 'Ho there!'

Voices, and perceived the Light approaching toward him. The Persons who attended the Light began some to laugh, others to sing, and others to hollow, at which the Woman testified some Fear, (for she had concealed her Suspicions of the Parson himself,) but *Adams* said, 'Be of good cheer, Damsel, and repose thy Trust in the same Providence, which hath hitherto protected thee, and never will forsake the Innocent.' These People who now approached were no other, Reader, than a Set of young Fellows, who came to these Bushes in pursuit of a Diversion which they call *Bird-batting*. This, if thou art ignorant of it (as perhaps if thou hast never travelled beyond *Kensington, Islington, Hackney*, or the *Borough*, thou mayst be) I will inform thee, is performed by holding a large Clap-Net before a Lanthorn, and at the same time, beating the Bushes: for the Birds, when they are disturbed from their Places of Rest, or Roost, immediately make to the Light, and so are enticed within the Net. *Adams* immediately told them, what had happened, and desired them, 'to hold the Lanthorn to the Face of the Man on the ground, for he feared he had *smote* him fatally.' But indeed his Fears were frivolous, for the Fellow, though he had been stunned by the last Blow he received, had long since recovered his Senses, and finding himself quit of *Adams*, had listened attentively to the Discourse between him and the young Woman; for whose Departure he had patiently waited, that he might likewise withdraw himself, having no longer Hopes of succeeding in his Desires, which were moreover almost as well cooled by Mr. *Adams*, as they could have been by the young Woman herself, had he obtained his utmost Wish. This Fellow, who had a Readiness at improving any Accident, thought he might now play a better part than that of a dead Man; and accordingly, the moment the Candle was held to his Face, he leapt up, and laying hold on *Adams*, cried out, 'No, Villain, I am not dead, though you and your wicked Whore might well think me so, after the barbarous Cruelties you have exercised on me. Gentlemen,' said he, 'you are luckily come to the Assistance of a poor Traveller, who would otherwise have been robbed and murdered by this vile Man and Woman, who led me hither out of my way from the High-Road, and both falling on me have used me as you see.' *Adams* was going to answer, when one of the young Fellows, cry'd, 'D——n them, let's carry them both before the Justice.' The poor Woman began to tremble, and *Adams* lifted up his Voice, but in vain. Three or four of them laid hands on him, and one holding the Lanthorn to his Face, they all agreed, *he had the most villainous Countenance* they ever beheld, and an Attorney's Clerk who was of the Company declared, *he was sure he had remembered him at the Bar*. As to the Woman, her Hair was dishevelled in the Struggle, and her Nose had bled, so that they could not perceive whether she was handsome or ugly: but they said her Fright plainly discovered her Guilt. And searching her Pockets, as they did those of *Adams* for Money, which the Fellow said he had lost, they found in her Pocket a Purse with some Gold in it, which abundantly convinced them, especially as the Fellow offered to swear to it. Mr. *Adams* was found to have no more than one Halfpenny about him. This the Clerk said, 'was a great Presumption that he was an old Offender, by cunningly giving all the Booty to the Woman.' To which all the rest readily assented.

This Accident promising them better Sport, than what they had proposed, they quitted their Intention of catching Birds, and unanimously resolved to proceed to the Justice with the Offenders. Being informed what a desperate Fellow *Adams* was, they tied his Hands behind him, and having hid their Nets among the Bushes, and the Lanthorn being carried before them, they placed the two Prisoners in their Front, and then began their March: *Adams* not only submitting patiently to his own Fate, but comforting and encouraging his Companion under her Sufferings.

Whilst they were on their way, the Clerk informed the rest, that this Adventure would prove a very beneficial one: for that they would be all entitled to their Proportions of 80 *l.* for apprehending the Robbers.[1] This occasion'd a Contention concerning the Parts which they had severally born in taking them; one insisting, 'he ought to have the greatest Share, for he had first laid his Hands on *Adams*;' another claiming a superiour Part for having first held the Lanthorn to the Man's Face, on the Ground, by which, he said, 'the whole was discovered.' The Clerk claimed four fifths of the Reward, for having proposed to search the Prisoners; and likewise the carrying them before the Justice: he said indeed, 'in strict Justice he ought to have the whole.' These Claims however they at last consented to refer to a future Decision, but seem'd all to agree that the Clerk was intitled to a Moiety. They then debated what Money should be allotted to

[1] See p. 71, n. 1.

the young Fellow, who had been employed only in holding the Nets. He very modestly said, 'that he did not apprehend any large Proportion would fall to his share; but hoped they would allow him something: he desired them to consider, that they had assigned their Nets to his Care, which prevented him from being as forward as any in laying hold of the Robbers, (for so these innocent People were called;) that if he had not occupied the Nets, some other must; concluding however that he should be contented with the smallest Share imaginable, and should think that rather their Bounty than his Merit.' But they were all unanimous in excluding him from any Part whatever, the Clerk particularly swearing, 'if they gave him a Shilling, they might do what they pleased with the rest; for he would not concern himself with the Affair.' This Contention was so hot, and so totally engaged the Attention of all the Parties, that a dextrous nimble Thief, had he been in Mr. *Adams's* situation, would have taken care to have given the Justice no Trouble that Evening. Indeed it required not the Art of a *Shepherd*[1] to escape, especially as the Darkness of the Night would have so much befriended him: but *Adams* trusted rather to his Innocence than his Heels, and without thinking of Flight, which was easy, or Resistance (which was impossible, as there were six lusty young Fellows, besides the Villain himself, present) he walked with perfect Resignation the way they thought proper to conduct him.

Adams frequently vented himself in Ejaculations during their Journey; at last poor *Joseph Andrews* occuring to his Mind, he could not refrain sighing forth his Name, which being heard by his Companion in Affliction, she cried, with some Vehemence, 'Sure I should know that Voice, you cannot certainly, Sir, be Mr. *Abraham Adams*?' 'Indeed Damsel,' says he, 'that is my Name; there is something also in your Voice, which persuades me I have heard it before.' 'La, Sir,' says she, 'don't you remember poor *Fanny*?' 'How *Fanny*!' answered *Adams*, 'indeed I very well remember you; what can have brought you hither?' 'I have told you Sir,' replied she, 'I was travelling towards *London*; but I thought you mentioned *Joseph Andrews*, pray what is become

[1] Jack Sheppard (1702–24), robber, highwayman, and escape-artist extraordinary. In the space of some five months before he was hanged in 1724, he broke prison four times. Defoe rushed into print the same year with *A Narrative of all the Robberies, Escapes, &c. of John Sheppard*, which went through several editions in rapid succession.

of him?' 'I left him, Child, this Afternoon,' said *Adams*, 'in the Stage-Coach, in his way towards our Parish, whither he is going to see you.' 'To see me? La, Sir,' answered *Fanny*, 'sure you jeer me; what should he be going to see me for?' 'Can you ask that?' replied *Adams*. 'I hope *Fanny* you are not inconstant; I assure you he deserves much better of you.' 'La! Mr. *Adams*,' said she, 'what is Mr. *Joseph* to me? I am sure I never had any thing to say to him, but as one Fellow-Servant might to another.' 'I am sorry to hear this,' said *Adams*, 'a vertuous Passion for a young Man, is what no Woman need be ashamed of. You either do not tell me Truth, or you are false to a very worthy Man.' *Adams* then told her what had happened at the Inn, to which she listened very attentively; and a Sigh often escaped from her, notwithstanding her utmost Endeavours to the contrary, nor could she prevent herself from asking a thousand Questions, which would have assured any one but *Adams*, who never saw farther into People than they desired to let him, of the Truth of a Passion she endeavoured to conceal. Indeed the Fact was, that this poor Girl having heard of *Joseph's* Misfortune by some of the Servants belonging to the Coach, which we have formerly mentioned to have stopped at the Inn while the poor Youth was confined to his Bed, that instant abandoned the Cow she was milking, and taking with her a little Bundle of Clothes under her Arm, and all the Money she was worth in her own Purse, without consulting any one, immediately set forward, in pursuit of One, whom, notwithstanding her shyness to the Parson, she loved with inexpressible Violence, though with the purest and most delicate Passion. This Shyness therefore, as we trust it will recommend her Character to all our Female Readers, and not greatly surprize such of our Males as are well acquainted with the younger part of the other Sex, we shall not give our selves any trouble to vindicate.

CHAPTER XI

What happened to them while before the Justice.
A Chapter very full of Learning.

THEIR Fellow-Travellers were so engaged in the hot Dispute
concerning the Division of the Reward for apprehending these
innocent People, that they attended very little to their Discourse.
They were now arrived at the Justice's House, and sent one of his
Servants in to acquaint his Worship, that they had taken two
Robbers, and brought them before him. The Justice, who was
just returned from a Fox-Chace, and had not yet finished his
Dinner, ordered them to carry the Prisoners into the Stable,
whither they were attended by all the Servants in the House, and
all the People of the Neighbourhood, who flock'd together to see
them with as much Curiosity as if there was something uncommon to be seen, or that a Rogue did not look like other People.

The Justice being now in the height of his Mirth and his Cups,
bethought himself of the Prisoners, and telling his Company he
believed they should have good Sport in their Examination, he
ordered them into his Presence. They had no sooner entered the
Room, than he began to revile them, saying, 'that Robberies on
the Highway were now grown so frequent, that People could not
sleep safely in their Beds, and assured them they both should be
made Examples of at the ensuing Assizes.' After he had gone on
some time in this manner, he was reminded by his Clerk, 'that
it would be proper to take the Deposition of the Witnesses against
them.' Which he bid him do, and he would light his Pipe in the
mean time. Whilst the Clerk was employed in writing down
the Depositions of the Fellow who had pretended to be robbed,
the Justice employed himself in cracking Jests on poor *Fanny*, in
which he was seconded by all the Company at Table. One asked,
'whether she was to be indicted for a *Highwayman*?' Another
whispered in her Ear, 'if she had not provided herself a great
Belly,[1] he was at her service.' A third said, 'he warranted she was
a Relation of *Turpin*.'[2] To which one of the Company, a great

---

[1] Pregnant women condemned to death could plead their condition in hopes that the
sentence would be mitigated or deferred.

[2] Dick Turpin (1705–39), a notorious highwayman, hanged in 1739.

Wit, shaking his Head and then his Sides, answered, 'he believed she was nearer related to *Turpis*;'[1] at which there was an universal Laugh. They were proceeding thus with the poor Girl, when somebody smoaking the Cassock, peeping forth from under the Great Coat of *Adams*, cried out, 'What have we here, a Parson?' 'How, Sirrah,' says the Justice, 'do you go a robbing in the Dress of a Clergyman? let me tell you, your Habit will not entitle you to the *Benefit of the Clergy*.'[2] 'Yes,' said the witty Fellow, 'he will have one Benefit of Clergy, he will be exalted above the Heads of the People,' at which there was a second Laugh. And now the witty Spark, seeing his Jokes take, began to rise in Spirits; and turning to *Adams*, challenged him to *cap* Verses, and provoking him by giving the first Blow, he repeated,

Molle meum levibus cord est vilebile Telis.[3]

Upon which *Adams*, with a Look full of ineffable Contempt, told him, he deserved scourging for his Pronuntiation. The witty Fellow answered, 'What do you deserve, Doctor, for not being able to answer the first time? Why, I'll give you one you Blockhead—with an *S*?

Si licet, ut fulvum spectatur in igdibus haurum.[4]

'What can'st not with an *M* neither? Thou art a pretty Fellow for a Parson—. Why did'st not steal some of the Parson's *Latin* as well as his Gown?' Another at the Table then answered, 'If he had, you would have been too hard for him; I remember you at the College a very Devil at this Sport, I have seen you

[1] Latin for 'shameful', 'disgraceful'.

[2] Originally, the clergy were exempt from trial by a secular court; since very few other people were literate, the ability to read was a convenient test of a clergyman, who could thereby gain his exemption. Later, on his first conviction, anyone who could read was granted 'benefit of clergy' and exempted from the sentence. But by the eighteenth century the privilege had been withdrawn from more and more offences, one of which was highway robbery. (Wood's *Institutes*, 7th ed. [1745], p. 415.)

[3] The wit's misquotation of Ovid, *Heroides*, xv. 79: '*molle meum levibusque cor est violabile telis*' ('My heart is tender and easily pierced by the light shaft'). In the Eton grammar, *Introduction to the Latin Tongue*, which he has studied unsuccessfully (see p. 147, n. 1), this verse is used to illustrate pronunciation (p. 115 of the 1758 edition).

[4] The wit's garbled version of Ovid, *Tristia*, I. v. 25: '*scilicet ut fulvum spectatur in ignibus aurum, | tempore sic duro est inspicienda fides*' ('Truly, as yellow gold is tested in fire, | So loyalty must be proved in time of stress'). Since the gentleman's error in saying *igdibus* for *ignibus* is in character, the correction in the fourth edition has been rejected as a sophistication.

catch a fresh Man: for no body that knew you, would engage with you.' 'I have forgot those things now,' cried the Wit, 'I believe I could have done pretty well formerly.—Let's see, what did I end with—an *M* again—ay—

Mars, Bacchus, Apollo, virorum.[1]

I could have done it once.'—'Ah! evil betide you, and so you can now,' said the other, 'no body in this County will undertake you.' *Adams* could hold no longer; 'Friend,' said he, 'I have a Boy not above eight Years old, who would instruct thee, that the last Verse runs thus:

Ut sunt Divorum, Mars, Bacchus, Apollo, virorum.'

'I'll hold thee a Guinea of that,' said the Wit, throwing the Money on the Table.—'And I'll go your halves,' cries the other. 'Done,' answered *Adams*, but upon applying to his Pocket, he was forced to retract, and own he had no Money about him; which set them all a laughing, and confirmed the Triumph of his Adversary, which was not moderate, any more than the Approbation he met with from the whole Company, who told *Adams* he must go a little longer to School, before he attempted to attack that Gentleman in *Latin*.

The Clerk having finished the Depositions, as well of the Fellow himself, as of those who apprehended the Prisoners, delivered them to the Justice; who having sworn the several Witnesses, without reading a Syllable, ordered his Clerk to make the *Mittimus*.[2]

Adams then said, 'he hoped he should not be condemned unheard.' 'No, no,' cries the Justice, 'you will be asked what you have to say for your self, when you come on your Trial, we are not trying you now; I shall only commit you to Goal: if you can prove your Innocence at *Size*, you will be found *Ignoramus*,[3] and

---

[1] Adams is more familiar with the Eton Latin grammar than his antagonist. In that textbook the chapter on the gender of nouns opens as follows: 'Propria *proper names* quæ *which* tribuuntur *are assigned* maribus *to the male kind* dicas *you may call* mascula *masculines*; ut *as*, sunt *are* Divorum *the names of the heathen Gods*; Mars *the God of war*, Bacchus *the God of wine*, Apollo *the God of wisdom*; Virorum *the names of men.* . .' (*Introduction to the Latin Tongue* [1758], p. 119).

[2] A writ from a justice of the peace to a jailer, directing him to take an offender into custody. (Jacob, *New Law-Dictionary*, 4th ed. [1739].)

[3] This term, meaning 'we are ignorant', was used by the grand jury when they judged the evidence against a person insufficient to bring him to trial. (Ibid.)

so no Harm done.' 'Is it no Punishment, Sir, for an innocent Man to lie several Months in Goal?' cries *Adams*: 'I beg you would at least hear me before you sign the *Mittimus*.' 'What signifies all you can say?' says the Justice, 'is it not here in black and white against you? I must tell you, you are a very impertinent Fellow, to take up so much of my time.—So make haste with his *Mittimus*.'

The Clerk now acquainted the Justice, that among other suspicious things, as a Penknife, &c. found in *Adams's* Pocket, they had discovered a Book written, as he apprehended, in Ciphers: for no one could read a Word in it. 'Ay,' says the Justice, 'this Fellow may be more than a common Robber, he may be in a Plot against the Government.—Produce the Book.' Upon which the poor Manuscript of *Æschylus*, which *Adams* had transcribed with his own Hand, was brought forth; and the Justice looking at it, shook his Head, and turning to the Prisoner, asked the Meaning of those Ciphers. 'Ciphers!' answer'd *Adams*, 'it is a Manuscript of *Æschylus*.' 'Who? who?' said the Justice. *Adams* repeated, '*Æschylus*.' 'That is an outlandish Name,' cried the Clerk. 'A fictitious Name rather, I believe,' said the Justice. One of the Company declared it looked very much like *Greek*. '*Greek*!' said the Justice, 'why 'tis all Writing.' 'Nay,' says the other, 'I don't positively say it is so: for it is a very long time since I have seen any *Greek*. There's one,' says he, turning to the Parson of the Parish, who was present, 'will tell us immediately.' The Parson taking up the Book, and putting on his Spectacles and Gravity together, muttered some Words to himself, and then pronounced aloud—'Ay indeed it is a *Greek* Manuscript, a very fine piece of Antiquity. I make no doubt but it was stolen from the same Clergyman from whom the Rogue took the Cassock.' 'What did the Rascal mean by his *Æschylus*?' says the Justice. 'Pooh!' answered the Doctor with a contemptuous Grin, 'do you think that Fellow knows any thing of this Book? *Æschylus*! ho! ho! ho! I see now what it is.—A Manuscript of one of the Fathers. I know a Nobleman who would give a great deal of Money for such a Piece of Antiquity.[1]—Ay, ay, Question and Answer. The

---

[1] De Castro (p. 369) and Dudden (i. 377) conjecture that this is a reference to Edward Harley (1689–1741), second Earl of Oxford, who completed the collection of manuscripts begun by his father and now in the British Museum. This identification is doubtful, however, not only because of the lack of more specific clues within the passage, but because of

Beginning is the Catechism in *Greek.*—Ay,—Ay,—*Pollaki toi*[1]
—What's your Name?'—'Ay, what's your Name?' says the
Justice to *Adams*, who answered, 'It is *Æschylus*, and I will main-
tain it.'—'O it is,' says the Justice; 'make Mr. *Æschylus* his
Mittimus. I will teach you to banter me with a false Name.'

One of the Company having looked stedfastly at *Adams*, asked
him, 'if he did not know Lady *Booby*?' Upon which *Adams* presently calling him to mind, answered in a Rapture, 'O Squire,
are you there? I believe you will inform his Worship I am
innocent.' 'I can indeed say,' replied the Squire, 'that I am very
much surprized to see you in this Situation;' and then addressing
himself to the Justice, he said, 'Sir, I assure you Mr. *Adams* is a
Clergyman as he appears, and a Gentleman of a very good Character. I wish you would enquire a little farther into this Affair: for
I am convinced of his Innocence.' 'Nay,' says the Justice, 'if he is
a Gentleman, and you are sure he is innocent, I don't desire to
commit him, not I; I will commit the Woman by herself, and
take your Bail for the Gentleman; look into the Book, Clerk, and
see how it is to take Bail; come—and make the *Mittimus* for the
Woman as fast as you can.' 'Sir,' cries *Adams*, 'I assure you she
is as innocent as myself.' 'Perhaps,' said the Squire, 'there may
be some Mistake; pray let us hear Mr. *Adams's* Relation.' 'With
all my heart,' answered the Justice, 'and give the Gentleman a
Glass to whet his Whistle before he begins. I know how to behave
myself to Gentlemen as well as another. No body can say I have
committed a Gentleman since I have been in the Commission.'
Adams then began the Narrative, in which, though he was very
prolix, he was uninterrupted, unless by several *Hums* and *Ha's*
of the Justice, and his Desire to repeat those Parts which seemed
to him most material. When he had finished; the Justice, who, on
what the Squire had said, believed every Syllable of his Story on
his bare Affirmation, notwithstanding the Depositions on Oath
to the contrary, began to let loose several *Rogues and Rascals*
against the Witness, whom he ordered to stand forth, but in vain:
the said Witness, long since finding what turn Matters were like

the chronology of events, both actual and fictional. Harley died on 16 June 1741: it is
unlikely that Fielding, in adding this passage to the second edition nearly a year later,
would have alluded to him as being still alive, or that, if he wished to be faithful to the
time-scheme of his story, which is set late in 1741, he would have had the parson do so.
  [1] The parson apparently misconstrues Æschylus' *Seven Against Thebes*, 227.

to take, had privily withdrawn, without attending the Issue. The Justice now flew into a violent Passion, and was hardly prevailed with not to commit the innocent Fellows, who had been imposed on as well as himself. He swore, 'they had best find out the Fellow who was guilty of Perjury, and bring him before him within two Days; or he would bind them all over to their good Behaviour.' They all promised to use their best Endeavours to that purpose, and were dismissed. Then the Justice insisted, that Mr. *Adams* should sit down and take a Glass with him; and the Parson of the Parish delivered him back the Manuscript without saying a Word; nor would *Adams*, who plainly discerned his Ignorance, expose it. As for *Fanny*, she was, at her own Request, recommended to the Care of a Maid-Servant of the House, who helped her to new dress, and clean herself.

The Company in the Parlour had not been long seated, before they were alarmed with a horrible Uproar from without, where the Persons who had apprehended *Adams* and *Fanny*, had been regaling, according to the Custom of the House, with the Justice's Strong Beer. These were all fallen together by the Ears, and were cuffing each other without any Mercy. The Justice himself sallied out, and with the Dignity of his Presence, soon put an end to the Fray. On his return into the Parlour, he reported, 'that the Occasion of the Quarrel, was no other than a Dispute, to whom, if *Adams* had been convicted, the greater Share of the Reward for apprehending him had belonged.' All the Company laughed at this, except *Adams*, who taking his Pipe from his Mouth fetched a deep Groan, and said, he was concerned to see so litigious a Temper in Men. That he remembered a Story something like it in one of the Parishes where his Cure lay: 'There was,' continued he, 'a Competition between three young Fellows, for the Place of the Clerk, which I disposed of, to the best of my Abilities, according to Merit: that is, I gave it to him who had the happiest Knack at setting a Psalm. The Clerk was no sooner established in his Place, than a Contention began between the two disappointed Candidates, concerning their Excellence, each contending, on whom, had they two been the only Competitors, my Election would have fallen. This Dispute frequently disturbed the Congregation, and introduced a Discord into the Psalmody, 'till I was forced to silence them both. But alas, the litigious Spirit could not be stifled; and being no longer

able to vent itself in singing, it now broke forth in fighting. It
produced many Battles, (for they were very near a Match;) and,
I believe, would have ended fatally, had not the Death of the
Clerk given me an Opportunity to promote one of them to his
Place; which presently put an end to the Dispute, and entirely
reconciled the contending Parties.' *Adams* then proceeded to make
some Philosophical Observations on the Folly of growing warm
in Disputes, in which neither Party is interested. He then applied
himself vigorously to smoaking; and a long Silence ensued, which
was at length broken by the Justice; who began to sing forth his
own Praises, and to value himself exceedingly on his nice Discernment in the Cause, which had lately been before him. He was
quickly interrupted by Mr. *Adams*, between whom and his Worship a Dispute now arose, whether he ought not, in strictness of
Law, to have committed him, the said *Adams*; in which the latter
maintained he ought to have been committed, and the Justice
as vehemently held he ought not. This had most probably produced a Quarrel, (for both were very violent and positive in their
Opinions) had not *Fanny* accidentally heard, that a young Fellow
was going from the Justice's House, to the very Inn where the
Stage-Coach in which *Joseph* was, put up. Upon this News, she
immediately sent for the Parson out of the Parlour. *Adams*, when
he found her resolute to go, (tho' she would not own the Reason,
but pretended she could not bear to see the Faces of those who
had suspected her of such a Crime,) was as fully determined to go
with her; he accordingly took leave of the Justice and Company,
and so ended a Dispute, in which the Law seemed shamefully to
intend to set a Magistrate and a Divine together by the ears.

CHAPTER XII

*A very delightful Adventure, as well to the Persons
concerned as to the good-natur'd Reader.*

ADAMS, *Fanny*, and the Guide set out together, about one in the
Morning, the Moon then just being risen. They had not gone
above a Mile, before a most violent Storm of Rain obliged them
to take shelter in an Inn, or rather Alehouse; where *Adams* immediately procured himself a good Fire, a Toast and Ale, and

a Pipe, and began to smoke with great Content, utterly forgetting every thing that had happened.

Fanny sat likewise down by the Fire; but was much more impatient at the Storm. She presently engaged the Eyes of the Host, his Wife, the Maid of the House, and the young Fellow who was their Guide; they all conceived they had never seen any thing half so handsome; and indeed, Reader, if thou art of an amorous Hue, I advise thee to skip over the next Paragraph; which to render our History perfect, we are obliged to set down, humbly hoping, that we may escape the Fate of *Pygmalion*:[1] for if it should happen to us or to thee to be struck with this Picture, we should be perhaps in as helpless a Condition as *Narcissus*;[2] and might say to ourselves, *Quod petis est nusquam.*[3] Or if the finest Features in it should set Lady —'s Image before our Eyes, we should be still in as bad Situation, and might say to our Desires, *Cœlum ipsum petimus stultitia.*[4]

Fanny was now in the nineteenth Year of her Age; she was tall and delicately shaped; but not one of those slender young Women, who seem rather intended to hang up in the Hall of an Anatomist, than for any other Purpose. On the contrary, she was so plump, that she seemed bursting through her tight Stays, especially in the Part which confined her swelling Breasts. Nor did her Hips want the Assistance of a Hoop to extend them. The exact Shape of her Arms, denoted the Form of those Limbs which she concealed; and tho' they were a little redden'd by her Labour, yet if her Sleeve slipt above her Elbow, or her Handkerchief discovered any part of her Neck, a Whiteness appeared which the finest *Italian* Paint would be unable to reach. Her Hair was of a Chesnut Brown, and Nature had been extremely lavish to her of it, which she had cut, and on *Sundays* used to curl down her Neck in the modern Fashion. Her Forehead was high, her Eye-brows arched, and rather full than otherwise. Her Eyes black and sparkling; her Nose, just inclining to the *Roman*; her Lips red and moist, and her Under-Lip, according to the Opinion of the Ladies, too pouting. Her Teeth were white, but not exactly even. The Small-Pox had left one only Mark on her Chin, which

---

[1] Cf. Ovid, *Metamorphoses*, x. 243–97.
[2] Cf. ibid., iii. 339–510.
[3] 'What you seek is nowhere' (ibid., iii. 433).
[4] 'In our folly we seek the very heavens' (Horace, *Odes*, I. iii. 38).

was so large, it might have been mistaken for a Dimple, had not
her left Cheek produced one so near a Neighbour to it, that the
former served only for a Foil to the latter. Her Complexion was
fair, a little injured by the Sun, but overspread with such a Bloom,
that the finest Ladies would have exchanged all their White for
it: add to these, a Countenance in which tho' she was extremely
bashful, a Sensibility appeared almost incredible; and a Sweetness, whenever she smiled, beyond either Imitation or Description. To conclude all, she had a natural Gentility, superior to the
Acquisition of Art, and which surprized all who beheld her.

This lovely Creature was sitting by the Fire with *Adams*, when
her Attention was suddenly engaged by a Voice from an inner
Room, which sung the following Song:

The SONG

SAY, Chloe, *where must the Swain stray*
  Who is by thy Beauties undone,
To wash their Remembrance away,
  To what distant Lethe *must run?*
The Wretch who is sentenc'd to die,
  May escape and leave Justice behind;
From his Country perhaps he may fly,
  But O can he fly from his Mind!

O Rapture! unthought of before,
  To be thus of Chloe *possest;*
Nor she, nor no Tyrant's hard Power,
  Her Image can tear from my Breast.
But felt not Narcissus *more Joy,*
  With his Eyes he beheld his lov'd Charms?
Yet what he beheld, the fond Boy
  More eagerly wish'd in his Arms.

How can it thy dear Image be,
  Which fills thus my Bosom with Woe?
Can aught bear Resemblance to thee,
  Which Grief and not Joy can bestow?
This Counterfeit snatch from my Heart,
  Ye Pow'rs, tho' with Torment I rave,
Tho' mortal will prove the fell Smart,
  I then shall find rest in my Grave.

Ah! see, the dear Nymph o'er the Plain,
    Comes smiling and tripping along,
A thousand Loves dance in her Train,
    The Graces around her all throng.
To meet her soft Zephyrus *flies,*
    And wafts all the Sweets from the Flow'rs;
Ah Rogue! whilst he kisses her Eyes,
    More Sweets from her Breath he devours.

My Soul, whilst I gaze, is on fire,
    But her Looks were so tender and kind,
My Hope almost reach'd my Desire,
    And left lame Despair far behind.
Transported with Madness I flew,
    And eagerly seiz'd on my Bliss;
Her Bosom but half she withdrew,
    But half she refus'd my fond Kiss.

Advances like these made me bold,
    I whisper'd her, Love,—*we're alone,*
The rest let Immortals unfold,
    No Language can tell but their own.
Ah! Chloe, *expiring, I cry'd,*
    How long I thy Cruelty bore?
Ah! Strephon, *she blushing reply'd,*
    You ne'er was so pressing before.

Adams had been ruminating all this Time on a Passage in *Æschylus*, without attending in the least to the Voice, tho' one of the most melodious that ever was heard; when casting his Eyes on *Fanny*, he cried out, 'Bless us, you look extremely pale.' 'Pale! Mr. *Adams*,' says she, 'O Jesus!' and fell backwards in her Chair. *Adams* jumped up, flung his *Æschylus* into the Fire, and fell a roaring to the People of the House for Help. He soon summoned every one into the Room, and the Songster among the rest: But, O Reader, when this Nightingale, who was no other than *Joseph Andrews* himself, saw his beloved *Fanny* in the Situation we have described her, can'st thou conceive the Agitations of his Mind? If thou can'st not, wave that Meditation to behold his Happiness, when clasping her in his Arms, he found Life and Blood returning into her Cheeks; when he saw her open her beloved Eyes, and heard her with the softest Accent whisper, 'Are you *Joseph Andrews?*' 'Art thou my *Fanny?*' he answered eagerly, and pulling her to his Heart, he imprinted numberless Kisses on her Lips, without considering who were present.

If Prudes are offended at the Lusciousness of this Picture, they may take their Eyes off from it, and survey Parson *Adams* dancing about the Room in a Rapture of Joy. Some Philosophers may perhaps doubt, whether he was not the happiest of the three; for the Goodness of his Heart enjoyed the Blessings which were exulting in the Breasts of both the other two, together with his own. But we shall leave such Disquisitions as too deep for us, to those who are building some favourite Hypotheses, which they will refuse no Metaphysical Rubbish to erect, and support: for our part, we give it clearly on the side of *Joseph*, whose Happiness was not only greater than the Parson's, but of longer Duration: for as soon as the first Tumults of *Adams's* Rapture were over, he cast his Eyes towards the Fire, where *Æschylus* lay expiring; and immediately rescued the poor Remains, to-wit, the Sheepskin Covering of his dear Friend, which was the Work of his own Hands, and had been his inseparable Companion for upwards of thirty Years.

Fanny had no sooner perfectly recovered herself, than she began to restrain the Impetuosity of her Transports; and reflecting on what she had done and suffered in the Presence of so many, she was immediately covered with Confusion; and pushing *Joseph* gently from her, she begged him to be quiet: nor would admit of either Kiss or Embrace any longer. Then seeing Mrs. *Slipslop* she curt'sied, and offered to advance to her; but that high Woman would not return her Curt'sies; but casting her Eyes another way, immediately withdrew into another Room, muttering as she went, she wondered *who the Creature was.*

CHAPTER XIII

*A Dissertation concerning high People and low People,
with Mrs.* Slipslop's *Departure in no very good Temper
of Mind, and the evil Plight in which she left*
Adams *and his Company.*

IT will doubtless seem extremely odd to many Readers, that Mrs. *Slipslop*, who had lived several Years in the same House with *Fanny*, should in a short Separation utterly forget her. And indeed the truth is, that she remembered her very well. As we would not willingly therefore, that any thing should appear unnatural in this our History, we will endeavour to explain the Reasons of her Conduct; nor do we doubt being able to satisfy the most curious Reader, that Mrs. *Slipslop* did not in the least deviate from the common Road in this Behaviour; and indeed, had she done otherwise, she must have descended below herself, and would have very justly been liable to Censure.

Be it known then, that the human Species are divided into two sorts of People, to-wit, *High* People and *Low* People. As by High People, I would not be understood to mean Persons literally born higher in their Dimensions than the rest of the Species, nor metaphorically those of exalted Characters or Abilities; so by Low People I cannot be construed to intend the Reverse. High People signify no other than People of Fashion, and low People those of no Fashion. Now this word *Fashion*, hath by long use lost its original Meaning, from which at present it gives us a very different Idea: for I am deceived, if by Persons of Fashion, we do not generally include a Conception of Birth and Accomplishments superior to the Herd of Mankind; whereas in reality, nothing more was originally meant by a Person of Fashion, than a Person who drest himself in the Fashion of the Times; and the Word really and truly signifies no more at this day. Now the World being thus divided into People of Fashion, and People of no Fashion, a fierce Contention arose between them, nor would those of one Party, to avoid Suspicion, be seen publickly to speak to those of the other; tho' they often held a very good Correspondence in private. In this Contention, it is difficult to say which Party succeeded:

for whilst the People of Fashion seized several Places to their own use, such as Courts, Assemblies, Operas, Balls, &c. the People of no Fashion, besides one Royal Place called his Majesty's Bear-Garden,[1] have been in constant Possession of all Hops, Fairs, Revels, &c. Two Places have been agreed to be divided between them, namely the Church and the Play-House; where they segregate themselves from each other in a remarkable Manner: for as the People of Fashion exalt themselves at Church over the Heads of the People of no Fashion; so in the Play-House they abase themselves in the same degree under their Feet. This Distinction I have never met with any one able to account for; it is sufficient, that so far from looking on each other as Brethren in the Christian Language, they seem scarce to regard each other as of the same Species. This the Terms *strange Persons*, *People one does not know*, *the Creature*, *Wretches*, *Beasts*, *Brutes*, and many other Appellations evidently demonstrate; which Mrs. *Slipslop* having often heard her Mistress use, thought she had also a Right to use in her turn: and perhaps she was not mistaken; for these two Parties, especially those bordering nearly on each other, to-wit the lowest of the High, and the highest of the Low, often change their Parties according to Place and Time; for those who are People of Fashion in one place, are often People of no Fashion in another: And with regard to Time, it may not be unpleasant to survey the Picture of Dependance like a kind of Ladder; as for instance, early in the Morning arises the Postillion, or some other Boy which great Families no more than great Ships are without, and falls to brushing the Clothes, and cleaning the Shoes of *John* the Footman, who being drest himself, applies his Hands to the same Labours for Mr. *Second-hand* the Squire's Gentleman; the Gentleman in the like manner, a little later in the Day, attends the Squire; the Squire is no sooner equipped, than he attends the Levee of my Lord; which is no sooner over, than my Lord himself is seen at the Levee of the Favourite, who after his Hour of Homage is at an end, appears himself to pay Homage to the Levee of his Sovereign. Nor is there perhaps, in this whole Ladder of Dependance, any one Step at a greater distance from the other, than the first from the second: so that to a Philosopher the Question might only seem whether you would chuse to be a

---

[1] The Bear-Garden in Hockley-in-the-Hole, Clerkenwell, was the scene of rough and violent sports—the baiting of bears and bulls, wrestling, cudgel-playing, and the like.

great Man at six in the Morning, or at two in the Afternoon. And yet there are scarce two of these, who do not think the least Familiarity with the Persons below them a Condescension, and if they were to go one Step farther, a Degradation.

And now, Reader, I hope thou wilt pardon this long Digression, which seemed to me necessary to vindicate the great Character of Mrs. *Slipslop*, from what low People, who have never seen high People, might think an Absurdity: but we who know them, must have daily found very high Persons know us in one Place and not in another, To-day, and not To-morrow; all which, it is difficult to account for, otherwise than I have here endeavour'd; and perhaps, if the Gods, according to the Opinion of some, made Men only to laugh at them, there is no part of our Behaviour which answers the End of our Creation better than this.

But to return to our History: *Adams*, who knew no more of all this than the Cat which sat on the Table, imagining Mrs. *Slipslop's* Memory had been much worse than it really was, followed her into the next Room, crying out, 'Madam *Slipslop*, here is one of your old Acquaintance: Do but see what a fine Woman she is grown since she left Lady *Booby's* Service.' 'I think I *reflect* something of her,' answered she with great Dignity, 'but I can't remember all the inferior Servants in our Family.' She then proceeded to satisfy *Adams's* Curiosity, by telling him, 'when she arrived at the Inn, she found a Chaise ready for her; that her Lady being expected very shortly in the Country, she was obliged to make the utmost haste, and in *Commensuration* of *Joseph's* Lameness, she had taken him with her;' and lastly, 'that the excessive *Virulence* of the Storm had driven them into the House where he found them.' After which, she acquainted *Adams* with his having left his Horse, and exprest some Wonder at his having strayed so far out of his Way, and at meeting him, as she said, 'in the Company of that Wench, who she feared was no better than she should be.'

The Horse was no sooner put into *Adams's* Head, but he was immediately driven out by this Reflection on the Character of *Fanny*. He protested, 'he believed there was not a chaster Damsel in the Universe. I heartily wish, I heartily wish,' cry'd he, (snapping his Fingers) 'that all her Betters were as good.' He then proceeded to inform her of the Accident of their meeting; but when he came to mention the Circumstance of delivering her from

the Rape, she said, 'she thought him properer for the Army than
the Clergy: that it did not become a Clergyman to lay violent
Hands on any one, that he should have rather prayed that she
might be strengthened.' *Adams* said, 'he was very far from being
ashamed of what he had done;' she replied, 'want of Shame was
not the *Currycuristick* of a Clergyman.' This Dialogue might have
probably grown warmer, had not *Joseph* opportunely entered the
Room, to ask leave of Madam *Slipslop* to introduce *Fanny*: but she
positively refused to admit any such Trollops; and told him, 'she
would have been burnt before she would have suffered him to get
into a Chaise with her; if she had once *respected* him of having his
Sluts way-laid on the Road for him,' adding, 'that Mr. *Adams*
acted a very pretty Part, and she did not doubt but to see him a
Bishop.' He made the best Bow he could, and cried out, 'I thank
you, Madam, for that Right Reverend Appellation, which I shall
take all honest Means to deserve.' 'Very honest Means,' returned
she with a Sneer, 'to bring good People together.' At these Words,
Adams took two or three Strides a-cross the Room, when the
Coachman came to inform Mrs. *Slipslop*, 'that the Storm was
over, and the Moon shone very bright.' She then sent for *Joseph*,
who was sitting without with his *Fanny*; and would have had him
gone with her: but he peremptorily refused to leave *Fanny* behind; which threw the good Woman into a violent Rage. She
said, 'she would inform her Lady what Doings were carrying on,
and did not doubt, but she would rid the Parish of all such People;'
and concluded a long Speech full of Bitterness and very hard
Words, with some Reflections on the Clergy, not decent to repeat: at last finding *Joseph* unmoveable, she flung herself into
the Chaise, casting a Look at *Fanny* as she went, not unlike that
which *Cleopatra* gives *Octavia* in the Play.[1] To say the truth, she
was most disagreeably disappointed by the Presence of *Fanny*;
she had from her first seeing *Joseph* at the Inn, conceived Hopes
of something which might have been accomplished at an Ale-
house as well as a Palace; indeed it is probable, Mr. *Adams* had
rescued more than *Fanny* from the Danger of a Rape that
Evening.

When the Chaise had carried off the enraged *Slipslop*; *Adams*,
Joseph, and *Fanny* assembled over the Fire; where they had a great
deal of innocent Chat, pretty enough; but as possibly, it would not

[1] Dryden's *All for Love*, III.

be very entertaining to the Reader, we shall hasten to the Morning; only observing that none of them went to bed that Night. *Adams*, when he had smoked three Pipes, took a comfortable Nap in a great Chair, and left the Lovers, whose Eyes were too well employed to permit any Desire of shutting them, to enjoy by themselves during some Hours, an Happiness which none of my Readers, who have never been in love, are capable of the least Conception of, tho' we had as many Tongues as *Homer* desired[1] to describe it with, and which all true Lovers will represent to their own Minds without the least Assistance from us.

Let it suffice then to say, that *Fanny* after a thousand Entreaties at last gave up her whole Soul to *Joseph*, and almost fainting in his Arms, with a Sigh infinitely softer and sweeter too, than any *Arabian* Breeze, she whispered to his Lips, which were then close to hers, 'O *Joseph*, you have won me; I will be yours for ever.' *Joseph*, having thanked her on his Knees, and embraced her with an Eagerness, which she now almost returned, leapt up in a Rapture, and awakened the Parson, earnestly begging him, 'that he would that Instant join their Hands together.' *Adams* rebuked him for his Request, and told him, 'he would by no means consent to any thing contrary to the Forms of the Church, that he had no Licence,[2] nor indeed would he advise him to obtain one. That the Church had prescribed a Form, namely the Publication of Banns, with which all good Christians ought to comply, and to the Omission of which, he attributed the many Miseries which befel great Folks in Marriage; concluding, *As many as are joined together otherwise than G——'s Word doth allow, are not joined together by G——, neither is their Matrimony lawful.*'[3] *Fanny* agreed with the Parson, saying to *Joseph* with a Blush, 'she assured him she would not consent to any such thing, and that she wondred

---

[1] In the *Iliad*, ii. 489, Homer wishes for ten tongues and ten mouths. Pope translated it as a thousand (Pope's *Iliad*, ii. 580–1), and Fielding remembered it as a hundred (see *Jonathan Wild*, IV. ix).

[2] To be married within the Church it was necessary either to procure a licence from the bishop or, more properly, to publish the banns three times. By law (7 & 8 William III, cap. 35) a parson marrying anyone without having satisfied one or the other of these conditions was liable to a forfeiture of £100. Before the Marriage Act of 1753, however, any contract made before witnesses was deemed valid for all except certain temporal purposes, such as a widow's right to claim dower.

[3] From 'The Form of Solemnization of Matrimony' in *The Book of Common Prayer*: 'For be ye well assured, that so many as are coupled together otherwise than Gods Word doth allow, are not joyned together by God, neither is their matrimony lawful.'

at his offering it.' In which Resolution she was comforted, and commended by *Adams*; and *Joseph* was obliged to wait patiently till after the third Publication of the Banns, which however, he obtained the Consent of *Fanny* in the presence of *Adams* to put in at their Arrival.

The Sun had been now risen some Hours, when *Joseph* finding his Leg surprisingly recovered, proposed to walk forwards; but when they were all ready to set out, an Accident a little retarded them. This was no other than the Reckoning which amounted to seven Shillings; no great Sum, if we consider the immense Quantity of Ale which Mr. *Adams* poured in. Indeed they had no Objection to the Reasonableness of the Bill, but many to the Probability of paying it; for the Fellow who had taken poor *Fanny's* Purse, had unluckily forgot to return it. So that the Account stood thus:

Mr. *Adams* and Company D^r.	o	7	o
In Mr. *Adams's* Pocket, ——————	o	o	$6\frac{1}{2}$[1]
In Mr. *Joseph's*, ——————	o	o	o
In Mrs. *Fanny's*, ——————	o	o	o
Balance ——————	o	6	$5\frac{1}{2}$

They stood silent some few Minutes, staring at each other, when *Adams* whipt out on his Toes, and asked the Hostess 'if there was no Clergyman in that Parish?' She answered, 'there was.' 'Is he wealthy?' replied he, to which she likewise answered in the Affirmative. *Adams* then snapping his Fingers returned overjoyed to his Companions, crying out, '*Eureka, Eureka*;' which not being understood, he told them in plain *English* 'they need give themselves no trouble; for he had a Brother in the Parish, who would defray the Reckoning, and that he would just step to his House and fetch the Money, and return to them instantly.'

---

[1] Fielding apparently forgets that in II. x Adams was said to have had 'no more than one Halfpenny about him'.

CHAPTER XIV

An Interview between Parson Adams *and Parson* Trulliber.

PARSON *Adams* came to the House of Parson *Trulliber*, whom he found stript into his Waistcoat, with an Apron on, and a Pail in his Hand, just come from serving his Hogs; for Mr. *Trulliber* was a Parson on *Sundays*, but all the other six might more properly be called a Farmer.[1] He occupied a small piece of Land of his own, besides which he rented a considerable deal more. His Wife milked his Cows, managed his Dairy, and followed the Markets with Butter and Eggs. The Hogs fell chiefly to his care, which he carefully waited on at home, and attended to Fairs; on which occasion he was liable to many Jokes, his own Size being with much Ale rendered little inferiour to that of the Beasts he sold. He was indeed one of the largest Men you should see, and could have acted the part of Sir *John Falstaff* without stuffing. Add to this, that the Rotundity of his Belly was considerably increased by the shortness of his Stature, his Shadow ascending very near as far in height when he lay on his Back, as when he stood on his Legs. His Voice was loud and hoarse, and his Accents extremely broad; to complete the whole, he had a Stateliness in his Gate, when he walked, not unlike that of a Goose, only he stalked slower.

Mr. *Trulliber* being informed that somebody wanted to speak with him, immediately slipt off his Apron, and clothed himself in an old Night-Gown, being the Dress in which he always saw his Company at home. His Wife who informed him of Mr. *Adams's* Arrival, had made a small Mistake; for she had told her Husband, 'she believed here was a Man come for some of his Hogs.' This Supposition made Mr. *Trulliber* hasten with the utmost expedition to attend his Guest; he no sooner saw *Adams*, than not in the least doubting the cause of his Errand to be what his Wife had imagined, he told him, 'he was come in very good

[1] As Fielding pointed out in *The Champion* (12 April 1740), in order that they might better attend to their spiritual offices, the clergy were forbidden by law (21 Henry VIII, cap. 13) to take lands to farm or to buy and sell in markets. The law, however, seems never to have been enforced.

time; that he expected a Dealer that very Afternoon;' and added, 'they were all pure and fat, and upwards of twenty Score a piece.' *Adams* answered, 'he believed he did not know him.' 'Yes, yes,' cry'd *Trulliber*, 'I have seen you often at *Fair*; why, we have dealt before now mun, I warrant you; yes, yes,' cries he, 'I remember thy Face very well, but won't mention a word more till you have seen them, tho' I have never sold thee a Flitch of such Bacon as is now in the Stye.' Upon which he laid violent Hands on *Adams*, and dragged him into the Hogs-Stye, which was indeed but two Steps from his Parlour Window. They were no sooner arrived there than he cry'd out, 'Do but handle them, step in, Friend, art welcome to handle them whether dost buy or no.' At which words opening the Gate, he pushed *Adams* into the Pig-Stye, insisting on it, that he should handle them, before he would talk one word with him. *Adams*, whose natural Complacence was beyond any artificial, was obliged to comply before he was suffered to explain himself, and laying hold on one of their Tails, the unruly Beast gave such a sudden spring, that he threw poor *Adams* all along in the Mire. *Trulliber* instead of assisting him to get up, burst into a Laughter, and entring the Stye, said to *Adams* with some contempt, *Why, dost not know how to handle a Hog?* and was going to lay hold of one himself; but *Adams*, who thought he had carried his Complacence far enough, was no sooner on his Legs, than he escaped out of the Reach of the Animals, and cry'd out, *nihil habeo cum Porcis*:[1] 'I am a Clergyman, Sir, and am not come to buy Hogs.' *Trulliber* answered, 'he was sorry for the Mistake; but that he must blame his Wife;' adding, 'she was a Fool, and always committed Blunders. He then desired him to walk in and clean himself, that he would only fasten up the Stye and follow him. *Adams* desired leave to dry his Great Coat, Wig, and Hat by the Fire, which *Trulliber* granted. Mrs. *Trulliber* would have brought him a Bason of Water to wash his Face, but her Husband bid her be quiet like a Fool as she was, or she would commit more Blunders, and then directed *Adams* to the Pump. While *Adams* was thus employed, *Trulliber* conceiving no great Respect for the Appearance of his Guest, fastened the Parlour-Door, and now conducted him into the Kitchin; telling him, he believed a Cup of Drink would do him no harm, and whispered his Wife to draw a little of the worst Ale. After a short Silence,

[1] 'I have nothing to do with swine.'

Adams said, 'I fancy, Sir, you already perceive me to be a Clergyman.' 'Ay, ay,' cries *Trulliber* grinning; 'I perceive you have some
Cassock; I will not venture to *caale* it a whole one.' *Adams*
answered, 'it was indeed none of the best; but he had the misfortune to tear it about ten Years ago in passing over a Stile.'
Mrs. *Trulliber* returning with the Drink, told her Husband 'she
fancied the Gentleman was a Traveller, and that he would be glad
to eat a bit.' *Trulliber* bid her 'hold her impertinent Tongue;' and
asked her 'if Parsons used to travel without Horses?' adding, 'he
supposed the Gentleman had none by his having no Boots on.'
'Yes, Sir, yes,' says *Adams*, 'I have a Horse, but I have left him
behind me.' 'I am glad to hear you have one,' says *Trulliber*; 'for
I assure you, I don't love to see Clergymen on foot; it is not seemly
nor suiting the Dignity of the Cloth.' Here *Trulliber* made a long
Oration on the Dignity of the Cloth (or rather Gown) not much
worth relating, till his Wife had spread the Table and set a Mess
of Porridge on it for his Breakfast. He then said to *Adams*, 'I
don't know, Friend, how you came to *caale* on me; however, as
you are here, if you think proper to eat a Morsel, you may.'
Adams accepted the Invitation, and the two Parsons sat down
together, Mrs. *Trulliber* waiting behind her Husband's Chair, as
was, it seems, her custom. *Trulliber* eat heartily, but scarce put
any thing in his Mouth without finding fault with his Wife's
Cookery. All which the poor Woman bore patiently. Indeed she
was so absolute an Admirer of her Husband's Greatness and
Importance, of which she had frequent Hints from his own
Mouth, that she almost carried her Adoration to an opinion of
his Infallibility. To say the truth, the Parson had exercised her
more ways than one; and the pious Woman had so well edified
by her Husband's Sermons, that she had resolved to receive the
good things of this World together with the bad.[1] She had indeed
been at first a little contentious; but he had long since got the
better, partly by her love for *this*, partly by her fear of *that*, partly
by her Religion, partly by the Respect he paid himself, and partly
by that which he received from the Parish: She had, in short,
absolutely submitted, and now worshipped her Husband as *Sarah*
did *Abraham*, calling him (not Lord but) Master.[2] Whilst they

---

[1] The reading of the third edition has been rejected as a sophistication. The original
version, which Fielding allowed to stand during his thorough revisions for the second
edition, seems in better accord with the irony in this passage.   [2] Cf. I Peter iii. 6.

were at Table, her Husband gave her a fresh Example of his
Greatness; for as she had just delivered a Cup of Ale to *Adams*,
he snatched it out of his Hand, and crying out, *I caal'd vurst*,
swallowed down the Ale. *Adams* denied it, and it was referred to
the Wife, who tho' her Conscience was on the side of *Adams*,
durst not give it against her Husband. Upon which he said, 'No,
Sir, no, I should not have been so rude to have taken it from you,
if you had *caal'd vurst*; but I'd have you know I'm a better Man
than to suffer the best He in the Kingdom to drink before me
in my own House, when I *caale vurst*.'

As soon as their Breakfast was ended, *Adams* began in the
following manner: 'I think, Sir, it is high time to inform you of
the business of my Embassy. I am a Traveller, and am passing
this way in company with two young People, a Lad and a Damsel,
my Parishioners, towards my own Cure: we stopt at a House
of Hospitality in the Parish, where they directed me to you, as
having the Cure.'—'Tho' I am but a Curate,' says *Trulliber*,
'I believe I am as warm[1] as the Vicar himself, or perhaps the
Rector of the next Parish too; I believe I could buy them both.'
'Sir,' cries *Adams*, 'I rejoice thereat. Now, Sir, my Business is,
that we are by various Accidents stript of our Money, and are
not able to pay our Reckoning, being seven Shillings. I therefore
request you to assist me with the Loan of those seven Shillings,
and also seven Shillings more, which peradventure I shall return
to you; but if not, I am convinced you will joyfully embrace
such an Opportunity of laying up a Treasure in a better Place
than any this World affords.'[2]

Suppose a Stranger, who entered the Chambers of a Lawyer,
being imagined a Client, when the Lawyer was preparing his
Palm for the Fee, should pull out a Writ against him. Suppose
an Apothecary, at the Door of a Chariot containing some great
Doctor of eminent Skill, should, instead of Directions to a
Patient, present him with a Potion for himself. Suppose a Minister
should, instead of a good round Sum, treat my Lord— or Sir—
or Esq;— with a good Broomstick. Suppose a civil Companion,
or a led Captain[3] should, instead of Virtue, and Honour, and
Beauty, and Parts, and Admiration, thunder Vice and Infamy,

---

[1] Rich.
[2] Cf. Matthew vi. 19–21, and many other passages in the New Testament.
[3] A sycophant or parasite.

and Ugliness, and Folly, and Contempt, in his Patron's Ears.
Suppose when a Tradesman first carries in his Bill, the Man of
Fashion should pay it; or suppose, if he did so, the Tradesman
should abate what he had overcharged on the Supposition of
waiting. In short—suppose what you will, you never can nor will
suppose any thing equal to the Astonishment which seiz'd on
Trulliber, as soon as *Adams* had ended his Speech. A while he
rolled his Eyes in Silence, some times surveying *Adams*, then his
Wife, then casting them on the Ground, then lifting them to
Heaven. At last, he burst forth in the following Accents. 'Sir,
I believe I know where to lay my little Treasure up as well as
another; I thank G— if I am not so warm as some, I am content; that is a Blessing greater than Riches; and he to whom that
is given need ask no more. To be content with a little is greater
than to possess the World, which a Man may possess without
being so.¹ Lay up my Treasure! what matters where a Man's
Treasure is, whose Heart is in the Scriptures?² there is the Treasure of a Christian.' At these Words the Water ran from *Adams's*
Eyes; and catching *Trulliber* by the Hand, in a Rapture, 'Brother,'
says he, 'Heavens bless the Accident by which I came to see you;
I would have walked many a Mile to have communed with you,
and, believe me, I will shortly pay you a second Visit: but my
Friends, I fancy, by this time, wonder at my stay, so let me have
the Money immediately.' *Trulliber* then put on a stern Look,
and cry'd out, 'Thou dost not intend to rob me?'³ At which the
Wife, bursting into Tears, fell on her Knees and roared out, 'O
dear Sir, for Heaven's sake don't rob my Master, we are but
poor People.' 'Get up for a Fool as thou art, and go about thy
Business,' said *Trulliber*, 'dost think the Man will venture his
Life? he is a Beggar and no Robber.' 'Very true indeed,' an-

¹ Trulliber mouths the platitudes of countless homilies, perhaps improvising, very
roughly, upon such scriptural texts as the following: 1 Timothy vi. 6–10, Philippians iv.
11, Hebrews xiii. 5, Proverbs xv. 16, xvi. 8, Ecclesiastes v. 10–12.

² Cf. Matthew vi. 21.

³ Thieves and sharpers sometimes disguised themselves as clergymen in order to win
the confidence of their victims. This practice, called 'preaching the parson,' was used early
in his career by the notorious criminal, Roger Johnson, whom Fielding introduces into
Jonathan Wild. Dressed as a clergyman and his servant, Johnson and an accomplice
travelled the country and, pretending to be short of ready cash, stopped at inns to be
directed to the homes of wealthy neighbours, of whom they would 'borrow' money on false
security. See *A Full and Particular Account of the Life and Notorious Transactions of Roger
Johnson* (1740), pp. 12–16.

swered *Adams*. 'I wish, with all my heart, the Tithing-Man[1] was
here,' cries *Trulliber*, ' I would have thee punished as a Vagabond
for thy Impudence. Fourteen Shillings indeed! I won't give thee
a Farthing. I believe thou art no more a Clergyman than the
Woman there, (pointing to his Wife) but if thou art, dost deserve
to have thy Gown stript over thy Shoulders, for running about
the Country in such a manner.' 'I forgive your Suspicions,' says
Adams, 'but suppose I am not a Clergyman, I am nevertheless thy
Brother, and thou, as a Christian, much more as a Clergyman,
art obliged to relieve my Distress.' 'Dost preach to me,' replied
Trulliber, 'dost pretend to instruct me in my Duty?' 'Ifacks, a
good Story,' cries Mrs. *Trulliber*, 'to preach to my Master.'
'Silence, Woman,' cries *Trulliber*; 'I would have thee know,
Friend, (addressing himself to *Adams*,) I shall not learn my Duty
from such as thee; I know what Charity is, better than to give to
Vagabonds.' 'Besides, if we were inclined, the Poors Rate[2] obliges
us to give so much Charity,' (cries the Wife.) 'Pugh! thou art a
Fool. Poors Reate! hold thy Nonsense,' answered *Trulliber*, and
then turning to *Adams*, he told him, 'he would give him nothing.'
'I am sorry,' answered *Adams*, 'that you do know what Charity
is, since you practise it no better; I must tell you, if you trust to
your Knowledge for your Justification, you will find yourself
deceived, tho' you should add Faith to it without good Works.'
'Fellow,' cries *Trulliber*, 'Dost thou speak against Faith in my
House? Get out of my Doors, I will no longer remain under the
same Roof with a Wretch who speaks wantonly of Faith and the
Scriptures.' 'Name not the Scriptures,' says *Adams*. 'How, not
name the Scriptures! Do you disbelieve the Scriptures?' cries
Tulliber. 'No, but you do,' answered *Adams*, 'if I may reason
from your Practice: for their Commands are so explicite, and their
Rewards and Punishments so immense, that it is impossible a
Man should stedfastly believe without obeying. Now, there is no
Command more express, no Duty more frequently enjoined than
Charity. Whoever therefore is void of Charity, I make no scruple
of pronouncing that he is no Christian.' 'I would not advise thee,
(says *Trulliber*) to say that I am no Christian. I won't take it of

[1] The parish constable.

[2] The Elizabethan Poor Law (43 Elizabeth, cap. 2) required the overseers of the poor in
each parish to levy a tax upon the inhabitants to provide for the indigent—to relieve the
impotent and to furnish enough stock to set the able-bodied to work.

you: for I believe I am as good a Man as thyself;' (and indeed, tho' he was now rather too corpulent for athletic Exercises, he had in his Youth been one of the best Boxers and Cudgel-players in the County.) His Wife seeing him clench his Fist, interposed, and begged him not to fight, but shew himself a true Christian, and take the Law of him. As nothing could provoke *Adams* to strike, but an absolute Assault on himself or his Friend; he smiled at the angry Look and Gestures of *Trulliber*; and telling him, he was sorry to see such Men in Orders, departed without farther Ceremony.

CHAPTER XV

An Adventure, the Consequence of a new Instance which Parson Adams *gave of his Forgetfulness.*

WHEN he came back to the Inn, he found *Joseph* and *Fanny* sitting together. They were so far from thinking his Absence long, as he had feared they would, that they never once miss'd or thought of him. Indeed, I have been often assured by both, that they spent these Hours in a most delightful Conversation: but as I never could prevail on either to relate it, so I cannot communicate it to the Reader.

Adams acquainted the Lovers with the ill Success of his Enterprize. They were all greatly confounded, none being able to propose any Method of departing, 'till *Joseph* at last advised calling in the Hostess, and desiring her to trust them; which *Fanny* said she despaired of her doing, as she was one of the sourest-fac'd Women she had ever beheld.

But she was agreeably disappointed; for the Hostess was no sooner asked the Question than she readily agreed; and with a Curt'sy and Smile, wished them a good Journey. However, lest *Fanny's* Skill in Physiognomy should be called in question, we will venture to assign one Reason, which might probably incline her to this Confidence and Good-Humour. When *Adams* said he was going to visit his Brother, he had unwittingly imposed on *Joseph* and *Fanny*; who both believed he had meant his natural Brother, and not his Brother in Divinity; and had so informed the

Hostess on her Enquiry after him. Now Mr. *Trulliber* had by his
Professions of Piety, by his Gravity, Austerity, Reserve, and the
Opinion of his great Wealth, so great an Authority in his Parish,
that they all lived in the utmost Fear and Apprehension of him.
It was therefore no wonder that the Hostess, who knew it was in
his Option whether she should ever sell another Mug of Drink,
did not dare to affront his supposed Brother by denying him
Credit.

They were now just on their Departure, when *Adams* recollected he had left his Great Coat and Hat at Mr. *Trulliber's*. As
he was not desirous of renewing his Visit, the Hostess herself,
having no Servant at home, offered to fetch it.

This was an unfortunate Expedient: for the Hostess was soon
undeceived in the Opinion she had entertained of *Adams*, whom
Trulliber abused in the grossest Terms, especially when he heard
he had had the Assurance to pretend to be his near Relation.

At her Return therefore, she entirely changed her Note. She
said, 'Folks might be ashamed of travelling about and pretending
to be what they were not. That Taxes were high, and for her part,
she was obliged to pay for what she had; she could not therefore
possibly, nor would she trust any body, no not her own Father.
That Money was never scarcer, and she wanted to make up a
Sum. That she expected therefore they should pay their Reckoning before they left the House.'

Adams was now greatly perplexed: but as he knew that he
could easily have borrowed such a Sum in his own Parish, and as
he knew he would have lent it himself to any Mortal in Distress;
so he took fresh Courage, and sallied out all round the Parish,
but to no purpose; he returned as pennyless as he went, groan-
ing and lamenting, that it was possible in a Country professing
Christianity, for a Wretch to starve in the midst of his Fellow-
Creatures who abounded.

Whilst he was gone, the Hostess who stayed as a sort of Guard
with *Joseph* and *Fanny* entertained them with the Goodness of
Parson *Trulliber*; and indeed he had not only a very good Character, as to other Qualities, in the Neighbourhood, but was reputed
a Man of great Charity: for tho' he never gave a Farthing, he
had always that Word in his Mouth.

Adams was no sooner returned the second time, than the Storm
grew exceeding high, the Hostess declaring among other things,

that if they offered to stir without paying her, she would soon overtake them with a Warrant.

Plato or *Aristotle*, or some body else hath said, THAT WHEN THE MOST EXQUISITE CUNNING FAILS, CHANCE OFTEN HITS THE MARK, AND THAT BY MEANS THE LEAST EXPECTED. *Virgil* expresses this very boldly:

> *Turne quod optanti Divûm promittere nemo*
> *Auderet, volvenda Dies en attulit ultro.*[1]

I would quote more great Men if I could: but my Memory not permitting me, I will proceed to exemplify these Observations by the following Instance.

There chanced (for *Adams* had not Cunning enough to contrive it) to be at that time in the Alehouse, a Fellow, who had been formerly a Drummer in an *Irish* Regiment, and now travelled the Country as a Pedlar. This Man having attentively listened to the Discourse of the Hostess, at last took *Adams* aside, and asked him what the Sum was for which they were detained. As soon as he was informed, he sighed and said, 'he was sorry it was so much: for that he had no more than six Shillings and Sixpence in his Pocket, which he would lend them with all his heart.' *Adams* gave a Caper, and cry'd out, 'it would do: for that he had Sixpence himself.' And thus these poor People, who could not engage the Compassion of Riches and Piety, were at length delivered out of their Distress by the Charity of a poor Pedlar.

I shall refer it to my Reader, to make what Observations he pleases on this Incident: it is sufficient for me to inform him, that after *Adams* and his Companions had returned him a thousand Thanks, and told him where he might call to be repaid, they all sallied out of the House without any Complements from their Hostess, or indeed without paying her any; *Adams* declaring, he would take particular Care never to call there again, and she on her side assuring them she wanted no such Guests.

---

[1] 'Turnus, what none of the gods would have dared to promise you as you wished, lo! rolling time has brought unasked' (*Aeneid*, ix. 6–7).

CHAPTER XVI

*A very curious Adventure, in which Mr. Adams gave
a much greater Instance of the honest Simplicity of his
Heart than of his Experience in the Ways
of this World.*

O u r Travellers had walked about two Miles from that Inn,
which they had more reason to have mistaken for a Castle, than
Don *Quixote* ever had any of those in which he sojourned; seeing
they had met with such Difficulty in escaping out of its Walls;
when they came to a Parish, and beheld a Sign of Invitation
hanging out. A Gentleman sat smoking a Pipe at the Door;
of whom *Adams* enquired the Road, and received so courteous
and obliging an Answer, accompanied with so smiling a Countenance, that the good Parson, whose Heart was naturally disposed
to Love and Affection, began to ask several other Questions;
particularly the Name of the Parish, and who was the Owner
of a large House whose Front they then had in prospect. The
Gentleman answered as obligingly as before; and as to the House,
acquainted him it was his own. He then proceeded in the following manner: 'Sir, I presume by your Habit you are a Clergyman:
and as you are travelling on foot, I suppose a Glass of good Beer
will not be disagreeable to you; and I can recommend my Landlord's within, as some of the best in all this County. What say
you, will you halt a little and let us take a Pipe together: there is
no better Tobacco in the Kingdom?' This Proposal was not dis-
pleasing to *Adams*, who had allayed his Thirst that Day, with
no better Liquor than what Mrs. *Trulliber's* Cellar had produced;
and which was indeed little superior either in Richness or Flavour
to that which distilled from those Grains her generous Husband
bestowed on his Hogs. Having therefore abundantly thanked the
Gentleman for his kind Invitation, and bid *Joseph* and *Fanny*
follow him, he entered the Ale-House, where a large Loaf and
Cheese and a Pitcher of Beer, which truly answered the Character
given of it, being set before them, the three Travellers fell to eating with Appetites infinitely more voracious than are to be found
at the most exquisite Eating-Houses in the Parish of *St. James's.*

The Gentleman expressed great Delight in the hearty and chearful Behaviour of *Adams*; and particularly in the Familiarity with which he conversed with *Joseph* and *Fanny*, whom he often called his Children, a Term, he explained to mean no more than his Parishioners; saying, he looked on all those whom God had entrusted to his Cure, to stand to him in that Relation. The Gentleman shaking him by the Hand highly applauded those Sentiments. 'They are indeed,' says he, 'the true Principles of a Christian Divine; and I heartily wish they were universal: but on the contrary, I am sorry to say the Parson of our Parish instead of esteeming his poor Parishioners as a part of his Family, seems rather to consider them as not of the same Species with himself. He seldom speaks to any unless some few of the richest of us; nay indeed, he will not move his Hat to the others. I often laugh when I behold him on *Sundays* strutting along the Church-Yard, like a Turky-Cock, through Rows of his Parishioners; who bow to him with as much Submission and are as unregarded as a Sett of servile Courtiers by the proudest Prince in *Christendom*. But if such temporal Pride is ridiculous, surely the spiritual is odious and detestable: if such a puffed up empty human Bladder strutting in princely Robes, justly moves one's Derision; surely in the Habit of a Priest it must raise our Scorn.'

'Doubtless,' answered *Adams*, 'your Opinion is right; but I hope such Examples are rare. The Clergy whom I have the honour to know, maintain a different Behaviour; and you will allow me, Sir, that the Readiness, which too many of the Laity show to contemn the Order, may be one reason of their avoiding too much Humility.' 'Very true indeed,' says the Gentleman; 'I find, Sir, you are a Man of excellent Sense, and am happy in this Opportunity of knowing you: perhaps, our accidental meeting may not be disadvantageous to you neither. At present, I shall only say to you, that the Incumbent of this Living is old and infirm; and that it is in my Gift. Doctor, give me your Hand; and assure yourself of it at his Decease.' *Adams* told him, 'he was never more confounded in his Life, than at his utter Incapacity to make any return to such noble and unmerited Generosity.' 'A mere Trifle, Sir,' cries the Gentleman, 'scarce worth your Acceptance; a little more than three hundred a Year. I wish it was double the Value for your sake.' *Adams* bowed, and cried from the Emotions of his Gratitude; when the other asked him, 'if he was married, or had any Children, besides those in the spiritual Sense he had mentioned.' 'Sir,' replied the Parson, 'I have a Wife and six at your service.' 'That is unlucky,' says the Gentleman; 'for I would otherwise have taken you into my own House as my Chaplain: however, I have another in the Parish, (for the Parsonage House is not good enough) which I will furnish for you. Pray does your Wife understand a Dairy?' 'I can't profess she does,' says *Adams*. 'I am sorry for it,' quoth the Gentleman; 'I would have given you half a dozen Cows, and very good Grounds to have maintained them.' 'Sir,' says *Adams*, in an Ecstacy, 'you are too liberal; indeed you are.' 'Not at all,' cries the Gentleman, 'I esteem Riches only as they give me an opportunity of doing Good; and I never saw one whom I had a greater Inclination to serve.' At which Words he shook him heartily by the Hand, and told him he had sufficient Room in his House to entertain him and his Friends. *Adams* begged he might give him no such Trouble, that they could be very well accommodated in the House where they were; forgetting they had not a Sixpenny Piece among them. The Gentleman would not be denied; and informing himself how far they were travelling, he said it was too long a Journey to take on foot, and begged that they would favour him, by suffering him to lend them a Servant and Horses; adding withal, that if they would do him the pleasure of their Company only two days, he would furnish them with his Coach and six. *Adams* turning to *Joseph*, said, 'How lucky is this Gentleman's goodness to you, who I am afraid would be scarce able to hold out on your lame Leg,' and then addressing the Person who made him these liberal Promises, after much bowing, he cried out, 'Blessed be the Hour which first introduced me to a Man of your Charity: you are indeed a Christian of the true primitive kind, and an honour to the Country wherein you live. I would willingly have taken a Pilgrimage to the holy Land to have beheld you: for the Advantages which we draw from your Goodness, give me little pleasure, in comparison of what I enjoy for your own sake; when I consider the Treasures you are by these means laying up for your self in a Country that passeth not away. We will therefore, most generous Sir, accept your Goodness, as well the Entertainment you have so kindly offered us at your House this Evening, as the Accommodation of your Horses To-morrow Morning.' He then began to search for his Hat, as did *Joseph* for his; and both they and *Fanny* were in order of Departure, when the Gentleman stopping short, and seeming to meditate by himself for the space of about a Minute, exclaimed thus: 'Sure never any thing was so unlucky; I have forgot that my House-Keeper was gone abroad, and hath locked up all my Rooms; indeed I would break them open for you, but shall not be able to furnish you with a Bed; for she hath likewise put away all my Linnen. I am glad it entered into my Head before I had given you the Trouble of walking there; besides, I believe you will find better accommodations here than you expect. Landlord, you can provide good Beds for these People, can't you?' 'Yes and please your Worship,' cries the Host, 'and such as no Lord or Justice of the Peace in the Kingdom need be ashamed to lie in.' 'I am heartily sorry,' says the Gentleman, 'for this Disappointment. I am resolved I will never suffer her to carry away the Keys again.' 'Pray, Sir, let it not make you uneasy,' cries *Adams*, 'we shall do very well here; and the Loan of your Horses is a Favour, we shall be incapable of making any Return to.' 'Ay!' said the Squire, 'the Horses shall attend you here at what Hour in the Morning you please.' And now after many Civilities too tedious to enumerate, many Squeezes by the Hand, with most affectionate Looks and Smiles on each other, and after appointing the Horses at seven the next Morning, the Gentleman took his Leave of them, and departed to his own House. *Adams* and his Companions returned to the Table, where the Parson smoaked another Pipe, and then they all retired to Rest.

Mr. *Adams* rose very early and called *Joseph* out of his Bed, between whom a very fierce Dispute ensued, whether *Fanny* should ride behind *Joseph*, or behind the Gentleman's Servant; *Joseph* insisting on it, that he was perfectly recovered, and was as capable of taking care of *Fanny*, as any other Person could be. But *Adams* would not agree to it, and declared he would not trust her behind him; for that he was weaker than he imagined himself to be.

This Dispute continued a long time, and had begun to be very hot, when a Servant arrived from their good Friend, to acquaint them, that he was unfortunately prevented from lending them any Horses; for that his Groom had, unknown to him, put his whole Stable under a Course of Physick.

This Advice presently struck the two Disputants dumb; *Adams*

cried out, 'Was ever any thing so unlucky as this poor Gentleman? I protest I am more sorry on his account, than my own.
You see, *Joseph*, how this good-natur'd Man is treated by his
Servants; one locks up his Linen, another physicks his Horses;
and I suppose by his being at this House last Night, the Butler
had locked up his Cellar. Bless us! how Good-nature is used in
this World! I protest I am more concerned on his account than
my own.' 'So am not I,' cries *Joseph*; 'not that I am much troubled
about walking on foot; all my Concern is, how we shall get out of
the House; unless God sends another Pedlar to redeem us. But
certainly, this Gentleman has such an Affection for you, that he
would lend you a larger Sum than we owe here; which is not
above four or five Shillings.' 'Very true, Child,' answered *Adams*;
'I will write a Letter to him, and will even venture to sollicit him
for three Half-Crowns; there will be no harm in having two or
three Shillings in our Pockets: as we have full forty Miles to
travel, we may possibly have occasion for them.'

Fanny being now risen, *Joseph* paid her a Visit, and left *Adams*
to write his Letter; which having finished, he dispatched a Boy
with it to the Gentleman, and then seated himself by the Door,
lighted his Pipe, and betook himself to Meditation.

The Boy staying longer than seemed to be necessary, *Joseph*
who with *Fanny* was now returned to the Parson, expressed some
Apprehensions, that the Gentleman's Steward had locked up his
Purse too. To which *Adams* answered, 'It might very possibly
be; and he should wonder at no Liberties which the Devil might
put into the Head of a wicked Servant to take with so worthy a
Master:' but added, 'that as the Sum was so small, so noble a
Gentleman would be easily able to procure it in the Parish; tho'
he had it not in his own Pocket. Indeed,' says he, 'if it was four
or five Guineas, or any such large Quantity of Money, it might
be a different matter.'

They were now sat down to Breakfast over some Toast and
Ale, when the Boy returned; and informed them, that the Gentleman was not at home. 'Very well,' cries *Adams*; 'but why, Child,
did you not stay 'till his return? Go back again, my good Boy,
and wait for his coming home: he cannot be gone far, as his
Horses are all sick; and besides, he had no Intention to go abroad;
for he invited us to spend this Day and To-morrow at his House.
Therefore, go back, Child, and tarry 'till his return home.' The

Messenger departed, and was back again with great Expedition; bringing an Account, that the Gentleman was gone a long Journey, and would not be at home again this Month. At these Words, *Adams* seemed greatly confounded, saying, 'This must be a sudden Accident, as the Sickness or Death of a Relation, or some such unforeseen Misfortune;' and then turning to *Joseph*, cried, 'I wish you had reminded me to have borrowed this Money last Night.' *Joseph* smiling, answered, 'he was very much deceived, if the Gentleman would not have found some Excuse to avoid lending it. I own,' says he, 'I was never much pleased with his professing so much Kindness for you at first sight: for I have heard the Gentlemen of our Cloth in *London* tell many such Stories of their Masters. But when the Boy brought the Message back of his not being at home, I presently knew what would follow; for whenever a Man of Fashion doth not care to fulfil his Promises, the Custom is, to order his Servants that he will never be at home to the Person so promised. In *London* they call it *denying him*. I have my self denied Sir *Thomas Booby* above a hundred times; and when the Man hath danced Attendance for about a Month, or sometimes longer, he is acquainted in the end, that the Gentleman is gone out of Town, and could do nothing in the Business.' 'Good Lord!' says *Adams*; 'What Wickedness is there in the Christian World? I profess, almost equal to what I have read of the *Heathens*. But surely, *Joseph*, your Suspicions of this Gentleman must be unjust; for, what a silly Fellow must he be, who would do the Devil's Work for nothing? and can'st thou tell me any Interest he could possibly propose to himself by deceiving us in his Professions?' 'It is not for me,' answered *Joseph*, 'to give Reasons for what Men do, to a Gentleman of your Learning.' 'You say right,' quoth *Adams*; 'Knowledge of Men is only to be learnt from Books, *Plato* and *Seneca* for that; and those are Authors, I am afraid Child, you never read.' 'Not I, Sir, truly,' answered *Joseph*; 'all I know is, it is a Maxim among the Gentlemen of our Cloth, that those Masters who promise the most perform the least; and I have often heard them say, they have found the largest Vailes in those Families, where they were not promised any. But, Sir, instead of considering any farther these Matters, it would be our wisest way to contrive some Method of getting out of this House: for the generous Gentleman, instead of doing us any Service, hath left us the whole

Reckoning to pay.' *Adams* was going to answer, when their Host
came in; and with a kind of Jeering-Smile said, 'Well, Masters!
the Squire hath not sent his Horses for you yet. Laud help me!
how easily some Folks make Promises!' 'How!' says *Adams*, 'have
you ever known him do any thing of this kind before?' 'Aye
marry have I,' answered the Host; 'it is no business of mine, you
know, Sir, to say any thing to a Gentleman to his face: but now
he is not here, I will assure you, he hath not his Fellow within
the three next Market-Towns. I own, I could not help laughing,
when I heard him offer you the Living; for thereby hangs a good
Jest. I thought he would have offered you my House next; for
one is no more his to dispose of than the other.' At these Words,
Adams blessing himself, declared, 'he had never read of such a
Monster; but what vexes me most,' says he, 'is, that he hath
decoyed us into running up a long Debt with you, which we are
not able to pay; for we have no Money about us; and what is
worse, live at such a distance, that if you should trust us, I am
afraid you would lose your Money, for want of our finding any
Conveniency of sending it.' 'Trust you, Master!' says the Host,
'that I will with all my heart; I honour the Clergy too much to
deny trusting one of them for such a Trifle; besides, I like your
fear of never paying me. I have lost many a Debt in my Lifetime; but was promised to be paid them all in a very short time.
I will score this Reckoning for the Novelty of it. It is the first
I do assure you of its kind. But what say you, Master, shall we
have t'other Pot before we part? It will waste but a little Chalk
more; and if you never pay me a Shilling, the Loss will not ruin
me.' *Adams* liked the Invitation very well; especially as it was
delivered with so hearty an Accent.—He shook his Host by the
Hand, and thanking him, said, 'he would tarry another Pot,
rather for the Pleasure of such worthy Company than for the
Liquor;' adding, 'he was glad to find some Christians left in the
Kingdom; for that he almost began to suspect that he was sojourn-
ing in a Country inhabited only by *Jews* and *Turks*.'

    The kind Host produced the Liquor, and *Joseph* with *Fanny*
retired into the Garden; where while they solaced themselves
with amorous Discourse, *Adams* sat down with his Host; and both
filling their Glasses and lighting their Pipes, they began that
Dialogue, which the Reader will find in the next Chapter.

CHAPTER XVII

A Dialogue between Mr. Abraham Adams *and his Host,*
which, by the Disagreement in their Opinions seemed
to threaten an unlucky Catastrophe, had it not been
timely prevented by the Return of the Lovers.

'Sir,' said the Host, 'I assure you, you are not the first to whom
our Squire hath promised more than he hath performed. He is so
famous for this Practice, that his Word will not be taken for
much by those who know him. I remember a young Fellow whom
he promised his Parents to make an Exciseman. The poor People,
who could ill afford it, bred their Son to Writing and Accounts,
and other Learning, to qualify him for the Place; and the Boy
held up his Head above his Condition with these Hopes; nor
would he go to plough, nor do any other kind of Work; and went
constantly drest as fine as could be, with two clean *Holland* Shirts
a Week, and this for several Years; 'till at last he followed the
Squire up to *London*, thinking there to mind him of his Promises:
but he could never get sight of him. So that being out of Money
and Business, he fell into evil Company, and wicked Courses;
and in the end came to a Sentence of Transportation, the News
of which broke the Mother's Heart. I will tell you another true
Story of him: There was a Neighbour of mine, a Farmer, who
had two Sons whom he bred up to the Business. Pretty Lads they
were; nothing would serve the Squire, but that the youngest
must be made a Parson. Upon which, he persuaded the Father to
send him to School, promising, that he would afterwards maintain
him at the University; and when he was of a proper Age, give
him a Living. But after the Lad had been seven Years at School,
and his Father brought him to the Squire with a Letter from his
Master, that he was fit for the University; the Squire, instead
of minding his Promise, or sending him thither at his Expence,
only told his Father, that the young Man was a fine Scholar; and
it was pity he could not afford to keep him at *Oxford* for four or
five Years more, by which Time, if he could get him a Curacy,
he might have him ordained.' The Farmer said, 'he was not a
Man sufficient to do any such thing.' 'Why then,' answered the

Squire; 'I am very sorry you have given him so much Learning; for if he cannot get his living by that, it will rather spoil him for any thing else; and your other Son who can hardly write his Name, will do more at plowing and sowing, and is in a better Condition than he: and indeed so it proved; for the poor Lad not finding Friends to maintain him in his Learning, as he had expected; and being unwilling to work, fell to drinking, though he was a very sober Lad before; and in a short time, partly with Grief, and partly with good Liquor, fell into a Consumption and died. Nay, I can tell you more still: There was another, a young Woman, and the handsomest in all this Neighbourhood, whom he enticed up to *London*, promising to make her a Gentlewoman to one of your Women of Quality: but instead of keeping his Word, we have since heard, after having a Child by her himself, she became a common Whore; then kept a Coffee-House in *Covent-Garden*, and a little after died of the *French* Distemper in a Goal. I could tell you many more Stories: but how do you imagine he served me myself? You must know, Sir, I was bred a Sea-faring Man, and have been many Voyages; 'till at last I came to be Master of a Ship myself, and was in a fair Way of making a Fortune, when I was attacked by one of those cursed *Guarda-Costas*, who took our Ships before the Beginning of the War;[1] and after a Fight wherein I lost the greater part of my Crew, my Rigging being all demolished, and two Shots received between Wind and Water, I was forced to strike. The Villains carried off my Ship, a Brigantine of 150 Tons, a pretty Creature she was, and put me, a Man, and a Boy, into a little bad Pink, in which with much ado, we at last made *Falmouth*; tho' I believe the *Spaniards* did not imagine she could possibly live a Day at Sea.

1 The alehouse-keeper, himself outspoken against the government (see p. 183, n. 1), alludes to an issue with which the Opposition had vexed Walpole for years. By treaty English ships had been forbidden all traffic in Spanish waters except for the trade in slaves; extensive smuggling began in the West Indies, and Spanish coastguard vessels, regarding the English as privateers, harassed and boarded British merchantmen. It was the captain of a *guarda-costa* who cut off the ear of Captain Richard Jenkins in 1731, an incident that later came to public notice and gave its name to the war with Spain that the government reluctantly declared on 19 October 1739. Criticism of Walpole's failure to protect English shipping and to pursue the war filled the Opposition journals: 'During a sixteen Years Peace with *Spain*', declared *Common Sense* (5 December 1741), 'were our Merchants continually plunder'd'; even after war had been declared English ships were being seized in the Channel 'almost within Sight of *Falmouth*' (*The Champion*, 25 March 1739/40). Fielding wrote *The Vernoniad*, a Patriot poem, to celebrate Admiral Vernon's victory at Porto Bello, a principal base of the *guarda-costas*.

Upon my return hither, where my Wife who was of this Country then lived, the Squire told me, he was so pleased with the Defence I had made against the Enemy, that he did not fear getting me promoted to a Lieutenancy of a Man of War, if I would accept of it, which I thankfully assured him I would. Well, Sir, two or three Years past, during which, I had many repeated Promises, not only from the Squire, but (as he told me) from the Lords of the Admiralty. He never returned from *London*, but I was assured I might be satisfied now, for I was certain of the first Vacancy; and what surprizes me still, when I reflect on it, these Assurances were given me with no less Confidence, after so many Disappointments, than at first. At last, Sir, growing weary and somewhat suspicious after so much delay, I wrote to a Friend in *London*, who I knew had some Acquaintance at the best House in the Admiralty; and desired him to back the Squire's Interest: for indeed, I feared he had sollicited the Affair with more Coldness than he pretended.—And what Answer do you think my Friend sent me?—Truly, Sir, he acquainted me, that the Squire had never mentioned my Name at the Admiralty in his Life; and unless I had much faithfuller Interest, advised me to give over my Pretensions, which I immediately did; and with the Concurrence of my Wife, resolved to set up an Alehouse, where you are heartily welcome: and so my Service to you; and may the Squire, and all such sneaking Rascals go to the Devil together.' 'Oh fie!' says *Adams*; 'Oh fie! He is indeed a wicked Man; but G— will, I hope, turn his Heart to Repentance. Nay, if he could but once see the Meanness of this detestable Vice; would he but once reflect that he is one of the most scandalous as well as pernicious Lyars; sure he must despise himself to so intolerable a degree, that it would be impossible for him to continue a Moment in such a Course. And to confess the Truth, notwithstanding the Baseness of this Character, which he hath too well deserved, he hath in his Countenance sufficient Symptoms of that *bona Indoles*, that Sweetness of Disposition which furnishes out a good Christian.' 'Ah! Master, Master, (says the Host,) if you had travelled as far as I have, and conversed with the many Nations where I have traded, you would not give any Credit to a Man's Countenance. Symptoms in his Countenance, quotha! I would look there perhaps to see whether a Man had had the Small-Pox, but for nothing else!' He spoke this with so little regard to the Parson's

Observation, that it a good deal nettled him; and taking the Pipe hastily from his Mouth, he thus answered:—'Master of mine, perhaps I have travelled a great deal farther than you without the Assistance of a Ship. Do you imagine sailing by different Cities or Countries is travelling? No.

Cælum non Animum mutant qui trans mare currunt.[1]

I can go farther in an Afternoon, than you in a Twelve-Month. What, I suppose you have seen the Pillars of *Hercules*, and perhaps the Walls of *Carthage*. Nay, you may have heard *Scylla*, and seen *Charybdis*; you may have entered the Closet where *Archimedes* was found at the taking *Syracuse*.[2] I suppose you have sailed among the *Cyclades*, and passed the famous Streights which take their name from the unfortunate *Helle*,[3] whose Fate is sweetly described by *Apollonius Rhodius*; you have past the very Spot, I conceive, where *Dædalus* fell into that Sea, his waxen Wings being melted by the Sun;[4] you have traversed the *Euxine* Sea, I make no doubt; nay, you may have been on the Banks of the *Caspian*, and called at *Colchis*, to see if there is ever another Golden Fleece.'—'Not I truly, Master,' answered the Host, 'I never touched at any of these Places.' 'But I have been at all these,' replied *Adams*. 'Then I suppose,' cries the Host, 'you have been at the *East Indies*, for there are no such, I will be sworn, either in the *West* or the *Levant*.' 'Pray where's the *Levant*?' quoth *Adams*, 'that should be in the *East Indies* by right.'[5]—'O ho! you are a pretty Traveller,' cries the Host, 'and not know the *Levant*. My service to

---

[1] 'Those who cross the sea change climate, but not their state of mind' (Horace, *Epistles*, I. xi. 27).

[2] When the Romans under Marcellus captured Syracuse in 212 B.C. a soldier came upon Archimedes and killed him as he was engaged in solving a mathematical problem, so abstracted that he was unaware of the sack of the city. Versions of the story appear in Cicero, *De Finibus Bonorum et Malorum*, v. 50; Livy, *History of Rome*, xxv. 31; Plutarch, 'Life of Marcellus'; and Valerius Maximus, *Factorum Dictorumque Memorabilium*, VIII. vii. 7—of these only the last mentions that Archimedes was killed inside his own house.

[3] Fleeing Thebes with her brother Phrixus on the back of a flying ram of golden fleece, Helle became dizzy and plunged into the straits now called the Dardanelles, but known to antiquity as the Hellespont. It was to recover the golden fleece of the ram that the Argonauts sailed for Colchis, a story recounted in the *Argonautica* of Apollonius Rhodius, who, however, devotes only two brief lines to the fate of Helle (i. 256–7).

[4] It was not Dædalus but his son Icarus who fell into that part of the Aegean Sea which bears his name. (Ovid, *Metamorphoses*, viii. 183–235.)

[5] The eastern part of the Mediterranean was called the Levant, a word derived from the French *lever*, to rise—hence the East with reference to the sun. Adams understands the etymology, but mistakes the location.

you, Master; you must not talk of these things with me! you must not tip us the Traveller; it won't go here.' 'Since thou art so dull to misunderstand me still,' quoth *Adams*, 'I will inform thee; the travelling I mean is in Books, the only way of travelling by which any Knowledge is to be acquired. From them I learn what I asserted just now, that Nature generally imprints such a Portraiture of the Mind in the Countenance, that a skilful Physiognomist will rarely be deceived. I presume you have never read the Story of *Socrates* to this purpose, and therefore I will tell it you. A certain Physiognomist asserted of *Socrates*, that he plainly discovered by his Features that he was a Rogue in his Nature. A Character so contrary to the Tenour of all this great Man's Actions, and the generally received Opinion concerning him, incensed the Boys of *Athens* so that they threw Stones at the Physiognomist, and would have demolished him for his Ignorance, had not *Socrates* himself prevented them by confessing the Truth of his Observations, and acknowledging that tho' he corrected his Disposition by Philosophy, he was indeed naturally as inclined to Vice as had been predicated of him.[1] Now, pray resolve me,—How should a Man know this Story, if he had not read it?' 'Well Master,' said the Host, 'and what signifies it whether a Man knows it or no? He who goes abroad as I have done, will always have opportunities enough of knowing the World, without troubling his head with *Socrates*, or any such Fellows.'—'Friend,' cries *Adams*, 'if a Man would sail round the World, and anchor in every Harbour of it, without Learning, he would return home as ignorant as he went out.' 'Lord help you,' answered the Host, 'there was my Boatswain, poor Fellow! he could scarce either write or read, and yet he would navigate a Ship with any Master of a Man of War; and a very pretty knowledge of Trade he had too.' 'Trade,' answered *Adams*, 'as *Aristotle* proves in his first Chapter of Politics, is below a Philosopher, and unnatural as it is managed now.'[2] The Host look'd

---

[1] Cicero, *Tusculan Disputations*, IV. xxxvii. 80, is the principal source of the story; he gives the name of the physiognomist as Zopyrus.

[2] *Politics*, I, esp. iii. 23, and iv. 5. Fielding would have agreed with Adams's second thought, that a tradesman is 'a very valuable Member of Society'. Though he assailed luxury and the bad manners of parvenus, Fielding throughout his career praised the honest merchant and tradesman, 'the most useful and valuable of all his Majesty's Subjects' (*The Champion*, 7 June 1740). In *The Journal of a Voyage to Lisbon* (Monday, 1 July) he wrote: 'There is, indeed, nothing so useful to man in general, nor so beneficial to particular

stedfastly at *Adams*, and after a Minute's silence asked him 'if
he was one of the Writers of the *Gazetteers*? for I have heard,'
says he, 'they are writ by Parsons.' '*Gazetteers*!' answer'd *Adams*.
'What is that?' 'It is a dirty News-Paper,' replied the Host,
'which hath been given away all over the Nation for these many
Years to abuse Trade and honest Men, which I would not suffer
to lie on my Table, tho' it hath been offered me for nothing.'¹
'Not I truly,' said *Adams*, 'I never write any thing but Sermons,
and I assure you I am no Enemy to Trade, whilst it is consistent
with Honesty; nay, I have always looked on the Tradesman,
as a very valuable Member of Society, and perhaps inferior to
none but the Man of Learning.' 'No, I believe he is not, nor to
him neither,' answered the Host. 'Of what use would Learning
be in a Country without Trade? What would all you Parsons do
to clothe your Backs and feed your Bellies? Who fetches you
your Silks and your Linens, and your Wines, and all the other
Necessaries of Life? I speak chiefly with regard to the Sailors.'
'You should say the Extravagancies of Life,' replied the Parson,
'but admit they were the Necessaries, there is something more
necessary than Life it self, which is provided by Learning; I
mean the Learning of the Clergy. Who clothes you with Piety,
Meekness, Humility, Charity, Patience, and all the other Christian Virtues? Who feeds your Souls with the Milk of brotherly
Love, and diets them with all the dainty Food of Holiness, which
at once cleanses them of all impure carnal Affections, and fattens

societies and individuals, as trade. This is that *alma mater*, at whose plentiful breast all
mankind are nourished.' He chose Heartfree, a tradesman, as the (moral) hero of *Jonathan
Wild*.

¹ Since 30 June 1735 *The Daily Gazetteer*, printed by Samuel Richardson and subsidized
by Walpole, had been the government's main organ for purposes of propaganda. It was
written pseudonymously by James Pitt ('Francis Osborne') and, later, Ralph Courteville
('R. Freeman'); among the 'Parsons' who contributed were Henry Bland, Dean of Durham,
and Francis Hare, Bishop of Chichester. Walpole bought up quantities of the newspaper
and had them distributed gratis throughout the country at an annual expense estimated at
£4,000–5,000, a fact which irked the Opposition: 'Paper, Print, Stamps, and Postage are
all given away, to force a Circulation; yet, after all, in many Places they are refus'd Admittance, and, in most others, serve only to light Pipes, or such other necessary Purposes, as
more emphatically express the Contempt they so notoriously deserve.' (*The Champion*,
3 January 1740/1.) Fielding, who naturally came under attack from 'the Gazetteers', began
satirizing them as early as *Pasquin* and *The Historical Register for 1736*, and, together with
James Ralph, he continued his criticism in *The Champion*. Ironically enough, after Fielding
abandoned that journal in June 1741, a rumour, which he denied, asserted that he had himself written for *The Daily Gazetteer* (see the Preface to the *Miscellanies*).

them with the truly rich Spirit of Grace?—Who doth this?' 'Ay, who indeed!' cries the Host; 'for I do not remember ever to have seen any such Clothing or such Feeding. And so in the mean time, Master, my service to you.' *Adams* was going to answer with some severity, when *Joseph* and *Fanny* returned, and pressed his Departure so eagerly, that he would not refuse them; and so grasping his Crabstick, he took leave of his Host, (neither of them being so well pleased with each other as they had been at their first sitting down together) and with *Joseph* and *Fanny*, who both exprest much Impatience, departed; and now all together renewed their Journey.

The History of the Adventures of

JOSEPH ANDREWS,

and of his Friend Mr. *Abraham Adams*

BOOK III

CHAPTER I

Matter prefatory in Praise of Biography.

NOTWITHSTANDING the Preference which may be vulgarly given to the Authority of those Romance-Writers, who intitle their Books, the History of *England*, the History of *France*, of *Spain*, &c. it is most certain, that Truth is only to be found in the Works of those who celebrate the Lives of Great Men, and are commonly called Biographers, as the others should indeed be termed Topographers or Chorographers: Words which might well mark the Distinction between them; it being the Business of the latter chiefly to describe Countries and Cities, which, with the Assistance of Maps, they do pretty justly, and may be depended upon: But as to the Actions and Characters of Men, their Writings are not quite so authentic, of which there needs no other Proof than those eternal Contradictions, occurring between two Topographers who undertake the History of the same Country: For instance, between my Lord *Clarendon* and Mr. *Whitlock*, between Mr. *Echard* and *Rapin*, and many others;[1] where Facts

---

[1] These historians were at the centre of a heated controversy, political in nature, that concerned the partisan depiction of the events of the Rebellion and of the Convention of 1689: written from the Tory point of view were *The True Historical Narrative of the Rebellion and Civil Wars in England* (1702–4) by Edward Hyde, Earl of Clarendon (1609–74), and *The History of England* (1707–18) by Laurence Echard (1670?–1730); written in defence of the Whigs were *Memorials of the English Affairs from the Beginning of the Reign of Charles I to the Happy Restoration of King Charles II* (1682) by Bulstrode Whitelocke (1605–75), and *Histoire d'Angleterre* (1723–5) by Paul de Rapin de Thoyras (1661–1725), translated by Nicholas Tindal, 1725–31. These histories occasioned a spate of polemical writing, equally biased, the nature of which may be judged from John Oldmixon's work: *Clarendon and Whitlock Compar'd. To which is occasionally added, A Comparison between the History of the Rebellion, and other Histories of the Civil War. Proving*

being set forth in a different Light, every Reader believes as he pleases, and indeed the more judicious and suspicious very justly esteem the whole as no other than a Romance, in which the Writer hath indulged a happy and fertile Invention. But tho' these widely differ in the Narrative of Facts; some ascribing Victory to the one, and others to the other Party: Some representing the same Man as a Rogue, to whom others give a great and honest Character, yet all agree in the Scene where the Fact is supposed to have happened; and where the Person, who is both a Rogue, and an honest Man, lived. Now with us Biographers the Case is different, the Facts we deliver may be relied on, tho' we often mistake the Age and Country wherein they happened: For tho' it may be worth the Examination of Critics, whether the Shepherd *Chrysostom*, who, as *Cervantes* informs us, died for Love of the fair *Marcella*, who hated him, was ever in *Spain*, will any one doubt but that such a silly Fellow hath really existed? Is there in the World such a Sceptic as to disbelieve the Madness of *Cardenio*, the Perfidy of *Ferdinand*, the impertinent Curiosity of *Anselmo*, the Weakness of *Camilla*, the irresolute Friendship of *Lothario*;[1] tho' perhaps as to the Time and Place where those several Persons lived, that good Historian may be deplorably deficient: But the most

---

very plainly, That the Editors of the Lord Clarendon's History, have hardly left one Fact, or one Character on the Parliament Side, fairly represented; That the Characters are all Satire, or Panegyrick, and the Facts adapted to the one, or the other, as suited best with their Design (1727). (See also, for the Whigs: Edward Calamy, *A Letter to Mr. Archdeacon Echard, Upon Occasion of his History of England* [1718]; John Oldmixon, *The Critical History of England, Ecclesiastical and Civil* [1724–30]; anon., *Remarks upon the Reverend Mr. Archdeacon Echard's History of England* [1724]; anon., *A Letter to Mr. Archdeacon Eachard* [1728]. For the Tories: Thomas Salmon, *The History of Great Britain and Ireland* [1725]; anon., *A Vindication of the Royal Family of the Stuarts, from the Aspersions Cast on them by Monsieur Rapin, Mr. Oldmixon, and Others* [1734]; John Davys, *Clarendon and Whitlock Farther Compar'd* [1739]; John Burton, *The Genuineness of Ld Clarendon's History of the Rebellion Printed at Oxford Vindicated* [1744].) Fielding's view of such 'Romance-Writers' was anticipated in Richard Savage's poem 'On False Historians' (*The Gentleman's Magazine*, xi [September 1741], 491–2, and *The London Magazine*, x [October 1741], 510–12).

[1] For the story of Chrysostome and Marcella, see *Don Quixote* (Motteux-Ozell version), Part 1, Book ii, Chapters 4–6; for Cardenio and Ferdinand, 1. iii. 9 ff.; for Anselmo, Camilla, and Lothario, whose story is contained in 'The Novel of the Curious Impertinent', 1. iv. 6–8. Fielding's great admiration for Cervantes, who, together with Lucian and Swift, comprised the 'great Triumvirate' of satirists (*The Covent-Garden Journal*, 4 February 1752), and who provided the model for 'The *Manner*' of *Joseph Andrews*, is well known. Fielding's praise of *Don Quixote*, however, was not unqualified: for his criticism of the 'loose' structure and 'incredible' adventures of Cervantes's novel, see the review of Charlotte Lennox's *The Female Quixote* in *The Covent-Garden Journal*, 24 March 1752.

known Instance of this kind is in the true History of *Gil-Blas,*
where the inimitable Biographer hath made a notorious Blunder
in the Country of Dr. *Sangrado,* who used his Patients as a Vint-
ner doth his Wine-Vessels, by letting out their Blood, and filling
them up with Water. Doth not every one, who is the least versed
in Physical History, know that *Spain* was not the Country in
which this Doctor lived? The same Writer hath likewise erred
in the Country of his Arch-bishop, as well as that of those great
Personages whose Understandings were too sublime to taste
any thing but Tragedy,[1] and in many others. The same Mistakes
may likewise be observed in *Scarron,*[2] the *Arabian Nights,* the
History of *Marianne* and *Le Paisan Parvenu,*[3] and perhaps some
few other Writers of this Class, whom I have not read, or do not
at present recollect; for I would by no means be thought to comprehend those Persons of surprising Genius, the Authors of immense Romances, or the modern Novel and *Atalantis* Writers;[4]
who without any Assistance from Nature or History, record
Persons who never were, or will be, and Facts which never did
nor possibly can happen: Whose Heroes are of their own Creation, and their Brains the Chaos whence all their Materials are
collected. Not that such Writers deserve no Honour; so far
otherwise, that perhaps they merit the highest: for what can
be nobler than to be as an Example of the wonderful Extent
of human Genius. One may apply to them what *Balzac* says
of *Aristotle,* that they are *a second Nature;*[5] for they have no

---

[1] For Dr. Sangrado's medical theory and practice, see *Gil Blas* (Smollett's translation),
II. iii–v; for the Archbishop of Grenada, VII. ii–iv. The last allusion is to the Marchioness of
Chaves and her fashionable literary society, who contemned productions of wit and humour,
preferring even the most trifling work so long as it was written in the serious style (IV. viii).

[2] *Le Roman comique* (1651–7), the well-known anti-romance by Paul Scarron (1610–60).
For another reference, see *The Opposition: A Vision.*

[3] *La Vie de Marianne* (1731–41) and *Le Paysan parvenu* (1735–6), novels by Pierre
Carlet de Chamblain de Marivaux (1688–1763).

[4] The specific allusion is to the scandalous *roman à clef, Secret Memoirs and Manners of
Several Persons of Quality, of Both Sexes. From the New Atalantis* (1709), by Mrs. Mary de
la Rivière Manley (1663–1724). This novel had a prominent place in the libraries not only
of Leonora in *The Spectator,* no. 37 (12 April 1711), but of several of Fielding's women: a
Miss Trifle in *The Champion* (26 April 1740) 'had the *Atalantis,* and several other entertaining
Pieces bound like a *Prayer-book*', with which she amused herself at church; both Shamela
(Letter XII) and Mrs. Fitzpatrick (*Tom Jones,* XI. vii) own copies. Satiric references to
the unnatural and immoral narratives of romance- and novel-writers frequently occur in
Fielding: see, for example, Mrs. Novel in *The Pleasures of the Town* (1730), *Tom Jones*
(IX. i), *Amelia* (VIII. v), and the Preface to *The Journal of a Voyage to Lisbon.*

[5] Cf. the second of *Deux Discours envoyez à Rome, à monseigneur le cardinal Bentivoglio*

Communication with the first; by which Authors of an inferiour Class, who can not stand alone, are obliged to support themselves as with Crutches; but these of whom I am now speaking, seem to be possessed of *those Stilts*, which the excellent *Voltaire* tells us in his Letters *carry the Genius far off, but with an irregular Pace.*[1] Indeed far out of the sight of the Reader,

Beyond the Realm of Chaos and old Night.[2]

But, to return to the former Class, who are contented to copy Nature, instead of forming Originals from the confused heap of Matter in their own Brains; is not such a Book as that which records the Atchievements of the renowned *Don Quixotte*, more worthy the Name of a History than even *Mariana's*;[3] for whereas the latter is confined to a particular Period of Time, and to a particular Nation; the former is the History of the World in general, at least that Part which is polished by Laws, Arts and Sciences; and of that from the time it was first polished to this day; nay and forwards, as long as it shall so remain.

I shall now proceed to apply these Observations to the Work before us; for indeed I have set them down principally to obviate some Constructions, which the Good-nature of Mankind, who are always forward to see their Friends Virtues recorded, may

(1627) by Jean-Louis Guez de Balzac (1594–1654). In defending an author's right to employ a certain boldness of style on occasion (he had himself been criticized for paying an extravagant compliment to Cardinal Richelieu), Balzac cites the example of Averroës, who had praised Aristotle as the perfection of Nature; a later philosopher, Balzac remarks, extended the hyperbole, calling him 'VNE SECONDE NATURE'. (See *Socrate chrestien, par le S*ʳ *de Balzac; & autres œuures du mesme autheur* [Paris, 1657], p. 330.)

[1] Cf. Letter XVIII ('On Tragedy') of *Letters Concerning the English Nation*, trans. J. Lockman (1733). Voltaire admires the power of English tragedy, but deplores its inflated language. He continues: 'But then it must be also confess'd, that the *Stilts* of the figurative Style on which the *English* Tongue is lifted up, raises the Genius at the same Time very far aloft, tho' with an irregular Pace' (p. 178).

[2] Fielding's faulty recollection of *Paradise Lost*, i. 542–3: 'A shout that tore Hell's Concave, and beyond / Frighted the reign of *Chaos* and old Night.' For the association of bad writing with the Miltonic realm of Chaos and Night, compare *The New Dunciad* (1742), which Pope was writing at Ralph Allen's house at the time of Fielding's visit late in 1741. (See the Introduction, p. xix.)

[3] *Historia general de España* (1601) by Juan de Mariana (1536–1623); English translation in 1699 by Captain John Stevens. In the Preface to the *Miscellanies* Fielding admits that he used this work as a source for his account of Julian the Apostate in *A Journey from This World to the Next*, where, in a footnote (i. xvii), he criticizes Mariana for confusing superstition and fact. According to the catalogue of his library Fielding owned a copy of Stevens's translation, from which he quotes, very roughly, in *The Covent-Garden Journal*, 4 November 1752.

put to particular parts. I question not but several of my Readers will know the Lawyer in the Stage-Coach, the Moment they hear his Voice. It is likewise odds, but the Wit and the Prude meet with some of their Acquaintance, as well as all the rest of my Characters. To prevent therefore any such malicious Applications, I declare here once for all, I describe not Men, but Manners; not an Individual, but a Species. Perhaps it will be answered, Are not the Characters then taken from Life? To which I answer in the Affirmative; nay, I believe I might aver, that I have writ little more than I have seen. The Lawyer is not only alive, but hath been so these 4000 Years,[1] and I hope G— will indulge his Life as many yet to come. He hath not indeed confined himself to one Profession, one Religion, or one Country; but when the first mean selfish Creature appeared on the human Stage, who made Self the Centre of the whole Creation; would give himself no Pain, incur no Danger, advance no Money to assist, or preserve his Fellow-Creatures; then was our Lawyer born; and whilst such a Person as I have described, exists on Earth, so long shall he remain upon it. It is therefore doing him little Honour, to imagine he endeavours to mimick some little obscure Fellow, because he happens to resemble him in one particular Feature, or perhaps in his Profession; whereas his Appearance in the World is calculated for much more general and noble Purposes; not to expose one pitiful Wretch, to the small and contemptible Circle of his Acquaintance; but to hold the Glass to thousands in their Closets, that they may contemplate their Deformity, and endeavour to reduce it, and thus by suffering private Mortification may avoid public Shame. This places the Boundary between, and distinguishes the Satirist from the Libeller; for the former privately corrects the Fault for the Benefit of the Person, like a Parent; the latter publickly exposes the Person himself, as an Example to others, like an Executioner.

There are besides little Circumstances to be considered, as the Drapery of a Picture, which tho' Fashion varies at different Times, the Resemblance of the Countenance is not by those means

---

[1] The revision in the second edition is curious. Fielding may have had in mind contemporary estimates of *historical* time (i.e. 4,000 years), calculated from the construction of the Tower of Babel and the dispersion of the nations. (See, for example, Thomas Stackhouse, *A New History of the Holy Bible, from the Beginning of the World, to the Establishment of Christianity*, 2nd. ed. [1742–4], I. 174.)

diminished. Thus, I believe, we may venture to say, Mrs. *Towwouse* is coeval with our Lawyer, and tho' perhaps during the Changes, which so long an Existence must have passed through, she may in her Turn have stood behind the Bar at an Inn, I will not scruple to affirm, she hath likewise in the Revolution of Ages sat on a Throne. In short where extreme Turbulency of Temper, Avarice, and an Insensibility of human Misery, with a Degree of Hypocrisy, have united in a female Composition, Mrs. *Towwouse* was that Woman; and where a good Inclination eclipsed by a Poverty of Spirit and Understanding, hath glimmer'd forth in a Man, that Man hath been no other than her sneaking Husband.

I shall detain my Reader no longer than to give him one Caution more of an opposite kind: For as in most of our particular Characters we mean not to lash Individuals, but all of the like sort; so in our general Descriptions, we mean not Universals, but would be understood with many Exceptions: For instance, in our Description of high People, we cannot be intended to include such, as whilst they are an Honour to their high Rank, by a well-guided Condescension, make their Superiority as easy as possible, to those whom Fortune chiefly hath placed below them. Of this number I could name a Peer[1] no less elevated by Nature than by Fortune, who whilst he wears the noblest Ensigns of Honour on his Person, bears the truest Stamp of Dignity on his Mind, adorned with Greatness, enriched with Knowledge, and embelished with Genius. I have seen this Man relieve with Generosity, while he hath conversed with Freedom, and be to the same Person a Patron and a Companion. I could name a Commoner[2] raised higher above the Multitude by superiour Talents,

[1] In all probability, Philip Dormer Stanhope, fourth Earl of Chesterfield (1694–1773), Fielding's patron and a leader of the Opposition against Walpole. *Pasquin* had furnished the title of Chesterfield's Patriot journal, *Common Sense*, in which, in the first leader (5 February 1736/7), Fielding is praised as 'an ingenious Dramatick Author'; and later that year, in the House of Lords, Chesterfield had vigorously opposed the passage of the theatrical Licensing Act, which Fielding's satires had precipitated. For his part, Fielding had dedicated *Don Quixote in England* (1734) to Chesterfield, and he paid him further compliments in the poems, *Of True Greatness* and *Of Good-Nature*. With the passage in *Joseph Andrews* compare the following eulogy from *An Essay on Conversation*: 'See the Earl of C[hesterfield] noble in his Birth, splendid in his Fortune, and embellished with every Endowment of Mind; how affable, how condescending! himself the only one who seems ignorant that he is every Way the greatest Person in the Room.'

[2] Ralph Allen (1693–1764), philanthropist and patron of letters. Allen made a fortune devising a system of cross-country posts for England and Wales, and then purchased the

than is in the power of his Prince to exalt him; whose Behaviour to those he hath obliged is more amiable than the Obligation itself, and who is so great a Master of Affability, that if he could divest himself of an inherent Greatness in his Manner, would often make the lowest of his Acquaintance forget who was the Master of that Palace, in which they are so courteously entertained. These are Pictures which must be, I believe, known: I declare they are taken from the Life, and not intended to exceed it. By those high People therefore whom I have described, I mean a Set of Wretches, who while they are a Disgrace to their Ancestors, whose Honours and Fortunes they inherit, (or perhaps a greater to their Mother, for such Degeneracy is scarce credible) have the Insolence to treat those with disregard, who are at least equal to the Founders of their own Splendor. It is, I fancy, impossible to conceive a Spectacle more worthy of our Indignation, than that of a Fellow who is not only a Blot in the Escutcheon of a great Family, but a Scandal to the human Species, maintaining a supercilious Behaviour to Men who are an Honour to their Nature, and a Disgrace to their Fortune.

And now, Reader, taking these Hints along with you, you may, if you please, proceed to the Sequel of this our true History.

CHAPTER II

A Night-Scene, wherein several wonderful Adventures befel Adams *and his Fellow-Travellers.*

I T was so late when our Travellers left the Inn or Ale-house, (for it might be called either) that they had not travelled many Miles before Night overtook them, or met them, which you please. The Reader must excuse me if I am not particular as to the Way they

valuable stone quarries at Combe Down. Of this stone he built the magnificent Palladian mansion—or 'Palace', as Fielding calls it—at Prior Park, Widcombe, near Bath; there in the late autumn of 1741, Fielding, together with Pope, seems to have been 'courteously entertained'. (See the Introduction, p. xix.) Fielding's long and friendly association with Allen, his benefactor, stems from this period. Allen later served as a model for Squire Allworthy of *Tom Jones*, and to him Fielding dedicated *Amelia*. In *A Journey from This World to the Next* (I. v) may be found another compliment on Allen's 'handsome' house; in *The Covent-Garden Journal* (11 April 1752) Axylus praises his charity.

took; for as we are now drawing near the Seat of the *Boobies*; and as that is a ticklish Name, which malicious Persons may apply according to their evil Inclinations to several worthy Country 'Squires, a Race of Men whom we look upon as entirely inoffensive, and for whom we have an adequate Regard, we shall lend no assistance to any such malicious Purposes.

Darkness had now overspread the Hemisphere, when *Fanny* whispered *Joseph*, 'that she begged to rest herself a little, for that she was so tired, she could walk no farther.' *Joseph* immediately prevailed with Parson *Adams*, who was as brisk as a Bee, to stop. He had no sooner seated himself, than he lamented the loss of his dear *Æschylus*; but was a little comforted, when reminded, that if he had it in his possession, he could not see to read.

The Sky was so clouded, that not a Star appeared. It was indeed, according to *Milton*, Darkness visible.[1] This was a Circumstance however very favourable to *Joseph*; for *Fanny*, not suspicious of being overseen by *Adams*, gave a loose to her Passion, which she had never done before; and reclining her Head on his Bosom, threw her Arm carelesly round him, and suffered him to lay his Cheek close to hers. All this infused such Happiness into *Joseph*, that he would not have changed his Turf for the finest Down in the finest Palace in the Universe.

Adams sat at some distance from the Lovers, and being unwilling to disturb them, applied himself to Meditation; in which he had not spent much time, before he discovered a Light at some distance, that seemed approaching towards him. He immediately hailed it, but to his Sorrow and Surprize it stopped for a moment and then disappeared. He then called to *Joseph*, asking him, 'if he had not seen the Light.' *Joseph* answered, 'he had.' 'And did you not mark how it vanished? (returned he) tho' I am not afraid of Ghosts, I do not absolutely disbelieve them.'

He then entered into a Meditation on those unsubstantial Beings, which was soon interrupted, by several Voices which he thought almost at his Elbow, tho' in fact they were not so extremely near. However, he could distinctly hear them agree on the Murther of any one they met. And a little after heard one of them say, 'he had killed a dozen since that day Fortnight.'

Adams now fell on his Knees, and committed himself to the

[1] *Paradise Lost*, i. 63.

care of Providence; and poor *Fanny*, who likewise heard those
terrible Words, embraced *Joseph* so closely, that had not he,
whose Ears were also open, been apprehensive on her account,
he would have thought no danger which threatned only himself
too dear a Price for such Embraces.

Joseph now drew forth his Penknife, and *Adams* having finished
his Ejaculations, grasped his Crabstick, his only Weapon, and
coming up to *Joseph* would have had him quit *Fanny*, and place
her in their Rear: but his Advice was fruitless, she clung closer
to him, not at all regarding the Presence of *Adams*, and in a sooth-
ing Voice declared, 'she would die in his Arms.' *Joseph* clasping
her with inexpressible Eagerness, whispered her, 'that he preferred Death in hers, to Life out of them.' *Adams* brandishing
his Crabstick, said, 'he despised Death as much as any Man,' and
then repeated aloud,

> '*Est hic, est animus lucis contemptor, et illum,*
> *Qui vita bene credat emi quo tendis, Honorem.*'[1]

Upon this the Voices ceased for a moment, and then one of
them called out, 'D—n you, who is there?' To which *Adams* was
prudent enough to make no Reply; and of a sudden he observed
half a dozen Lights, which seemed to rise all at once from the
Ground, and advance briskly towards him. This he immediately
concluded to be an Apparition, and now beginning to conceive
that the Voices were of the same kind, he called out, 'In the
Name of the L—d what would'st thou have?' He had no sooner
spoke, than he heard one of the Voices cry out, 'D—n them, here
they come;' and soon after heard several hearty Blows, as if a
number of Men had been engaged at Quarterstaff. He was just
advancing towards the Place of Combat, when *Joseph* catching
him by the Skirts, begged him that they might take the Opportunity of the dark, to convey away *Fanny* from the Danger which
threatned her. He presently complied, and *Joseph* lifting up
Fanny, they all three made the best of their way, and without
looking behind them or being overtaken, they had travelled full
two Miles, poor *Fanny* not once complaining of being tired; when
they saw far off several Lights scattered at a small distance from

[1] 'Here is a spirit that scorns the light [life], and believes that honour which you pursue
to be well bought with a life' (Virgil, *Aeneid*, ix. 205–6). Adams substitutes *illum* for *istum*
in the original.

each other, and at the same time found themselves on the Descent of a very steep Hill. *Adams's* Foot slipping, he instantly
disappeared, which greatly frightned both *Joseph* and *Fanny*; indeed, if the Light had permitted them to see it, they would scarce
have refrained laughing to see the Parson rolling down the Hill,
which he did from top to bottom, without receiving any harm.
He then hollowed as loud as he could, to inform them of his
safety, and relieve them from the Fears which they had conceived
for him. *Joseph* and *Fanny* halted some time, considering what
to do; at last they advanced a few Paces, where the Declivity
seemed least steep; and then *Joseph* taking his *Fanny* in his Arms,
walked firmly down the Hill, without making a false step, and
at length landed her at the bottom, where *Adams* soon came to
them.

Learn hence, my fair Countrywomen, to consider your own
Weakness, and the many Occasions on which the strength of
a Man may be useful to you; and duly weighing this, take care,
that you match not yourselves with the spindle-shanked Beaus
and Petit Maîtres of the Age, who instead of being able like
Joseph Andrews, to carry you in lusty Arms through the rugged
ways and downhill Steeps of Life, will rather want to support
their feeble Limbs with your Strength and Assistance.

Our Travellers now moved forwards, whither the nearest
Light presented itself, and having crossed a common Field, they
came to a Meadow, whence they seemed to be at a very little
distance from the Light, when, to their grief, they arrived at the
Banks of a River. *Adams* here made a full stop, and declared he
could swim, but doubted how it was possible to get *Fanny* over;
to which *Joseph* answered, 'if they walked along its Banks they
might be certain of soon finding a Bridge, especially as by the
number of Lights they might be assured a Parish was near.'
'Odso, that's true indeed,' said *Adams*, 'I did not think of that.'
Accordingly *Joseph's* Advice being taken, they passed over two
Meadows, and came to a little Orchard, which led them to a
House. *Fanny* begged of *Joseph* to knock at the Door, assuring
him, 'she was so weary that she could hardly stand on her Feet.'
Adams who was foremost performed this Ceremony, and the
Door being immediately opened, a plain kind of a Man appeared
at it; *Adams* acquainted him, 'that they had a young Woman with
them, who was so tired with her Journey, that he should be much

obliged to him, if he would suffer her to come in and rest herself.'
The Man, who saw *Fanny* by the Light of the Candle which he
held in his Hand, perceiving her innocent and modest Look,
and having no Apprehensions from the civil Behaviour of *Adams*,
presently answered, that the young Woman was very welcome
to rest herself in his House, and so were her Company. He then
ushered them into a very decent Room, where his Wife was sitting
at a Table; she immediately rose up, and assisted them in setting
forth Chairs, and desired them to sit down, which they had
no sooner done, than the Man of the House asked them if they
would have any thing to refresh themselves with? *Adams* thanked
him, and answered, he should be obliged to him for a Cup of his
Ale, which was likewise chosen by *Joseph* and *Fanny*. Whilst he
was gone to fill a very large Jugg with this Liquor, his Wife told
Fanny she seemed greatly fatigued, and desired her to take something stronger than Ale; but she refused, with many thanks, saying it was true, she was very much tired, but a little Rest she
hoped would restore her. As soon as the Company were all seated,
Mr. *Adams*, who had filled himself with Ale, and by publick
Permission had lighted his Pipe; turned to the Master of the
House, asking him, 'if evil Spirits did not use to walk in that
Neighbourhood?' To which receiving no answer, he began to
inform him of the Adventure which they had met with on the
Downs; nor had he proceeded far in his Story, when somebody
knocked very hard at the Door. The Company expressed some
Amazement, and *Fanny* and the good Woman turned pale; her
Husband went forth, and whilst he was absent, which was some
time, they all remained silent looking at one another, and heard
several Voices discoursing pretty loudly. *Adams* was fully persuaded that Spirits were abroad, and began to meditate some
Exorcisms; *Joseph* a little inclined to the same Opinion: *Fanny*
was more afraid of Men, and the good Woman herself began to
suspect her Guests, and imagined those without were Rogues
belonging to their Gang. At length the Master of the House
returned, and laughing, told *Adams* he had discovered his Apparition; that the Murderers were Sheep-stealers, and the twelve
Persons murdered were no other than twelve Sheep. Adding that
the Shepherds had got the better of them, had secured two, and
were proceeding with them to a Justice of Peace. This Account
greatly relieved the Fears of the whole Company; but *Adams*

muttered to himself, 'he was convinced of the truth of Apparitions for all that.'

They now sat chearfully round the Fire, 'till the Master of the House having surveyed his Guests, and conceiving that the Cassock, which having fallen down, appeared under *Adams's* Great-Coat, and the shabby Livery on *Joseph Andrews*, did not well suit with the Familiarity between them, began to entertain some suspicions, not much to their Advantage: addressing himself therefore to *Adams*, he said, 'he perceived he was a Clergyman by his Dress, and supposed that honest Man was his Footman.' 'Sir,' answered *Adams*, 'I am a Clergyman at your Service; but as to that young Man, whom you have rightly termed honest, he is at present in no body's Service, he never lived in any other Family than that of Lady *Booby*, from whence he was discharged, I assure you, for no Crime.' *Joseph* said, 'he did not wonder the Gentleman was surprized to see one of Mr. *Adams's* Character condescend to so much goodness with a poor Man.' 'Child,' said *Adams*, 'I should be ashamed of my Cloth, if I thought a poor Man, who is honest, below my notice or my familiarity. I know not how those who think otherwise, can profess themselves followers and servants of him who made no distinction, unless, peradventure, by preferring the Poor to the Rich. Sir,' said he, addressing himself to the Gentleman, 'these two poor young People are my Parishioners, and I look on them and love them as my Children. There is something singular enough in their History, but I have not now time to recount it.' The Master of the House, notwithstanding the Simplicity which discovered itself in *Adams*, knew too much of the World to give a hasty Belief to Professions. He was not yet quite certain that *Adams* had any more of the Clergyman in him than his Cassock. To try him therefore further, he asked him, 'if Mr. *Pope* had lately published any thing new?' *Adams* answered, 'he had heard great Commendations of that Poet, but that he had never read, nor knew any of his Works.' 'Ho! ho!' says the Gentleman to himself, 'have I caught you?' 'What,' said he, 'have you never seen his *Homer*?'[1] *Adams* answered, 'he had never read any Translation of

---

[1] Pope's brilliant, if free, translation of the *Iliad* in heroic couplets was published in six volumes, 1715–20; in 1725–6 a version of the *Odyssey* followed in which Pope was assisted by William Broome and Elijah Fenton. Later in his career Fielding's opinion of the accuracy, not the literary quality, of Pope's *Homer* seems to have been qualified: in *Amelia*

the Classicks.' 'Why truly,' reply'd the Gentleman, 'there is a Dignity in the *Greek* Language which I think no modern Tongue can reach.' 'Do you understand *Greek*, Sir?' said *Adams* hastily. 'A little, Sir,' answered the Gentleman. 'Do you know, Sir,' cry'd *Adams*, 'where I can buy an *Æschylus?* an unlucky Misfortune lately happened to mine.' *Æschylus* was beyond the Gentleman, tho' he knew him very well by Name; he therefore returning back to *Homer*, asked *Adams* 'what Part of the *Iliad* he thought most excellent.' *Adams* return'd, 'his Question would be properer, what kind of Beauty was the chief in Poetry, for that *Homer* was equally excellent in them all.

'And indeed,' continued he, 'what *Cicero* says of a complete Orator, may well be applied to a great Poet; *He ought to comprehend all Perfections.*[1] *Homer* did this in the most excellent degree; it is not without Reason therefore that the Philosopher, in the 22d Chapter of his Poeticks, mentions him by no other Appellation than that of *The Poet*:[2] He was the Father of the Drama, as well as the Epic: Not of Tragedy only, but of Comedy also; for his *Margites*, which is deplorably lost, bore, says *Aristotle*, the

(VIII. v) Captain Booth declares that 'tho' it is certainly a noble Paraphrase, and of itself a fine Poem, yet, in some Places, it is no Translation at all'. Earlier, however, Fielding had nothing but the highest praise for it. In *The Champion* (12 June 1740), after having quoted in a previous number (31 May) from the notes to the *Odyssey* and *Iliad*, he defended Pope's 'divine Translation of the *Iliad*, which I have lately with *no Disadvantage to the Translator* COMPARED with the Original'; in *A Journey from This World to the Next* (I. viii) he introduced Homer himself, who 'asked much after Mr. *Pope,* and said he was very desirous of seeing him: for that he had read his *Iliad* in his Translation with almost as much delight, as he believed he had given others in the Original'. It is of course not surprising that Fielding should have considered Pope 'the greatest Poet of his Time', whose 'Works will be coeval with the Language in which they are writ' (*The Champion*, 27 November 1739). For more on Fielding's relations with Pope, see S. J. Sackett, 'Fielding and Pope', *N & Q,* N.S. vi (June 1959), 200–4, and Battestin, 'Lord Hervey's Role in *Joseph Andrews*', *PQ,* xlii (1963), 235–9.

1 Cf. *De Oratore*, i. 6, translated as follows by William Guthrie in 1742: 'no Man can deserve the Praise of an accomplish'd Orator, without a perfect Knowledge of all the Arts, and every thing that is great. . . .'

2 *Poetics*, xxii. 9. The references specifically to the content of Chapters xxii and (later) xxiv of the *Poetics* suggest that, in writing this learned passage, Fielding did not resort to either of the two most convenient modern translations available to him: André Dacier's French version (Paris, 1692) or the anonymous English version (1705) based on Dacier. In both these works the remarks of Aristotle to which Parson Adams alludes are found, respectively, in Chapter xxiii. 4 and in Chapter xxv. 6. Adams's citations do tally, however, with the chapter divisions used in Guillaume Du Val's Greek–Latin text of the *Poetics* in *Aristotelis Opera Omnia* (Paris, 1629), of which Fielding owned a copy. (The chapter divisions in Du Val are identical with those in the Loeb Classical Library translation.)

same Analogy to Comedy, as his *Odyssey* and *Iliad* to Tragedy.[1]
To him therefore we owe *Aristophanes*, as well as *Euripides*,
Sophocles, and my poor *Æschylus*. But if you please we will confine ourselves (at least for the present) to the *Iliad*, his noblest
Work; tho' neither *Aristotle*, nor *Horace* give it the Preference,
as I remember, to the *Odyssey*. First then as to his Subject, can
any thing be more simple, and at the same time more noble?
He is rightly praised by the first of those judicious Critics, for not
chusing the whole War,[2] which, tho' he says, it hath a compleat
Beginning and End, would have been too great for the Understanding to comprehend at one View. I have therefore often
wondered why so correct a Writer as *Horace* should in his Epistle
to *Lollius* call him the *Trojani Belli Scriptorem*.[3] Secondly, his
Action, termed by *Aristotle Pragmaton Systasis*;[4] is it possible for
the Mind of Man to conceive an Idea of such perfect Unity, and
at the same time so replete with Greatness? And here I must
observe what I do not remember to have seen noted by any, the
Harmotton, that agreement of his Action to his Subject: For as the
Subject is Anger, how agreeable is his Action, which is War? from
which every Incident arises, and to which every Episode immediately relates. Thirdly, His Manners, which *Aristotle* places
second in his Description of the several Parts of Tragedy, and
which he says are included in the Action;[5] I am at a loss whether
I should rather admire the Exactness of his Judgment in the nice
Distinction, or the Immensity of his Imagination in their Variety.
For, as to the former of these, how accurately is the sedate, injured
Resentment of *Achilles* distinguished from the hot insulting Passion of *Agamemnon*? How widely doth the brutal Courage of
Ajax differ from the amiable Bravery of *Diomedes*; and the Wisdom of *Nestor*, which is the Result of long Reflection and Experience, from the Cunning of *Ulysses*, the Effect of Art and Subtilty
only? If we consider their Variety, we may cry out with *Aristotle*
in his 24th Chapter,[6] that no Part of this divine Poem is destitute
of Manners. Indeed I might affirm, that there is scarce a Character in human Nature untouched in some part or other. And as
there is no Passion which he is not able to describe, so is there

---

[1] *Poetics*, iv. 12.   [2] Ibid., xxiii. 5.
[3] 'Writer of the Trojan War' (Horace, *Epistles*, I. ii. 1).
[4] 'Arrangement of the incidents' (*Poetics*, vi. 12).
[5] Ibid., vi. 9, 19, and vi. 13.   [6] Ibid., xxiv. 14. (See p. 197, n. 2.)

none in his Reader which he cannot raise. If he hath any superior
Excellence to the rest, I have been inclined to fancy it is in the
Pathetick. I am sure I never read with dry Eyes, the two Episodes,
where *Andromache* is introduced,[1] in the former lamenting the
Danger, and in the latter the Death of *Hector*. The Images are so
extremely tender in these, that I am convinced, the Poet had the
worthiest and best Heart imaginable. Nor can I help observing
how short *Sophocles* falls of the Beauties of the Original, in that
Imitation of the dissuasive Speech of *Andromache*, which he hath
put into the Mouth of *Tecmessa*.[2] And yet *Sophocles* was the greatest Genius who ever wrote Tragedy, nor have any of his Succes-
sors in that Art, that is to say, neither *Euripides* nor *Seneca* the
Tragedian been able to come near him. As to his Sentiments and
Diction, I need say nothing; the former are particularly remarkable for the utmost Perfection on that Head, namely Propriety;
and as to the latter, *Aristotle*, whom doubtless you have read over
and over, is very diffuse.[3] I shall mention but one thing more,
which that great Critic in his Division of Tragedy calls *Opsis*,[4]
or the Scenery, and which is as proper to the Epic as to the Drama,
with this difference, that in the former it falls to the share of the
Poet, and in the latter to that of the Painter. But did ever Painter
imagine a Scene like that in the 13th and 14th Iliads? where
the Reader sees at one View the Prospect of *Troy*, with the Army
drawn up before it; the *Grecian* Army, Camp, and Fleet, *Jupiter*
sitting on Mount *Ida*, with his Head wrapt in a Cloud, and a
Thunderbolt in his Hand looking towards *Thrace*; *Neptune* driving
through the Sea, which divides on each side to permit his Passage,
and then seating himself on Mount *Samos*: The Heavens opened,
and the Deities all seated on their Thrones. This is Sublime! This
is Poetry!' *Adams* then rapt out a hundred *Greek* Verses, and with
such a Voice, Emphasis and Action, that he almost frighten'd
the Women; and as for the Gentleman, he was so far from entertaining any further suspicion of *Adams*, that he now doubted
whether he had not a Bishop in his House. He ran into the most
extravagant Encomiums on his Learning, and the Goodness of his
Heart began to dilate to all the Strangers. He said he had great
Compassion for the poor young Woman, who looked pale and
faint with her Journey; and in truth he conceived a much higher

[1] *Iliad*, vi. 407–39, and xxiv. 723–45.   [2] *Ajax*, 485–524.
[3] *Poetics*, xix. 1–xxii. 19.   [4] Ibid., vi. 9; cf. vi. 28.

Opinion of her Quality than it deserved. He said, he was sorry he could not accommodate them all: But if they were contented with his Fire-side, he would sit up with the Men, and the young Woman might, if she pleased, partake his Wife's Bed, which he advis'd her to; for that they must walk upwards of a Mile to any House of Entertainment, and that not very good neither. *Adams*, who liked his Seat, his Ale, his Tobacco and his Company, persuaded *Fanny* to accept this kind Proposal, in which Sollicitation he was seconded by *Joseph*. Nor was she very difficultly prevailed on; for she had slept little the last Night, and not at all the preceding, so that Love itself was scarce able to keep her Eyes open any longer. The Offer therefore being kindly accepted, the good Woman produced every thing eatable in her House on the Table, and the Guests being heartily invited, as heartily regaled themselves, especially Parson *Adams*. As to the other two, they were Examples of the Truth of that physical Observation, that Love, like other sweet Things, is no Whetter of the Stomach.

Supper was no sooner ended, than *Fanny* at her own Request retired, and the good Woman bore her Company. The Man of the House, *Adams* and *Joseph*, who would modestly have withdrawn, had not the Gentleman insisted on the contrary, drew round the Fire-side, where *Adams*, (to use his own Words) replenished his Pipe, and the Gentleman produced a Bottle of excellent Beer, being the best Liquor in his House.

The modest Behaviour of *Joseph*, with the Gracefulness of his Person, the Character which *Adams* gave of him, and the Friendship he seemed to entertain for him, began to work on the Gentleman's Affections, and raised in him a Curiosity to know the Singularity which *Adams* had mentioned in his History. This Curiosity *Adams* was no sooner informed of, than with *Joseph's* Consent, he agreed to gratify it, and accordingly related all he knew, with as much Tenderness as was possible for the Character of Lady *Booby*; and concluded with the long, faithful and mutual Passion between him and *Fanny*, not concealing the Meanness of her Birth and Education. These latter Circumstances entirely cured a Jealousy which had lately risen in the Gentleman's Mind, that *Fanny* was the Daughter of some Person of Fashion, and that *Joseph* had run away with her, and *Adams* was concerned in the Plot. He was now enamour'd of his Guests, drank their Healths with great Cheerfulness, and return'd many Thanks to

Adams, who had spent much Breath; for he was a circumstantial Teller of a Story.

Adams told him it was now in his power to return that Favour; for his extraordinary Goodness, as well as that Fund of Literature he was Master of*, which he did not expect to find under such a Roof, had raised in him more Curiosity than he had ever known. 'Therefore,' said he, 'if it be not too troublesome, Sir, your History, if you please.'

The Gentleman answered, he could not refuse him what he had so much Right to insist on; and after some of the common Apologies, which are the usual Preface to a Story, he thus began.

CHAPTER III

In which the Gentleman relates the
History of his Life.

S I R, I am descended of a good Family, and was born a Gentleman. My Education was liberal, and at a public School, in which

---

* The Author hath by some been represented to have made a Blunder here: For *Adams* had indeed shewn some Learning, (say they) perhaps all the Author had; but the Gentleman hath shewn none, unless his Approbation of Mr. *Adams* be such: But surely it would be preposterous in him to call it so. I have however, notwithstanding this Criticism which I am told came from the Mouth of a great Orator,[1] in a public Coffee-House, left this Blunder as it stood in the first Edition. I will not have the Vanity to apply to any thing in this Work, the Observation which M. *Dacier* makes in her Preface to her *Aristophanes*:[2] *Je tiens pour une Maxime constante qu'une Beauté médiocre plait plus generalement qu'une Beauté sans défaut.* Mr. *Congreve* hath made such another Blunder in his *Love for Love*,[3] where *Tattle* tells Miss *Prue, She should admire him as much for the Beauty he commends in her, as if he himself was possest of it.*

---

[1] Possibly John 'Orator' Henley (see p. 235, n. 4).

[2] In the Preface to *Le Plutus et les Nuées d'Aristophane* (Paris, 1684), translated by Mme Anne Lefèvre Dacier (1654–1720). Fielding added this passage to the second edition at a time when he was consulting Mme Dacier's work for his own (and William Young's) translation of *Plutus*. His familiarity with Mme Dacier's criticism and translations (especially her *Homer*) is attested by several other references, the most complimentary of which occurs in *A Journey from This World to the Next* (I. viii), where she is introduced in Elysium sitting on Homer's lap. (See also *The Champion*, 4 December 1739; *Tom Jones* [VII. xii]; and *The Covent-Garden Journal*, 8 February and 21 October 1752.)

[3] In *Love for Love* (1695), II. ii, Tattle advises Miss Prue: 'If I tell you you are handsome, you must deny it, and say I flatter you. But you must think yourself more charming than I speak you: and like me, for the beauty which I say you have, as much as if I had it myself.'

I proceeded so far as to become Master of the *Latin*, and to be tolerably versed in the *Greek* Language. My Father died when I was sixteen, and left me Master of myself. He bequeathed me a moderate Fortune, which he intended I should not receive till I attained the Age of twenty-five: For he constantly asserted that was full early enough to give up any Man entirely to the Guidance of his own Discretion. However, as this Intention was so obscurely worded in his Will, that the Lawyers advised me to contest the Point with my Trustees, I own I paid so little Regard to the Inclinations of my dead Father, which were sufficiently certain to me, that I followed their Advice, and soon succeeded: For the Trustees did not contest the Matter very obstinately on their side. 'Sir,' said *Adams*, 'May I crave the Favour of your Name?' The Gentleman answer'd, 'his Name was *Wilson*,' and then proceeded.

I stay'd a very little while at School after his Death; for being a forward Youth, I was extremely impatient to be in the World: For which I thought my Parts, Knowledge, and Manhood thoroughly qualified me. And to this early Introduction into Life, without a Guide, I impute all my future Misfortunes; for besides the obvious Mischiefs which attend this, there is one which hath not been so generally observed. The first Impression which Mankind receives of you, will be very difficult to eradicate. How unhappy, therefore, must it be to fix your Character in Life, before you can possibly know its Value, or weigh the Consequences of those Actions which are to establish your future Reputation?

A little under seventeen I left my School and went to *London*, with no more than six Pounds in my Pocket. A great Sum as I then conceived; and which I was afterwards surprized to find so soon consumed.

The Character I was ambitious of attaining, was that of a fine Gentleman; the first Requisites to which, I apprehended were to be supplied by a Taylor, a Periwig-maker, and some few more Tradesmen, who deal in furnishing out the human Body. Notwithstanding the Lowness of my Purse, I found Credit with them more easily than I expected, and was soon equipped to my Wish. This I own then agreeably surprized me; but I have since learn'd, that it is a Maxim among many Tradesmen at the polite End of the Town to deal as largely as they can, reckon as high as they can, and arrest as soon as they can.

The next Qualifications, namely Dancing, Fencing, Riding the great Horse, and Musick, came into my head; but as they required Expence and Time, I comforted myself, with regard to Dancing, that I had learned a little in my Youth, and could walk a Minuet genteelly enough; as to Fencing, I thought my Good-Humour would preserve me from the Danger of a Quarrel; as to the Horse, I hoped it would not be thought of; and for Musick, I imagined I could easily acquire the Reputation of it; for I had heard some of my School-fellows pretend to Knowledge in Operas, without being able to sing or play on the Fiddle.

Knowledge of the Town seemed another Ingredient; this I thought I should arrive at by frequenting publick Places. Accordingly I paid constant Attendance to them all; by which means I was soon Master of the fashionable Phrases, learn'd to cry up the fashionable Diversions, and knew the Names and Faces of the most fashionable Men and Women.

Nothing now seemed to remain but an Intrigue, which I was resolved to have immediately; I mean the Reputation of it; and indeed I was so successful, that in a very short time I had half a dozen with the finest Women in Town.

At these Words *Adams* fetched a deep Groan, and then blessing himself, cry'd out, *Good Lord! What wicked Times these are?*

Not so wicked as you imagine, continued the Gentleman; for I assure you, they were all Vestal Virgins for any thing which I knew to the contrary. The Reputation of Intriguing with them was all I sought, and was what I arriv'd at: and perhaps I only flattered myself even in that; for very probably the Persons to whom I shewed their Billets, knew as well as I, that they were Counterfeits, and that I had written them to myself.

'*WRITE Letters to yourself!*' said *Adams* staring!

O Sir, answered the Gentleman, *It is the very Error of the Times.* Half our modern Plays have one of these Characters in them.[1] It is incredible the Pains I have taken, and the absurd Methods I employed to traduce the Character of Women of Distinction. When another had spoken in Raptures of any one, I have

[1] Perhaps the most famous instance of such a character in the drama is Petulant in Congreve's *Way of the World* (1700). By underscoring, typographically, the exchange here, Fielding seems to call attention to a private joke at the expense of Adams's original, William Young. For a contemporary account of Young's having written a letter of invitation to himself and having then been discovered through his own absence of mind, see the Introduction, p. xxi, n. 2.

answered, 'D—n her, she! We shall have her at *H—d's*[1] very soon.' When he hath reply'd, 'he thought her virtuous,' I have answered, 'Ay, thou wilt always think a Woman virtuous, till she is in the Streets, but you and I, *Jack* or *Tom*, (turning to another in Company) know better.' At which I have drawn a Paper out of my Pocket, perhaps a Taylor's Bill, and kissed it, crying at the same time, *By Gad I was once fond of her.*

'Proceed, if you please, but do not swear any more,' said *Adams.*

Sir, said the Gentleman, I ask your Pardon. Well, Sir, in this Course of Life I continued full three Years,—'What Course of Life?' answered *Adams*; 'I do not remember you have yet mentioned any.'—Your Remark is just, said the Gentleman smiling, I should rather have said, in this Course of doing nothing. I remember some time afterwards I wrote the Journal of one Day, which would serve, I believe, as well for any other, during the whole Time; I will endeavour to repeat it to you.

In the Morning I arose, took my great Stick, and walked out in my green Frock with my Hair in Papers, (*a Groan from* Adams) and sauntered about till ten.

Went to the Auction; told Lady — she had a dirty Face; laughed heartily at something Captain — said; I can't remember what, for I did not very well hear it; whispered Lord —; bowed to the Duke of —; and was going to bid for a Snuff-box; but did not, for fear I should have had it.

From 2 to 4, drest myself.	A Groan.
4 to 6, dined.	A Groan.
6 to 8, Coffee-house.	
8 to 9, *Drury-Lane* Play-house.	
9 to 10, *Lincoln's-Inn-Fields.*	
10 to 12, Drawing-Room.	A great Groan.

At all which Places nothing happened worth Remark. At which *Adams* said with some Vehemence, 'Sir, this is below the

---

[1] Mother Haywood (also Heywood or Hayward), whom Fielding in a note to *Juvenal's Sixth Satire Modernised in Burlesque Verse* identifies as 'a useful Woman in the Parish of Covent-Garden', was the keeper of a fashionable brothel. At the time of her death on 11 December 1743 she was reputed to have been worth £10,000 (*Gentleman's Magazine*, xiii [December 1743], 668). The scene of *Miss Lucy in Town*, produced in May 1742, is set in her establishment, Fielding, in the original version, calling her Mrs. Haycock. (See also *A Letter to a Noble Lord* [1742].) For another contemporary reference, see Whitehead's poem, *Manners: A Satire* (1739).

Life of an Animal, hardly above Vegetation; and I am surprized
what could lead a Man of your Sense into it.' What leads us into
more Follies than you imagine, Doctor, answered the Gentleman;
Vanity: For as contemptible a Creature as I was, and I assure you,
yourself cannot have more Contempt for such a Wretch than I
now have, I then admir'd myself, and should have despised a
Person of your present Appearance (you will pardon me) with
all your Learning, and those excellent Qualities which I have
remarked in you. *Adams* bowed, and begged him to proceed.
After I had continued two Years in this Course of Life, said the
Gentleman, an Accident happened which obliged me to change
the Scene. As I was one day at *St. James's* Coffee-house,[1] making
very free with the Character of a young Lady of Quality, an
Officer of the Guards who was present, thought proper to give
me the lye. I answered, I might possibly be mistaken; but I
intended to tell no more than the Truth. To which he made no
Reply, but by a scornful Sneer. After this I observed a strange
Coldness in all my Acquaintance; none of them spoke to me first,
and very few returned me even the Civility of a Bow. The Company I used to dine with, left me out, and within a Week I found
myself in as much Solitude at *St. James's*, as if I had been in a
Desart. An honest elderly Man, with a great Hat and long Sword,
at last told me, he had a Compassion for my Youth, and therefore
advised me to shew the World I was not such a Rascal as they
thought me to be. I did not at first understand him: But he
explained himself, and ended with telling me, if I would write
a Challenge to the Captain, he would out of pure Charity go to
him with it. 'A very charitable Person truly!' cried *Adams*.
I desired till the next Day, continued the Gentleman, to consider
on it, and retiring to my Lodgings, I weighed the Consequences
on both sides as fairly as I could. On the one, I saw the Risk of
this Alternative, either losing my own Life, or having on my
hands the Blood of a Man with whom I was not in the least
angry. I soon determined that the Good which appeared on the
other, was not worth this Hazard. I therefore resolved to quit
the Scene, and presently retired to the *Temple*, where I took
Chambers. Here I soon got a fresh Set of Acquaintance, who
knew nothing of what had happened to me. Indeed they were not

---

[1] Situated on the south-west corner of St. James's Street, this was a favourite meeting
place for Whigs and officers of the palace guards.

greatly to my Approbation; for the Beaus of the *Temple* are only
the Shadows of the others. They are the Affectation of Affectation. The Vanity of these is still more ridiculous, if possible, than
of the others. Here I met with smart Fellows who drank with
Lords they did not know, and intrigued with Women they never
saw. *Covent-Garden* was now the farthest Stretch of my Ambition,
where I shone forth in the Balconies at the Play-houses, visited
Whores, made Love to Orange-Wenches, and damned Plays.
This Career was soon put a stop to by my Surgeon, who convinced me of the Necessity of confining myself to my Room for
a Month. At the End of which, having had Leisure to reflect,
I resolved to quit all further Conversation with Beaus and Smarts
of every kind, and to avoid, if possible, any Occasion of returning
to this Place of Confinement. 'I think,' said *Adams*, 'the Advice
of a Month's Retirement and Reflection was very proper; but
I should rather have expected it from a Divine than a Surgeon.'
The Gentleman smiled at *Adams's* Simplicity, and without explaining himself farther on such an odious Subject went on thus:
I was no sooner perfectly restored to Health, than I found my
Passion for Women, which I was afraid to satisfy as I had done,
made me very uneasy; I determined therefore to keep a Mistress.
Nor was I long before I fixed my Choice on a young Woman,
who had before been kept by two Gentlemen, and to whom I was
recommended by a celebrated Bawd. I took her home to my
Chambers, and made her a Settlement, during Cohabitation. This
would perhaps have been very ill paid: However, she did not
suffer me to be perplexed on that account; for before Quarter-
day, I found her at my Chambers in too familiar Conversation
with a young Fellow who was drest like an Officer, but was indeed
a City Apprentice. Instead of excusing her Inconstancy, she
rapped out half a dozen Oaths, and snapping her Fingers at me,
swore she scorned to confine herself to the best Man in *England*.
Upon this we parted, and the same Bawd presently provided her
another Keeper. I was not so much concerned at our Separation,
as I found within a Day or two I had Reason to be for our Meeting: For I was obliged to pay a second Visit to my Surgeon. I was
now forced to do Penance for some Weeks, during which Time
I contracted an Acquaintance with a beautiful young Girl, the
Daughter of a Gentleman, who after having been forty Years
in the Army, and in all the Campaigns under the Duke of *Marl-*

borough,[1] died a Lieutenant on Half-Pay; and had left a Widow with this only Child, in very distrest Circumstances: they had only a small Pension from the Government, with what little the Daughter could add to it by her Work; for she had great Excellence at her Needle. This Girl was, at my first Acquaintance with her, sollicited in Marriage by a young Fellow in good Circumstances. He was Apprentice to a Linen-draper, and had a little Fortune sufficient to set up his Trade. The Mother was greatly pleased with this Match, as indeed she had sufficient Reason. However, I soon prevented it. I represented him in so low a Light to his Mistress, and made so good an Use of Flattery, Promises, and Presents, that, not to dwell longer on this Subject than is necessary, I prevailed with the poor Girl, and convey'd her away from her Mother! In a word, I debauched her.—(At which Words, *Adams* started up, fetch'd three Strides cross the Room, and then replaced himself in his Chair.) You are not more affected with this Part of my Story than myself: I assure you it will never be sufficiently repented of in my own Opinion: But if you already detest it, how much more will your Indignation be raised when you hear the fatal Consequences of this barbarous, this villainous Action? If you please therefore, I will here desist.—'By no means,' cries *Adams*, 'Go on, I beseech you, and Heaven grant you may sincerely repent of this and many other things you have related.' —I was now, continued the Gentleman, as happy as the Possession of a fine young Creature, who had a good Education, and was endued with many agreeable Qualities, could make me. We liv'd some Months with vast Fondness together, without any Company or Conversation more than we found in one another: But this could not continue always; and tho' I still preserved a great Affection for her, I began more and more to want the Relief of other Company, and consequently to leave her by degrees, at last, whole Days to herself. She failed not to testify some

---

[1] John Churchill, first Duke of Marlborough (1650–1722), victorious commander of the British forces against France, 1702–11. In frequent references to the controversial hero of the Whigs, Fielding, whose father had fought under Marlborough at Blenheim and whose mother's family was related to the Churchills by marriage, was adulatory. (See, for example, *Of True Greatness, The Vernoniad, A Journey from This World to the Next* [1. iv], *The True Patriot* [24 December 1745], and *A Proper Answer to a Late Scurrilous Libel* [1747].) In April 1742 Fielding published his *Full Vindication of the Dutchess Dowager of Marlborough,* written in behalf of Sarah, Marlborough's widow, who had herself been active in the Opposition to Walpole.

Uneasiness on these Occasions, and complained of the melancholy
Life she led; to remedy which, I introduced her into the Acquaintance of some other kept Mistresses, with whom she used to play
at Cards, and frequent Plays and other Diversions. She had not
liv'd long in this Intimacy, before I perceived a visible Alteration in her Behaviour; all her Modesty and Innocence vanished
by degrees, till her Mind became thoroughly tainted. She affected
the Company of Rakes, gave herself all manner of Airs, was never
easy but abroad, or when she had a Party at my Chambers. She
was rapacious of Money, extravagant to Excess, loose in her
Conversation; and if ever I demurred to any of her Demands,
Oaths, Tears, and Fits, were the immediate Consequences. As
the first Raptures of Fondness were long since over, this Behaviour
soon estranged my Affections from her; I began to reflect with
pleasure that she was not my Wife, and to conceive an Intention
of parting with her, of which having given her a Hint, she took
care to prevent me the Pains of turning her out of doors, and
accordingly departed herself, having first broken open my Escru-
tore, and taken with her all she could find, to the Amount of
about 200 *l.* In the first Heat of my Resentment, I resolved to
pursue her with all the Vengeance of the Law: But as she had the
good Luck to escape me during that Ferment, my Passion afterwards cooled, and having reflected that I had been the first
Aggressor, and had done her an Injury for which I could make
her no Reparation, by robbing her of the Innocence of her Mind;
and hearing at the same time that the poor old Woman her
Mother had broke her Heart, on her Daughter's Elopement from
her, I, concluding myself her Murderer ('As you very well might,'
cries *Adams*, with a Groan;) was pleased that God Almighty had
taken this Method of punishing me, and resolved quietly to submit to the Loss. Indeed I could wish I had never heard more of
the poor Creature, who became in the end an abandoned Pro-
fligate; and after being some Years a common Prostitute, at last
ended her miserable Life in *Newgate.*—Here the Gentleman
fetch'd a deep Sigh, which Mr. *Adams* echo'd very loudly, and
both continued silent looking on each other for some Minutes.
At last the Gentleman proceeded thus: I had been perfectly constant to this Girl, during the whole Time I kept her: But she
had scarce departed before I discovered more Marks of her
Infidelity to me, than the Loss of my Money. In short, I was

forced to make a third Visit to my Surgeon, out of whose hands
I did not get a hasty Discharge.

I now forswore all future Dealings with the Sex, complained
loudly that the Pleasure did not compensate the Pain, and railed
at the beautiful Creatures, in as gross Language as *Juvenal* himself formerly reviled them in.[1] I looked on all the Town-Harlots
with a Detestation not easy to be conceived, their Persons appeared
to me as painted Palaces inhabited by Disease and Death: Nor
could their Beauty make them more desirable Objects in my
Eyes, than Gilding could make me covet a Pill, or golden Plates
a Coffin. But tho' I was no longer the absolute Slave, I found some
Reasons to own myself still the Subject of Love. My Hatred
for Women decreased daily; and I am not positive but Time
might have betrayed me again to some common Harlot, had I
not been secured by a Passion for the charming *Saphira*; which
having once entered upon, made a violent Progress in my Heart.
Saphira was Wife to a Man of Fashion and Gallantry, and one
who seemed, I own, every way worthy of her Affections, which
however he had not the Reputation of having. She was indeed
a *Coquette achevée*. 'Pray Sir,' says *Adams*, 'What is a Coquette?
I have met with the Word in *French* Authors, but never could
assign any Idea to it. I believe it is the same with *une Sotte*,
Anglicé *a Fool*.' Sir, answer'd the Gentleman, perhaps you are
not much mistaken: but as it is a particular kind of Folly, I will
endeavour to describe it. Were all Creatures to be ranked in the
Order of Creation, according to their Usefulness, I know few
Animals that would not take place of a Coquette; nor indeed hath
this Creature much Pretence to any thing beyond Instinct: for
tho' sometimes we might imagine it was animated by the Passion
of Vanity, yet far the greater part of its Actions fall beneath even
that low Motive; For instance, several absurd Gestures and
Tricks, infinitely more foolish than what can be observed in the
most ridiculous Birds and Beasts, and which would persuade the
Beholder that the silly Wretch was aiming at our Contempt. Indeed its Characteristick is Affectation, and this led and governed
by Whim only: for as Beauty, Wisdom, Wit, Good-nature,

---

[1] An allusion to Juvenal's *Sixth Satire*, a diatribe against women. Part of this satire
Fielding 'Modernised in Burlesque Verse' and included in the *Miscellanies* of 1743. In the
Preface he remarks that this imitation was first sketched out before he was twenty, while he,
like Mr. Wilson, was smarting from an injury done him by a young lady.

Politeness and Health are sometimes affected by this Creature; so
are Ugliness, Folly, Nonsense, Ill-nature, Ill-breeding and Sickness likewise put on by it in their Turn. Its Life is one constant
Lye, and the only Rule by which you can form any Judgment
of them is, that they are never what they seem. If it was possible
for a Coquette to love (as it is not, for if ever it attains this Passion,
the Coquette ceases instantly) it would wear the Face of Indifference if not of hatred to the beloved Object; you may therefore
be assured, when they endeavour to persuade you of their liking,
that they are indifferent to you at least. And indeed this was the
Case of my *Saphira*, who no sooner saw me in the number of her
Admirers, than she gave me what is commonly called Encouragement; she would often look at me, and when she perceived me
meet her Eyes, would instantly take them off, discovering at the
same time as much Surprize and Emotion as possible. These
Arts failed not of the Success she intended; and as I grew more
particular to her than the rest of her Admirers, she advanced in
proportion more directly to me than to the others. She affected
the low Voice, Whisper, Lisp, Sigh, Start, Laugh, and many
other Indications of Passion, which daily deceive thousands.
When I play'd at Whisk with her, she would look earnestly at
me, and at the same time lose Deal or revoke; then burst into a
ridiculous Laugh, and cry, 'La! I can't imagine what I was
thinking of.' To detain you no longer, after I had gone through a
sufficient Course of Gallantry, as I thought, and was thoroughly
convinced I had raised a violent Passion in my Mistress; I sought
an Opportunity of coming to an Eclaircissement with her. She
avoided this as much as possible, however great Assiduity at
length presented me one. I will not describe all the Particulars of
this Interview; let it suffice, that when she could no longer pretend not to see my Drift, she first affected a violent Surprize, and
immediately after as violent a Passion: She wondered what I had
seen in her Conduct, which could induce me to affront her in this
manner: And breaking from me the first Moment she could,
told me, I had no other way to escape the Consequence of her
Resentment, than by never seeing, or at least speaking to her
more. I was not contented with this Answer; I still pursued her,
but to no purpose, and was at length convinced that her Husband
had the sole Possession of her Person, and that neither he nor
any other had made any Impression on her Heart. I was taken

off from following this *Ignis Fatuus* by some Advances which
were made me by the Wife of a Citizen, who tho' neither very
young nor handsome, was yet too agreeable to be rejected by my
amorous Constitution. I accordingly soon satisfy'd her, that she
had not cast away her Hints on a barren or cold Soil; on the
contrary, they instantly produced her an eager and desiring Lover.
Nor did she give me any Reason to complain; she met the
Warmth she had raised with equal Ardour. I had no longer a
Coquette to deal with, but one who was wiser than to prostitute
the noble Passion of Love to the ridiculous Lust of Vanity. We
presently understood one another; and as the Pleasures we sought
lay in a mutual Gratification, we soon found and enjoyed them.
I thought myself at first greatly happy in the possession of this
new Mistress, whose Fondness would have quickly surfeited a
more sickly Appetite, but it had a different Effect on mine; she
carried my Passion higher by it than Youth or Beauty had been
able: But my Happiness could not long continue uninterrupted.
The Apprehensions we lay under from the Jealousy of her Husband, gave us great Uneasiness. 'Poor Wretch! I pity him,'
cry'd *Adams*. He did indeed deserve it, said the Gentleman, for
he loved his Wife with great Tenderness, and I assure you it is a
great Satisfaction to me that I was not the Man who first seduced
her Affections from him. These Apprehensions appeared also too
well grounded; for in the End he discovered us, and procur'd
Witnesses of our Caresses. He then prosecuted me at Law, and
recovered 3000 *l*. Damages, which much distressed my Fortune
to pay: and what was worse, his Wife being divorced, came upon
my hands. I led a very uneasy Life with her; for besides that my
Passion was now much abated, her excessive Jealousy was very
troublesome. At length Death delivered me from an Inconvenience, which the Consideration of my having been the Author of
her Misfortunes, would never suffer me to take any other Method
of discarding.

I now bad adieu to Love, and resolved to pursue other less
dangerous and expensive Pleasures. I fell into the Acquaintance
of a Set of jolly Companions, who slept all Day and drank all
Night: Fellows who might rather be said to consume Time than
to live. Their best Conversation was nothing but Noise: Singing, Hollowing, Wrangling, Drinking, Toasting, Sp—wing,[1]

[1] i.e. spewing.

Smoking, were the chief Ingredients of our Entertainment. And yet bad as these were, they were more tolerable than our graver Scenes, which were either excessive tedious Narratives of dull common Matters of Fact, or hot Disputes about trifling Matters, which commonly ended in a Wager. This Way of Life the first serious Reflection put a period to, and I became Member of a Club frequented by young Men of great Abilities.[1] The Bottle was now only called in to the Assistance of our Conversation, which rolled on the deepest Points of Philosophy. These Gentlemen were engaged in a Search after Truth, in the Pursuit of which they threw aside all the Prejudices of Education, and governed themselves only by the infallible Guide of Human Reason. This

---

[1] In the account of Wilson's club Fielding satirizes the so-called Freethinkers, who are defined as follows by Philomath in *The Covent-Garden Journal* (16 September 1752): 'by a Freethinker I mean a Man who in the Old Testament, as well as in all other Writings, makes use of his Reason as a Guide, and will believe nothing contradictory to that or common Sense, and who does not put faith in Matters he does not comprehend.' Their professed rationalism notwithstanding, the members of Wilson's club subscribe, according to the occasion, to contradictory theories of morality:

(1) The principles that flattered Wilson's opinion of himself and lured him to join the society are those of Shaftesbury, who insisted that by the proper exercise of reason and the cultivation of an innate moral sense, one will love '*Right*, for its own sake, and on the account of its own natural Beauty and Worth' (*An Inquiry concerning Virtue, or Merit*, ι. iii. 1; in *Characteristicks*, 5th ed. [1732], ii. 42); 'Obedience to the Rule of Right', he asserted, is best motivated by one's awareness of '*the Excellence of the Object*, not the *Reward* or *Punishment*' offered by Christianity (*The Moralists*, ii. iii; in ibid. ii. 273). Fielding's best satiric representation of the inadequacy of such Deistic principles as a moral imperative is the character of Square in *Tom Jones*, whose favourite phrase is '*the natural Beauty of Virtue*', and who measures all actions 'by the *unalterable Rule of Right*, and the *eternal Fitness of Things*' (iii. iii).

(2) Used to justify the immoral behaviour of Wilson's club-members, the arguments about the relativity of good and evil and about one's 'Right from Nature' to indulge one's appetites are drawn from Hobbes and Mandeville, those 'Political Philosophers', as Fielding called them in *The Champion* (22 January 1739/40), whose views were diametrically opposed to those of Shaftesbury. In the *Leviathan* Hobbes, discussing the *Jus Naturale*, declared that there is a 'naturall Right of every man to everything' (i. xiv); the words *good* and *evil*, he asserted, 'are ever used with relation to the person that useth them: There being nothing simply and absolutely so; nor any common Rule of Good and Evill, to be taken from the nature of the objects themselves' (i. vi). In *A Search into the Nature of Society* Mandeville similarly observed that 'things are only Good and Evil in reference to something else, and according to the Light and Position they are placed in' (*The Fable of the Bees*, ed. F. B. Kaye [1924], i. 367).

For more extensive satire against such societies of Freethinkers, see *The Covent-Garden Journal* (28 January and 11 February 1752) on the Robinhoodians and the Hell-Fire Club. Fielding's continuing opposition both to the principles and to what he believed to be the pernicious influence of Deism is attested by his ambitious, if unfinished, attempt to refute Bolingbroke's *Essays* in the final year of his life.

great Guide, after having shewn them the Falshood of that very antient but simple Tenet, that there is such a Being as a Deity in the Universe, helped them to establish in his stead a certain *Rule of Right*, by adhering to which they all arrived at the utmost Purity of Morals. Reflection made me as much delighted with this Society, as it had taught me to despise and detest the former. I began now to esteem myself a Being of a higher Order than I had ever before conceived, and was the more charmed with this Rule of Right, as I really found in my own Nature nothing repugnant to it. I held in utter Contempt all Persons who wanted any other Inducement to Virtue besides her intrinsick Beauty and Excellence; and had so high an Opinion of my present Companions, with regard to their Morality, that I would have trusted them with whatever was nearest and dearest to me. Whilst I was engaged in this delightful Dream, two or three Accidents happen'd successively, which at first much surprized me. For, one of our greatest Philosophers, or *Rule of Right-men* withdrew himself from us, taking with him the Wife of one of his most intimate Friends. Secondly, Another of the same Society left the Club without remembring to take leave of his Bail. A third having borrowed a Sum of Money of me, for which I received no Security, when I asked him to repay it, absolutely denied the Loan. These several Practices, so inconsistent with our golden Rule, made me begin to suspect its Infallibility; but when I communicated my Thoughts to one of the Club, he said 'there was nothing absolutely good or evil in itself; that Actions were denominated good or bad by the Circumstances of the Agent. That possibly the Man who ran away with his Neighbour's Wife might be one of very good Inclinations, but over-prevailed on by the Violence of an unruly Passion, and in other Particulars might be a very worthy Member of Society: That if the Beauty of any Woman created in him an Uneasiness, he had a Right from Nature to relieve himself;' with many other things, which I then detested so much, that I took Leave of the Society that very Evening, and never returned to it again. Being now reduced to a State of Solitude, which I did not like, I became a great Frequenter of the Play-houses, which indeed was always my favourite Diversion, and most Evenings past away two or three Hours behind the Scenes, where I met with several Poets, with whom I made Engagements at the Taverns. Some of the Players were likewise of our Parties. At these Meetings we were generally entertain'd by the Poets with reading their Performances, and by the Players with repeating their Parts: Upon which Occasions, I observed the Gentleman who furnished our Entertainment, was commonly the best pleased of the Company; who, tho' they were pretty civil to him to his Face, seldom failed to take the first Opportunity of his Absence to ridicule him. Now I made some Remarks, which probably are too obvious to be worth relating. 'Sir,' says *Adams*, 'your Remarks if you please.' First then, says he, I concluded that the general Observation, that Wits are most inclined to Vanity, is not true. Men are equally vain of Riches, Strength, Beauty, Honours, *&c.* But, these appear of themselves to the Eyes of the Beholders, whereas the poor Wit is obliged to produce his Performance to shew you his Perfection, and on his Readiness to do this that vulgar opinion I have before mentioned is grounded: But doth not the Person who expends vast Sums in the Furniture of his House, or the Ornaments of his Person, who consumes much Time, and employs great Pains in dressing himself, or who thinks himself paid for Self-Denial, Labour, or even Villany by a Title or a Ribbon, sacrifice as much to Vanity as the poor Wit, who is desirous to read you his Poem or his Play? My second Remark was, that Vanity is the worst of Passions, and more apt to contaminate the Mind than any other: For as Selfishness is much more general than we please to allow it, so it is natural to hate and envy those who stand between us and the Good we desire. Now in Lust and Ambition these are few; and even in Avarice we find many who are no Obstacles to our Pursuits; but the vain Man seeks Pre-eminence; and every thing which is excellent or praise-worthy in another, renders him the Mark of his Antipathy. *Adams* now began to fumble in his Pockets, and soon cried out, 'O la! I have it not about me.'—Upon this the Gentleman asking him what he was searching for, he said he searched after a Sermon, which he thought his Master-piece, against Vanity. 'Fie upon it, fie upon it,' cries he, 'why do I ever leave that Sermon out of my Pocket? I wish it was within five Miles, I would willingly fetch it, to read it to you.' The Gentleman answered, that there was no need, for he was cured of the Passion. 'And for that very Reason,' quoth *Adams*, 'I would read it, for I am confident you would admire it: Indeed, I have never been a greater Enemy to any Passion than that silly one of Vanity.' The

Gentleman smiled, and proceeded—From this Society I easily
past to that of the Gamesters, where nothing remarkable happened, but the finishing my Fortune, which those Gentlemen soon
helped me to the End of. This opened Scenes of Life hitherto
unknown; Poverty and Distress with their horrid Train of Duns,
Attorneys, Bailiffs, haunted me Day and Night. My Clothes grew
shabby, my Credit bad, my Friends and Acquaintance of all
kinds cold. In this Situation the strangest Thought imaginable
came into my Head; and what was this, but to write a Play?
for I had sufficient Leisure; Fear of Bailiffs confined me every
Day to my Room; and having always had a little Inclination and
something of a Genius that way, I set myself to work, and within
few Months produced a Piece of five Acts, which was accepted
of at the Theatre. I remembred to have formerly taken Tickets
of other Poets for their Benefits long before the Appearance of
their Performances, and resolving to follow a Precedent, which
was so well suited to my present Circumstances; I immediately
provided myself with a large Number of little Papers. Happy indeed would be the State of Poetry, would these Tickets pass current at the Bakehouse, the Ale-House, and the Chandler's-Shop:
But alas! far otherwise; no Taylor will take them in Payment for Buckram, Stays, Stay-tape; nor no Bailiff for Civility-
Money. They are indeed no more than a Passport to beg with, a
Certificate that the Owner wants five Shillings, which induces
well-disposed Christians to Charity. I now experienced what is
worse than Poverty, or rather what is the worst Consequence of
Poverty, I mean Attendance and Dependance on the Great. Many
a Morning have I waited Hours in the cold Parlours of Men of
Quality, where after seeing the lowest Rascals in Lace and Embroidery, the Pimps and Buffoons in Fashion admitted, I have
been sometimes told on sending in my Name, that my Lord
could not possibly see me this Morning: A sufficient Assurance
that I should never more get entrance into that House. Sometimes I have been at last admitted, and the great Man hath
thought proper to excuse himself, by telling me he was *tied up*.
'*Tied up*,' says *Adams*, 'pray what's that?' Sir, says the Gentleman, the Profit which Booksellers allowed Authors for the best
Works, was so very small, that certain Men of Birth and Fortune
some Years ago, who were the Patrons of Wit and Learning,
thought fit to encourage them farther, by entring into voluntary

Subscriptions for their Encouragement. Thus *Prior, Rowe, Pope,* and some other Men of Genius, received large Sums for their Labours from the Public.[1] This seemed so easy a Method of getting Money, that many of the lowest Scriblers of the Times ventured to publish their Works in the same Way; and many had the Assurance to take in Subscriptions for what was not writ, nor ever intended.[2] Subscriptions in this manner growing infinite, and a kind of Tax on the Public; some Persons finding it not so easy a Task to discern good from bad Authors, or to know what Genius was worthy Encouragement, and what was not, to prevent the Expence of Subscribing to so many, invented a Method to excuse themselves from all Subscriptions whatever; and this was to receive a small Sum of Money in consideration of giving a large one if ever they subscribed; which many have done, and many more have pretended to have done, in order to silence all Sollicitation. The same Method was likewise taken with Play-house Tickets, which were no less a public Grievance; and this is what they call being *tied up* from subscribing. 'I can't say but the Term is apt enough, and somewhat typical,' said *Adams*; 'for a Man of large Fortune, who ties himself up, as you call it, from the Encouragement of Men of Merit, ought to be tied up in reality.' Well, Sir, says the Gentleman, to return to my Story. Sometimes I have received a Guinea from a Man of Quality, given with as ill a Grace as Alms are generally to the meanest Beggar, and purchased too with as much Time spent in Attendance, as, if it had been spent in honest Industry, might have brought me more Profit with infinitely more Satisfaction. After about two Months spent in this disagreeable way with the utmost Mortification, when I was pluming my Hopes on the Prospect

[1] Bernard Lintot published Nicholas Rowe's *Tragedy of Jane Shore* by subscription in 1714. Pope's *Homer*, issued by Lintot in the same manner, earned its author about £9,000. From Jacob Tonson's subscription publication of his *Poems on Several Occasions* in 1719 Matthew Prior received some 4,000 guineas.

[2] By the middle of the century such dishonest practices were bringing this lucrative method of publication into bad repute. Richard Savage's Iscariot Hackney, for example, printed proposals for subscription, received money, and gave receipts, 'without any intention of delivering the book' (*An Author to be Let* [1729], in *Works* [1777], ii. 273). Fielding, who made a handsome profit from the subscription publication of the *Miscellanies* in 1743, severely criticized those who abused the practice: 'there seems at first Sight', he wrote in *The Jacobite's Journal* (30 April 1748), 'to be but little Difference between taking a Purse upon the Highway, and soliciting Subscriptions for Books, which are never intended to be published. . . .' See also the revised version of *The Author's Farce* (II. iv) and *Amelia* (VIII. v).

of a plentiful Harvest from my Play, upon applying to the Prompter to know when it came into Rehearsal, he informed me he had received Orders from the Managers to return me the Play again; for that they could not possibly act it that Season; but if I would take it and revise it against the next, they would be glad to see it again. I snatch'd it from him with great Indignation, and retired to my Room, where I threw myself on the Bed in a Fit of Despair—'You should rather have thrown yourself on your Knees,' says *Adams*; 'for Despair is sinful.' As soon, continued the Gentleman, as I had indulged the first Tumult of my Passion, I began to consider coolly what Course I should take, in a Situation without Friends, Money, Credit or Reputation of any kind. After revolving many things in my Mind, I could see no other Possibility of furnishing myself with the miserable Necessaries of Life than to retire to a Garret near the *Temple*, and commence Hackney-writer to the Lawyers; for which I was well qualify'd, being an excellent Penman. This Purpose I resolved on, and immediately put it in execution. I had an Acquaintance with an Attorney who had formerly transacted Affairs for me, and to him I applied: But instead of furnishing me with any Business, he laugh'd at my Undertaking, and told me 'he was afraid I should turn his Deeds into Plays, and he should expect to see them on the Stage.' Not to tire you with Instances of this kind from others, I found that *Plato* himself did not hold Poets in greater Abhorrence[1] than these Men of Business do. Whenever I durst venture to a Coffee-house, which was on *Sundays* only,[2] a Whisper ran round the Room, which was constantly attended with a Sneer —*That's Poet Wilson*: for I know not whether you have observed it, but there is a Malignity in the Nature of Man, which when not weeded out, or at least covered by a good Education and Politeness, delights in making another uneasy or dissatisfied with himself. This abundantly appears in all Assemblies, except those which are filled by People of Fashion, and especially among the younger People of both Sexes, whose Birth and Fortunes place them just without the polite Circles; I mean the lower Class of

---

[1] In discussing the education of the Guardians in *The Republic,* Plato recommended the strict censorship of poetry, which lied about the nature of the gods and appealed to the emotions rather than to the intellect.

[2] Sunday arrests were unlawful, except for treason, felony, or breach of the peace. (29 Charles II, cap. 7.)

the Gentry, and the higher of the mercantile World, who are in reality the worst bred part of Mankind. Well, Sir, whilst I continued in this miserable State, with scarce sufficient Business to keep me from starving, the Reputation of a Poet being my Bane, I accidentally became acquainted with a Bookseller, who told me 'it was a Pity a Man of my Learning and Genius should be obliged to such a Method of getting his Livelihood; that he had a Compassion for me, and if I would engage with him, he would undertake to provide handsomely for me.' A Man in my Circumstances, as he very well knew, had no Choice. I accordingly accepted his Proposal with his Conditions, which were none of the most favourable, and fell to translating with all my Might. I had no longer reason to lament the want of Business; for he furnished me with so much, that in half a Year I almost writ myself blind. I likewise contracted a Distemper by my sedentary Life, in which no part of my Body was exercised but my right Arm, which rendered me incapable of writing for a long time. This unluckily happening to delay the Publication of a Work, and my last Performance not having sold well, the Bookseller declined any further Engagement, and aspersed me to his Brethren as a careless, idle Fellow. I had however, by having half-work'd and half-starv'd myself to death during the Time I was in his Service, saved a few Guineas, with which I bought a Lottery-Ticket, resolving to throw myself into Fortune's Lap,[1] and try if she would make me amends for the Injuries she had done me at the Gaming-Table. This Purchase being made left me almost pennyless; when, as if I had not been sufficiently miserable, a Bailiff in Woman's Clothes got Admittance to my Chamber, whither he was directed by the Bookseller. He arrested me at my Taylor's

---

[1] From 1694 to 1826 state lotteries were held at intervals to raise money for such purposes as the construction of Westminster Bridge and the establishment of the British Museum. This system, which encouraged gambling even among the poor and which led to profiteering by unscrupulous ticket-mongers, was satirized by Fielding, especially in his ballad-opera, *The Lottery* (1732), and in *The Champion*, 3 January 1739/40.

In 1741 draws for the Westminster Bridge lottery began at Stationers' Hall on 23 November and ended on 29 December (*The Champion*, 24 November and 31 December); they were attacked by the Opposition as 'a Sort of *State-Traps* set up to catch necessitous and unwary People with the Hopes of golden Mountains' (*The Craftsman*, 28 November; see also *The Champion*, 24 December). Mr. Wilson's comparison of the lottery to Dame Fortune was of course familiar: one ticket-seller offered his customers gratis '*exceeding beautiful Schemes of the Lottery, and a Copper-plate Picture, representing* Fortune *throwing a* BAG OF GOLD, amongst the *Adventurers, who buy Tickets at his Office*'. (*The Craftsman*, 28 November 1741.)

Suit, for thirty-five Pounds; a Sum for which I could not procure
Bail, and was therefore conveyed to his House, where I was locked
up in an upper Chamber.[1] I had now neither Health (for I was
scarce recovered from my Indisposition) Liberty, Money, or
Friends; and had abandoned all Hopes, and even the Desire of
Life. 'But this could not last long,' said *Adams*, 'for doubtless the
Taylor released you the moment he was truly acquainted with
your Affairs; and knew that your Circumstances would not permit you to pay him.' Oh, Sir, answered the Gentleman, he knew
that before he arrested me; nay, he knew that nothing but Incapacity could prevent me paying my Debts; for I had been his
Customer many Years, had spent vast Sums of Money with him,
and had always paid most punctually in my prosperous Days:
But when I reminded him of this, with Assurances that if he would
not molest my Endeavours, I would pay him all the Money I
could, by my utmost Labour and Industry, procure, reserving
only what was sufficient to preserve me alive: He answered, His
Patience was worn out; that I had put him off from time to time;
that he wanted the Money; that he had put it into a Lawyer's
hands; and if I did not pay him immediately, or find Security,
I must lie in Goal and expect no Mercy. 'He may expect Mercy,'
cries *Adams* starting from his Chair, 'where he will find none.
How can such a Wretch repeat the Lord's Prayer, where the
Word which is translated, I know not for what Reason, *Tres-
passes*, is in the Original *Debts*? And as surely as we do not forgive
others their Debts when they are unable to pay them; so surely
shall we ourselves be unforgiven, when we are in no condition of
paying.' He ceased, and the Gentleman proceeded. While I was
in this deplorable Situation a former Acquaintance, to whom I

---

[1] The practice of imprisonment for debt was a feature of English law (and inhumanity)
that Fielding attacked often and severely. The best gloss on the passage in *Joseph Andrews*
is an impassioned leader appearing in *The True Patriot* for 3 December 1745: there Fielding
distinguishes between two kinds of debtors—those whose debts are the result of extravagance
and fraud, and those who are merely unfortunate and willing to repay their creditors; to
prosecute the latter, to 'add Chains to Poverty, and rob those of the Benefit of wholesome
Air who have scarce any other Food or Comfort', serves only to gratify a malicious appetite
for revenge, and is an outrage against Christianity for which the creditor, as Parson Adams
had earlier warned, 'must himself contract so bitter a Debt to the Justice of an avenging
GOD'. See also *The Champion* (16 and 19 February 1739/40); *Of Good-Nature*; *Jonathan
Wild* (I. iv); *A Journey from This World to the Next* (I. xxii—where tailors, one of whom
imprisoned Mr. Wilson, are satirized for prosecuting debtors); *The Jacobite's Journal* (26
December 1747 and 14 May 1748); *Tom Jones* (VII. iii); and *Amelia* (VIII. i–ii).

had communicated my Lottery-Ticket, found me out, and making me a Visit with great Delight in his Countenance, shook me heartily by the Hand, and wished me Joy of my good Fortune: 'For,' says he, 'your Ticket is come up a Prize of 3000 *l.*' *Adams* snapt his Fingers at these Words in an Ecstasy of Joy; which however did not continue long: For the Gentleman thus proceeded. Alas! Sir, this was only a Trick of Fortune to sink me the deeper: For I had disposed of this Lottery-Ticket two Days before to a Relation, who refused lending me a Shilling without it, in order to procure myself Bread. As soon as my Friend was acquainted with my unfortunate Sale, he began to revile me, and remind me of all the ill Conduct and Miscarriages of my Life. He said, 'I was one whom Fortune could not save, if she would; that I was now ruined without any Hopes of Retrieval, nor must expect any Pity from my Friends; that it would be extreme Weakness to compassionate the Misfortunes of a Man who ran headlong to his own Destruction.' He then painted to me in as lively Colours as he was able, the Happiness I should have now enjoyed, had I not foolishly disposed of my Ticket. I urg'd the Plea of Necessity: But he made no Answer to that, and began again to revile me, till I could bear it no longer, and desired him to finish his Visit. I soon exchanged the Bailiff's House for a Prison; where, as I had not Money sufficient to procure me a separate Apartment, I was crouded in with a great number of miserable Wretches, in common with whom I was destitute of every Convenience of Life, even that which all the Brutes enjoy, wholesome Air. In these dreadful Circumstances I applied by Letter to several of my old Acquaintance, and such to whom I had formerly lent Money without any great Prospect of its being returned, for their Assistance; but in vain. An Excuse instead of a Denial was the gentlest Answer I received.—Whilst I languished in a Condition too horrible to be described, and which in a Land of Humanity, and, what is much more Christianity, seems a strange Punishment for a little Inadvertency and Indiscretion. Whilst I was in this Condition, a Fellow came into the Prison, and enquiring me out deliver'd me the following Letter:

Sir,

   My Father, to whom you sold your Ticket in the last Lottery, died the same Day in which it came up a Prize, as you have possibly heard, and left me sole Heiress of all his Fortune. I am so much touched with your present Circumstances, and the Uneasiness you must feel at having been driven to dispose of what might have made you happy, that I must desire your Acceptance of the inclosed, and am

Your humble Servant,

Harriet Hearty

And what do you think was inclosed? 'I don't know,' cried *Adams*: 'Not less than a Guinea, I hope.'—Sir, it was a Bank-Note for 200 *l.*—'200 *l.*!' says *Adams*, in a Rapture.—No less, I assure you, answered the Gentleman; a Sum I was not half so delighted with, as with the dear Name of the generous Girl that sent it me; and who was not only the best, but the handsomest Creature in the Universe; and for whom I had long had a Passion, which I never durst disclose to her. I kiss'd her Name a thousand times, my Eyes overflowing with Tenderness and Gratitude, I repeated—. But not to detain you with these Raptures, I immediately acquired my Liberty, and having paid all my Debts, departed with upwards of fifty Pounds in my Pocket, to thank my kind Deliverer. She happened to be then out of Town, a Circumstance which, upon Reflection, pleased me; for by that means I had an Opportunity to appear before her in a more decent Dress. At her Return to Town within a Day or two, I threw myself at her Feet with the most ardent Acknowledgments, which she rejected with an unfeigned Greatness of Mind, and told me, I could not oblige her more than by never mentioning, or if possible, thinking on a Circumstance which must bring to my Mind an Accident that might be grievous to me to think on. She proceeded thus: 'What I have done is in my own eyes a Trifle, and perhaps infinitely less than would have become me to do. And if you think of engaging in any Business, where a larger Sum may be serviceable to you, I shall not be over-rigid, either as to the Security or Interest.' I endeavoured to express all the Gratitude in my power to this Profusion of Goodness, tho' perhaps it was my Enemy, and began to afflict my Mind with more Agonies, than all the Miseries I had underwent; it affected me with severer Reflections than Poverty, Distress, and Prisons united had been able to make me feel: For, Sir, these Acts and Professions of Kindness, which were sufficient to have raised in a good Heart the most violent Passion of Friendship to one of the

same, or to Age and Ugliness in a different Sex, came to me
from a Woman, a young and beautiful Woman, one whose Perfections I had long known; and for whom I had long conceived
a violent Passion, tho' with a Despair, which made me endeavour
rather to curb and conceal, than to nourish or acquaint her with
it. In short, they came upon me united with Beauty, Softness, and
Tenderness, such bewitching Smiles.——O Mr. *Adams*, in that
Moment, I lost myself, and forgetting our different Situations,
nor considering what Return I was making to her Goodness, by
desiring her who had given me so much, to bestow her All,
I laid gently hold on her Hand, and conveying it to my Lips,
I prest it with inconceivable Ardour; then lifting up my swimming
Eyes, I saw her Face and Neck overspread with one Blush; she
offered to withdraw her Hand, yet not so as to deliver it from
mine, tho' I held it with the gentlest Force. We both stood
trembling, her Eyes cast on the ground, and mine stedfastly
fixed on her. Good G——, what was then the Condition of my
Soul! burning with Love, Desire, Admiration, Gratitude, and
every tender Passion, all bent on one charming Object. Passion
at last got the better of both Reason and Respect, and softly
letting go her Hand, I offered madly to clasp her in my Arms;
when a little recovering herself, she started from me, asking me
with some Shew of Anger, 'if she had any Reason to expect this
Treatment from me.' I then fell prostrate before her, and told
her, 'if I had offended, my Life was absolutely in her power,
which I would in any manner lose for her sake. Nay, Madam,
(said I) you shall not be so ready to punish me, as I to suffer.
I own my Guilt. I detest the Reflection that I would have sacrificed your Happiness to mine. Believe me, I sincerely repent my
Ingratitude, yet believe me too, it was my Passion, my unbounded
Passion for you, which hurried me so far; I have loved you
long and tenderly; and the Goodness you have shewn me, hath
innocently weighed down a Wretch undone before. Acquit me
of all mean mercenary Views, and before I take my Leave of you
for ever, which I am resolved instantly to do, believe me, that
Fortune could have raised me to no height to which I could not
have gladly lifted you. O curst be Fortune.'——'Do not,' says she,
interrupting me with the sweetest Voice, 'Do not curse Fortune,
since she hath made me happy, and if she hath put your Happiness in my power, I have told you, you shall ask nothing in

Reason which I will refuse.' 'Madam,' said I, 'you mistake me if you imagine, as you seem, my Happiness is in the power of Fortune now. You have obliged me too much already; if I have any Wish, it is for some blest Accident, by which I may contribute with my Life to the least Augmentation of your Felicity. As for my self, the only Happiness I can ever have, will be hearing of your's; and if Fortune will make that complete, I will forgive her all her Wrongs to me.' 'You may, indeed,' answered she, smiling, 'For your own Happiness must be included in mine. I have long known your Worth; nay, I must confess,' said she, blushing, 'I have long discovered that Passion for me you profess, notwithstanding those Endeavours which I am convinced were unaffected, to conceal it; and if all I can give with Reason will not suffice,—take Reason away,—and now I believe you cannot ask me what I will deny.'—She uttered these Words with a Sweetness not to be imagined. I immediately started, my Blood which lay freezing at my Heart, rushed tumultuously through every Vein. I stood for a Moment silent, then flying to her, I caught her in my Arms, no longer resisting,—and softly told her, she must give me then herself.—O Sir,—Can I describe her Look? She remained silent and almost motionless several Minutes. At last, recovering herself a little, she insisted on my leaving her, and in such a manner that I instantly obeyed: You may imagine, however, I soon saw her again.—But I ask pardon, I fear I have detained you too long in relating the Particulars of the former Interview. 'So far otherwise,' said *Adams*, licking his Lips, 'that I could willingly hear it over again.' Well, Sir, continued the Gentleman, to be as concise as possible, within a Week she consented to make me the happiest of Mankind. We were married shortly after; and when I came to examine the Circumstances of my Wife's Fortune; (which I do assure you I was not presently at Leisure enough to do) I found it amounted to about six thousand Pounds, most part of which lay in Effects; for her Father had been a Wine-Merchant, and she seemed willing, if I liked it, that I should carry on the same Trade. I readily and too inconsiderately undertook it: For not having been bred up to the Secrets of the Business, and endeavouring to deal with the utmost Honesty and Uprightness, I soon found our Fortune in a declining Way, and my Trade decreasing by little and little: For my Wines which I never adulterated after their Importation, and were sold as neat as they came over, were universally decried by the Vintners, to whom I could not allow them quite as cheap as those who gained double the Profit by a less Price. I soon began to despair of improving our Fortune by these means; nor was I at all easy at the Visits and Familiarity of many who had been my Acquaintance in my Prosperity, but denied, and shunned me in my Adversity, and now very forwardly renewed their Acquaintance with me. In short, I had sufficiently seen, that the Pleasures of the World are chiefly Folly, and the Business of it mostly Knavery; and both, nothing better than Vanity: The Men of Pleasure tearing one another to pieces, from the Emulation of spending Money, and the Men of Business from Envy in getting it. My Happiness consisted entirely in my Wife, whom I loved with an inexpressible Fondness, which was perfectly returned; and my Prospects were no other than to provide for our growing Family; for she was now big of her second Child; I therefore took an Opportunity to ask her Opinion of entering into a retired Life, which after hearing my Reasons, and perceiving my Affection for it, she readily embraced. We soon put our small Fortune, now reduced under three thousand Pounds, into Money, with part of which we purchased this little Place, whither we retired soon after her Delivery, from a World full of Bustle, Noise, Hatred, Envy, and Ingratitude, to Ease, Quiet, and Love. We have here liv'd almost twenty Years, with little other Conversation than our own, most of the Neighbourhood taking us for very strange People; the Squire of the Parish representing me as a Madman, and the Parson as a Presbyterian; because I will not hunt with the one, nor drink with the other. 'Sir,' says *Adams*, 'Fortune hath I think paid you all her Debts in this sweet Retirement.' Sir, replied the Gentleman, I am thankful to the great Author of all Things for the Blessings I here enjoy. I have the best of Wives, and three pretty Children, for whom I have the true Tenderness of a Parent; but no Blessings are pure in this World. Within three Years of my Arrival here I lost my eldest Son. (*Here he sighed bitterly.*) 'Sir,' says *Adams*, 'we must submit to Providence, and consider Death is common to all.' We must submit, indeed, answered the Gentleman; and if he had died, I could have borne the Loss with Patience: But alas! Sir, he was stolen away from my Door by some wicked travelling People whom they call *Gipsies*; nor could I ever with the most diligent

Search recover him. Poor Child! he had the sweetest Look, the exact Picture of his Mother; at which some Tears unwittingly dropt from his Eyes, as did likewise from those of *Adams*, who always sympathized with his Friends on those Occasions. Thus, Sir, said the Gentleman, I have finished my Story, in which if I have been too particular, I ask your Pardon; and now, if you please, I will fetch you another Bottle; which Proposal the Parson thankfully accepted.

CHAPTER IV

A Description of Mr. Wilson's *Way of Living. The*
tragical Adventure of the Dog, and other
grave Matters.

THE Gentleman returned with the Bottle, and *Adams* and he sat some time silent, when the former started up and cried, '*No, that won't do.*' The Gentleman enquired into his Meaning; he answered, 'he had been considering that it was possible the late famous King *Theodore*[1] might have been that very Son whom he lost;' but added, 'that his Age could not answer that Imagination. However,' says he, 'G— disposes all things for the best, and very probably he may be some Great Man, or Duke, and may one day or other revisit you in that Capacity.' The Gentleman answered, he should know him amongst ten thousand, for he had a Mark on his left Breast, of a Strawberry, which his Mother had given him by longing for that Fruit.

That beautiful young Lady, the *Morning*, now rose from her Bed, and with a Countenance blooming with fresh Youth and Sprightliness, like Miss *—, with soft Dews hanging on her pouting Lips, began to take her early Walk over the eastern Hills; and presently after, that gallant Person the Sun stole softly from his Wife's Chamber to pay his Addresses to her; when the

* *Whoever the Reader pleases.*

[1] Theodore Stephen, Baron von Neuhof (1686–1756), a German adventurer, crowned as Theodore I of Corsica in 1736, but expelled by the Genoese in 1738. He fled to England, where he was imprisoned for debt but eventually released and supported by benefactors for the rest of his life. See also *The Historical Register for the Year 1736* (I. i).

Gentleman ask'd his Guest if he would walk forth and survey his little Garden, which he readily agreed to, and *Joseph* at the same time awaking from a Sleep in which he had been two Hours buried, went with them. No Parterres, no Fountains, no Statues embellished this little Garden. Its only Ornament was a short Walk, shaded on each side by a Filbert Hedge, with a small Alcove at one end, whither in hot Weather the Gentleman and his Wife used to retire and divert themselves with their Children, who played in the Walk before them: But tho' Vanity had no Votary in this little Spot, here was variety of Fruit, and every thing useful for the Kitchin, which was abundantly sufficient to catch the Admiration of *Adams*, who told the Gentleman he had certainly a good Gardener. Sir, answered he, that Gardener is now before you; whatever you see here, is the Work solely of my own Hands. Whilst I am providing Necessaries for my Table, I like-wise procure myself an Appetite for them. In fair Seasons I seldom pass less than six Hours of the twenty-four in this Place, where I am not idle, and by these means I have been able to pre-serve my Health ever since my Arrival here without Assistance from Physick. Hither I generally repair at the Dawn, and exer-cise myself whilst my Wife dresses her Children, and prepares our Breakfast, after which we are seldom asunder during the residue of the Day; for when the Weather will not permit them to accompany me here, I am usually within with them; for I am neither ashamed of conversing with my Wife, nor of playing with my Children: to say the Truth, I do not perceive that Inferiority of Understanding which the Levity of Rakes, the Dulness of Men of Business, or the Austerity of the Learned would persuade us of in Women. As for my Woman, I declare I have found none of my own Sex capable of making juster Observations on Life, or of delivering them more agreeably; nor do I believe any one possessed of a faithfuller or braver Friend. And sure as this Friendship is sweetened with more Delicacy and Tenderness, so is it confirmed by dearer Pledges than can attend the closest male Alliance: For what Union can be so fast, as our common Interest in the Fruits of our Embraces? Perhaps, Sir, you are not yourself a Father; if you are not, be assured you cannot conceive the Delight I have in my Little-Ones. Would you not despise me, if you saw me stretched on the Ground, and my Children playing round me? 'I should reverence the Sight,' quoth *Adams*, 'I myself

am now the Father of six, and have been of eleven, and I can say
I never scourged a Child of my own, unless as his School-master,
and then have felt every Stroke on my own Posteriors. And as
to what you say concerning Women, I have often lamented my
own Wife did not understand *Greek*.'—The Gentleman smiled,
and answered, he would not be apprehended to insinuate that his
own had an Understanding above the Care of her Family, on the
contrary, says he, my *Harriet* I assure you is a notable Housewife, and the House-keepers of few Gentlemen understand
Cookery or Confectionary better; but these are Arts which she
hath no great Occasion for now: however, the Wine you commended so much last Night at Supper, was of her own making,
as is indeed all the Liquor in my House, except my Beer, which
falls to my Province. ('And I assure you it is as excellent,' quoth
Adams, 'as ever I tasted.') We formerly kept a Maid-Servant,
but since my Girls have been growing up, she is unwilling to
indulge them in Idleness; for as the Fortunes I shall give them
will be very small, we intend not to breed them above the Rank
they are likely to fill hereafter, nor to teach them to despise or ruin
a plain Husband. Indeed I could wish a Man of my own Temper,
and a retired Life, might fall to their Lot: for I have experienced
that calm serene Happiness which is seated in Content, is inconsistent with the Hurry and Bustle of the World. He was proceeding thus, when the Little Things, being just risen, ran eagerly
towards him, and asked him Blessing: They were shy to the
Strangers, but the eldest acquainted her Father that her Mother
and the young Gentlewoman were up, and that Breakfast was
ready. They all went in, where the Gentleman was surprized at
the Beauty of *Fanny*, who had now recovered herself from her
Fatigue, and was entirely clean drest; for the Rogues who had
taken away her Purse, had left her her Bundle. But if he was so
much amazed at the Beauty of this young Creature, his Guests
were no less charmed at the Tenderness which appeared in the
Behaviour of Husband and Wife to each other, and to their Children, and at the dutiful and affectionate Behaviour of these to their
Parents. These Instances pleased the well-disposed Mind of
Adams equally with the Readiness which they exprest to oblige
their Guests, and their Forwardness to offer them the best of
every thing in their House; and what delighted him still more,
was an Instance or two of their Charity: for whilst they were at

Breakfast, the good Woman was called forth to assist her sick Neighbour, which she did with some Cordials made for the public Use; and the good Man went into his Garden at the same time, to supply another with something which he wanted thence, for they had nothing which those who wanted it were not welcome to. These good People were in the utmost Cheerfulness, when they heard the Report of a Gun, and immediately afterwards a little Dog, the Favourite of the eldest Daughter, came limping in all bloody, and laid himself at his Mistress's Feet: The poor Girl, who was about eleven Years old, burst into Tears at the sight, and presently one of the Neighbours came in and informed them, that the young Squire, the Son of the Lord of the Manor, had shot him as he past by, swearing at the same time he would prosecute the Master of him for keeping a Spaniel; for that he had given Notice he would not suffer one in the Parish. The Dog, whom his Mistress had taken into her Lap, died in a few Minutes, licking her Hand. She exprest great Agony at his Loss, and the other Children began to cry for their Sister's Misfortune, nor could *Fanny* herself refrain. Whilst the Father and Mother attempted to comfort her, *Adams* grasped his Crab Stick, and would have sallied out after the Squire, had not *Joseph* with-held him. He could not however bridle his Tongue—He pronounced the Word *Rascal* with great Emphasis, said he deserved to be hanged more than a Highwayman, and wish'd he had the scourging him. The Mother took her Child, lamenting and carrying the dead Favourite in her Arms out of the Room, when the Gentleman said, this was the second time this Squire had endeavoured to kill the little Wretch, and had wounded him smartly once before, adding, he could have no Motive but Ill-nature; for the little thing, which was not near as big as one's Fist, had never been twenty Yards from the House in the six Years his Daughter had had it. He said he had done nothing to deserve this Usage: but his Father had too great a Fortune to contend with. That he was as absolute as any Tyrant in the Universe, and had killed all the Dogs, and taken away all the Guns in the Neighbourhood, and not only that, but he trampled down Hedges, and rode over Corn and Gardens, with no more Regard than if they were the Highway. 'I wish I could catch him in my Garden,' said *Adams*; 'tho' I would rather forgive him riding through my House than such an ill-natur'd Act as this.'

The Cheerfulness of their Conversation being interrupted by this Accident, in which the Guests could be of no service to their kind Entertainer, and as the Mother was taken up in administring Consolation to the poor Girl, whose Disposition was too good hastily to forget the sudden Loss of her little Favourite, which had been fondling with her a few Minutes before; and as *Joseph* and *Fanny* were impatient to get home and begin those previous Ceremonies to their Happiness which *Adams* had insisted on, they now offered to take their Leave. The Gentleman importuned them much to stay Dinner: but when he found their Eagerness to depart, he summoned his Wife, and accordingly having performed all the usual Ceremonies of Bows and Curtsies, more pleasant to be seen than to be related, they took their Leave, the Gentleman and his Wife heartily wishing them a good Journey, and they as heartily thanking them for their kind Entertainment. They then departed, *Adams* declaring that this was the Manner in which the People had lived in the Golden Age.

CHAPTER V

A Disputation on Schools, held on the Road between
Mr. Abraham Adams *and* Joseph; *and a Discovery*
not unwelcome to them both.

O u r Travellers having well refreshed themselves at the Gentleman's House, *Joseph* and *Fanny* with Sleep, and Mr. *Abraham Adams* with Ale and Tobacco, renewed their Journey with great Alacrity; and, pursuing the Road in which they were directed, travelled many Miles before they met with any Adventure worth relating. In this Interval, we shall present our Readers with a very curious Discourse, as we apprehend it, concerning public Schools, which pass'd between Mr. *Joseph Andrews* and Mr. *Abraham Adams.*

They had not gone far, before *Adams* calling to *Joseph*, asked him if he had attended to the Gentleman's Story; he answered, 'to all the former Part.' 'And don't you think,' says he, 'he was a very unhappy Man in his Youth?' 'A very unhappy Man indeed,' answered the other. '*Joseph*,' cries *Adams*, screwing up his Mouth,

'I have found it; I have discovered the Cause of all the Misfortunes which befel him. A public School, *Joseph*, was the Cause of all the Calamities which he afterwards suffered. Public Schools are the Nurseries of all Vice and Immorality. All the wicked Fellows whom I remember at the University were bred at them. —Ah Lord! I can remember as well as if it was but yesterday, a Knot of them; they called them King's Scholars,[1] I forget why— very wicked Fellows! *Joseph*, you may thank the Lord you were not bred at a public School, you would never have preserved your Virtue as you have. The first Care I always take, is of a Boy's Morals, I had rather he should be a Blockhead than an Atheist or a Presbyterian. What is all the Learning of the World compared to his immortal Soul? What shall a Man take in exchange for his Soul? But the Masters of great Schools trouble themselves about no such thing. I have known a Lad of eighteen at the University, who hath not been able to say his Catechism; but for my own part, I always scourged a Lad sooner for missing that than any other Lesson. Believe me, Child, all that Gentleman's Misfortunes arose from his being educated at a public School.'

'It doth not become me,' answer'd *Joseph*, 'to dispute any thing, Sir, with you, especially a matter of this kind; for to be sure you must be allowed by all the World to be the best Teacher of a School in all our County.' 'Yes, that,' says *Adams*, 'I believe, is granted me; that I may without much Vanity pretend to—nay I believe I may go to the next County too—but *gloriari non est meum*.'[2]—'However, Sir, as you are pleased to bid me speak,' says *Joseph*, 'you know, my late Master, Sir *Thomas Booby*, was bred at a public School, and he was the finest Gentleman in all the Neighbourhood. And I have often heard him say, if he had a hundred Boys he would breed them all at the same Place. It was his Opinion, and I have often heard him deliver it, that a Boy taken from a public School, and carried into the World, will learn more in one Year there, than one of a private Education will in five. He used to say, the School itself initiated him a great way, (I remember that was his very Expression) for great Schools are little Societies, where a Boy of any Observation may see in

---

[1] Scholars on the foundation at Westminster who attend either Christ Church, Oxford, or Trinity College, Cambridge. Adams probably refers to Oxford, since that was the university of his original, the Reverend William Young. (See Introduction, p. xxi, n. 2.)

[2] 'It is not for me to boast.'

Epitome what he will afterwards find in the World at large.' '*Hinc illæ lachrymæ*;[1] for that very Reason,' quoth *Adams*, 'I prefer a private School, where Boys may be kept in Innocence and Ignorance: for, according to that fine Passage in the Play of *Cato*, the only *English* Tragedy I ever read,

> *If Knowledge of the World must make Men Villains,*
> *May* Juba *ever live in Ignorance.*[2]

Who would not rather preserve the Purity of his Child, than wish him to attain the whole Circle of Arts and Sciences; which, by the bye, he may learn in the Classes of a private School? for I would not be vain, but I esteem myself to be second to none, *nulli secundum*, in teaching these things; so that a Lad may have as much Learning in a private as in a public Education.' 'And with Submission,' answered *Joseph*, 'he may get as much Vice, witness several Country Gentlemen, who were educated within five Miles of their own Houses, and are as wicked as if they had known the World from their Infancy. I remember when I was in the Stable, if a young Horse was vicious in his Nature, no Correction would make him otherwise; I take it to be equally the same among Men: if a Boy be of a mischievous wicked Inclination, no School, tho' ever so private, will ever make him good; on the contrary, if he be of a righteous Temper, you may trust him to *London*, or wherever else you please, he will be in no danger of being corrupted. Besides, I have often heard my Master say, that the Discipline practised in public Schools was much better than that in private.' —'You talk like a Jackanapes,' says *Adams*, 'and so did your Master. Discipline indeed! because one Man scourges twenty or thirty Boys more in a Morning than another, is he therefore a better Disciplinarian? I do presume to confer in this Point with all who have taught from *Chiron's* time to this Day; and, if I was Master of six Boys only, I would preserve as good Discipline amongst them as the Master of the greatest School in the World. I say nothing, young Man; remember, I say nothing; but if Sir *Thomas* himself had been educated nearer home, and under the Tuition of somebody, remember, I name nobody, it might have been better for him—but his Father must institute him in the

---

[1] 'Hence proceed all those tears' (Horace, *Epistles*, I. xix. 41).

[2] Adams slightly alters Juba's reply to Syphax in Addison's *Cato*, II. v: 'If Knowledge of the World makes Man perfidious, / May *Juba* ever live in Ignorance!'

Knowledge of the World. *Nemo mortalium omnibus horis sapit.*[1]
Joseph seeing him run on in this manner asked pardon many
times, assuring him he had no Intention to offend. 'I believe you
had not, Child,' said he, 'and I am not angry with you: but for
maintaining good Discipline in a School; for this,——' And then
he ran on as before, named all the Masters who are recorded in
old Books, and preferred himself to them all. Indeed if this good
Man had an Enthusiasm, or what the Vulgar call a Blind-side, it
was this: He thought a Schoolmaster the greatest Character in
the World, and himself the greatest of all Schoolmasters, neither
of which Points he would have given up to *Alexander the Great*
at the Head of his Army.[2]

Adams continued his Subject till they came to one of the
beautifullest Spots of Ground in the Universe. It was a kind of
natural Amphitheatre, formed by the winding of a small Rivulet,
which was planted with thick Woods, and the Trees rose gradually above each other by the natural Ascent of the Ground they
stood on; which Ascent, as they hid with their Boughs, they
seemed to have been disposed by the Design of the most skillful
Planter. The Soil was spread with a Verdure which no Paint
could imitate, and the whole Place might have raised romantic
Ideas in elder Minds than those of *Joseph* and *Fanny*, without the
Assistance of Love.

Here they arrived about Noon, and *Joseph* proposed to *Adams*
that they should rest a while in this delightful Place, and refresh
themselves with some Provisions which the Good-nature of Mrs.
Wilson had provided them with. *Adams* made no Objection to the
Proposal, so down they sat, and pulling out a cold Fowl, and
a Bottle of Wine, they made a Repast with a Cheerfulness which
might have attracted the Envy of more splendid Tables. I should
not omit, that they found among their Provision a little Paper,
containing a piece of Gold, which *Adams* imagining had been put
there by mistake, would have returned back, to restore it; but he
was at last convinced by *Joseph*, that Mr. *Wilson* had taken this
handsome way of furnishing them with a Supply for their Jour-

---

[1] 'No man is wise all the time' (Pliny, *Natural History*, VII. xl. 131).

[2] An allusion to Diogenes' proud defiance of Alexander at Corinth. (See Cicero, *Tusculan Disputations*, v. xxxii. 92.) This famous confrontation between philosopher and conqueror, both of whom were in Fielding's view guilty of pride, is commented upon in *Of True Greatness* and dramatized at length in *A Dialogue between Alexander the Great and Diogenes the Cynic*, included in Fielding's *Miscellanies*.

ney, on his having related the Distress which they had been in, when they were relieved by the Generosity of the Pedlar. *Adams* said, he was glad to see such an Instance of Goodness, not so much for the Conveniency which it brought them, as for the sake of the Doer, whose Reward would be great in Heaven.[1] He likewise comforted himself with a Reflection, that he should shortly have an Opportunity of returning it him; for the Gentleman was within a Week to make a Journey into *Somersetshire*, to pass through *Adams's* Parish, and had faithfully promised to call on him: A Circumstance which we thought too immaterial to mention before; but which those who have as great an Affection for that Gentleman as ourselves will rejoice at, as it may give them Hopes of seeing him again. Then *Joseph* made a Speech on Charity, which the Reader, if he is so disposed, may see in the next Chapter; for we scorn to betray him into any such Reading, without first giving him Warning.

CHAPTER VI

Moral Reflections by Joseph Andrews, *with the Hunting Adventure, and Parson* Adams's *miraculous Escape.*

'I have often wondered, Sir,' said *Joseph*, 'to observe so few Instances of Charity among Mankind; for tho' the Goodness of a Man's Heart did not incline him to relieve the Distresses of his Fellow-Creatures, methinks the Desire of Honour should move him to it.[2] What inspires a Man to build fine Houses, to purchase fine Furniture, Pictures, Clothes, and other things at a great Expence, but an Ambition to be respected more than other People? Now would not one great Act of Charity, one Instance of redeeming a poor Family from all the Miseries of Poverty, restoring an unfortunate Tradesman by a Sum of Money to the means of procuring a Livelihood by his Industry, discharging an undone Debtor from his Debts or a Goal, or any such like

---

[1] Cf. Matthew v. 12 and Luke vi. 23, 35.

[2] The sentiment of course is old, but with Joseph Andrews's argument that charity, not wealth or fashionableness, is the source of true honour, compare especially Isaac Barrow, 'The Duty and Reward of Bounty to the Poor' (1671), *Works*, ed. Napier, i. 90–94.

Example of Goodness, create a Man more Honour and Respect than he could acquire by the finest House, Furniture, Pictures or Clothes that were ever beheld? For not only the Object himself, who was thus relieved, but all who heard the Name of such a Person must, I imagine, reverence him infinitely more than the Possessor of all those other things: which when we so admire, we rather praise the Builder, the Workman, the Painter, the Laceman, the Taylor, and the rest, by whose Ingenuity they are produced, than the Person who by his Money makes them his own. For my own part, when I have waited behind my Lady in a Room hung with fine Pictures, while I have been looking at them I have never once thought of their Owner, nor hath any one else, as I ever observed; for when it hath been asked whose Picture that was, it was never once answered, the Master's of the House, but *Ammyconni, Paul Varnish, Hannibal Scratchi*, or *Hogarthi*,[1] which I suppose were the Names of the Painters: but if it was asked, who redeemed such a one out of Prison? who lent such a ruined Tradesman Money to set up? who cloathed that Family of poor small Children? it is very plain, what must be the Answer. And besides, these great Folks are mistaken, if they imagine they get any Honour at all by these means; for I do not remember I ever was with my Lady at any House where she commended the House or Furniture, but I have heard her at her return home make sport and jeer at whatever she had before commended: and I have been told by other Gentlemen in Livery, that it is the same in their Families: but I defy the wisest Man in the World to turn a true good Action into Ridicule.[2] I defy him to do it. He who should endeavour it, would be laughed at himself, instead of making others laugh. Nobody scarce doth any Good, yet they all agree in praising those who do. Indeed it is strange that all Men should consent in commending Goodness, and no Man endeavour to deserve that Commendation; whilst, on the contrary, all rail at Wickedness, and all are as eager to be what they

---

[1] Joseph's garbled versions of the names of celebrated painters, the first three Italian: Jacopo Amigoni (1675–1752), Paolo Veronese (1528–88), and Annibale Carracci (1560–1609). Amigoni lived in England from 1730 to 1739 and, among other works, painted the Queen's portrait. The last name is, of course, another compliment to Hogarth (see p. 6, n. 1). For an earlier reference to Carracci, see *The Universal Gallant* (IV. i).

[2] Cf. Shaftesbury, *Sensus Communis: An Essay on the Freedom of Wit and Humour,* IV. i; in *Characteristics,* 5th ed. (1732), i. 129: 'One may defy the World to turn real *Bravery* or *Generosity* into Ridicule.'

abuse. This I know not the Reason of, but it is as plain as Day-
light to those who converse in the World, as I have done these
three Years.' 'Are all the great Folks wicked then?' says *Fanny*.
'To be sure there are some Exceptions,' answered *Joseph*. 'Some
Gentlemen of our Cloth report charitable Actions done by their
Lords and Masters, and I have heard 'Squire *Pope*, the great
Poet, at my Lady's Table, tell Stories of a Man that lived at
a Place called *Ross*,[1] and another at the *Bath*, one *Al—Al—*I
forget his Name, but it is in the Book of Verses.[2] This Gentleman hath built up a stately House too, which the 'Squire likes
very well; but his Charity is seen farther than his House, tho' it
stands on a Hill, ay, and brings him more Honour too. It was his
Charity that put him in the Book, where the 'Squire says he puts
all those who deserve it; and to be sure, as he lives among all the
great People, if there were any such, he would know them.'—
This was all of Mr. *Joseph Andrews's* Speech which I could get
him to recollect, which I have delivered as near as was possible in
his own Words, with a very small Embellishment. But I believe
the Reader hath not been a little surprized at the long Silence of
Parson *Adams*, especially as so many Occasions offer'd themselves
to exert his Curiosity and Observation. The truth is, he was fast
asleep, and had so been from the beginning of the preceding Narrative: and indeed if the Reader considers that so many Hours
had past since he had closed his Eyes,[3] he will not wonder at his
Repose, tho' even *Henley* himself, or as great an Orator (if any
such be) had been in his *Rostrum* or Tub before him.[4]

---

[1] Pope celebrates the benevolence of 'the Man of Ross', John Kyrle (1634?–1724), in his
Epistle to Bathurst, ll. 250–90.

[2] Ralph Allen again (see p. 190, n. 2), whom Pope compliments for his charity in
Epilogue to the Satires, Dialogue I. 135–6: 'Let humble ALLEN, with an aukward Shame, /
Do good by stealth, and blush to find it Fame.' See the Dedication of *Tom Jones*, where
Fielding quotes the last line.

[3] This statement, added to the second edition, corrects an error which Fielding had
noticed too late to revise before the publication of the first edition, but in time to prefix the
following apology: 'Among other Errors, the Reader is desired to excuse this: That in the
Second Volume, Mr. *Adams*, is, by Mistake, mentioned to have sat up two subsequent
Nights; when in reality, a Night of Rest intervened' (I. A10ᵛ). The night of rest to which
Fielding refers was spent in the inn, II. xvi; before that, Adams had merely taken 'a comfortable Nap' in a chair (II. xiii).

[4] John 'Orator' Henley (1692–1756) was an eccentric priest and 'Zany', as Pope called
him (*Dunciad*, iii. 206), who left the Church in 1726 to preach in Newport market and,
later, in his 'chapel' in Portman Street, Lincoln's Inn Fields. On Sundays Henley declaimed
in an absurdly eloquent style on some theological subject, on Wednesdays on some other

Joseph, who, whilst he was speaking, had continued in one Attitude, with his Head reclining on one side, and his Eyes cast on the Ground, no sooner perceived, on looking up, the Position of *Adams*, who was stretched on his Back, and snored louder than the usual braying of the Animal with long Ears; than he turned towards *Fanny*, and taking her by the Hand, began a Dalliance, which, tho' consistent with the purest Innocence and Decency, neither he would have attempted, nor she permitted before any Witness. Whilst they amused themselves in this harmless and delightful manner, they heard a Pack of Hounds approaching in full Cry towards them, and presently afterwards saw a Hare pop forth from the Wood, and crossing the Water, land within a few Yards of them in the Meadows. The Hare was no sooner on Shore, than it seated itself on its hinder Legs, and listened to the Sound of the Pursuers. *Fanny* was wonderfully pleased with the little Wretch, and eagerly longed to have it in her Arms, that she might preserve it from the Dangers which seemed to threaten it: but the rational part of the Creation do not always aptly distinguish their Friends from their Foes; what wonder then if this silly Creature, the moment it beheld her, fled from the Friend who would have protected it, and traversing the Meadows again, past the little Rivulet on the opposite side. It was however so spent and weak, that it fell down twice or thrice in its way. This affected the tender Heart of *Fanny*, who exclaimed with Tears in her Eyes against the Barbarity of worrying a poor innocent defenceless Animal out of its Life, and putting it to the extremest Torture for Diversion. She had not much time to make Reflections of this kind, for on a sudden the Hounds rushed through the Wood, which resounded with their Throats, and the Throats of their *Retinue*, who *attended* on them on horseback. The Dogs now past the Rivulet, and pursued the Footsteps of the Hare;

topic, charging a shilling admission; his pulpit or 'Tub' was elegantly covered with velvet adorned with fleurs-de-lis. From 1730 to 1741 he edited *The Hyp-Doctor*, a pro-ministerial journal. (See *The Champion*, 13 December 1739 and 14 February 1739/40.) Fielding satirized Henley as 'Dr. Orator' in *The Author's Farce*; and in the proceedings of the first Court of Criticism in *The Jacobite's Journal* (16 January 1748), a petition from 'Orator Handlie . . . praying to be Crier of the Court, offering to write, preach, or swear any thing, and to profess any Party or Religion, at a cheap rate', is rejected. Since the epithet was inescapably associated with his name, Henley may be the 'great Orator' who, missing the point of Fielding's humour, publicly criticized Adams's praise of Mr. Wilson's learning and thus led Fielding to add a facetious footnote to the second edition of *Joseph Andrews* (see p. 201).

five Horsemen attempted to leap over, three of whom succeeded, and two were in the Attempt thrown from their Saddles into the Water; their Companions and their own Horses too proceeded after their Sport, and left their Friends and Riders to invoke the Assistance of Fortune, or employ the more active means of Strength and Agility for their Deliverance. *Joseph* however was not so unconcerned on this Occasion; he left *Fanny* for a moment to herself, and ran to the Gentlemen, who were immediately on their Legs, shaking their Ears, and easily with the help of his Hand attained the Bank, (for the Rivulet was not at all deep) and without staying to thank their kind Assister, ran dripping across the Meadow, calling to their Brother Sportsmen to stop their Horses: but they heard them not.

The Hounds were now very little behind their poor reeling, staggering Prey, which fainting almost at every Step, crawled through the Wood, and had almost got round to the Place where *Fanny* stood, when it was overtaken by its Enemies; and being driven out of the Covert was caught, and instantly tore to pieces before *Fanny's* Face, who was unable to assist it with any Aid more powerful than Pity; nor could she prevail on *Joseph*, who had been himself a Sportsman in his Youth, to attempt any thing contrary to the Laws of Hunting, in favour of the Hare, which he said was killed fairly.

The Hare was caught within a Yard or two of *Adams*, who lay asleep at some distance from the Lovers, and the Hounds in devouring it, and pulling it backwards and forwards, had drawn it so close to him, that some of them (by Mistake perhaps for the Hare's Skin) laid hold of the Skirts of his Cassock; others at the same time applying their Teeth to his Wig, which he had with a Handkerchief fastened to his Head, they began to pull him about; and had not the Motion of his Body had more effect on him than seemed to be wrought by the Noise, they must certainly have tasted his Flesh, which delicious Flavour might have been fatal to him: But being roused by these Tuggings, he instantly awaked, and with a Jerk delivering his Head from his Wig, he with most admirable Dexterity recovered his Legs, which now seemed the only Members he could entrust his Safety to. Having therefore escaped likewise from at least a third Part of his Cassock, which he willingly left as his *Exuviæ* or Spoils to the Enemy, he fled with the utmost speed he could summon to his Assistance. Nor let this be any Detraction from the Bravery of his Character; let the Number of the Enemies, and the Surprize in which he was taken, be considered; and if there be any Modern so outragiously brave, that he cannot admit of Flight in any Circumstance whatever, I say (but I whisper that softly, and I solemnly declare, without any Intention of giving Offence to any brave Man in the Nation) I say, or rather I whisper that he is an ignorant Fellow, and hath never read *Homer* nor *Virgil*, nor knows he any thing of *Hector* or *Turnus*;[1] nay, he is unacquainted with the History of some great Men living, who, tho' as brave as Lions, ay, as Tigers, have run away the Lord knows how far, and the Lord knows why, to the Surprize of their Friends, and the Entertainment of their Enemies. But if Persons of such heroick Disposition are a little offended at the Behaviour of *Adams*, we assure them they shall be as much pleased with what we shall immediately relate of *Joseph Andrews*. The Master of the Pack was just arrived, or, as the Sportsmen call it, *Come in*, when *Adams* set out, as we have before mentioned. This Gentleman was generally said to be a great Lover of Humour; but not to mince the matter, especially as we are upon this Subject, he was a great *Hunter of Men*: indeed he had hitherto followed the Sport only with Dogs of his own Species; for he kept two or three Couple of barking Curs for that Use only. However, as he thought he had now found a Man nimble enough, he was willing to indulge himself with other Sport, and accordingly crying out, *Stole away*, encouraged the Hounds to pursue Mr. *Adams*, swearing it was the largest Jack Hare he ever saw; at the same time hallooing and hooping as if a conquered Foe was flying before him; in which he was imitated by these two or three Couple of Human, or rather two-leg'd Curs on horseback which we have mentioned before.

Now thou, whoever thou art, whether a Muse, or by what other Name soever thou chusest to be called, who presidest over Biography, and hast inspired all the Writers of Lives in these our Times: Thou who didst infuse such wonderful Humour into the Pen of immortal *Gulliver*,[2] who hast carefully guided the Judg-

---

[1] *Iliad*, xxii; *Aeneid*, xii.

[2] Fielding's admiration for Swift, who, together with Lucian and Cervantes, comprised the 'great Triumvirate' of satirists (*The Covent-Garden Journal*, 4 February 1752), is perhaps best indicated in the words of the obituary appearing in *The True Patriot* (5 November 1745): there Swift is called 'A Genius who deserves to be ranked among the first whom the World ever saw. He possessed the Talents of a *Lucian*, a *Rabelais*, and a *Cervantes*, and

ment, whilst thou hast exalted the nervous manly Style of thy
Mallet:[1] Thou who hadst no Hand in that Dedication, and Preface, or the Translations which thou wouldst willingly have struck
out of the Life of *Cicero*:[2] Lastly, Thou who without the Assistance of the least Spice of Literature, and even against his Inclination, hast, in some Pages of his Book, forced *Colley Cibber*[3] to write
English; do thou assist me in what I find myself unequal to. Do
thou introduce on the Plain, the young, the gay, the brave *Joseph
Andrews*, whilst Men shall view him with Admiration and Envy;
tender Virgins with Love and anxious Concern for his Safety.

No sooner did *Joseph Andrews* perceive the Distress of his
Friend, when first the quick-scenting Dogs attacked him, than
he grasped his Cudgel[4] in his right Hand, a Cudgel which his
Father had of his Grandfather, to whom a mighty strong Man
of *Kent*[5] had given it for a Present in that Day, when he broke
three Heads on the Stage. It was a Cudgel of mighty Strength
and wonderful Art, made by one of Mr. *Deard's* best Workmen,[6]

in his Works exceeded them all. He employed his Wit to the noblest Purposes, in ridiculing
as well Superstition in Religion as Infidelity, and the several Errors and Immoralities which
sprung up from time to time in his Age; and lastly, in the Defence of his Country, against
several pernicious Schemes of wicked Politicians.' In *The Champion* (20 March 1739/40)
Fielding paid Swift the compliment of imitation, presenting, in the manner of Gulliver,
'Some Extracts Out of the Voyages of Mr. Job Vinegar'.

[1] David Mallet (1705–65), Scotch poet and dramatist and a member of the literary
Opposition to Walpole. Here Fielding refers to Mallet's biography, *The Life of Francis
Bacon*, written for Millar's edition of Bacon's works (1740) and dedicated to the Earl of
Chesterfield.

[2] *The History of the Life of Marcus Tullius Cicero* by the Cambridge theologian and
librarian, Conyers Middleton (1683–1750), was published in February 1741. Fielding was
irritated both by Middleton's fulsome dedication of the work to John, Lord Hervey, and by
his condescending disparagement, in the Preface, of *Observations on the Life of Cicero* (1731),
a work by Fielding's friend and patron, George Lyttelton. (That Fielding was not alone
in his hostility to Middleton's biography is evident from a pamphlet by an anonymous
Oxonian, also derisively critical of Middleton's Dedication, Preface, and his translations:
see *The Death of M—l—n in the Life of Cicero* [1741].) In *Shamela* Fielding had parodied
Middleton's Dedication, and later in *Joseph Andrews* (IV. ix) he roughly paraphrased a
passage from it in describing the unprincipled politics of Beau Didapper, for whom Hervey
was the original (see p. 313, n. 1). In time Fielding's attitude seems to have softened: he
concluded the Preface to *An Enquiry into the Causes of the late Increase of Robbers* (1751) by
quoting 'a fine observation' from Middleton's work.   [3] See p. 18, n. 3.

[4] Cf. the account of Achilles' shield in the *Iliad*, xviii.

[5] William Joy (d. 1734), called 'Samson, the strong man of Kent', performed remarkable
feats of strength in the early part of the century.

[6] William Deard, or Deards (d. 17 June 1761), was a fashionable London jeweller, toy-
maker, and pawnbroker; in 1740 his shop was located in Fleet Street, opposite St. Dunstan's
Church (by 1744 he had moved to the Strand). Facetious or satiric references to Deard

whom no other Artificer can equal; and who hath made all those
Sticks which the Beaus have lately walked with about the Park[1]
in a Morning: But this was far his Master-piece; on its Head was
engraved a Nose and Chin, which might have been mistaken for
a Pair of Nut-crackers. The Learned have imagined it designed
to represent the *Gorgon*: but it was in fact copied from the Face
of a certain long *English* Baronet[2] of infinite Wit, Humour, and
Gravity. He did intend to have engraved here many Histories:
As the first Night of Captain *B*—'*s* Play,[3] where you would have
seen Criticks in Embroidery transplanted from the Boxes to
the Pit, whose ancient Inhabitants were exalted to the Galleries,
where they played on Catcalls. He did intend to have painted an
Auction-Room, where Mr. *Cock*[4] would have appeared aloft in
his Pulpit, trumpeting forth the Praises of a *China* Bason; and
with Astonishment wondering that *Nobody bids more for that fine,
that superb*—He did intend to have engraved many other things,
but was forced to leave all out for want of room.

abound in Fielding's works: see, for example, *The Temple Beau* (1730), IV. vi; *The Miser*
(1733), II. i; *The Vernoniad; Jonathan Wild* (II. iii); and *The Covent-Garden Journal*,
4 January 1752; Deard is doubtless the 'eminent' or 'celebrated' toyman referred to in
A Journey from This World to the Next (I. i) and *Tom Jones* (XII. iv).

    [1] The Mall in St. James's Park, near the royal palace, was the fashionable promenade
of the day.

    [2] An ironic reference to 'Long' Sir Thomas Robinson (1700?–77) of Rokeby Park,
from 1735 commissioner of the Excise under Walpole until his appointment as Governor
of Barbados late in 1741; he was created baronet on 10 March 1730/1. Robinson was very
tall and very dull; witness, for example, Chesterfield's verses on him: 'Unlike my subject
now shall be my song; / It shall be witty and it shan't be long.' He was also extravagant,
managing to ruin himself by the lavish balls he gave for the beau-monde (see the account
of one of these, attended by three hundred of the nobility and gentry and lasting until six
in the morning, in *The Daily Advertiser*, 5 December 1741).

    [3] Charles Bodens (d. 19 June 1753), officer in the Coldstream Footguards and Gentleman
Usher to the King. His play, *The Modish Couple*, seems not to have been his at all, but
rather the work of Lord Hervey and the Prince of Wales, who wished to conceal their
authorship and so persuaded Bodens, who was also the court pimp, to stand in their stead.
But knowledge of the ruse apparently leaked to the public, and when the play opened on
10 January 1732 it was roundly damned. Fielding, who wrote the epilogue for the play,
makes another satiric reference to it in *Pasquin*, v. i. (For a full account, see Charles B.
Woods, 'Captain B—'s Play', *Harvard Studies and Notes in Philology and Literature*, xv
[1933], 243–55.)

    [4] Christopher Cock (d. 10 December 1748) was a well-known auctioneer whose head-
quarters, located after 1737 in the Grand Piazza, Covent Garden, were a fashionable resort.
In *The Historical Register for the Year 1736*, Act II, Fielding satirically dramatized an
auction presided over by one Christopher Hen; other references to him occur in *The
Champion*, 19 February 1739/40, and in *Juvenal's Sixth Satire Modernised in Burlesque
Verse*.

No sooner had *Joseph* grasped this Cudgel in his Hands, than
Lightning darted from his Eyes; and the heroick Youth, swift
of Foot, ran with the utmost speed to his Friend's assistance. He
overtook him just as *Rockwood* had laid hold of the Skirt of his
Cassock, which being torn hung to the ground. Reader, we would
make a Simile on this Occasion, but for two Reasons: The first
is, it would interrupt the Description, which should be *rapid* in
this Part; but that doth not weigh much, many Precedents occurring for such an Interruption: The second, and much the greater
Reason is, that we could find no Simile adequate to our Purpose: For indeed, what Instance could we bring to set before our
Reader's Eyes at once the Idea of Friendship, Courage, Youth,
Beauty, Strength, and Swiftness; all which blazed in the Person
of *Joseph Andrews*. Let those therefore that describe Lions and
Tigers, and Heroes fiercer than both, raise their Poems or Plays
with the Simile of *Joseph Andrews*, who is himself above the reach
of any Simile.

Now *Rockwood* had laid fast hold on the Parson's Skirts, and
stopt his Flight; which *Joseph* no sooner perceived, than he
levelled his Cudgel at his Head, and laid him sprawling. *Jowler*
and *Ringwood* then fell on his Great-Coat, and had undoubtedly
brought him to the Ground, had not *Joseph*, collecting all his
Force given *Jowler* such a Rap on the Back, that quitting his
Hold he ran howling over the Plain: A harder Fate remained for
thee, O *Ringwood*. *Ringwood* the best Hound that ever pursued
a Hare, who never threw his Tongue but where the Scent was
undoubtedly true; good at *trailing*; and *sure in a Highway*, no
Babler, no *Over-runner*, respected by the whole Pack: For, whenever he opened, they knew the Game was at hand. He fell by the
Stroke of *Joseph*. *Thunder*, and *Plunder*, and *Wonder*, and *Blunder*,
were the next Victims of his Wrath, and measured their Lengths
on the Ground. Then *Fairmaid*, a Bitch which Mr. *John Temple*[1]
had bred up in his House, and fed at his own Table, and lately
sent the Squire fifty Miles for a Present, ran fiercely at *Joseph*,
and bit him by the Leg; no Dog was ever fiercer than she, being
descended from an *Amazonian* Breed, and had worried Bulls in

[1] Probably the Hon. John Temple, Esq. (1680–1752), younger brother of Henry Temple,
first Viscount Palmerston. Through his marriage with his cousin Elizabeth, grand-
daughter of Sir William Temple, he acquired the estate at Moor Park, Surrey—approxi-
mately fifty miles from the scene of Adams's 'roasting'.

her own Country, but now waged an unequal Fight; and had shared the Fate of those we have mentioned before, had not *Diana* (the Reader may believe it or not, as he pleases) in that Instant interposed, and in the Shape of the Huntsman snatched her Favourite up in her Arms.

The Parson now faced about, and with his Crab Stick felled many to the Earth, and scattered others, till he was attacked by *Cæsar* and pulled to the Ground; then *Joseph* flew to his Rescue, and with such Might fell on the Victor, that, O eternal Blot to his Name! *Cæsar* ran yelping away.

The Battle now raged with the most dreadful Violence, when lo the Huntsman, a Man of Years and Dignity, lifted his Voice, and called his Hounds from the Fight; telling them, in a Language they understood, that it was in vain to contend longer; for that Fate had decreed the Victory to their Enemies.

Thus far the Muse hath with her usual Dignity related this prodigious Battle, a Battle we apprehend never equalled by any Poet, Romance or Life-writer whatever, and having brought it to a Conclusion she ceased; we shall therefore proceed in our ordinary Style with the Continuation of this History. The Squire and his Companions, whom the Figure of *Adams* and the Gallantry of *Joseph* had at first thrown into a violent Fit of Laughter, and who had hitherto beheld the Engagement with more Delight than any Chace, Shooting-match, Race, Cock-fighting, Bull or Bear-baiting had ever given them, began now to apprehend the Danger of their Hounds, many of which lay sprawling in the Fields. The Squire therefore having first called his Friends about him, as Guards for Safety of his Person, rode manfully up to the Combatants, and summoning all the Terror he was Master of, into his Countenance, demanded with an authoritative Voice of *Joseph*, what he meant by assaulting his Dogs in that Manner. *Joseph* answered with great Intrepidity, that they had first fallen on his Friend; and if they had belonged to the greatest Man in the Kingdom, he would have treated them in the same Way; for whilst his Veins contained a single Drop of Blood, he would not stand idle by, and see that Gentleman (*pointing to* Adams) abused either by Man or Beast; and having so said, both he and *Adams* brandished their wooden Weapons, and put themselves into such a Posture, that the Squire and his Company thought proper to preponderate, before they offered to revenge the Cause of their four-footed Allies.

At this Instant *Fanny*, whom the Apprehension of *Joseph's* Danger had alarmed so much, that forgetting her own she had made the utmost Expedition, came up. The Squire and all the Horsemen were so surprized with her Beauty, that they immediately fixed both their Eyes and Thoughts solely on her, every one declaring he had never seen so charming a Creature. Neither Mirth nor Anger engaged them a Moment longer; but all sat in silent Amaze. The Huntsman only was free from her Attraction, who was busy in cutting the Ears of the Dogs, and endeavouring to recover them to Life; in which he succeeded so well, that only two of no great Note remained slaughtered on the Field of Action. Upon this the Huntsman declared, ''twas well it was no worse; for his part he could not blame the Gentleman, and wondered his Master would encourage the Dogs to hunt *Christians*; that it was the surest way to spoil them, to make them follow *Vermin* instead of sticking to a Hare.'

The Squire being informed of the little Mischief that had been done; and perhaps having more Mischief of another kind in his Head, accosted Mr. *Adams* with a more favourable Aspect than before: he told him he was sorry for what had happened; that he had endeavoured all he could to prevent it, the Moment he was acquainted with his Cloth, and greatly commended the Courage of his Servant; for so he imagined *Joseph* to be. He then invited Mr. *Adams* to Dinner, and desired the young Woman might come with him. *Adams* refused a long while; but the Invitation was repeated with so much Earnestness and Courtesy, that at length he was forced to accept it. His Wig and Hat, and other Spoils of the Field, being gathered together by *Joseph*, (for otherwise probably they would have been forgotten;) he put himself into the best Order he could; and then the Horse and Foot moved forward in the same Pace towards the Squire's House, which stood at a very little distance.

Whilst they were on the Road, the lovely *Fanny* attracted the Eyes of all; they endeavoured to outvie one another in Encomiums on her Beauty; which the Reader will pardon my not relating, as they had not any thing new or uncommon in them: So must he likewise my not setting down the many curious Jests which were made on *Adams*, some of them declaring that

Parson-hunting was the best Sport in the World: Others commending his standing at Bay, which they said he had done as well as
any Badger; with such like Merriment, which tho' it would ill
become the Dignity of this History, afforded much Laughter and
Diversion to the Squire, and his facetious Companions.

CHAPTER VII

*A Scene of Roasting very nicely adapted to the
present Taste and Times.*

THEY arrived at the Squire's House just as his Dinner was ready.
A little Dispute arose on the account of *Fanny*, whom the Squire
who was a Batchelor, was desirous to place at his own Table; but
she would not consent, nor would Mr. *Adams* permit her to be
parted from *Joseph*: so that she was at length with him consigned
over to the Kitchin, where the Servants were ordered to make him
drunk; a Favour which was likewise intended for *Adams*: which
Design being executed, the Squire thought he should easily
accomplish, what he had, when he first saw her, intended to
perpetrate with *Fanny*.

It may not be improper, before we proceed farther to open a
little the Character of this Gentleman, and that of his Friends.
The Master of this House then was a Man of a very considerable
Fortune; a Batchelor, as we have said, and about forty Years of
Age: He had been educated (if we may here use that Expression)
in the Country, and at his own Home, under the Care of his
Mother and a Tutor, who had Orders never to correct him nor
to compel him to learn more than he liked, which it seems was
very little, and that only in his Childhood; for from the Age of
fifteen he addicted himself entirely to Hunting and other rural
Amusements, for which his Mother took care to equip him with
Horses, Hounds, and all other Necessaries: and his Tutor endeavouring to ingratiate himself with his young Pupil, who would,
he knew, be able handsomely to provide for him, became his
Companion, not only at these Exercises, but likewise over a
Bottle, which the young Squire had a very early Relish for. At
the Age of twenty, his Mother began to think she had not ful-

filled the Duty of a Parent; she therefore resolved to persuade her Son, if possible, to that which she imagined would well supply all that he might have learned at a publick School or University. This is what they commonly call *Travelling*; which, with the help of the Tutor who was fixed on to attend him, she easily succeeded in. He made in three Years the Tour of *Europe*, as they term it, and returned home, well furnish'd with *French* Clothes, Phrases and Servants, with a hearty Contempt for his own Country; especially what had any Savour of the plain Spirit and Honesty of our Ancestors. His Mother greatly applauded herself at his Return; and now being Master of his own Fortune, he soon procured himself a Seat in Parliament, and was in the common Opinion one of the finest Gentlemen of his Age: But what distinguished him chiefly, was a strange Delight which he took in every thing which is ridiculous, odious, and absurd in his own Species; so that he never chose a Companion without one or more of these Ingredients, and those who were marked by Nature in the most eminent Degree with them, were most his Favourites: if he ever found a Man who either had not or endeavoured to conceal these Imperfections, he took great pleasure in inventing Methods of forcing him into Absurdities, which were not natural to him, or in drawing forth and exposing those that were; for which purpose he was always provided with a Set of Fellows whom we have before called Curs; and who did indeed no great Honour to the Canine Kind: Their Business was to hunt out and display every thing that had any Savour of the above mentioned Qualities, and especially in the gravest and best Characters: But if they failed in their Search, they were to turn even Virtue and Wisdom themselves into Ridicule for the Diversion of their Master and Feeder. The Gentlemen of Curlike Disposition, who were now at his House, and whom he had brought with him from *London*, were an old Half-pay Officer, a Player, a dull Poet, a Quack Doctor, a scraping Fidler, and a lame *German* Dancing-Master.

As soon as Dinner was served, while Mr. *Adams* was saying Grace, the Captain conveyed his Chair from behind him; so that when he endeavoured to seat himself, he fell down on the Ground; and thus compleated Joke the first, to the great Entertainment of the whole Company. The second Joke was performed by the Poet, who sat next him on the other side, and took an Opportunity, while poor *Adams* was respectfully drinking to the Master of the

House, to overturn a Plate of Soup into his Breeches; which, with the many Apologies he made, and the Parson's gentle Answers, caused much Mirth in the Company. Joke the third was served up by one of the Waiting-men, who had been ordered to convey a Quantity of Gin into Mr. *Adams's* Ale, which he declaring to be the best Liquor he ever drank, but rather too rich of the Malt, contributed again to their Laughter. Mr. *Adams*, from whom we had most of this Relation, could not recollect all the Jests of this kind practised on him, which the inoffensive Disposition of his own Heart made him slow in discovering; and indeed, had it not been for the Information which we received from a Servant of the Family, this Part of our History, which we take to be none of the least curious, must have been deplorably imperfect; tho' we must own it probable, that some more Jokes were (as they call it) *cracked* during their Dinner; but we have by no means been able to come at the Knowledge of them. When Dinner was removed, the Poet began to repeat some Verses, which he said were made *extempore*. The following is a Copy of them, procured with the greatest difficulty.

An extempore *Poem on Parson* Adams.

Did ever Mortal such a Parson view;
His Cassock old, his Wig not over-new?
Well might the Hounds have him for Fox mistaken,
In Smell more like to that, than rusty Bacon*.
But would it not make any Mortal stare,
To see this Parson taken for a Hare?
Could Phœbus *err thus grossly, even he*
For a good Player might have taken thee.

At which Words the Bard whip'd off the Player's Wig, and received the Approbation of the Company, rather perhaps for the Dexterity of his Hand than his Head. The Player, instead of re-torting the Jest on the Poet, began to display his Talents on the same Subject. He repeated many Scraps of Wit out of Plays, reflecting on the whole Body of the Clergy, which were received with great Acclamations by all present. It was now the Dancing-Master's Turn to exhibit his Talents; he therefore addressing himself to *Adams* in broken *English*, told him, 'he was a Man ver

---

* All Hounds that will hunt Fox or other Vermin, will hunt a Piece of rusty Bacon trailed on the Ground.

well made for de Dance, and he suppose by his Walk, dat he had
learn of some great Master. He said it was ver pretty Quality
in Clergyman to dance;' and concluded with desiring him to
dance a Minuet, telling him, 'his Cassock would serve for Petticoats; and that he would himself be his Partner.' At which Words,
without waiting for an Answer, he pulled out his Gloves, and the
Fiddler was preparing his Fiddle. The Company all offered the
Dancing-Master Wagers that the Parson outdanced him, which
he refused, saying, 'he believed so too; for he had never seen any
Man in his Life who looked de Dance so well as de Gentleman:'
He then stepped forwards to take _Adams_ by the Hand, which the
latter hastily withdrew, and at the same time clenching his Fist,
advised him not to carry the Jest too far, for he would not endure
being put upon. The Dancing-master no sooner saw the Fist than
he prudently retired out of it's reach, and stood aloof mimicking
Adams, whose Eyes were fixed on him, not guessing what he was
at, but to avoid his laying hold on him, which he had once
attempted. In the mean while, the Captain perceiving an Opportunity pinned a Cracker or Devil to the Cassock, and then lighted
it with their little smoking Candle. _Adams_ being a Stranger to
this Sport, and believing he had been blown up in reality, started
from his Chair, and jumped about the Room, to the infinite Joy
of the Beholders, who declared he was the best Dancer in the
Universe. As soon as the Devil had done tormenting him, and
he had a little recovered his Confusion, he returned to the Table,
standing up in the Posture of one who intended to make a Speech.
They all cried out, _Hear him_, _Hear him_; and he then spoke in the
following manner: 'Sir, I am sorry to see one to whom Providence
hath been so bountiful in bestowing his Favours, make so ill and
ungrateful a Return for them; for tho' you have not insulted me
yourself, it is visible you have delighted in those that do it, nor
have once discouraged the many Rudenesses which have been
shewn towards me; indeed towards yourself, if you rightly understood them; for I am your Guest, and by the Laws of Hospitality entitled to your Protection. One Gentleman hath thought
proper to produce some Poetry upon me, of which I shall only
say, that I had rather be the Subject than the Composer. He hath
pleased to treat me with Disrespect as a Parson; I apprehend my
Order is not the Object of Scorn, nor that I can become so, unless by being a Disgrace to it, which I hope Poverty will never be

called. Another Gentleman indeed hath repeated some Sentences, where the Order itself is mentioned with Contempt. He says they are taken from Plays. I am sure such Plays are a Scandal to the Government which permits them, and cursed will be the Nation where they are represented. How others have treated me, I need not observe; they themselves, when they reflect, must allow the Behaviour to be as improper to my Years as to my Cloth. You found me, Sir, travelling with two of my Parishioners, (I omit your Hounds falling on me; for I have quite forgiven it, whether it proceeded from the Wantonness or Negligence of the Huntsman,) my Appearance might very well persuade you that your Invitation was an Act of Charity, tho' in reality we were well provided; yes, Sir, if we had had an hundred Miles to travel, we had sufficient to bear our Expences in a noble manner.' (At which Words he produced the half Guinea which was found in the Basket.) 'I do not shew you this out of Ostentation of Riches, but to convince you I speak Truth. Your seating me at your Table was an Honour which I did not ambitiously affect; when I was here, I endeavoured to behave towards you with the utmost Respect; if I have failed, it was not with Design, nor could I, certainly, so far be guilty as to deserve the Insults I have suffered. If they were meant therefore either to my Order or my Poverty (and you see I am not very poor) the Shame doth not lie at my door, and I heartily pray, that the Sin may be averted from your's.' He thus finished, and received a general Clap from the whole Company. Then the Gentleman of the House told him, 'he was sorry for what had happened; that he could not accuse him of any Share in it: That the Verses were, as himself had well observed, so bad, that he might easily answer them; and for the Serpent, it was undoubtedly a very great Affront done him by the Dancing-Master, for which if he well thrashed him, as he deserved, (the Gentleman said) he should be very much pleased to see it;' (in which probably he spoke Truth.) *Adams* answered, 'whoever had done it, it was not his Profession to punish him that way; but for the Person whom he had accused, I am a Witness, (says he) of his Innocence, for I had my Eye on him all the while. Whoever he was, God forgive him, and bestow on him a little more Sense as well as Humanity.' The Captain answer'd with a surly Look and Accent, 'that he hoped he did not mean to reflect on him; d—n him, he had as much *Imanity* as another, and if any Man said he had not, he would convince him of his Mistake by cutting his Throat.' *Adams* smiling, said, 'he believed he had spoke right by Accident.' To which the Captain returned, 'What do you mean by my speaking right? if you was not a Parson, I would not take these Words; but your Gown protects you. If any Man who wears a Sword had said so much, I had pulled him by the Nose before this.' *Adams* replied, 'if he attempted any Rudeness to his Person, he would not find any Protection for himself in his Gown;' and clenching his Fist, declared he had threshed many a stouter Man. The Gentleman did all he could to encourage this warlike Disposition in *Adams*, and was in hopes to have produced a Battle: But he was disappointed; for the Captain made no other Answer than, 'It is very well you are a Parson,' and so drinking off a Bumper to old Mother Church, ended the Dispute.

Then the Doctor, who had hitherto been silent, and who was the gravest, but most mischievous Dog of all, in a very pompous Speech highly applauded what *Adams* had said; and as much discommended the Behaviour to him; he proceeded to Encomiums on the Church and Poverty; and lastly recommended Forgiveness of what had past to *Adams*, who immediately answered, 'that every thing was forgiven;' and in the Warmth of his Goodness he filled a Bumper of strong Beer, (a Liquor he preferred to Wine) and drank a Health to the whole Company, shaking the Captain and the Poet heartily by the Hand, and addressing himself with great Respect to the Doctor; who indeed had not laughed outwardly at any thing that past, as he had a perfect Command of his Muscles, and could laugh inwardly without betraying the least Symptoms in his Countenance. The Doctor now began a second formal Speech, in which he declaimed against all Levity of Conversation; and what is usually called Mirth. He said, 'there were Amusements fitted for Persons of all Ages and Degrees, from the Rattle to the discussing a Point of Philosophy, and that Men discovered themselves in nothing more than in the Choice of their Amusements; for,' says he, 'as it must greatly raise our Expectation of the future Conduct in Life of Boys, whom in their tender Years we perceive instead of Taw or Balls, or other childish Play-things, to chuse, at their Leisure-Hours, to exercise their Genius in Contentions of Wit, Learning, and such like; so must it inspire one with equal Contempt of a Man, if we should discover him playing at Taw or other childish Play.' *Adams* highly

commended the Doctor's Opinion, and said, 'he had often wondered at some Passages in ancient Authors, where *Scipio*, *Lælius*,
and other great Men were represented to have passed many
Hours in Amusements of the most trifling kind.'[1] The Doctor
reply'd, 'he had by him an old *Greek* Manuscript where a favourite
Diversion of *Socrates* was recorded.' 'Ay,' says the Parson eagerly,
'I should be most infinitely obliged to you for the Favour of
perusing it.' The Doctor promised to send it him, and farther
said, 'that he believed he could describe it. I think,' says he, 'as
near as I can remember, it was this. There was a Throne erected,
on one side of which sat a King, and on the other a Queen, with
their Guards and Attendants ranged on both sides; to them was
introduced an Ambassador, which Part *Socrates* always used to
perform himself; and when he was led up to the Footsteps of the
Throne, he addressed himself to the Monarchs in some grave
Speech, full of Virtue and Goodness, and Morality, and such
like. After which, he was seated between the King and Queen,
and royally entertained. This I think was the chief part.—Perhaps
I may have forgot some Particulars; for it is long since I read it.'
Adams said, 'it was indeed a Diversion worthy the Relaxation of
so great a Man; and thought something resembling it should be
instituted among our great Men, instead of Cards and other idle
Pass-time, in which he was informed they trifled away too much
of their Lives.' He added, 'the Christian Religion was a nobler
Subject for these Speeches than any *Socrates* could have invented.'
The Gentleman of the House approved what Mr. *Adams* said,
and declared, 'he was resolved to perform the Ceremony this very
Evening.' To which the Doctor objected, as no one was prepared
with a Speech, 'Unless,' said he, (turning to *Adams* with a Gravity
of Countenance which would have deceived a more knowing
Man) 'you have a Sermon about you, Doctor.'—'Sir,' says *Adams*,
'I never travel without one, for fear what may happen.' He was
easily prevailed on by his worthy Friend, as he now called the
Doctor, to undertake the Part of the Ambassador; so that the
Gentleman sent immediate Orders to have the Throne erected;
which was performed before they had drank two Bottles: And

---

[1] Scipio Africanus Minor (*c.* 185–129 B.C.) and Caius Lælius, 'the Wise' (b. *c.* 186 B.C.).
In *De Oratore*, ii. 6, Cicero relates that for relaxation these close friends would go on excur-
sions into the country and take pleasure in such boyish amusements as gathering mussels
and shells. See also *Tom Jones*, VII. i.

perhaps the Reader will hereafter have no great reason to admire the Nimbleness of the Servants. Indeed, to confess the Truth, the Throne was no more than this; there was a great Tub of Water provided, on each side of which were placed two Stools raised higher than the Surface of the Tub, and over the Whole was laid a Blanket; on these Stools were placed the King and Queen, namely, the Master of the House, and the Captain. And now the Ambassador was introduced, between the Poet and the Doctor, who having read his Sermon to the great Entertainment of all present, was led up to his Place, and seated between their Majesties. They immediately rose up, when the Blanket wanting its Supports at either end, gave way, and soused *Adams* over Head and Ears in the Water; the Captain made his Escape, but unluckily the Gentleman himself not being as nimble as he ought, *Adams* caught hold of him before he descended from his Throne, and pulled him in with him, to the entire secret Satisfaction of all the Company. *Adams* after ducking the Squire twice or thrice leapt out of the Tub, and looked sharp for the Doctor, whom he would certainly have convey'd to the same Place of Honour; but he had wisely withdrawn: he then searched for his Crabstick, and having found that, as well as his Fellow-Travellers, he declared he would not stay a moment longer in such a House. He then departed, without taking leave of his Host, whom he had exacted a more severe Revenge on, than he intended: For as he did not use sufficient care to dry himself in time, he caught a Cold by the Accident, which threw him into a Fever, that had like to have cost him his Life.

CHAPTER VIII

Which some Readers will think too short, and others too long.

ADAMS, and *Joseph*, who was no less enraged than his Friend, at the Treatment he met with, went out with their Sticks in their Hands; and carried off *Fanny*, notwithstanding the Opposition of the Servants, who did all, without proceeding to Violence, in their power to detain them. They walked as fast as they could, not so much from any Apprehension of being pursued, as that

Mr. *Adams* might by Exercise prevent any harm from the Water. The Gentleman who had given such Orders to his Servants concerning *Fanny*, that he did not in the least fear her getting away, no sooner heard that she was gone, than he began to rave, and immediately dispatched several with Orders, either to bring her back, or never return. The Poet, the Player, and all but the Dancing-master and Doctor went on this Errand.

The Night was very dark, in which our Friends began their Journey; however they made such Expedition, that they soon arrived at an Inn, which was at seven Miles Distance. Here they unanimously consented to pass the Evening, Mr. *Adams* being now as dry as he was before he had set out on his Embassy.

This Inn, which indeed we might call an Ale-house, had not the Words, *The New Inn*, been writ on the Sign, afforded them no better Provision than Bread and Cheese, and Ale; on which, however, they made a very comfortable Meal; for Hunger is better than a *French* Cook.

They had no sooner supped, than *Adams* returning Thanks to the Almighty for his Food, declared he had eat his homely Commons, with much greater Satisfaction than his splendid Dinner, and exprest great Contempt for the Folly of Mankind, who sacrificed their Hopes of Heaven to the Acquisition of vast Wealth, since so much Comfort was to be found in the humblest State and the lowest Provision. 'Very true, Sir,' says a grave Man who sat smoking his Pipe by the Fire, and who was a Traveller as well as himself. 'I have often been as much surprized as you are, when I consider the Value which Mankind in general set on Riches, since every day's Experience shews us how little is in their power; for what indeed truly desirable can they bestow on us? Can they give Beauty to the Deformed, Strength to the Weak, or Health to the Infirm? Surely if they could, we should not see so many ill-favoured Faces haunting the Assemblies of the Great, nor would such numbers of feeble Wretches languish in their Coaches and Palaces. No, not the Wealth of a Kingdom can purchase any Paint, to dress pale Ugliness in the Bloom of that young Maiden, nor any Drugs to equip Disease with the Vigour of that young Man. Do not Riches bring us Sollicitude instead of Rest, Envy instead of Affection, and Danger instead of Safety? Can they prolong their own Possession, or lengthen his Days who enjoys them? So far otherwise, that the Sloth, the Luxury, the

Care which attend them, shorten the Lives of Millions, and bring them with Pain and Misery, to an untimely Grave. Where then is their Value, if they can neither embellish, or strengthen our Forms, sweeten or prolong our Lives? Again—Can they adorn the Mind more than the Body? Do they not rather swell the Heart with Vanity, puff up the Cheeks with Pride, shut our Ears to every Call of Virtue, and our Bowels to every Motive of Compassion!' 'Give me your Hand, Brother,' said *Adams* in a Rapture; 'for I suppose you are a Clergyman.' 'No truly,' answered the other, (indeed he was a Priest of the Church of *Rome*; but those who understand our Laws[1] will not wonder he was not over-ready to own it.) 'Whatever you are,' cries *Adams*, 'you have spoken my Sentiments: I believe I have preached every Syllable of your Speech twenty times over: For it hath always appeared to me easier for a Cable Rope (which by the way is the true rendering of that Word we have translated *Camel*) to go through the Eye of a Needle, than for a rich Man to get into the Kingdom of Heaven.'[2] 'That, Sir,' said the other, 'will be easily granted you by Divines, and is deplorably true: But as the Prospect of our Good at a distance doth not so forcibly affect us, it might be of some Service to Mankind to be made thoroughly sensible, which I think they might be with very little serious Attention, that even the Blessings of this World, are not to be purchased with Riches. A Doctrine in my Opinion, not only metaphysically, but if I may so say, mathematically demonstrable; and which I have been always so perfectly convinced of, that I have a Contempt for nothing so much as for Gold.' *Adams* now began a long Discourse; but as most which he said occurs among many Authors, who have

---

[1] Laws against Roman Catholics in England were severe, though not often enforced. By law their priests were liable to a fine of £200 and could be charged with high treason for saying mass—a regulation that was implemented by the offer of a £100 reward for the apprehension of offenders. For keeping a school, priests could suffer perpetual imprisonment. (See 23 Elizabeth, cap. 1; and 11 & 12 William III, cap. 4.) And laymen, if they refused to deny even the spiritual authority of the Pope, were subject to the penalties of recusancy: they could be fined £20 a month for not attending church, and, together with many other restrictions, they were forbidden to practice law or medicine or to hold any public office, to prosecute suits at law, or even to travel over five miles from their usual residence without a special licence. Even so, there was a general fear that 'Papist' priests in disguise were operating everywhere in England—holding mass, converting the people to Catholicism, and acting as spies for France. (See, for example, the letter from 'Anti-Pope' in *The Champion*, 23 July 1741.)

[2] Adams's emendation of Matthew xix. 24 had been proposed by other biblical scholars, but it is not generally approved.

treated this Subject, I shall omit inserting it. During its Continuance *Joseph* and *Fanny* retired to Rest, and the Host likewise left the Room. When the *English* Parson had concluded, the *Romish* resumed the Discourse, which he continued with great Bitterness and Invective; and at last ended by desiring *Adams* to lend him eighteen Pence to pay his Reckoning; promising, if he never paid him, he might be assured of his Prayers. The good Man answered, that eighteen Pence would be too little to carry him any very long Journey; that he had half a Guinea in his Pocket, which he would divide with him. He then fell to searching his Pockets, but could find no Money: For indeed the Company with whom he dined, had past one Jest upon him which we did not then enumerate, and had picked his Pocket of all that Treasure which he had so ostentatiously produced.

'Bless me,' cry'd *Adams*, 'I have certainly lost it, I can never have spent it. Sir, as I am a Christian I had a whole half Guinea in my Pocket this Morning, and have not now a single Halfpenny of it left. Sure the Devil must have taken it from me.' 'Sir,' answered the Priest smiling, 'You need make no Excuses; if you are not willing to lend me the Money, I am contented.' 'Sir,' cries *Adams*, 'if I had the greatest Sum in the World; ay, if I had ten Pounds about me, I would bestow it all to rescue any Christian from Distress. I am more vexed at my Loss on your account than my own. Was ever any thing so unlucky? because I have no Money in my Pocket, I shall be suspected to be no Christian.' 'I am more unlucky,' quoth the other, 'if you are as generous as you say: For really a Crown would have made me happy, and conveyed me in plenty to the Place I am going, which is not above twenty Miles off, and where I can arrive by to-morrow Night. I assure you I am not accustomed to travel Pennyless. I am but just arrived in *England*, and we were forced by a Storm in our Passage to throw all we had overboard. I don't suspect but this Fellow will take my Word for the Trifle I owe him; but I hate to appear so mean as to confess myself without a Shilling to such People: For these, and indeed too many others know little Difference in their Estimation between a Beggar and a Thief.' However, he thought he should deal better with the Host that Evening than the next Morning; he therefore resolved to set out immediately, notwithstanding the Darkness; and accordingly as soon as the Host returned he communicated to him the Situation of his Affairs; upon which the Host scratching his Head, answered, 'Why, I do not know, Master, if it be so, and you have no Money, I must trust I think, tho' I had rather always have ready Money if I could; but, marry, you look like so honest a Gentleman, that I don't fear your paying me, if it was twenty times as much.' The Priest made no Reply, but taking leave of him and *Adams*, as fast as he could, not without Confusion, and perhaps with some Distrust of *Adams's* Sincerity, departed.

He was no sooner gone than the Host fell a shaking his Head, and declared if he had suspected the Fellow had no Money, he would not have drawn him a single Drop of Drink; saying, he despaired of ever seeing his Face again; for that he looked like a confounded Rogue. 'Rabbit the Fellow,' cries he, 'I thought by his talking so much about Riches, that he had a hundred Pounds at least in his Pocket.' *Adams* chid him for his Suspicions, which he said were not becoming a Christian; and then without reflecting on his Loss, or considering how he himself should depart in the Morning, he retired to a very homely Bed, as his Companions had before; however, Health and Fatigue gave them a sweeter Repose than is often in the power of Velvet and Down to bestow.

CHAPTER IX

Containing as surprizing and bloody Adventures as can be found in this, or perhaps any other authentic History.

IT was almost Morning when *Joseph Andrews*, whose Eyes the Thoughts of his dear *Fanny* had opened, as he lay fondly meditating on that lovely Creature, heard a violent knocking at the Door over which he lay; he presently jumped out of Bed, and opening the Window, was asked if there were no Travellers in the House; and presently by another Voice, If two Men and a young Woman had not taken up their Lodgings there that Night. Tho' he knew not the Voices, he began to entertain a Suspicion of the Truth; for indeed he had received some Information from one of the Servants of the Squire's House, of his Design; and answered in the Negative. One of the Servants who knew the Host well, called out to him by his Name, just as he had opened another Window, and asked him the same Question; to which he answered in the Affirmative. 'O ho!' said another; 'Have we found you?' And ordered the Host to come down and open his Door. *Fanny,* who was as wakeful as *Joseph,* no sooner heard all this, than she leap'd from her Bed, and hastily putting on her Gown and Petticoats, ran as fast as possible to *Joseph's* Room, who then was almost drest; he immediately let her in, and embracing her with the most passionate Tenderness, bid her fear nothing: For he would die in her Defence. 'Is that a Reason why I should not fear,' says she, 'when I should lose what is dearer to me than the whole World?' *Joseph* then kissing her Hand, said he could almost thank the Occasion which had extorted from her a Tenderness she would never indulge him with before. He then ran and waked his Bedfellow *Adams,* who was yet fast asleep, notwithstanding many Calls from *Joseph*: But was no sooner made sensible of their Danger than he leaped from his Bed, without considering the Presence of *Fanny,* who hastily turned her Face from him, and enjoyed a double Benefit from the dark, which as it would have prevented any Offence to an Innocence less pure, or a Modesty less delicate, so it concealed even those Blushes which were raised in her.

Adams had soon put on all his Clothes but his Breeches, which in the Hurry he forgot; however, they were pretty well supplied by the length of his other Garments: And now the House-Door being opened, the Captain, the Poet, the Player, and three Servants came in. The Captain told the Host, that two Fellows who were in his House had run away with a young Woman, and desired to know in which Room she lay. The Host, who presently believed the Story, directed them, and instantly the Captain and Poet, jostling one another, ran up. The Poet, who was the nimblest, entering the Chamber first, searched the Bed and every other part, but to no purpose; the Bird was flown, as the impatient Reader, who might otherwise have been in pain for her, was before advertised. They then enquired where the Men lay, and were approaching the Chamber, when *Joseph* roared out in a loud Voice, that he would shoot the first Man who offered to attack the Door. The Captain enquired what Fire-Arms they had; to which the Host answered, he believed they had none; nay, he was almost convinced of it: For he had heard one ask the other in

the Evening, what they should have done, if they had been overtaken when they had no Arms; to which the other answered, they
would have defended themselves with their Sticks as long as they
were able, and G— would assist a just Cause. This satisfied the
Captain, but not the Poet, who prudently retreated down Stairs,
saying it was his Business to record great Actions, and not to do
them. The Captain was no sooner well satisfied that there were
no Fire-Arms, than bidding Defiance to Gunpowder, and swearing he loved the Smell of it, he ordered the Servants to follow
him, and marching boldly up, immediately attempted to force
the Door, which the Servants soon helped him to accomplish.
When it was opened, they discovered the Enemy drawn up three
deep; *Adams* in the Front, and *Fanny* in the Rear. The Captain
told *Adams*, that if they would go all back to the House again,
they should be civilly treated: but unless they consented, he
had Orders to carry the young Lady with him, whom there was
great Reason to believe they had stolen from her Parents; for
notwithstanding her Disguise, her Air, which she could not conceal, sufficiently discovered her Birth to be infinitely superiour
to theirs. *Fanny* bursting into Tears, solemnly assured him he was
mistaken; that she was a poor helpless Foundling, and had no
Relation in the World which she knew of; and throwing herself on her Knees, begged that he would not attempt to take her
from her Friends, who she was convinced would die before they
would lose her, which *Adams* confirmed with Words not far from
amounting to an Oath. The Captain swore he had no leisure to
talk, and bidding them thank themselves for what happened, he
ordered the Servants to fall on, at the same time endeavouring to
pass by *Adams* in order to lay hold on *Fanny*; but the Parson interrupting him, received a Blow from one of them, which without
considering whence it came, he returned to the Captain, and gave
him so dextrous a Knock in that part of the Stomach which is
vulgarly called the Pit, that he staggered some Paces backwards.
The Captain, who was not accustomed to this kind of play,
and who wisely apprehended the Consequence of such another
Blow, two of them seeming to him equal to a Thrust through the
Body, drew forth his Hanger, as *Adams* approached him, and was
levelling a Blow at his Head, which would probably have silenced
the Preacher for ever, had not *Joseph* in that Instant lifted up a
certain huge Stone Pot of the Chamber with one Hand, which six

Beaus could not have lifted with both,[1] and discharged it, together with the Contents, full in the Captain's Face. The uplifted Hanger dropped from his Hand, and he fell prostrate on the Floor *with a lumpish Noise, and his Halfpence rattled in his Pocket*;[2] the red Liquour which his Veins contained, and the white Liquor which the Pot contained, ran in one Stream down his Face and his Clothes. Nor had *Adams* quite escaped, some of the Water having in its Passage shed its Honours on his Head, and began to trickle down the Wrinkles or rather Furrows of his Cheeks, when one of the Servants snatching a Mop out of a Pail of Water which had already done its Duty in washing the House, pushed it in the Parson's Face; yet could not he bear him down; for the Parson wresting the Mop from the Fellow with one Hand, with the other brought his Enemy as low as the Earth, having given him a Stroke over that part of the Face, where, in some Men of Pleasure, the natural and artificial Noses are conjoined.[3]

Hitherto Fortune seemed to incline the Victory on the Travellers side, when, according to her Custom, she began to shew the Fickleness of her Disposition: for now the Host entering the Field, or rather Chamber, of Battle, flew directly at *Joseph*, and darting his Head into his Stomach (for he was a stout Fellow, and an expert Boxer) almost staggered him; but *Joseph* stepping one Leg back, did with his left Hand so chuck him under the Chin that he reeled. The Youth was pursuing his Blow with his right Hand, when he received from one of the Servants such a Stroke with a Cudgel on his Temples, that it instantly deprived him of Sense, and he measured his Length on the Ground.

Fanny rent the Air with her Cries, and *Adams* was coming to the assistance of *Joseph*: but the two Serving-Men and the Host now fell on him, and soon subdued him, tho' he fought like a Madman, and looked so black with the Impressions he had received from the Mop, that *Don Quixotte* would certainly have taken him for an inchanted *Moor*. But now follows the most tragical Part; for the Captain was risen again, and seeing *Joseph* on

---

[1] Cf. *Aeneid*, xii. 896–902, where Turnus pauses in his flight to hurl a huge stone at Aeneas: 'This scarce twice six chosen men could uplift upon their shoulders, men of such frames as earth now begets' (trans. H. R. Fairclough, Loeb Classical Library, 1918).

[2] Fielding's mock-heroic adaptation of a line that recurs in the *Iliad*: δούπησεν δὲ πεσών, ἀράβησε δὲ τεύχε᾿ ἐπ᾿ αὐτῷ ('He fell with a thud, and his armour clanged upon him').

[3] The venereal disease often attacked and destroyed the nose.

the Floor, and *Adams* secured, he instantly laid hold on *Fanny*, and with the Assistance of the Poet and Player, who hearing the Battle was over, were now come up, dragged her, crying and tearing her Hair, from the Sight of her *Joseph*, and with a perfect Deafness to all her Entreaties, carried her down Stairs by Violence, and fastened her on the Player's Horse; and the Captain mounting his own, and leading that on which this poor miserable Wretch was, departed without any more Consideration of her Cries than a Butcher hath of those of a Lamb; for indeed his Thoughts were only entertained with the Degree of Favour which he promised himself from the Squire on the Success of this Adventure.

The Servants who were ordered to secure *Adams* and *Joseph* as safe as possible, that the 'Squire might receive no Interruption to his Design on poor *Fanny*, immediately by the Poet's Advice tied *Adams* to one of the Bed-posts, as they did *Joseph* on the other side, as soon as they could bring him to himself; and then leaving them together, back to back, and desiring the Host not to set them at liberty, nor go near them till he had farther Orders, they departed towards their Master; but happened to take a different Road from that which the Captain had fallen into.

CHAPTER X

A Discourse between the Poet and Player; of no other
Use in this History, but to divert the Reader.

BEFORE we proceed any farther in this Tragedy, we shall leave Mr. *Joseph* and Mr. *Adams* to themselves, and imitate the wise Conductors of the Stage; who in the midst of a grave Action entertain you with some excellent piece of Satire or Humour called a Dance. Which Piece indeed is therefore danced, and not spoke, as it is delivered to the Audience by Persons whose thinking Faculty is by most People held to lie in their Heels; and to whom, as well as Heroes, who think with their Hands, Nature hath only given Heads for the sake of Conformity, and as they are of use in Dancing, to hang their Hats on.[1]

---

[1] Although entr'acte dancing and singing were regular features in all theatres of the period (a notable exception being the Haymarket when Fielding was in control), this passage

The Poet addressing the Player, proceeded thus: 'As I was saying' (for they had been at this Discourse all the time of the Engagement, above Stairs) 'the Reason you have no good new Plays is evident; it is from your Discouragement of Authors. Gentlemen will not write, Sir, they will not write without the Expectation of Fame or Profit, or perhaps both. Plays are like Trees which will not grow without Nourishment; but like Mushrooms, they shoot up spontaneously, as it were, in a rich Soil. The Muses, like Vines, may be pruned, but not with a Hatchet. The Town, like a peevish Child, knows not what it desires, and is always best pleased with a Rattle. A Farce-Writer hath indeed some Chance for Success; but they have lost all Taste for the Sublime. Tho' I believe one Reason of their Depravity is the Badness of the Actors. If a Man writes like an Angel, Sir, those Fellows know not how to give a Sentiment Utterance.' 'Not so fast,' says the Player, 'the modern Actors are as good at least as their Authors, nay, they come nearer their illustrious Predecessors, and I expect a *Booth*[1] on the Stage again, sooner than a *Shakespear* or an *Otway*; and indeed I may turn your Observation against you, and with Truth say, that the Reason no Authors are encouraged, is because we have no good new Plays.' 'I have not affirmed the contrary,' said the Poet, 'but I am surprized you grow so warm; you cannot imagine yourself interested in this Dispute, I hope you have a better Opinion of my Taste, than to apprehend I squinted at yourself. No, Sir, if we had six such Actors as you, we should soon rival the *Bettertons* and *Sandfords*[2] of former Times; for, without a Compliment to you, I think it impossible for any one to have excelled you in most of your Parts. Nay, it is solemn Truth, and I have heard many, and all great Judges, express as much; and you will pardon me if I tell you, I think every time I have seen you lately, you have constantly

---

may be another allusion to the 'entertainments' of John Rich (see p. 36, n. 1), which Fielding burlesqued in *Tumble-Down Dick, or Phaeton in the Suds*. In ironically dedicating the published version of that play (1744) to 'Mr. John Lun', Fielding made a joke similar to the one that concludes this paragraph, pretending that he could not tell the reason for Rich's success: '(whether owing to your Heels or your Head, I will not determine)'.

[1] Barton Booth (1681–1733) was considered, after Betterton, the best of the tragedians before Garrick; perhaps his greatest successes were in the roles of Othello and Cato.

[2] Thomas Betterton (1635–1710) was the most celebrated tragedian of his time. Samuel Sandford (*fl.* 1661–1700) excelled as a stage villain.

acquired some new Excellence, like a Snowball. You have deceived me in my Estimation of Perfection, and have outdone what I thought inimitable.' 'You are as little interested,' answer'd the Player, 'in what I have said of other Poets; for d——n me, if there are not manly Strokes, ay whole Scenes, in your last Tragedy, which at least equal *Shakespear*. There is a Delicacy of Sentiment, a Dignity of Expression in it, which I will own many of our Gentlemen did not do adequate Justice to. To confess the Truth, they are bad enough, and I pity an Author who is present at the Murder of his Works.'—'Nay, it is but seldom that it can happen,' returned the Poet, 'the Works of most modern Authors, like dead-born Children, cannot be murdered. It is such wretched half-begotten, half-writ, lifeless, spiritless, low, groveling Stuff, that I almost pity the Actor who is oblig'd to get it by heart, which must be almost as difficult to remember as Words in a Language you don't understand.' 'I am sure,' said the Player, 'if the Sentences have little Meaning when they are writ, when they are spoken they have less. I know scarce one who ever lays an Emphasis right, and much less adapts his Action to his Character. I have seen a tender Lover in an Attitude of fighting with his Mistress, and a brave Hero suing to his Enemy with his Sword in his Hand—I don't care to abuse my Profession, but rot me if in my Heart I am not inclined to the Poet's Side.' 'It is rather generous in you than just,' said the Poet; 'and tho' I hate to speak ill of any Person's Production; nay I never do it, nor will—but yet to do Justice to the Actors, what could *Booth* or *Betterton* have made of such horrible Stuff as *Fenton's Mariamne*, *Frowd's Philotas*, or *Mallet's Eurydice*,[1] or those low, dirty, last Dying-Speeches, which a Fellow in the City or *Wapping*, your *Dillo* or *Lillo*,[2] what was his Name, called Tragedies?'—'Very well, Sir,' says the Player, 'and pray what do you think of such Fellows as

---

[1] Tragedies performed, respectively, in 1723, 1731, and 1731; the authors are Elijah Fenton (1683–1730), Philip Frowde (d. 1738), and David Mallet (see p. 239, n. 1). The plays by Fenton and Mallet were quite successful, but Frowde's lugubrious performance died after six nights.

[2] George Lillo (1693–1739), a London jeweller, was the author of the successful 'domestic' tragedy, *The London Merchant; or The History of George Barnwell* (1731). In 1736 Fielding, who became a close friend of Lillo, accepted his *Fatal Curiosity* for the Haymarket Theatre and wrote the prologue. In a eulogy of Lillo appearing in *The Champion* (26 February 1739/40), shortly after the dramatist's death, Fielding wrote: 'His FATAL CURIOSITY, which is a Master-Piece in its Kind, and inferior only to *Shakspeare's* best Pieces, gives him a Title to be call'd, the best Tragic Poet of his Age. . . .'

Quin[1] and *Delane*,[2] or that face-making Puppy young *Cibber*,[3] that ill-looked Dog *Macklin*,[4] or that saucy Slut Mrs. *Clive*?[5] What work would they make with your *Shakespeares*, *Otways* and *Lees*? How would those harmonious Lines of the last come from their Tongues?

> *—No more; for I disdain*
> *All Pomp when thou art by—far be the Noise*
> *Of Kings and Crowns from us, whose gentle Souls*
> *Our kinder Fates have steer'd another way.*
> *Free as the Forest Birds we'll pair together,*
> *Without rememb'ring who our Fathers were:*
> *Fly to the Arbors, Grots and flowry Meads,*
> *There in soft Murmurs interchange our Souls,*
> *Together drink the Crystal of the Stream,*
> *Or taste the yellow Fruit which Autumn yields.*
> *And when the golden Evening calls us home,*
> *Wing to our downy Nests and sleep till Morn.*[6]

'Or how would this Disdain of *Otway*,

> *Who'd be that foolish, sordid thing, call'd Man?*[7]

[1] James Quin (1693–1766) was the leading actor between the retirement of Booth and the emergence of Garrick. For Fielding's complimentary references to Quin, see 'To John Hayes, Esq.', 'Essay on Conversation', *The Jacobite's Journal* (6 February 1748), and *The Covent-Garden Journal* (31 March 1752).

[2] Dennis Delane (d. 1750) was popular as a tragedian.

[3] Colley Cibber's disreputable son, Theophilus (1703–58), was, like his father, a successful comedian. He acted in several of Fielding's plays and became, in turn, the subject of satire in two of them, as Marplay Junior in the revised version of *The Author's Farce* and as Pistol in *The Historical Register for the Year 1736*. Other satiric references to Theophilus Cibber may be found in *The Champion* (10 December 1739, 17 May and 6 September 1740).

[4] Charles Macklin (1697–1797) acted in several of Fielding's comedies, but was best known for his portrayal of Shylock. For Fielding's *The Wedding Day* (February 1743) Macklin wrote and delivered the prologue, wherein, perhaps recalling the passage in *Joseph Andrews*, he amusingly makes Fielding insult his 'good long, dismal, mercy-begging Face'.

[5] Catherine 'Kitty' Clive (1711–85) was a favourite comic actress, much admired for her fine singing voice. She acted in several of Fielding's plays; Fielding, who claimed to have been the first to recognize her talents, dedicated *The Intriguing Chambermaid* to her in 1734 and was extravagant in praising her: 'in Comedy', he declared in *The Jacobite's Journal* (30 January 1748), Mrs. Clive 'is certainly the best Actress the World ever produced'. For other references see the Preface to *The Mock Doctor* (1732), Letter XL of *Familiar Letters between the Principal Characters in David Simple* (1747), *The Jacobite's Journal* (6 February 1748), *Tom Jones* (IX. i), *The Covent-Garden Journal* (11 January and 8 February 1752).

[6] The player quotes, with reasonable accuracy, from Nathaniel Lee's *Theodosius: or The Force of Love* (1680), II. i, where Varanes protests his love for Athenais.

[7] The line from Otway's *The Orphan: or, The Unhappy Marriage* (1680), I. i, reads: 'Who'd be that sordid foolish thing call'd Man . . . ?'

'Hold, hold, hold,' said the Poet, 'Do repeat that tender Speech in the third Act of my Play which you made such a Figure in.'—'I would willingly,' said the Player, 'but I have forgot it.'—'Ay, you was not quite perfect enough in it when you play'd it,' cries the Poet, 'or you would have had such an Applause as was never given on the Stage; an Applause I was extremely concerned for your losing.'—'Sure,' says the Player, 'if I remember, that was hiss'd more than any Passage in the whole Play.'—'Ay your speaking it was hiss'd,' said the Poet. 'My speaking it!' said the Player.—'I mean your not speaking it,' said the Poet. 'You was out, and then they hiss'd.'—'They hiss'd, and then I was out, if I remember,' answer'd the Player; 'and I must say this for myself, that the whole Audience allowed I did your Part Justice, so don't lay the Damnation of your Play to my account.' 'I don't know what you mean by Damnation,' reply'd the Poet. 'Why you know it was acted but one Night,' cried the Player. 'No,' said the Poet, 'you and the whole Town know I had Enemies; the Pit were all my Enemies, Fellows that would cut my Throat, if the Fear of Hanging did not restrain them. All Taylors, Sir, all Taylors.'—'Why should the Taylors be so angry with you?' cries the Player. 'I suppose you don't employ so many in making your Clothes.' 'I admit your Jest,' answered the Poet, 'but you remember the Affair as well as myself; you know there was a Party in the Pit and Upper-Gallery, would not suffer it to be given out again; tho' much, ay infinitely, the Majority, all the Boxes in particular, were desirous of it; nay, most of the Ladies swore they never would come to the House till it was acted again—Indeed I must own their Policy was good, in not letting it be given out a second time; for the Rascals knew if it had gone a second Night, it would have run fifty: for if ever there was Distress in a Tragedy —I am not fond of my own Performance; but if I should tell you what the best Judges said of it—Nor was it entirely owing to my Enemies neither, that it did not succeed on the Stage as well as it hath since among the polite Readers; for you can't say it had Justice done it by the Performers.'—'I think,' answer'd the Player, 'the Performers did the Distress of it Justice: for I am sure we were in Distress enough, who were pelted with Oranges all the last Act; we all imagined it would have been the last Act of our Lives.'

The Poet, whose Fury was now raised, had just attempted to

answer, when they were interrupted, and an end put to their Discourse by an Accident; which, if the Reader is impatient to know, he must skip over the next Chapter, which is a sort of Counterpart to this, and contains some of the best and gravest Matters in the whole Book, being a Discourse between Parson *Abraham Adams* and Mr. *Joseph Andrews.*

CHAPTER XI

Containing the Exhortations of Parson Adams to his Friend in Affliction;[1] *calculated for the Instruction and Improvement of the Reader.*

JOSEPH no sooner came perfectly to himself, than perceiving his Mistress gone, he bewailed her Loss with Groans, which would have pierced any Heart but those which are possessed by some People, and are made of a certain Composition not unlike Flint in its Hardness and other Properties; for you may strike Fire from them which will dart through the Eyes, but they can never distil one Drop of Water the same way. His own, poor Youth, was of a softer Composition; and at those Words, *O my dear Fanny! O my Love! shall I never, never see thee more?* his Eyes overflowed with Tears, which would have become any but a Hero. In a word, his Despair was more easy to be conceived than related.—

Mr. *Adams,* after many Groans, sitting with his Back to *Joseph,* began thus in a sorrowful Tone: 'You cannot imagine, my good Child, that I entirely blame these first Agonies of your Grief; for, when Misfortunes attack us by Surprize, it must require infinitely more Learning than you are master of to resist them: but it is the Business of a Man and a Christian to summon Reason as quickly as he can to his Aid; and she will presently teach him Patience and Submission. Be comforted, therefore,

---

[1] Cf. Fielding's essay, *Of the Remedy of Affliction for the Loss of Our Friends* (1743). On this essay, its place in the tradition of the *consolatio,* and the relation of Adams's 'Exhortations' to both, see H. K. Miller, *Essays on Fielding's 'Miscellanies'* (Princeton, 1961), pp. 228–71. With Adams's explanation of the duty of submission to providence, cf. Tillotson's sermon, 'The wisdom of God in his providence' (*Works* [1757], viii. 140–60).

Child, I say be comforted. It is true you have lost the prettiest,
kindest, loveliest, sweetest young Woman: One with whom you
might have expected to have lived in Happiness, Virtue and
Innocence. By whom you might have promised yourself many
little Darlings, who would have been the Delight of your Youth,
and the Comfort of your Age. You have not only lost her, but
have reason to fear the utmost Violence which Lust and Power
can inflict upon her. Now indeed you may easily raise Ideas of
Horror, which might drive you to Despair.'—'O I shall run
mad,' cries *Joseph*, 'O that I could but command my Hands to
tear my Eyes out and my Flesh off.'—'If you would use them to
such Purposes, I am glad you can't,' answer'd *Adams*. 'I have
stated your Misfortune as strong as I possibly can; but on the
other side, you are to consider you are a Christian, that no
Accident happens to us without the Divine Permission, and that
it is the Duty of a Man, much more of a Christian, to submit.
We did not make ourselves; but the same Power which made us,
rules over us, and we are absolutely at his Disposal; he may do
with us what he pleases, nor have we any Right to complain.
A second Reason against our Complaint is our Ignorance; for
as we know not future Events, so neither can we tell to what
Purpose any Accident tends; and that which at first threatens
us with Evil, may in the end produce our Good. I should indeed
have said our Ignorance is twofold (but I have not at present
time to divide properly) for as we know not to what purpose any
Event is ultimately directed; so neither can we affirm from what
Cause it originally sprung. You are a Man, and consequently a
Sinner; and this may be a Punishment to you for your Sins;
indeed in this Sense it may be esteemed as a Good, yea as the
greatest Good, which satisfies the Anger of Heaven, and averts
that Wrath which cannot continue without our Destruction.
Thirdly, Our Impotency of relieving ourselves, demonstrates the
Folly and Absurdity of our Complaints: for whom do we resist?
or against whom do we complain, but a Power from whose Shafts
no Armour can guard us, no Speed can fly? A Power which
leaves us no Hope, but in Submission.'—'O Sir,' cried *Joseph*,
'all this is very true, and very fine; and I could hear you all day,
if I was not so grieved at Heart as now I am.' 'Would you take
Physick,' says *Adams*, 'when you are well, and refuse it when you
are sick? Is not Comfort to be administred to the Afflicted, and

not to those who rejoice, or those who are at ease?'—'O you have
not spoken one Word of Comfort to me yet,' returned *Joseph*.
'No!' cries *Adams*, 'What am I then doing? what can I say to
comfort you?'—'O tell me,' cries *Joseph*, 'that *Fanny* will escape
back to my Arms, that they shall again inclose that lovely Creature, with all her Sweetness, all her untainted Innocence about
her.'—'Why perhaps you may,' cries *Adams*; 'but I can't promise you what's to come. You must with perfect Resignation
wait the Event; if she be restored to you again, it is your Duty to
be thankful, and so it is if she be not: *Joseph*, if you are wise, and
truly know your own Interest, you will peaceably and quietly
submit to all the Dispensations of Providence; being thoroughly
assured, that all the Misfortunes, how great soever, which happen
to the Righteous, happen to them for their own Good.—Nay, it
is not your Interest only, but your Duty to abstain from immoderate Grief; which if you indulge, you are not worthy the
Name of a Christian.'—He spoke these last Words with an Accent
a little severer than usual; upon which *Joseph* begged him not to
be angry, saying he mistook him, if he thought he denied it was his
Duty; for he had known that long ago. 'What signifies knowing
your Duty, if you do not perform it?' answer'd *Adams*. 'Your
Knowledge encreases your Guilt—O *Joseph*, I never thought you
had this Stubbornness in your Mind.' *Joseph* replied, 'he fancied
he misunderstood him, which I assure you,' says he, 'you do, if
you imagine I endeavour to grieve; upon my Soul I don't.' *Adams*
rebuked him for swearing, and then proceeded to enlarge on the
Folly of Grief, telling him, all the wise Men and Philosophers,
even among the Heathens, had written against it, quoting several
Passages from *Seneca*,[1] and the *Consolation*, which tho' it was not
Cicero's, was, he said, as good almost as any of his Works,[2] and
concluded all by hinting, that immoderate Grief in this Case
might incense that Power which alone could restore him his

---

[1] Seneca's consolatory works include: *De consolatione ad Marciam, Ad Polybium*, and
Epistulae morales ad Lucilium (LXIII, XCVIII, and XCIX).

[2] In all probability the reference is not to Boethius' *Consolation of Philosophy*, but to the
pseudo-Ciceronian *Consolation*, which Arthur Murphy says Fielding was in the habit of
reading in times of affliction (see *An Essay on the Life and Genius of Henry Fielding, Esq*; in
Works [4v., 1762], i. 48). About 1583 a work purporting to be Cicero's lost consolation on
the death of Tullia was published in Venice under his name; it went through many editions
and was translated into French, but doubts immediately arose regarding its authenticity.
In 1741 Conyers Middleton could observe that the *Consolation* was 'undoubtedly spurious'.
(See *The Life of Cicero* [1741], ii. 188.)

Fanny. This Reason, or indeed rather the Idea which it raised of
the Restoration of his Mistress, had more effect than all which the
Parson had said before; and for a moment abated his Agonies:
but when his Fears sufficiently set before his Eyes the Danger
that poor Creature was in, his Grief returned again with repeated
Violence, nor could *Adams* in the least asswage it; tho' it may be
doubted in his Behalf, whether *Socrates* himself could have prevailed any better.

They remained some time in silence; and Groans and Sighs
issued from them both, at length *Joseph* burst out into the
following Soliloquy:

> *Yes, I will bear my Sorrows like a Man,*
> *But I must also feel them as a Man.*
> *I cannot but remember such things were,*
> *And were most dear to me—*[1]

Adams asked him what Stuff that was he repeated?—To which
he answer'd, they were some Lines he had gotten by heart out
of a Play.—'Ay, there is nothing but Heathenism to be learn'd
from Plays,' reply'd he—'I never heard of any Plays fit for a
Christian to read, but *Cato* and the *Conscious Lovers*;[2] and I must
own in the latter there are some things almost solemn enough for
a Sermon.' But we shall now leave them a little, and enquire after
the Subject of their Conversation.

CHAPTER XII

More Adventures, which we hope will as much please as surprize the Reader.

NEITHER the facetious Dialogue which pass'd between the Poet
and Player, nor the grave and truly solemn Discourse of Mr.
Adams, will, we conceive, make the Reader sufficient Amends for
the Anxiety which he must have felt on the account of poor *Fanny,*
whom we left in so deplorable a Condition. We shall therefore now

---

[1] Cf. *Macbeth,* IV. iii. 258–62, where Macduff laments the murder of his wife and children.

[2] Addison's neo-classical tragedy, *Cato,* was produced in 1713; Richard Steele's moralizing comedy, *The Conscious Lovers,* in 1722.

proceed to the Relation of what happened to that beautiful and innocent Virgin, after she fell into the wicked Hands of the Captain.

The Man of War having convey'd his charming Prize out of the Inn a little before Day, made the utmost Expedition in his power towards the Squire's House, where this delicate Creature was to be offered up a Sacrifice to the Lust of a Ravisher. He was not only deaf to all her Bewailings and Entreaties on the Road, but accosted her Ears with Impurities, which, having been never before accustomed to them, she happily for herself very little understood. At last he changed this Note, and attempted to sooth and mollify her, by setting forth the Splendor and Luxury which would be her Fortune with a Man who would have the Inclination, and Power too, to give her whatever her utmost Wishes could desire; and told her he doubted not but she would soon look kinder on him, as the Instrument of her Happiness, and despise that pitiful Fellow, whom her Ignorance only could make her fond of. She answered, She knew not whom he meant, she never was fond of any pitiful Fellow. 'Are you affronted, Madam,' says he, 'at my calling him so? but what better can be said of one in a Livery, notwithstanding your Fondness for him?' She returned, That she did not understand him, that the Man had been her Fellow-Servant, and she believed was as honest a Creature as any alive; but as for Fondness for Men—'I warrant ye,' cries the Captain, 'we shall find means to persuade you to be fond; and I advise you to yield to gentle ones; for you may be assured that it is not in your power by any Struggles whatever to preserve your Virginity two Hours longer. It will be your Interest to consent; for the 'Squire will be much kinder to you if he enjoys you willingly than by force.'—At which Words she began to call aloud for Assistance (for it was now open Day) but finding none, she lifted her Eyes to Heaven, and supplicated the Divine Assistance to preserve her Innocence. The Captain told her, if she persisted in her Vociferation, he would find a means of stopping her Mouth. And now the poor Wretch perceiving no Hopes of Succour, abandoned herself to Despair, and sighing out the Name of *Joseph, Joseph!* a River of Tears ran down her lovely Cheeks, and wet the Handkerchief which covered her Bosom. A Horseman now appeared in the Road, upon which the Captain threatened her violently if she complained; however, the moment they approached each other, she begged him with the utmost Earnestness to relieve a distressed Creature, who was in the hands of a Ravisher. The Fellow stopt at those Words; but the Captain assured him it was his Wife, and that he was carrying her home from her Adulterer. Which so satisfied the Fellow, who was an old one, (and perhaps a married one too) that he wished him a good Journey, and rode on. He was no sooner past, than the Captain abused her violently for breaking his Commands, and threaten'd to gagg her; when two more Horsemen, armed with Pistols, came into the Road just before them. She again sollicited their Assistance; and the Captain told the same Story as before. Upon which one said to the other—'That's a charming Wench! *Jack*; I wish I had been in the Fellow's Place whoever he is.' But the other, instead of answering him, cried out eagerly, 'Zounds, I know her:' and then turning to her said, 'Sure you are not *Fanny Goodwill*?'—'Indeed, indeed I am,' she cry'd—'O *John*, I know you now—Heaven hath sent you to my Assistance, to deliver me from this wicked Man, who is carrying me away for his vile Purposes—O for G—'s sake rescue me from him.' A fierce Dialogue immediately ensued between the Captain and these two Men, who being both armed with Pistols, and the Chariot which they attended being now arrived, the Captain saw both Force and Stratagem were vain, and endeavoured to make his Escape; in which however he could not succeed. The Gentleman who rode in the Chariot, ordered it to stop, and with an Air of Authority examined into the Merits of the Cause; of which being advertised by *Fanny*, whose Credit was confirmed by the Fellow who knew her, he ordered the Captain, who was all bloody from his Encounter at the Inn, to be conveyed as a Prisoner behind the Chariot, and very gallantly took *Fanny* into it; for, to say the truth, this Gentleman (who was no other than the celebrated Mr. *Peter Pounce*, and who preceded the Lady *Booby* only a few Miles, by setting out earlier in the Morning) was a very gallant Person, and loved a pretty Girl better than any thing, besides his own Money, or the Money of other People.

The Chariot now proceeded towards the Inn, which as *Fanny* was informed lay in their way, and where it arrived at that very time while the Poet and Player were disputing below Stairs, and *Adams* and *Joseph* were discoursing back to back above: just at that Period to which we brought them both in the two preceding Chapters, the Chariot stopt at the Door, and in an instant *Fanny* leaping from it, ran up to her *Joseph*.—O Reader, conceive if thou canst, the Joy which fired the Breasts of these Lovers on this Meeting; and, if thy own Heart doth not sympathetically assist thee in this Conception, I pity thee sincerely from my own: for let the hard-hearted Villain know this, that there is a Pleasure in a tender Sensation beyond any which he is capable of tasting.

Peter being informed by *Fanny* of the Presence of *Adams*, stopt to see him, and receive his Homage; for, as *Peter* was an Hypocrite, a sort of People whom Mr. *Adams* never saw through, the one paid that Respect to his seeming Goodness which the other believed to be paid to his Riches; hence Mr. *Adams* was so much his Favourite, that he once lent him four Pounds thirteen Shillings and Sixpence, to prevent his going to Goal, on no greater Security than a Bond and Judgment,[1] which probably he would have made no use of, tho' the Money had not been (as it was) paid exactly at the time.

It is not perhaps easy to describe the Figure of *Adams*; he had risen in such a violent Hurry, that he had on neither Breeches nor Stockings; nor had he taken from his Head a red spotted Handkerchief, which by Night bound his Wig, that was turned inside out, around his Head. He had on his torn Cassock, and his Great-Coat; but as the remainder of his Cassock hung down below his Great-Coat; so did a small Strip of white, or rather whitish Linnen appear below that; to which we may add the several Colours which appeared on his Face, where a long Piss-burnt Beard, served to retain the Liquor of the Stone Pot, and that of a blacker hue which distilled from the Mop.—This Figure, which *Fanny* had delivered from his Captivity, was no sooner spied by *Peter*, than it disordered the composed Gravity of his Muscles; however he advised him immediately to make himself clean, nor would accept his Homage in that Pickle.

The Poet and Player no sooner saw the Captain in Captivity, than they began to consider of their own Safety, of which Flight presented itself as the only means; they therefore both of them mounted the Poet's Horse, and made the most expeditious Retreat in their power.

The Host, who well knew Mr. *Pounce* and the Lady *Booby's* Livery, was not a little surprized at this change of the Scene, nor

---

[1] A certificate binding a person to pay a certain sum of money and assigning his chattels as security for the debt.

was his Confusion much helped by his Wife, who was now just risen, and having heard from him the Account of what had past, comforted him with a decent Number of Fools and Blockheads, asked him why he did not consult her, and told him he would never leave following the nonsensical Dictates of his own Numscull, till she and her Family were ruined.

Joseph being informed of the Captain's Arrival, and seeing his *Fanny* now in Safety, quitted her a moment, and running down stairs, went directly to him, and stripping off his Coat challenged him to fight; but the Captain refused, saying he did not understand Boxing. He then grasped a Cudgel in one Hand, and catching the Captain by the Collar with the other, gave him a most severe Drubbing, and ended with telling him, he had now had some Revenge for what his dear *Fanny* had suffered.

When Mr. *Pounce* had a little regaled himself with some Provision which he had in his Chariot, and Mr. *Adams* had put on the best Appearance his Clothes would allow him, *Pounce* ordered the Captain into his Presence; for he said he was guilty of Felony, and the next Justice of Peace should commit him: but the Servants (whose Appetite for Revenge is soon satisfied) being sufficiently contented with the Drubbing which *Joseph* had inflicted on him, and which was indeed of no very moderate kind, had suffered him to go off, which he did, threatening a severe Revenge against *Joseph*, which I have never heard he thought proper to take.

The Mistress of the House made her voluntary Appearance before Mr. *Pounce*, and with a thousand Curt'sies told him, 'she hoped his Honour would pardon her Husband, who was a very *nonsense* Man, for the sake of his poor Family; that indeed if he could be ruined alone, she should be very willing of it, *for because as why*, his Worship very well knew he deserved it: but she had three poor small Children, who were not capable to get their own Living; and if her Husband was sent to Goal, they must all come to the Parish;[1] for she was a poor weak Woman, continually a breeding, and had no time to work for them. She therefore hoped his Honour would take it into his Worship's Consideration, and forgive her Husband this time; for she was sure he never intended any Harm to Man, Woman, or Child; and if it was not for that

---

[1] To seek relief of the parish, which, under the Poor Law, was obliged to provide for its poor (see p. 167, n. 2).

Block-Head of his own, the Man in some things was well enough; for she had had three Children by him in less than three Years, and was almost ready to cry out the fourth time.' She would have proceeded in this manner much longer, had not *Peter* stopt her Tongue, by telling her he had nothing to say to her Husband, nor her neither. So, as *Adams* and the rest had assured her of Forgiveness, she cried and curt'sied out of the Room.

Mr. *Pounce* was desirous that *Fanny* should continue her Journey with him in the Chariot, but she absolutely refused, saying she would ride behind *Joseph*, on a Horse which one of Lady *Booby's* Servants had equipped him with. But alas! when the Horse appeared, it was found to be no other than that identical Beast which Mr. *Adams* had left behind him at the Inn, and which these honest Fellows who knew him had redeemed. Indeed whatever Horse they had provided for *Joseph*, they would have prevailed with him to mount none, no not even to ride before his beloved *Fanny*, till the Parson was supplied; much less would he deprive his Friend of the Beast which belonged to him, and which he knew the moment he saw, tho' *Adams* did not: however, when he was reminded of the Affair, and told that they had brought the Horse with them which he left behind, he answered—*Bless me! and so I did.*

Adams was very desirous that *Joseph* and *Fanny* should mount this Horse, and declared he could very easily walk home. 'If I walked alone,' says he, 'I would wage a Shilling, that the *Pedestrian* out-stripped the *Equestrian* Travellers: but as I intend to take the Company of a Pipe, peradventure I may be an Hour later.' One of the Servants whispered *Joseph* to take him at his Word, and suffer the old Put to walk if he would: This Proposal was answered with an angry Look and a peremptory Refusal by *Joseph*, who catching *Fanny* up in his Arms, aver'd he would rather carry her home in that manner, than take away Mr. *Adams's* Horse, and permit him to walk on foot.

Perhaps, Reader, thou hast seen a Contest between two Gentlemen, or two Ladies quickly decided, tho' they have both asserted they would not eat such a nice Morsel, and each insisted on the other's accepting it; but in reality both were very desirous to swallow it themselves. Do not therefore conclude hence, that this Dispute would have come to a speedy Decision: for here both Parties were heartily in earnest, and it is very probable, they

would have remained in the Inn-yard to this day, had not the
good *Peter Pounce* put a stop to it; for finding he had no longer
hopes of satisfying his old Appetite with *Fanny*, and being desirous
of having some one to whom he might communicate his Grandeur, he told the Parson he would convey him home in his Chariot.
This Favour was by *Adams*, with many Bows and Acknowledgments, accepted, tho' he afterwards said, 'he ascended the Chariot
rather that he might not offend, than from any Desire of riding
in it, for that in his heart he preferred the *Pedestrian* even to the
Vehicular Expedition.' All matters being now settled, the Chariot
in which rode *Adams* and *Pounce* moved forwards; and *Joseph*
having borrowed a Pillion from the Host, *Fanny* had just seated
herself thereon, and had laid hold on the Girdle which her Lover
wore for that purpose, when the wise Beast, who concluded that
one at a time was sufficient, that two to one were odds, &c. discovered much Uneasiness at this double Load, and began to
consider his hinder as his Fore-legs, moving the direct contrary
way to that which is called forwards. Nor could *Joseph* with all
his Horsemanship persuade him to advance: but without having
any regard to the lovely Part of the lovely Girl which was on his
Back, he used such Agitations, that had not one of the Men come
immediately to her Assistance, she had in plain *English* tumbled
backwards on the Ground. This Inconvenience was presently
remedied by an Exchange of Horses, and then *Fanny* being again
placed on her Pillion, on a better natured, and somewhat a better
fed Beast, the Parson's Horse finding he had no longer Odds
to contend with, agreed to march, and the whole Procession
set forwards for *Booby-Hall*, where they arrived in a few Hours
without any thing remarkable happening on the Road, unless
it was a curious Dialogue between the Parson and the Steward;
which, to use the Language of a late Apologist, a Pattern to all
Biographers, *waits for the Reader in the next Chapter.*[1]

[1] At the close of Chapter iv of his *Apology*, Cibber refers to 'those several Vehicles [i.e. his
accounts of the actors], which you will find waiting in the next Chapter, to carry you thro'
the rest of the Journey, at your Leisure' (2nd ed., 1740, p. 100).

CHAPTER XIII

A curious Dialogue which passed between Mr. Abraham
Adams *and Mr.* Peter Pounce, *better worth reading
than all the Works of* Colley Cibber *and many others.*

THE Chariot had not proceeded far, before Mr. *Adams* observed
it was a very fine Day. 'Ay, and a very fine Country too,' answered
Pounce. 'I should think so more,' returned *Adams*, 'if I had not
lately travelled over the *Downs*, which I take to exceed this and all
other Prospects in the Universe.' 'A fig for Prospects,' answered
Pounce, 'one Acre here is worth ten there; and for my own part,
I have no Delight in the Prospect of any Land but my own.'
'Sir,' said *Adams*, 'you can indulge yourself with many fine Prospects
of that kind.' 'I thank God I have a little,' replied the other,
'with which I am content, and envy no Man: I have a little,
Mr. *Adams*, with which I do as much good as I can.' *Adams*
answered, that Riches without Charity were nothing worth; for
that they were only a Blessing to him who made them a Blessing
to others. 'You and I,' said *Peter*, 'have different Notions of
Charity. I own, as it is generally used, I do not like the Word, nor
do I think it becomes one of us Gentlemen; it is a mean Parson-
like Quality; tho' I would not infer many Parsons have it neither.'
'Sir,' said *Adams*, 'my Definition of Charity is a generous Disposition to relieve the Distressed.'[1] 'There is something in that
Definition,' answered *Peter*, 'which I like well enough; it is, as
you say, a Disposition—and does not so much consist in the Act
as in the Disposition to do it; but alas, Mr. *Adams*, Who are
meant by the Distressed? Believe me, the Distresses of Mankind
are mostly imaginary, and it would be rather Folly than Goodness
to relieve them.' 'Sure, Sir,' replied *Adams*, 'Hunger and Thirst,
Cold and Nakedness, and other Distresses which attend the Poor,

[1] Cf. Isaac Barrow in 'The Duty and Reward of Bounty to the Poor': '. . . that we
should be always, in affection and disposition of mind, ready to part with anything we have
for the succour of our poor brethren'; Barrow continues, however, by making explicit what
Adams only implies: 'that to the utmost of our ability (according to moral estimation
prudently rated) upon all occasions we should really express that disposition in our
practice . . . .' (*Works*, ed. Napier, i. 14.) Fielding quotes this passage in *The Covent-Garden
Journal*, 16 May 1752.

can never be said to be imaginary Evils.' 'How can any Man complain of Hunger,' said *Peter*, 'in a Country where such excellent Sallads are to be gathered in almost every Field? or of Thirst, where every River and Stream produces such delicious Potations? And as for Cold and Nakedness, they are Evils introduced by Luxury and Custom. A Man naturally wants Clothes no more than a Horse or any other Animal, and there are whole Nations who go without them: but these are things perhaps which you, who do not know the World—' 'You will pardon me, Sir,' returned *Adams*; 'I have read of the *Gymnosophists*.'[1] 'A plague of your *Jehosaphats*,' cried *Peter*; 'the greatest Fault in our Constitution is the Provision made for the Poor, except that perhaps made for some others. Sir, I have not an Estate which doth not contribute almost as much again to the Poor as to the Land-Tax, and I do assure you I expect to come myself to the Parish in the end.' To which *Adams* giving a dissenting Smile, *Peter* thus proceeded: 'I fancy, Mr. *Adams*, you are one of those who imagine I am a Lump of Money; for there are many who I fancy believe that not only my Pockets, but my whole Clothes, are lined with Bank-Bills; but I assure you, you are all mistaken: I am not the Man the World esteems me. If I can hold my Head above Water, it is all I can. I have injured myself by purchasing. I have been too liberal of my Money. Indeed I fear my Heir will find my Affairs in a worse Situation than they are reputed to be. Ah! he will have reason to wish I had loved Money more, and Land less. Pray, my good Neighbour, where should I have that Quantity of Riches the World is so liberal to bestow on me? Where could I possibly, without I had stole it, acquire such a Treasure?' 'Why truly,' says *Adams*, 'I have been always of your Opinion; I have wondered as well as yourself with what Confidence they could report such things of you, which have to me appeared as mere Impossibilities; for you know, Sir, and I have often heard you say it, that your Wealth is of your own Acquisition, and can it be credible that in your short time you should have amassed such a heap of Treasure as these People will have you worth? Indeed had you inherited an Estate like Sir *Thomas Booby*, which had descended in your Family for many Generations, they might have had a colour for their Assertions.' 'Why, what do they say I am worth?' cries *Peter* with a malicious Sneer. 'Sir,' answered

[1] A sect of ascetic Hindu philosophers who wore little clothing and ate no meat.

Adams, 'I have heard some aver you are not worth less than twenty thousand Pounds.' At which *Peter* frowned. 'Nay, Sir,' said *Adams*, 'you ask me only the Opinion of others, for my own part I have always denied it, nor did I ever believe you could possibly be worth half that Sum.' 'However, Mr. *Adams*,' said he, squeezing him by the Hand, 'I would not sell them all I am worth for double that Sum; and as to what you believe, or they believe, I care not a Fig, no not a Fart. I am not poor because you think me so, nor because you attempt to undervalue me in the Country. I know the Envy of Mankind very well, but I thank Heaven I am above them. It is true my Wealth is of my own Acquisition. I have not an Estate like Sir *Thomas Booby*, that hath descended in my Family through many Generations; but I know the Heirs of such Estates who are forced to travel about the Country like some People in torn Cassocks, and might be glad to accept of a pitiful Curacy for what I know. Yes, Sir, as shabby Fellows as yourself, whom no Man of my Figure, without that Vice of Good-nature about him, would suffer to ride in a Chariot with him.' 'Sir,' said *Adams*, 'I value not your Chariot of a Rush; and if I had known you had intended to affront me, I would have walked to the World's End on foot ere I would have accepted a place in it. However, Sir, I will soon rid you of that Inconvenience,' and so saying, he opened the Chariot-Door without calling to the Coachman, and leapt out into the Highway, forgetting to take his Hat along with him; which however Mr. *Pounce* threw after him with great violence. *Joseph* and *Fanny* stopt to bear him Company the rest of the way, which was not above a Mile.

The History of the Adventures of
JOSEPH ANDREWS,
and of his Friend Mr. *Abraham Adams*

BOOK IV

CHAPTER I

The Arrival of Lady Booby *and the rest at* Booby-Hall.

THE Coach and Six, in which Lady *Booby* rode, overtook the other Travellers as they entered the Parish. She no sooner saw *Joseph*, than her Cheeks glow'd with red, and immediately after became as totally pale. She had in her Surprize almost stopt her Coach; but recollected herself timely enough to prevent it. She entered the Parish amidst the ringing of Bells, and the Acclamations of the Poor, who were rejoiced to see their Patroness returned after so long an Absence, during which time all her Rents had been drafted to *London*, without a Shilling being spent among them, which tended not a little to their utter impoverishing; for if the Court would be severely missed in such a City as *London*, how much more must the Absence of a Person of great Fortune be felt in a little Country Village, for whose Inhabitants such a Family finds a constant Employment and Supply; and with the Offalls of whose Table the infirm, aged, and infant Poor are abundantly fed, with a Generosity which hath scarce a visible Effect on their Benefactor's Pockets?

But if their Interest inspired so publick a Joy into every Countenance, how much more forcibly did the Affection which they bore Parson *Adams* operate upon all who beheld his Return. They flocked about him like dutiful Children round an indulgent Parent, and vyed with each other in Demonstrations of Duty and Love. The Parson on his side shook every one by the Hand, enquiring heartily after the Healths of all that were absent, of their Children and Relations, and exprest a Satisfaction in his Face, which nothing but Benevolence made happy by its Objects could infuse.

Nor did *Joseph* and *Fanny* want a hearty Welcome from all who saw them. In short, no three Persons could be more kindly received, as indeed none ever more deserved to be universally beloved.

Adams carried his Fellow-Travellers home to his House, where he insisted on their partaking whatever his Wife, whom with his Children he found in Health and Joy, could provide. Where we shall leave them, enjoying perfect Happiness over a homely Meal, to view Scenes of greater Splendor but infinitely less Bliss.

Our more intelligent Readers will doubtless suspect by this second Appearance of Lady *Booby* on the Stage, that all was not ended by the Dismission of *Joseph*; and to be honest with them, they are in the right; the Arrow had pierced deeper than she imagined; nor was the Wound so easily to be cured. The Removal of the Object soon cooled her Rage, but it had a different Effect on her Love; that departed with his Person; but this remained lurking in her Mind with his Image. Restless, interrupted Slumbers, and confused horrible Dreams were her Portion the first Night. In the Morning, Fancy painted her a more delicious Scene; but to delude, not delight her: for before she could reach the promised Happiness, it vanished, and left her to curse, not bless the Vision.

She started from her Sleep, her Imagination being all on fire with the Phantom, when her Eyes accidentally glancing towards the Spot where yesterday the real *Joseph* had stood, that little Circumstance raised his Idea in the liveliest Colours in her Memory. Each Look, each Word, each Gesture rushed back on her Mind with Charms which all his Coldness could not abate. Nay, she imputed that to his Youth, his Folly, his Awe, his Religion, to every thing, but what would instantly have produced Contempt, want of Passion for the Sex; or, that which would have roused her Hatred, want of Liking to her.

Reflection then hurried her farther, and told her she must see this beautiful Youth no more, nay, suggested to her, that she herself had dismissed him for no other Fault, than probably that of too violent an Awe and Respect for herself; and which she ought rather to have esteemed a Merit, the Effects of which were besides so easily and surely to have been removed; she then

blamed, she cursed the hasty Rashness of her Temper; her Fury
was vented all on herself, and *Joseph* appeared innocent in her
Eyes. Her Passion at length grew so violent that it forced her on
seeking Relief, and now she thought of recalling him: But Pride
forbad that, Pride which soon drove all softer Passions from her
Soul, and represented to her the Meanness of him she was fond
of. That Thought soon began to obscure his Beauties; Contempt
succeeded next, and then Disdain, which presently introduced
her Hatred of the Creature who had given her so much Uneasiness. These Enemies of *Joseph* had no sooner taken Possession
of her Mind, than they insinuated to her a thousand things in his
Disfavour; every thing but Dislike of her Person; a Thought,
which as it would have been intolerable to her, she checked the
moment it endeavoured to arise. Revenge came now to her
Assistance; and she considered her Dismission of him stript, and
without a Character, with the utmost Pleasure. She rioted in the
several kinds of Misery, which her Imagination suggested to her,
might be his Fate; and with a Smile composed of Anger, Mirth, and
Scorn, viewed him in the Rags in which her Fancy had drest him.

Mrs. *Slipslop* being summoned, attended her Mistress, who
had now in her own Opinion totally subdued this Passion. Whilst
she was dressing, she asked if that Fellow had been turned away
according to her Orders. *Slipslop* answered, she had told her
Ladyship so, (as indeed she had)—'And how did he behave?'
replied the Lady. 'Truly Madam,' cries *Slipslop*, 'in such a manner
that *infected* every body who saw him. The poor Lad had but
little Wages to receive: for he constantly allowed his Father and
Mother half his Income; so that when your Ladyship's Livery
was stript off, he had not wherewithal to buy a Coat, and must
have gone naked, if one of the Footmen had not *incommodated*
him with one; and whilst he was standing in his Shirt, (and to
say truth, he was an *amorous* Figure) being told your Ladyship
would not give him a Character, he sighed, and said he had done
nothing willingly to offend; that for his part he should always
give your Ladyship a good Character where-ever he went; and
he pray'd God to bless you; for you was the best of Ladies, tho'
his Enemies had set you against him: I wish you had not turned
him away; for I believe you have not a faithfuller Servant in the
House.'—'How came you then,' replied the Lady, 'to advise me
to turn him away?' 'I, Madam,' said *Slipslop*, 'I am sure you will

do me the Justice to say, I did all in my power to prevent it; but I saw your Ladyship was angry; and it is not the business of us upper Servants to *hint or fear* on those occasions.'—'And was it not you, audacious Wretch,' cried the Lady, 'who made me angry? Was it not your Tittle-tattle, in which I believe you belyed the poor Fellow, which incensed me against him? He may thank you for all that hath happened; and so may I for the Loss of a good Servant, and one who probably had more Merit than all of you. Poor Fellow! I am charmed with his Goodness to his Parents. Why did not you tell me of that, but suffer me to dismiss so good a Creature without a Character? I see the Reason of your whole Behaviour now as well as your Complaint; you was jealous of the Wenches.' 'I jealous!' said *Slipslop*, 'I assure you I look upon myself as his Betters; I am not Meat for a Footman I hope.' These Words threw the Lady into a violent Passion, and she sent *Slipslop* from her Presence, who departed tossing her Nose and crying, 'Marry come up! there are some People more jealous than I, I believe.' Her Lady affected not to hear the Words, tho' in reality she did, and understood them too. Now ensued a second Conflict, so like the former, that it might savour of Repetition to relate it minutely. It may suffice to say, that Lady *Booby* found good Reason to doubt whether she had so absolutely conquered her Passion, as she had flattered herself; and in order to accomplish it quite, took a Resolution more common than wise, to retire immediately into the Country. The Reader hath long ago seen the Arrival of Mrs. *Slipslop*, whom no Pertness could make her Mistress resolve to part with; lately, that of Mr. *Pounce*, her Fore-runners; and lastly, that of the Lady herself.

The Morning after her Arrival being *Sunday*, she went to Church, to the great Surprize of every body, who wondered to see her Ladyship, being no very constant Churchwoman, there so suddenly upon her Journey. *Joseph* was likewise there; and I have heard it was remarked, that she fixed her Eyes on him much more than on the Parson; but this I believe to be only a malicious Rumour. When the Prayers were ended Mr. *Adams* stood up, and with a loud Voice pronounced: *I publish the Banns of Marriage between* Joseph Andrews *and* Frances Goodwill, *both of this Parish*, &c. Whether this had any Effect on Lady *Booby* or no, who was then in her Pew, which the Congregation could not see into, I could never discover: But certain it is, that in about a quarter of an Hour she stood up, and directed her Eyes to that part of the Church where the Women sat, and persisted in looking that way during the Remainder of the Sermon, in so scrutinizing a manner, and with so angry a Countenance, that most of the Women were afraid she was offended at them.

The moment she returned home, she sent for *Slipslop* into her Chamber, and told her, she wondered what that impudent Fellow *Joseph* did in that Parish? Upon which *Slipslop* gave her an Account of her meeting *Adams* with him on the Road, and likewise the Adventure with *Fanny*. At the Relation of which, the Lady often changed her Countenance; and when she had heard all, she ordered Mr. *Adams* into her Presence, to whom she behaved as the Reader will see in the next Chapter.

CHAPTER II

A Dialogue between Mr. Abraham Adams *and the Lady* Booby.

MR. *Adams* was not far off; for he was drinking her Ladyship's Health below in a Cup of her Ale. He no sooner came before her, than she began in the following manner: 'I wonder, Sir, after the many great Obligations you have had to this Family,' (with all which the Reader hath, in the Course of this History, been minutely acquainted) 'that you will ungratefully show any Respect to a Fellow who hath been turned out of it for his Misdeeds. Nor doth it, I can tell you, Sir, become a Man of your Character, to run about the Country with an idle Fellow and Wench. Indeed, as for the Girl, I know no harm of her. *Slipslop* tells me she was formerly bred up in my House, and behaved as she ought, till she hankered after this Fellow, and he spoiled her. Nay, she may still perhaps do very well, if he will let her alone. You are therefore doing a monstrous thing, in endeavouring to procure a Match between these two People, which will be to the Ruin of them both.'—'Madam,' says *Adams*, 'if your Ladyship will but hear me speak, I protest I never heard any harm of Mr. *Joseph Andrews*; if I had, I should have corrected him for it: For I never have, nor will encourage the Faults of those under my Cure. As for the young Woman, I assure your Ladyship I have as good an

Opinion of her as your Ladyship yourself, or any other can have. She is the sweetest-tempered, honestest, worthiest, young Creature; indeed as to her Beauty, I do not commend her on that account, tho' all Men allow she is the handsomest Woman, Gentle or Simple, that ever appeared in the Parish.' 'You are very impertinent,' says she, 'to talk such fulsome Stuff to me. It is mighty becoming truly in a Clergyman to trouble himself about handsome Women, and you are a delicate Judge of Beauty, no doubt. A Man who hath lived all his Life in such a Parish as this, is a rare Judge of Beauty. Ridiculous! Beauty indeed,—a Country Wench a Beauty.—I shall be sick whenever I hear Beauty mentioned again.—And so this Wench is to stock the Parish with Beauties, I hope.—But, Sir, our Poor is numerous enough already; I will have no more Vagabonds settled here.' 'Madam,' says *Adams*, 'your Ladyship is offended with me, I protest without any Reason. This Couple were desirous to consummate long ago, and I dissuaded them from it; nay, I may venture to say, I believe, I was the sole Cause of their delaying it.' 'Well,' says she, 'and you did very wisely and honestly too, notwithstanding she is the greatest Beauty in the Parish.'—'And now, Madam,' continued he, 'I only perform my Office to Mr. *Joseph*.'—'Pray don't Mister such Fellows to me,' cries the Lady. 'He,' said the Parson, 'with the Consent of *Fanny*, before my Face, put in the Banns.' —'Yes,' answered the Lady, 'I suppose the Slut is forward enough; *Slipslop* tells me how her Head runs on Fellows; that is one of her Beauties, I suppose. But if they have put in the Banns, I desire you will publish them no more without my Orders.' 'Madam,' cries *Adams*, 'if any one puts in sufficient Caution, and assigns a proper Reason against them, I am willing to surcease.' —'I tell you a Reason,' says she, 'he is a Vagabond, and he shall not settle here, and bring a Nest of Beggars into the Parish; it will make us but little Amends that they will be Beauties.' 'Madam,' answered *Adams*, 'with the utmost Submission to your Ladyship, I have been informed by Lawyer *Scout*, that any Person who serves a Year, gains a Settlement[1] in the Parish where he

---

[1] There were several ways of gaining a legal settlement in a parish—e.g. by owning a house or land in the parish, by renting a tenement of at least £10 a year, by paying the parish rates, by executing an annual office in the parish, etc. Among these, 'Living as a hired Servant for a Year in the Parish, being unmarried, &c. and Serving or being bound as an Apprentice in a Parish, all make a legal Settlement.' (See Jacob, *New Law-Dictionary*, 4th ed. [1739], s.v. 'Poor'.) In discussing the laws of settlement in *An Enquiry into the Causes*

serves.' 'Lawyer *Scout*,' replied the Lady, 'is an impudent Cox-comb; I will have no Lawyer *Scout* interfere with me. I repeat to you again, I will have no more Incumbrances brought on us; so I desire you will proceed no farther.' 'Madam,' returned *Adams*, 'I would obey your Ladyship in every thing that is lawful; but surely the Parties being poor is no Reason against their marrying. G—d forbid there should be any such Law. The Poor have little Share enough of this World already; it would be barbarous indeed to deny them the common Privileges, and innocent Enjoyments which Nature indulges to the animal Creation.' 'Since you under-stand yourself no better,' cries the Lady, 'nor the Respect due from such as you to a Woman of my Distinction, than to affront my Ears by such loose Discourse, I shall mention but one short Word; It is my Orders to you, that you publish these Banns no more; and if you dare, I will recommend it to your Master, the Doctor, to discard you from his Service. I will, Sir, notwith-standing your poor Family; and then you and the greatest Beauty in the Parish may go and beg together.' 'Madam,' answered *Adams*, 'I know not what your Ladyship means by the Terms *Master* and *Service*. I am in the Service of a Master who will never discard me for doing my Duty: And if the Doctor (for indeed I have never been able to pay for a Licence)[1] thinks proper to turn me out from my Cure, G— will provide me, I hope, another. At least, my Family as well as myself have Hands; and he will prosper, I doubt not, our Endeavours to get our Bread honestly with them. Whilst my Conscience is pure, I shall never fear what Man can do unto me.'—'I condemn my Humility,' said the Lady, 'for demeaning myself to converse with you so long. I shall take other Measures; for I see you are a Confederate with them. But the sooner you leave me, the better; and I shall give Orders that my Doors may no longer be open to you, I will suffer no Parsons who run about the Country with Beauties to be entertained

---

of the late Increase of Robbers, Fielding identifies the statute as 3 & 4 William & Mary, cap. 11.

[1] Adams's poverty has rendered his status in the Church technically illegal. Before he could legally officiate, a curate had to obtain a licence to preach and be admitted to his cure by the bishop of the diocese or by an ordinary with episcopal jurisdiction. (See William Watson, *The Clergy-Man's Law: or, The Complete Incumbent*, 4th ed. [1747], pp. 147, 208–9, and 338.) The cost of a licence might be as little as 18 shillings or as much as £3; in 1734 a jury allowed a fee of £2. 14s. 4d. (See Richard Burn, *Ecclesiastical Law*, 6th ed. [London, 1797], ii. 267; cited by Amory, p. 26, n. 27.)

here.'—'Madam,' said *Adams*, 'I shall enter into no Person's Doors against their Will: But I am assured, when you have enquired farther into this matter, you will applaud, not blame my Proceeding; and so I humbly take my leave;' which he did with many Bows, or at least many Attempts at a Bow.

CHAPTER III

What past between the Lady and Lawyer Scout.

I N the Afternoon the Lady sent for Mr. *Scout*, whom she attacked most violently for intermeddling with her Servants, which he denied, and indeed with Truth; for he had only asserted accidentally, and perhaps rightly, that a Year's Service gained a Settlement; and so far he owned he might have formerly informed the Parson, and believed it was Law. 'I am resolved,' said the Lady, 'to have no discarded Servants of mine settled here; and so, if this be your Law, I shall send to another Lawyer.' *Scout* said, 'if she sent to a hundred Lawyers, not one nor all of them could alter the Law. The utmost that was in the power of a Lawyer, was to prevent the Law's taking effect; and that he himself could do for her Ladyship as well as any other: And I believe,' says he, 'Madam, your Ladyship not being conversant in these Matters hath mistaken a Difference: For I asserted only, that a Man who served a Year was settled. Now there is a material Difference between being settled in Law and settled in Fact; and as I affirmed generally he was settled, and Law is preferable to Fact, my Settlement must be understood in Law, and not in Fact! And suppose, Madam, we admit he was settled in Law, what use will they make of it, how doth that relate to Fact? He is not settled in Fact; and if he be not settled in Fact, he is not an Inhabitant; and if he is not an Inhabitant, he is not of this Parish; and then undoubtedly he ought not to be published here; for Mr. *Adams* hath told me your Ladyship's Pleasure, and the Reason, which is a very good one, to prevent burdening us with the Poor, we have too many already; and I think we ought to have an Act to hang or transport half of them. If we can prove in Evidence, that he is not settled in Fact, it is another matter. What

I said to Mr. *Adams*, was on a Supposition that he was settled in Fact; and indeed if that was the Case, I should doubt.'—'Don't tell me your *Facts* and your *ifs*,' said the Lady, 'I don't understand your Gibberish: You take too much upon you, and are very impertinent in pretending to direct in this Parish, and you shall be taught better, I assure you, you shall. But as to the Wench, I am resolved she shall not settle here; I will not suffer such Beauties as these to produce Children for us to keep.'—'Beauties indeed! your Ladyship is pleased to be merry,'—answered *Scout*. —'Mr. *Adams* described her so to me,' said the Lady. '—Pray what sort of Dowdy is it, Mr. *Scout?*'—'The ugliest Creature almost I ever beheld, a poor dirty Drab, your Ladyship never saw such a Wretch.'—'Well but, dear Mr. *Scout*, let her be what she will,—these ugly Women will bring Children you know; so that we must prevent the Marriage.'—'True, Madam,' replied *Scout*, 'for the subsequent Marriage co-operating with the Law, will carry Law into Fact. When a Man is married, he is settled in Fact; and then he is not removeable.[1] I will see Mr. *Adams*, and I make no doubt of prevailing with him. His only Objection is doubtless that he shall lose his Fee: But that being once made easy, as it shall be, I am confident no farther Objection will remain. No, no, it is impossible: but your Ladyship can't discommend his Unwillingness to depart from his Fee. Every Man ought to have a proper Value for his Fee. As to the matter in question, if your Ladyship pleases to employ me in it, I will venture to promise you Success. The Laws of this Land are not so vulgar, to permit a mean Fellow to contend with one of your Ladyship's Fortune. We have one sure Card, which is to carry him before Justice *Frolick*, who, upon hearing your Ladyship's Name, will commit him without any farther Questions. As for the dirty Slut, we shall have nothing to do with her: for if we get rid of the Fellow, the ugly Jade will—' 'Take what Measures you please, good Mr. *Scout*,' answered the Lady, 'but I wish you could rid the Parish of both; for *Slipslop* tells me such Stories of this Wench, that I abhor the Thoughts of her; and tho' you say she is such an ugly Slut, yet you know, dear Mr. *Scout*, these forward Creatures who run after Men, will always find some as

---

[1] If a man married, even before he had gained a legal settlement by serving a year, he could not be removed from the parish. (See Jacob, *New Law-Dictionary*, 4th ed. [1739], s.v. 'Poor'.)

forward as themselves: So that, to prevent the Increase of Beggars, we must get rid of her.'—'Your Ladyship is very much in the right,' answered *Scout*, 'but I am afraid the Law is a little deficient in giving us any such Power of Prevention; however the Justice will stretch it as far as he is able, to oblige your Ladyship. To say truth, it is a great Blessing to the Country that he is in the Commission; for he hath taken several Poor off our hands, that the Law would never lay hold on. I know some Justices who make as much of committing a Man to *Bridewell*[1] as his Lordship at *Size* would of hanging him: But it would do a Man good to see his Worship our Justice commit a Fellow to *Bridewell*; he takes so much pleasure in it: And when once we ha' un there, we seldom hear any more o' un. He's either starved or eat up by Vermin in a Month's time.'—Here the Arrival of a Visitor put an end to the Conversation, and Mr. *Scout* having undertaken the Cause, and promised it Success, departed.

This *Scout* was one of those Fellows, who without any Knowledge of the Law, or being bred to it, take upon them, in defiance of an Act of Parliament,[2] to act as Lawyers in the Country, and are called so. They are the Pests of Society, and a Scandal to a Profession, to which indeed they do not belong; and which owes to such kind of Rascallions the Ill-will which weak Persons bear towards it. With this Fellow, to whom a little before she would not have condescended to have spoken, did a certain Passion for *Joseph*, and the Jealousy and Disdain of poor innocent *Fanny*, betray the Lady *Booby*, into a familiar Discourse, in which she inadvertently confirmed many Hints, with which *Slipslop*, whose Gallant he was, had pre-acquainted him; and whence he had taken an Opportunity to assert those severe Falshoods of little *Fanny*, which possibly the Reader might not have been well able to account for, if we had not thought proper to give him this Information.

---

[1] In London, Bridewell Hospital, rebuilt in 1720, was a house of correction for minor offenders such as whores and vagabonds, who were set to work beating hemp and supported on a penny-loaf of bread a day. In Fielding's opinion commitment to this prison was a severe punishment which, instead of reforming prisoners, generally confirmed and improved them in the practice of vice; during his tenure as magistrate he, like his own Squire Allworthy (*Tom Jones*, I. ix), refused to commit any but the most abandoned offenders to Bridewell. (See *An Enquiry into the Causes of the late Increase of Robbers* and *The Covent-Garden Journal* [1 August 1752].)

[2] See 2 George II. cap. 23 (1729), called 'An Act for the better Regulation of Attorneys and Solicitors.' According to the terms of this statute, pettyfoggers such as Scout were liable to a fine of £50 for practising law without being duly qualified.

CHAPTER IV

*A short Chapter, but very full of Matter; particularly
the Arrival of Mr.* Booby *and his Lady.*

ALL that Night and the next Day, the Lady *Booby* past with the
utmost Anxiety; her Mind was distracted, and her Soul tossed up
and down by many turbulent and opposite Passions. She loved,
hated, pitied, scorned, admired, despised the same Person by
Fits, which changed in a very short Interval. On *Tuesday* Morning, which happened to be a Holiday,[1] she went to Church,
where, to her surprize, Mr. *Adams* published the Banns again
with as audible a Voice as before. It was lucky for her, that as
there was no Sermon, she had an immediate Opportunity of
returning home, to vent her Rage, which she could not have concealed from the Congregation five Minutes; indeed it was not
then very numerous, the Assembly consisting of no more than
Adams, his Clerk, his Wife, the Lady, and one of her Servants.
At her Return she met *Slipslop*, who accosted her in these Words:
—'O Meam, what doth your Ladyship think? To be sure Lawyer
Scout hath carried *Joseph* and *Fanny* both before the Justice. All
the Parish are in Tears, and say they will certainly be hanged: For
no body knows what it is for.'—'I suppose they deserve it,' says
the Lady. 'What dost thou mention such Wretches to me?'—
'O dear Madam,' answer'd *Slipslop*, 'is it not a pity such a *graceless*
young Man should die a *virulent* Death? I hope the Judge will
take *Commensuration* on his Youth. As for *Fanny*, I don't think
it signifies much what becomes of her; and if poor *Joseph* hath
done any thing, I could venture to swear she *traduced* him to it:
Few Men ever come to *fragrant* Punishment, but by those nasty
Creatures who are a Scandal to our *Sect*.' The Lady was no more
pleased at this News, after a moment's Reflection, than *Slipslop*
herself: For tho' she wished *Fanny* far enough, she did not desire
the Removal of *Joseph*, especially with her. She was puzzled how
to act, or what to say on this Occasion, when a Coach and six
drove into the Court, and a Servant acquainted her with the
Arrival of her Nephew *Booby* and his Lady. She ordered them to

[1] See Introduction, p. xxvi.

be conducted into a Drawing-Room, whither she presently re-paired, having composed her Countenance as well as she could; and being a little satisfied that the Wedding would by these means be at least interrupted; and that she should have an Oppor-tunity to execute any Resolution she might take, for which she saw herself provided with an excellent Instrument in *Scout*.

The Lady *Booby* apprehended her Servant had made a Mis-take, when he mentioned Mr. *Booby's* Lady; for she had never heard of his Marriage: but how great was her Surprize, when at her entering the Room, her Nephew presented his Wife to her, saying, 'Madam, this is that charming *Pamela*, of whom I am convinced you have heard so much.' The Lady received her with more Civility than he expected; indeed with the utmost: For she was perfectly polite, nor had any Vice inconsistent with Good-breeding. They past some little time in ordinary Discourse, when a Servant came and whispered Mr. *Booby*, who presently told the Ladies he must desert them a little on some Business of Con-sequence; and as their Discourse during his Absence would afford little Improvement or Entertainment to the Reader, we will leave them for a while to attend Mr. *Booby*.

CHAPTER V

*Containing Justice Business; Curious Precedents of
Depositions, and other Matters necessary to be perused
by all Justices of the Peace and their Clerks.*

THE young Squire and his Lady were no sooner alighted from their Coach, than the Servants began to enquire after Mr. *Joseph*, from whom they said their Lady had not heard a Word to her great Surprize, since he had left Lady *Booby's*. Upon this they were instantly informed of what had lately happened, with which they hastily acquainted their Master, who took an immediate Resolution to go himself, and endeavour to restore his *Pamela* her Brother, before she even knew she had lost him.

The Justice, before whom the Criminals were carried, and who lived within a short Mile of the Lady's House, was luckily Mr. *Booby's* Acquaintance, by his having an Estate in his Neigh-

bourhood. Ordering therefore his Horses to his Coach, he set
out for the Judgment-Seat, and arriv'd when the Justice had
almost finished his Business. He was conducted into a Hall,
where he was acquainted that his Worship would wait on him in
a moment; for he had only a Man and a Woman to commit to
Bridewell first. As he was now convinced he had not a Minute
to lose, he insisted on the Servants introducing him directly into
the Room where the Justice was then executing his Office, as he
called it. Being brought thither, and the first Compliments being
past between the Squire and his Worship, the former asked the
latter what Crime those two young People had been guilty of.
'No great Crime,' answered the Justice. 'I have only ordered them
to *Bridewell* for a Month.' 'But what is their Crime?' repeated
the Squire. 'Larceny, an't please your Honour,' said *Scout.* 'Ay,'
says the Justice, 'a kind of felonious larcenous thing. I believe
I must order them a little Correction too, a little Stripping and
Whipping.' (Poor *Fanny,* who had hitherto supported all with
the Thoughts of her *Joseph's* Company, trembled at that Sound;
but indeed without reason, for none but the Devil himself would
have executed such a Sentence on her.) 'Still,' said the Squire,
'I am ignorant of the Crime, the Fact I mean.' 'Why, there it
is in Peaper,' answered the Justice, shewing him a Deposition,
which in the Absence of his Clerk he had writ himself, of which
we have with great difficulty procured an authentick Copy; and
here it follows *verbatim et literatim.*[1]

The Depusition of James Scout, *Layer, and* Thomas Trotter,
*Yeoman, taken befor mee, on of his Magesty's Justasses of the Piece
for* Zumersetshire.

'These Deponants saith, and first *Thomas Trotter* for himself saith,
that on the   of this instant *October,* being Sabbath-Day,[2]
betwin the Ours of 2 and 4 in the afternoon, he zeed *Joseph
Andrews* and *Francis Goodwill* walk akross a certane Felde belung-
ing to Layer *Scout,* and out of the Path which ledes thru the said
Felde, and there he zede *Joseph Andrews* with a Nife cut one
Hassel-Twig, of the value, as he believes, of 3 half pence, or
thereabouts; and he saith, that the said *Francis Goodwill* was

---

[1] 'Word for word and letter for letter.'

[2] In 1741 Sundays in October fell on the 4th, 11th, 18th, and 25th of the month. For
reasons discussed in the Introduction (p. xxvi) it is impossible to fix a more precise date.

likewise walking on the Grass out of the said Path in the said
Felde, and did receive and karry in her Hand the said Twig, and
so was cumfarting, eading and abatting to the said *Joseph* therein.
And the said *James Scout* for himself says, that he verily believes
the said Twig to be his own proper Twig, &c.'

'Jesu!' said the Squire, 'would you commit two Persons to
Bridewell for a Twig?' 'Yes,' said the Lawyer, 'and with great
Lenity too; for if we had called it a young Tree they would have
been both hanged.'—'Harkee, (says the Justice, taking aside the
Squire) I should not have been so severe on this Occasion, but
Lady *Booby* desires to get them out of the Parish; so Lawyer
Scout will give the Constable Orders to let them run away, if they
please; but it seems they intend to marry together, and the Lady
hath no other means, as they are legally settled there, to prevent
their bringing an Incumbrance on her own Parish.' 'Well,' said
the Squire, 'I will take care my Aunt shall be satisfied in this
Point; and likewise I promise you, *Joseph* here shall never be any
Incumbrance on her. I shall be oblig'd to you therefore, if, instead
of *Bridewell*, you will commit them to my Custody.'—'O to be
sure, Sir, if you desire it,' answer'd the Justice; and without more
ado, *Joseph* and *Fanny* were delivered over to Squire *Booby*, whom
Joseph very well knew; but little ghest how nearly he was related
to him. The Justice burnt his *Mittimus*. The Constable was sent
about his Business. The Lawyer made no Complaint for want of
Justice, and the Prisoners, with exulting Hearts, gave a thousand
Thanks to his Honour Mr. *Booby*, who did not intend their
Obligations to him should cease here; for ordering his Man to
produce a Cloakbag which he had caused to be brought from
Lady *Booby's* on purpose, he desired the Justice that he might have
Joseph with him into a Room; where ordering his Servant to take
out a Suit of his own Clothes, with Linnen and other Necessaries,
he left *Joseph* to dress himself, who not yet knowing the Cause
of all this Civility, excused his accepting such a Favour, as long
as decently he could. Whilst *Joseph* was dressing, the Squire repaired to the Justice, whom he found talking with *Fanny*; for
during the Examination she had lopped her Hat over her Eyes,
which were also bathed in Tears, and had by that means concealed
from his Worship what might perhaps have rendered the Arrival
of Mr. *Booby* unnecessary, at least for herself. The Justice no

sooner saw her Countenance cleared up, and her bright Eyes shining through her Tears, than he secretly cursed himself for having once thought of *Bridewell* for her. He would willingly have sent his own Wife thither, to have had *Fanny* in her place. And conceiving almost at the same instant Desires and Schemes to accomplish them, he employed the Minutes whilst the Squire was absent with *Joseph*, in assuring her how sorry he was for having treated her so roughly before he knew her Merit; and told her, that since Lady *Booby* was unwilling that she should settle in her Parish, she was heartily welcome to his, where he promised her his Protection, adding, that he would take *Joseph* and her into his own Family, if she liked it; which Assurance he confirmed with a Squeeze by the Hand. She thanked him very kindly, and said, 'she would acquaint *Joseph* with the Offer, which he would certainly be glad to accept; for that Lady *Booby* was angry with them both; tho' she did not know either had done any thing to offend her: but imputed it to Madam *Slipslop*, who had always been her Enemy.'

The Squire now returned, and prevented any farther Continuance of this Conversation; and the Justice out of a pretended Respect to his Guest, but in reality from an Apprehension of a Rival; (for he knew nothing of his Marriage,) ordered *Fanny* into the Kitchin, whither she gladly retired; nor did the Squire, who declined the Trouble of explaining the whole matter, oppose it.

It would be unnecessary, if I was able, which indeed I am not, to relate the Conversation between these two Gentlemen, which rolled, as I have been informed, entirely on the Subject of Horse-racing. *Joseph* was soon drest in the plainest Dress he could find, which was a blue Coat and Breeches, with a Gold Edging, and a red Waistcoat with the same; and as this Suit, which was rather too large for the Squire, exactly fitted him; so he became it so well, and looked so genteel, that no Person would have doubted its being as well adapted to his Quality as his Shape; nor have suspected, as one might when my Lord—, or Sir—, or Mr.— appear in Lace or Embroidery, that the Taylor's Man wore those Clothes home on his Back, which he should have carried under his Arm.

The Squire now took leave of the Justice, and calling for *Fanny*, made her and *Joseph*, against their Wills, get into the Coach with him, which he then ordered to drive to Lady *Booby's*.—It had

moved a few Yards only, when the Squire asked *Joseph*, if he
knew who that Man was crossing the Field; for, added he, 'I
never saw one take such Strides before.' *Joseph* answered eagerly,
'O Sir, it is Parson *Adams*.'—'O la, indeed, and so it is,' said
Fanny; 'poor Man he is coming to do what he could for us. Well,
he is the worthiest best natur'd Creature.'—'Ay,' said *Joseph*,
'God bless him; for there is not such another in the Universe.'—
'The best Creature living sure,' cries *Fanny*. 'Is he?' says the
Squire, 'then I am resolved to have the best Creature living in
my Coach,' and so saying he ordered it to stop, whilst *Joseph* at
his Request hollowed to the Parson, who well knowing his Voice,
made all the haste imaginable, and soon came up with them;
he was desired by the Master, who could scarce refrain from
Laughter at his Figure, to mount into the Coach, which he with
many Thanks refused, saying he could walk by its side, and he'd
warrant he kept up with it; but he was at length over-prevailed on.
The Squire now acquainted *Joseph* with his Marriage; but he
might have spared himself that Labour; for his Servant, whilst
Joseph was dressing, had performed that Office before. He continued to express the vast Happiness he enjoyed in his Sister,
and the Value he had for all who belonged to her. *Joseph* made
many Bows, and exprest as many Acknowledgments; and Parson
Adams, who now first perceived *Joseph's* new Apparel, burst into
Tears with Joy, and fell to rubbing his Hands and snapping his
Fingers, as if he had been mad.

They were now arrived at the Lady *Booby's*, and the Squire
desiring them to wait a moment in the Court, walked in to his
Aunt, and calling her out from his Wife, acquainted her with
Joseph's Arrival; saying, 'Madam, as I have married a virtuous
and worthy Woman, I am resolved to own her Relations, and
shew them all a proper Respect; I shall think myself therefore
infinitely obliged to all mine, who will do the same. It is true, her
Brother hath been your Servant; but he is now become my
Brother; and I have one Happiness, that neither his Character,
his Behaviour or Appearance give me any reason to be ashamed
of calling him so. In short, he is now below, drest like a Gentleman, in which Light I intend he shall hereafter be seen; and you
will oblige me beyond Expression, if you will admit him to be
of our Party; for I know it will give great Pleasure to my Wife,
tho' she will not mention it.'

This was a stroke of Fortune beyond the Lady *Booby's* Hopes or Expectation; she answered him eagerly, 'Nephew, you know how easily I am prevailed on to do any thing which *Joseph Andrews* desires—Phoo, I mean which you desire me, and as he is now your Relation, I cannot refuse to entertain him as such.' The Squire told her, he knew his Obligation to her for her Compliance, and going three Steps, returned and told her—he had one more Favour, which he believed she would easily grant, as she had accorded him the former. 'There is a young Woman—' 'Nephew,' says she, 'don't let my Good-nature make you desire, as is too commonly the Case, to impose on me. Nor think, because I have with so much Condescension agreed to suffer your Brother-in-law to come to my Table, that I will submit to the Company of all my own Servants, and all the dirty Trollops in the Country.' 'Madam,' answer'd the Squire, 'I believe you never saw this young Creature. I never beheld such Sweetness and Innocence joined with such Beauty, and withal so genteel.' 'Upon my Soul, I won't admit her,' reply'd the Lady in a Passion; 'the whole World shan't prevail on me, I resent even the Desire as an Affront, and—' The Squire, who knew her Inflexibility, interrupted her, by asking Pardon, and promising not to mention it more. He then returned to *Joseph*, and she to *Pamela*. He took *Joseph* aside and told him, he would carry him to his Sister; but could not prevail as yet for *Fanny*. *Joseph* begged that he might see his Sister alone, and then be with his *Fanny*; but the Squire knowing the Pleasure his Wife would have in her Brother's Company, would not admit it, telling *Joseph* there would be nothing in so short an Absence from *Fanny*, whilst he was assured of her Safety; adding, he hoped he could not so easily quit a Sister whom he had not seen so long, and who so tenderly loved him— *Joseph* immediately complied; for indeed no Brother could love a Sister more; and recommending *Fanny*, who rejoiced that she was not to go before Lady *Booby*, to the Care of Mr. *Adams*, he attended the Squire up stairs, whilst *Fanny* repaired with the Parson to his House, where she thought herself secure of a kind Reception.

CHAPTER VI

Of which you are desired to read no more
than you like.

T H E Meeting between *Joseph* and *Pamela* was not without Tears
of Joy on both sides; and their Embraces were full of Tenderness
and Affection. They were however regarded with much more
Pleasure by the Nephew than by the Aunt, to whose Flame they
were Fewel only; and this was increased by the Addition of Dress,
which was indeed not wanted to set off the lively Colours in which
Nature had drawn Health, Strength, Comeliness, and Youth.
In the Afternoon *Joseph*, at their Request, entertained them with
the Account of his Adventures, nor could Lady *Booby* conceal her
Dissatisfaction at those Parts in which *Fanny* was concerned,
especially when Mr. *Booby* launched forth into such rapturous
Praises of her Beauty. She said, applying to her Niece, that she
wondered her Nephew, who had pretended to marry for Love,
should think such a Subject proper to amuse his Wife with:
adding, that for her part, she should be jealous of a Husband who
spoke so warmly in praise of another Woman. *Pamela* answer'd,
indeed she thought she had cause; but it was an Instance of
Mr. *Booby's* aptness to see more Beauty in Women than they
were Mistresses of. At which Words both the Women fixed their
Eyes on two Looking-Glasses; and Lady *Booby* replied that Men
were in the general very ill Judges of Beauty; and then whilst
both contemplated only their own Faces, they paid a cross Compliment to each other's Charms. When the Hour of Rest approached, which the Lady of the House deferred as long as
decently she could, she informed *Joseph* (whom for the future we
shall call Mr. *Joseph*, he having as good a Title to that Appellation as many others, I mean that incontested one of good Clothes)
that she had ordered a Bed to be provided for him; he declined
this Favour to his utmost; for his Heart had long been with his
Fanny; but she insisted on his accepting it, alledging that the
Parish had no proper Accommodation for such a Person, as he
was now to esteem himself. The Squire and his Lady both joining
with her, Mr. *Joseph* was at last forced to give over his Design
of visiting *Fanny* that Evening, who on her side as impatiently

expected him till Midnight, when in complacence to Mr. *Adams's*
Family, who had sat up two Hours out of Respect to her, she
retired to Bed, but not to sleep; the Thoughts of her Love kept
her waking, and his not returning according to his Promise,
filled her with Uneasiness; of which however she could not
assign any other Cause than merely that of being absent from him.

Mr. *Joseph* rose early in the Morning, and visited her in whom
his Soul delighted. She no sooner heard his Voice in the Parson's
Parlour, than she leapt from her Bed, and dressing herself in a
few Minutes, went down to him. They past two Hours with
inexpressible Happiness together, and then having appointed
Monday, by Mr. *Adams's* permission, for their Marriage, Mr.
Joseph returned according to his Promise, to Breakfast at the
Lady *Booby's*, with whose Behaviour since the Evening we shall
now acquaint the Reader.

She was no sooner retired to her Chamber than she asked *Slipslop* what she thought of this wonderful Creature her Nephew
had married. 'Madam?' said *Slipslop*, not yet sufficiently understanding what Answer she was to make. 'I ask you,' answer'd the
Lady, 'what you think of the Dowdy, my Niece I think I am to
call her?' *Slipslop*, wanting no further Hint, began to pull her to
pieces, and so miserably defaced her, that it would have been
impossible for any one to have known the Person. The Lady
gave her all the Assistance she could, and ended with saying—
'I think, *Slipslop*, you have done her Justice; but yet, bad as she is,
she is an Angel compared to this *Fanny*.' *Slipslop* then fell on
Fanny, whom she hack'd and hew'd in the like barbarous manner,
concluding with an Observation that there was always something
in those low-life Creatures which must eternally distinguish them
from their Betters. 'Really,' said the Lady, 'I think there is one
Exception to your Rule, I am certain you may ghess who I
mean.'—'Not I, upon my word, Madam,' said *Slipslop*.—'I mean
a young Fellow; sure you are the dullest Wretch,' said the Lady.
—'O la, I am indeed—Yes truly, Madam, he is an *Accession*,'
answer'd *Slipslop*.—'Ay, is he not, *Slipslop*?' returned the Lady.
'Is he not so genteel that a Prince might without a Blush acknowledge him for his Son. His Behaviour is such that would not
shame the best Education. He borrows from his Station a Condescension in every thing to his Superiors, yet unattended by
that mean Servility which is called Good-Behaviour in such

Persons. Every thing he doth hath no mark of the base Motive of Fear, but visibly shews some Respect and Gratitude, and carries with it the Persuasion of Love—And then for his Virtues; such Piety to his Parents, such tender Affection to his Sister, such Integrity in his Friendship, such Bravery, such Goodness, that if he had been born a Gentleman, his Wife would have possest the most invaluable Blessing.'—'To be sure, Ma'am,' says *Slipslop*. —'But as he is,' answered the Lady, 'if he had a thousand more good Qualities, it must render a Woman of Fashion contemptible even to be suspected of thinking of him, yes I should despise myself for such a Thought.' 'To be sure, Ma'am,' said *Slipslop*. 'And why to be sure?' reply'd the Lady, 'thou art always one's Echo. Is he not more worthy of Affection than a dirty Country Clown, tho' born of a Family as old as the Flood, or an idle worthless Rake, or little puisny Beau of Quality? And yet these we must condemn ourselves to, in order to avoid the Censure of the World; to shun the Contempt of others, we must ally ourselves to those we despise; we must prefer Birth, Title and Fortune to real Merit. It is a Tyranny of Custom, a Tyranny we must comply with: For we People of Fashion are the Slaves of Custom.'— 'Marry come up!' said *Slipslop*, who now well knew which Party to take, 'if I was a Woman of your Ladyship's Fortune and Quality, I would be a Slave to no body.'—'Me,' said the Lady, 'I am speaking, if a young Woman of Fashion who had seen nothing of the World should happen to like such a Fellow.—Me indeed; I hope thou dost not imagine—' 'No, Ma'am, to be sure,' cried *Slipslop*.—'No! what no?' cried the Lady. 'Thou art always ready to answer, before thou hast heard one. So far I must allow he is a charming Fellow. Me indeed! No, *Slipslop*, all Thoughts of Men are over with me.—I have lost a Husband, who—but if I should reflect, I should run mad.—My future Ease must depend upon Forgetfulness. *Slipslop*, let me hear some of thy Nonsense to turn my Thoughts another way. What dost thou think of Mr. *Andrews*?' 'Why I think,' says *Slipslop*, 'he is the handsomest most properest Man I ever saw; and if I was a Lady of the greatest Degree, it would be well for some Folks. Your Ladyship may talk of Custom if you please; but I am *confidous* there is no more Comparison between young Mr. *Andrews*, and most of the young Gentlemen who come to your Ladyship's House in *London*; a Parcel of *Whipper-snapper* Sparks: I would sooner marry our old Parson *Adams*. Never tell me what People say, whilst I am happy in the Arms of him I love. Some Folks rail against other Folks, because other Folks have what some Folks would be glad of.'—'And so,' answered the Lady, 'if you was a Woman of Condition, you would really marry Mr. *Andrews?*'—'Yes, I assure your Ladyship,' replied *Slipslop*, 'if he would have me.'—'Fool, Idiot,' cries the Lady, 'if he would have a Woman of Fashion! Is that a Question?' 'No truly, Madam,' said *Slipslop*, 'I believe it would be none, if *Fanny* was out of the way; and I am *confidous* if I was in your Ladyship's Place, and liked Mr. *Joseph Andrews*, she should not stay in the Parish a moment. I am sure Lawyer *Scout* would send her packing, if your Ladyship would but say the Word.' This last Speech of *Slipslop* raised a Tempest in the Mind of her Mistress. She feared *Scout* had betrayed her, or rather that she had betrayed herself. After some Silence and a double Change of her Complexion; first to pale and then to red, she thus spoke: 'I am astonished at the Liberty you give your Tongue. Would you insinuate, that I employed *Scout* against this Wench, on the account of the Fellow?' 'La Ma'am,' said *Slipslop*, frighted out of her Wits. 'I *assassinate* such a Thing!' 'I think you dare not,' answered the Lady, 'I believe my Conduct may defy Malice itself to assert so cursed a Slander. If I had ever discovered any Wantonness, any Lightness in my Behaviour: If I had followed the Example of some whom thou hast I believe seen, in allowing myself indecent Liberties, even with a Husband: But the dear Man who is gone (*here she began to sob*) was he alive again, (*then she produced Tears*) could not upbraid me with any one Act of Tenderness or Passion. No, *Slipslop*, all the time I cohabited with him, he never obtained even a Kiss from me, without my expressing Reluctance in the granting it. I am sure he himself never suspected how much I loved him.—Since his Death, thou knowest, tho' it is almost six Weeks (it wants but a Day) ago,[1] I have not admitted one Visitor, till this Fool my Nephew arrived. I have confined myself quite to one Party of Friends.—And can such a Conduct as this fear to be arraigned? To be accused not

[1] Either Lady Booby wishes to exaggerate the duration of mourning, or Fielding again forgets the chronology of his story. Joseph set out on his journey from London on the seventh day after Sir Thomas Booby's death (I. v); the journey itself required eleven days; Lady Booby makes the above observation on the third day after the arrival at her country-seat: a total of *three* weeks less a day. (For an account of the time-scheme of *Joseph Andrews*, see Dudden, i. 344–50.)

only of a Passion which I have always despised; but of fixing it on such an Object, a Creature so much beneath my Notice.'—'Upon my word, Ma'am,' says *Slipslop*, 'I do not understand your Ladyship, nor know I any thing of the matter.'—'I believe indeed thou dost not understand me.—Those are Delicacies which exist only in superior Minds; thy coarse Ideas cannot comprehend them. Thou art a low Creature, of the *Andrews* Breed, a Reptile of a lower Order, a Weed that grows in the common Garden of the Creation.'—'I assure your Ladyship,' says *Slipslop*, whose Passions were almost of as high an Order as her Lady's, 'I have no more to do with *Common Garden*¹ than other Folks. Really, your Ladyship talks of Servants as if they were not born of the Christian *Specious*. Servants have Flesh and Blood as well as Quality; and Mr. *Andrews* himself is a Proof that they have as good, if not better. And for my own Part, I can't perceive my *Dears** are coarser than other People's; and I am sure, if Mr. *Andrews* was a *Dear* of mine, I should not be ashamed of him in company with Gentlemen; for whoever hath seen him in his new Clothes, must confess he looks as much like a Gentleman as any body. Coarse, quotha! I can't bear to hear the poor young Fellow run down neither; for I will say this, I never heard him say an ill Word of any body in his Life. I am sure his Coarseness doth not lie in his Heart; for he is the best-natur'd Man in the World; and as for his Skin, it is no coarser than other People's, I am sure. His Bosom when a Boy was as white as driven Snow; and where it is not covered with Hairs, is so still. Ifaukins! if I was Mrs. *Andrews*, with a hundred a Year, I should not envy the best She who wears a Head. A Woman that could not be happy with such a Man, ought never to be so: For if he can't make a Woman happy, I never yet beheld the Man who could. I say again I wish I was a great Lady for his sake, I believe when I had made a Gentleman of him, he'd behave so, that no body should *deprecate* what I had done; and I fancy few would venture to tell him he was no Gentleman to his Face, nor to mine neither.' At which Words, taking up the Candles, she asked her Mistress, who had been some time in her Bed, if she had any farther Commands; who

---

* Meaning perhaps Ideas.

¹ The colloquial name for Covent Garden, a disreputable district. Cf. *The Covent-Garden Journal*, 11 February 1752: 'one General DRAWCANSIR . . . set up his Standard in the Common Gardens. . . .'

mildly answered she had none; and telling her, she was a comical
Creature, bid her Good-night.

CHAPTER VII

*Philosophical Reflections, the like not to be found in
any light* French *Romance. Mr.* Booby's *grave Advice
to* Joseph, *and* Fanny's *Encounter with a Beau.*

HABIT, my good Reader, hath so vast a Prevalence over the
human Mind, that there is scarce any thing too strange or too
strong to be asserted of it. The Story of the Miser, who from long
accustoming to cheat others, came at last to cheat himself, and
with great Delight and Triumph, picked his own Pocket of a
Guinea, to convey to his Hoard, is not impossible or improbable.
In like manner, it fares with the Practisers of Deceit, who from
having long deceived their Acquaintance, gain at last a Power
of deceiving themselves, and acquire that very Opinion (however
false) of their own Abilities, Excellencies and Virtues, into which
they have for Years perhaps endeavoured to betray their Neighbours. Now, Reader, to apply this Observation to my present
Purpose, thou must know, that as the Passion generally called
Love, exercises most of the Talents of the Female or fair
World; so in this they now and then discover a small Inclination
to Deceit; for which thou wilt not be angry with the beautiful
Creatures, when thou hast considered, that at the Age of seven
or something earlier, Miss is instructed by her Mother, that
Master is a very monstrous kind of Animal, who will, if she suffers
him to come too near her, infallibly eat her up, and grind her to
pieces. That so far from kissing or toying with him of her own
accord, she must not admit him to kiss or toy with her. And lastly,
that she must never have any Affection towards him; for if she
should, all her Friends in Petticoats would esteem her a Traitress,
point at her, and hunt her out of their Society. These Impressions
being first received, are farther and deeper inculcated by their
School-mistresses and Companions; so that by the Age of Ten
they have contracted such a Dread and Abhorrence of the above
named Monster, that whenever they see him, they fly from him as

the innocent Hare doth from the Greyhound. Hence to the Age of fourteen or fifteen, they entertain a mighty Antipathy to Master; they resolve and frequently profess that they will never have any Commerce with him, and entertain fond Hopes of passing their Lives out of his reach, of the Possibility of which they have so visible an Example in their good Maiden Aunt. But when they arrive at this Period, and have now past their second Climacteric, when their Wisdom grown riper, begins to see a little farther; and from almost daily falling in Master's way, to apprehend the great Difficulty of keeping out of it; and when they observe him look often at them, and sometimes very eagerly and earnestly too, (for the Monster seldom takes any notice of them till at this Age) they then begin to think of their Danger; and as they perceive they cannot easily avoid him, the wiser Part bethink themselves of providing by other Means for their Security. They endeavour by all the Methods they can invent to render themselves so amiable in his Eyes, that he may have no Inclination to hurt them; in which they generally succeed so well, that his Eyes, by frequent languishing, soon lessen their Idea of his Fierceness, and so far abate their Fears, that they venture to parley with him; and when they perceive him so different from what he hath been described, all Gentleness, Softness, Kindness, Tenderness, Fondness, their dreadful Apprehensions vanish in a moment; and now (it being usual with the human Mind to skip from one Extreme to its Opposite, as easily, and almost as suddenly, as a Bird from one Bough to another;) Love instantly succeeds to Fear: But as it happens to Persons, who have in their Infancy been thoroughly frightned with certain no Persons called Ghosts, that they retain their Dread of those Beings, after they are convinced that there are no such things; so these young Ladies, tho' they no longer apprehend devouring, cannot so entirely shake off all that hath been instilled into them; they still entertain the Idea of that Censure which was so strongly imprinted on their tender Minds, to which the Declarations of Abhorrence they every day hear from their Companions greatly contribute. To avoid this Censure therefore, is now their only care; for which purpose they still pretend the same Aversion to the Monster: And the more they love him, the more ardently they counterfeit the Antipathy. By the continual and constant Practice of which Deceit on others, they at length impose on themselves, and really believe they hate what they love. Thus indeed it happened to Lady *Booby*, who loved *Joseph* long before she knew it; and now loved him much more than she suspected. She had indeed, from the time of his Sister's Arrival in the Quality of her Niece; and from the Instant she viewed him in the Dress and Character of a Gentleman, began to conceive secretly a Design which Love had concealed from herself, 'till a Dream betrayed it to her.

She had no sooner risen than she sent for her Nephew; when he came to her, after many Compliments on his Choice, she told him, 'he might perceive in her Condescension to admit her own Servant to her Table, that she looked on the Family of *Andrews* as his Relations, and indeed her's; that as he had married into such a Family, it became him to endeavour by all Methods to raise it as much as possible; at length she advised him to use all his Art to dissuade *Joseph* from his intended Match, which would still enlarge their Relation to Meanness and Poverty; concluding, that by a Commission in the Army, or some other genteel Employment, he might soon put young Mr. *Andrews* on the foot of a Gentleman; and that being once done, his Accomplishments might quickly gain him an Alliance, which would not be to their Discredit.'

Her Nephew heartily embraced this Proposal; and finding Mr. *Joseph* with his Wife, at his Return to her Chamber, he immediately began thus: 'My Love to my dear *Pamela*, Brother, will extend to all her Relations; nor shall I shew them less Respect than if I had married into the Family of a Duke. I hope I have given you some early Testimonies of this, and shall continue to give you daily more. You will excuse me therefore, Brother, if my Concern for your Interest makes me mention what may be, perhaps, disagreeable to you to hear: But I must insist upon it, that if you have any Value for my Alliance or my Friendship, you will decline any Thoughts of engaging farther with a Girl, who is, as you are a Relation of mine, so much beneath you. I know there may be at first some Difficulty in your Compliance, but that will daily diminish; and you will in the end sincerely thank me for my Advice. I own, indeed, the Girl is handsome: But Beauty alone is a poor Ingredient, and will make but an uncomfortable Marriage.' 'Sir,' said *Joseph*, 'I assure you her Beauty is her least Perfection; nor do I know a Virtue which that young Creature is not possest of.' 'As to her Virtues,' answered Mr. *Booby*, 'you can be yet but a slender Judge of them: But if she had never so many, you will find her Equal in these among her Superiors in Birth and Fortune, which now you are to esteem on a footing with yourself; at least I will take care they shall shortly be so, unless you prevent me by degrading yourself with such a Match, a Match I have hardly patience to think of; and which would break the Hearts of your Parents, who now rejoice in the Expectation of seeing you make a Figure in the World.' 'I know not,' replied *Joseph*, 'that my Parents have any power over my Inclinations; nor am I obliged to sacrifice my Happiness to their Whim or Ambition: Besides, I shall be very sorry to see that the unexpected Advancement of my Sister, should so suddenly inspire them with this wicked Pride, and make them despise their Equals, I am resolved on no account to quit my dear *Fanny*, no, tho' I could raise her as high above her present Station as you have raised my Sister.' 'Your Sister, as well as myself,' said *Booby*, 'are greatly obliged to you for the Comparison: But, Sir, she is not worthy to be compared in Beauty to my *Pamela*; nor hath she half her Merit. And besides, Sir, as you civilly throw my Marriage with your Sister in my Teeth, I must teach you the wide Difference between us; my Fortune enabled me to please myself; and it would have been as overgrown a Folly in me to have omitted it, as in you to do it.' 'My Fortune enables me to please myself likewise,' said *Joseph*; 'for all my Pleasure is centred in *Fanny*, and whilst I have Health, I shall be able to support her with my Labour in that Station to which she was born, and with which she is content.' 'Brother,' said *Pamela*, 'Mr. *Booby* advises you as a Friend; and, no doubt, my Papa and Mamma will be of his Opinion, and will have great reason to be angry with you for destroying what his Goodness hath done, and throwing down our Family again, after he hath raised it. It would become you better, Brother, to pray for the Assistance of Grace[1] against such a Passion, than to indulge it.'— 'Sure, Sister, you are not in earnest; I am sure she is your Equal at least.'—'She was my Equal,' answered *Pamela*, 'but I am no longer *Pamela Andrews*, I am now this Gentleman's Lady, and as such am above her—I hope I shall never behave with an unbecoming Pride; but at the same time I shall always endeavour to know myself, and question not the Assistance of Grace to that purpose.' They were now summoned to Breakfast, and thus ended their

[1] See p. 46, n. 1.

Discourse for the present, very little to the Satisfaction of any of the Parties.

Fanny was now walking in an Avenue at some distance from the House, where *Joseph* had promised to take the first Opportunity of coming to her. She had not a Shilling in the World, and had subsisted ever since her Return entirely on the Charity of Parson *Adams*. A young Gentleman attended by many Servants, came up to her, and asked her if that was not the Lady *Booby's* House before him? This indeed he well knew; but had framed the Question for no other Reason than to make her look up and discover if her Face was equal to the Delicacy of her Shape. He no sooner saw it, than he was struck with Amazement. He stopt his Horse, and swore she was the most beautiful Creature he ever beheld. Then instantly alighting, and delivering his Horse to his Servant, he rapt out half a dozen Oaths that he would kiss her; to which she at first submitted, begging he would not be rude: but he was not satisfied with the Civility of a Salute, nor even with the rudest Attack he could make on her Lips, but caught her in his Arms and endeavoured to kiss her Breasts, which with all her Strength she resisted; and as our Spark was not of the *Herculean* Race, with some difficulty prevented. The young Gentleman being soon out of breath in the Struggle, quitted her, and remounting his Horse called one of his Servants to him, whom he ordered to stay behind with her, and make her any Offers whatever, to prevail on her to return home with him in the Evening; and to assure her he would take her into Keeping. He then rode on with his other Servants, and arrived at the Lady's House, to whom he was a distant Relation, and was come to pay a Visit.

The trusty Fellow, who was employ'd in an Office he had been long accustomed to, discharged his Part with all the Fidelity and Dexterity imaginable; but to no purpose. She was entirely deaf to his Offers, and rejected them with the utmost Disdain. At last the Pimp, who had perhaps more warm Blood about him than his Master, began to sollicit for himself; he told her, tho' he was a Servant, he was a Man of some Fortune, which he would make her Mistress of—and this without any Insult to her Virtue, for that he would marry her. She answer'd, if his Master himself, or the greatest Lord in the Land would marry her, she would refuse him. At last being weary with Persuasions, and on fire with Charms which would have almost kindled a Flame in the Bosom of an antient Philosopher, or modern Divine, he fastened his Horse to the Ground, and attacked her with much more Force than the Gentleman had exerted. Poor *Fanny* would not have been able to resist his Rudeness any long time, but the Deity who presides over chaste Love sent her *Joseph* to her Assistance. He no sooner came within sight, and perceived her struggling with a Man, than like a Cannon-Ball, or like Lightning, or any thing that is swifter, if any thing be, he ran towards her, and coming up just as the Ravisher had torn her Handkerchief from her Breast, before his Lips had touched that Seat of Innocence and Bliss, he dealt him so lusty a Blow in that part of his Neck which a Rope would have become with the utmost Propriety, that the Fellow staggered backwards, and perceiving he had to do with something rougher than the little, tender, trembling Hand of *Fanny*, he quitted her, and turning about saw his Rival, with Fire flashing from his Eyes, again ready to assail him; and indeed before he could well defend himself or return the first Blow, he received a second, which had it fallen on that part of the Stomach to which it was directed, would have been probably the last he would have had any Occasion for; but the Ravisher lifting up his Hand, drove the Blow upwards to his Mouth, whence it dislodged three of his Teeth; and now not conceiving any extraordinary Affection for the Beauty of *Joseph's* Person, nor being extremely pleased with this method of Salutation, he collected all his Force, and aimed a Blow at *Joseph's* Breast, which he artfully parry'd with one Fist, so that it lost its Force entirely in Air. And stepping one Foot backward, he darted his Fist so fiercely at his Enemy, that had he not caught it in his Hand (for he was a Boxer of no inferiour Fame) it must have tumbled him on the Ground. And now the Ravisher meditated another Blow, which he aimed at that part of the Breast where the Heart is lodged, *Joseph* did not catch it as before, yet so prevented its Aim, that it fell directly on his Nose, but with abated Force. *Joseph* then moving both Fist and Foot forwards at the same time, threw his Head so dextrously into the Stomach of the Ravisher, that he fell a lifeless Lump on the Field, where he lay many Minutes breathless and motionless.

When *Fanny* saw her *Joseph* receive a Blow in his Face, and Blood running in a Stream from him, she began to tear her Hair, and invoke all human and divine Power to his Assistance. She was not, however, long under this Affliction, before *Joseph* having

conquered his Enemy, ran to her, and assured her he was not
hurt; she then instantly fell on her Knees and thanked G——, that
he had made *Joseph* the means of her Rescue, and at the same time
preserved him from being injured in attempting it. She offered
with her Handkerchief to wipe his Blood from his Face; but he
seeing his Rival attempting to recover his Legs, turned to him
and asked him if he had enough; to which the other answer'd he
had; for he believed he had fought with the Devil, instead of a
Man, and loosening his Horse, said he should not have attempted
the Wench if he had known she had been so well provided for.

Fanny now begged *Joseph* to return with her to Parson *Adams*,
and to promise that he would leave her no more; these were
Propositions so agreeable to *Joseph*, that had he heard them he
would have given an immediate Assent: but indeed his Eyes were
now his only Sense; for you may remember, Reader, that the
Ravisher had tore her Handkerchief from *Fanny's* Neck, by
which he had discovered such a Sight; that *Joseph* hath declared
all the Statues he ever beheld were so much inferiour to it in
Beauty, that it was more capable of converting a Man into a
Statue, than of being imitated by the greatest Master of that Art.
This modest Creature, whom no Warmth in Summer could ever
induce to expose her Charms to the wanton Sun, a Modesty
to which perhaps they owed their inconceivable Whiteness, had
stood many Minutes bare-necked in the Presence of *Joseph*, before her Apprehension of his Danger, and the Horror of seeing
his Blood would suffer her once to reflect on what concerned herself; till at last, when the Cause of her Concern had vanished,
an Admiration at his Silence, together with observing the fixed
Position of his Eyes, produced an Idea in the lovely Maid, which
brought more Blood into her Face than had flowed from *Joseph's*
Nostrils. The snowy Hue of her Bosom was likewise exchanged
to Vermillion at the instant when she clapped her Handkerchief
round her Neck. *Joseph* saw the Uneasiness she suffered, and
immediately removed his Eyes from an Object, in surveying
which he had felt the greatest Delight which the Organs of Sight
were capable of conveying to his Soul. So great was his Fear of
offending her, and so truly did his Passion for her deserve the
noble Name of Love.

Fanny being recovered from her Confusion, which was almost equalled by what *Joseph* had felt from observing it, again

mention'd her Request; this was instantly and gladly complied with, and together they crossed two or three Fields, which brought them to the Habitation of Mr. *Adams*.

CHAPTER VIII

A Discourse which happened between Mr. Adams, *Mrs.* Adams, Joseph *and* Fanny; *with some Behaviour of Mr.* Adams, *which will be called by some few Readers, very low, absurd, and unnatural.*

THE Parson and his Wife had just ended a long Dispute when the Lovers came to the Door. Indeed this young Couple had been the Subject of the Dispute; for Mrs. *Adams* was one of those prudent People who never do any thing to injure their Families, or perhaps one of those good Mothers who would even stretch their Conscience to serve their Children. She had long entertained hopes of seeing her eldest Daughter succeed Mrs. *Slipslop*, and of making her second Son an Exciseman by Lady *Booby's* Interest. These were Expectations she could not endure the Thoughts of quitting, and was therefore very uneasy to see her Husband so resolute to oppose the Lady's Intention in *Fanny's* Affair. She told him, 'it behoved every Man to take the first Care of his Family; that he had a Wife and six Children, the maintaining and providing for whom would be Business enough for him without intermeddling in other Folks Affairs; that he had always preached up Submission to Superiours, and would do ill to give an Example of the contrary Behaviour in his own Conduct; that if Lady *Booby* did wrong, she must answer for it herself, and the Sin would not lie at their Door; that *Fanny* had been a Servant, and bred up in the Lady's own Family, and consequently she must have known more of her than they did, and it was very improbable if she had behaved herself well, that the Lady would have been so bitterly her Enemy; that perhaps he was too much inclined to think well of her because she was handsome, but handsome Women were often no better than they should be; that G— made ugly Women as well as handsome ones, and that if a Woman had Virtue, it

signified nothing whether she had Beauty or no.' For all which
Reasons she concluded, he should oblige the Lady and stop the
future Publication of the Banns: but all these excellent Arguments had no effect on the Parson, who persisted in doing his
Duty without regarding the Consequence it might have on his
worldly Interest; he endeavoured to answer her as well as he
could, to which she had just finished her Reply, (for she had
always the last Word every where but at Church) when *Joseph*
and *Fanny* entered their Kitchin, where the Parson and his Wife
then sat at Breakfast over some Bacon and Cabbage. There
was a Coldness in the Civility of Mrs. *Adams*, which Persons of
accurate Speculation might have observed, but escaped her present Guests; indeed it was a good deal covered by the Heartiness
of *Adams*, who no sooner heard that *Fanny* had neither eat nor
drank that Morning, than he presented her a Bone of Bacon he
had just been gnawing, being the only Remains of his Provision,
and then ran nimbly to the Tap, and produced a Mug of small
Beer, which he called Ale, however it was the best in his House.
Joseph addressing himself to the Parson, told him the Discourse
which had past between Squire *Booby*, his Sister and himself,
concerning *Fanny*: he then acquainted him with the Dangers
whence he had rescued her, and communicated some Apprehensions on her account. He concluded, that he should never have
an easy Moment till *Fanny* was absolutely his, and begged that
he might be suffered to fetch a Licence, saying, he could easily
borrow the Money. The Parson answered, that he had already
given his Sentiments concerning a Licence, and that a very few
Days would make it unnecessary. '*Joseph*,' says he, 'I wish this
Haste doth not arise rather from your Impatience than your Fear:
but as it certainly springs from one of these Causes, I will examine
both. Of each of these therefore in their Turn; and first, for the
first of these, namely, Impatience. Now, Child, I must inform
you, that if in your purposed Marriage with this young Woman,
you have no Intention but the Indulgence of carnal Appetites,
you are guilty of a very heinous Sin. Marriage was ordained for
nobler Purposes, as you will learn when you hear the Service
provided on that Occasion read to you. Nay perhaps, if you are
a good Lad, I shall give you a Sermon *gratis*, wherein I shall
demonstrate how little Regard ought to be had to the Flesh on
such Occasions. The Text will be, Child, *Matthew* the 5th, and

Part of the 28th Verse,[1] *Whosoever looketh on a Woman so as to lust after her.* The latter Part I shall omit, as foreign to my Purpose. Indeed all such brutal Lusts and Affections are to be greatly subdued, if not totally eradicated, before the Vessel can be said to be consecrated to Honour. To marry with a View of gratifying those Inclinations is a Prostitution of that holy Ceremony, and must entail a Curse on all who so lightly undertake it. If, therefore, this Haste arises from Impatience, you are to correct, and not give way to it. Now as to the second Head which I proposed to speak to, namely, Fear. It argues a Diffidence highly criminal of that Power in which alone we should put our Trust, seeing we may be well assured that he is able not only to defeat the Designs of our Enemies, but even to turn their Hearts. Instead of taking therefore any unjustifiable or desperate means to rid ourselves of Fear, we should resort to Prayer only on these Occasions, and we may be then certain of obtaining what is best for us. When any Accident threatens us, we are not to despair, nor when it overtakes us, to grieve; we must submit in all things to the Will of Providence, and not set our Affections so much on any thing here, as not to be able to quit it without Reluctance. You are a young Man, and can know but little of this World; I am older, and have seen a great deal. All Passions are criminal in their Excess, and even Love itself, if it is not subservient to our Duty, may render us blind to it. Had *Abraham* so loved his Son *Isaac*,[2] as to refuse the Sacrifice required, is there any of us who would not condemn him? *Joseph*, I know your many good Qualities, and value you for them: but as I am to render an Account of your Soul, which is committed to my Cure, I cannot see any Fault without reminding you of it. You are too much inclined to Passion, Child, and have set your Affections so absolutely on this young Woman, that if G—— required her at your hands, I fear you would reluctantly part with her. Now believe me, no Christian ought so to set his Heart on any Person or Thing in this World, but that whenever it shall be required or taken from him in any manner by Divine Providence, he may be able, peaceably, quietly, and contentedly to resign it.' At which Words one came

---

[1] The latter part of Matthew v. 28, which Adams omits, reveals the inappropriateness of the text to the subject of sexual love *in marriage*: 'But I say unto you, That whosoever looketh on a woman to lust after her hath committed adultery with her already in his heart.'

[2] Genesis xxii. 1–18.

hastily in and acquainted Mr. *Adams* that his youngest Son was drowned. He stood silent a moment, and soon began to stamp about the Room and deplore his Loss with the bitterest Agony. *Joseph*, who was overwhelmed with Concern likewise, recovered himself sufficiently to endeavour to comfort the Parson; in which Attempt he used many Arguments that he had at several times remember'd out of his own Discourses both in private and publick, (for he was a great Enemy to the Passions, and preached nothing more than the Conquest of them by Reason and Grace) but he was not at leisure now to hearken to his Advice. 'Child, Child,' said he, 'do not go about Impossibilities. Had it been any other of my Children I could have born it with patience; but my little Prattler, the Darling and Comfort of my old Age—the little Wretch to be snatched out of Life just at his Entrance into it; the sweetest, best-temper'd Boy, who never did a thing to offend me. It was but this Morning I gave him his first Lesson in *Quæ Genus.*[1] This was the very Book he learnt, poor Child! it is of no further use to thee now. He would have made the best Scholar, and have been an Ornament to the Church—such Parts and such Goodness never met in one so young.' 'And the handsomest Lad too,' says Mrs. *Adams*, recovering from a Swoon in *Fanny's* Arms. —'My poor *Jacky*,[2] shall I never see thee more?' cries the Parson. —'Yes, surely,' says *Joseph*, 'and in a better Place, you will meet again never to part more.'—I believe the Parson did not hear these Words, for he paid little regard to them, but went on lamenting whilst the Tears trickled down into his Bosom. At last he cry'd out, 'Where is my little Darling?' and was sallying out, when to his great Surprize and Joy, in which I hope the Reader will sympathize, he met his Son in a wet Condition indeed, but alive, and running towards him. The Person who brought the News of his Misfortune, had been a little too eager, as People sometimes are, from I believe no very good Principle, to relate ill News; and seeing him fall into the River, instead of running to his Assistance, directly ran to acquaint his Father of a Fate which he had concluded to be inevitable, but whence the Child was relieved by the same poor Pedlar who had relieved his Father

[1] In the Eton Latin grammar (*Introduction to the Latin Tongue* [1758]) the section treating the gender and declension of heteroclite or irregular nouns begins '*Quæ genus aut flexum variant* . . . .'

[2] Fielding's slip: Adams later calls his son Dicky.

before from a less Distress. The Parson's Joy was now as extravagant as his Grief had been before; he kissed and embraced his Son a thousand times, and danced about the Room like one frantick; but as soon as he discovered the Face of his old Friend the Pedlar, and heard the fresh Obligation he had to him, what were his Sensations? not those which two Courtiers feel in one another's Embraces; not those with which a great Man receives the vile, treacherous Engines of his wicked Purposes; not those with which a worthless younger Brother wishes his elder Joy of a Son, or a Man congratulates his Rival on his obtaining a Mistress, a Place, or an Honour.—No, Reader, he felt the Ebullition, the Overflowings of a full, honest, open Heart towards the Person who had conferred a real Obligation, and of which if thou can'st not conceive an Idea within, I will not vainly endeavour to assist thee.

When these Tumults were over, the Parson taking *Joseph* aside, proceeded thus—'No, *Joseph*, do not give too much way to thy Passions, if thou dost expect Happiness.'—The Patience of *Joseph*, nor perhaps of *Job*, could bear no longer; he interrupted the Parson, saying, 'it was easier to give Advice than take it, nor did he perceive he could so entirely conquer himself, when he apprehended he had lost his Son, or when he found him recover'd.' —'Boy,' reply'd *Adams*, raising his Voice, 'it doth not become green Heads to advise grey Hairs—Thou art ignorant of the Tenderness of fatherly Affection; when thou art a Father thou wilt be capable then only of knowing what a Father can feel. No Man is obliged to Impossibilities, and the Loss of a Child is one of those great Trials where our Grief may be allowed to become immoderate.' 'Well, Sir,' cries *Joseph*, 'and if I love a Mistress as well as you your Child, surely her Loss would grieve me equally.' 'Yes, but such Love is Foolishness, and wrong in itself, and ought to be conquered,' answered *Adams*, 'it savours too much of the Flesh.' 'Sure, Sir,' says *Joseph*, 'it is not sinful to love my Wife, no not even to doat on her to Distraction!' 'Indeed but it is,' says *Adams*. 'Every Man ought to love his Wife, no doubt; we are commanded so to do; but we ought to love her with Moderation and Discretion.'—'I am afraid I shall be guilty of some Sin, in spight of all my Endeavours,' says *Joseph*; 'for I shall love without any Moderation, I am sure.'—'You talk foolishly and childishly,' cries *Adams*. 'Indeed,' says Mrs. *Adams*, who had listened to the latter part of their Conversation, 'you talk more foolishly yourself. I hope, my Dear, you will never preach any such Doctrine as that Husbands can love their Wives too well. If I knew you had such a Sermon in the House, I am sure I would burn it; and I declare if I had not been convinced you had loved me as well as you could, I can answer for myself I should have hated and despised you. Marry come up! Fine Doctrine indeed! A Wife hath a Right to insist on her Husband's loving her as much as ever he can: And he is a sinful Villain who doth not. Doth he not promise to love her, and to comfort her, and to cherish her, and all that? I am sure I remember it all, as well as if I had repeated it over but Yesterday, and shall never forget it. Besides, I am certain you do not preach as you practise; for you have been a loving and a cherishing Husband to me, that's the truth on't; and why you should endeavour to put such wicked Nonsense into this young Man's Head, I cannot devise. Don't hearken to him, Mr. *Joseph*, be as good a Husband as you are able, and love your Wife with all your Body and Soul too.' Here a violent Rap at the Door put an end to their Discourse, and produced a Scene which the Reader will find in the next Chapter.

CHAPTER IX

A Visit which the good Lady Booby *and her polite Friend paid to the Parson.*

THE Lady *Booby* had no sooner had an Account from the Gentleman of his meeting a wonderful Beauty near her House, and perceived the Raptures with which he spoke of her, than immediately concluding it must be *Fanny*, she began to meditate a Design of bringing them better acquainted; and to entertain Hopes that the fine Clothes, Presents and Promises of this Youth, would prevail on her to abandon *Joseph*: She therefore proposed to her Company a Walk in the Fields before Dinner, when she led them towards Mr. *Adams's* House; and as she approached it, told them, if they pleased she would divert them with one of the most ridiculous Sights they had ever seen, which was an old foolish Parson, who, she said laughing, kept a Wife and six Brats on a Salary of about twenty Pounds a Year; adding, that there was not such another ragged Family in the Parish. They all readily agreed to this Visit, and arrived whilst Mrs. *Adams* was declaiming, as in the last Chapter. Beau *Didapper*, which was the Name of the young Gentleman we have seen riding towards Lady *Booby's*, with his Cane mimicked the Rap of a *London* Footman at the Door. The People within; namely, *Adams*, his Wife, and three Children, *Joseph*, *Fanny*, and the Pedlar, were all thrown into Confusion by this Knock; but *Adams* went directly to the Door, which being opened, the Lady *Booby* and her Company walked in, and were received by the Parson with about two hundred Bows; and by his Wife with as many Curt'sies; the latter telling the Lady, 'she was ashamed to be seen in such a Pickle, and that her House was in such a Litter: But that if she had expected such an Honour from her Ladyship, she should have found her in a better manner.' The Parson made no Apologies, tho' he was in his Half-Cassock and a Flannel Night-Cap. He said, 'they were heartily welcome to his poor Cottage,' and turning to Mr. *Didapper*, cried out, *Non mea renidet in Domo Lacunar*:[1] The Beau answered, 'he did not understand *Welch*;' at which the Parson stared, and made no Reply.

Mr. *Didapper*, or Beau *Didapper*, was a young Gentleman of about four Foot five Inches in height. He wore his own Hair, tho' the Scarcity of it might have given him sufficient Excuse for a Periwig. His Face was thin and pale: The Shape of his Body and Legs none of the best; for he had very narrow Shoulders, and no Calf; and his Gait might more properly be called hopping than walking. The Qualifications of his Mind were well adapted to his Person. We shall handle them first negatively. He was not entirely ignorant: For he could talk a little *French*, and sing two or three *Italian* Songs: He had lived too much in the World to be bashful, and too much at Court to be proud: He seemed not much inclined to Avarice; for he was profuse in his Expences: Nor had he all the Features of Prodigality; for he never gave a Shilling:— No Hater of Women; for he always dangled after them; yet so little subject to Lust, that he had, among those who knew him best, the Character of great Moderation in his Pleasures. No Drinker of Wine; nor so addicted to Passion, but that a hot Word or two from an Adversary made him immediately cool.

---

[1] From Horace, *Odes*, II. xviii. 1–2: '*Non ebur neque aureum | mea renidet in domo lacunar*' ('No ivory or golden cornice glitters in my home').

Now, to give him only a Dash or two on the affirmative Side: 'Tho' he was born to an immense Fortune, he chose, for the pitiful and dirty Consideration of a Place of little consequence, to depend entirely on the Will of a Fellow, whom they call a Great-Man; who treated him with the utmost Disrespect, and exacted of him a plenary Obedience to his Commands; which he implicitly submitted to, at the Expence of his Conscience, his Honour, and of his Country; in which he had himself so very large a Share.'[1] And to finish his Character, 'As he was entirely well satisfied with his own Person and Parts, so he was very apt to ridicule and laugh at any Imperfection in another.'[2] Such was the little Person or rather Thing that hopped after Lady *Booby* into Mr. *Adams's* Kitchin.

The Parson and his Company retreated from the Chimney-side, where they had been seated, to give room to the Lady and hers. Instead of returning any of the Curt'sies or extraordinary Civility of Mrs. *Adams*, the Lady turning to Mr. *Booby*, cried out, '*Quelle Bête! Quel Animal!*' And presently after discovering *Fanny* (for she did not need the Circumstance of her standing by *Joseph* to assure the Identity of her Person) she asked the Beau, 'whether he did not think her a pretty Girl?'—'Begad, Madam,' answered he, ''tis the very same I met.' 'I did not imagine,'

[1] John, Lord Hervey, the original of Beau Didapper, was the subject of the fulsome Dedication to Conyers Middleton's *Life of Cicero* (see p. 239, n. 2), which Fielding had earlier parodied in Conny Keyber's Dedication to *Shamela*. The first of the passages in quotation marks above is Fielding's condensed and inverted version of two paragraphs in which Middleton celebrates Hervey's patriotism; Fielding specifically echoes the phrasing at the beginning and end of Middleton's encomium: 'though born to the first honors of Your country'; and 'born to so large a share of the property, as well as the honors of the nation'. (See the Dedication to *The Life of Cicero* [1741], I. ix–xi.) On Hervey and his role in *Joseph Andrews*, see Introduction, p. xxiii, n. 2.

[2] In *Verses Address'd to the Imitator of the First Satire of the Second Book of Horace* (1733) Hervey, together with Lady Mary Wortley Montagu, cruelly ridiculed not only Pope's poetry and morals, but his birth and crooked body. Pope replied in *A Letter to a Noble Lord* (written in 1733 and privately circulated), satirizing Hervey under the name of Fannius, an enemy of Horace. In the second of the passages in quotation marks above, Fielding combines and paraphrases Pope's statements: (1) 'This *Fannius* was, it seems, extremely fond both of his *Poetry* and his *Person*, which appears by the pictures and *Statues* he caused to be made of himself, and by his great diligence to propagate *bad Verses* at *Court*, and get them admitted into the library of *Augustus*' (Pope's *Works*, ed. Warburton [1751], viii. 263); (2) '. . . it is *improper*, nay *unchristian*, to expose the *personal* defects of our brother: that both such perfect forms as yours, and such unfortunate ones as mine, proceed from the hand of the same *Maker*; who *fashioneth his Vessels* as he pleaseth, and that it is not from their *shape* we can tell whether they are made for *honour* or *dishonour*' (viii. 268). On Hervey and Pope, see Introduction, p. xxiii, n. 2.

replied the Lady, 'you had so good a Taste.' 'Because I never liked you, I warrant,' cries the Beau. 'Ridiculous!' said she, 'you know you was always my Aversion.' 'I would never mention Aversion,' answered the Beau, 'with that Face*; dear Lady *Booby*, wash your Face before you mention Aversion, I beseech you.' He then laughed and turned about to coquette it with *Fanny*.

Mrs. *Adams* had been all this time begging and praying the Ladies to sit down, a Favour which she at last obtained. The little Boy to whom the Accident had happened, still keeping his Place by the Fire, was chid by his Mother for not being more mannerly: But Lady *Booby* took his part, and commending his Beauty, told the Parson he was his very Picture. She then seeing a Book in his Hand, asked, 'if he could read?' 'Yes,' cried *Adams*, 'a little *Latin*, Madam, he is just got into *Quæ Genus*.'—'A Fig for *quere genius*,' answered she, 'let me hear him read a little *English*.'—'*Lege, Dick, Lege*,' said *Adams*: But the Boy made no Answer, till he saw the Parson knit his Brows; and then cried, 'I don't understand you, Father.' 'How, Boy,' says *Adams*, 'What doth *Lego* make in the imperative Mood? *Legito*, doth it not?' 'Yes,' answered *Dick*.—'And what besides?' says the Father. '*Lege*,' quoth the Son, after some hesitation. 'A good Boy,' says the Father: 'And now, Child, What is the *English* of *Lego*?'—To which the Boy, after long puzzling, answered, he could not tell. 'How,' cries *Adams* in a Passion,—'What hath the Water washed away your Learning? Why, what is *Latin* for the *English* Verb *read*? Consider before you speak.'—The Child considered some time, and then the Parson cried twice or thrice, '*Le—*, *Le—*.'—*Dick* answered, '*Lego*.'—'Very well;—and then, what is the *English*,' says the Parson, 'of the Verb *Lego*?'—'*To read*,' cried *Dick*.—'Very well,' said the Parson, 'a good Boy, you can do well, if you will take pains.—I assure your Ladyship he is not much above eight Years old, and is out of his *Propria quæ Maribus*[2]

* Lest this should appear unnatural to some Readers, we think proper to acquaint them, that it is taken verbatim from very polite Conversation.[1]

[1] Cf. Vanbrugh's *A Journey to London* (1728), IV. i. Captain Toupee replies to Lady Loverule, who wishes to engage him in a game of Hazard: 'What, with that Face? Go, go wash it, go wash it, and put on some handsome things; you lookt a good likely Woman last Night' (p. 48).

[2] See p. 147, n. 1.

already.—Come, *Dick*, read to her Ladyship;'—which she again
desiring, in order to give the Beau Time and Opportunity with
Fanny, *Dick* began as in the following Chapter.

CHAPTER X

*The History of two Friends, which may afford an useful
Lesson to all those Persons, who happen to take up
their Residence in married Families.*

'Leonard and *Paul* were two Friends.'—'Pronounce it *Lennard*,
Child,' cry'd the Parson.—'Pray, Mr. *Adams*,' says Lady *Booby*,
'let your Son read without Interruption.' *Dick* then proceeded.
'*Lennard* and *Paul* were two Friends, who having been educated
together at the same School, commenced a Friendship which they
preserved a long time for each other. It was so deeply fixed in both
their Minds, that a long Absence, during which they had maintained no Correspondence, did not eradicate nor lessen it: But it
revived in all its Force at their first Meeting, which was not till
after fifteen Years Absence, most of which Time *Lennard* had
spent in the *East-Indi-es*.'—'Pronounce it short *Indies*,' says
Adams.—'Pray, Sir, be quiet,' says the Lady.—The Boy repeated—'in the *East-Indies*, whilst *Paul* had served his King
and Country in the Army. In which different Services, they had
found such different Success, that *Lennard* was now married,
and retired with a Fortune of thirty thousand Pound; and *Paul*
was arrived to the Degree of a Lieutenant of Foot; and was not
worth a single Shilling.
  'The Regiment in which *Paul* was stationed, happened to be
ordered into Quarters, within a small distance from the Estate
which *Lennard* had purchased; and where he was settled. This
latter, who was now become a Country Gentleman and a Justice
of Peace, came to attend the Quarter-Sessions, in the Town where
his old Friend was quartered, soon after his Arrival. Some Affair
in which a Soldier was concerned, occasioned *Paul* to attend the
Justices. Manhood, and Time, and the Change of Climate had
so much altered *Lennard*, that *Paul* did not immediately recollect
the Features of his old Acquaintance: But it was otherwise with

Lennard. He knew *Paul* the moment he saw him; nor could he contain himself from quitting the Bench, and running hastily to embrace him. *Paul* stood at first a little surprized; but had soon sufficient Information from his Friend, whom he no sooner remembred, than he returned his Embrace with a Passion which made many of the Spectators laugh, and gave to some few a much higher and more agreeable Sensation.

'Not to detain the Reader with minute Circumstances, *Lennard* insisted on his Friend's returning with him to his House that Evening; which Request was complied with, and Leave for a Month's Absence for *Paul*, obtained of the commanding Officer.

'If it was possible for any Circumstance to give any addition to the Happiness which *Paul* proposed in this Visit, he received that additional Pleasure, by finding on his Arrival at his Friend's House, that his Lady was an old Acquaintance which he had formerly contracted at his Quarters; and who had always appeared to be of a most agreeable Temper. A Character she had ever maintained among her Intimates, being of that number, every Individual of which is called quite the best sort of Woman in the World.

'But good as this Lady was, she was still a Woman; that is to say, an Angel and not an Angel—' 'You must mistake, Child,' cries the Parson, 'for you read Nonsense.' 'It is so in the Book,' answered the Son. Mr. *Adams* was then silenc'd by Authority, and *Dick* proceeded—'For tho' her Person was of that kind to which Men attribute the Name of Angel, yet in her Mind she was perfectly Woman. Of which a great degree of Obstinacy gave the most remarkable, and perhaps most pernicious Instance.

'A Day or two past after *Paul's* Arrival before any Instances of this appear'd; but it was impossible to conceal it long. Both she and her Husband soon lost all Apprehension from their Friend's Presence, and fell to their Disputes with as much Vigour as ever. These were still pursued with the utmost Ardour and Eagerness, however trifling the Causes were whence they first arose. Nay, however incredible it may seem, the little Consequence of the matter in Debate was frequently given as a Reason for the Fierceness of the Contention, as thus: *If you loved me, sure you would never dispute with me such a Trifle as this.* The Answer to which is very obvious; for the Argument would hold equally on both sides, and was constantly retorted with some Addition, as—*I am sure I have much more Reason to say so, who am in the right.* During all these Disputes, *Paul* always kept strict Silence, and preserved an even Countenance without shewing the least visible Inclination to either Party. One day, however, when Madam had left the Room in a violent Fury, *Lennard* could not refrain from referring his Cause to his Friend. Was ever any thing so unreasonable, says he, as this Woman? What shall I do with her? I doat on her to Distraction; nor have I any Cause to complain of more than this Obstinacy in her Temper; whatever she asserts she will maintain against all the Reason and Conviction in the World. Pray give me your Advice.—First, says *Paul*, I will give my Opinion, which is flatly that you are in the wrong; for supposing she is in the wrong, was the Subject of your Contention anywise material? What signified it whether you was married in a red or yellow Waistcoat? for that was your Dispute. Now suppose she was mistaken, as you love her you say so tenderly, and I believe she deserves it, would it not have been wiser to have yielded, tho' you certainly knew yourself in the right, than to give either her or yourself any Uneasiness? For my own part, if ever I marry, I am resolved to enter into an Agreement with my Wife, that in all Disputes (especially about Trifles) that Party who is most convinced they are right, shall always surrender the Victory: by which means we shall both be forward to give up the Cause. I own, said *Lennard*, my dear Friend, shaking him by the Hand, there is great Truth and Reason in what you say; and I will for the future endeavour to follow your Advice. They soon after broke up the Conversation, and *Lennard* going to his Wife, asked her pardon, and told her his Friend had convinced him he had been in the wrong. She immediately began a vast Encomium on *Paul*, in which he seconded her, and both agreed he was the worthiest and wisest Man upon Earth. When next they met, which was at Supper, tho' she had promised not to mention what her Husband told her, she could not forbear casting the kindest and most affectionate Looks on *Paul*, and asked him with the sweetest Voice, whether she should help him to some Potted-Woodcock?—Potted Partridge, my Dear, you mean, says the Husband. My Dear, says she, I ask your Friend if he will eat any potted Woodcock; and I am sure I must know, who potted it. I think I should know too, who shot them, reply'd the Husband,

and I am convinced I have not seen a Woodcock this Year; however, tho' I know I am in the right I submit, and the potted Partridge is potted Woodcock, if you desire to have it so. It is equal to me, says she, whether it is one or the other; but you would persuade one out of one's Senses; to be sure you are always in the right in your own Opinion; but your Friend I believe knows which he is eating. *Paul* answered nothing, and the Dispute continued as usual the greatest part of the Evening. The next Morning the Lady accidentally meeting *Paul*, and being convinced he was her Friend, and of her side, accosted him thus: —I am certain, Sir, you have long since wonder'd at the Unreasonableness of my Husband. He is indeed in other respects a good sort of Man; but so positive, that no Woman but one of my complying Temper could possibly live with him. Why last Night now, was ever any Creature so unreasonable?—I am certain you must condemn him—Pray answer me, was he not in the wrong? *Paul*, after a short Silence, spoke as follows: I am sorry, Madam, that as Good-manners obliges me to answer against my Will, so an Adherence to Truth forces me to declare myself of a different Opinion. To be plain and honest, you was entirely in the wrong; the Cause I own not worth disputing, but the Bird was undoubtedly a Partridge. O Sir, reply'd the Lady, I cannot possibly help your Taste.—Madam, returned *Paul*, that is very little material; for had it been otherwise, a Husband might have expected Submission.—Indeed! Sir, says she, I assure you!— Yes, Madam, cry'd he, he might from a Person of your excellent Understanding; and pardon me for saying such a Condescension would have shewn a Superiority of Sense even to your Husband himself.—But, dear Sir, said she, why should I submit when I am in the right?—For that very Reason, answer'd he, it would be the greatest Instance of Affection imaginable: for can any thing be a greater Object of our Compassion than a Person we love, in the wrong? Ay, but I should endeavour, said she, to set him right. Pardon me, Madam, answered *Paul*, I will apply to your own Experience, if you ever found your Arguments had that effect. The more our Judgments err, the less we are willing to own it: for my own part, I have always observed the Persons who maintain the worst side in any Contest, are the warmest. Why, says she, I must confess there is Truth in what you say, and I will endeavour to practice it. The Husband then coming in, *Paul* departed. And *Lennard* approaching his Wife with an Air of Good-humour, told her he was sorry for their foolish Dispute the last Night: but he was now convinced of his Error. She answered smiling, she believed she owed his Condescension to his Complacence; that she was ashamed to think a Word had past on so silly an Occasion, especially as she was satisfy'd she had been mistaken. A little Contention followed, but with the utmost Goodwill to each other, and was concluded by her asserting that *Paul* had thoroughly convinced her she had been in the wrong. Upon which they both united in the Praises of their common Friend.

'*Paul* now past his time with great Satisfaction; these Disputes being much less frequent as well as shorter than usual: but the Devil, or some unlucky Accident in which perhaps the Devil had no hand, shortly put an end to his Happiness. He was now eternally the private Referee of every Difference; in which after having perfectly as he thought established the Doctrine of Submission, he never scrupled to assure both privately that they were in the right in every Argument, as before he had followed the contrary Method. One day a violent Litigation happened in his Absence, and both Parties agreed to refer it to his Decision. The Husband professing himself sure the Decision would be in his favour, the Wife answer'd, he might be mistaken; for she believed his Friend was convinced how seldom she was to blame—and that if he knew all.—The Husband reply'd—My Dear, I have no desire of any Retrospect, but I believe if you knew all too, you would not imagine my Friend so entirely on your side. Nay, says she, since you provoke me, I will mention one Instance. You may remember our Dispute about sending *Jacky* to School in cold Weather, which Point I gave up to you from mere Compassion, knowing myself to be in the right, and *Paul* himself told me afterwards, he thought me so. My Dear, replied the Husband, I will not scruple your Veracity; but I assure you solemnly, on my applying to him, he gave it absolutely on my side, and said he would have acted in the same manner. They then proceeded to produce numberless other Instances, in all which *Paul* had, on Vows of Secrecy, given his Opinion on both sides. In the Conclusion, both believing each other, they fell severely on the Treachery of *Paul*, and agreed that he had been the occasion of almost every Dispute which had fallen out between them. They then became extremely loving, and so full of Condescension on both sides, that they vyed with each other in censuring their own Conduct, and jointly vented their Indignation on *Paul*, whom the Wife, fearing a bloody Consequence, earnestly entreated her Husband to suffer quietly to depart the next Day, which was the time fixed for his Return to Quarters, and then drop his Acquaintance.

'However ungenerous this Behaviour in *Lennard* may be esteemed, his Wife obtained a Promise from him (tho' with difficulty) to follow her Advice; but they both exprest such unusual Coldness that day to *Paul*, that he, who was quick of Apprehension, taking *Lennard* aside, prest him so home, that he at last discovered the Secret. *Paul* acknowledged the Truth, but told him the Design with which he had done it—To which the other answered, he would have acted more friendly to have let him into the whole Design; for that he might have assured himself of his Secrecy. *Paul* reply'd, with some Indignation, he had given him a sufficient Proof how capable he was of concealing a Secret from his Wife. *Lennard* returned with some Warmth—He had more reason to upbraid him, for that he had caused most of the Quarrels between them by his strange Conduct, and might (if they had not discovered the Affair to each other) have been the Occasion of their Separation. *Paul* then said—' But something now happened, which put a stop to *Dick's* Reading, and of which we shall treat in the next Chapter.

CHAPTER XI

In which the History is continued.

JOSEPH ANDREWS had borne with great Uneasiness the Impertinence of Beau *Didapper* to *Fanny*, who had been talking pretty freely to her, and offering her Settlements; but the Respect to the Company had restrained him from interfering, whilst the Beau confined himself to the Use of his Tongue only; but the said Beau watching an Opportunity whilst the Ladies Eyes were disposed another way, offered a Rudeness to her with his Hands; which *Joseph* no sooner perceived than he presented him with so sound a Box on the Ear, that it conveyed him several Paces from

where he stood. The Ladies immediately skreamed out, rose from
their Chairs, and the Beau, as soon as he recovered himself, drew
his Hanger, which *Adams* observing, snatched up the Lid of a
Pot in his left Hand, and covering himself with it as with a Shield,
without any Weapon of Offence in his other Hand, stept in
before *Joseph*, and exposed himself to the enraged Beau, who
threatened such Perdition and Destruction, that it frighted the
Women, who were all got in a huddle together, out of their Wits;
even to hear his Denunciations of Vengeance. *Joseph* was of a
different Complexion, and begged *Adams* to let his Rival come
on; for he had a good Cudgel in his Hand, and did not fear him.
Fanny now fainted into Mrs. *Adams's* Arms, and the whole Room
was in Confusion, when Mr. *Booby* passing by *Adams*, who lay
snug under the Pot-Lid, came up to *Didapper*, and insisted on
his sheathing the Hanger, promising he should have Satisfaction;
which *Joseph* declared he would give him, and fight him at any
Weapon whatever. The Beau now sheathed his Hanger, and
taking out a Pocket-Glass, and vowing Vengeance all the Time,
re-adjusted his Hair; the Parson deposited his Shield, and *Joseph*
running to *Fanny*, soon brought her back to Life. Lady *Booby*
chid *Joseph* for his Insult on *Didapper*; but he answered he would
have attacked an Army in the same Cause. 'What Cause?' said
the Lady. 'Madam,' answered *Joseph*, 'he was rude to that young
Woman.'—'What,' says the Lady, 'I suppose he would have
kissed the Wench; and is a Gentleman to be struck for such an
Offer? I must tell you, *Joseph*, these Airs do not become you.'—
'Madam,' said Mr. *Booby*, 'I saw the whole Affair, and I do not
commend my Brother; for I cannot perceive why he should take
upon him to be this Girl's Champion.'—'I can commend him,'
says *Adams*, 'he is a brave Lad; and it becomes any Man to be
the Champion of the Innocent; and he must be the basest
Coward, who would not vindicate a Woman with whom he is on
the Brink of Marriage.'—'Sir,' says Mr. *Booby*, 'my Brother is
not a proper Match for such a young Woman as this.'—'No,'
says Lady *Booby*, 'nor do you, Mr. *Adams*, act in your proper
Character, by encouraging any such Doings; and I am very much
surprized you should concern yourself in it. I think your Wife
and Family your properer Care.'—'Indeed, Madam, your Ladyship says very true,' answered Mrs. *Adams*, 'he talks a pack of
Nonsense, that the whole Parish are his Children. I am sure I

don't understand what he means by it; it would make some Women suspect he had gone astray: but I acquit him of that; I can read Scripture as well as he; and I never found that the Parson was obliged to provide for other Folks Children; and besides he is but a poor Curate, and hath little enough, as your Ladyship knows, for me and mine.'—'You say very well, Mrs. *Adams*,' quoth the Lady *Booby*, who had not spoke a Word to her before, 'you seem to be a very sensible Woman; and I assure you, your Husband is acting a very foolish Part, and opposing his own Interest; seeing my Nephew is violently set against this Match: and indeed I can't blame him; it is by no means one suitable to our Family.' In this manner the Lady proceeded with Mrs. *Adams*, whilst the Beau hopped about the Room, shaking his Head; partly from Pain, and partly from Anger; and *Pamela* was chiding *Fanny* for her Assurance, in aiming at such a Match as her Brother.—Poor *Fanny* answered only with her Tears, which had long since begun to wet her Handkerchief; which *Joseph* perceiving, took her by the Arm, and wrapping it in his, carried her off, swearing he would own no Relation to any one who was an Enemy to her he lov'd more than all the World. He went out with *Fanny* under his left Arm, brandishing a Cudgel in his right, and neither Mr. *Booby* nor the Beau thought proper to oppose him. Lady *Booby* and her Company made a very short stay behind him; for the Lady's Bell now summoned them to dress; for which they had just time before Dinner.

Adams seemed now very much dejected, which his Wife perceiving, began to apply some matrimonial Balsam. She told him he had Reason to be concerned; for that he had probably ruined his Family with his foolish Tricks: But perhaps he was grieved for the Loss of his two Children, *Joseph* and *Fanny*. His eldest Daughter went on:—'Indeed Father, it is very hard to bring Strangers here to eat your Children's Bread out of their Mouths. —You have kept them ever since they came home; and for any thing I see to the contrary may keep them a Month longer: Are you obliged to give her Meat, tho'f she was never so handsome? But I don't see she is so much handsomer than other People. If People were to be kept for their Beauty, she would scarce fare better than her Neighbours, I believe.—As for Mr. *Joseph*, I have nothing to say, he is a young Man of honest Principles, and will pay some time or other for what he hath: But for the Girl,

—Why doth she not return to her Place she ran away from? I would not give such a Vagabond Slut a Halfpenny, tho' I had a Million of Money; no, tho' she was starving.' 'Indeed but I would,' cries little *Dick*; 'and Father, rather than poor *Fanny* shall be starved, I will give her all this Bread and Cheese.'—(*Offering what he held in his Hand.*)—*Adams* smiled on the Boy, and told him he rejoiced to see he was a Christian; and that if he had a Halfpenny in his Pocket he would have given it him; telling him, it was his Duty to look upon all his Neighbours as his Brothers and Sisters, and love them accordingly. 'Yes, Papa,' says he, 'I love her better than my Sisters; for she is handsomer than any of them.' 'Is she so, Saucebox?' says the Sister, giving him a Box on the Ear, which the Father would probably have resented, had not *Joseph*, *Fanny*, and the Pedlar, at that Instant, returned together.—*Adams* bid his Wife prepare some Food for their Dinner; she said, 'truly she could not, she had something else to do.' *Adams* rebuked her for disputing his Commands, and quoted many Texts of Scripture[1] to prove, *that the Husband is the Head of the Wife, and she is to submit and obey.* The Wife answered, 'it was Blasphemy to talk Scripture out of Church; that such things were very proper to be said in the Pulpit: but that it was prophane to talk them in common Discourse.' *Joseph* told Mr. *Adams* 'he was not come with any Design to give him or Mrs. *Adams* any trouble; but to desire the Favour of all their Company to the *George* (an Alehouse in the Parish,) where he had bespoke a Piece of Bacon and Greens for their Dinner.' Mrs. *Adams*, who was a very good sort of Woman, only rather too strict in Œconomicks, readily accepted this Invitation, as did the Parson himself by her Example; and away they all walked together, not omitting little *Dick*, to whom *Joseph* gave a Shilling, when he heard of his intended Liberality to *Fanny*.

[1] Cf. Ephesians v. 22–24; Colossians iii. 18; 1 Peter iii. 1, 5–6.

CHAPTER XII

*Where the good-natur'd Reader will see something
which will give him no great Pleasure.*

THE Pedlar had been very inquisitive from the time he had first
heard that the great House in this Parish belonged to the Lady
Booby; and had learnt that she was the Widow of Sir *Thomas*, and
that Sir *Thomas* had bought *Fanny*, at about the Age of three or
four Years, of a travelling Woman; and now their homely but
hearty Meal was ended, he told *Fanny*, he believed he could
acquaint her with her Parents. The whole Company, especially
she herself, started at this Offer of the Pedlar's.—He then proceeded thus, while they all lent their strictest Attention: 'Tho'
I am now contented with this humble way of getting my Livelihood, I was formerly a Gentleman; for so all those of my Profession are called. In a word, I was a Drummer in an *Irish* Regiment
of Foot. Whilst I was in this honourable Station, I attended an
Officer of our Regiment into *England* a recruiting. In our March
from *Bristol* to *Froome* (for since the Decay of the Woollen Trade,
the clothing Towns have furnished the Army with a great number
of Recruits)[1] we overtook on the Road a Woman who seemed to
be about thirty Years old, or thereabouts, not very handsome; but
well enough for a Soldier. As we came up to her, she mended her
Pace, and falling into Discourse with our Ladies (for every Man
of the Party, namely, a Serjeant, two private Men, and a Drum,
were provided with their Woman, except myself) she continued
to travel on with us. I perceiving she must fall to my Lot, advanced presently to her, made Love to her in our military way,
and quickly succeeded to my Wishes. We struck a Bargain within
a Mile, and lived together as Man and Wife to her dying Day.'

---

[1] The situation to which the pedlar refers was a recurrent theme in Opposition journals
at the time Fielding was writing *Joseph Andrews*. Consider, for example, *The Champion* for
31 October 1741, under 'HOME NEWS': 'From Froom, the great Cloathing Town in Somersetshire, we hear, That through the Decay of Trade, and Decrease of the Woollen Manufacture, above a Thousand young Fellows, for want of Employ, have inlisted themselves
into the Service out of that Neighbourhood, in fourteen Weeks only, since the Commence-
ment of the War.' Similar notices appeared in *Common Sense*, 10 January 1741; *The
Champion*, 15 October 1741; and *The Universal Spectator, and Weekly Journal*, 17 October
1741. (See also, p. 112, n. 3.)

—'I suppose,' says *Adams* interrupting him, 'you were married with a Licence: For I don't see how you could contrive to have the Banns published while you were marching from Place to Place.'—'No, Sir,' said the Pedlar, 'we took a Licence to go to Bed together, without any Banns.'—'Ay, ay,' said the Parson, '*ex Necessitate*, a Licence may be allowable enough; but surely, surely, the other is the more regular and eligible Way.'—The Pedlar proceeded thus, 'She returned with me to our Regiment, and removed with us from Quarters to Quarters, till at last, whilst we lay at *Galloway*, she fell ill of a Fever, and died. When she was on her Death-bed she called me to her, and crying bitterly, declared she could not depart this World without discovering a Secret to me, which she said was the only Sin which sat heavy on her Heart. She said she had formerly travelled in a Company of Gipsies, who had made a Practice of stealing away Children; that for her own part, she had been only once guilty of the Crime; which she said she lamented more than all the rest of her Sins, since probably it might have occasioned the Death of the Parents: For, added she, it is almost impossible to describe the Beauty of the young Creature, which was about a Year and half old when I kidnapped it. We kept her (for she was a Girl) above two Years in our Company, when I sold her myself for three Guineas to Sir *Thomas Booby* in *Somersetshire*. Now, you know whether there are any more of that Name in this County.'—'Yes,' says *Adams*, 'there are several *Boobys* who are Squires; but I believe no Baronet now alive, besides it answers so exactly in every Point there is no room for Doubt; but you have forgot to tell us the Parents from whom the Child was stolen.'—'Their Name,' answered the Pedlar, 'was *Andrews*. They lived about thirty Miles from the Squire; and she told me, that I might be sure to find them out by one Circumstance; for that they had a Daughter of a very strange Name, *Paměla* or *Pamēla*; some pronounced it one way, and some the other.' *Fanny*, who had changed Colour at the first mention of the Name, now fainted away, *Joseph* turned pale, and poor *Dicky* began to roar; the Parson fell on his Knees and ejaculated many Thanksgivings that this Discovery had been made before the dreadful Sin of Incest was committed; and the Pedlar was struck with Amazement, not being able to account for all this Confusion, the Cause of which was presently opened by the Parson's Daughter, who was the only unconcerned Person; (for the Mother was chaffing *Fanny's* Temples, and taking the utmost care of her) and indeed *Fanny* was the only Creature whom the Daughter would not have pitied in her Situation; wherein, tho' we compassionate her ourselves, we shall leave her for a little while, and pay a short Visit to Lady *Booby*.

CHAPTER XIII

The History returning to the Lady Booby, *gives some Account of the terrible Conflict in her Breast between Love and Pride; with what happened on the present Discovery.*

T H E Lady sat down with her Company to Dinner: but eat nothing. As soon as her Cloth was removed, she whispered *Pamela*, that she was taken a little ill, and desired her to entertain her Husband and Beau *Didapper*. She then went up into her Chamber, sent for *Slipslop*, threw herself on the Bed, in the Agonies of Love, Rage, and Despair; nor could she conceal these boiling Passions longer, without bursting. *Slipslop* now approached her Bed, and asked how her Ladyship did; but instead of revealing her Disorder, as she intended, she entered into a long Encomium on the Beauty and Virtues of *Joseph Andrews*; ending at last with expressing her Concern, that so much Tenderness should be thrown away on so despicable an Object as *Fanny*. *Slipslop* well knowing how to humour her Mistress's Frenzy, proceeded to repeat, with Exaggeration if possible, all her Mistress had said, and concluded with a Wish, that *Joseph* had been a Gentleman, and that she could see her Lady in the Arms of such a Husband. The Lady then started from the Bed, and taking a Turn or two cross the Room, cry'd out with a deep Sigh,—*Sure he would make any Woman happy.*—'Your Ladyship,' says she, 'would be the happiest Woman in the World with him.—A fig for Custom and Nonsense. What *vails* what People say? Shall I be afraid of eating Sweetmeats, because People may say I have a sweet Tooth? If I had a mind to marry a Man, all the World should not hinder me. Your Ladyship hath no Parents to *tutelar* your *Infections*; besides he is of your Ladyship's Family now, and as good a

Gentleman as any in the Country; and why should not a Woman
follow her Mind as well as a Man? Why should not your Ladyship marry the Brother, as well as your Nephew the Sister? I am
sure, if it was a *fragrant* Crime I would not persuade your Ladyship to it.'—'But, dear *Slipslop*,' answered the Lady, 'if I could
prevail on myself to commit such a Weakness, there is that cursed
Fanny in the way, whom the Idiot, O how I hate and despise
him—' 'She, a little ugly Mynx,' cries *Slipslop*, 'leave her to me.
—I suppose your Ladyship hath heard of *Joseph's fitting* with one
of Mr. *Didapper's* Servants about her; and his Master hath
ordered them to carry her away by force this Evening. I'll take
care they shall not want Assistance. I was talking with his Gentleman, who was below just when your Ladyship sent for me.'—
'Go back,' says the Lady *Booby*, 'this Instant; for I expect Mr.
Didapper will soon be going. Do all you can; for I am resolved
this Wench shall not be in our Family; I will endeavour to return
to the Company; but let me know as soon as she is carried off.'
Slipslop went away, and her Mistress began to arraign her own
Conduct in the following Manner:

'What am I doing? How do I suffer this Passion to creep
imperceptibly upon me! How many Days are past since I could
have submitted to ask myself the Question?—Marry a Footman!
Distraction! Can I afterwards bear the Eyes of my Acquaintance? But I can retire from them; retire with one in whom I
propose more Happiness than the World without him can give
me! Retire—to feed continually on Beauties, which my inflamed
Imagination sickens with eagerly gazing on; to satisfy every
Appetite, every Desire, with their utmost Wish.—Ha! and do I
doat thus on a Footman! I despise, I detest my Passion.—Yet
why? Is he not generous, gentle, kind?—Kind to whom? to the
meanest Wretch, a Creature below my Consideration. Doth he
not?—Yes, he doth prefer her; curse his Beauties, and the little
low Heart that possesses them; which can basely descend to this
despicable Wench, and be ungratefully deaf to all the Honours
I do him.—And can I then love this Monster? No, I will tear
his Image from my Bosom, tread on him, spurn him. I will have
those pitiful Charms which now I despise, mangled in my sight;
for I will not suffer the little Jade I hate to riot in the Beauties
I contemn. No, tho' I despise him myself; tho' I would spurn
him from my Feet, was he to languish at them, no other should

taste the Happiness I scorn. Why do I say Happiness? To me it would be Misery.—To sacrifice my Reputation, my Character, my Rank in Life, to the Indulgence of a mean and a vile Appetite. —How I detest the Thought! How much more exquisite is the Pleasure resulting from the Reflection of Virtue and Prudence, than the faint Relish of what flows from Vice and Folly! Whither did I suffer this improper, this mad Passion to hurry me, only by neglecting to summon the Aids of Reason to my Assistance? Reason, which hath now set before me my Desires in their proper Colours, and immediately helped me to expel them. Yes, I thank Heaven and my Pride, I have now perfectly conquered this un-worthy Passion; and if there was no Obstacle in its way, my Pride would disdain any Pleasures which could be the Consequence of so base, so mean, so vulgar—' *Slipslop* returned at this Instant in a violent Hurry, and with the utmost Eagerness, cry'd out,—'O, Madam, I have strange News. *Tom* the Footman is just come from the *George*; where it seems *Joseph* and the rest of them are a *jinketting*; and he says, there is a strange Man who hath discovered that *Fanny* and *Joseph* are Brother and Sister.'—'How, *Slipslop*,' cries the Lady in a Surprize.—'I had not time, Madam,' cries *Slipslop*, 'to enquire about *Particles*, but *Tom* says, it is most certainly true.'

This unexpected Account entirely obliterated all those admir-able Reflections which the supreme Power of Reason had so wisely made just before. In short, when Despair, which had more share in producing the Resolutions of Hatred we have seen taken, began to retreat, the Lady hesitated a Moment, and then for-getting all the Purport of her Soliloquy, dismissed her Woman again, with Orders to bid *Tom* attend her in the Parlour, whither she now hastened to acquaint *Pamela* with the News. *Pamela* said, she could not believe it: For she had never heard that her Mother had lost any Child, or that she had ever had any more than *Joseph* and herself. The Lady flew into a violent Rage with her, and talked of Upstarts and disowning Relations, who had so lately been on a level with her. *Pamela* made no answer: But her Hus-band, taking up her Cause, severely reprimanded his Aunt for her Behaviour to his Wife; he told her, if it had been earlier in the Evening, she should not have staid a Moment longer in her House; that he was convinced, if this young Woman could be proved her Sister, she would readily embrace her as such; and he himself would do the same: He then desired the Fellow might be sent for, and the young Woman with him; which Lady *Booby* immediately ordered, and thinking proper to make some Apology to *Pamela* for what she had said, it was readily accepted, and all things reconciled.

The Pedlar now attended, as did *Fanny*, and *Joseph* who would not quit her; the Parson likewise was induced, not only by Curiosity, of which he had no small Portion, but by his Duty, as he apprehended, to follow them: for he continued all the way to exhort them, who were now breaking their Hearts, to offer up Thanksgivings, and be joyful for so miraculous an Escape.

When they arrived at *Booby-Hall*, they were presently called into the Parlour, where the Pedlar repeated the same Story he had told before, and insisted on the Truth of every Circumstance; so that all who heard him were extremely well satisfied of the Truth, except *Pamela*, who imagined, as she had never heard either of her Parents mention such an Accident, that it must be certainly false; and except the Lady *Booby*, who suspected the Falshood of the Story, from her ardent Desire that it should be true; and *Joseph* who feared its Truth, from his earnest Wishes that it might prove false.

Mr. *Booby* now desired them all to suspend their Curiosity and absolute Belief or Disbelief, till the next Morning, when he expected old Mr. *Andrews* and his Wife to fetch himself and *Pamela* home in his Coach, and then they might be certain of perfectly knowing the Truth or Falshood of this Relation; in which he said, as there were many strong Circumstances to induce their Credit, so he could not perceive any Interest the Pedlar could have in inventing it, or in endeavouring to impose such a Falshood on them.

The Lady *Booby*, who was very little used to such Company, entertained them all, *viz.* Her Nephew, his Wife, her Brother and Sister, the Beau, and the Parson, with great Good-humour at her own Table. As to the Pedlar, she ordered him to be made as welcome as possible, by her Servants. All the Company in the Parlour, except the disappointed Lovers, who sat sullen and silent, were full of Mirth: For Mr. *Booby* had prevailed on *Joseph* to ask Mr. *Didapper's* pardon; with which he was perfectly satisfied. Many Jokes past between the Beau and the Parson, chiefly on each other's Dress; these afforded much Diversion to the

Company. *Pamela* chid her Brother *Joseph* for the Concern which he exprest at discovering a new Sister. She said, if he loved *Fanny* as he ought, with a pure Affection, he had no Reason to lament being related to her.—Upon which *Adams* began to discourse on *Platonic* Love; whence he made a quick Transition to the Joys in the next World, and concluded with strongly asserting that there was no such thing as Pleasure in this. At which *Pamela* and her Husband smiled on one another.

This happy Pair proposing to retire (for no other Person gave the least Symptom of desiring Rest) they all repaired to several Beds provided for them in the same House; nor was *Adams* himself suffered to go home, it being a stormy Night. *Fanny* indeed often begged she might go home with the Parson; but her Stay was so strongly insisted on, that she at last, by *Joseph's* Advice, consented.

CHAPTER XIV

Containing several curious Night-Adventures, in which Mr. Adams *fell into many Hair-breadth 'Scapes, partly owing to his Goodness, and partly to his Inadvertency.*

ABOUT an Hour after they had all separated (it being now past three in the Morning) Beau *Didapper*, whose Passion for *Fanny* permitted him not to close his Eyes, but had employed his Imagination in Contrivances how to satisfy his Desires, at last hit on a Method by which he hoped to effect it. He had ordered his Servant to bring him word where *Fanny* lay, and had received his Information; he therefore arose, put on his Breeches and Nightgown, and stole softly along the Gallery which led to her Apartment; and being come to the Door, as he imagined it, he opened it with the least Noise possible, and entered the Chamber. A Savour now invaded his Nostrils which he did not expect in the Room of so sweet a young Creature, and which might have probably had no good effect on a cooler Lover. However, he groped out the Bed with difficulty; for there was not a Glimpse of Light, and opening the Curtains, he whispered in *Joseph's* Voice (for he was an excellent Mimick) 'Fanny, my Angel, I am come to inform thee that I have discovered the Falshood of the Story we last Night heard. I am no longer thy Brother, but thy Lover; nor will I be delayed the Enjoyment of thee one Moment longer. You have sufficient Assurances of my Constancy not to doubt my marrying you, and it would be want of Love to deny me the possession of thy Charms.'—So saying, he disencumbered himself from the little Clothes he had on, and leaping into Bed, embraced his Angel, as he conceived her, with great Rapture. If he was surprized at receiving no Answer, he was no less pleased to find his Hug returned with equal Ardour. He remained not long in this sweet Confusion; for both he and his Paramour presently discovered their Error. Indeed it was no other than the accomplished *Slipslop* whom he had engaged; but tho' she immediately knew the Person whom she had mistaken for *Joseph*, he was at a loss to guess at the Representative of *Fanny*. He had so little seen or taken notice of this Gentlewoman, that Light itself would have afforded him no Assistance in his Conjecture. Beau *Didapper* no sooner had perceived his Mistake, than he attempted to escape from the Bed with much greater Haste than he had made to it; but the watchful *Slipslop* prevented him. For that prudent Woman being disappointed of those delicious Offerings which her Fancy had promised her Pleasure, resolved to make an immediate Sacrifice to her Virtue. Indeed she wanted an Opportunity to heal some Wounds which her late Conduct had, she feared, given her Reputation; and as she had a wonderful Presence of Mind, she conceived the Person of the unfortunate Beau to be luckily thrown in her way to restore her Lady's Opinion of her impregnable Chastity. At that instant therefore, when he offered to leap from the Bed, she caught fast hold of his Shirt, at the same time roaring out, 'O thou Villain! who hast attacked my Chastity, and I believe ruined me in my Sleep; I will swear a Rape against thee, I will prosecute thee with the utmost Vengeance.' The Beau attempted to get loose, but she held him fast, and when he struggled, she cry'd out, 'Murther! Murther! Rape! Robbery! Ruin!' At which Words Parson *Adams*, who lay in the next Chamber, wakeful and meditating on the Pedlar's Discovery, jumped out of Bed, and without staying to put a rag of Clothes on, hastened into the Apartment whence the Cries proceeded. He made directly to the Bed in the dark, where laying hold of the Beau's Skin (for *Slipslop* had torn his Shirt almost off)

and finding his Skin extremely soft, and hearing him in a low
Voice begging *Slipslop* to let him go, he no longer doubted but
this was the young Woman in danger of ravishing, and immediately falling on the Bed, and laying hold on *Slipslop's* Chin,
where he found a rough Beard, his Belief was confirmed; he therefore rescued the Beau, who presently made his Escape, and then
turning towards *Slipslop*, receiv'd such a Cuff on his Chops, that
his Wrath kindling instantly, he offered to return the Favour so
stoutly, that had poor *Slipslop* received the Fist, which in the dark
past by her and fell on the Pillow, she would most probably have
given up the Ghost.—*Adams* missing his Blow, fell directly on
Slipslop, who cuffed and scratched as well as she could; nor was
he behind-hand with her, in his Endeavours, but happily the
Darkness of the Night befriended her—She then cry'd she was
a Woman; but *Adams* answered she was rather the Devil, and if
she was, he would grapple with him; and being again irritated
by another Stroke on his Chops, he gave her such a Remembrance in the Guts, that she began to roar loud enough to be
heard all over the House. *Adams* then seizing her by the Hair (for
her Double-clout had fallen off in the Scuffle) pinned her Head
down to the Bolster, and then both called for Lights together.
The Lady *Booby*, who was as wakeful as any of her Guests, had
been alarmed from the beginning; and, being a Woman of a bold
Spirit, she slipt on a Nightgown, Petticoat and Slippers, and taking
a Candle, which always burnt in her Chamber, in her Hand,
she walked undauntedly to *Slipslop's* Room; where she entred
just at the instant as *Adams* had discovered, by the two Mountains which *Slipslop* carried before her, that he was concerned
with a Female. He then concluded her to be a Witch, and said
he fancied those Breasts gave suck to a Legion of Devils. *Slipslop*
seeing Lady *Booby* enter the Room, cried, *Help! or I am ravished*,
with a most audible Voice, and *Adams* perceiving the Light,
turned hastily and saw the Lady (as she did him) just as she came
to the Feet of the Bed, nor did her Modesty, when she found the
naked Condition of *Adams*, suffer her to approach farther.—She
then began to revile the Parson as the wickedest of all Men, and
particularly railed at his Impudence in chusing her House for the
Scene of his Debaucheries, and her own Woman for the Object
of his Bestiality. Poor *Adams* had before discovered the Countenance of his Bedfellow, and now first recollecting he was naked, he

was no less confounded than Lady *Booby* herself, and immediately whipt under the Bed-clothes, whence the chaste *Slipslop* endeavoured in vain to shut him out. Then putting forth his Head, on which, by way of Ornament, he wore a Flannel Nightcap, he protested his Innocence, and asked ten thousand Pardons of Mrs. *Slipslop* for the Blows he had struck her, vowing he had mistaken her for a Witch. Lady *Booby* then, casting her Eyes on the Ground, observed something sparkle with great Lustre, which, when she had taken it up, appeared to be a very fine pair of Diamond Buttons for the Sleeves. A little farther she saw lie the Sleeve itself of a Shirt with laced Ruffles. 'Heyday!' says she, 'what is the meaning of this?'—'O, Madam,' says *Slipslop*, 'I don't know what hath happened, I have been so terrified. Here may have been a dozen Men in the Room.' 'To whom belongs this laced Shirt and Jewels?' says the Lady.—'Undoubtedly,' cries the Parson, 'to the young Gentleman whom I mistook for a Woman on coming into the Room, whence proceeded all the subsequent Mistakes; for if I had suspected him for a Man, I would have seized him had he been another *Hercules*, tho' indeed he seems rather to resemble *Hylas*.'[1] He then gave an Account of the Reason of his rising from Bed, and the rest, till the Lady came into the Room; at which, and the Figures of *Slipslop* and her Gallant, whose Heads only were visible at the opposite Corners of the Bed, she could not refrain from Laughter, nor did *Slipslop* persist in accusing the Parson of any Motions towards a Rape. The Lady therefore desired him to return to his Bed as soon as she was departed, and then ordering *Slipslop* to rise and attend her in her own Room, she returned herself thither. When she was gone, *Adams* renewed his Petitions for Pardon to Mrs. *Slipslop*, who with a most Christian Temper not only forgave, but began to move with much Curtesy towards him, which he taking as a Hint to be gone, immediately quitted the Bed, and made the best of his way towards his own; but unluckily instead of turning to the right, he turned to the left, and went to the Apartment where *Fanny* lay, who (as the Reader may remember) had not slept a wink the preceding Night, and who was so hagged out with what had happen'd to her in the Day, that notwithstanding all Thoughts of her *Joseph*, she was fallen

[1] Hylas—Hercules' 'Favourite Youth', as he is called in the notes to *Plutus*, v. i—was so beautiful that he was drowned by a nymph, who fell in love with him and pulled him into her spring. (See the *Argonautica*, i. 1207 ff.)

into so profound a Sleep, that all the Noise in the adjoining Room had not been able to disturb her. *Adams* groped out the Bed, and turning the Clothes down softly, a Custom Mrs. *Adams* had long accustomed him to, crept in, and deposited his Carcase on the Bedpost, a Place which that good Woman had always assigned him.

As the Cat or Lapdog of some lovely Nymph for whom ten thousand Lovers languish, lies quietly by the side of the charming Maid, and ignorant of the Scene of Delight on which they repose, meditates the future Capture of a Mouse, or Surprizal of a Plate of Bread and Butter: so *Adams*, lay by the side of *Fanny*, ignorant of the Paradise to which he was so near, nor could the Emanation of Sweets which flowed from her Breath, overpower the Fumes of Tobacco which played in the Parson's Nostrils. And now Sleep had not overtaken the good Man, when *Joseph*, who had secretly appointed *Fanny* to come to her at the break of Day, rapped softly at the Chamber-Door, which when he had repeated twice, *Adams* cry'd, *Come in, whoever you are*. *Joseph* thought he had mistaken the Door, tho' she had given him the most exact Directions; however, knowing his Friend's Voice, he opened it, and saw some female Vestments lying on a Chair. *Fanny* waking at the same instant, and stretching out her Hand on *Adams's* Beard, she cry'd out,—'O Heavens! where am I?' 'Bless me! where am I?' said the Parson. Then *Fanny* skreamed, *Adams* leapt out of Bed, and *Joseph* stood, as the Tragedians call it, like the *Statue of Surprize*.[1] 'How came she into my Room?' cry'd Adams. 'How came you into hers?' cry'd *Joseph*, in an Astonishment. 'I know nothing of the matter,' answered *Adams*, 'but that she is a Vestal for me. As I am a Christian, I know not whether she is a Man or Woman. He is an Infidel who doth not believe in Witchcraft. They as surely exist now as in the Days of *Saul*.[2] My Clothes are bewitched away too, and *Fanny's* brought into their place.' For he still insisted he was in his own Apartment; but *Fanny* denied it vehemently, and said his attempting to persuade *Joseph* of such a Falshood, convinced her of his wicked Designs. 'How!' said *Joseph*, in a Rage, 'Hath he offered any Rudeness to you?'—She answered, she could not accuse him of any more than villainously stealing to Bed to her, which she thought Rudeness sufficient, and what no Man

[1] See p. 40, n. 1.
[2] The encounter between Saul and the Witch of Endor is told in 1 Samuel xxviii. 7–25.

would do without a wicked Intention. *Joseph's* great Opinion of *Adams* was not easily to be staggered, and when he heard from *Fanny* that no Harm had happened, he grew a little cooler; yet still he was confounded, and as he knew the House, and that the Women's Apartments were on this side Mrs. *Slipslop's* Room, and the Men's on the other, he was convinced that he was in *Fanny's* Chamber. Assuring *Adams*, therefore, of this Truth, he begged him to give some Account how he came there. *Adams* then, standing in his Shirt, which did not offend *Fanny* as the Curtains of the Bed were drawn, related all that had happened, and when he had ended, *Joseph* told him, it was plain he had mistaken, by turning to the right instead of the left. 'Odso!' cries *Adams*, 'that's true, as sure as Sixpence, you have hit on the very thing.' He then traversed the Room, rubbing his Hands, and begged *Fanny's* pardon, assuring her he did not know whether she was Man or Woman. That innocent Creature firmly believing all he said, told him, she was no longer angry, and begged *Joseph* to conduct him into his own Apartment, where he should stay himself, till she had put her Clothes on. *Joseph* and *Adams* accordingly departed, and the latter soon was convinced of the Mistake he had committed; however, whilst he was dressing himself, he often asserted he believed in the Power of Witchcraft notwithstanding, and did not see how a Christian could deny it.

CHAPTER XV

The Arrival of Gaffar and Gammar Andrews, with another Person, not much expected; and a perfect Solution of the Difficulties raised by the Pedlar.

As soon as *Fanny* was drest, *Joseph* returned to her, and they had a long Conversation together, the Conclusion of which was, that if they found themselves to be really Brother and Sister, they vowed a perpetual Celibacy, and to live together all their Days, and indulge a *Platonick* Friendship for each other.

The Company were all very merry at Breakfast, and *Joseph* and *Fanny* rather more cheerful than the preceding Night. The Lady *Booby* produced the Diamond Button, which the Beau most readily owned, and alledged that he was very subject to walk in his Sleep. Indeed he was far from being ashamed of his Amour, and rather endeavoured to insinuate that more than was really true had past between him and the fair *Slipslop*.

Their Tea was scarce over, when News came of the Arrival of old Mr. *Andrews* and his Wife. They were immediately introduced and kindly received by the Lady *Booby*, whose Heart went now pit-a-pat, as did those of *Joseph* and *Fanny*. They felt perhaps little less Anxiety in this Interval than *Œdipus* himself whilst his Fate was revealing.

Mr. *Booby* first open'd the Cause, by informing the old Gentleman that he had a Child in the Company more than he knew of, and taking *Fanny* by the Hand, told him, this was that Daughter of his who had been stolen away by Gypsies in her Infancy. Mr. *Andrews*, after expressing some Astonishment, assured his Honour that he had never lost a Daughter by Gypsies, nor ever had any other Children than *Joseph* and *Pamela*. These Words were a Cordial to the two Lovers; but had a different effect on Lady *Booby*. She ordered the Pedlar to be called, who recounted his Story as he had done before.—At the end of which, old Mrs. *Andrews* running to *Fanny*, embraced her, crying out, *She is, she is my Child*. The Company were all amazed at this Disagreement between the Man and his Wife; and the Blood had now forsaken the Cheeks of the Lovers, when the old Woman turning to her Husband, who was more surprized than all the rest, and having a little recovered her own Spirits, delivered herself as follows. 'You may remember, my Dear, when you went a Serjeant to *Gibraltar* you left me big with Child, you staid abroad you know upwards of three Years. In your Absence I was brought to bed, I verily believe of this Daughter, whom I am sure I have reason to remember, for I suckled her at this very Breast till the Day she was stolen from me. One Afternoon, when the Child was about a Year, or a Year and half old, or thereabouts, two Gipsy Women came to the Door, and offered to tell my Fortune. One of them had a Child in her Lap; I shewed them my Hand, and desired to know if you was ever to come home again, which I remember as well as if it was but yesterday, they faithfully promised me you should—I left the Girl in the Cradle, and went to draw them a Cup of Liquor, the best I had; when I returned with the Pot (I am sure I was not absent longer than whilst I am telling

it to you) the Women were gone. I was afraid they had stolen
something, and looked and looked, but to no purpose, and Heaven
knows I had very little for them to steal. At last hearing the
Child cry in the Cradle, I went to take it up—but *O the living!*
how was I surprized to find, instead of my own Girl that I had
put into the Cradle, who was as fine a fat thriving Child as you
shall see in a Summer's Day, a poor sickly Boy, that did not seem
to have an Hour to live. I ran out, pulling my Hair off, and crying
like any mad after the Women, but never could hear a Word of
them from that Day to this. When I came back, the poor Infant
(which is our *Joseph* there, as stout as he now stands) lifted up
its Eyes upon me so piteously, that to be sure, notwithstanding
my Passion, I could not find in my heart to do it any mischief.
A Neighbour of mine happening to come in at the same time, and
hearing the Case, advised me to take care of this poor Child, and
G— would perhaps one day restore me my own. Upon which I
took the Child up, and suckled it to be sure, all the World as if
it had been born of my own natural Body. And as true as I am
alive, in a little time I loved the Boy all to nothing as if it had been
my own Girl.—Well, as I was saying, Times growing very hard,
I having two Children, and nothing but my own Work, which
was little enough, G— knows, to maintain them, was obliged to
ask Relief of the Parish; but instead of giving it me, they removed
me, by Justices Warrants,[1] fifteen Miles to the Place where I now
live, where I had not been long settled before you came home.
Joseph (for that was the Name I gave him myself—the Lord
knows whether he was baptized or no, or by what Name) *Joseph*,
I say, seemed to me to be about five Years old when you returned;
for I believe he is two or three Years older than our Daughter
here; (for I am thoroughly convinced she is the same) and when
you saw him you said he was a chopping Boy, without ever minding his Age; and so I seeing you did not suspect any thing of the
matter, thought I might e'en as well keep it to myself, for fear
you should not love him as well as I did. And all this is veritably
true, and I will take my Oath of it before any Justice in the
Kingdom.'

[1] Under the Poor Law (see p. 167, n. 2) a parish was obliged to care for its poor—i.e.
those who had gained a legal settlement (see p. 282, n. 1). Otherwise, by the provisions of
13 & 14 Charles II, cap. 12, a poor person could be removed by warrant of two justices of
the peace to the parish where he was last legally settled. Fielding discusses the laws of settlement and removal in *An Enquiry into the Causes of the late Increase of Robbers.*

The Pedlar, who had been summoned by the Order of Lady *Booby*, listened with the utmost Attention to Gammar *Andrews's* Story, and when she had finished, asked her if the supposititious Child had no Mark on its Breast? To which she answered, 'Yes, he had as fine a Strawberry as ever grew in a Garden.' This *Joseph* acknowledged, and unbuttoning his Coat, at the Intercession of the Company, shewed to them. 'Well,' says Gaffar *Andrews*, who was a comical sly old Fellow, and very likely desired to have no more Children than he could keep, 'you have proved, I think, very plainly that this Boy doth not belong to us; but how are you certain that the Girl is ours?' The Parson then brought the Pedlar forward, and desired him to repeat the Story which he had communicated to him the preceding Day at the Alehouse; which he complied with, and related what the Reader, as well as Mr. *Adams*, hath seen before. He then confirmed, from his Wife's Report, all the Circumstances of the Exchange, and of the Strawberry on *Joseph's* Breast. At the Repetition of the Word *Strawberry*, *Adams*, who had seen it without any Emotion, started, and cry'd, *Bless me! something comes into my Head*. But before he had time to bring any thing out, a Servant called him forth. When he was gone, the Pedlar assured *Joseph*, that his Parents were Persons of much greater Circumstances than those he had hitherto mistaken for such; for that he had been stolen from a Gentleman's House, by those whom they call Gypsies, and had been kept by them during a whole Year, when looking on him as in a dying Condition, they had exchanged him for the other healthier Child, in the manner before related. He said, as to the Name of his Father, his Wife had either never known or forgot it; but that she had acquainted him he lived about forty Miles from the Place where the Exchange had been made, and which way, promising to spare no Pains in endeavouring with him to discover the Place.

But Fortune, which seldom doth good or ill, or makes Men happy or miserable by halves, resolved to spare him this Labour. The Reader may please to recollect, that Mr. *Wilson* had intended a Journey to the West, in which he was to pass through Mr. *Adams's* Parish, and had promised to call on him. He was now arrived at the Lady *Booby's* Gates for that purpose, being directed thither from the Parson's House, and had sent in the Servant whom we have above seen call Mr. *Adams* forth. This had no sooner mentioned the Discovery of a stolen Child, and had uttered the word *Strawberry*, than Mr. *Wilson*, with Wildness in his Looks, and the utmost Eagerness in his Words, begged to be shewed into the Room, where he entred without the least Regard to any of the Company but *Joseph*, and embracing him with a Complexion all pale and trembling, desired to see the Mark on his Breast; the Parson followed him capering, rubbing his Hands, and crying out, *Hic est quem quæris, inventus est, &c.*[1] *Joseph* complied with the Request of Mr. *Wilson*, who no sooner saw the Mark, than abandoning himself to the most extravagant Rapture of Passion, he embraced *Joseph*, with inexpressible Extasy, and cried out in Tears of Joy, *I have discovered my Son, I have him again in my Arms*. *Joseph* was not sufficiently apprized yet, to taste the same Delight with his Father, (for so in reality he was;) however, he returned some Warmth to his Embraces: But he no sooner perceived from his Father's Account, the Agreement of every Circumstance, of Person, Time, and Place, than he threw himself at his Feet, and embracing his Knees, with Tears begged his Blessing, which was given with much Affection, and received with such Respect, mixed with such Tenderness on both sides, that it affected all present: But none so much as Lady *Booby*, who left the Room in an Agony, which was but too much perceived, and not very charitably accounted for by some of the Company.

CHAPTER XVI

Being the last. In which this true History is brought to a happy Conclusion.

FANNY was very little behind her *Joseph*, in the Duty she exprest towards her Parents; and the Joy she evidenced in discovering them. Gammar *Andrews* kiss'd her, and said she was heartily glad to see her: But for her part she could never love any one better than *Joseph*. Gaffar *Andrews* testified no remarkable

---

[1] 'Here is the one whom you seek; he is found.' In his elation Adams seems to combine allusions to Matthew xxviii. 5–6 ('*Jesum, qui crucifixus est, quæritus;* | *non est hic, surrexit enim. . . .*'), and to Luke xv. 24 ('*hic filius meus mortuus erat, et revixit; perierat, et inventus est*'): the first is the angel's announcement to the women at the tomb that Christ was risen (see, too, Mark xvi. 5–6, Luke xxiv. 4–6, and John xx. 15, where Christ Himself addresses Mary Magdalene, using the singular form, '*quem quæris*'); the second is the father's jubilant declaration at the return of the Prodigal Son.

Emotion, he blessed and kissed her, but complained bitterly, that he wanted his Pipe, not having had a Whiff that Morning.

Mr. *Booby*, who knew nothing of his Aunt's Fondness, imputed her abrupt Departure to her Pride, and Disdain of the Family into which he was married; he was therefore desirous to be gone with the utmost Celerity: And now, having congratulated Mr. *Wilson* and *Joseph* on the Discovery, he saluted *Fanny*, called her Sister, and introduced her as such to *Pamela*, who behaved with great Decency on the Occasion.

He now sent a Message to his Aunt, who returned, that she wished him a good Journey; but was too disordered to see any Company: He therefore prepared to set out, having invited Mr. *Wilson* to his House, and *Pamela* and *Joseph* both so insisted on his complying, that he at last consented, having first obtained a Messenger from Mr. *Booby*, to acquaint his Wife with the News; which, as he knew it would render her completely happy, he could not prevail on himself to delay a moment in acquainting her with.

The Company were ranged in this manner. The two old People with their two Daughters rode in the Coach, the Squire, Mr. *Wilson*, *Joseph*, Parson *Adams*, and the Pedlar proceeded on Horseback.

In their way *Joseph* informed his Father of his intended Match with *Fanny*; to which, tho' he expressed some Reluctance at first, on the Eagerness of his Son's Instances he consented, saying if she was so good a Creature as she appeared, and he described her, he thought the Disadvantages of Birth and Fortune might be compensated. He however insisted on the Match being deferred till he had seen his Mother; in which *Joseph* perceiving him positive, with great Duty obeyed him, to the great delight of Parson *Adams*, who by these means saw an Opportunity of fulfilling the Church Forms, and marrying his Parishioners without a Licence.

Mr. *Adams* greatly exulting on this Occasion, (for such Ceremonies were Matters of no small moment with him) accidentally gave Spurs to his Horse, which the generous Beast disdaining, for he was high of Mettle, and had been used to more expert Riders than the Gentleman who at present bestrode him: for whose Horsemanship he had perhaps some Contempt, immediately ran away full speed, and played so many antic Tricks, that he tumbled the Parson from his Back; which *Joseph* perceiving, came to his Relief. This Accident afforded infinite Merriment to the Servants, and no less frighted poor *Fanny*, who beheld him as he past by the Coach; but the Mirth of the one, and Terror of the other were soon determined, when the Parson declared he had received no Damage.

The Horse having freed himself from his unworthy Rider, as he probably thought him, proceeded to make the best of his way: but was stopped by a Gentleman and his Servants, who were travelling the opposite way; and were now at a little distance from the Coach. They soon met; and as one of the Servants delivered *Adams* his Horse, his Master hailed him, and *Adams* looking up, presently recollected he was the Justice of Peace before whom he and *Fanny* had made their Appearance. The Parson presently saluted him very kindly; and the Justice informed him, that he had found the Fellow who attempted to swear against him and the young Woman the very next day, and had committed him to *Salisbury* Goal, where he was charged with many Robberies.

Many Compliments having past between the Parson and the Justice, the latter proceeded on his Journey, and the former having with some disdain refused *Joseph's* Offer of changing Horses; and declared he was as able a Horseman as any in the Kingdom, re-mounted his Beast; and now the Company again proceeded, and happily arrived at their Journey's End, Mr. *Adams* by good Luck, rather than by good Riding, escaping a second Fall.

The Company arriving at Mr. *Booby's* House, were all received by him in the most courteous, and entertained in the most splendid manner, after the Custom of the old *English* Hospitality, which is still preserved in some very few Families in the remote Parts of *England*. They all past that Day with the utmost Satisfaction; it being perhaps impossible to find any Set of People more solidly and sincerely happy. *Joseph* and *Fanny* found means to be alone upwards of two Hours, which were the shortest but the sweetest imaginable.

In the Morning, Mr. *Wilson* proposed to his Son to make a Visit with him to his Mother; which, notwithstanding his dutiful Inclinations, and a longing Desire he had to see her, a little concerned him as he must be obliged to leave his *Fanny*: But the Goodness of Mr. *Booby* relieved him; for he proposed to send his own Coach and six for Mrs. *Wilson*, whom *Pamela* so very earnestly invited, that Mr. *Wilson* at length agreed with the Entreaties of Mr. *Booby* and *Joseph*, and suffered the Coach to go empty for his Wife.

On *Saturday* Night the Coach return'd with Mrs. *Wilson*, who added one more to this happy Assembly. The Reader may imagine much better and quicker too than I can describe, the many Embraces and Tears of Joy which succeeded her Arrival. It is sufficient to say, she was easily prevailed with to follow her Husband's Example, in consenting to the Match.

On *Sunday* Mr. *Adams* performed the Service at the Squire's Parish Church, the Curate of which very kindly exchanged Duty, and rode twenty Miles to the Lady *Booby's* Parish, so to do; being particularly charged not to omit publishing the Banns, being the third and last Time.

At length the happy Day arrived, which was to put *Joseph* in the possession of all his Wishes. He arose and drest himself in a neat, but plain Suit of Mr. *Booby's*, which exactly fitted him; for he refused all Finery; as did *Fanny* likewise, who could be prevailed on by *Pamela* to attire herself in nothing richer than a white Dimity Night-Gown. Her Shift indeed, which *Pamela* presented her, was of the finest Kind, and had an Edging of Lace round the Bosom; she likewise equipped her with a Pair of fine white Thread Stockings, which were all she would accept; for she wore one of her own short round-ear'd Caps, and over it a little Straw Hat, lined with Cherry-coloured Silk, and tied with a Cherry-coloured Ribbon. In this Dress she came forth from her Chamber, blushing, and breathing Sweets; and was by *Joseph*, whose Eyes sparkled Fire, led to Church, the whole Family attending, where Mr. *Adams* performed the Ceremony; at which nothing was so remarkable, as the extraordinary and unaffected Modesty of *Fanny*, unless the true Christian Piety of *Adams*, who publickly rebuked Mr. *Booby* and *Pamela* for laughing in so sacred a Place, and so solemn an Occasion. Our Parson would have done no less to the highest Prince on Earth: For tho' he paid all Submission and Deference to his Superiors in other Matters, where the least Spice of Religion intervened, he immediately lost all Respect of Persons. It was his Maxim, That he was a Servant of the Highest, and could not, without departing from his Duty, give up the least Article of his Honour, or of his Cause, to the greatest earthly Potentate. Indeed he always asserted, that Mr. *Adams* at Church with his Surplice on, and Mr. *Adams* without that Ornament, in any other place, were two very different Persons.

When the Church Rites were over, *Joseph* led his blooming Bride back to Mr. *Booby's* (for the Distance was so very little, they did not think proper to use a Coach) the whole Company attended them likewise on foot; and now a most magnificent Entertainment was provided, at which Parson *Adams* demonstrated an Appetite surprizing, as well as surpassing every one present. Indeed the only Persons who betrayed any Deficiency on this Occasion, were those on whose account the Feast was provided. They pampered their Imaginations with the much more exquisite Repast which the Approach of Night promised them; the Thoughts of which filled both their Minds, tho' with different Sensations; the one all Desire, while the other had her Wishes tempered with Fears.

At length, after a Day past with the utmost Merriment, corrected by the strictest Decency; in which, however, Parson *Adams*, being well filled with Ale and Pudding, had given a Loose to more Facetiousness than was usual to him: The happy, the blest Moment arrived, when *Fanny* retired with her Mother, her Mother-in-law, and her Sister. She was soon undrest; for she had no Jewels to deposite in their Caskets, nor fine Laces to fold with the nicest Exactness. Undressing to her was properly discovering, not putting off Ornaments: For as all her Charms were the Gifts of Nature, she could divest herself of none. How, Reader, shall I give thee an adequate Idea of this lovely young Creature! the Bloom of Roses and Lillies might a little illustrate her Complexion, or their Smell her Sweetness: but to comprehend her entirely, conceive Youth, Health, Bloom, Beauty, Neatness, and Innocence in her Bridal-Bed; conceive all these in their utmost Perfection, and you may place the charming *Fanny's* Picture before your Eyes.

Joseph no sooner heard she was in Bed, than he fled with the utmost Eagerness to her. A Minute carried him into her Arms, where we shall leave this happy Couple to enjoy the private Rewards of their Constancy; Rewards so great and sweet, that I apprehend *Joseph* neither envied the noblest Duke, nor *Fanny* the finest Duchess that Night.

The third Day, Mr. *Wilson* and his Wife, with their Son and Daughter returned home; where they now live together in a State of Bliss scarce ever equalled. Mr. *Booby* hath with unprecedented Generosity given *Fanny* a Fortune of two thousand

Pound, which *Joseph* hath laid out in a little Estate in the same Parish with his Father, which he now occupies, (his Father having stock'd it for him;) and *Fanny* presides, with most excellent Management in his Dairy; where, however, she is not at present very able to bustle much, being, as Mr. *Wilson* informs me in his last Letter, extremely big with her first Child.

Mr. *Booby* hath presented Mr. *Adams* with a Living of one hundred and thirty Pounds a Year. He at first refused it, resolving not to quit his Parishioners, with whom he hath lived so long: But on recollecting he might keep a Curate at this Living, he hath been lately inducted into it.

The Pedlar, besides several handsome Presents both from Mr. *Wilson* and Mr. *Booby*, is, by the latter's Interest, made an Excise-man; a Trust which he discharges with such Justice, that he is greatly beloved in his Neighbourhood.

As for the Lady *Booby*, she returned to *London* in a few days, where a young Captain of Dragoons, together with eternal Parties at Cards, soon obliterated the Memory of *Joseph*.

Joseph remains blest with his *Fanny*, whom he doats on with the utmost Tenderness, which is all returned on her side. The Happiness of this Couple is a perpetual Fountain of Pleasure to their fond Parents; and what is particularly remarkable, he declares he will imitate them in their Retirement; nor will be prevailed on by any Booksellers, or their Authors, to make his Appearance in *High-Life*.[1]

---

[1] An allusion primarily to Richardson's two-volume sequel to *Pamela* (7 December 1741), which traces the fortunes of its heroine 'In her *EXALTED CONDITION*', in a series of letters '*between Her, and Persons of* Figure *and* Quality, *upon the most Important and Entertaining Subjects, In* GENTEEL LIFE'. By choosing the words '*High-Life*', however, Fielding put an edge on the mischief here by recalling an amusing quarrel between Richardson and some rival booksellers (namely, Richard Chandler, Caesar Ward, John Wood, Charles Woodward, and Thomas Waller), who had hired an undistinguished hack, John Kelly, to write the spurious continuation of *Pamela* called *Pamela's Conduct in High Life* (May 1741). This work, advertised in *The Champion*, embarrassed and irritated Richardson, forcing him to undertake his own genuine sequel, and goading him to expose and discredit 'the honest *High-Life Men*' in several announcements in the newspapers. (See, for example, *The Daily Gazetteer*, 1, 4 June and 11 July; *The London Evening-Post*, 23–25 June.) A second volume of the *High-Life* appeared in September, by which time still another pretended sequel, called *Pamela in High Life: Or, Virtue Rewarded,* printed for one Mary Kingman, began to be issued in numbers. (For a complete account of the affair, see McKillop, *Samuel Richardson* [1936], pp. 51-57, and Kreissman, *Pamela-Shamela* [1960], pp. 66–69.)

APPENDIXES

APPENDIX I

List of Substantive Emendations

6. 5–6 copying] 3;   Copy 1–2
8. 8–9 there . . . distinguishing them] 3;   they require some Difficulty in distinguishing; 1–2
17. 18–20 farther, and to . . . and so, by . . . World, he may] 3;   farther, to . . . and by . . . World, may 1–2
20. 8 desirable and becoming] 3;   desirable, as becoming 1–2
22. 26 at divine] 2;   a divine 1
23. 31 privately] 4;   *om.* 1–3
24. 1 *Joey*] 2;   who 1
24. 6–8 He . . . employed] 2;   That he had ever . . . Family, employed 1
25. 4–5 more . . . profited] 2;   more Books, had profited 1
25. 8 through] 2;   by 1
25. 12 *The*] 2;   *om.* 1
25. 15–25 Knight . . . impoverish'd himself.] 2;   Knight on Suits, which he then had for Tithes with seven Tenants of his Manor, in order to set aside a Modus, by which the Parson proposed an Advantage of several Shillings *per annum*, and by these Suits had greatly impoverished himself, and utterly undone the poor Tenants. 1
26. 7–10 *Adams* . . . desiring her] 2;   To her therefore, *Adams* mentioned the Case of young *Andrews*, and desired her 1
26. 18 any such] 2;   such a 1
26. 18 She is] 2;   She he is 1
27. 37 on] 2;   at 1
29. 20 I am] 2;   I I am 1
30. 7 against] 2;   again 1
30. 39 that] 2;   the 1
32. 11 a Maiden] 3;   an antient Maiden 1–2
34. 3 leave him] 3;   break off 1–2
34. 8 VII] 3;   VI 1–2
34. 21 Another] 3;   One other 1–2
37. 16 VIII] 3;   VII 1–2
38. 37 full,] 2;   ∼ₐ 1
39. 23 and] 2;   *om.* 1
39. 24 guilty—Consider] 2;   guilty. And consider 1
39. 32 for] 3;   and 1–2
39. 34–35 with . . . Eyes,] 2;   *om.* 1
39. 36 as] 3;   but 1–2

42. 1–3 answered . . . ordered] 2;　was going to speak, when she refused to hear him, and ordered 1
42. 18 IX] 3;　VIII 1–2
43. 13 in which] 2;　which 1
43. 13 indulge her] 2;　indulge to her 1
45. 1 *Joseph* was,] 2;　*Joey,* was 1
45. 27 Doubt] 2;　Doubts 1
46. 1 X] 3;　IX 1–2
46. 22 hath] 2;　has 1
46. 24 Example] 2;　Examples 1
47. 32 that] 2;　this 1
48. 1 XI] 3;　X 1–2
48. 3–4 made, that . . . *He*] 3;　made, to indicate our Idea of a simple Fellow, *That he* 1–2
49. 16 this] 2;　that 1
49. 34 a] 2;　the 1
50. 10 *Thomas*] 2;　*John* 1
51. 1 XII] 3;　XI 1–2
51. 3 *to*] 3;　by 1–2
51. 6 to which . . . whither] 3;　whither . . . where 1–2
53. 25 great Coats] 2;　*om.* 1
55. 24 repeated] 2;　repeat 1
55. 25 sung] 2;　sing 1
56. 7 there?] 3;　~, 1–2
56. 9 lend] 2;　lend to 1
56. 23 hath] 2;　has 1
56. 24 doth] 2;　does 1
57. 19 XIII] 3;　XII 1–2
58. 6 , said he,] 2;　*om.* 1
58. 7 *would have been*] 2;　*would be* 1
59. 5 if Heaven had] 3;　would Heaven have 1–2
59. 16 , as he said,] 2;　*om.* 1
59. 28 bad] 2;　bid 1
60. 19 said that was enough, and] 2;　*om.* 1
61. 1 XIV] 3;　XIII 1–2
61. 7 took] 2;　he took 1
61. 35 peeked] 5;　pecked 1–2; picked 3–4
62. 31 have] 2;　*om.* 1
63. 18 caught] 2;　got 1
63. 23 told] 2;　he told 1
63. 30 he] 2;　*om.* 1
64. 5 to it] 3;　on it 1–2
64. 6 Men] 3;　Man 1–2

64. 18 and if] 2;   and that if 1
64. 19 desired] 2;   he desired 1
66. 3 XV] 3;   XIV 1–2
66. 21–26 Mrs. *Tow-wouse* . . . House.'] 2;   *om.* 1
67. 3–4 them; in which . . . clenching] 2;   them; which Resolution,
    Mr. *Adams*, in clenching 1
67. 26 bad] 2;   bid 1
68. 5 he knew] 2;   knew 1
68. 16 after this he] 4;   *om.* 1–3
68. 31 as to] 2;   to 1
70. 9 XVI] 3;   XV 1–2
70. 26 call] 3;   should call 1–2
70. 26 latter] 2;   young Fellow 1
71. 4 But human Life, as] 2;   But as it 1
71. 6 very] 2;   human Life very 1
72. 2–3 ; which . . . Evidence] 2;   *om.* 1
73. 1 home] 2;   *om.* 1
73. 5 into] 2;   in 1
73. 23 undoubtedly] 2;   certainly 1
74. 40 used . . . it] 2;   used in Setting 1
75. 2 and where] 3;   whither 1–2
75. 11–12 I would . . . Cloth;] 2;   *om.* 1
75. 25 nine] 4;   three 1–3
76. 10 said] 2;   says 1
77. 12 Woman] 2;   Women 1
79. 1 XVII] 3;   XVI 1–2
79. 23–25 'So that . . . you.'] 2;   *om.* 1
82. 7 things] 3;   *om.* 1–2
82. 10 to his] 2;   in to his 1
85. 2–4 , tho' . . . sort] 2;   *om.* 1
85. 10 ; my Be— . . . than me] 2;   *om.* 1
85. 25 she . . . pleased] 2;   he was not pleased 1
85. 28–30 , and at . . . leave her] 2;   We will therefore leave her in this
    Temper 1
86. 1 XVIII] 3;   XVII 1–2
86. 7 unfortunately] 2;   unhappily 1
86. 9 them] 2;   *om.* 1
86. 15 and Drawers . . . whom] 2;   Drawers, and others, all of which 1
86. 18 but] 3;   about 1–2
87. 23 when, as] 2;   when 1
88. 14 squeezed her] 2;   squeezed it 1
88. 24–25 of: Since . . . every] 2;   of. ¶ As every 1
89. 22 not] 2;   and not 1

90. 25–32 To mention . . . Sanction] 2;   These have the Sanction 1

91. 2–3 , according . . . Critics,] 2;   *om.* 1

91. 5 hath so long lain] 2;   so long lay 1

92. 24 different ways] 2;   *om.* 1

92. 25–26 with his Friend] 2;   *om.* 1

92. 27–29 was, that . . . left] 2;   was no other than the forgetting to put up the Sermons, which were indeed left 1

93. 4–33 This Discovery . . . the Bill was called for, which,] 2;   The Bill was now called for, and 1

93. 34 Sum] 2;   Sum which 1

93. 36 be surprized] 2;   be too much surprized 1

94. 10 Persons] 2;   two Persons 1

94. 40 of his Clerk] 2;   *om.* 1

95. 7–13 was willing . . . when he honestly] 2;   would probably have been willing to give him Credit 'till next time, had not *Joseph*, when he honestly 1

95. 15 Mrs. . . . water; she . . . she] 2;   Mr. . . . water, and he . . . he 1

95. 20 Mrs.] 2;   Mr. 1

95. 25–31 'What (says . . . cried *Tow-wouse.*] 2;   Then I cannot part with the Horse, replied *Tow-wouse.* 1

96. 18 dry] 2;   have dried 1

96. 25 bad] 2;   bid 1

97. 14 former] 2;   first 1

97. 28 then] 2;   now 1

98. 1 House] 2;   Horse 1

99. 8 Gentlemen] 3;   Gentleman 1–2

100. 26 what Passengers] 2;   whom 1

101. 2 *Adams*] 2;   him 1

101. 5 , but short,] 2;   *om.* 1

101. 21 *Thomas's*] 2;   *John's* 1

101. 28–32 I am . . . are no Secrets] 2;   'They are no Secrets 1

101. 33 be] 2;   *om.* 1

101. 34 the Boy's] 2;   his 1

102. 13 Mistress . . . Master] 2;   Master . . . Mistress 1

102. 22 justly . . . unfortunate] 2;   call a Woman justly unfortunate 1

102. 30 their] 2;   this 1

102. 37 more] 2;   the more 1

103. 2 allure;] 2;   ~ ᴧ 1

103. 4 , who] 2;   *om.* 1

104. 28 is it] 2;   it is 1

106. 3–5 this delicate . . . requires] 2;   a Passion which requires 1

106. 36 *This Letter . . . former.] 2;   *om.* 1

107. 18 possibly] 2;   possible 1

108. 10 *Florella*] 2; *Howella* 1
108. 40 *Leonora*] 2; her 1
109. 17 confounded] 2; awaked 1
109. 19 childish] 3; childest 1–2
110. 2 his] 2; this 1
111. 4–6 If I . . . What Happiness!—] 2; *om.* 1
112. 4 you shall have no] 2; you, he shall give you no 1
112. 10 began] 2; begun 1
112. 17 except the] 2; except their 1
112. 19–20 especially as . . . Interest,] 2; *om.* 1
113. 3 Room. Here 'tis] 3; Room; 'tis 1–2
113. 7–8 'She must . . . *Lais* herself.'] 2; *om.* 1
114. 14 'Tis] 3; It's 1–2
114. 15 is] 3; as 1–2
115. 38 regain the Affections of] 3; reconcile herself to 1–2
116. 5–6 Gentleman? No other . . . on him.] 2; Gentleman?— 1
116. 7 regaining the Affections of] 3; reconciling yourself to 1–2
118. 17 had been . . . Master's] 2; had likewise been his Trade 1
118. 21–23 as his Legs . . . fall, and] 2; *om.* 1
119. 23–24 , (having . . . *Adams*)] 2; *om.* 1
119. 27 perceiving, *Adams*] 2; *Adams* perceiving, 1
120. 3 saluted . . . trickled] 3; saluting his Countenance, trickled 1–2
120. 26 to *Italy*] 2; *om.* 1
121. 14–15 *Damnata . . . Viterbo.*] 2; *om.* 1
122. 8–9 who . . . Dignity,] 2; *om.* 1
122. 21 suppose] 2; supposed 1
122. 33–35 crying, as . . . *Boniface.*'] 2; crying: *Tutta è Pace; so send in my Dinner, good* Boniface. 1
124. 34–35 Remarks?ₐ . . . Prude.'] 3; ~ ?' . . . ~·ₐ 1–2
127. 22 but when . . . imagined] 3; but *Bellarmine* when he imagined 1–2
128. 9–10 from that Subject] 2; *om.* 1
129. 4 *L'Amour*] 2; *Amour* 1
129. 24 , said the Lady,] 2; *om.* 1
129. 27 hears] 2; heard 1
129. 27 nor] 2; or 1
130. 21 forwards] 2; on 1
131. 2 'Very little.'] W; very little. 1–5
132. 32 bad] 2; bid 1
133. 14 too] 2; *om.* 1
133. 16 Curacy. Well] 3; ~.' '~ 1–2
134. 23 believe I] 2; believe I I 1
135. 18 as much] 3; much 1–2
138. 10 hasten] 2; hastened 1

140. 9–19 THE Silence ... Enemy, wisely weighing] 2; WHILST *Adams* was wisely weighing 1

140. 20–21 the two ... Chapter] 2; these two Methods of proceeding 1

140. 25 : At length] 2; ; *om.* 1

141. 4 (for she ... himself,)] 2; *om.* 1

144. 20 the Coach] 3; that Coach 1–2

148. 8–149. 5 The Clerk ... banter me with a false Name.'] 2; *om.* 1

148. 26 and putting] 3; putting 2

149. 28 uninterrupted] 2; uninterrupted too 1

150. 9–12 ; and the Parson ... expose it] 2; *om.* 1

150. 36–37 on whom ... my Election] 2; they two only had been the Competitors on whom my Election 1

152. 14 Lady] 2; a Lady 1

155. 20–21 which ... Hands, and] 2; who 1

155. 31 immediately] 3; she immediately 1–2

156. 12 her Conduct] 2; this her Conduct 1

158. 1 two in the Afternoon] 2; twelve 1

158. 10 all which] 2; for all which 1

158. 28 *Virulence*] 2; Violence 1

160. 8 desired] 2; had 1

162. 10 managed] 2; waited in 1

162. 23 he stalked] 2; *om.* 1

162. 29 here was] 2; he was 1; there was 5

163. 39 Ale] 2; Cyder 1

164. 3 *caale*] 2; call 1

164. 18 *caale*] 2; call 1

165. 3 *caal'd*] 2; *called* 1

165. 8 *caal'd*] 2; *called* 1

165. 10 *caale*] 2; *call* 1

168. 5 a true] 2; the true 1

169. 1–2 by his Professions ... Gravity] 2; by his Piety, Gravity 1

169. 7 to affront] 2; affront 1

169. 21 nor would she] 3; nor she would not 1–2

169. 26 Sum in] 2; Sum at 1

169. 37–38 : for tho' ... Mouth] 2; *om.* 1

172. 13 few of] 2; few 1

172. 27 contemn] 3; condemn 1–2

173. 14 a greater] 2; greater 1

173. 32 willingly] 2; willing 1

173. 33 to have] 2; to to have 1

174. 5 hath] 2; has 1

174. 7 hath] W; has 1–5

176. 19 hath] 2; has 1

177. 3 hath] 2;   has 1
177. 8 hath] 2;   has 1
178. 21–22 I will . . . him:] 2;   *om.* 1
178. 27 a proper] 2;   proper 1
179. 10 Nay . . . still:] 2;   *om.* 1
179. 24 being] 2;   *om.* 1
179. 26 , a pretty Creature she was,] 2;   ; *om.* 1
180. 38 Countenance,ₐ quotha!ₐₐ I] 5;   ~,' ~! '~ 1–3; ~, ~!' '~ 4
182. 14 incensed . . . threw] 2;   that the Boys of *Athens* threw 1
185. 10–11 the Works of those who] 2;   their Works who 1
186. 2–8 and indeed . . . Character, yet all agree] 2;   but all agree 1
186. 7 to whom others give] 4;   while others give him 2–3
186. 8 the Fact] 2;   it 1
186. 9–10 ; and where . . . lived] 2;   *om.* 1
187. 3 *Sangrado*] 4;   *Sanglardo* 1–3
187. 5–7 Doth not . . . lived?] 2;   *om.* 1
187. 10 and in many] 2;   and perhaps in many 1
187. 15 Persons . . . Genius,] 2;   great Genius's 1
188. 9 the confused] 2;   their confused 1
189. 11 4000] 2;   5000 1
189. 23–24 Purposes; not] 2;   Purposes, than 1
189. 24 and contemptible] 2;   *om.* 1
190. 15 the like] 2;   that like 1
190. 21 chiefly hath] 3;   hath chiefly 1–2
191. 8 and not] 3;   nor are 1–2
191. 13 are at least] 3;   have been 1–2
193. 4 which . . . himself] 2;   *om.* 1
195. 5 that] 2;   *om.* 1
197. 4–5 cry'd *Adams*,] 2;   *om.* 1
197. 12 , continued he,] 2;   *om.* 1
197. 13 *He*] 2;   who 1
197. 14 *Homer*] 2;   Indeed *Homer* 1
199. 7–13 Nor can I . . . come near him.] 2;   *om.* 1
199. 9 which] 3;   with 2
199. 30 *Adams*] 2;   He 1
199. 30–32 and with . . . he was so far] 2;   'till the Gentleman was so far 1
199. 34–36 He ran . . . Strangers] 2;   The Goodness of his Heart began therefore to dilate without any further Restraint 1
200. 10–11 ; for she . . . was scarce able] 2;   , Love itself being scarce able 1
200. 14 and] 2;   while 1
201. 17–27 *The Author . . . possest of it.*] 2;   *om.* 1
201. 24 *plait*] 3;   *plaire* 2

202. 38 the polite] 2;   that polite 1
203. 31 *very*] 2;   *om.* 1
204. 30 A great Groan.] 2;   *om.* 1
204. 32 *Adams* said] 2;   *Adams* having fetched a great Groan, said 1
205. 22 , with . . . Sword,] 2;   *om.* 1
206. 12–13 all further . . . every kind] 2;   any further . . . all kinds 1
206. 27 that account] 2;   this account 1
206. 37 forced] 3;   oblig'd 1–2
208. 29 was pleased] 2;   I was pleased 1
210. 23–24 La! . . . thinking of] 2;   I would not have you guess what I was thinking of for the World 1
210. 30 when] 4;   till 1–3
211. 16 Beauty] 2;   Vanity 1
211. 30 delivered me from] 4;   rid me of 1–3
211. 34 bad] 2;   bid 1
212. 6 I became] 2;   I now became 1
214. 40 silly] 3;   simple 1–2
216. 5–7 had the Assurance . . . not writ, nor ever intended] 3;   had even the Assurance . . . never writ nor intended 1–2
218. 18 a Work] 2;   the Work 1
218. 23 saved] 3;   amassed 1–2
219. 14 Assurances] 2;   Assurance 1
220. 7 a Trick] 2;   the Trick 1
220. 35 came into] 3;   came one day into 1–2
221. 35–36 ; it affected . . . Reflections] 2;   , *om.* 1
223. 9 own Happiness . . . mine] 2;   own must be included in it 1
224. 4 to despair] 2;   so despair 1
225. 1 Child] 2;   *Jacky* 1
226. 20–21 and exercise] 3;   where I exercise 1–2
226. 40 I myself] 2;   and I myself 1
227. 9 the House-keepers . . . Gentlemen] 4;   few Gentlemen's House-keepers 1–3
227. 14–15 ('And I . . . tasted.')] 2;   *om.* 1
227. 35 at the dutiful] 2;   the dutiful 1
229. 18 V] 3;   IV 1–2
229. 33 Part] 2;   Parts 1
230. 3 afterwards] 2;   after 1
231. 1 afterwards] 2;   after 1
232. 16 and the Trees] 2;   whose Trees 1
232. 19–20 Design . . . Planter] 3;   most skillful Design of the Planter 1–2
232. 32–33 imagining had . . . restore it] 3;   imagining it had . . . deliver them 1–2
233. 4 brought them] 2;   brought to them 1

233. 4 as for] 3;   but for 1–2
233. 17 VI] 3;   V 1–2
233. 20 *Joseph*] 2;   he 1
234. 15 *Scratchi*] 2;   *Scarachi* 1
234. 19 small] 3;   little 1–2
234. 21–22 I ever was] 3;   I have ever been 1–2
235. 12 too] 3;   *om.* 1–2
235. 13 in the Book] 3;   upon the Book 1–2
235. 23 so many Hours] 2;   two Nights 1
236. 6 a Dalliance] 2;   Dalliance 1
236. 18 rational] 3;   sensible and human 1–2
236. 20–21 beheld . . . who] 2;   beheld, fled from her who 1
236. 30 *Retinue*, who *attended*] 2;   Attendants who waited 1
237. 28 Cassock;] 3;   ∼, 1–2
240. 7 long] 2;   *om.* 1
241. 28–29 : For . . . they knew] 4;   , who, whenever he opened, knew 1–3
242. 2 those] 3;   these 1–2
243. 7–8 her, every one declaring] 2;   her. Every one declared 1
244. 6 VII] 3;   VI 1–2
244. 23 may . . . Expression] 4;   may use the Expression 1–3; may here use the Expression 5
246. 4 served up . . . Waiting-men] 2;   performed by one of the Serving-men 1
247. 11–12 the latter] 2;   he 1
247. 26–27 standing . . . Speech. They] 3;   and standing . . . Speech, they 1–2
248. 23 not very] 2;   not so very 1
248. 31–32 the Gentleman said] 4;   *om.* 1–3
248. 39 hoped he] 2;   hoped he he 1
249. 10 this] 2;   the 1
251. 10–11 seated . . . Majesties. They] 3;   being seated . . . Majesties, they 1–2
251. 23 taking . . . exacted] 2;   exacted . . . taken 1
251. 28 VIII] 3;   VII 1–2
254. 30–31 Pennyless. I am but] 3;   Pennyless: But am 1–2
255. 6 but] 2;   *om.* 1
255. 22 IX] 3;   VIII 1–2
256. 25 his other Garments] 2;   the rest 1
256. 27 two] 2;   the two 1
256. 31–32 Poet, . . . nimblest, . . . first,] 3;   ∼∧ . . . ∼∧ . . . Chamber, first∧ 1;   ∼∧ . . . ∼∧ . . . Chamber∧ first, 2
258. 13 from . . . Hand] 2;   out of his Hands 1

258. 34 was risen] 2; being risen 1
259. 15 Bed-posts, as] 3; Bed-posts, with his Hands behind him, as 1–2
259. 21 X] 3; IX 1–2
264. 7 XI] 3; X 1–2
264. 20 any but] 4; any thing but 1–3
265. 16 , much more of a Christian,] 4; and a Christian 1–3
266. 8–14 You must . . . Good.—Nay] 2; The Doctrine I teach you is a certain Security—nay 1
266. 24 says he,] 2; *om.* 1
266. 30 , he said,] 2; *om.* 1
266. 31 hinting] 2; saying 1
267. 24 XII] 3; XI 1–2
268. 17–23 She knew not. . . . Fondness for Men] 2; the Riches of the World could not make her amends for the Loss of him; nor would she be persuaded to exchange him for the greatest Prince upon Earth 1
268. 24 to be fond] 2; *om.* 1
269. 15 *John*] 2; *Thomas* 1
269. 30 the celebrated] 2; *om.* 1
270. 9–11 the one paid . . . hence] 3; this paid that Respect to his Goodness which the other attributed to be paid to his Riches; and hence 1–2
270. 18–20 a violent Hurry . . . that was turned] 4; a Hurry, that he had on neither Breeches, Garters, nor Stockings; nor had he . . . his Wig, turned 1–3
270. 25–26 where a long . . . served] 2; *viz.* a Piss-burnt Beard, which served 1
271. 2–3 heard from him . . . comforted] 3; heard the Account of what had past from him, comforted 1–2
271. 12 gave] 3; he gave 1–2
271. 20–23 being sufficiently . . . had suffered] 3; were sufficiently . . . and had suffered 1–2
272. 9–273. 28 but she absolutely . . . set forwards for *Booby-Hall*] 2; and she absolutely refused, being determined to ride behind *Joseph*, on a Horse which one of Lady *Booby's* Servants had equipped him with. (This was indeed the same which *Adams* had left behind him at the Inn, and was by these honest Men who knew him, redeemed:) if any means could be contrived of conveying Mr. *Adams* with them; whose Company *Pounce*, when he found he had no longer hopes of satisfying his old Appetite with *Fanny*, desired in his Vehicle. So that all matters being settled to the Content of every one, *Adams* and *Pounce* mounting the Chariot, and *Fanny* being placed on a Pillion, which *Joseph* borrowed of the Host, they all set forwards for *Booby-Hall* 1
274. 1 XIII] 3; XII 1–2
275. 33 of your own] 3; your own 1–2

276. 12 hath] 4;   has 1–3
277. 30–31 enquiring] 4;   enquired 1–3
279. 32 an *amorous*] 2;   a lovely 1
281. 24 doth it . . . become a Man] 2;   is it . . . becoming in a Man 1
283. 2 *Scout*] 2;   *Snout* 1
283. 4 farther] 2;   further 1
283. 23 out] 4;   *om.* 1–3
283. 31–284. 1 you, I will suffer . . . here.'—] 2;   you.' 1
284. 34–285. 8 If we can prove . . . to produce Children] 2;   'Truly,' said the Lady, 'they are a grievous Load, and unless we had an Employment for them, it would be Charity to send them where they might have something to do. At least, I am sure we ought to prevent the farther Growth of the Evil, and not let such Beauties as these produce Children 1
285. 23 from] 3;   with 1–2
285. 29 *Frolick*] 3;   *Trolick* 1–2
285. 30–32 As for the dirty . . . Jade will] 2;   *om.* 1
288. 8 mentioned] 3;   had mentioned 1–2
289. 5 a Woman] 2;   Woman 1
289. 7 into] 2;   to 1
289. 8 was then] 2;   then was 1
292. 16 up] 2;   *om.* 1
292. 30–32 own her . . . infinitely] 2;   shew a proper Respect, and own her Relations, and I shall think myself infinitely 1
293. 35 thought herself secure] 2;   was certain 1
294. 8 this was increased] 4;   being assisted 1–3
294. 12 the Account] 4;   an Account 1–3
295. 7 *Joseph*] 2;   *Joseph* however 1
295. 31 may] 2;   must 1
296. 14 born] 2;   he's born 1
296. 25 of the World] 2;   in the World 1
298. 32 *deprecate*] 2;   discommend 1
299. 34 Dread] 3;   Dread of, 1–2
301. 7 a Dream] 2;   Dream 1
302. 32 indulge it] 3;   indulge 1–2
302. 35 Lady] 3;   Wife 1–2
304. 3–4 would not . . . but] 4;   would have been able to resist his Rudeness a very short time, when 1–2; would not have been able to resist his Rudeness a short time, but 3
304. 32 yet] 3;   but 1–2
306. 3 the Habitation of] 2;   *om.* 1
307. 15 Bacon] 3;   Bacon which 1–2
307. 37–308. 3 Nay perhaps. . . . Indeed] 2;   *om.* 1

308. 19–20 and not set . . . quit it] 4;   and set our Affections so much on nothing here that we cannot quit it 1–3
310. 36 her] 2;   them 1
313. 8 of his Country] 2;   his Country 1
314. 9 at last] 3;   had at last 1–2
316. 27 Mind] 2;   Passions 1
316. 28 gave] 2;   was 1
316. 29 Instance] 2;   *om.* 1
319. 10 common] 2;   com- 1
321. 19 re-adjusted] 3;   he re-adjusted 1–2
322. 28–29 had probably . . . Tricks] 4;   had most probably ruined his Family with his Tricks 1–2; had probably ruined his Family with his Tricks almost 3
323. 22 in common] 2;   in in common 1
327. 18 own] 3;   *om.* 1–2
328. 32 any more] 3;   more 1–2
329. 8–9 but by . . . apprehended] 4;   but his Duty, as he apprehended it 1–3
329. 26 perfectly] 4;   certainly 1–3
331. 12 Error] 3;   mutual Deceit 1–2
333. 34 lay] 3;   *om.* 1–2
334. 25 Tragedians call] 3;   Tragedian calls 1–2
334. 37 any] 3;   *om.* 1–2
341. 16–17 the Justice] 2;   Justice 1

APPENDIX II

List of Accidentals Emendations

4. 14 Diction,] W;   ~; 1–5
6. 17 *Ridiculous*] 2;   *ridiculous* 1
17. 26 read,] 2;   ~ₐ 1
18. 1 Youth;] 4;   ~, 1–3
18. 14 Amiable] 2;   amiable 1
24. 9 *Whole Duty of Man*] W;   Whole Duty of Man 1–5
25. 8 Waiting-Gentlewoman] 2;   waiting Gentlewoman 1
25. 13 only,] 2;   ~ₐ 1
28. 4 *my*ₐ] 2;   ~, 1
28. 6 *Footman? . . . Tittle.*] W; ~, . . . ~? 1–5
29. 35 *Joey?*] 2;   ~. 1
30. 3 blushed.] W;   ~, 1–5
30. 28 Don't you?] 2;   ~, 1
35. 12 Lady,] W;   ~! 1–5
36. 30 Delight!] 2;   ~. 1
39. 25 *laying her Hand carelessly upon his*] 2;   laying . . . his 1
42. 34 *Particle*] 2;   Particle 1
43. 23 Mistress? . . . Lady.] 2;   ~, . . . ~? 1
47. 33 Morning.] 2;   ~, 1
50. 12 Livery,] 2;   ~ₐ 1
53. 11 *a little*] 2;   a little 1
62. 15–16 of Wounds? . . . *Tow-wouse.*] 2;   ~, . . . ~? 1
62. 17 Gentleman. 'A] 2;   ~, 'a 1
62. 23 Sir.] W;   ~, 1–5
63. 3 you,] W;   ~. 1–5
63. 14 Method.—] 2;   ~, 1
69. 1 *Barnabas*ₐ] 2;   ~, 1
72. 13 *Suckbribe?*] W;   ~; 1–5
72. 16 Room.] W;   ~ₐ 1–5
75. 8 arrived.] 2;   ~, 1
84. 4 *Leviathan*] W;   Leviathan 1–5
85. 1 *She-Dog*] W;   *She Dog* 1–5
85. 7 She-Dog, and] 2;   ~? And 1
85. 17 *She-Dog*] W;   *She Dog* 1–5
99. 26 of? . . . *Adams.*] W;   ~,' . . . ~? 1–5
100. 11 Soul?] 5;   ~, 1–4
104. 32 be? . . . *Leonora.*] W;   ~, . . . ~? 1–5

107. 23 Imagination,] 3;   ~ˌ 1–2
108. 19 Company;] 2;   ~, 1
110. 19 thought] 2;   Thought 1
110. 35 She] 2;   she 1
114. 28 Gentleman?' 'D—n] 2;   ~? d—n 1
119. 19 believed] 2;   belived 1
122. 33 *Italian*] 3;   Italian 2
123. 32 with,] 3;   ~ˌ 1–2
128. 27 Days] 2;   Day's 1
130. 13 *Aye,*] 2;   ~ˌ 1
131. 11 *Sir*] W;   Sir 1–5
133. 3 *Courtly*] 3;   *Courtley* 1–2
137. 14 Bullets?] 2;   ~. 1
138. 28–29 *that he had done his Business*] 2;   that . . . Business 1
138. 29 *that*] W;   that 1–5
138. 29–30 *he had sent him to the Shades below*] 2;   he . . . below 1
138. 30 *that he was dead*] 2;   that . . . dead 1
143. 34 hither?] 2;   ~. 1
144. 4–5 that?' . . . *Adams.*] 2;   ~,' . . . ~? 1
146. 23 Gown?] 2;   ~. 1
149. 4 Justice;] W;   ~, 2–5
149. 19 *Mittimus*] 2;   Mittimus 1
149. 33 *Rogues and Rascals*] 3;   Rogues and Rascals 1–2
152. 15 our Desires] 3;   our-Desires 1–2
154. 6 *Flow'rs;*] 2;   ~ˌ 1
156. 21 Low] 2;   low 1
156. 35 theyˌ often] 2;   ~; ~ 1
160. 29 Parson,] 2;   ~ˌ 1
161. 26 *Eureka, Eureka;*] 2;   Ευρηκα, Ευρηκα, 1
162. 7 *Sundays*] 2;   Sundays 1
163. 21 *Hog?*] 2;   ~: 1
164. 12 me.] 2;   ~; 1
167. 18 Fool.] 3;   ~, 1–2
180. 13 delay,] 2;   ~. 1
181. 22 sworn,] 2;   ~ˌ 1
181. 23 where's the *Levant?*] 3;   ~, 1–2
186. 16 existed?] 2;   ~. 1
187. 25 *a second Nature*] 2;   a second Nature 1
192. 31 vanished?] 3;   ~, 1–2
194. 32 saidˌ *Adams*] 2;   ~, ~ 1
197. 3 Sir?] W;   ~, 1–5
197. 5 *Æschylus?*] 4;   ~, 1–2; ~; 3
197. 8 *Iliad*] 3;   Iliad 1–2

197. 13–14 *He ought to comprehend all Perfections*] 2;   who ought . . . Per-
    fections 1
198. 1 *Odyssey*] 3;   Odyssey 1–2
198. 1 *Iliad*] 3;   Iliad 1–2
198. 4 *Iliad*] 3;   Iliad 1–2
198. 6 *Odyssey*] 3;   Odyssey 1–2
198. 32 only?] 3;   ~. 1–2
201. 24 *Beauté*] 3;   *Beautè* 2
201. 24 *médiocre*] W;   *mediocre* 2–5
201. 24 *Beauté*] 3;   *Beautè* 2
204. 11 Life?] 3;   ~, 1–2
204. 18 Adams] 2;   *Adams* 1
208. 28 I,] 2;   ~ₐ 1
209. 23 Anglicé] W;   Anglicè 1–5
211. 39 Hollowing] 2;   hollowing 1
213. 25–32 'there . . . himself;'] 2;   there . . . himself; 1
214. 35 Pocket?] 3;   ~; 1–2
217. 15 *Temple*] 3;   Temple 1–2
219. 17 alive:] 2;   ~. 1
221. 9 200 *l.* !' . . . Rapture.] W;   ~ₐ' . . . ~! 1–5
226. 17 twenty-four] 3;   twenty four 1–2
228. 4 thence,] 2;   ~ₐ 1
230. 26 *meum.*' —] W;   ~ₐₐ — 1–5
231. 10 School?] 2;   ~: 1
237. 10 Bank,] W;   ~; 1–5
242. 25–26 Bear-baiting] 2;   Bear-Baiting 1
248. 36 Innocence, for] 2;   ~. For 1
258. 12 him down;] 2;   ~; ~ₐ 1
262. 12 *Arbors,*] 2;   *Arbor'sₐ* 1
269. 15 *Goodwill?*] W;   ~ₐ 1–2; ~. 3–5
270. 23 Great-Coat] 2;   Great Coat 1
275. 28 Treasure?] 3;   ~. 1–2
280. 27 *Pounce,*] 2;   ~ₐ 1
290. 23 *Mittimus*] W;   Mittimus 1–5
290. 25 Hearts,] 2;   ~; 1
294. 31 him;] W;   ~, 1–2; ~. 3–5
295. 18 Madam?] W;   ~! 1–5
297. 5 *Andrews?*] 3;   ~. 1–2
301. 6 Loveₐ] 2;   ~, 1
307. 7–8 Reply, (for . . . Church)] 2;   Reply; for . . . Church, 1
308. 21 World;] 2;   ~, 1
308. 26 knowₐ] 2;   ~, 1
314. 21 besides?] 3;   ~, 1–2

314. 27 *read?*] 3;   ~. 1–2
314. 30 *Lego?*] W;   ~. 1–4; ~, 5
317. 39 know,] 2;   ~ₐ 1
317. 40 too,] 5;   ~ₐ 1–4
318. 33 wrong?] 2;   ~. 1
323. 12 Saucebox?] 2;   ~, 1
325. 32 Name,] 3;   ~ₐ 1–2
325. 32 *Paměla*; some] 2;   ~, Some 1
325. 40 (for] 2;   ₐfor 1
327. 3 Sister?] 3;   ~. 1–2
327. 30 whom?] 3;   ~, 1–2
337. 17 sure,] 2;   ~ₐ 1
338. 18 *Strawberry*] 3;   Strawberry 1–2
339. 2 *Strawberry*] 3;   Strawberry 1–2
343. 24 Creature!] 2;   ~; 1

APPENDIX III

Word-Division

1. *End-of-the-Line Hyphenation in the Wesleyan Edition*

(NOTE. The following compounds, hyphenated at the end of the line in the Wesleyan edition, are hyphenated within the line in the copy-text. Hyphenated compounds in which both elements are capitalized are not included.)

10. 20	good-|natur'd	177. 22	Life-|time
20. 22	Cudgel-|player	206. 27	Quarter-|day
21. 29	Dog-|kennel	216. 16	Play-|house
22. 22	Tea-|table	218. 21	half-|starv'd
32. 11	Forty-|five	242. 25	Bear-|baiting
37. 12	inside-|out	254. 29	to-|morrow
60. 30	good-|natured	274. 20	Parson-|like
68. 9	Chicken-|broth	288. 14	Good-|breeding
119. 29	out-|done	313. 14	Chimney-|side
155. 19	Sheep-|skin	319. 7	Good-|will
157. 19	to-|wit		

2. *End-of-the-Line Hyphenation in the Copy-Text*

(NOTE. The following compounds, or possible compounds, are hyphenated at the end of the line in the copy-text. The form in which they have been given in the Wesleyan edition, as listed below, represents the usual practice of the copy-text insofar as it may be ascertained from other appearances.)

10. 37	Good-natur'd	187. 8	Arch-bishop
43. 7	Marry-come-up	202. 33	Periwig-maker
45. 7	hoodwinked	209. 36	Good-nature
49. 14	Twelve-month's	221. 31	over-rigid
51. 29	Cudgel-playing	227. 2	School-master
56. 25	Ale-house	228. 21	with-held
59. 27	Heartstrings	228. 24	Highwayman
69. 25	with-hold	238. 29	two-leg'd
75. 2	*Syder-and*	241. 27	*Highway*
85. 3	above-mentioned	242. 19	Life-writer
98. 16	Twelve-month	245. 30	Curlike
129. 23	*Ourasho*	247. 8	outdanced
151. 31	*good-natur'd*	250. 23	Pass-time

251. 20	Crabstick	305. 24	bare-necked
254. 32	overboard	319. 2	Good-humour
270. 5	hard-hearted	323. 2	Halfpenny
276. 24	Highway	333. 11	Heyday
299. 33	School-mistresses	342. 22	Cherry-coloured

3. *Special Cases*

(NOTE. The following compounds, or possible compounds, are hyphenated at the end of the line in both the Wesleyan edition and the copy-text.)

67. 22	three-pence-half-|penny
114. 17	well-|bred
159. 33	Ale-|house
228. 37	High-|way
231. 22	where-|ever

APPENDIX IV

Historical Collation

3. 26 nor] or 4–5
4. 17 Descriptions] Description 3–5
4. 29 to] *om. text* 4–5 (*cw* to)
6. 5–6 copying] Copy 1–2
8. 8–9 there . . . distinguishing them] they require some Difficulty in distinguishing; 1–2
9. 24 Objects] Object 3–5
10. 18 few very] very few 5
17. 18–20 farther, and to . . . and so, by . . . World, he may] farther, to . . . and by . . . World, may 1–2
20. 8 desirable and becoming] desirable, as becoming 1–2
21. 27 call] calls 5
22. 26 at divine] a divine 1
23. 13 hath past] has past 5
23. 31 privately] *om.* 1–3
24. 1 *Joey*] who 1
24. 6–8 He . . . employed] That he had ever . . . Family, employed 1
25. 4–5 more . . . profited] more Books, had profited 1
25. 8 through] by 1
25. 12 The] *om.* 1
25. 15–25 Knight . . . impoverish'd himself.] Knight on Suits, which he then had for Tithes with seven Tenants of his Manor, in order to set aside a Modus, by which the Parson proposed an Advantage of several Shillings *per annum*, and by these Suits had greatly impoverished himself, and utterly undone the poor Tenants. 1
26. 7–10 *Adams* . . . desiring her] To her therefore, *Adams* mentioned the Case of young *Andrews*, and desired her 1
26. 18 any such] such a 1
26. 18 She is] She he is 1
27. 25–26 Town-Air] the Town-Air 2–5
27. 37 on] at 1
28. 26 these] those 3–5
29. 8 *never*] *ever* 4–5
29. 14 Women] the Women 3–5
29. 20 I am] I I am 1
30. 7 against] again 1
30. 28 are either] either are 4–5

30. 39 that] the 1

32. 3 next-door] the next-door 4–5

32. 11 a Maiden] an antient Maiden 1–2

32. 28 was] *om.* 2–3

32. 35 pay] to pay 4–5

33. 35 had] has 3–5

34. 3 leave him] break off 1–2

34. 3–4 defer . . . to some] to defer . . . till some 4–5

34. 8 VII] VI 1–2

34. 21 Another] One other 1–2

34. 26–27 have before] had before 4–5

37. 16 VIII] VII 1–2

38. 11 that] the 4–5

38. 37 full,] ~∧ 1

39. 11 not, perhaps,] perhaps not 3–5

39. 23 and] *om.* 1

39. 24 guilty—Consider] guilty. And consider 1

39. 32 for] and 1–2

39. 34–35 with . . . Eyes,] *om.* 1

39. 36 as] but 1–2

41. 26 hath] has 5

42. 1–3 answered . . . ordered] was going to speak, when she refused to hear
    him, and ordered 1

42. 11 infinite] infinitely 5

42. 18 IX] VIII 1–2

43. 12 that] the 4–5

43. 13 in which] which 1

43. 13 indulge her] indulge to her 1

44. 5 turn] to turn 5

45. 1 *Joseph* was,] *Joey,* was 1

45. 27 Doubt] Doubts 1

45. 30 was . . . to make] was our present Business only to make 3–5

46. 1 X] IX 1–2

46. 17 I] *om.* 5

46. 22 hath] has 1

46. 24 Example] Examples 1

47. 17 *Premiums*] *Præmium* 3–5

47. 32 that] this 1

48. 1 XI] X 1–2

48. 3–4 made, that . . . *He*] made, to indicate our Idea of a simple **Fellow,**
    That he 1–2

48. 21 been formerly] formerly been 3–5

48. 36 a uniform] an uniform 3–5

49. 16 this] that 1
49. 34 a] the 1
50. 10 *Thomas*] *John* 1
51. 1 XII] XI 1–2
51. 3 *to*] by 1–2
51. 6 to which . . . whither] whither . . . where 1–2
51. 11 hopes] Hope 5
53. 25 great Coats] *om.* 1
54. 29 the more] more 3–5
55. 24 repeated] repeat 1
55. 25 sung] sing 1
56. 7 there?] ∼, 1–2
56. 9 lend] lend to 1
56. 23 hath] has 1
56. 24 doth] does 1
57. 3 had washed] and washed 4–5
57. 9 he ever] ever he 3–5
57. 11 had] *om.* 3–5
57. 17 Circumstance] Circumstances 3–5
57. 19 XIII] XII 1–2
58. 6 , said he,] *om.* 1
58. 7 *would have been*] *would be* 1
59. 5 if Heaven had] would Heaven have 1–2
59. 16 , as he said,] *om.* 1
59. 28 bad] bid 1
59. 32 of parting] of of parting 3
59. 36 Passion] Passions 3–5
60. 19 said that was enough, and] *om.* 1
61. 1 XIV] XIII 1–2
61. 7 took] he took 1
61. 25–26 not to be fallen] to be fallen not 3–5
61. 35 peeked] pecked 1–2; picked 3–4
62. 31 have] *om.* 1
63. 13 *occurrite*] *accurrite* 2–5
63. 18 caught] got 1
63. 23 told] he told 1
63. 30 he] *om.* 1
64. 5 to it] on it 1–2
64. 6 Men] Man 1–2
64. 18 and if] and that if 1
64. 19 desired] he desired 1
66. 3 XV] XIV 1–2
66. 21–26 Mrs. *Tow-wouse* . . . House.'] *om.* 1

66. 35 greater] great 4–5
67. 3–4 them; in which . . . clenching] them; which Resolution, Mr.
    Adams, in clenching 1
67. 26 bad] bid 1
68. 5 he knew] knew 1
68. 16 after this he] *om.* 1–3
68. 31 as to] to 1
69. 8 be] have 4–5
70. 9 XVI] XV 1–2
70. 22 Fellows] Fellow 3
70. 26 call] should call 1–2
70. 26 latter] young Fellow 1
71. 4 But human Life, as] But as it 1
71. 6 very] human Life very 1
72. 2–3 ; which . . . Evidence] *om.* 1
72. 16 *John*ʌ] ~, 4–5
73. 1 home] *om.* 1
73. 5 into] in 1
73. 23 undoubtedly] certainly 1
74. 22 shot] shoot 3–5
74. 40 used . . . it] used in Setting 1
75. 2 and where] whither 1–2
75. 11–12 I would . . . Cloth;] *om.* 1
75. 19 the Exciseman's] Exciseman's 4–5
75. 25 nine] three 1–3
76. 10 said] says 1
76. 11 amount] amount to 4–5
77. 12 Woman] Women 1
78. 14 a way] away 5
79. 1 XVII] XVI 1–2
79. 18 assured him] assured them 4
79. 23–25 'So that . . . you.'] *om.* 1
82. 7 things] *om.* 1–2
82. 10 to his] in to his 1
82. 10 to set] set 3–5
82. 22 for] or 2
83. 18 make] makes 5
85. 2–4 , tho' . . . sort] *om.* 1
85. 10 ; me Be— . . . than me] *om.* 1
85. 25 she . . . pleased] he was not pleased 1
85. 28–30 , and at . . . leave her] We will therefore leave her in this Temper 1
86. 1 XVIII] XVII 1–2
86. 7 unfortunately] unhappily 1

86. 9 them] *om.* 1
86. 15 and Drawers . . . whom] Drawers, and others, all of which 1
86. 18 but] about 1–2
86. 20 any] an 2–5
87. 12 sometimes of] sometimes 3–5
87. 23 when, as] when 1
88. 14 squeezed her] squeezed it 1
88. 15 whispering] whispered 3–5
88. 24–25 of : Since . . . every] of. ¶ As every 1
89. 22 not] and not 1
90. 25–32 To mention . . . Sanction] These have the Sanction 1
91. 2–3 , according . . . Critics,] *om.* 1
91. 5 hath so long lain] so long lay 1
92. 14 doth] does 3–5
92. 24 different ways] *om.* 1
92. 25–26 with his Friend] *om.* 1
92. 27–29 was, that . . . left] was no other than the forgetting to put up the Sermons, which were indeed left 1
93. 4–33 This Discovery . . . the Bill was called for, which,] The Bill was now called for, and 1
93. 26 return] turn 5
93. 34 Sum] Sum which 1
93. 36 be surprized] be too much surprized 1
94. 10 Persons] two Persons 1
94. 40 of his Clerk] *om.* 1
95. 7–13 was willing . . . when he honestly] would probably have been willing to give him Credit 'till next time, had not *Joseph*, when he honestly 1
95. 15 Mrs. . . . water; she . . . she] Mr. . . . water, and he . . . he 1
95. 20 Mrs.] Mr. 1
95. 25–31 'What (says . . . cried *Tow-wouse.*] Then I cannot part with the Horse, replied *Tow-wouse.* 1
95. 39 this] his 4–5
96. 3 had miss'd] miss'd 3–5
96. 18 dry] have dried 1
96. 25 bad] bid 1
97. 2 *two*] *the* 5
97. 14 former] first 1
97. 28 then] now 1
98. 1 House] Horse 1
99. 8 Gentlemen] Gentleman 1–2
99. 15 believe] believed 4
99. 18 as] *om.* 4–5

100. 26 what Passengers] whom 1
100. 26 had] had got 5
101. 2 *Adams*] him 1
101. 5 , but short,] *om.* 1
101. 12 a Coach] the Coach 5
101. 21 *Thomas's*] *John's* 1
101. 28–32 I am . . . are no Secrets] 'They are no Secrets 1
101. 33 be] *om.* 1
101. 34 the Boy's] his 1
102. 13 Mistress . . . Master] Master . . . Mistress 1
102. 22 justly . . . unfortunate] call a Woman justly unfortunate 1
102. 30 their] this 1
102. 37 more] the more 1
103. 2 allure;] ~∧ 1
103. 4 , who] *om.* 1
104. 28 is it] it is 1
106. 3–5 this delicate . . . requires] a Passion which requires 1
106. 29 by] to 4–5
106. 36 *This Letter . . . former.] *om.* 1
107. 8 Inconveniences] Inconveniencies 3–5
107. 18 possibly] possible 1
107. 19 that] and 4–5
108. 10 *Florella*] *Howella* 1
108. 40 *Leonora*] her 1
109. 17 confounded] awaked 1
109. 19 childish] childest 1–2
109. 29 which] that 3–5
110. 2 his] this 1
111. 4–6 If I . . . What Happiness!—] *om.* 1
111. 18 Preferments] Preferment 3–5
111. 26 will not they] will they not 5
112. 4 you shall have no] you, he shall give you no 1
112. 10 began] begun 1
112. 17 except the] except their 1
112. 19–20 especially as . . . Interest,] *om.* 1
113. 3 Room. Here 'tis] Room; 'tis 1–2
113. 7–8 'She must . . . *Lais* herself.'] *om.* 1
114. 14 'Tis] It's 1–2
114. 15 is] as 1–2
115. 38 regain the Affections of] reconcile herself to 1–2
116. 5–6 Gentleman? No other . . . on him.] Gentleman?— 1
116. 7 regaining the Affections of] reconciling yourself to 1–2
117. 13 farther] further 2–5

118. 17 had been . . . Master's] had likewise been his Trade 1
118. 21–23 as his Legs . . . fall, and] *om.* 1
119. 23–24 , (having . . . *Adams*)] *om.* 1
119. 24 repeating] repeated 5
119. 27 perceiving, *Adams*] *Adams* perceiving, 1
119. 32 likewise] *om.* 3–5
120. 3 saluted . . . trickled] saluting his Countenance, trickled 1–2
120. 4 down] down to 4–5
120. 18 a use] an Use 3–5
120. 26 to *Italy*] *om.* 1
121. 4 Miss] Mrs. 4–5
121. 14–15 *Damnata . . . Viterbo.*] *om.* 1
122. 5 Puddings] Pudding 2
122. 8–9 who . . . Dignity,] *om.* 1
122. 21 suppose] supposed 1
122. 33–35 crying, as . . . *Boniface.*'] crying: *Tutta è Pace; so send in my Dinner, good* Boniface. 1
124. 11 That] The 4–5
124. 26 swearing of] ~, to 3–4; ~ₐ to 5
124. 34–35 Remarks?ₐ . . . Prude.'] ~?' . . . ~.ₐ 1–2
125. 11 hath no] hath not 2–5
126. 12 these] those 3–5
127. 22 but when . . . imagined] but *Bellarmine* when he imagined 1–2
128. 9–10 from that Subject] *om.* 1
128. 14 then] that 5
128. 15 Inclination at present,] Inclination, at presentₐ 3–5
128. 37 incapable . . . delivering] incapable my self of delivering 3–5
128. 39 *Ah jamais*] *A jamais* 3–5
128. 39 *Ah Diable*] *Au Diable* 3–5
129. 4 *L'Amour*] *Amour* 1
129. 24 , said the Lady,] *om.* 1
129. 27 hears] heard 1
129. 27 nor] or 1
130. 21 forwards] on 1
131. 2 'Very little.'] very little 1–5
132. 32 bad] bid 1
133. 14 too] *om.* 1
133. 16 Curacy. Well] ~.' '~ 1–2
133. 29 Chaplain] a Chaplain 5
134. 12 now was] was now 5
134. 17 knew] know 4–5
134. 23 believe I] believe I I 1
135. 18 as much] much 1–2

137. 9 says *Adams*] said *Adams* 5
138. 7 espies] spies 5
138. 10 hasten] hastened 1
140. 9–19 THE Silence ... Enemy, wisely weighing] WHILST *Adams* was wisely weighing 1
140. 20–21 the two ... Chapter] these two Methods of proceeding 1
140. 25 : At length] ; *om.* 1
141. 4 (for she ... himself,)] *om.* 1
141. 10 thou art] you are 5
144. 20 the Coach] that Coach 1–2
145. 7 sent] had sent 3–5
145. 13 People of] People in 4–5
145. 16 being now] now being 3–5
145. 24 by] by by 3
146. 19 S?] ~. 3–5
146. 20 *igdibus*] *ignibus* 4–5
147. 7 County] Country 3–5
148. 8–149. 5 The Clerk ... banter me with a false Name.'] *om.* 1
148. 11–12 this Fellow] the Fellow 4–5
148. 22 Nay] No 4–5
148. 26 and putting] putting 2
149. 28 uninterrupted] uninterrupted too 1
150. 9–12 ; and the Parson ... expose it] *om.* 1
150. 36–37 on whom ... my Election] they two only had been the Competitors on whom my Election 1
151. 10 broken] broke 4–5
151. 33 then just being] being then just 3–5
152. 13 *Quod*] *Quid* 2
152. 14 Lady] a Lady 1
155. 13 Hypotheses] Hypothesis 3–5
155. 20–21 which ... Hands, and] who 1
155. 31 immediately] she immediately 1–2
156. 12 her Conduct] this her Conduct 1
157. 33–34 his Hour] the Hour 4–5
158. 1 two in the Afternoon] twelve 1
158. 10 all which] for all which 1
158. 15–16 of all this] of this 3–5
158. 28 *Virulence*] Violence 1
160. 8 desired] had 1
162. 10 managed] waited in 1
162. 23 he stalked] *om.* 1
162. 29 here was] he was 1; there was 5
163. 39 Ale] Cyder 1

164. 3 *caale*] call 1
164. 18 *caale*] call 1
164. 31 good . . . bad] bad . . . good 3–5
165. 3 *caal'd*] *called* 1
165. 4 it, and it] it; it 3–5
165. 8 *caal'd*] *called* 1
165. 10 *caale*] *call* 1
165. 15 towards] towards to 3–4
166. 11 lay my little Treasure up] lay up my little Treasure 3–5
168. 5 a true] the true 1
168. 9 farther] further 2–5
169. 1–2 by his Professions . . . Gravity] by his Piety, Gravity 1
169. 7 to affront] affront 1
169. 21 nor would she] nor she would not 1–2
169. 26 Sum in] Sum at 1
169. 37–38 : for tho' . . . Mouth] *om.* 1
170. 3 *Plato* or] *Plato* and 4–5
172. 13 few of] few 1
172. 21 justly] just 4
172. 27 contemn] condemn 1–2
173. 10 says] said 2–5
173. 14 a greater] greater 1
173. 32 willingly] willing 1
173. 33 to have] to to have 1
173. 38 as well] as well as 3
174. 4 have forgot] had forgot 3–5
174. 5 hath] has 1
174. 7 hath] has 1–5
174. 10 expect] expected 4–5
174. 22 Smiles on] Smiles at 4–5
174. 30 insisting] insisted 5
176. 19 hath] has 1
177. 3 hath] has 1
177. 8 hath] has 1
178. 14 do] to 3–5
178. 21–22 I will . . . him:] *om.* 1
178. 27 a proper] proper 1
179. 10 Nay . . . still:] *om.* 1
179. 24 being] *om.* 1
179. 26 , a pretty Creature she was,] ; *om.* 1
180. 38 Countenance,$_\wedge$ quotha!$_{\wedge\wedge}$ I] ~,' ~! '~ 1–3; ~, ~!' '~ 4
182. 14 incensed . . . threw] that the Boys of *Athens* threw 1
182. 14 so$_\wedge$] ~, 3–5

182. 19 predicated] predicted 5
182. 25 would sail] should sail 3–5
185. 10 only to be found]; to be found only 3–5
185. 10–11 the Works of those who] their Works who 1
186. 2–8 and indeed . . . Character, yet all agree] but all agree 1
186. 7 to whom others give] while others give him 2–3
186. 8 the Fact] it 1
186. 9–10 ; and where . . . lived] *om.* 1
186. 21 that good] the good 4–5
187. 3 *Sangrado*] *Sanglardo* 1–3
187. 5–7 Doth not . . . lived?] *om.* 1
187. 10 and in many] and perhaps in many 1
187. 15 Persons . . . Genius,] great Genius's 1
188. 5 *with an irregular*] *without any regular* 4–5
188. 9 the confused] their confused 1
189. 2 hear] heard 4–5
189. 11 4000] 5000 1
189. 14 on] upon 4–5
189. 23–24 Purposes; not] Purposes, than 1
189. 24 and contemptible] *om.* 1
190. 15 the like] that like 1
190. 21 chiefly hath] hath chiefly 1–2
191. 4 would] he would 4–5
191. 6 Palace] Place 4–5
191. 8 and not] nor are 1–2
191. 13 are at least] have been 1–2
191. 25 Ale-house] Ale-hose 2
193. 4 which . . . himself] *om.* 1
193. 9 their Rear] the Rear 3–5
194. 3 frightned] frighted 4–5
194. 8 relieve] to relieve 4–5
194. 21 Steeps] Steps 4–5
194. 23 whither] where 3–5
194. 25 whence] where 3–5
194. 38 a Man] Man 3–5
195. 5 that] *om.* 1
195. 24 his Story] the Story 4–5
197. 4–5 cry'd *Adams,*] *om.* 1
197. 12 , continued he,] *om.* 1
197. 13 *He*] who 1
197. 14 *Homer*] Indeed *Homer* 1
199. 7–13 Nor can I . . . come near him.] *om.* 1
199. 8 how short *Sophocles* falls] how *Sophocles* falls short 3–5

199. 9 which] with 2

199. 30 *Adams*] He 1

199. 30–32 and with . . . he was so far] 'till the Gentleman was so far 1

199. 34–36 He ran . . . Strangers] The Goodness of his Heart began therefore to dilate without any further Restraint 1

200. 10–11 ; for she . . . was scarce able] , Love itself being scarce able 1

200. 14 and] while 1

201. 17–27 *The Author . . . possest of it.*] om. 1

201. 24 *plait*] *plaire* 2

202. 38 the polite] that polite 1

203. 31 *very*] om. 1

203. 34 Character] Characters 4–5

204. 11 yet] om. 3–5

204. 30 A great Groan.] om. 1

204. 32 *Adams* said] *Adams* having fetched a great Groan, said 1

205. 22 , with . . . Sword,] om. 1

205. 33 least] east 4

205. 35 therefore resolved] resolved therefore 5

206. 12–13 all further . . . every kind] any further . . . all kinds 1

206. 27 that account] this account 1

206. 37 forced] oblig'd 1–2

208. 29 was pleased] I was pleased 1

210. 23–24 La! . . . thinking of] I would not have you guess what I was thinking of for the World 1

210. 30 when] till 1–3

211. 16 Beauty] Vanity 1

211. 30 delivered me from] rid me of 1–3

211. 34 bad] bid 1

212. 2 these] they 3

212. 6 I became] I now became 1

214. 17 or] or in 4–5

214. 40 silly] simple 1–2

216. 5–7 had the Assurance . . . not writ, nor ever intended] had even the Assurance . . . never writ nor intended 1–2

218. 6 a Pity] pity 3–5

218. 18 a Work] the Work 1

218. 23 saved] amassed 1–2

218. 28 Woman's] Women's 5

219. 14 Assurances] Assurance 1

220. 7 a Trick] the Trick 1

220. 12 remind] to remind 4–5

220. 17 his own] my own 5

220. 35 came into] came one day into 1–2

221. 35–36 ; it affected . . . Reflections] , *om.* 1
223. 9 own Happiness . . . mine] own must be included in it 1
224. 4 to despair] so despair 1
224. 6 denied] had denied 4–5
225. 1 Child] *Jacky* 1
225. 18 lost] had lost 3–5
225. 22 amongst] among 4–5
226. 20–21 and exercise] where I exercise 1–2
226. 34 is it] it is 5
226. 35 Interest] Interests 5
226. 40 I myself] and I myself 1
227. 9 the House-keepers . . . Gentlemen] few Gentlemen's House-keepers 1–3
227. 14–15 ('And I . . . tasted.')] *om.* 1
227. 34 Husband] the Husband 3–5
227. 35 at the dutiful] the dutiful 1
228. 1 forth] for 4–5
228. 17 his Loss] her Loss 4–5
229. 18 V] IV 1–2
229. 25 in] into 4–5
229. 33 Part] Parts 1
230. 3 afterwards] after 1
230. 7 called] call 4–5
230. 12 of the World] in the World 5
231. 1 afterwards] after 1
232. 16 and the Trees] whose Trees 1
232. 19–20 Design . . . Planter] most skillful Design of the Planter 1–2
232. 32–33 imagining had . . . restore it] imagining it had . . . deliver them 1–2
233. 4 brought them] brought to them 1
233. 4 as for] but for 1–2
233. 17 VI] V 1–2
233. 20 *Joseph*] he 1
234. 8 Laceman] Lacemaker 3–5
234. 15 *Scratchi*] *Scarachi* 1
234. 19 small] little 1–2
234. 21–22 I ever was] I have ever been 1–2
235. 12 too] *om.* 1–2
235. 13 in the Book] upon the Book 1–2
235. 23 so many Hours] two Nights 1
236. 5 than] then 4
236. 6 a Dalliance] Dalliance 1
236. 18 rational] sensible and human 1–2

236. 20–21 beheld . . . who] beheld, fled from her who 1
236. 30 *Retinue, who attended*] Attendants who waited 1
237. 5 employ] to employ 4–5
237. 28 Cassock;] ~, 1–2
237. 30 they] *om.* 3–5
240. 7 long] *om.* 1
240. 17 all out] out all 5
241. 1 this] his 5
241. 28–29 : For . . . they knew] , who, whenever he opened, knew 1–3
242. 2 those] these 1–2
242. 36 Drop] Droop 2
243. 7–8 her, every one declaring] her. Every one declared 1
244. 6 VII] VI 1–2
244. 23 may . . . Expression] may use the Expression 1–3; may here use the Expression 5
245. 37 thus] this 4–5
246. 4 served up . . . Waiting-men] performed by one of the Serving-men 1
247. 11–12 the latter] he 1
247. 26–27 standing . . . Speech. They] and standing . . . Speech, they 1–2
247. 39 Object] Subject 5
248. 12 were] are 5
248. 23 not very] not so very 1
248. 31 thrashed] threshed 2–5
248. 31–32 the Gentleman said] *om.* 1–3
248. 37 was] has 5
248. 39 hoped he] hoped he he 1
249. 4 you was] you you was 3
249. 10 this] the 1
250. 34 the Ambassador] an Ambassador 4–5
251. 10–11 seated . . . Majesties. They] being seated . . . Majesties, they 1–2
251. 23 taking . . . exacted] exacted . . . taken 1
251. 28 VIII] VII 1–2
254. 30–31 Pennyless. I am but] Pennyless: But am 1–2
255. 6 but] *om.* 1
255. 22 IX] VIII 1–2
256. 25 his other Garments] the rest 1
256. 27 two] the two 1
256. 31–32 Poet, . . . nimblest, . . . first,] ~ₐ . . . ~ₐ . . . Chamber, firstₐ 1; ~ₐ . . . ~ₐ . . . Chamberₐ first, 2
258. 13 from . . . Hand] out of his Hands 1
258. 34 was risen] being risen 1
259. 10 only entertained] entertained only 3–5
259. 15 Bed-posts, as] Bed-posts, with his Hands behind him, as 1–2

259. 18 go] to go 2–5
259. 21 X] IX 1–2
261. 30 Sir] *om.* 3–5
263. 17 know I had Enemies] had Enemies 2; were Enemies 3; were my Enemies 4–5
263. 24 would not] that would not 4–5
263. 35 done it] done 4–5
264. 7 XI] X 1–2
264. 20 any but] any thing but 1–3
265. 13 strong] strongly 5
265. 16 , much more of a Christian,] and a Christian 1–3
266. 8–14 You must . . . Good.—Nay] The Doctrine I teach you is a certain Security—nay 1
266. 24 says he,] *om.* 1
266. 30 , he said,] *om.* 1
266. 31 hinting] saying 1
267. 24 XII] XI 1–2
267. 28 Player] the Player 5
268. 10 this] his 4–5
268. 16 only could] could only 4–5
268. 17–23 She knew not. . . . Fondness for Men] the Riches of the World could not make her amends for the Loss of him; nor would she be persuaded to exchange him for the greatest Prince upon Earth 1
268. 24 to be fond] *om.* 1
269. 15 *John*] *Thomas* 1
269. 30 the celebrated] *om.* 1
270. 9–11 the one paid . . . hence] this paid that Respect to his Goodness which the other attributed to be paid to his Riches; and hence 1–2
270. 18–20 a violent Hurry . . . that was turned] a Hurry, that he had on neither Breeches, Garters, nor Stockings; nor had he . . . his Wig, turned 1–3
270. 23 Strip] Stripe 2–5
270. 25–26 where a long . . . served] *viz.* a Piss-burnt Beard, which served 1
271. 2–3 heard from him . . . comforted] heard the Account of what had past from him, comforted 1–2
271. 12 gave] he gave 1–2
271. 20–23 being sufficiently . . . had suffered] were sufficiently . . . and had suffered 1–2
272. 9–273. 28 but she absolutely . . . set forwards for *Booby-Hall*] and she absolutely refused, being determined to ride behind *Joseph*, on a Horse which one of Lady *Booby's* Servants had equipped him with. (This was indeed the same which *Adams* had left behind him at the Inn, and was by these honest Men who knew him, redeemed:) if any means could

be contrived of conveying Mr. *Adams* with them; whose Company *Pounce*, when he found he had no longer hopes of satisfying his old Appetite with *Fanny*, desired in his Vehicle. So that all matters being settled to the Content of every one, *Adams* and *Pounce* mounting the Chariot, and *Fanny* being placed on a Pillion, which *Joseph* borrowed of the Host, they all set forwards for *Booby-Hall* 1

272. 21 left] had left 5
272. 24 this Horse] his Horse 5
273. 13 laid hold on] laid hold of 3–5
274. 1 XIII] XII 1–2
274. 17 only a Blessing] a Blessing only 3–5
275. 4 produces] produce 4–5
275. 33 of your own] your own 1–2
276. 12 hath] has 1–3
276. 14 the Heirs] Heirs 3–5
277. 10 than] that 4
277. 10 with red] withered 3
277. 30–31 enquiring] enquired 1–3
279. 13 her] bear 3–5
279. 32 an *amorous*] a lovely 1
280. 2 it is] is is 4
280. 3 those] these 4–5
280. 12 your Complaint] of your Complaint 4–5
280. 34 believe] believed 4–5
281. 24 doth it . . . become a Man] is it . . . becoming in a Man 1
282. 13 Poor is] Poor are 4–5
282. 28 sufficient] a sufficient 4–5
283. 2 *Scout*] *Snout* 1
283. 4 farther] further 1
283. 19 Terms] Term 2–5
283. 23 out] *om.* 1–3
283. 31–284. 1 you, I will suffer . . . here.'—] you.' 1
284. 16 nor] or 3–5
284. 34–285. 8 If we can prove . . . to produce Children] 'Truly,' said the Lady, 'they are a grievous Load, and unless we had an Employment for them, it would be Charity to send them where they might have something to do. At least, I am sure we ought to prevent the farther Growth of the Evil, and not let such Beauties as these produce Children 1
285. 23 from] with 1–2
285. 29 *Frolick*] *Trolick* 1–2
285. 30–32 As for the dirty . . . Jade will] *om.* 1
286. 8 lay] have lain 4–5

286. 12–13 un . . . un] um . . . um 3
287. 6 by many] with many 5
287. 28 *fragrant*] a *fragrant* 4–5
288. 8 mentioned] had mentioned 1–2
289. 5 a Woman] Woman 1
289. 7 into] to 1
289. 8 was then] then was 1
289. 18 her] *om.* 2–5
290. 8 we] he 5
290. 27 here] there 4–5
290. 36 lopped] looped 4–5
291. 12 it] *om.* 2–3
292. 16 up] *om.* 1
292. 30–32 own her . . . infinitely] shew a proper Respect, and own her
    Relations, and I shall think myself infinitely 1
293. 35 thought herself secure] was certain 1
294. 8 this was increased] being assisted 1–3
294. 12 the Account] an Account 1–3
294. 13 was] were 4–5
295. 7 *Joseph*] *Joseph* however 1
295. 31 may] must 1
296. 14 born] he's born 1
296. 25 of the World] in the World 1
296. 26 dost] didst 4–5
296. 27 cried *Slipslop*] cries *Slipslop* 3–5
298. 5 Those] These 4–5
298. 31 had made] made 4–5
298. 32 *deprecate*] discommend 1
299. 34 Dread] Dread of, 1–2
301. 7 a Dream] Dream 1
302. 26 was] *om.* 3
302. 32 indulge it] indulge 1–2
302. 35 Lady] Wife 1–2
303. 4 where] when 4–5
304. 3–4 would not . . . but] would have been able to resist his Rudeness a
    very short time, when 1–2; would not have been able to resist his
    Rudeness a short time, but 3
304. 11 his Neck] the Neck 5
304. 32 yet] but 1–2
306. 3 the Habitation of] *om.* 1
306. 7 *be*] *he* 4
307. 15 Bacon] Bacon which 1–2
307. 37–308. 3 Nay perhaps. . . . Indeed] *om.* 1

308. 19–20 and not set . . . quit it] and set our Affections so much on nothing here that we cannot quit it 1–3
309. 33 seeing] having seen 4–5
310. 20 take] to take 4–5
310. 36 her] them 1
311. 26 than] then 4–5
313. 8 of his Country] his Country 1
314. 9 at last] had at last 1–2
316. 27 Mind] Passions 1
316. 28 gave] was 1
316. 29 Instance] *om.* 1
317. 14 anywise] anyways 3–4; any ways 5
317. 15 yellow] a yellow 5
318. 1 convinced] convinced that 3–5
318. 28 a Superiority] such a Superiority 5
318. 32 a Person] the Person 5
319. 1 an Air] the Air 4–5
319. 10 common] com- 1
321. 7 frighted] frightened 4–5
321. 15 the Hanger] his Hanger 4–5
321. 19 re-adjusted] he re-adjusted 1–2
322. 28–29 had probably . . . Tricks] had most probably ruined his Family with his Tricks 1–2; had probably ruined his Family with his Tricks almost 3
322. 31 to bring] to to bring 3
323. 22 in common] in in common 1
325. 20 half] a Half 3–5
327. 18 own] *om.* 1–2
327. 39 I despise] despise 5
328. 29 whither] where 4–5
328. 32 had ever had] had ever 5
328. 32 any more] more 1–2
329. 8–9 but by . . . apprehended] but his Duty, as he apprehended it 1–3
329. 26 perfectly] certainly 1–3
330. 30 not] nor 4
331. 5 doubt my marrying] doubt of my marrying 4; doubt of marrying 5
331. 12 Error] mutual Deceit 1–2
331. 40 torn] tore 4–5
333. 34 lay] *om.* 1–2
334. 25 Tragedians call] Tragedian calls 1–2
334. 27 an Astonishment] Astonishment 5
334. 37 any] *om.* 1–2

336. 37 yesterday,] ~; 5
338. 11 ours] yours 4–5
339. 17 than] then 4
340. 34 high of] of high 5
341. 16–17 the Justice] Justice 1
343. 21 nicest] utmost 4–5
344. 1 Pound] Pounds 5

APPENDIX V

Bibliographical Description of the
First Five Editions

(1) THE FIRST EDITION (22 February 1742), 2 vols., 12°

Title-page: A facsimile of the title-page of the first edition introduces the present text. A unique feature of the title is the inclusion of the word 'of' in the seventh line: 'And of his FRIEND'.

Collation: Vol. I. 12°: A¹⁰ B–O¹², $6(—G6) signed (missigning L3 as L5), 166 leaves, pp. *i–ii* iii–xix *xx*, *1* 2–308 *309–312* (misnumbering 308 as 306)

Vol. II. 12°: π² A–N¹², $6(—D6) signed (missigning A3 as B3, A5 as B5), 158 leaves, pp. *i–iv*, *1* 2–310 *311–312* (misnumbering 214 as 241, 267 as 276)

Contents: Vol. I: A1 title (verso blank), A2 preface, A10ᵛ erratum, B1 text (Books I–II), O11–12 publisher's advertisements.

Vol. II: π1 publisher's advertisements (recto blank), π2 title (verso blank), A1 text (Books III–IV), N12 publisher's advertisements.

Notes: (1) This description is based on the copy of the first edition in the British Museum, checked against the copy in Princeton and a microfilm of the Bodleian copy.

(2) Two instances of duplicate chapter numberings occur: thus there are two chapters VI in Book I and two chapters IV in Book III. As a result the subsequent chapters in these two books are misnumbered in sequence.

(2) THE SECOND EDITION (10 June 1742), 2 vols., 12°

Title-page: THE | HISTORY | OF THE | ADVENTURES | OF | *JOSEPH ANDREWS,* | And his FRIEND | Mr. *ABRAHAM ADAMS.* | Written in Imitation of | The *Manner* of CERVANTES, | Author of *Don Quixote.* | [*rule*] | The SECOND EDITION: | Revifed and Corrected with *Alterations* and | *Additions* by the AUTHOR. | [*rule*] | IN TWO VOLUMES. | [*rule*] | VOL. I. | [*double rule*] | *LONDON:* | Printed for A. MILLAR, over-againft | *St. Clement's Church,* in the *Strand.* | M.DCC.XLII.

Collation: Vol. I. 12°: A–O¹², \$6(—G6) signed, 168 leaves, pp. *i–ii*
iii–xxii *xxiii–xxiv*, *1* 2–308 *309–312*

Vol. II. 12°: ᵖA⁴ A–M¹² N⁸, \$6(—B6) signed, 156 leaves,
pp. *i–ii* iii–vii *viii*, *1* 2–304 (misnumbering 189 as 199)

Contents: Vol. I: A1 title (verso blank), A2 preface, A9 contents of
vol. I, A12 publisher's advertisements, B1 text (Books I–II), O11–12
publisher's advertisements.

Vol. II: ᵖA1 title (verso blank), ᵖA2 contents of vol. II (ᵖA4ᵛ blank),
A1 text (Books III–IV).

Notes: (1) This description is based on the copy of the second edition in
the British Museum, checked against the copy in Princeton and the
present editor's personal copy.

(2) This is the first edition to include a table of contents (in each
volume), and the first edition to include Book and Chapter references
in the headlines (e.g., 'Book III. / Ch. 2.').

(3) Errors in chapter numbering as in the first edition. The headlines
designate Book I, Chapter ¹VI, as part of Chapter V, and Book III,
Chapter ¹IV, as part of Chapter III. Errors in the headlines include
the following (roman and arabic numerals refer to the volume and page
unless otherwise indicated): I, 213, misnumbers 'Ch. 7' as 'Ch. 8'; II,
122–144 (signature F), misnumbers 'Book III' as 'Book II'; II, 161,
misnumbers 'Ch. 11' as 'Ch. 12'; II, 242–264 (signature L), misnumbers
'Book IV' as 'Book III'; II, 257, misnumbers 'Ch. 11' as 'Ch. 10'.

(3) THE THIRD EDITION (21–28 March 1743), 2 vols., 12°

Title-page: THE | HISTORY | OF THE | ADVENTURES |
OF | *JOSEPH ANDREWS*, | And his FRIEND | Mr. *ABRAHAM
ADAMS*. | Written in Imitation of | The *Manner* of CERVANTES, |
Author of *Don Quixote*. | [*rule*] | By HENRY FIELDING, Efquire. |
[*rule*] | The THIRD EDITION, illuftrated with CUTS. | [*rule*] | IN TWO
VOLUMES. | [*rule*] | VOL. I. | [*double rule*] | LONDON: |
Printed for A. MILLAR, oppofite to *Katharine* | *Street*, in the *Strand*.
M.DCC.XLIII.

Collation: Vol. I. 12°: π⁴ A⁶ B–K¹² L⁶, \$6 signed, 124 leaves, pp. *i–xx*,
1 2–226 *227–228* [Note: excluded from this formula are five engravings, inserted opposite pp. 30, 76, 136, 168, 198.]

Vol. II. 12°: *A⁴*(—A4[?]) B–K¹² L⁴ *M*1(=A4[?]), \$6 signed, 116
leaves, pp. *i–vi*, *1* 2–226 [Note: excluded from this formula are seven
engravings, inserted opposite pp. 57, 71, 88, 106, 142, 177, 223.]

Contents: Vol. I: π1 title (verso blank), π2 contents of vol. I, A1 preface,
B1 text (Books I–II), L6 publisher's advertisements.

Vol. II: A1 title (verso blank), A2 contents of vol. II, B1 text (Books III–IV).

Notes: (1) This description is based on the copy of the third edition in the Bodleian Library, checked against the copy in Princeton. The British Museum copy of Volume I is variant, A6 occurring between π1 and π2.

(2) The third edition, containing twelve engravings by J. Hulett, is the first illustrated edition of *Joseph Andrews*, the first edition to bear Fielding's name on the title-page, and the first edition to correct the errors in chapter numbering mentioned in the notes to editions one and two.

(4) THE FOURTH EDITION (29 October 1748 [the title-page reads 1749]), 2 vols., 12°

Title-page: As in third edition, except after author's name and rule as follows: 'Illuſtrated with CUTS. | [*rule*] | The FOURTH EDITION, reviſed and corrected. | [*rule*] | IN TWO VOLUMES. | [*double rule*] | LONDON: |' etc. The date is given: 'M.DCC.XLIX.'

Collation: Vol. I. 12°: π⁴ A⁶ B–K¹² L⁶, $6(—E6) signed, 124 leaves, pp. *i–xx*, *1* 2–226 *227–228* (misnumbering 89 as 98) [Note: excluded from this formula are five engravings, inserted opposite pp. 30, 76, 136, 168, 198.]

Vol. II. 12°: *A*⁴(—A4[?]) B–K¹² L⁴ *M*1(=A4[?]), $6 signed, 116 leaves, pp. *i–vi*, *1* 2–226 (misnumbering 62 as 64) [Note: excluded from this formula are seven engravings, inserted opposite pp. 57, 71, 88, 106, 142, 177, 223.]

Contents: Vol. I: π1 title (verso blank), π2 contents of vol. I, A1 preface, B1 text (Books I–II), L6 publisher's advertisements.

Vol. II: A1 title (verso blank), A2 contents of vol. II, B1 text (Books III–IV).

Note: (1) This description is based on the copy of the fourth edition in the British Museum, checked against the copy in Yale.

(5) THE FIFTH EDITION (19 December 1751), 2 vols., 12°

Title-page: As in fourth edition, except for the substitution of the appropriate edition number ('FIFTH') and the date, 'M.DCC.LI.'

Collation: Vol. I. 12°: π*A*⁴ A⁶ B–K¹² L⁶, $6 signed, 124 leaves, pp. *i–xx*, *1* 2–226 *227–228* (misnumbering 220 as 200, 225 as 209) [Note: excluded from this formula are five engravings, inserted opposite pp. 30, 76, 136, 168, 198.]

Vol. II. 12°: A^4(—A4[?]) B–K^{12} L^4 M1(=A4[?]), \$6 signed, 116 leaves, pp. *i–vi*, *1* 2–226 [Note: excluded from this formula are seven engravings, inserted opposite pp. 57, 71, 88, 106, 142, 177, 223.]

Contents: Vol. I: $^\pi$A1 title (verso blank), $^\pi$A2 contents of vol. I, A1 preface, B1 text (Books I–II), L6 publisher's advertisements.

Vol. II: A1 title (verso blank), A2 contents of vol. II, B1 text (Books III–IV).

Note: (1) This description is based on the copy of the fifth edition in the British Museum, checked against the copy at Yale.

The Murphy Editions

THE so-called 'Murphy editions' of *Joseph Andrews*, contained in the octavo and quarto printings of *The Works of Henry Fielding, Esq;* (1762),[1] are curious enough on several grounds to warrant brief consideration. For one thing, the texts of most modern editions of the novel are ultimately based on one or the other of these editions, despite the fact that they appeared some eight years after Fielding's death. Bibliographically, certain unusual features of the *Works* complicate the task of the editor. Comparison of the Murphy texts with earlier editions of *Joseph Andrews* indicates, for example, that the octavo (though called 'The SECOND EDITION' on the title-page) must be granted priority.[2] The quarto, which was printed from the rearranged standing type of the octavo—a process so difficult that many passages were bungled and required resetting—is a very corrupt text. The octavo, therefore, is the only one of the two versions that need concern us, and there are cogent reasons for denying any authority even to this text.

Unlike preceding editions of *Joseph Andrews*, which occurred in a direct line of descent, each set from the immediately preceding single-edition copy-text, the Murphy octavo was based on Volume I of the fourth edition and on Volume II of the third edition; thus the text of Books III and IV of the novel does not incorporate any of Fielding's final revisions. Moreover, besides being the first editor of *Joseph Andrews* to modernize the accidentals

---

[1] In April 1762 *The Works of Henry Fielding, Esq; With the Life of the Author* by Arthur Murphy was published by Andrew Millar in two editions simultaneously—one in four volumes quarto, the other in eight volumes octavo. The Murphy texts of *Joseph Andrews* are included in Volume II of the quarto and in Volume IV of the octavo.

[2] Collation discloses fifty-two substantive readings common to both the octavo and the quarto but not found in any of the first six editions of *Joseph Andrews*—a clear indication that the two texts are dependent, that one was based on the other. The vast majority of these variants are obviously the result of compositorial error or sophistication. In another fifty-two instances the quarto and the octavo differ; in fifty of these the octavo exactly agrees with the reading of Murphy's copy-texts and must therefore have preceded the quarto. Thus, to cite only two of many examples, 'her dear Horatio', the reading of the octavo and the copy-text, becomes in the quarto 'her Horatio' (8°: IV. 262.12; 4°: II. 469.4); 'and a young woman' becomes 'and a woman' (8°: IV. 429.12; 4°: II. 546.25).

It should be noted that Millar assigned the *Works* to more than one printer and that the order of priority evident from an examination of the texts of *Joseph Andrews* does not necessarily obtain for all volumes. For the volumes printed by William Strahan (namely, according to his ledger, Volume I of the quarto and Volumes I–II of the octavo), Professor Woods found that the quarto is closer to Murphy's copy-texts than the octavo.

of the text with regard to capitalization and italics, Murphy (or the compositor) took further liberties with the original, introducing several substantive changes of his own. Of these the great majority are obvious corruptions of Fielding's intentions. At least three, however, are bold enough to raise the question of authenticity. Two changes occur in the speech of Mrs. Slipslop: where Fielding, probably through an oversight, allowed her to step out of character by correctly using the words 'Compassion' (125.3) and 'distinguish' (295.29), Murphy altered these to the malapropisms, 'compulsion' and 'exstinguish'. A third change, more puzzling, substitutes 'canvas' for 'Stays' (215.22).[1] These corrections, however, are exactly the sort that Murphy, who was no very scrupulous editor, might well have permitted himself to make. The weight of evidence is solidly against our assuming that Murphy had access to a copy of the novel revised by Fielding, as he probably did have when preparing the text of *Amelia*. In preparing *Amelia* for the press, Murphy was doubtless using a marked copy of the novel that Fielding had entrusted to Millar to be used when a second edition was called for, an occasion that did not present itself until the publication of the *Works* in 1762. On the other hand, by 1748 Fielding had completed extensive revisions of *Joseph Andrews*; in neither the fifth edition nor the sixth (published by Millar in the year of Murphy's text) is there any evidence of Fielding's correcting hand.

For these reasons all of Murphy's alterations have been excluded from the present text. In the interest of rendering the textual history of *Joseph Andrews* as complete as possible, however, a sample of these variants is given below. The readings from Murphy that follow are common to both the octavo and the quarto texts, with three exceptions found in the quarto version only and designated 'M4°'.

3.3   with] from[2]
18.6   obtained] attained M4°
41.31   *John*] om.
100.24   gone] going
125.3   Compassion] compulsion
134.12   in my good] with my good

[1] Several reasons, none very satisfactory, might explain this substitution: (1) in *Joseph Andrews*, 11. i, Fielding had already used the phrase, 'Buckram, Stays, and Stay-tape', in reference to a tailor's bill; Murphy may have wished to avoid the repetition. (2) Since stays were used principally in corsets, it might have seemed more appropriate for a poet to purchase canvas from his tailor; stay-tape, on the other hand, was often used with buckram in the manufacture of men's coats. (3) Murphy's revision results in a combination of items that may have been conventional: the *O.E.D.* (s.v. 'Stay-tape') quotes the following phrase from Ned Ward's *London Spy*, iv (1706), 91—'To find Canvas, Stay-Tape, and Buckram in a Taylors Bill.'

[2] The sixth edition (1762), which is otherwise based on the fifth edition (1751), also reads 'from'.

145.25   Deposition] depositions
145.28   Depositions] deposition
166.9–10   to Heaven] up to heaven
187.21   collected] selected
215.22   Stays] canvas
219.21   lie] die M4°
255.31   their Lodgings there] there their lodging
290.36   lopped] flopped
295.29   distinguish] exstinguish
311.22   *good*] *polite* M4°
333.31   be gone] begin
342.30   so solemn] on so solemn

PRINTED IN GREAT BRITAIN
AT THE UNIVERSITY PRESS, OXFORD
BY VIVIAN RIDLER
PRINTER TO THE UNIVERSITY